W9-AKJ-527

# MONSTER HUNTER
# VENDETTA

## Larry Correia

MONSTER HUNTER VENDETTA

This is a work of fiction. All the characters and events portrayed in this book are fictional, and any resemblance to real people or incidents is purely coincidental.

Copyright © 2010 by Larry Correia.

All rights reserved, including the right to reproduce this book or portions thereof in any form.

A Baen Book

Baen Publishing Enterprises
P.O. Box 1403
Riverdale, NY 10471
www.baen.com

ISBN: 978-1-4391-3391-0

Cover art by Alan Pollack
Team Haven patch by Rabbit Boyett

First printing, October 2010
Third printing, May 2013

Distributed by Simon & Schuster
1230 Avenue of the Americas
New York, NY 10020

Pages by Joy Freeman (www.pagesbyjoy.com)
Printed in the United States of America

This novel is dedicated to Diamantine.

# Acknowledgments

Thanks to the members of Reader Force Alpha for the feedback and corrections. You guys know everything. Special thanks to Kathy Jackson and Bob Westover for the proofing, Rabbit Boyett for patch art, Toni Weisskopf and her amazing crew at Baen, and the caffeine of a thousand vanilla Cokes.

"When monsters have nightmares,
they're dreaming about us."

—MHI Company Handbook

# CHAPTER 1

It was less than a year ago that the illusion shattered and I got my welcome to the real world. Up until that point I considered myself perfectly average, living a normal life, with a regular career. That all changed the night my accounting supervisor turned into a werewolf and tried to eat me. Now there are basically two ways to deal with such a problem. Most people confronted with something so hideously impossible tend to curl up into the fetal position and die. On the other hand, those of us destined to become Monster Hunters simply take care of business. He almost ended my life but I tossed him out a fourteen-story window. He died, I didn't. That makes me the winner.

After that initial encounter I was approached with a job offer. Apparently survivors like me aren't that common, and as a result killing a monster is a real résumé builder. I was recruited by Monster Hunter International, the premier eradication company in the business. We protect mankind from the unnatural forces that come crawling out from our darkest nightmares, and in return, we get paid the big bucks.

It wasn't that long after I started my new job that MHI came up against an unfathomable evil from the past. It took everything we had to survive, but in the end, the Cursed One was defeated and I literally saved the world.

I was employee of the month.


The biggest chupacabra in the pack was only four feet tall, but what they lacked in mass, they made up for in sheer ferocity. Being unable to get to their dinner was making them even surlier than usual. The peasant girl had been futilely tinkering with the engine of her broken-down Chevy Vega when the first chupacabra had come sniffing onto the jungle road. Her screams at seeing the little demon-lizard-insect thing hop down the dirt lane like a demented miniature kangaroo had driven it into a frenzy, and she had barely managed to dive into the car ahead of its snapping jaws. Her continued cries from behind the locked doors of the old rust bucket had attracted the rest of the pack, and now there were a dozen of the creatures clambering on the car.

Chupacabras do not normally attack people. The puncture tubes that jut from their mouths could pierce a human skull like a screwdriver through a milk jug, but instinctively they stick to preying on small animals. Once a chupacabra pack has tasted human blood, however, they absolutely will not stop, and killings become more and more frequent. From what I have seen in this business, people must be either extremely tasty, or addictive, like monster crack.

The creatures were scratching and clawing at the car's windows and roof. The girl just kept on screaming. She had a remarkably good set of lungs for this kind of thing, which is why we'd picked her. Her cries spurred the monsters on, and they all began to shriek as well, echoing across the dark jungle canopy for miles.

The four-footer jumping up and down on the hood of the Vega was pissed. It had to be the pack's alpha male, and it couldn't figure out why the glass wasn't breaking. I watched it carefully through the night-vision monocular.

"I think he suspects something," Trip Jones whispered.

I nodded. They might be clever for creatures with brains the size of tangerines, but the goat-suckers had never run into bulletproof glass before. Finally the alpha hopped off the car and scurried over to the side of the road. I almost keyed my radio, but he hesitated there, looking for something, and came up with a rock. He crawled back on the hood, raised the rock, and started banging away at the windshield. The others cheered and hooted him on.

"Hey, I didn't know suckers knew how to use tools," Milo Anderson said over the radio. He was positioned on the other side of the road. All of us were wearing ghillie suits over our body armor and had been lying in the underbrush being eaten by insects for hours. The foul-smelling grease that we had rubbed on ourselves earlier to hide our smell from the chupacabras' sensitive noses also served as seasoning for the region's bugs.

My radio crackled. "We'll have to update the database," Julie Shackleford replied, the roar of the chopper's engine could be heard behind her. "Tool use . . . That's fascinating."

Apparently our fake peasant, Holly Newcastle, didn't think it was nearly as fascinating from her position as bait in the front seat of the Vega. The theatrical screaming stopped for a moment. "Uh, guys..." The rest of us could hear the glass cracking in the background. "Guys?"

We had three members of Monster Hunter International hiding in the brush, one in the decoy car, two more on the rapidly approaching attack helicopter, carefully positioned claymores along the roadside, piles of guns, thousands of rounds of ammo, state of the art night-vision and thermal-imaging equipment, a lot of attitude, and a general dislike of evil beasties.

I keyed my microphone.

"Execute."

My name is Owen Zastava Pitt and I kill monsters for a living.

"This is Harbinger," the familiar voice said through the phone, sounding a little groggy. I must have woken him. "What time is it?"

"It's almost midnight here," I answered, which meant that it was like one or two in the morning in Alabama. I was never very good at remembering time zones.

There was a brief pause. "So somebody's either got eaten, or you completed the contract."

"Mission accomplished, chief. Julie's dropping the evidence off at the mayor's office and arranging the funds transfer." The evidence consisted of a burlap sack full of severed chupacabra heads. "It was a big pack. Smoked them all."

"Nice." This had been a lucrative job. The Mexican resort depended on tourism, so when people started getting their organs liquefied and drained, it was bad for business, especially since it was happening during their busy season. It was spring break, after all. "Everybody okay?"

"They're good." Loud music drifted in through the open window of my hotel room. There was a wild party going on around the Olympic-sized pool, populated mostly by American college students engaged in all manner of drunken debauchery. "Looking forward to payday I bet."

"Rush jobs always pay well. How'd the team do?" Earl asked. I knew what he really wanted to ask was how his team did without him. The timing of the mission had just not worked out, as there were very few places that were safe for him during the full moon.

"They were awesome. It was beautiful." Exploding chupacabras were not what most people would find artistic, but I knew Earl would understand. He was after all, the Director of Operations for a company whose mission statement actually read: *Evil looms. Cowboy up. Kill it. Get paid.*

"Wish I could've been there, but you know how it is. Good work, Z."

That comment made me swell with pride. My boss wasn't known for giving compliments. This had been the first operation that I had been allowed to plan entirely, and it had been a success. Well, I had the very experienced Julie and Milo there to make sure I didn't screw it up, but I had still done pretty damn good. "Thanks, Earl. See you tomorrow."

"'Night, kid. Tell Julie I love her, and next time, call me in the *morning*."

I tossed the sat-phone on the bed next to my body

armor and weapons. I still needed to clean my guns
before I packed them up for the return flight. It had
been humid out in the forest, and rust was my enemy.
But right now I didn't feel like doing the work, I just
wanted to gloat. Picking up my heavy Kevlar suit, I
paused to brush some chupacabra juice off the patch
stuck on the arm. It was a little green Happy Face
with devil horns. Just a simple logo, but for me it
represented a lot of hard work. It was MHI's unofficial logo, and the only Hunters who got to wear it
were the ones chosen for Harbinger's personal team.
I grinned and dropped the armor back on the bed.
I'd earned that patch a few times over.

The complimentary hotel room was extremely nice,
way nicer than the roach motels that MHI usually
seemed to stay in, but I was still too charged up
from today's mission to relax. I opened the glass doors
and stepped onto the balcony. The hip-hop music
was louder now, and the cloud that drifted up from
the pool area was strong enough to give a DEA dog
a seizure. My room was on the second floor. There
had to be a couple hundred people down there, most
of them young Americans. An obnoxious crowd had
gathered around the DJ table, and a film crew was
doing an interview with some rapper who was about
to host a wet tee shirt contest or something. An ine-
briated young woman screamed, lifted her shirt, and
flashed me. I waved stupidly. *Good old spring break*.

Life was good. Monster Hunter International was
the best private monster hunting company on the
planet. I had not even been doing this for a year, but
already I was planning and executing operations in
foreign countries, and I had just been complimented

by the most experienced Hunter in the world. Not bad for a guy who was basically just an accountant who happened to be handy with a gun.

The wood deck was cool under my bare feet. I leaned on the balcony, directly above the stenciled sign that stated in both English and Spanish that it was not safe to lean on the balcony, and did a quick search of the swim-suited, dancing throng. I could not see any of my team. That wasn't really a surprise though.

Milo and Skippy were probably checking the chopper for the trip home tomorrow. Neither one would be into this scene, especially Skippy, because he wasn't human and was very uncomfortable around crowds. Milo's wife was pregnant and due any time now, so he just wanted to get home as fast as he could. Trip was definitely not the party type. He had picked up the only fantasy novel available in the hotel gift shop, some ridiculous L.H. Franzibald thing, and was probably squirreled away in his room reading like usual. He is such a nerd—and that's coming from an accountant. Holly definitely gave the impression of being a party girl, but with her, who knew? You could tell me that Holly was helping the nuns at the local orphanage or you could tell me that she was dancing on the bar for tips, and either story would be equally plausible.

Julie would be coming straight back here when she finished harassing the local officials for our money. I had planned on going with her, but since I had been the one to saw off the goat-suckers' heads, Julie had *ordered* me to return here and take a shower. Chupacabras are rather nasty little buggers. My girlfriend—correction, fiancée—would be back soon enough. I was still getting used to the idea of being engaged.

We'd skip the party scene. For me personally, I had spent too many years bouncing rowdy drunks to ever want to *be* a rowdy drunk.

It was satisfying to know that it had been me and my friends who had kept any of the tourists below from being killed. Certainly some of them were going to be dead from alcohol poisoning by tomorrow morning, but that sounded like a personal problem to me. As long as none of them were eaten by chupacabras, it was out of my hands.

My back-patting was interrupted by a hard knock on the door. Julie had probably finished collecting our paycheck and returned. I was looking forward to having some alone time with her. If I had been thinking, I would have lit some candles and put on some romantic music or something to take advantage of our free pseudo-vacation, but I was never very good at thinking of those kinds of things beforehand. I left the balcony, closed the double doors, drew the thick curtains mostly shut, and started across the suite. The bass continued to thump through the glass. "Who is it?" I shouted.

"Is that Owen Zastava Pitt?" came the muffled response.

*Shoot. Not Julie.* The voice was unfamiliar. Frowning, I paused by the bed, picked up one of my STI pistols, the long-slide .45, and held it down by my leg. I was paranoid back when I was an accountant. As a Monster Hunter I took paranoia to whole new levels. We were registered here under the Shackleford name, and Julie was the one who had done the negotiating with the resort. I couldn't think of anyone other than my teammates here who would know my name. "Yeah? What do you want?"

"Mr. Pitt, I've traveled a long way to meet you." The voice had an English accent, not one of those prim and proper *Masterpiece Theater* ones, but more like someone who had grown up on the tough side of town. "May I come in?"

One thing that I had learned in this job, you *never* give an invitation to the unknown. "Look, dude, whatever you're selling, I don't want any." Moving as quietly as possible, I went to the peephole. The mystery man's face was distorted through the bubble glass. The hall lights must have gone out, and he was cloaked in shadow. I could only see eyes and the outline of a face. He did not look like the friendly type, but then again, neither was I.

He must have caught the darkening of the peephole, and automatically glanced up, scowling as if he was thinking really hard about something. There was no way he could see me, but I felt shivers go down my spine as I just *knew* he was staring me down. "Ah, yes. You are the one."

The door shook in its frame.

Startled, I jumped back and raised my pistol. The shaking increased in intensity, threatening to vibrate the door to pieces. There was a crack as wood broke. I snapped the STI into position. "Back off. I'm warning you!"

Every light bulb in the room popped. Sparks flew from the wall sconces, plunging the room into darkness. There was a splintering noise as the doorframe cracked. Truly freaked out at this point, I jerked the trigger and fired two quick rounds through the center of the door. I knew that the sturdy hotel door would barely slow the 230-grain silver/lead bullets, and whoever was pulling my door off the hinges surely must have been hit. The door quit shaking.

Instinctively, I moved back. I had dealt with enough supernatural bullshit by this point of my life that it just seemed like the reasonable thing to do. Hunching down behind the bed, I wished that I was wearing my armor instead of a pair of shorts and a tee shirt. The music from the pool area continued, cranked so absurdly loud that the other guests had probably not even heard the gunshots.

Blinking rapidly as my eyes adjusted to the sudden gloom, my pistol pointed at the door, I waited. There was an M3 flashlight mounted on the dust cover of my .45. I put my finger on the activation switch. Anything that came through that door was going to get lit up, both with blinding light and bullets, maybe even in that order. "Come on . . ." I muttered under my breath.

There was a terrible boom and the door flew from its hinges and crashed to the floor. A giant shape flowed into the room, so vast and tall that it gave the impression of having to duck to clear the frame. It straightened up, towering above me, formless and terrifying, with the consistency of smoke, a blob of pitch-black intimidation. I had never seen anything like it before.

I activated the flashlight, flooding the room with brilliant white light. I blinked in surprise. The giant shadow was gone, and a normal man stood glaring at me. He was skinny, tough-looking, probably in his mid-thirties, with a nearly shaved head, and a mean scowl. He was dressed in black jeans and a gray hooded sweatshirt, casual enough to fit in with the crowd outside. He held up one hand to protect his eyes.

"Don't move," I ordered, hunkered low behind the bed, my glowing tritium front sight centered in the middle of his chest.

"So this is the great Hunter," he said calmly. "For somebody who's supposed to be so extraordinarily important, you seem rather unimpressive." He swept his hand downward sharply. The bulb in my flashlight exploded.

"Neat trick," I said as I pulled the trigger.

But he was already gone. Giant hands wrapped around my biceps, jerked me to my feet and slung me into the wall. A brutal chill flowed up my arm as he yanked the gun from my hand, almost taking my trigger finger with it. I threw an elbow but touched nothing. He hit me again, low in my side, and it rocked me. The blow was cold as ice and hard as a hammer. I gasped in pain.

I'm not exaggerating when I say that I am a mean son of a bitch when it comes to fighting. I can throw down against the best of them, and I had done it in the dark before. There was no time for thought, only action. I came back quick, lashing out at where my opponent should have been. I stumbled into the bed. There was a swish of air as he moved around me: I threw a back fist and missed, and was rewarded with a mighty blow to my shoulders. I kicked out, only to have something cold and impossibly big latch onto my leg. He pulled hard. Off balance, I fell, grunting on impact. This hotel had some solid floors.

He grabbed me by the front of my shirt and lifted me with ease. I tried to grasp his hands to apply a wristlock, but there was nothing there. He crushed me against the wall with brute force, pushing me through a layer of drywall.

"I'm taking you with me, Hunter, whether you like it or not." The Englishman's voice seemed to radiate from all around me. There was a frigid weight pushing against my chest as I swung my forearm through it in vain. The darkness swirled around my arm like smoke, and the pressure increased on my lungs, making it impossible to breathe. My back slid up the wall and I left the ground. I panicked, lashed out with my feet, my knees, my elbows, my fists, but it was like moving through water. Whatever had me trapped was incorporeal, and I was blacking out.

"It's useless," he chuckled through my futile strikes. "I can't believe you're the one. This is pathetic. I was at least expecting a fight. Can you truly be the one who defeated Lord Machado?"

That name. *Not again. No, not again.* The bad chemical taste of fear was suddenly in my mouth.

My body was hoisted effortlessly into the air, and tossed casually across the room. I slammed into the wall near the bathroom and crumpled to the carpet. My head was swimming but I immediately began to crawl toward my stash of weapons on the bed. Now that I was a few feet away, I could see the giant shadow shape moving across the room, almost as if it were pacing, agitated. My assailant continued to speak. "You must be important though. It took some time for the message to reach me. I was shocked to receive something from the other side. You have no idea how rare it is for the Old Ones to take the time to communicate with this world. Oh, the Dread Overlord is going to be happy when I deliver you. I don't know how you managed to get on his bad books, but you're bloody well fucked."

As the big shadow moved, it passed in front of the sliver of light emanating from the balcony curtains. The shape was gone, and it was just the man again, but as he left the light, his body seemed to drift into smoke and the shadow returned.

*Light.* I need light. Whatever he was, he only seemed to have a body in the light. "The Old Ones can kiss my ass ... Stupid mollusks." I reached the bed, but the shadow was on me in an instant, freezing tendrils clamped around my wrist. He jerked me around and dragged me across the floor toward the exit.

"Time to go. The Overlord awaits."

I thrashed, fought, but only managed to give myself a nasty carpet burn.

There was a flicker of green light across the room. The black force around my wrist coalesced into normal human fingers. He was flesh again. The shadow man frowned.

Fireworks. They were setting off fireworks at the party.

My bare foot collided with his ribs. He stumbled back from the brutal kick, falling through the bathroom door. With no time to spare, I leapt up, reached the bed, and searched through the dark for a weapon. My hand closed around the leather-wrapped handle of my Ganga Ram, a Himalayan kukri. I jerked the massive knife from the scabbard.

A metallic screeching noise came from the shadows of the bathroom as something was torn free. The next firework blossomed red. The illumination was just enough for me to see the flash of a large white object hurtling at me. Flinging myself down, I could feel the wind as the toilet barely missed my head. It shattered the balcony door, tore through the curtains, and flew into the night.

More light from the party flooded into the room. The black shape glided out of the bathroom toward me, but it shrunk into the form of the Englishman as he left the shadows. He charged with a roar. "Oh, it's on now," I grunted as I got back to my feet and drove my knife forward. His face registered the shock as the curved blade of the Ganga Ram slammed through his ribs and out his back. He looked down in surprise. I twisted the blade with all my might, cutting upward through his torso.

I've managed to hack a few things to death with this knife over the last year. I should have been splattered with blood, but there was nothing, no liquid at all; it was like I was sawing through a bone-in ham. He glared back up, eyebrows creasing together in rage as more fireworks exploded outside, and clamped a brutal hand around my throat. The air to my brain was choked off as he hoisted me off the floor.

With a foot of steel driven through his guts, he shouted in my face. "I tried to be polite, and now you have to make me do this the hard way. I wanted to deliver you to the Old Ones with your mind in one piece, but *nooo,* you have to be difficult..." I continued to saw the blade back and forth, searching for his heart, but he didn't seem to notice. "Fine then. We'll just devour your brain and give the Old Ones a vegetable. They don't respect humans enough to know the difference anyway." He paused as his neck suddenly ballooned up like a puffer fish. "Snack time, little friend..." He opened his mouth wide, tilting his head back, and some *thing* came up his throat, black claws pushing past his lips, tiny red eyes blinking into existence over a circular mouth filled with fishhook teeth, crawling, struggling upward, heading right for my face, and strangely enough, I somehow could tell it was hungry.

*Screw that!*

I yanked the kukri out of his chest, lifted it high overhead, and swung down, chopping his hand off at the wrist. I fell to the floor, gasping for air as the pressure was released from my throat. His running shoe collided with my stomach as he punted me across the room. I rolled painfully to a stop by the balcony, realized that his severed hand was still clawing at my neck, and tore it away. The little shadow monster crawling out of the Englishman's mouth shrieked in an insanely high pitch as he seemed to choke it back down, and with a hard swallow, it was gone. He raised the stump of his ruined arm. Writhing shadow leapt from the end, instantly twisting and re-forming into a new hand. He balled the fresh hand into a fist, lowered his head, and started toward me.

A man has to know his limitations, and I was way out of my league on this one. Instantly back to my feet, I ran for the balcony, bare feet crunching on a piece of broken glass. "Ouch! Ouch!" Heedless of the danger, I vaulted over the railing and plummeted into the party below.

Landing brutally hard, lightning cascading up my legs, I crashed through a rosebush and onto the porcelain shards of the broken toilet. I lay there, gasping for a moment. As a very large man, gymnastic feats were not really my specialty. I struggled through the plants and tumbled onto the tile by the pool, scattering college students like bowling pins. My left ankle throbbed from the impact, but I stood, hobbling, and raised my kukri, which I had somehow managed not to impale myself on.

I roared up at my room, "Come and get me!" The shadow man was leaning on the railing, glowering down at me, fireworks exploding overhead. There was enough light down here that I somehow knew he wasn't going to follow. Several partygoers shrieked, spilled their beers, and ran as I shook my kukri with one hand and extended my middle finger with the other. "Yeah, I thought so, you pansy!"

"This isn't over," the Englishman shouted over the music. He turned his attention away from me for a moment, and nodded at someone on the far side of the party. I had no idea who or what he was signaling, but it probably wasn't the wet tee shirt contest. He returned his attention to me and smiled. "Well done. For now...but, dead or alive, I'll deliver you to the Dread Overlord eventually."

"Better things than you have tried."

"Farewell, Hunter. We *will* meet again...assuming you live through the next few minutes, that is." He faded back into the shadows and was gone.

If I could get to my radio, I could rouse the team and chase this puke down. I took a step forward, flinching violently as the pressure hit a piece of broken glass impaled in my heel. Swearing, I paused to yank the tiny shard out and toss it into the bushes.

"Oh, man, dude, are you okay?" one of the bystanders asked stupidly. "You totally like fell out the window!"

I snarled. He cringed back. The partiers gave me a wide berth. I glared at them angrily and anyone

who was even vaguely contemplating saying anything
retreated a few more feet. Turning my attention to
gathering reinforcements, I started limping for the
entrance, but there was a commotion on the far side
of the pool. Some of the partygoers were screaming
now, real cries of terror that could be heard even
above the din of the dance music. I turned back
toward them, dripping blood, holding a giant knife,
and bellowed, "What now?"

Zombies. Lots of zombies.

The party was officially over.

Someone had backed a package truck up to the
entrance of the pool area. The rear doors were open
and corpses were tumbling out. These undead were in
an advanced state of decomposition. Their flesh was
rotten and sloughing off. Many of them were missing
eyes, noses, and ears. There were so many that they
must have been literally stacked on top of each other
inside the truck's hold.

There are many different variations of undead,
with your basic zombie being the simplest of all. A
zombie is just an animated corpse, wandering around
in search of one thing: flesh. The big problem with
zombies is that they multiply like rabbits. Their bites
are always eventually fatal, and the bitten always rise
as zombies themselves. Their poison travels instantly
through the nervous system, and not even amputation of the bitten limb can stop the transformation.
Basically, they're a major pain in the ass, the Monster
Hunter's equivalent to cockroaches. Usually stupid, and
normally slow, zombies are not much of a challenge
for an experienced Hunter, provided that said Hunter
has a decent gun and friends with guns. I was pretty

much alone, had just gotten the crap kicked out of me, and was armed with only a knife. The kukri was a great big freaking knife, mind you, but still it was only a knife. Not a good recipe for success.

I could have run away. Even with one ankle already swelling, there was no way they could have caught me. I could rally my team and come back to the pool with some real armament. That would be the safe thing to do. But as I watched, one of the tourists, a guy just barely out of his teens, was pulled down by some of the corpses. They descended on him like a pack of dogs, and his screaming and kicking stopped in an instant. The zombies were falling out the back of the truck into a pile, but spurred on by the nearness of meat, they were driving themselves to their feet and lumbering into the mob. The tourists panicked as they saw their friends getting disemboweled right in front of them. Hundreds of people began to crash into each other, trying to shove their way to safety. The small and the weak were smashed underfoot, just more zombie fodder.

The smell of decay hit my nostrils.

MHI was a private company. We weren't cops. We weren't the Fed's Monster Control Bureau. We were contractors, mercenaries. We had no obligation to protect the innocent unless they were paying us to do it. To jump in was suicide.

"Aw…damn it." I raised my Ganga Ram and charged the truck of undead. I pushed past the fleeing partiers. There were lots of them, but I'm a big man, and when I pick a direction, I'm hard to stop. My bare feet slipped on the water that splashed onto the tile as the crowd knocked people into the pool. The patio was packed. You could feel the panic of the herd.

The mostly sober were able to flee, but those that had been in the water were sitting ducks. A young woman was trying to climb out, but one of the zombies had grabbed her by the hair and was tugging her toward its jagged mouth, maggots wriggling in its face. I lopped the creature's arm off at the elbow. The girl flew back with a splash. The zombie turned automatically toward me and I removed the top of its head right above the eye sockets. It went limp. It pays to know your monsters. With zombies, destroy the brain, and they go right down.

Another zombie saw me, locked on, and charged. This one had been an old woman once. "Whoa!" I jumped back as it swiped at me. These zombies were fast. I had dealt with regular zombies before, but I'd only heard rumors of faster ones. It kept coming, head bent, lipless mouth open and snapping. If those teeth broke my skin, I was worse than dead. I shattered one of its knees in a cloud of dust with my bloody heel and it toppled into the pool.

Hacking and slashing, zombies to the front, zombies to the side. *Have to protect these kids.* An ironic thought considering most of them were about my age. A man went down with one of the undead on his back, biting at his neck. They were too far away; I wouldn't make it in time. I spied a half-empty beer bottle lying on its side, scooped it up and threw it at the creature. The bottle shattered over the thing's skull, but it was far too distracted by food. The man screamed as the zombie latched onto his throat. The scream bubbled off into a gurgle.

I lowered my shoulder and dived, crashing into the undead, feeling its bones snap beneath papery skin. I rolled to my knees much faster than it did, and with a brutal chop sent the zombie's head spinning away from its neck. My blade came away coated in spider webs and blackened ooze with the consistency of mud. These zombies were far from fresh. I gagged on the stink.

The creatures were everywhere. There must have been fifty in that truck, and already they were multiplying, as some of the tourists' bodies began to convulse. The music was still playing. Fireworks were still erupting. The scene was utter chaos. If we didn't stop these things now, we were going to have a full-fledged outbreak, right in a population center, and that's a nightmare. A nearby girl, obviously stoned out of her mind, began to giggle and point at the sillier looking zombies, oblivious to the other one that was heading right for her. Friggin' stoners. I started toward her.

A hand locked around my injured ankle with a grip like iron. Looking down, I saw the man who had been bitten. He pulled at me, his mouth open, hungry, his brain already dead, his system now overcome with only one impulse . . . food . . . *me*. That was near instantaneous reanimation after death, the sign of a bad strain. "Sorry, dude." I bent over and smashed open the top of his head. I was instantly splattered with brains. After two swings he quit moving. The fresh ones are harder to shut down. The distraction distracted me long enough that by the time I was done, stoner chick was missing her nose. "Damn it!"

There was a gunshot. A security guard had come out from the hotel to see what the commotion was. His eyes were wide, staring as the creatures soaked up bullets and kept coming. One of the shots missed and, thankfully, put the bleating stereo out of commission.

The patio was now quiet except for the moaning of the recently deceased and the screams of the fleeing.

"Shoot them in the head! *Cabeza!*" I shouted, leaping over dead and twitching bodies, running for the hapless guard. "*Despidalos en las cabezas!*" I took the nearest zombie from behind, driving my blade through its dusty throat and wrenching the head aside. The security guard fell to his knees, his hands stretched in front of him as a zombie in a yellowed wedding dress bore down on him. *Too far.* My Ganga Ram was not balanced for throwing, but I hurled it end over end to strike the zombie in the head.

Unfortunately it hit handle first. That got the creature's attention long enough. I reached it as it turned its attention back to the guard, grabbed it by the bottom of its rotting jaw and the top of its head and wrenched the skull until the spine broke and its open eye sockets were staring at me. The zombie flopped to the ground. *Apparently that works too.*

Breathing hard, I picked up my knife. The pool, which now had a definite pink tint to it, was cleared out except for a few zombies wandering around the bottom and a couple of torn bodies bobbing on the surface. Everything that was still alive had run. The remaining original zombies were venturing into the resort, chasing after the scattering crowds, spreading their curse. The recently dead were just starting to rise and would be following shortly. The resort was right on the edge of town, and there were fifty thousand people sleeping down there. This could get real ugly, real fast.

The guard crossed himself as he surveyed the blood-soaked patio. "*Madre de Dios!*" I had to remind myself that regular people were always shocked by how fast the carnage happened. I guess I'd kind of gotten used to it.

"Yeah, okay, if you aren't going to use that..." I retrieved his gun. It was an ancient Smith Military & Police revolver, in obviously neglected condition. I opened the rusty cylinder and ejected the empties. "Um...*cartuchos?*" The guard reached into his pocket with one shaking hand, and dropped six tarnished .38 specials cartridges onto the ground. He got up and ran for the exit. I can't say I blamed him. I knelt down and gathered up the cartridges.

"Z! Look out!" There was a sharp crack of a gunshot and something warm splattered all over my back. The fresh corpse fell onto the patio, skull smashed wide open. "Zombies? How the hell are there zombies?"

"Holly. I'm glad to see you," I answered as I snapped the cylinder shut on the old revolver. Holly Newcastle was running across the tile, rifle in hand, and about half of her armor flapping unbuckled around her torso. "We got a problem."

"Ya think?" she exclaimed, as she turned and mercilessly blasted the rising undead tourists. Holly had certainly become a better shot over the last year. I stuck my fingers in my ears to block out the deafening noise. She had put in her electronic earpieces, but mine were still up in my room. Her .308 Vepr was a loud rifle. "I was down on the beach, saw a bunch of people come out screaming, so I grabbed my stuff. What the hell's going on? Where are the others?" I realized she was wearing nothing but a yellow bikini and flip-flops under her hastily donned vest.

"I don't know." I heard a chattering noise from the street on the other side of the parked truck, a suppressed subgun. "Well, there's Trip. Looks like he's got that end covered." I surveyed the area. There were two other paths out of the pool area between the buildings. "You follow those, I'll go this way. I don't have my radio, so try to raise the others. We've got to take them all before it spreads out of control."

"Got it," she said as she rocked a fresh magazine into her gun. "So how would you tell the locals, Go inside, lock your doors, there are zombies out . . . I knew I should have taken Spanish."

"*Vaya adentro. Cierren sus puertas.* Um . . . didn't exactly cover this in high school . . ." I speak five languages fluently—Spanish isn't one of them. "*Hay muertos andandos afuera.* And one more thing, watch out for an Englishman, blond guy, short hair, mean-looking, dark clothing," I ordered. "If you see him, shoot him a *lot*. And use your flashlight."

"Huh?" I knew that Holly had no moral compunctions about killing anybody, but even she usually needed a reason.

"I'll explain later, but these are his zombies."

"Got it." She turned and ran toward the latest screams.

I went in the other direction, up the stairs, and back into the hotel. The building was nice, new, modern, and up until a few minutes ago, very clean. There was a splattering of fluids, fresh blood, and discarded tissue from the undead staining the carpet. I held the Smith in my right and my kukri in my left as I followed the obvious trail. I kicked myself for not asking Holly if she had a spare gun. My pulse pounded in my head, and I tried to keep scanning every corner, waiting for something to pop out.

I heard a series of loud booms ahead of me, coming

from the direction of the front desk. Somebody had a shotgun. I ran faster, pain throbbing in my twisted ankle with each step. I could hear the hungry moaning. They were right ahead of me.

The undead were clustered together, trying to force their way through the main doors and out into the crowded streets. There were at least a dozen of them, some old, some new, all ugly. A lone uniformed *Federale* stood in their way, blasting them with a pump shotgun. Their bodies were falling, creating a choke point at the entrance. His shotgun clicked empty, and too terrified to notice, he kept on pumping and dry-firing.

I charged the undead from behind. I had no idea how off the sights on the Smith were, so I used it as a contact weapon. *Press muzzle into zombie's head. Pull trigger. Repeat.* One of the six corroded cartridges failed to fire, but another pull of the trigger put my last bullet through the lucky monster's sinuses. Flinging the empty revolver at the head of another zombie, I stepped over the fallen bodies and started swinging away with my knife.

The rearmost creatures moved against me, reaching, chomping, eyes wide. They were new, and only minutes before had been guests of the resort, happy, carefree, normal kids, with normal lives. I shoved those thoughts aside and went about my gruesome business. My knife was heavy, curved. It was designed for taking off limbs, and I put it to work.

*Teeth.* Snapping closed inches from my arms. I reversed my blade and cleaved the jaw off of a zombie with a Chico State tee shirt. I realized I was screaming, bellowing something incomprehensible. The cop had regained his senses enough to reload his shotgun.

He fired and I was concussively sprayed with brains. I stepped aside, hoping not to catch a stray piece of buckshot, and the final zombies followed me, having zeroed in on the scent of my flesh.

There were three of them, and they were piling on top of each other to reach me. I backed away, swinging at anything that presented itself, leaving fingers and the occasional hand on the ground. The zombies didn't seem to notice. My feet slipped on the now sodden carpet and I slid against the check-in desk. Lunging forward, I slammed the tip of my knife through a nasal cavity, and then jumped back as the final two grabbed at me. My knife handle, slick with gore, slipped from my fingers, still lodged in the falling zombie's skull. Now I was really hosed.

I grabbed the desk and vaulted over it, landing painfully on the other side. The zombies flung themselves at the counter and started to wiggle over, their fingers and stumps flailing at me. Lying on my back, I kicked one of the things in the face hard enough to put bone fragments through its brain, launching it back over the counter. I leaned forward, swatted aside the last zombie's arm, avoided the snapping teeth, grabbed it by the side of the head and twisted. The blood-soaked mess was too slippery for a solid grasp, so I shoved my thumbs through the squishy eye sockets for leverage and twisted violently to the side. There was a brutal crunch and the final undead flopped down, twitching.

"I . . . hate . . . zombies . . ." I lay on the floor in a rapidly spreading pool of blood as the last corpse was drained by gravity. The lobby was quiet. The clock on the wall read 12:21. I gradually pushed myself up and glanced over the counter. It looked clear. There was a pile of bodies heaped in the entryway, but none of them had made it to the street. Gunfire could be heard in multiple directions now, so hopefully my team had gotten on the outbreak quick enough to keep it contained. The sucky part now was going to be isolating the bitten survivors. I had to get to my radio.

The Mexican cop stepped gingerly through the shattered window. His Mossberg was shaking and he was hyperventilating. I recognized the feeling, the feeling that a regular person gets when they find out that the world they live in was not really as it was supposed to be. It could be a real bummer. I walked slowly around the counter, my dripping hands open in front of me. I knew that I had to look terrible, covered in all manner of disgusting stuff, and I didn't want him to mistake me for another zombie.

"Hey, *amigo*. I'm a friend," I said calmly.

He looked at me in shock, leveled the muzzle at my chest and pulled the trigger. The click of the firing pin landing on the empty chamber was extremely loud. I jumped about two feet straight up.

"Whoa! I'm human! Easy!" I shouted, raising my hands high. "I'm one of the good guys. *Soy un hombre bueno.*"

He nodded slowly, some comprehension dawning in his shocked eyes. I nodded back. Sirens approached. A green truck with *Policia* on the side screeched to a halt in front of the hotel and men with M-16s jumped out of the back. I looked back to the cop, ready to congratulate him on a job well done, but the last thing I saw was the butt of his shotgun sailing toward my forehead.

# CHAPTER 2

"Do you know what the penalty for having illegal firearms in Mexico are, *Señor* Pitt?"

"Like a million years per bullet?" I responded. The police interrogator shook his head sadly, nodded at his subordinate, and my head snapped back as the junior policeman hit me. He was wearing some sort of weighted leather glove, and it hurt pretty bad. I leaned my head forward and spit blood on the plastic table. Somehow I had managed to cultivate a hobby of being beaten up by law enforcement officers. On the bright side, this guy was a featherweight compared to my old buddy Special Agent Franks. Now that guy knew how to beat a confession out of somebody.

"You are being held on suspicion of murder, *Señor* Pitt. I have over seventy bodies to explain, and somebody *will* be held accountable. I assure you that our justice system is not as lenient as your own." I didn't think that that many tourists had been bitten, so they must be charging me for the original zombies too. I suppose the fact that they had obviously been dead for months wasn't going to help me.

I had no idea where I was, or how long I had been out, having woken up in the back of a truck with a sack tied over my head. Since the air tasted like burning tires, I was guessing that I had been taken inland, and if I had been unconscious long enough, I might even be in Mexico City. The interrogator's English was excellent. He was short, pudgy, with a bad comb-over, but his manner indicated that he was not a man to be trifled with. "Now why did you have multiple firearms and illegal military equipment in your room?"

"About that, any chance I can get some of those guns back? The shotgun and the matching set of .45s? Those have sentimental value...." I went back to the question before he had the chance to signal the other cop to hit me again. "Really, like I already said, contact the consulate. We have written permission from your government. I'm here as an independent security consultant. Our weapons were allowed per the terms of the contract."

"And what exactly was your duty in Mexico?"

"I already told you I'm not at liberty to disclose that." The Mexican government had a policy similar to the United States' official position: Monsters Do Not Exist. The rules are idiotic, but for those of us who made our living cashing in on these governments' bounties for unnatural creatures, we always had to be careful to tiptoe around the truth with the general public. It may have been evil, it may have been stupid, but it was policy. And the people who enforced that policy had no problem shooting people like me if we talked too much. "Just call your superiors. This is all a misunderstanding."

He nodded at the other police officer, and I braced myself for the impact. This time he hit me above the kidney. I grunted. It hurt, but he didn't really drive the fist in there. When you're hitting somebody in the body, you need to punch *through* the target, not at it. *Amateur.*

"We already contacted them." The interrogator took out a pack of cigarettes, shook one out, and lit it with a gold-plated Zippo. "Sadly, they said that they had no knowledge of you, your organization, or why you are here."

It sounded like MHI had just been disavowed. *Not good.* "Well...there's been a mistake then."

"Certainly, merely just a, how would you say? Clerical error." He nodded, and this time I was pelted across the back of my head. At least the guy hitting me was getting some variety. This was bad, very bad. There was no way that the Mexican government had just forgotten about a team of American Monster Hunters. They were going to deny that they had ever contacted us. Better that than to admit there were supernatural creatures on their soil. They were probably already spinning some story to cover up the zombie outbreak and I was willing to bet that my team wasn't going to fit in with the official version of events.

"I can show you our copies of the contract, signed by your state governor. All I need is one phone call."

"I think not. My superiors and the governor's office have already confirmed that they have signed nothing. You are a liar and I'm tiring of this game."

Options were starting to run thin and I didn't want to spend the rest of my life in a Mexican jail. So I guess that meant it was time to see if the interrogator could handle the truth. "Okay, I'll talk."

"I'm waiting."

I gestured with my head at the other cop. It was the best I could do since my forearms and ankles had been zip-tied to the sturdy chair. "Does this guy speak English?"

The interrogator held up his thumb and forefinger. "*Un poco*, a little."

My whole body ached. At least if I could get rid of Cop #2 they'd quit hitting me for a while. "You might want him to wait outside. You don't want what I'm about to tell you to get out, if you know what I mean."

The interrogator slowly exhaled a thick cloud of smoke. The three of us were in a small, plain room. The only furniture was my chair, his chair, and a cheap plastic table. There was a bloody phonebook, a pair of needle-nose pliers, and a five-gallon bucket of water sitting in the corner. I didn't want to guess what those were for. Finally he gestured for the younger cop to leave. I heard the snap of a crisp salute, and then the opening and closing of the door behind me.

"Any chance we can settle this with some good old-fashioned bribery?" I asked. "My company's very generous."

"*Mordida?* Maybe if I only had one or two bodies. But this many? And half of them Americans? I'm afraid not. You see, someone must be executed for this. Tell me what I want to know, and it might not be you."

"Gotcha. Figured as much, but you never know until you ask. I didn't think you had the death penalty here."

He shrugged. "There is the *unofficial* death penalty. So let us continue, *Señor* Pitt. Who are you?"

"I work for a company called Monster Hunter International. We're based out of Alabama. We specialize in discreetly handling monster-related problems." He stared at me blankly. "Monsters...For example we were paid to come here to deal with a pack of goat-suckers."

"Chupacabras?" he asked slowly.

"Yes. A few weeks ago, some hikers were killed at the resort, and once those things taste people, they don't go back. We were hired because it was thought more deaths would be detrimental to tourism." I suppose a massive zombie attack rendered that a moot point. "The company I work for is considered the best in the world when it comes to dealing with things like this."

"I see...and the reason that I have never heard of this is..." His voice betrayed no emotion.

"Government-mandated secrecy. Those of us who have monster experience are usually warned by the authorities to keep our mouths shut. That has been the policy for forever. If the regular population were to know that all of the stuff from the myths, and the fairy tales, and the bad movies was real, well, you can imagine the panic and the trouble it would cause."

"And you believe this?"

I paused. I didn't know if he asked if I believed in the government's policies, or if I believed in what I was just telling him. I decided to run with the first option. "No, I think the policy is stupid. People should know the truth. Instead, to keep the problem in check, most governments have some sort of system to keep the unnatural populations down. In my country there is a bounty system administered by the Treasury Department. It's called PUFF."

"Puff?"

"Perpetual Unearthly Forces Fund. It pays money to any private citizen who kills a monster on the PUFF list. My company specializes in working the PUFF list, and also in private contracts from municipalities, companies, and private individuals, like your wealthy resort owners. See, lots of important people know about monsters, but they have to keep it on the down low, if you know what I mean. So they call people like us. Let's see, PUFF was started by Teddy Roosevelt, uh . . . he was our president back in—"

"I know who Theodore Roosevelt was. I attended UCLA."

"Go Trojans," I said.

"You're thinking of the wrong school." He sighed and rubbed his temple with his fingers. "Please continue . . ."

"I guess you don't want to hear the history of professional Monster Hunting . . ."

He casually examined the end of his burning cigarette. "No, I really want to know about last night." He glanced absently at his watch. "Fourteen hours ago. What happened at the hotel. There were many deaths, and I wish to know why."

"That was not our doing."

"I have witnesses who saw you chopping people up with a machete."

"Those weren't people. Those were zombies."

"Zombies . . ."

"Yes. The walking dead. The man who created them, the man you are looking for is an Englishman."

I proceeded to give him a rough description of the real villain. I didn't know what the Englishman was, but he'd been there for me, which meant that the carnage at the hotel was partially my fault. "Bastard works for the Old Ones," I muttered under my breath.

"What is an Old One, *Señor* Pitt?" The interrogator casually reached under his chair and pulled out a manila file folder.

Screw it. It was obvious he thought I was nuts, might as well give him a good reason. I just needed to stay in one piece long enough for my team to find me. "They're a race of ancient creatures. Evil and ugly."

He pulled an ornate pen from his pocket and began to make notes in the folder. "And how will we know when we find these Old Ones?"

My father had always warned me that I didn't know when to shut up. "The real thing? They're hard to miss. The ones you have to worry about are their servants. Last summer..." I caught myself.

"Last summer what?"

I shrugged. He already thought I was a complete whackadoo, so what did I have to lose? Crazy prisoners probably got their own cells. I was guessing that you wouldn't stick them out with the regular population. "Remember last summer, with the missing five minutes?"

"Yes," he replied. Of course he did. Everybody on Earth had experienced it. Five minutes of time had been erased as if they had never existed. It had caused a global panic. People had instantly found themselves where they had been five minutes before, but with the memory of what had transpired during that missing time still intact. Pandemonium ensued.

Thousands had been born twice, others had died twice, and others still, like myself, had died, only to have those moments erased to be given another chance.

"That was caused by the Old Ones. Last summer, one of their minions arranged for them to break into this world."

"And did these . . . Old Ones . . . succeed?"

I snorted. "Of course not. If they had, you would have known it. But that rift in time, the missing five minutes, was caused by somebody screwing around with one of their ancient artifacts." I didn't mention that that had been me, or that apparently I was the only human in the world with the ability to do so. They had manipulated me in the hopes that I would open the door for them, and they had almost succeeded.

The interrogator leaned back heavily in his chair. "Scientists are now saying that it had something to do with solar radiation. Increased activity causing a distortion in the atmosphere, along with psychological delusions of missing time caused by imbalances in our brain chemistry."

"Yeah, I saw that on the Discovery Channel too, but I'm telling you, it was the Old Ones. That was no delusion. Those things are out there, and they are some bad mothers. This guy with the zombies, he works for them, and if he works for them, then we've got a serious problem on our hands."

"Do we?" He continued writing. From my zip-tied vantage point, I couldn't see what his notes said, but I was sure that it was something to the effect that I was totally screwed and was going to be enjoying a long stay in the Mexican penal system.

"Yes. They'll stop at nothing to get what they want.

Those undead you had crawling all over that resort were a joke compared to what these things can whip up." He cocked his head to the side and studied me intently. I could tell that I had lost him, but at least they weren't hitting me with that phonebook. "Talk to a doctor, take a look at those bodies. They've been dead for a lot longer than a day, but they were moving around. I'm sure you have plenty of witnesses to that. You do a little looking, and you can probably find the cemetery where all those bodies were stolen from."

He clicked his pen and dropped it back in his pocket. "I don't know how you dug up all of those corpses and spread them out like you did, but let me assure you, *Señor* Pitt, pretending to be insane will not get you off in this country. I have had enough of your nonsense. You disgust me, and your fairy tales will not save you. You are nothing but a filthy murderer, and you think that you can come here and spin these ridiculous lies? Do you think we are stupid?" He stood, adjusted his tie, and spit in my face. I could not move my arm to wipe it away, and I could feel it slowly drip down my forehead and into my eyes. The beating was one thing, but that was too much. If I hadn't been tied to the chair, I would have broken the interrogator in half. The door opened behind me and other policemen entered the room. The interrogator switched back to Spanish, but I could understand him relatively well.

"I've had enough for today. We'll work on him again in the morning. Put this piece of shit in Section Six with the other animals. Let them teach him some humility."

◆          ◆          ◆

Section Six was one large room, subdivided into a bunch of ten-foot-square pens, each enclosed with thick iron bars and chain-link fencing. There was a path between the pens where the guards patrolled with truncheons ready. Small naked bulbs dangled in each alley. There were two sets of cots in each cell, with anywhere from five to seven prisoners shoved into each. My cell had all of the comforts of home, including a bucket, and not much else. You can guess what the bucket was for.

It was dark, and it stunk of sweat, and fear, and violence. I don't think that Amnesty International ever spent much time in this place. I sat cross-legged in the corner of one of the cells. The four other men who shared my tiny space sat across from me, glaring sullenly. Section Six seemed to be where they kept all of the badasses, lunatics, and that general selection of humanity that you just didn't invite to the church picnic. There were incoherent cries and shouts all across the large space. It was not exactly pleasant.

A stocky man with one milky eye, and missing an ear, whispered to his buddy in Spanish. "You think he understands us?"

"I don't know...he don't look too smart," answered the prettier of the two, an obese man with a spider web tattooed across his face. "Look at him. He's got to be messed up in the head. He just keeps staring at us."

The reason I was staring at them was because I had to really concentrate to understand what they were saying. I had practiced up on my Spanish before taking this trip. I have a gift for languages, but the gutter slang these guys spoke was terrible by any standard. I could keep up, barely. Strangely enough, having magically learned archaic Portuguese last summer was really helping.

"They said he was an American."

"He ain't one of us, so I don't care," said the third, a skinny guy who sounded like he had tuberculosis. "Soon as he goes to sleep, I'm gonna shiv him good."

"Jorge, now why are you gonna go and do that?"

Jorge shrugged. "I like stabbing people."

"I don't know, man. He's one big dude. Look at him. That ain't no regular American who got drunk in some whorehouse and wound up here. That dude is gonna tear you up, man. He's got muscles like a *luchador*."

I just kept glaring. I figured my best bet was to appear as mean as possible. A wise old gunfighter had once told me that if you looked like food, you were going to get eaten, and I really didn't want to end up as prison food.

My body ached, and I was in a really foul mood. They had not even treated my cuts from when I had jumped off the balcony, and they were now big grisly scabs that I was sure were going to end up infected. My left ankle was badly swollen, the little puncture in my heel was driving me nuts, and most embarrassingly, after I had been squirted down with a fire hose and had lice poison dumped on me, the biggest set of prison clothes they had for me were about two sizes too small. Not a lot of 4X convicts in Mexico, apparently. The last thing you want to do when you are already in a bad mood is try to wear pants that are too tight.

"I'm telling you, man, I think he understands us. Look at those eyes. He's crazy pissed."

"See, that's why I need to hurry up and shiv him."

"Jorge, he's gonna rip your balls off."

"Shut up, Mateo, quit being such a wimp."

My options were rather limited. I was in jail. The Mexican government was denying that they had given me permission to be here with enough munitions to arm a small rebellion. I had no idea where my team was, or what shape they were in, or even if they had all survived the outbreak. There was some sort of crazy shadow freak out looking to snag me for the Old Ones. I hadn't been offered a lawyer or a phone call, so I doubted that MHI knew where I was either. And the lice powder really itched.

"What do you think, Esteban?" asked Spider Web Face.

The last man looked up from his bunk. He was older, and had obviously been through some rough times. He had scars all along his face and arms, his hair was gray and long, and his skin had the texture of leather. I knew that he had to be somebody special, since he got his own bunk, and none of this band of thugs messed with him. He studied me silently, and the others waited for him to pass judgment.

Finally he spoke, not to them, but rather to me, loud enough that everyone could hear. "I heard from one of the guards, you hacked up like a hundred people with a machete, arms and legs and heads everywhere, even ate some of them. Killed some cops too. Burned a hotel down. Took twenty *Federales* to take you out...You speak Spanish?"

"*Un poco.*"

"I figured you did." He put his head back down.

"Oh shit, man," said Jorge. "I was just kidding

about the shiv thing. You know, mess with the new guy and all that."

I gave Jorge my most menacing look. He cowered back into the corner. Now, most people would not react well to being put into the ultraviolent, dog-eat-dog world that was a prison full of murderers and psychopaths, but hey, I'd killed a werewolf with my bare hands. I figured that I would fit in just fine here.

"Say, Esteban," I asked over the shouting from the next cell. "Where are we?"

"You don't know?" His eyes peeked out from under his mane of hair. I could tell he was a sharp one.

"Nah ... I was pretty worn out from chopping up all those people. You know how it is." If you have a rep, you might as well run with it.

"You're in Tijira Prison. This, my friend, is a very bad place."

"I've seen worse," I lied.

"I'm sure you have. Me personally, I'm here because I avenged my wife's honor against the filthy tyrants, but alas, I failed. May God rest her soul," he said solemnly. Some of the thugs crossed themselves.

"Sorry to hear that."

Without skipping a beat he switched to English. "Naw, just pulling your leg. I'm from San Diego. I was flying coke across the border, got back to TJ, didn't have enough to pay the right people, and they stuck me in here rather than just shooting me. Some days I wish they would have just killed me and got it over with. These morons here think I'm Zorro or something so they leave me alone. If a Yankee wants to survive in here, you need a reputation, so I'll back you up, you back me up."

"Good deal." I held out my hand. He reached over and shook it with a firm grip. "Owen Zastava Pitt."

"Zapato? Like a shoe?"

"No, Zastava. It's Serbian."

"You don't look Serbian."

In other words, I was way too brown. "I'm a little bit of everything." That much was true. I always checked the Other box on any official type forms. "Look, Esteban..."

"You can call me Steve, the Esteban thing is for these guys." He nodded his head at the other criminals. "The story is that I shot it out with the cops and the army to avenge them burning my village or something. If you don't get respect in here, you don't last long."

"Okay, Steve, my company will get me out of here. We're worth a lot of money, and can get the best lawyers. I just need to survive long enough for that to happen, so I appreciate the help. You scratch my back, I scratch yours, know what I mean?"

"That's cool. I'm still waiting for trial myself. I haven't even been arraigned yet. I'm hoping I get my turn in front of the judge before too long."

"How long have you been here?"

He looked up at the ceiling as he gave it some thought.

"Three years come June."

A cold weight settled into the bottom of my stomach. "No kidding?"

"No kidding. Welcome to Tijira."

They had taken my watch, but I guessed that it was about 9 P.M. when the guards killed most of the lights in Section Six. Steve, or Esteban as the local fauna knew him, and I were still talking quietly, me to pass the nervous time, and him because I was the first other American he had seen in a year. The previous guy had lasted all of thirty minutes before somebody had decided they didn't particularly like gringos in their jail. Steve said that it had taken weeks for the bloodstains to fade. He was a nice enough guy for a prison-hardened drug smuggler, and talking to him sure beat talking to One Ear, Jorge, or Spider Web.

"So, Owen, you got a wife?"

"Nope, but I'm engaged."

"That's great. What's she like?"

I tried to make myself more comfortable on the bug-ridden cot. Since I was now the new boss of this cell, I got the luxury accommodations. Sometimes being a muscle-bound behemoth paid dividends. Poor One Ear had to sleep on the floor now. "She's awesome. Smart, funny, tough, brave. Her name's Julie. Julie Shackleford."

"Is she hot?"

"Dude . . . please."

"Sorry, but I've kind of been in jail for a while," he explained. "It's been so damn long since I've seen a woman . . ." He trailed off. I just hoped that MHI hurried up and found me soon. I did not sign on to this gig to end up spending my golden years in a place like this. "So what's she look like?" he asked as he lay back on his bunk and closed his eyes. I admit, I could have been offended, but more than anything, I just felt pity.

"Well, she's pretty," I answered. That was an understatement. I had been infatuated with her since the day that we had met. Julie was the best thing that had ever happened to me, and almost losing her had been the worst. "Real tall for a girl, actually. Kind of buff; she works out a lot. Long brown hair, has the prettiest brown eyes I've ever seen, wears glasses..."

"Chicks with glasses are hot."

"I'm with you there, bro, I'm with you there. In fact, she's probably out there looking for me right now."

"Here? In Mexico?"

"Of course. She's a Monster Hunter too."

"Look, I already said that I would back you on the whole crazy-machete-killer thing. You don't need to keep up the monster movie shtick."

I laughed out loud. Tubercular Jorge grumbled at me from his corner. "I wasn't joking. She's a Hunter, and she's good, real good. On the business end, she does most of our contract negations, and she's a real expert when it comes to monster lore. On the operational side she's our team sharpshooter. I've seen her plug a lindwyrm through the eyestalk from a moving helicopter. And tell you what, she can run a pistol like you wouldn't believe. Anyways, I'm a lucky guy. Somehow I've got a Southern belle, sniper, art babe to fall in love with me. I don't know how I pulled that off." That much was true. I still couldn't figure out exactly how a blundering schlub like me had managed to impress somebody like her.

Julie had been one of the first Hunters that I had met. She had come to my home to recruit me while I was still recovering from my initial monster encounter. It had been love at first sight. For me at least. Thankfully, she had come around eventually. All I had had to do was take on all the armies of evil and save the world to impress her.

"Sounds like you guys make a...interesting couple."
Steve sounded slightly nervous.

"In fact she's been doing this way longer than I
have. The company is a family business, her grandpa
is the CEO. They've been into this for over a hundred
years now. She was born for it. Killing monsters is
what the Shacklefords eat, sleep, live and breathe."

"Sounds like you have some psycho in-laws."

There was a long uncomfortable pause as I thought
about what to say. I rubbed the huge welt on my
forehead from the shotgun butt. How would I describe
my soon-to-be relatives?

"Oh, touched a nerve, I see."

"You have no idea," I muttered. If there was an
international award for who had the worst mother-in-
law, I would be a sure winner. "Her parents used to be
Hunters too, really good people from what I understand,
but...ah hell, you wouldn't believe me if I told you."

"Oh come on, like I believe any of your crap anyway."

"Never mind them. Let's just say that they're pure
evil now."

"They can't be that bad. I'm sure over time you
guys will be able to work out your differences."

"I wouldn't bet on it," I responded. I rolled over
on my side as something that felt suspiciously like a
centipede crawled between my shoulder blades.

The few remaining light bulbs flickered a few
times then died. A murmur rose from the prisoners.
"Power's out again," Steve stated the obvious. There
was an electric wailing sound in the distance, high-
pitched and whiny. It sounded three times and then
died abruptly. "Guess not. That's the alarm." Steve
rose from his cot and went to the bars. All the other

men were moving as well. Anything that broke the monotony of Section Six was a major deal for them. "Something's up."

I sat up. "What's going on?"

"I don't know, man." He turned to rapid-fire Spanish and ordered the thugs to quiet down. They sullenly obeyed.

The room was very dark. I felt a tinge of fear. Maybe the shadow man had come back for me. There were only a few small windows set high in the walls of the large space, but the moon was fat and bright tonight, so some pale light was spilling down in beams. I scanned the bars. I could see the movement of men in the other cages, stalking, curious, nervous.

*Gunfire.*

I stood. If I knew anything in this world, I knew guns, and that was the sharp crack of a high-powered rifle. Then another, and another, then the gun was silent.

"Somebody trying to break out?" Jorge asked as he absently scratched himself. "Don't sound like he made it too far."

It was quiet. Even the crazies who had been blubbering constantly had shut up.

"Man, nobody makes it over the wall here. Poor fool," One Ear said.

More gunfire. Now there were other rifles, some of them crackling through long bursts of full-auto, and the thumping of shotguns. A flashlight briefly illuminated the cell and then swung wildly away as a guard sprinted past us. The prisoners began to yell at him, but he just kept running until the flashlight disappeared as he left the room.

Could it be Julie and my team, come to rescue me? No way. Not like this. We killed monsters. We tried real hard not to hurt people. If they knew I was here, the rescue would involve lawyers and bribery, not guns. Something else was going on. It had to be the guy from the hotel.

"Anybody got a light?" I shouted. "A lighter, a flashlight, anything."

"Huh?"

"Something that can make light. Sparks, fire, I don't care. Anything."

Jorge held up a lighter. "It'll cost you." He smiled maliciously.

I was across the cell in an instant. He tried to move his hand back, but I locked onto his wrist. He tried to struggle so I wrapped my other hand around the precious lighter. I broke his thumb as I yanked it free. He squealed.

"Shut it!" I shouted. I turned to Steve. His eyes were very wide in the moonlight. "Whatever happens, stay calm. If you see some freaky shit, stay calm. If a great big shadow comes to get me, use this." I pressed the lighter into his hand. "Wait 'til he comes in our cell. His attention will be on me. Just flick it on. Then I can hit him. Understand?"

"What are you talking about?" The gunfire was becoming more sporadic, as if there were fewer guards left able to shoot. There were several pops from a small caliber pistol, seemingly just outside in the hallway leading into Section Six. Somebody in the hall began to scream. I snapped my head in that direction. The scream tapered off into a gurgle and then nothing.

"Just do it." I stepped back from Steve and oriented

myself toward the entrance, preparing for battle. There was no way I was getting taken to the Old Ones. I rotated my head and cracked the vertebrae in my neck. My adrenaline was beginning to flow, my breathing unconsciously quickening, filling my blood with extra oxygen. My vision tunneled in on the gray shape of the door, and the sounds of the room seemed to become muted. Outwardly I was calm. Inside I was terrified. If the shadow man came for me here, I had nowhere to run.

The others were worried now. They knew that something was horribly amiss. I heard prayers coming from men who looked like they had not spoken to God in a very long time. The temperature began to drop. Section Six had been warm and humid. It came so suddenly that it took precious seconds for my mind to recognize the brutal, unnatural cold. My breath hissed out as steam in the moonlight. The other men in my cell began to unconsciously crowd in the corner away from the entrance.

The heavy iron door that secured Section Six creaked open on rusted hinges. A hush fell over the room. A lone figure stepped into the blue moonlight. High heels clicked on the concrete floor. I could make out a familiar feminine shape silhouetted in the faint light, and for a split second I thought it was Julie. Tall, perfectly proportioned, shapely, but the supernatural cold told me I was wrong. A larger figure entered the room behind the woman. A broad-shouldered man, almost as tall as me.

"Oh no," I said with much greater volume than I intended.

"Owen, what the hell's going on?" Steve was terrified,

and he was hard to understand over the chattering of his teeth. The temperature had dropped to near freezing.

Approaching, they passed directly under one of the windows. I was right. It was *them*. The woman started toward my cell, walking delicately down the path between the cages. She was achingly beautiful, perfect. But sex appeal to a vampire was like one of those deep ocean fish with the bioluminescent light bulbs dangling over their jaws, just an efficient way to catch their prey. The heels continued to click. The brute glided silently behind her. I didn't take my eyes off of the approaching pair. "Remember when I told you about my in-laws?"

Steve nodded quickly in the dark.

"They're here."

Some poor idiot who hadn't seen a woman in decades made a horrible mistake. Unable to control himself with the ethereal beauty passing before him, he opened his big stupid mouth. The language was such profane slang that I couldn't have translated it even if I had been able to understand the lowest level of gutter Spanish.

Susan Shackleford paused before answering the man. "You'd like that, wouldn't you?" Her Southern accent was obvious, her voice perfect. When she smiled I could see the white of her teeth. Chills ran down my spine.

"Yeah, *puta*, I show you good time!" Some of his buddies whooped for him. These guys must have already forgotten the hundreds of rounds of gunfire that had just been expended. Well, it wasn't the cream of the intellectual crop that ended up in places like this.

The big figure stopped. "That's my wife you're talkin' about, asshole." In the poor light, it was hard to tell what happened next. The prisoner was standing in the center of his cell, well out of reach from the bars. Yet somehow Ray Shackleford reached through the tight barrier, grabbed him by the neck, and pulled the prisoner *through* the bars. Iron bent and bones shattered. The man screamed in agony before his heart exploded as it was jerked through the two-inch gap. He ended up dangling a few feet above the ground, mangled top half in the alleyway, pelvis and kicking legs still inside the cell. A puddle began to widen under the twitching corpse.

"Thank you, honey. That was downright chivalrous."

"You're welcome, dear."

The population of Section Six exploded. Everyone surged against the far corners of their cells, pushing against bars or chain link. Dozens of voices rose into the night air, panic, confusion, terror.

"Y'all be QUIET!" Ray bellowed. I involuntarily covered my ears as the shockwave hit. His voice shook the building. Dust fell from the ceiling.

Now there was only whimpering and crying. The prisoners knew that something terribly inhuman was in their presence. The vampires approached slowly. "Owen. Good to see you again." Susan smiled at me. Her eyes seemed to glow pale in the dark.

"Heya, kid. How's it hanging?" Ray waved.

"Susan . . . Ray . . ." I nodded at them. Every joint in my body ached with fear. I was a dead man, or worse. Much worse.

I had fought Susan twice before. Both times I had been lucky to escape with my life. She was a Master vampire, strongest of all the undead. The first time we had squared off she had taken a twenty-second burst from a flamethrower and a direct hit with a grenade, and had walked away. The second time she had only been turned aside by the faith of Milo Anderson. Compared to Milo, my faith sucked. She could move faster than the human eye could track, tear a man's head off with her pinky finger, and I had personally put half a dozen silver shotgun slugs through her skull with no effect. If Susan wanted to kill me, there wasn't a damn thing that I could do about it.

Steve began to flick the lighter.

"What, you want an encore or something?" Ray laughed. "'Freebird'! Whoo!"

"If you've come for me, I'm not going down without a fight," I snarled.

"You've got *cojones*, kid," Ray said. "I'll give you that. See, dear, I told you he was a good match for Julie. She always had the best killer instinct of our kids." He gestured at me. I had only known Ray for a brief time, and that had been after I had sprung him from an insane asylum. The last time that I had seen Ray he had still been human, barely alive, and rapidly bleeding to death from the savage wound Susan had inflicted on him, so I had to admit that he looked a lot better now. "If we wanted to off you, we would've done it already."

"Wrong. You can't come into a home if you aren't invited. And this is currently my home," I said as I gestured around my cell. Though many of their limitations were a mystery, I knew that at least some of the vampire legends were true. "So back off!" I ordered with a lot more confidence than I felt.

Susan sighed. She approached the bars and leaned against them. It was shocking how much she looked like her daughter, only Susan was inhumanly perfect. Her fingernails were painted bright red and showed up like beacons in the dark. I took an involuntary step back. "Owen, honey, don't lawyer up on me now." She absently flicked one finger towards Jorge. Her piercing eyes didn't waver from mine. "Can I come in?"

The prisoner gasped as she invaded his mind with all the subtlety of a battering ram. His eyes rolled back into his head and he began to convulse violently. I started toward him, but I was too late. "*Si!*" he sputtered, then toppled over, dead.

"See? If you weren't so damn obstinate he'd still be alive. No great loss, weak mind, easily controlled, and so disease ridden I wouldn't have drunk him if I was starving." She drew her long fingers away from the bars, and then slowly pushed her face against the iron. She seemed to compress into the space. The gap was only a few inches across, but Susan slid through easily. She stepped into the cell and then casually brushed the dust from her skin-tight dress.

One Ear screamed like a little girl.

I waited for her to make her move, though realistically if I even saw her coming it was only because she wanted to play with her food. Susan looked down at one of the cots in disgust, shrugged, then sat on it. She crossed her legs, briefly showing off entirely too much thigh, and placed her hands on her knees. Ray frowned.

"Sit. We need to talk."

I looked at her stupidly.

She gestured at the other cot. "I ain't here to hurt you. I'm here with a business proposition."

"You've got to be kidding me...." I said.

Susan's gaze did not waver. "Ray, you told me he

was smarter than he looks." She began to absently drum her fingers on her knee, impatient.

"He is, but it takes him a minute to warm up." Ray folded his arms and leaned against one of the other cells. The hardened prisoners huddled in the far corner. Ray assessed them like I would size up steaks in the meat department. "Hey, honey, how about Mexican for dinner?"

"Sure, just pick a good one.... Look, Owen, I promised a truce, and I'm good for it. You didn't come looking for me, and I can respect that. I'm prepared to leave you and my precious daughter alone, just like I said before. That isn't why I'm here. Please sit. We don't have much time before their reinforcements arrive and you don't want to force me to kill a bunch more innocents. Do you?"

I backed up and slowly sat, careful to keep my eyes on her the whole time. Susan Shackleford emanated predatory danger. Every instinct in my body screamed for me to fight or flee. I tried to steady my voice. "Okay...."

"So how've you been?" she asked, trying to sound casual. Was it possible that this was awkward for her too? I never really wondered if the undead had societal niceties. Apparently Southern politeness really did die hard. "Wedding still on for August?"

"Yep. We're fine. So how are you guys? Still dead and evil? Ray still insane?"

"No, he's much better now." She uncrossed her long legs and leaned forward, pouting. "So much for being pleasant."

"Pleasant would be you doing us all a favor and going for a long walk on a sunny day."

"Kid," Ray growled. "Your terminal smart-assitude is starting to piss me off. You better show a little more respect."

He had a point. "It isn't anything personal. We don't want anything to do with you. Leave me alone."

Susan sighed. "Fine. Let's cut to the chase. I want to hire MHI. I've got a job for you to do."

My mouth dropped open. "Serious?"

"Duh. You think I came to this shit hole for fun? I'm serious. Not hiring MHI as much as hiring you in particular. And this is a mutually beneficial arrangement. The man, or used-to-be-a-man, that attacked you yesterday, I want to help you destroy him."

That didn't make sense. "Why?"

"He's your enemy. He's trying to suck up to the Old Ones, so he means to deliver you to the Dread Overlord itself."

I licked my lips. "Susan, last time we met, *you* were a servant of the Old Ones."

"Wrong. I owe no loyalty to those things. Jaeger forced me to serve Lord Machado. I was as much of a pawn as you were. When you killed Jaeger and his boss, I was freed from their servitude. I serve only myself now. I hated those crusty ancient bastards."

"Right. . . . You're no ordinary vamp, Susan. We both know that. You're too young to be a Master, but you are. Somehow you became way stronger than you should be, and I think I know how." From my own experience with the Old Ones' magic, I knew the kind of gifts and curses that they could bestow.

"Owen, you're an idiot. Don't strain yourself thinking so hard." Just for a moment, the turn of her head, the sound of her voice, it was almost as if I was speaking with Julie, but with a hiss, it was gone. She waved her hands dismissively. "Sure, I'm powerful, more powerful than the dusty old vampires that came before me. The decrepit coots should never have turned a Monster Hunter into a vampire. The source of my power is my business, but I give you my word that I'm not with the Old Ones. My offer is to help you... and in so doing, help myself."

"Why? What's in it for you?"

"That guy after you? He's a necromancer, a wizard with powers over the undead," Susan said.

"Even you?"

"Perhaps, but I'm not in a particular hurry to find out. I've been a slave before, and I don't intend to let that happen again. He's building an army, and I don't feel like getting drafted. Basically, this necromancer is a threat to me, to all the independent dead."

I snorted. "Even more than MHI? If I recall correctly, we kicked your ass pretty good last time."

"Wrong again. Goody-two-shoes Milo banished me last time. If we tangle again, I'm taking him out first, and he won't see me coming. So don't push it unless you want his blood on your hands too."

That made me furious. I clenched my teeth. *Nobody* threatens my friends.

"Just so you know, when you get angry, you broadcast your thoughts like you had a loudspeaker. Try anything stupid and I'll just kill you and save the necromancer the trouble. Relax, Ray," Susan said soothingly to her husband. Ray must have heard my thoughts, as he had silently moved up to the bars. He moved just on the other side, like a lion at the zoo. He didn't look as disheveled and crazy as when he was human, but now his square face was drawn, angry, and extremely dangerous. He was as protective of his wife in death as he had been in life. Whereas Susan was cold and calculating, the newly undead and far-less-powerful Ray was barely restrained crazy bottled in room-temperature flesh. I forced myself to calm down before Ray pulled me through the bars like the earlier prisoner.

"That's better. Now listen close," Susan ordered. "After our little altercation last summer, you drew the attention of the boss king of the Old Ones itself. That's quite a feat for a mere blood bag. You're a marked man now. This guy trying to kill you? He thinks popping you will score him big points. If he brings you in, he'll be rewarded with all sorts of power. And that's bad news."

*She's scared of him.* "For you and me both."

"As much as it pains me to admit it, yeah."

This whole thing was unsettling. Only a fool would trust a vampire. Ray was still glowering at me. The other prisoners were whimpering and trying to hide. What she was saying made sense in a way. If she was working with the shadow man, it wasn't like she needed any elaborate hoax to catch me. "How about you tell me who he is and where to find him?"

Susan shook her head. "I'm still working on that. I've got some suspicions, and you'll be the first to know if I'm right. But you ain't ready to face him yet. His magic makes him untouchable."

"So how do I beat him? I'm all about killing stuff."

"What? I'm supposed to do all the work?" Susan's sultry laugh was creepy. "I don't know exactly. You'll need to figure that out yourself."

"Well, fat lot of good you vampires are."

"Stuff it." She reached into the fold of her dress and produced a small white handkerchief. "As you surely know by now, since you survived Koriniha's little test, you're a very special man, Owen. Only one human born every five hundred years has the gifts you do. I know more about you than you do about yourself. Ray has been doing research again . . ."

"Last time he did that he almost sucked Alabama into another dimension. You sure you want to let him do that?"

"Hey, I'm a pro," Ray said, in mock embarrassment. "I was still learning then."

Susan ignored us. "He thinks you'll be able to destroy the necromancer. You have abilities beyond your understanding." She unwrapped the small package and dropped a tiny object into her palm. Her bright red nails curled around it like a Venus flytrap. "I'm going to give you a present, a little something to unlock your true potential. That way when you face the Old Ones' pet magician again, you'll be able to finish him and do us both a favor. Understand?"

"What is it?" I asked hesitantly. I knew a little bit about my abilities, and though I didn't understand them, I knew enough to be deathly afraid of them.

She opened her hand. There was a tiny sliver in her palm, a rock chip. It began to emit a faint glow, reflecting on her pale skin. Then it seemed to pulse as a bit of living darkness flashed across it. Recoiling, I fell off the bed and crashed into the bars. I pushed against one of the prisoners and whoever it was scurried away from me.

"Keep it away!" I shouted. I don't know how she got a piece of Koriniha's artifact, but I recognized it immediately for what it was. I *felt* it. The *Kumaresh Yar*. It existed before our world. It exists to destroy our world, but to be used to its full potential, it needs to be activated by someone like me. And now a piece of it was here, dangerously close.

I was shaking. "You don't know how dangerous it is, to everybody, everything. I can't use that thing. I'll kill us all."

"Don't worry. This is only a small fragment. Ray's worked some spells on it, so it should be safe . . . mostly. I'm gonna use this to help you," Susan said. I blinked and she was standing, hovering over me, the tiny shard of the dreaded artifact of the Old Ones held out like a talisman only inches away. "Ray's research says that this probably won't kill you, but it will put you in touch with a little bit of that power you experienced before. The last thing I want to do is make a Hunter stronger, but you're my best bet to get rid of this necromancer."

Ray suddenly twitched, looking at the ceiling. "Better hurry, dear. We've got company coming. Sounds like the Feds."

"I hear them," she answered. She pushed the shard toward my forehead. I tried to swat her arm away. I might as well have been hitting the bars of the cell. I shoved as hard as I could, but she was far stronger than I was. She ignored the flying fists, intent on her mission. "Don't worry, honey, this won't hurt a bit."

"No!" The tiny chunk of the *Kumaresh Yar* touched my skin. The world exploded in pain. Black lightning crackled across Section Six and sparked across the chain link. It was as if someone had driven a glowing-hot ice pick through my brain, and then twisted until it pierced out the base of my skull. I screamed as a cascade of strange visions tore through my mind, pummeling me with disjointed alien memories.

Something inside of me woke up.

Fueled by the artifact, I struck Susan. This time it had the desired effect. She flew back and crashed into the bars. The pain and pressure subsided. I rolled onto my side, limp, eyelids heavy, barely able to breathe.

"Hot damn!" Susan exclaimed. She had left a human-shaped impression in the iron. Most of the prisoners were openly crying for their mothers now. The last of the rampant black electricity dissipated, but left a smell in the air like a chemical fire. Susan rotated her neck and arms as the bones knit back together. "That was unexpected."

"Told you it would work," Ray said smugly. "Now let's go. Feds are almost here, and I ain't up to taking on somebody like Agent Franks."

Susan held up one hand to silence her husband. She rewrapped the shard and put it away. I no longer had the strength to hold up my head, and it slowly flopped to the concrete. I watched as her high heels clicked toward me. She stopped and squatted down. I felt her nails caress the back of my neck. She bent down and her cold lips pressed against my ear. Her voice was barely a whisper. "One last thing. The thing that saved Julie, the Guardian's mark on her neck. You know that it'll eventually kill her, don't you? It's from the other side, where everything comes with a price. When that time comes, my earlier offer stands. When either of you is ready for immortality, call my name and I'll be there. That's what family is for."

I struggled to keep my eyes open. So weak . . . so

very cold. I could barely move. Susan kissed me gently on the top of my head.

"So what about dinner?" Ray sounded petulant.

"This one here smells disease-free. Grab him. Let's go."

The last thing I heard before the darkness came was Steve screaming for somebody to help him.

My strength gradually returned. Feeling tingled back into my limbs. Fighting back waves of nausea and dizziness, I pushed myself to my hands and knees. *What had Susan done to me?* The bars of my cell had been bent wide open so Ray could extract Steve alive. Perhaps if I hurried, a part of me thought, maybe I could save him. The logical part of my brain already knew the truth. He was long gone. The temperature was already returning to normal.

One Ear grabbed me by the arm. "The devil took him! Poor Esteban. You brought this on us!" He cocked one meaty fist back to pummel me. I was too weak to defend myself. The prisoner flinched as a shot rang out. Plaster dust rained down from the ceiling. One Ear raised his open hands over his head as multiple flashlight beams converged on us.

"I may not speak the language, but I'm assuming a 10mm into the ceiling is pretty universal for *cut it out*." The voice spoke in clearly enunciated English.

Squinting into the super-bright weapon-mounted lights, I could make out several dark shapes. "Myers? Is that you?"

"I'm afraid so. You're coming with us, Pitt. Consider yourself extradited. Okay, men, fall back. Watch out, vampires on premises."

Gloved hands grabbed me by each arm and dragged me out of the cell. Flashlight beams stabbed in every direction as more armed men formed a perimeter around me. Their uniforms consisted of black body armor and every bit of high-tech tactical gear known to man. Feds. Not *Federales*, but rather United States federal agents, specifically the men of the Monster Control Bureau of the U.S. Department of Justice. Deadly professionals, every last one, and you would be hard pressed to find a bigger bunch of assholes.

"Pitt, what's your status?" Special Agent Myers snapped. Unlike the other Feds, Myers was wearing his standard uniform of a cheap suit and skinny tie. No matter how important a lawman he was, and last I had heard, he was the interim director of the whole top-secret agency, he would always look like a junior college English professor to me.

"Susan and Ray Shackleford are here," I gasped. Myers and I had a bit of history. He and his partner, Agent Franks, had been the representatives of the government who had visited me in the hospital after my very first monster encounter. They had threatened my life if I didn't keep quiet that day, and they had come very close to fulfilling that promise on a few other occasions. I suppose you could say that I did not have a very good working relationship with the government.

Myers spoke into his radio. "We've recovered the target, all teams return to extract. We have at least two vampires. One Master. Repeat one Master. The dark-haired female Caucasian is the Master. The large white-haired male is the lesser, but is still very dangerous. If you see her, do not hesitate, because she

sure won't." He stepped past the corpse that Ray had
pulled through the bars. There was still some residual
twitching. The agents pulling me along slipped as their
boots lost traction in the spreading puddle of blood.

I never thought that I would think of these guys as
a sight for sore eyes. "Glad to see you too, Myers,"
I said cheerfully.

"Shut up. You have no idea how much trouble
you've caused me." Myers sounded frustrated. My
legs were starting to wobble less, so I tried to walk
rather than be baggage. The Feds just kept on pulling. "I was sent to find you at the resort, but when
I arrived, there had been a zombie outbreak. I found
your team, but they had no idea where you were. It
took a lot of diplomatic work to track you here. And
then we roll up to find this mess. You're not an easy
man to find."

*Why had Myers been looking for me?*

The hallway outside Section Six was splattered with
the bodies of dead guards. Even as jaded as I am to
this kind of thing, I had to look away. These people
had done nothing to deserve the vampires' wrath. The
Feds kept Myers and me in the center of a protective
diamond formation as we hurried outward. The Fed
on point led us quickly through the maze of winding
passages. There were many confused survivors, guards,
loose prisoners, and staff all wandering around in the
dark, but nobody challenged the squadron of well
armed Americans. Good thing too, because I had seen
how trigger-happy the Monster Control Bureau was.

The courtyard was engulfed in chaos. One guard
tower was on fire. The main truck gate was wide
open, with one of the heavy gates lying broken and

splintered in the road. Denim-clad prisoners were
running out the opening and fleeing into the dark.
Torn shapes sat in the moonlight or dangled from
the razor-wire fence. Those must have been the men
who had tried to stop Susan.

Three black Suburbans were parked directly in
front of the exit, engines running. A large man in
drab black armor was waiting for us, a stubby F2000
rifle looking tiny in his massive arms. The man was
broad and muscled like an NFL linebacker. He was
a frightening apparition. Something about this particular Fed emanated a nonchalant capacity to deliver
unbelievable pain. His dark face scowled from under
a pair of night vision goggles when he saw me being
dragged out of the building.

"Franks, my brother, what's up?" I shouted. Special Agent Franks of the Monster Control Bureau
particularly seemed to hate my guts. On the day that
it becomes expedient for the government to end my
life, I somehow know that it will be Agent Franks
who'll get the job.

"Too bad," he muttered.

"What's too bad?" I asked as the Feds shoved
me through the open door of the waiting Suburban.

"We got here in time." He slammed the door
after me.

# CHAPTER 3

"Owen!"

I blinked my bleary eyes as they tried to adjust to the lighted interior of the Suburban. Suddenly I was squished against the door as someone hugged me tight.

"Julie?" She was as beautiful as ever. I hadn't been exaggerating when I had described her to my poor dead cellmate. Tall, brunette, gorgeous, way smarter than I am, talented, and tough as nails. Julie is the spitting image of her mother, only alive and not filled with soul-crushing evil. "Oh, man! I'm sure glad to see you." I hugged her and ran a filthy hand across her cheek. Being a tough guy, I tried not to cry like a sissy in front of the federal agents. She held me tight. She must have thought that she had lost me. I sure did hate that feeling.

She tilted her head back and kissed me. *Man, I'm glad to be out of jail.* Finally she broke away, removed her glasses and wiped a tiny bit of moisture from her eyes. "You taste like chemicals."

"Lice powder. What's going on?"

"I should ask you that. What happened at the resort? There were zombies, and then you disappeared, and then the Feds showed up looking for you."

"It's complicated, I'll try to explain, but is the team okay? And what are you doing with these guys?"

"Everybody's fine. I made Myers bring me when I found out he was looking for you. Oh, Owen, I'm just glad you're safe."

The driver's side door opened and Agent Franks squeezed his bulk behind the wheel. Myers slid into the passenger side. The interior light died when he closed the door. Myers turned to face us over the seat.

"You didn't make me do anything. I *let* you come," he snapped.

"I hoped we could use her to ID your body," Franks said emotionlessly. That made two complete sentences in one night, which was pretty good for Franks. Sadly, both of them had something to do with wishing for my death. I suppose I just have that effect on some people. Franks slammed the big vehicle into gear and gunned it out through the gate in a spray of gravel. Prisoners caught in the headlights had to jump out of the way to avoid being run down. Myers turned back around and spoke into his radio, ordering the other two vehicles to watch for an ambush. The gates of Tijira Prison faded into the background.

"And the zombie outbreak? Did we get it contained in time?" I had to know. It was stupid, but I felt like it was my fault.

"There were only a few more casualties after you were arrested. A *Girls Gone Wild* video crew had their brains eaten . . . so no significant losses," Myers stated.

"What happened? How did you end up here?"

Julie asked. "And what happened to your head? That lump is huge."

"Shotgun butt." I dismissed it with a wave. Unfortunately for me, traumatic brain injuries were a relatively common occurrence. "I'll explain later. I saw your mom and dad."

"What?" Julie's voice rose an octave. "Here? Now?" She turned and watched out the window. "Not again..." Normally Julie's Alabama accent was very faint, except for when she got excited, or in this case, scared. Susan and Ray would be a dark spot in our life until they finally got staked and chopped.

"I think they're gone for now." I put my arm over her shoulder and pulled her close and whispered in her ear. "I'll fill you in on what they said, but I don't want these pricks to hear." She nodded and her hand moved to the black mark on the side of her neck, an unconscious habit that she had picked up when she was under a great deal of stress. To most people, the mark looked like a thick, black, line tattoo. In actuality it was something entirely different. Susan's parting words had been about how the mark that had saved Julie was going to eventually kill her. *Not if I can help it.*

"Pitt, at the resort, did you see him?" Myers queried, back to business.

"Him who?" I decided to play stupid. I knew that the Feds had not rescued me out of the goodness of their hearts and I wanted to know why.

"The leader of the Condition. The necromancer."

"English guy, turns into a giant shadow when the lights go out, throws toilets at people, that one?"

Myers got excited. "Did you see his face?"

"A little, but it was dark."

"I'll have you talk to a sketch artist on the flight home. You're now the only person we know of who has seen him in person."

"What's the Condition?" Julie asked.

"The Sanctified Church of the Temporary Mortal Condition. They're a death cult. A real bunch of nut-job whackos. They've been around forever, but only over the last year have they really shown up on our radar. The man who attacked you, he's their leader."

"A church? Why don't you just go burn their compound down? You guys are Feds after all."

Myers either didn't get the jab, or he chose to ignore it. "We would if we could. But the Condition is good. They work in cells. Their higher-level operatives are known as the Exalted Order of the Shadows. We can't isolate their leaders, or even most of their ranking members. As far as we can tell they're dabbling in some real hard-core black magic. And they're connected . . . businessmen, politicians, the media, even movie stars. This cult is now our number one priority."

"Let me guess. They worship the Old Ones?"

"Yes. And they're out to get you specifically," he said, pausing briefly in thought. "How did you know that they were connected to those things?"

I didn't say anything.

Myers turned around and glared at me. "Look, Pitt, if you have information, you need to share it. These guys are bad news, their leader is secret enemy number one, and right now I'm your best chance to survive them." He tried to look friendly, and mostly failed. "I know that we've gotten off on the wrong foot, but I'm trying to help you here."

"Why?"

"That's our job. We're supposed to protect and defend the taxpayers." He smiled, and in the dark I wasn't sure if the government man or Susan had been more intimidating, but for totally different reasons. One because it represented a soulless entity with the power to suck the very blood from the innocent, and the other because it was a vampire. The Suburban continued to accelerate down the rutted road.

"Bullshit."

Myers shrugged. He was smart enough not to waste his time. "All right, let me level with you. You are currently our only in against this cult. Just about everybody we've tried to infiltrate has ended up zombified or worse. I've finally got a man inside, but he's low on their totem pole and they won't reveal anything to him. We can't get any of the known members to turn snitch, and if they seem to think about it, they're never seen again. But the Condition's fixated on you, and through you, it gives us a way to capture some of them for questioning."

I put my face in my palm. "Oh, come on. Why does everything seem to have it in for me personally?" I figured I knew why I was the target of the Old Ones. I had been responsible for thwarting their invasion, but the Feds did not know that. I was sure of that much, because if the Feds knew what I had pulled off, up to and including time travel, then I had no doubt that my brain would be sitting in a glass jar in some government lab being poked with electrodes to see how it worked.

"About that . . ." Myers looked away, a little sheepish. "Sorry."

I'd screwed up their invasion plans by not falling in line. I had no idea what Myers had to be sorry about. "Huh?"

"It was a misunderstanding," he said. I waited for the explanation. Myers took his time, actually seeming a bit embarrassed. "See, when MHI was fighting Lord Machado's minions, we decided to play it safe . . . So we . . . kind of . . . dropped a nuke on the area."

"You did what?" Julie shouted. "You tried to nuke Alabama?"

"Only a little one. It was for the best," he said defensively. "We didn't think you were going to succeed. I was certain that the bad guys were going to win, and I couldn't allow that. You know what would have happened then."

"Gee whiz, thanks, Myers. I was right there, and I didn't see a mushroom cloud, so I'm assuming you screwed up."

He shrugged. "When the bomb struck, the rift had already been opened. It passed through cleanly and detonated on the other side, inside the Old Ones' reality. It must have made them angry and from what our intel is telling us, it even hurt the big cheese of Old Ones. For some reason they think that you're the one that sent the weapon . . . Hence, the interdimensional hit out for you. Sorry."

"I don't think *sorry* covers the indiscriminate use of nuclear weapons, jackass." No wonder the Old Ones were blaming me. Not only had I wrecked their invasion, they also thought that I had attacked them in their own world as well. I've made a lot of people angry throughout the course of my life, but I'd never hit a 10,000-foot-tall crustacean with an atom bomb before.

"So, what now?" Julie snapped. "We just wait for this cult to come and kill my fiancé? I don't think so."

Myers shook his head. "We're going to fly you home. I want you to go about your business, and wait for the cult to make their move. I'll provide a protective detail to guard you, and when the cult strikes, we'll be ready."

"Why don't I just go hide out somewhere? Lay low for a while?" It was a rhetorical question. I was not the running type.

"They'll find you. The Condition aren't normal nut jobs. Unfortunately the stuff they believe in actually works. No. I want you in the open. And they are going to have to crawl out from under their rock to get you, and when they do..." Myers' slammed his fist into his palm. It was actually not a very intimidating mannerism from a person who looked like a junior college English professor.

"So after they kill me, you swoop in and arrest them?"

Franks finally spoke. "They won't kill you."

"And why not?"

Franks didn't answer. Myers patted the terse man on the shoulder. "You'll be safe because you'll be under the personal protection of my best men, led by Agent Franks himself. His primary mission is to keep you alive."

The very idea was preposterous. Franks? Protecting me? "Screw that," I sputtered. "I'll take my chance with the zombies."

"I've never failed a mission," Franks said simply.

"And what about the Natchy Bottom?"

"Doesn't count," Franks replied. I saw his cold

eyes flick to the rearview mirror. He watched me for a moment before returning his attention to the road. Franks had gotten just as dead as the rest of us before I had managed to erase five minutes of time. He had put up an amazing fight and had taken inhuman amounts of damage before going down, but he had still lost.

"I can protect myself," I stated.

"MHI can protect him," Julie added. "We're better at this than you federal guys anyway."

"Civilians," Franks muttered as he swung the wheel hard and took a sharp right onto a less traveled road. I didn't know if he meant us or the other drivers.

"You don't have a choice. Your country needs you, Pitt," Myers said.

"Needs me as bait! I'm not down with that. Get yourself a different worm for that hook, Myers. I don't trust your people at all. And it'll be a cold day in hell before I put my life in the hands of that jackbooted thug." I gestured angrily at Franks. The big agent ignored me.

"You're going to let us protect you from the Condition, or we will make life very difficult for MHI. If you think you had it bad last time around, just push me and see what happens this time," Myers threatened. "You've used up your political goodwill from last summer, Harbinger isn't Congress' golden boy anymore, and my agency has been moved from Justice to Homeland Security."

"Didn't know that..." Julie said. Top-secret, shadow-government reorganizations didn't usually end up in the papers.

"Which means I'm now authorized to screw with

your company more than ever before." Myers had once been a member of Monster Hunter International before he had left and joined the government. I did not know what had caused him to leave, but he certainly packed a bitter hate for us ever since. MHI had been shut down once before by executive order and I knew that some factions of the government were just itching for us to give them an excuse to do it again. "I'm prepared to take this all the way. Are you? Think on it."

Julie muttered something profane about Myers' ancestry under her breath. We both knew the senior Fed wasn't bluffing. The dark Mexican countryside flashed by outside the window as I glared at my reflection. This certainly sucked. In the previous twenty-four hours I had been attacked by a shadow necromancer and his zombies, beaten by *Federales*, deloused, visited by vampires, reunited with a shard of the most evil artifact in the known world, been targeted by a death cult, and had it topped off by being placed under the protection of a man who could best be described as *not* a member of the Owen Z. Pitt fan club.

No one spoke for a long time. Finally Myers turned back around to watch the road, knowing in his little black bureaucrat's heart that he had us beat. Julie rested her head on my shoulder. I grabbed her hand and squeezed. We had faced worse together.

Or so I thought.

"What's on your mind?" I asked quietly.

Julie had pulled me aside once we had disembarked at the small airport. A U.S. Air Force C-130 Hercules was refueling nearby, and soon we would be on our way back to the States. The night sky was bright under the nearly full moon and I could make out the shape of Agent Franks shadowing us thirty feet away. He was scanning the chain link fence, looking for anything moving in the desert scrub. The man certainly took his job seriously. They were running some sort of loud compressor near the aircraft, so I wasn't worried about him overhearing us. Julie and I stood in the darkness behind a diminutive aircraft hangar while we talked about the day's events.

"This is crap," she hissed. "I'm so sick and tired of the Feds." She was obviously upset, and her pretty features were drawn into a hard scowl.

"And..." I prompted. I knew her too well. There was obviously something else.

She grimaced. "And what the hell were my parents doing here? I hate to say it, but when they offered a truce, I actually believed it. If they ever did anything against us, Earl would make it his life's work to track them down. I at least thought they had the sense of self-preservation to avoid that."

"Believe it or not, I think the truce is still in effect...." I briefly explained the nature of Susan's visit, but I'm ashamed to say that I held something back. I did not mention Susan's promise that Julie was going to die from the mark. I felt bad for withholding information, and I would tell her, but just not yet. For all I knew, Susan was lying, scheming, trying to find some way to unite more of her family into her dark world, the evil bitch.

"A shard of the artifact? How? It disappeared in Childersburg. I always assumed that the Feds got it when they cordoned off the area. How did my mom end up with part of it?"

I shrugged. "Beats me. All I know is that it hurt like hell when she touched me with it. I'm scared to death of that thing."

"Do you think..." She searched for the words. "Could it be starting again?"

"I don't know," I answered. I hugged her tight. I was terrified of the things that artifact had done, and could do, and more especially, what it *allowed* me to do. I'd rather kill myself than risk turning those things loose. "I just don't know."

"Oh, Owen...I've got a bad feeling about this. I thought I'd lost you."

"I'm not going anywhere. I promise." Saying that made me think of another promise. "I lost my gear. The pistols you gave me...your brother's pistols. They meant a lot—"

She stopped me flat. "We can replace the guns. I can't replace you."

Franks shouted at us, "It's time." As if to accentuate his words, the big engines turned over and the props began to roar.

"He's such an asshole." Julie mumbled into my shoulder. She pushed slowly away, and we started toward the waiting plane. "Speaking of which..." She raised her voice, "Agent Franks!"

The Fed nodded in her direction.

"At DeSoya Caverns, last summer, I asked if you had taken care of my father, I asked if you had let him turn into a vampire, and if you had let him escape. Since Owen just saw him, I'm assuming that you lied to me." Julie was intimidating when she was angry.

I don't think Franks' brain was wired with the

capability of being intimidated. Franks shrugged. "Classified," he said simply, turned and walked toward the plane.

"Oh, hanging out with him is just going to be a blast, won't it?" she asked.

"And for a while there I thought that me and Franks had come to terms. . . ." We walked under the runway lights. The C-130 was drastically loud. The other Feds were carrying their gear up the loading ramp.

"Mr. Pitt? Ms. Shackleford?" A black-clad agent approached us. He had removed his helmet and balaclava and had tucked them under one arm. This one was young, and seemed friendly enough. His skin was deeply tanned, his neatly buzzed hair black, and his eyes twinkled when he smiled. There was a squat but heavy-looking duffle bag slung over one shoulder. He shouted to be heard over the engines. "I'm Agent Torres. I'm on your protective detail. It's an honor to meet you." He held out one gloved hand, and surprised, I shook it. It was not normal for the Feds to be nice to MHI personnel.

"You must be new," I shouted.

"Yes. Just assigned to the Bureau. I came over from Border Patrol." He shook Julie's hand as well, and his face betrayed his surprise at the impressive strength in her handshake. I had had that reaction the first time I met her as well. "Ms. Shackleford, I read up on your family in the Monster Control academy. Wow, all I can say is, wow . . . You guys are amazing. Your great-grandfather was one of the pioneers of Monster Hunting. This is a real honor."

"Well, thanks," Julie stammered. Apparently I wasn't the only one surprised at meeting a friendly agent. My usual encounters with them involved bullying, threats, intimidation, and the occasional fist fight.

He unslung the duffle bag and handed it to me. "I think this belongs to you."

The bag was as heavy as it looked. I unzipped it, peered inside, and was greeted with a wonderful sight. "Abomination!" I shouted. I put the bag down and pulled out my customized Saiga shotgun. I pulled back the charging handle to check the chamber and the bolt was as slick as ever. It was a brutal weapon, a shortened, full-auto, magazine-fed 12-gauge, complete with underslung 40mm grenade launcher, EO-Tech holographic optic, and—the *pièce de résistance*—a side-folding, silver-inlaid bayonet. Abomination and I had been through some serious things together. It wasn't just my gun, it was damn near my friend.

"And my STIs...And my armor!" I was really geeking out now. My two .45s, built originally for Julie's brother Ray, had been put back in their holsters. The only thing missing was my Ganga Ram, last seen lodged in a zombie's skull. "No freaking way. This is awesome." In my defense, you don't get very far in my line of work unless you really get to know and love your equipment. "I thought these babies were gone forever...how did you find them?"

Torres seemed rather proud of himself. "My team secured the perimeter at the prison. I found this bag in the hands of a fat *Federale,* dead in the parking lot. Looked like he was planning on taking these home, but he'd been ripped apart, you know, and the bag was open, and when I shined my light on it, I saw this." He pointed at the Happy Face patch. "And I've heard how hard it is to earn one of those! I figured if you were still alive, you were going to want your gear back." He shrugged. "No biggie."

I had to resist the urge to hug him. "Thanks, Agent Torres. I appreciate it."

"Consider it a professional courtesy. Hey, I'm going to help guard you for awhile. Just call me Anthony." He shook my hand again. "Really nice to meet you guys. I've got to go." He smiled, waved, looking almost like an embarrassed teenager, and ran to rejoin his team on the ramp.

I turned to look at Julie. She was as perplexed as I was. She mouthed the word "damn." I put Abomination back in the bag and zipped it shut. When I picked up the duffle, the weight seemed familiar and reassuring.

"Maybe this won't be as bad as we thought," I said. "I didn't know the Monster Control Bureau employed anybody nice."

"He must have slipped past Human Resources."

Cazador, Alabama. Population 682. A pretty much run-of-the-mill little village nestled deep in the woods south of Montgomery. A quick drive through town—and there was no such thing as a long drive through Cazador—wouldn't reveal much except the catfish plant, a few stores, and a pair of churches. But a few miles out of town was the headquarters compound of Monster Hunter International. The main office building was two stories on the surface, and built like a medieval fortress. From the air it looked like a wide, squat bullfrog. The other buildings were spread out—a hangar for our plane and chopper, the sunk-in bunker that was the armory, Milo's prefab workshop, the body shack, and a handful of small buildings that served as the barracks for the Newbie training classes. A tall, chain link fence which was topped with razor wire and coated with kudzu enclosed an area largely made up of bulldozer-pushed berms of red clay soil. MHI's shooting range facilities were top notch.

The Air Force plane came in low over the thick forest surrounding the compound. For a brief instant I saw Skippy's village flash by underneath, then the mostly hidden homes were gone. Seconds later the tires chirped as we hit runway.

"Hey!" the Fed shouted. His voice sounded nasal through the intercom headset. "Mr. Pitt. Pay attention."

"Huh?" I glanced away from the window. The sun was rising, and the view had been nice. The Fed showed me his laptop screen with a picture of the man who had attacked me at the resort: a lean face, square jaw, intense eyes, short hair. "Yep, that's pretty close."

The agent swiveled the laptop back so he could look at the screen. "What about it isn't right?"

"I don't know. It was dark, and he was beating the living hell out of me." Plus it was hard to explain that I had not seen a soul inside when I had looked through the man's eyes. How exactly do you convey that to a sketch artist? "Besides the little demon-leech monster thingy that crawled out his mouth, that's good enough."

The C-130 rolled to a stop near our hangar. I removed the ice pack from my swollen forehead and unbuckled my harness. The Monster Control Bureau had been nice enough to clean my cuts, wrap my ankle, and provide some pain-killers. I was in a pretty happy place. Yep, the government issues good pain-killers.

The drugs had even made the uncomfortable web seats, temperature swings, and noise bearable.

The hydraulics that powered the loading ramp made a truly impressive amount of noise as it was lowered to the ground. Most of the agents were already standing, preparing to exit the plane. Many of them looked slightly nervous. The last time they had been here had been to secure the compound and arrest Julie and me. In the aftermath many of them had gotten royally beaten by a slightly perturbed Earl Harbinger. I recognized a few of them, including one agent who had a slightly crooked nose. If I recalled correctly, I think that I might have given him that nose. He scowled at me, then flipped me the bird, low enough that I would see, but that it wouldn't come to Myers' or Franks' attention. Yep. That would be the guy. Grabbing my bag, I stood and headed for the ramp. Julie was right behind me. We would be damned if we waited for the government men.

A few Hunters were already waiting for us on the tarmac. Earl Harbinger still appeared to be in his forties, and I knew that if I died of old age, by that time he might look fifty. Wearing that same old leather bomber jacket that was like an MHI fixture, Earl stood stiffly, his arms folded in front of his chest, his cold blue eyes examining the plane and its occupants. He was really just an average-looking guy, not big, not particularly intimidating in any physical way, but he emanated a certain old-school toughness, a wily competence that smelled of tobacco smoke and pure animal cunning. Earl Harbinger was not a man to trifle with, and that was only taking into account his human side.

Trip Jones stared grimly at the descending ramp, his dark features drawn into an intense frown. Normally Trip was probably the happiest, most easygoing and likable person whom I had ever known, but his last encounter with Feds had involved a massive beatdown, with him being on the receiving end of the beating, so he was understandably distrusting. Trip was from Florida, Jamaican by ethnicity, devout Baptist by belief, and MHI moral compass by default. Trip was our Samaritan, our good guy, if you will. He was a Hunter because he was innately a hero. Comparing myself to my friend always made me feel guilty because I knew that I could never be the kind of man that he was.

Holly Newcastle could best be described as hot, both in looks and temperament. Fiery by nature, always looking something like a villainess from a Bond movie. Only a fool would underestimate her. Our former stripper liked to play up the dumb blond angle whenever it was convenient, but she was sharp as a tack, mean as hell, and probably the most merciless Hunter I knew. She regarded the plane with a mischievous grin. If Trip was a Hunter because he was a hero, Holly was a Hunter because it was the best legal avenue she had to inflict violence on the forces of evil, and she was damn good at it.

Earl's face lit up when he saw Julie and me coming down the ramp. After Susan had disappeared and Ray had gone into seclusion, Earl had been like a father to Julie and her brothers. The man looked relieved, yet exhausted, but he always looked tired the next few days after a full moon. Being locked in a concrete cell while you attack the walls in a psychotic rage all night will do that to you. He gave Julie a quick hug.

"Jules, Owen, welcome back..." He stuck out his hand and shook mine with his standard eye-watering and bone-crushing grip. Trip and Holly descended on me, clapping me on the back and demanding to know what had happened. The three of us had started out in the same class of Newbies, so we had been through some crazy things together. It was good to be among friends again. Other Hunters approached in the distance, drawn to the commotion and the sight of the massive plane. A lone figure, dressed from head to toe in black, watched from near the hangar. He waved awkwardly when he saw me, then slunk back into the building as the Feds disembarked. Skippy did not like crowds, or most people for that matter, but especially hated anyone from the government. The Feds clustered around the ramp, bunched up, checking out the compound, a few of the experienced ones no doubt taking stock for the day when the political winds changed and they finally got the order to shut us down by any means necessary.

The plane's engines died and the runway was suddenly very quiet. The two groups stood separated, like the freshmen boys and girls at a high school dance. Finally Myers and Franks broke away and crossed the divide. Myers' imitation-silk tie flapped over his shoulder in the wind. The two stopped in front of Earl. Nobody offered to shake hands.

"Earl..." Myers said.

"Well, if it isn't Special Agent Dwayne Myers," Earl responded, just oozing contempt. *Myers' first name was Dwayne?* I learned something new every day. "And his faithful sidekick, Mongo." The quiet brute nodded slightly. I did not think Franks actually liked anyone, but he did seem to slightly respect those who might present a challenge in a physical confrontation. Now, Harbinger versus Franks? I would pay serious money to watch that one because I didn't care how tough the Fed was, I'm pretty sure if he caught Earl in a bad mood, they would have to scrape Franks up and carry him out in a couple trash bags.

"I'm guessing you got the call?" the senior agent queried. Myers' voice and attitude was cold. I knew that he despised Harbinger, as Myers used to work for him, and though I did not know the specifics, I certainly knew that there was some bad history between the two.

"I did. And I don't like it one bit. Are all these"— Harbinger gestured contemptuously toward the Feds— "the 'protective detail'? Because if you're going for subtle, that ain't it."

"No. I'm leaving four handpicked agents. They'll shadow Pitt and try to look like your people . . . so sloppy . . . and unprofessional. The rest of us will be on standby. We'll be staging out of Montgomery until this is resolved. I'm expecting MHI's full assistance. The legality of continued private Monster Hunting is coming under congressional review next session and you wouldn't want me to testify that you didn't want to cooperate."

"Oh, we're the spirit of cooperation . . . So now why don't you take your goons and get the hell off my land?"

"Believe me, I can't wait. But take this. You should at least know what you're up against." Myers held out a manila folder. "I don't think you realize the magnitude of the threat that's coming for you."

It was hard to believe that Myers had once been one of us. The very thought made me cringe. I reached for the folder, and as I did so my fingertips touched the agent's thumb. Black lightning crashed behind my eyes.

I was sitting on a wooden bench. The delicious smell of sizzling beef drifted from the nearby barbeque. It was nearing sundown, and the heat had broken under the soft Alabama breeze. Fireflies danced in the nearby forest.

"Dwayne, how do you want your burger?"

"Medium," I answered without hesitation.

"Gotcha..." Big Ray Shackleford answered as he squished the patties with a spatula. "Honey?" The flames hissed as the grease dripped through the grill.

"Rare. No, super rare." Susan Shackleford was sitting on a lawn chair to my right. She sighed as she tried to get comfortable. She was eight months' pregnant and having a hard time. I tried not to stare at Susan. Even heavy with child, she was still the best-looking woman I had ever known, but she was also my best friend's wife. "On second thought... How about you just kind of warm up the outside?"

"Can do." Ray took a second to wipe his meaty hands on his apron and then took a long pull from his beer. He set it down with a satisfied grunt. Ray cut an imposing figure, big, muscular, confident, pretty much everything that I wasn't. "Earl? Dorcas?"

"Rare." Harbinger was sitting at the picnic table. I was still intimidated by my boss, but now that he had picked me to be on his team and had let me in on the family secret, I felt much more comfortable in his presence.

"Medium, Ray. And I mean medium. Not all black and crispy. Don't screw it up again. Damn boy, but I ain't never known nobody to burn up a good piece of meat like you."

Dorcas was also at the picnic table, busy cleaning her .45 Long Colt on top of a piece of newspaper. She was kind of like our mother figure. A bitter crone of a mother figure for sure, but I knew that she loved us in her own demented redneck way. "Damn, idiot. Should have let me cook."

"Yes, ma'am," Ray responded automatically. I don't think that I will ever get used to these Southerners and their incessant politeness to their elders. "Hood?"

"Well done, please." The voice came from behind me. Hood was the youngest member of the team, and supposedly I was his trainer. In actuality he was so on the ball that sometimes it was like he was teaching me. I had even overheard Harbinger talking about how he had never met somebody with a better gift for Monster Hunting. Not bad for a fat kid from Birmingham.

"Since you're the Newbie, you're lucky if you get grill scrapings." Ray laughed hard and drained the rest of his beer. "Julie! Get daddy another beer!"

"Okay!" the little girl shouted. She leapt gracefully off the nearby tire swing and ran for the house, her ponytail whipping behind her. She was only eight, but already I could tell that she was going to be the spitting image of her mom and sharp as her dad. That one was going to be a heartbreaker. She disappeared into the massive old plantation house with a slam of the screen door.

I glanced around at the other Monster Hunters.

Grandpa Shackleford was engaged in an animated conversation with some other Hunters about how Ronald Reagan was the most pro-Monster Hunting president we'd had since Eisenhower. He kept swinging his hook for emphasis. That red-headed teenager that Earl had saved in Idaho recently, Milo, was doodling on some scrap of paper, probably about some other weird invention that he had come up with. A few others were drifting up, summoned by the smell of the barbeque, and Ray began to shout questions at each of them. The MHI staff were in a good mood, and rightly so. The case that we had just cracked had been a tough one, and we were feeling invincible.

"Yo, Myers," Ray said.

"Yeah, buddy?"

"We kicked some ass today, didn't we?"

I leaned back on the bench and stretched my bad arm. A vampire had wrecked my rotator cuff and ruined my shot at ever pitching in the majors, but if I hadn't had that encounter all those years ago, then I would never have gotten to become a part of this. I looked at the patch sewn on my sleeve as I turned my arm, just a little green happy face with horns. It wasn't much, but it meant a lot to me.

"We sure did, Ray. We sure did."

These people were my family.

"What are you staring at?" Myers asked me belligerently.

Reality came crashing back. Glancing around, runway, big airplane, my friends, and a bunch of scowling Feds, I was at the compound, out on the tarmac, but I had just been at a barbeque ... at Julie's house, only

it had been a long time ago...and I had been...
*Agent Myers? What the hell?* "Nothing...."

Myers shook his head and released the folder, probably thinking that I was a complete moron. I must
have been out of it for just a few seconds. "Like I was
saying, you need to know what you're up against. Do
you have someplace where we could talk in private?"

Harbinger nodded. "Let's go." He motioned to the
main building. All of the Feds began to follow and he
raised his hand. "No, just the *protective detail*. The
rest of you assholes can stay on the plane." My boss
didn't wait for any sort of disagreement, he just spun
on his heel and led the way. I did note, however, that
he was grinding his teeth together rather violently.

Still reeling from what had just happened, I reached
out and grabbed Julie's hand. Nothing happened. No
flash of black lightning, no visions. She looked at me
strangely.

"Z, are you okay?" Holly asked me. "You look kind
of flushed."

I shook my head. I couldn't say anything in front
of the Feds, but the last time I had lived someone
else's memories, Lord Machado's to be precise, it had
been powered by the same artifact that Susan had just
exposed me to again. "No, I'm fine. Must have been
the flight....Let's get this over with."

Franks regarded me suspiciously as I walked after
Harbinger and Myers. Finally, he nodded at three
other agents. They picked up their gear and followed.

The group entered the main building, passing quickly
through the entryway, as Earl was walking at a pace
that indicated he wanted to get this done with. Agent

Franks made note of the portcullis chained above us, almost approvingly.

"Welcome home, Z. Milo told me you'd killed yourself a mess of zombies," Dorcas, our secretary, receptionist, and semi-retired Hunter, said from behind her massive desk. She looked like a typical matronly Southern grandma, except for the Ruger Redhawk bulging from the shoulder holster underneath her knit sweater. "I can always count on you for a good killin' story or two, about the only entertainment I get around here nowadays."

"Yes, ma'am, I'll tell you all about it after this meeting."

When she spied the Feds coming up behind me, her smile vanished, and her eyes narrowed so dangerously that they turned into little slits. For a second it looked like she thought about going for that magnum. "Myers . . ." she spat.

"Dorcas," the senior Fed responded slowly.

"How's the traitor business treating you?"

Myers was unperturbed. "Good, good . . . How's your leg?"

"It's made of plastic. How'd you think it's doing?"

"Yes, of course . . . Forgot. See you around." Myers nodded smugly and followed Earl down the hallway. The hate-filled look that Dorcas cast after us almost peeled the paint off the walls. I paused for a moment. Our receptionist was usually cranky—hell, she was prepared to commit murder if any of the other employees messed with her lunch in the cafeteria fridge—but I had never seen her like that before.

I waited until the Feds were out of earshot. "What's that about?"

She sneered. "Old times . . . me and Judas there have a score to settle."

"What'd he do?"

"He saved my life . . ." Dorcas shook her head and went back to answering the phones. "Now get. I've got work to do."

I caught up with the others as they were entering the smaller conference room we had set aside on the first floor. It was going to be a tight fit, but apparently Harbinger didn't want to give the Feds access to the nicer room on the second floor. Myers had stopped Earl in the hallway right in front of the wall of silver memorial plaques and was speaking. "Just you, Shackleford, and Pitt. I have some very sensitive information, and it's on a need-to-know basis. My men will stay out here."

"Negative." My boss gestured at Trip and Holly. "They're on my personal team. Anything you can say to me, you can say to them."

"Your team?" Myers grew furious. His face turned red and he raised his voice. "The *great* Earl Harbinger? Not keeping secrets from his team? That's new." It was a surprising change in demeanor. The small man went to the memorial wall and started scanning back through the names, obviously looking for one in particular. He finally found the one he wanted, chronologically over a dozen deaths before the large number from the Christmas Party of '95, and stabbed his finger into it. "No secrets? So, you've told your team about Marty then?"

Earl did not respond for several seconds. All the Feds except for Franks appeared surprised at their commander's sudden emotional outburst. Franks looked bored. The Hunters were confused. Finally my boss sighed, apparently not prepared to debate the point. It was shocking to see him back down on his own turf. "You two, wait outside. Don't let these guys touch anything," He pointed at the rest of the protective detail. Trip and Holly knew not to argue. They stepped aside.

I stopped to read the indicated plaque as the others entered the conference room. The plaque had a small picture of a young man with a sly grin on his chubby face.

### A. MARTIN HOOD
1/14/1960-10/17/1986

Nothing really set it apart from the other four hundred and some-odd other plaques on the wall. I went into the meeting.

# CHAPTER 4

Franks and Myers sat on one side of the table, Earl, Julie, and I on the other. The senior Fed still seemed uncharacteristically angry. He gestured to the folder that he had given me. "Open it."

"Why the secrecy?" Julie asked.

"Open it," Myers repeated. I dropped it on the table between us and flipped through the thick stack of papers. The top sheet was a sketch artist's interpretation of the shadow man from the flight home. "The Sanctified Church of the Temporary Mortal Condition, or Condition for short, was founded ten years ago," Myers stated, as if he had given this briefing a few times. "They didn't come up on our radar for a while. We thought they were just another bunch of scam artists taking money from gullible morons, until they released this . . ." He pulled out a sheet of paper and handed it to Harbinger.

"A proclamation heralding the return of the Old Ones . . ." Earl frowned, "It's a bunch of crap about welcoming our new overlords back to Earth." He held up the paper, "And a really bad drawing of some sort of sky squid." I had seen that particular shape once before, while my disembodied spirit slugged it out with Lord Machado for control of space and time, only the picture didn't do it justice. In real life the Dread Overlord was as big across as ten aircraft carriers parked in a line.

"Check the date." Franks spoke for the first time.

Julie leaned in to see. "That was printed two days before Lord Machado tried to use the artifact in Childersburg, one day before we got killed in Natchy Bottom...So, they knew beforehand?"

"Yes, and once the whole world got to travel through time for five minutes, it really helped the Condition's recruiting," Myers said. I was still really glad that the government didn't know that was my fault. "They're growing, and the word is out that their leader, this guy"—Myers tapped the artist's rendition of the shadow man—"is building an army to help prepare the Earth for the Old Ones' return. Monster Control Bureau agents were sent to investigate, but we've had almost no luck and I've lost some good men. The Condition is brutal, devious, and their magic actually works, so our intel is extremely limited."

"Who are they?" Julie asked.

Myers picked out another sheet. "These are some of the members we know about, but they're just useful idiots, celebrities and suckers they're scamming money off of to fund their operations. We've investigated them thoroughly. As usual, they don't have a clue what they're into. Publically, the Condition is just another oddball religion. They preach about ending the greedy tyranny of man and building a perfect utopia on Earth, under the wise leadership of the benevolent Old Ones, of course."

My side of the table gave a collective snort. We'd all dealt with those things before.

"I take it you can understand why my superiors are so concerned. This church has been recruiting monsters, various types of undead, and they even found a shoggoth somewhere."

Earl picked up the picture of the Englishman. "So I take it you can't find this asshole?"

"They call him their Shadow Lord. He's an enigma. All of their leadership is cloaked in secrecy. Finding him is where Pitt comes in. They'll be forced to send some of their operatives to get him, and when they do, we'll take them. My orders are to shut this church down, no matter what. I just need an in."

"What? Worshipping giant space mollusks that want to enslave humanity isn't cool? What's next, you guys going to pick on the Scientologists?" I asked sarcastically.

"I'm sensing some serious First Amendment issues on this one," Julie offered.

"ACLU's gonna be pissed," Harbinger responded.

I laughed. Franks leaned forward, flipped through the stack, and pulled out a glossy crime-scene photo. He shoved it at me. It was, or had been, a woman. She had been brutally torn to bits. The laughter died off.

"Oh . . . That's terrible," Julie said.

"That was our last undercover agent to infiltrate the inner circle of the Condition, Special Agent Ashley Patterson. They left her on the front steps of her kids' day care like that," Myers said. "She was still living at the time this picture was taken. They used necromancy so she could suffer longer than was humanly possible."

*Ouch.* I had seen a lot of terrible things in the last year, but that made even my stomach lurch. That was a whole new level of cruel.

"Friend of mine..." Franks stated.

It was a somber moment, but that idea just struck me as odd. "You have friends?" I blurted.

Franks scowled at me but Myers continued. "Agent Patterson did find this." The next picture appeared to be of a large piece of pink skin that had been engraved with a knife or something to leave very crude writing. "Apparently you can't just send a message from the other side. They had to slice the note onto one of their living minions and then launch it through a portal. It can be very messy."

"Gross." Julie adjusted her glasses and tried to make out the words carved on the piece of meat. "To all minions of...I can't make out the next word... Overlord? Find and utterly destroy the human Hunter known as...Owen Zastava Pitt..."

"What!" I exclaimed. "Let me see that..." Sure enough, there was my name, etched onto some sacrifice. This was too much. The Dread Overlord had declared jihad. This thing was terrifying. It was huge. "An alien *god* has a vendetta against me? Oh, that's just awesome."

"Yeah," Franks said. "Awesome." I swear the bastard almost smiled. Almost.

"So now we wait for the Condition to come to us," Myers said proudly. "It turns out the Old Ones never bother to communicate with their followers here, so this message was a big deal. Capturing Pitt is now the cultists' primary goal. They'll do anything to get him. Any attack they launch gives us one more lead that we don't currently have."

I turned back to the picture of the MCB agent. She was in five pieces and still *alive*. I did not want to end up as a crime-scene photo. "Your plan sucks."

"This file contains everything we know about the Condition, their assets, their methods. We'll be ready for them to make their move. In the meantime, you just go about your business and pretend we're not here."

"Okay, so why the secrecy?" Earl asked sharply. "Or was your little tantrum out in the hallway just to prove a point?"

The senior Fed shook his head. "Marty was my friend."

"Mine too . . ."

"Then maybe you should have thought of that before you murdered him," Myers snapped.

Earl flashed with anger, shoved his chair away from the table and stood, glaring down at Myers. His fist hit the table hard enough to crack the wood. "It was an accident!"

I've got to hand it to him, Myers didn't so much as flinch, and since I knew he also knew what Earl was capable of when he was angry, that was especially impressive. "What, are you going to *accidentally* kill me too?" Franks' hand inched toward his holstered Glock, surely loaded with silver bullets, ready to plug Earl if he should so much as twitch, and for a moment the little conference room teetered on the edge of violence. "Do it. And it'll be the end of MHI once and for all." The college professor was locked in a staring contest with the werewolf and the killing machine got ready to shoot everybody.

"Enough." Julie was calm as she spoke. "Earl, sit, please. Agent Myers, we're cooperating fully. You two can murder each other over personal business later. We've got work to do." Harbinger pulled his chair back to the table. He was really ticked. Franks put his big hands back on the table. Since I was sitting next to her, I was the only one who saw Julie discreetly return her compact .45 to her lap. She had been prepared to shoot Franks under the table, Han Solo style. My God, I love this woman.

It took a moment for everyone to calm down. I don't know what had transpired between the two men, but Earl was still flushed as Myers pulled out a final piece of paper. "As for the secrecy, we've been eavesdropping on the Condition's communications—wire taps, reading their mail, the usual."

"Shocking," I muttered.

Myers dropped the bomb. "The Condition has a spy inside of MHI."

The three of us glanced at each other. The idea was absurd. "Horse shit," Earl snapped. "I know my men."

"We have several messages in here that reference a mole. You've been infiltrated. How many people have you hired since the battle with Lord Machado?"

We looked to Julie. She was the one who kept track of logistics. "Two training classes, twenty-six Newbies in total, made it through to hiring, with another fifty currently going through." And the three of us knew that of those fifty, we would be lucky if half of them made it through training and this current class had been the biggest that we had ever had. MHI had been drastically short-handed since we had been allowed to reopen. We had been cranking through classes as quickly as possible. "You honestly think one of our new employees is working for the Condition?"

"In their mind, your company is what stopped the second coming. What do you think? You can't trust your senior people either. Keep in mind what kind of things you're dealing with. The Old Ones are powerful, and it wouldn't take much to flip someone you've known for a long time."

"Yeah, you know all about betraying people, don't you, Dwayne?" Earl said. Myers' nostrils flared, but he didn't respond. Earl continued, "I think you're full of it. You hate MHI, and you just want to spread doubt and get us mistrusting each other. I know how you operate. This is all about getting us shut down, but the people you answer to said we're sticking around, and that just pisses you off no end, don't it?"

"For now." Before Myers could say more, his phone rang. It was still set on that annoying version of "Take Me Out to the Ballgame." Glaring at Earl, he answered, listened for a moment, then stood, cupping the phone so the caller wouldn't hear. "We're done here," Myers did his best to act unruffled and professional. "All I require is your full cooperation against the Condition. Go about your regular business and Agent Franks will stay close to Pitt at all times. The Congressional Subcommittee on Unearthly Forces expects MHI to be willing to work with the government. Go against them, I dare you, because then I'll get my wish and MHI will be finished."

"Prick," Earl sullenly murmured under his breath. "You've got the file. Do whatever you want with it. I don't care. Either way, I win. I can show myself out." Myers adjusted his tie and buttoned his cheap suit. "I'll be in touch."

"So that's it. Just keep doing our job like nothing special is happening?" I asked in exasperation. I was still having a difficult time liking this *plan*. If you could call being a sitting duck a plan.

"As for your job, I wouldn't worry too much about hunting monsters," Myers said, "because the monsters will be hunting you." The senior agent left the room without looking back.

I glanced at Earl. He was grinding his teeth again. Julie was baffled and tired. She closed the file. We had a strange symbiotic relationship with the government. We lived off their bounties, chafed at their rules, and had to put up with a lot of their crap, but this was something entirely new.

It was uncomfortably silent for a solid minute. Franks looked across the table at three scowling Monster Hunters and asked nonchalantly, "So, what you got to eat around here?"

"Julie, could you show our *guest* to the cafeteria?" Harbinger asked. "Owen and I need to talk ... alone." Julie stood. Franks hesitated, his mind probably running through the potential of me being assassinated should he walk twenty feet down the hallway. Finally, he relented, shoved his bulk back from the table and followed Julie.

I waited until the door had closed. "Well ... this sucks."

"It's a load of crap, is what it is," he spat. "I got the call this morning. Cooperate or else. So, I guess we ain't got much choice. Stupid government ... Now what exactly happened in Mexico?" Earl Harbinger was the most experienced Hunter in the world. If anyone would know what to do, it was him. I told him everything I could think of, having learned last summer that even the seemingly irrelevant details counted. He rubbed his face wearily when I told him about being exposed to the artifact. He stopped me after the part about how Susan had told me that the mark was going to kill Julie.

"Did you tell Julie about that?" He ran his thumb down the outside of his neck. I shook my head in the negative. "Good. Don't. Susan's a liar, and I wouldn't put it past her trying to manipulate you two into doing something stupid. It probably ain't as bad as she's making it out."

"I'm still worried about her."

"Understandable. But Julie will be fine. I know a thing or two about curses, and no matter what happens, she's a survivor. She gets that from me . . . If you were to die, she'd get by fine. She's a Shackleford. On the other hand, if you lost her, you'd fall apart, and for some reason, she's taken a shine to you. So that alone will keep her around. She's stubborn like that."

I didn't know what to say to that. It was odd having ultimate badass, Earl Harbinger, trying to reassure me that everything was going to be okay. Yet, I could tell that he was as nervous as I was. He loved Julie like she was his own child, but then Earl was back to business. "What else?"

"Well . . . I don't know how to explain it, but I had a vision, or something, just a few minutes ago."

Harbinger cringed. "Not this shit again . . ." I couldn't blame him. Last time I had visions, I had almost destroyed the world.

"Well, this one was different than before, but kind of the same. I think it was some sort of flash because of the artifact. Last time I had visions, I lived through parts of the Cursed One's life. But this time, it was just some weird little thing from Myers, of all people, when I touched his hand outside, and it wasn't even any big deal. It was just some random memory, where you guys were all eating burgers or something, but it was real . . . I think." My boss reached over and poked me hard in the arm with one finger. "Ouch! Hey, quit it."

"Anything?" he asked. I looked at him strangely. "What? I don't know how all this weirdo magic stuff works either. What else happened?"

"That's about it, and now you know what I do. No, I take that back. You know more than I do. What's the deal with you two anyway?"

Earl paused for a long time, trying to think of what to say. "It don't matter."

That pissed me off. I had put it on the line for this company. "Oh, Myers seems to think that it does, and it looks like I'm stuck in the middle of your feud. I've bled, killed, and even died with this company. I think I've earned the right to know a few of MHI's deep dark secrets at this point."

He just looked defeated now. "It's no big secret, just not something I'm proud of. There was a Hunter named Hood once, good buddy of Myers and your father-in-law to be. They were real tight, like you, Trip, and Holly are now. Until I . . . I killed him by accident."

"On a mission?" It wasn't unheard of. We made our living off the judicious use of firearms, high explosives, and pointy things in a real dynamic environment. Bad things happened occasionally. Hell, Holly had nearly blown up Trip once.

Earl shook his head. "No...look, it don't matter. It was my fault and I made sure that it could never happen again. It was just a stupid mistake. But that's when Myers left us, and he's hated my guts ever since. He held me responsible, and by extension, all of MHI. I just...just don't want to talk about it."

I believed him. I could honestly say that I had never actually seen him look remorseful before. The look was gone in an instant, and replaced with his usual gruff exterior. He coughed. "No need to worry about that. What's done is done. Myers can kiss off. First priority, we need to keep you from getting capped by some death cult. If I let you get killed, Julie would never shut up about it." He held up his hand and tapped his thumb and fingers together for the universal sign for nagging.

"Gee, thanks."

"Aw, just messing with you. We're down to the last few days of this training class, and they're looking remarkably good. I've got some experienced Hunters running it, but they could probably use some help." None of the senior Hunters liked taking time off paying jobs to pull training duty, especially since training didn't involve collecting any bounties, and seldom involved any killing, which were the two main reasons most of us got into this business to start with. "As of right now, you're off active duty. You're going to stay at the compound and help with training."

"What?" I shouted. Harbinger's personal team was kind of like MHI's mobile strike force. We mostly bounced around, assisting local teams as they needed it. It was considered the sweetest gig in the company by many, and with the level of monster activity around the country being what it was, we were almost always busy. "No way. I should be out there working cases. Our team's due to get called up anytime now."

"The rest of us are. You ain't. Not until this blows over. Look, Owen, it's not anything personal. I would do the same thing for any of my men, and you would too, should you get your own team someday." I had noticed that since I was planning on marrying his great-granddaughter and heiress-apparent, Harbinger had taken an interest in my leadership skills. "Provided you live that long."

"That's not fair," I muttered.

"Fair? Boy, you're in the wrong business if you want *fair*. What's not fair is all of us getting killed walking into an ambush meant for you. The compound is the safest place for you to be, surrounded by firepower. No monster has had the guts to attack the compound in fifty years."

"I can take care of myself, Earl." I insisted. "This is bull—"

He cut me off. "Decision's final, Hunter." His tone suggested that he was not about to listen to me. Earl had been running this gang of type-A personality mercenary killers since my grandfather was in diapers. Nothing I said here was going to sway him once he had picked a course of action.

"What's to keep them from sending an army of zombies against the compound? He did it in Mexico."

"This place has been warded," he explained. It was obvious that I didn't get it. He sighed and backed up.

"You know how vampires can't come into a place unless they've been invited? Well, we've got something even better than that covering the compound. No undead can enter here, period. And if this guy's main weapon is bossing around undead, this is the safest place you can be. No transdimensional creatures either, which rules out anything sent directly from the Old Ones."

"How's that work?" I asked.

"Beats me, but it does. We found a ward stone a long time ago, and set it up here. Any undead that cross the threshold of this property just explode. It's really kind of neat. Don't go spreading that around, though, because once in a while some undead come by with a bone to pick, and it's fun to watch them blow up when they cross the gate."

"I don't like it . . ." I muttered.

Harbinger pulled out a pack of Marlboros and shook one into his hand. "I didn't say that I'm going to make you sit here forever, did I? Don't worry. We'll figure out a way to deal with this cult. The Feds might not be able to handle it, but they're a bunch of bureaucratic twits. I'll call in some favors and we'll start working our sources out on the dark side. We'll find them ourselves, then take care of this problem, MHI style . . ."

"Which usually involves chainsaws," I said happily.

"Yes. Yes, it does." He flipped open his MHI logo Zippo and lit his cigarette, indicating that this was bothering him more than he was letting on. He usually didn't smoke inside the main building unless he was under a lot of stress. "In the meantime, you lay low here at home base."

"If the compound's so safe then what about this spy?"

"I think Myers is a liar," Harbinger answered, a little too quickly. "But...I didn't get this old by not being paranoid. Look, you think getting stuck on training duty is a joke, fine. Congratulations, you're now responsible for rooting out this mole if there is one."

Now I figured he was just humoring me. "And just how am I supposed to do that?"

Harbinger shoved the Feds' file folder toward me. "I don't know yet. Use your imagination. I'll gather the others that I know we can trust, and you can meet me in the main conference room at six. Ditch the federal weasels on the way. In the meantime, don't let Franks screw around with any of our stuff. I don't trust that guy."

"Okay, first off, we need to set some ground rules," I spoke slowly and avoided using big words so Franks wouldn't be confused. Past history indicated that when he got confused, he tended to hit me. He and the three other Feds were sitting across from me in the MHI cafeteria. Franks was on his fourth sandwich and apparently had a metabolism like a blast furnace. The other agents—Torres, Herzog, and Archer—listened intently. The one thing I could say for the Feds, they did take their jobs really seriously. "You don't need to be so close. Here at the compound, I'm safe."

Franks snorted. Agent Torres actually raised his hand, which made me feel a little silly. I pointed at him.

"Owen. May I call you that?" I nodded. My friends around here usually just called me Z, but it would be a cold day in hell before I ranked anybody from the MCB as a friend. "I know this is awkward, but we're just here to help." Torres was the youngest, and seemed sincere. He did seem to really respect MHI, which was abnormal. After the meeting, Holly had told me that she thought he was the cutest too, which had caused me to roll my eyes so hard that I had actually hurt myself. He had given me back my precious guns though, so I was inclined to not *totally* hate him.

"When people from the government tell me they're just here to help, I get nervous. You're supposed to blend in, right? We've got a giant Newbie class going on now, the compound's crowded, and always having four of you walking in formation around me looking like a bunch of storm troopers isn't going to help."

Archer spoke. "So what do you expect us to do? Just sit back and wait for the Condition to murder you?" Archer was tall, but unlike most of the overly buffed MCB, he was skinny. The average Fed made your average Hunter look pretty dumpy. But Archer was thin, with an angular nose, and a large Adam's apple. He had one of those haircuts that worked if you were a Marine, but otherwise just made you look kind of silly, with the buzzed sides, and the perfectly straight flattop, so symmetrical that it had to have been done with surveying gear.

"Look, Pitt, we don't want to be here any more than you want us to be," Herzog said. She was the first female MCB agent I had met, all of five feet tall, and built like a bulldog, complete with jowls. She also had the worst attitude. "We all know this is a bullshit assignment, and I don't know what we did to piss Myers off to get stuck doing this scut work, no offense, sir," she nodded at Franks, who stopped chewing long enough to grunt an affirmation. "We

should be out killing monsters, and taking down the
Condition the old-fashioned way. Beating the ever-
livin' hell out of everyone in it until somebody squeals
where the bosses are, and then putting a bullet in
the brain of every last one of the squid-worshipping
fanatics. We kneecap enough of these assholes and cut
off enough thumbs, somebody will talk. They always
do. We need to be out there putting the fear of God
into these freaks, not babysitting...*you*."

Torres had mentioned Border Patrol at the airstrip.
Archer had an 82nd Airborne tat on his forearm. All the
MCB types apparently started out in regular government
jobs, so I had to know. "Herzog, who were you with
before being recruited by the Monster Control Bureau?"

"Internal Revenue Service."

*God help us.* "Oh...well...okay then." That made
sense. I had a sneaking suspicion that she had once
audited my old job. Somebody from the IRS had
actually taken the time to draw frowny faces in red
ink on a depreciation schedule that I had filled out.
She seemed like the type. "Look, personally I agree.
I would much rather have you out there doing your
thing, cutting thumbs off and whatnot, and not following me around. Like this, you're going to stick
out. This just isn't going to work."

"The only Hunters who know who we really are
are Harbinger and his immediate people," Torres
suggested to Franks. "We can blend in with the new
recruits. Nobody, including the Condition's spy, will
ever even know we're on site unless Owen needs us."

"You three, maybe...but everybody knows of Franks,"
I pointed out. I didn't add that his reputation for brutality had an almost urban legend quality to it in Monster

Hunting circles. "He'll have to go, I don't know, live in the forest or something."

Torres was undeterred. "Okay, then the cover story can be that Agent Franks is a liaison, assigned here to build camaraderie between private sector and governmental Hunters." The man was just chock full of helpful suggestions, though I still liked my live-in-the-forest idea better. Franks nodded slowly, as if the idea of him being an ambassador of goodwill made any sense whatsoever. "We stay out of your way, we're still accomplishing our mission, everybody's happy."

"Everybody saw your great big airplane land today."

"Nobody was close except for your friends. We can say it was for Agent Franks. The rest of us are late additions to the class."

I bit my lip. Torres had a point. "That'll work, but there's one more thing."

"Oh, I'm sorry, is putting our lives on the line to protect you from the forces of evil *inconvenient*?" Herzog asked, just oozing sympathy.

"Yeah, it is." I had no patience for this nonsense. I didn't ask for their help. "Inside this, the main building, you're not allowed past the first floor. When I'm working here at the compound, my room is upstairs. Upstairs is off limits. The basement is off limits." Really, I didn't care, but I knew that MHI had a lot of things stashed around here that they really didn't want the government to know about. Hell, I still didn't now what was in half of the basement. Plus it was one more way for me to be a pain in the ass to Franks' Goon Squad. I can't help it. I really do have an antiauthoritarian streak.

"That's not going to make our mission any easier," Torres suggested gently.

"You want to blend in with the Newbies? They aren't allowed past the first floor either until they've graduated training. Deal with it."

"Myers warned us that you'd be difficult," Archer said, raising his voice slightly. "So that's how it's going to be then. Who the hell are you to—"

I raised my hand and cut him off. "You want to go upstairs, get a warrant. Otherwise, shut it, Buzz Cut. We all know why you're here, and that's to capture some assassins. You couldn't care less what happens to me. So worst-case scenario, I get killed, then you can mop up and your boss is happy. This whole damn thing is his fault anyway, and I don't have to have you all crowding my personal space." That seemed to really piss off Herzog and Archer. Torres looked like it hurt his feelings that I would question his honest intentions. He was almost like a governmental version of Trip.

Surprisingly enough, Franks didn't argue, he just kept chewing, taking the time to savor the Wonder Bread and bologna. Finally he swallowed and wiped his mouth with the back of one massive hand. "Whatever . . . It's your funeral." He glanced across his team and nonchalantly ordered, "It's settled. Hang back until someone tries to kidnap Pitt. Interrogate the survivors."

Somehow that didn't give me a real good feeling.

The file on the Sanctified Church of the Temporary Mortal Condition was fat with color photos, weird intel, and disturbing reports. I had spent the last three hours poring over the notes, and the more I read, the more worried I got. It had grown dark outside and stuffy inside the second-floor conference room.

"Man, what a bunch of jerks," Milo Anderson said

as he leaned back in his chair, holding a sheet of paper in front of his bushy red beard, eyes darting back and forth behind thick round glasses as he read through the list of the various atrocities. "I never knew there were this many ways to sacrifice a virgin!"

"Better watch out, Trip," Holly muttered under her breath as she flipped through the pages, her shoes up on the conference table, absently chewing a pencil between her teeth. "They're coming to get you."

Trip studiously ignored her and kept on reading factoids about the people who wanted to bundle me up and ship me across the universe to be devoured by a giant mollusk. Harbinger had said that he was going to bring in the people he trusted, and apparently, that was pretty much everybody who would normally be here anyway, which wasn't exactly surprising. When you spend this much time risking life and limb with people, they aren't just coworkers, they're family. And apparently, having one of that family personally threatened gets taken pretty damn seriously.

"So which of y'all's got a plan on how we kill all these folks on here?" Dorcas asked, holding up the list of the suspected cultists. She slurped noisily from her coffee mug. Normally our senior-citizen receptionist wouldn't be in a team planning meeting, but she had taken an almost grandmotherly liking to me over the last year. Either that or she was just itching to shoot somebody.

"We're Monster Hunter International, not Doofus Hunter International," Julie said soothingly. "We're not interested in these chumps. Most of them probably don't even know what they're involved in. Besides, knowing the government, their intel is probably wrong on half these names anyway. Sorry, Dorcas."

"Tempting though . . ." Holly said, glancing at the list. "I hate that guy's movies."

"Terrible actor," Trip agreed.

Albert Lee was the last to arrive. He limped into the room carrying a stack of books hastily gathered from the archives under one arm and balancing his cane in the other. Lee had worked as our archivist ever since his leg had been severely injured at DeSoya Caverns. Though mighty handy on demolitions, his real calling was in research. He put the heavy books down and then thumped me hard on the back. "Good to see you made it home, man," he said with a grin.

I shook his offered hand. "Good to be home, Al."

"Wait 'til you see what I found. Dude, you are *so* screwed," he said as he sat down next to me, his metal leg brace creaking audibly. I felt bad whenever it seemed to cause him discomfort, which was often. I had been serving as his team leader when he had taken that hit and I still held myself responsible. Realistically, there was nothing that I could have done differently, but that's still how I felt. Lee, a tough former Marine, had never uttered a single word about it, except to joke about how it had finally given him an excuse to buy a badass sword cane.

The room was relatively full. Earl Harbinger, Julie Shackleford, Milo Anderson, Trip Jones, and Holly Newcastle were normal fixtures, as they made up the backbone of my team. In addition, Skippy, our pilot, and leader of our orc contingent, was standing quietly at the back of the room, still wearing his hood and goggles, unwilling to take a seat at the table, even among his friends. It wasn't that Skippy was unsociable, it was just that being around humans was always painfully awkward for him. And compared to most of his people, he was the life of the party.

The only other active Hunter present was someone I only knew in passing, and had never personally worked with, other than briefly last year when all of MHI was gathered for DeSoya Caverns. Her name was Esmeralda Paxton, Seattle team lead, and she was the one who had drawn the duty of training this Newbie class. Paxton was probably only a little over five feet tall, in her early forties, with auburn hair tied up in a bun, and wearing wire-rimmed glasses. She had on a folksy patchwork vest, a fashion that really didn't seem to fit in with all the hardened killers. She looked more likely to bake up a plate of chocolate-chip cookies than to stake a vampire, but Earl trusted her enough to lead a team in one of the most active parts of the country, and Julie's very own younger brother had been assigned to her care, so apparently she was a lot more dangerous than her motherly looks indicated. She had not spoken much yet, but continued to study the material intently.

Raymond Shackleford the Third, semi-retired super Hunter, whom Julie referred to as Grandpa, and the rest of us normally just called Boss, was sitting at his customary seat at the head of the table. He had aged quite a bit during the time I had known him. His white hair was getting wispier, the scarred side of his face around his eye patch was beginning to droop, and I was sad to notice that his nagging cough had gotten worse since we had left for Mexico. He was more of a symbolic leader. Earl Harbinger, real name Raymond Shackleford the Second, ran the day-to-day operations of the company, but there was no way that the Boss was going to sit out on a death threat against one of his Hunters. Missing his right hand, he banged his stainless-steel hook on the table to get everyone's attention.

He cleared his throat. "All right, people. What's the consensus?"

"Z's hosed," Trip suggested.

"Thank you, Mr. Jones. All in favor?"

The entire table said "Aye," then laughed at my expense. "Thanks, guys," I muttered. Julie patted my hand under the table.

"All right, enough of that tomfoolery," the Boss ordered. "Threat assessment?"

"Very bad, sir," Lee hoisted the first book. "Nobody knows who this necromancer is. I've been reading up on them today, and that title can be used for anybody who dabbles in death magic, animating the dead, all the way up to some really bad men who've done some terrible things."

"What kind of terrible?"

"Pretty much anything you can think of. The last MHI case I can find involving one was in Haiti, 1978. There was a high body count on that one," Lee replied.

"I remember that," the Boss said. "That was the man who had all those doppelgangers working for him, replaced all the city authorities, and then held himself a big old massacre." We'd learned a bit about doppelgangers in training, but hadn't spent much time on them since nobody had seen one for decades. They were perfect mimics, and historically, the mysterious creatures had caused all sorts of trouble. "Good thing we haven't had to deal with those cursed shapeshifters since."

"No, you're thinking of Cuba in '53," Harbinger corrected his son. "Haiti was the one where the necromancer sewed all those bodies together into that giant flesh golem."

"My memory ain't what it used to be," the Boss replied simply. I noted that Harbinger looked a little sad at that. It had to be difficult to see your loved ones age a decade for every one of yours.

"Either way you get the point. This could be potentially really ugly. Historically they've raised the dead, invented totally new kinds of undead, opened portals to other dimensions, that kind of thing," Lee said. "And I'm assuming it gets worse." Our archivist pulled on a pair of surgical gloves before opening the largest, dustiest, and oldest book. The cover was bound in ornate leather and the pages were hand-inked on yellowed parchment. Lee was very careful, almost delicate, in order to not damage the ancient tome. "The Feds' notes mentioned that the Condition has a pet shoggoth, so I figured I would see what one of those could do..." The drawing was of a horrible, bulbous, lumpy, asymmetrical thing, with far too many mouths and eyes. I was really hoping that the artist had been exaggerating. "There are passing references to them in different places. This one is in Arabic, but it had the most info on them."

"Nasty...What's it do?" Holly asked.

The Boss and Harbinger exchanged a quick glance. The Boss spoke first. "They're a pain in the rear, is what they are. My brother Leroy and I fought one once, right here in Cazador. It moved into the forest years back. Stinky, messy beast, started eating townsfolk and livestock. I tried to kill it, but it got away."

"You never told me you'd hunted a shoggoth, Grandpa." Julie leaned across me to see the book. "I didn't know those still existed." Julie frowned as she studied the picture. "Wait a second...*Mr. Trash Bags*?"

"Who's Mr. Trash Bags?" I asked.

Her mouth fell open as she recognized it. Julie pointed at the old book. "Right there! That's Mr. Trash Bags! He was my imaginary friend when I was a little girl. We used to play games together in the forest. He was big and cuddly and sweet. You know how imaginary friends are. But that's totally him, Mr. Trash Bags. I was like six years old, but I still remember."

She had to be pulling my leg. "Your imaginary friend was a blob?"

"Sorry, Jules. He wasn't imaginary," Earl said apologetically. "And you were four. We never could figure out why it didn't just eat you. You cried for days after we chased it off."

Julie leaned back, looking flustered. "Wow...that...that really sucks," my fiancée said slowly. "He was such a nice...*thing*."

"Yes, and that's why I didn't tell you," her Grandpa said. "I figured you didn't need to know that your best friend was a soul-sucking creature from the great beyond. I hope you understand, my dear. Please, carry on, Mr. Lee."

Lee appeared a little surprised that one of his managers had been friends with a horrific blob. "Uh... yeah. Shoggoths are basically servants, manual laborers to the Old Ones. They do their bidding, run errands, eat people, dig tunnels, that kind of thing. To quote the original author, who's only referred to as the Mad Arab, 'To look upon their hideous thousand eyes is to invite horror and the suffering of infinite madness, within tombs of blackness where the innocent are devoured for eternity.' And so on."

"He seemed really nice..." Julie said hesitantly. "This is a major bummer..."

"They're amorphous. They can change shape quickly, but they're about fifteen feet across and weigh around two tons," Earl said. "They can communicate, but they're relatively stupid. Just brute force, steamrollers, made out of tar and eyeballs. And they eat everything." *Except for a four-year-old girl, luckily.* Julie seemed to be taking it well, but she came from a long line of Hunters who were proud of their flexible minds. Harbinger continued. "Fire chased it off last time. Milo, I want all the flamethrowers checked out and ready to go."

Julie rubbed her neck. "Well, that just makes me sad."

Now it was my turn to pat her hand under the table.

Esmeralda Paxton raised her hand politely to cut in. "You have more problems than just a shoggoth, not that those aren't terrible enough, mind you. One of these intercepted e-mail messages mentions, and I quote, 'The High Priest is prepared to use Force and Violence to satisfy the requests of the great Old Ones, no matter what the cost.'"

"Well, he did hit me with a toilet," I pointed out. "That's pretty damn violent."

She shook her head. "Force and Violence are capitalized."

I looked at her stupidly. "Cultists are bad at grammar?"

"They're proper nouns?" Trip asked. "Those are names."

Esmeralda smiled and pointed at Trip. "Bingo. And if this is who I'm thinking of, the Los Alamos team fought them once before, back when I was a Newbie."

Harbinger thought about it for a moment, scowling. "Cratos and Bia? It can't be. That was twenty years ago."

"Seventeen years. Please don't try and age me prematurely, Earl," the petite woman scolded him. "I'm not a little old lady yet, though I do eventually plan on being a surprisingly aggressive little old lady. They use the old Greek names for Force and Violence. They've been around for a really long time. Some say they're immortals."

"Everything's immortal," Earl stated, "until you figure out how to kill it."

"My team tracked them across southern Europe. They were easy to follow, since they made a mess wherever they went. We even managed to ambush them once, only to discover that they were virtually indestructible. Then they vanished into thin air. We never did get to collect those bounties."

"So, what are Force and Violence?" Julie asked. "I don't remember this kind."

"We're not sure what they are," Esmeralda explained. "Physically, they seemed similar to ogres, but they're smarter, or at least the female, Bia, is rather clever. The male, Cratos, is dumb as a rock, but unbelievably strong. They're either ancient or they took their names from minor gods in the Greek pantheon to give that impression."

"Ancient Greece, like Zeus comes down from Olympus and turns into a giant horny swan, kind of stuff?"

I asked. "Because, you know, this stuff wasn't weird enough already."

Earl leaned back in his chair, deep in thought. "Don't mock ancient Greek monsters. A minotaur near cost me my life, once. There's nothing tougher than a giant bull-man with bulletproof hide . . . I made a coat out of him."

"Well, we don't really know what they are. But they're monsters that show up every so often and go on a killing spree. The weirdest thing was that they didn't just kill people, they killed other monsters too. Their behavior was a mystery. This message might not even refer to the same creatures, but I just thought I should point it out," Esmeralda said. "If we run into two humanoids, and one's twelve feet tall and bright red, and the other's about eight feet tall, and purple—"

"Stop." Skippy suddenly cut her off. His gravelly voice made me jump. He had been so quiet that I had forgotten he was even in the room. The orc walked up to the table awkwardly and stared at Esmeralda, goggles tilting to the side. "Skippy . . . knows. Knows these . . ." He said some unpronounceable word in his own language. "Like you, Harb Anger, like MHI . . . they hunt. But bad. They bad things. No honor . . . Not hunt, to protect . . . hunt for kill. Hunt for make suffer. Hunt my people. Many *Urks* die." Skippy bowed his hooded head toward us, his shielded eyes inscrutable as ever. Speaking English always seemed painful to him. "Enemies . . . pay to kill many *Urks*." He said that same word again.

"What's that mean?" Trip asked. My friend had spent a lot of time at Skippy's village over the last few months, fascinated by the tribe, and had been picking up a lot of the orcish language.

Skippy stood awkwardly, tilting his head to one side, trying to find the words in English. "Think you call...*Hit Men.*"

"Assassins..." Esmeralda nodded thoughtfully. "That makes sense. We never did know why they attacked where they did, but there did seem to be a definite pattern. Then when their work was done, they just disappeared."

"This just keeps getting better and better. Ogre hit men..." I muttered. This Condition was just full of fun. "So, they're like the monster version of us?"

"No!" the orc responded with surprising intensity. Skippy shook his head vehemently. "Not like MHI. No honor!"

"How are they different, Skippy?" Trip asked calmly.

The orc continued to shake his head, agitated. Skippy seemed really offended by the idea that his adopted clan was anything at all like these things. "You, Hunters, paid money...for kill monster. These two...They kill, but paid...paid in *souls.* Eat the soul, live forever." Skippy finished talking and then retreated quietly back into the corner, seemingly embarrassed by saying so much. The others continued to talk back and forth in excited tones. Hunters tend to get pumped at the prospect of taking down something new.

My attention was diverted from the conversation as the conference room door swung open and another person walked in. I recognized him immediately, but was taken completely by surprise. The others didn't seem to notice.

The newcomer was about as tall as I was, but where I was hulking, he was lean, and where I was ugly, he was movie-star handsome. He was wearing standard issue MHI body armor only his was in black, had been tailored to fit better, and it still apparently had that magic ability to never get dirty. The spot where the green Happy Face with horns patch had been on his arm was blank Velcro now, but other than that, he looked exactly the same as the day he'd resigned.

"Hey, everyone, sorry I'm late. We had to wrap up today's training first. We started the Newbies on long-range rifle." Grant Jefferson, *former* Hunter, apologized as he walked up to the table. "I came as soon as I could, Earl. Why is Agent Franks guarding the staircase?"

I hadn't seen him since last summer. I glanced at Julie and she was as surprised to see her ex-boyfriend here as I was.

"Have a seat, Grant, I'll catch you up later," Earl said, gesturing at an open spot across the table from me.

He wasn't the only one who needed some catching up. "Hey, Grant. Why are you *here*, exactly?" I asked, probably a little louder than I needed to. The bad acoustics of the conference room were probably what made me sound a little more perturbed that I should have been. *Acoustics. Yeah.*

"Oh, hi, Julie," Grant said, easily ignoring me as he smoothly slid into the chair. He casually put his armored elbows on the table. "When did you get back from Mexico?" His tone was friendly.

"This afternoon . . ." she said slowly. I didn't know which was more of a surprise for her, Grant or Mr. Trash Bags. "MCB flew us back."

"Sorry I missed you earlier. Your brother is still out on the line. He said to tell you he'll catch up soon." Grant pretended to notice me for the first time. "Pitt, good to see you," he lied politely.

I grunted something noncommittal.

He turned his attention right back to Julie. "And congratulations to you two on getting engaged. That's just *great*." His fake smile was very convincing.

"Thanks." Julie was not deterred by small talk. "What are you doing here?"

Grant raised his eyebrows. "No one told you?"

"Aw, crap. Forgot," Earl said quickly. "It's been a busy few days. While you were in Mexico, Grant came by, asked for his old job back." I glared at Trip and Holly. They'd gotten back yesterday. Apparently they had forgotten to mention Grant's rehiring during all the excitement. They knew how well the two of us got along. Trip made eye contact and shrugged, as if to say *whoops*. "We're so shorthanded, I was glad to have the help."

"I guess the whole Hollywood thing didn't work out for you, huh?" I asked suspiciously.

He just smiled. His perfectly capped white teeth looked almost like Tic-Tacs. "No. It was fun, but Hunting is my true calling. I'm glad to be home."

I bit my tongue. *Home?* Sure, he had seen some horrible things while in the clutches of the Cursed One's seven Master vampires, but everybody had been as nice as possible to him in the aftermath, and he had still walked away, a quitter.

"Well . . . it's good to have you back," Julie said civilly. Their breakup had been a bit on the icy side. I hadn't been there for the actual "discussion" part, though I had been there when she'd knocked him out with the butt of an M14. Julie had never wanted to talk about it, so I had left it alone. With Grant gone, it had been one topic of conversation that we'd just mutually avoided.

"Where's your team patch?" I asked, being a complete jackass. Grant's hand subconsciously flicked to his arm, and just briefly he let slip a scowl. The golden boy never could handle failure.

Earl, sensing tension, spoke again, "I've assigned Grant to help Esmeralda with training for now. When the other team leads come in at graduation in a few days, we'll find a spot for him on one of the teams. We need all the experienced Hunters we can get out there in the field."

"Glad to help," Grant replied, still glaring at me. I smiled, noting that his once perfect nose had healed with a slight bend from when I had broken it.

"Yes, yes, back to business," said the Boss, who apparently could not care less about our petty personal dramas. "Anything else we need to know about this Condition?" Nobody had mentioned the potential spy. Earl caught my eye and shook his head slightly so the others wouldn't notice. Apparently we were keeping that part a secret.

"We're dealing with an organization that has a couple hundred human members, tops," Earl said. "And most of them are going to be fanatics rather than professionals in this *exalted order* of assholes. Their leader's powers are useless here, so we should be relatively safe from a direct assault. Unless he sends his other non-undead monsters against us, and if that happens, we'll just button up and deal with them. In the meantime we need to prepare for any other threats he comes up with. None of you will breathe a word of this to anyone outside of this room. We'll come up with a plan for this Condition." He began to rattle off duties. "Everyone, keep an eye on Franks. I don't trust him. Lee, see what you can find out about these ogre things from the archives. Julie, Dorcas, I want you to contact all the team leads, give them a brief rundown about this cult and see if any of them can scare up any local intel. Milo, Trip, Holly, go see the elves, check if they've had any dealings with them."

Holly groaned out loud.

"I really do know them better than anybody, I guess." Milo squinted toward me. "My wife's about to have a baby, and if I'm off talking to trailer park elves about you when she goes into labor with my first child, I'm holding you personally responsible."

I nodded slowly, not really sure how I was going to help with that.

Earl continued. "Esmeralda, Owen will be helping you with training. Don't let his goofiness fool you. He's actually a decent firearms instructor."

"I certainly could use another hand," she said.

"And you'll be adding three undercover federal agents to your class," Earl added. I believe that Esmeralda actually groaned louder than Holly had about the elves. Apparently the Seattle team leader got along with the government as well as everyone else at MHI. "Yeah, I know. Just pretend they aren't here."

"Damn Feds, on my property," the Boss murmured. I swear that if he wasn't such a gentleman, he would have spit on the floor. The government paid a large portion of the bills through PUFF, but that didn't mean we had to enjoy working with their Hunters.

"Can I at least be extra mean to them?" Esmeralda asked.

Harbinger smiled that predatory way only werewolves can. "But of course."

"I've got just the thing." Esmeralda grinned back. "Milo, we'll need some more cow entrails for another Gut Crawl tomorrow. It wouldn't be fair if our late arrivals missed out on that."

"I don't have anything fresh," Milo stated.

"Even better..."

# CHAPTER 5

I settled into a routine over the next few days. Whenever I was working at the compound, I slept in a small room on the top floor directly across from Julie's temporary room. Some of Harbinger's team had their own homes off site, mostly in nearby Cazador, but I had been living at the old Shackleford family estate, or at least I had until Earl had decreed it was safer for me to stay here. The routine started early; Esmeralda and her Hunters had the Newbies up and running by six. I'd shower and head downstairs for breakfast where, inevitably, Agent Franks was sitting in a chair at the base of the stairs waiting for me. We had assigned him a private room, but as of yet, I was unaware if he had actually used it. The giant apparently never slept, and if he did, I was willing to bet it was with one eye open. Each morning since we'd gotten back he had been in the exact same spot, in a folding chair stolen from the cafeteria, back against the wall, waiting. And each morning, he would just nod at me when I would appear, as if he had heard me long before I had come down, and had been waiting patiently.

Franks had gone incognito. After the first day, I had pointed out that if he was supposedly some sort of liaison, he probably wouldn't be wandering around wearing his full suit of armor, with his assault rifle slung on his back, and what looked like about fifty pounds of ancillary gear. Apparently, he had agreed. So now Franks was in his other uniform, a cheap black suit, with a black clip-on tie, and a white dress shirt that had never been intended to be buttoned around a neck as thick as his. I had spotted him carrying at least two full-size Glocks, and I was guessing he had a grenade in each coat pocket, but for Franks, that was real low profile.

"Mornin', Sunshine," I said sarcastically, inwardly wishing that he would just go away.

He glowered for a moment, apparently impatient that nothing had tried to murder me yet. He adjusted the grenades in his pockets, checked his clip-on, and stood. As usual, Franks didn't have much to say. I started for the cafeteria, Franks trailing sullenly a few feet behind.

Today was going to be much like yesterday. After breakfast, I needed to catch up on paperwork, then I was supposed to run the range and teach the Newbies how to shoot better—hopefully at the targets and not at each other by accident, which got harder to do as the exercises got more complicated. Esmeralda had me doing that for most of the day.

"Any new intel from your people?" I asked Agent Franks over breakfast. We were alone in the large cafeteria. The Newbie class was out on their run, and

Harbinger's team were mostly still working on the jobs he had assigned to them. I knew that Trip, Holly, and Milo had road-tripped it to Corinth yesterday to shake down the elves at the Enchanted Forest Trailer Park. Lucky them.

"No," he said sullenly over a mouthful of bacon. Franks chewed with his mouth open. Loudly.

"Any idea when this cult might make their move?"

"No."

"Think they're scared because I'm here?"

He shrugged.

"Anything interesting happen last night?"

"No."

Being by nature the kind of person who is uncomfortable with long silences, I kept trying. "If we're going to be hanging out, we might as well get to know each other some. I've known you for a while now." I didn't need to mention that our first meeting had been with him pointing a gun at my head, and our second had involved him beating the ever-living hell out of me. "And I don't even know what your first name is."

He didn't respond for a long time. "Agent."

So much for being friendly. "So, Agent, got any hobbies? Chia Pet farm? Collect Pokemon cards?"

I could feel the disdain. The power-lifter veins in his forehead bulged slightly as I annoyed him. "No."

That was pretty much the same as every other conversation I'd had with Franks. Apparently the government had not issued him a personality. The man was a hulking, violent, silent enigma. I sighed, and went back to the routine.

◈          ◈          ◈

My office was on the top floor. I suppose that it was technically the Monster Hunter International Finance Department, but that seemed a bit pretentious a title for just me and a computer with Quickbooks Pro installed on it. I guess that I was the *interim* finance department, since I'd finally talked Earl into hiring a full-time bookkeeper, but I'd been too busy to follow up on it, so in the meantime, it was all me.

The accounting for MHI wasn't nearly as complicated as my old job. I managed to mostly keep everything up to date between missions. Before I'd come on it had been a real mess. Apparently killing and math were mutually exclusive skill sets for most people, but I'd gotten the books cleaned up. I'd steered us through an IRS audit a few months ago and that had been almost as hard as defeating Lord Machado.

The books were rough. I wasn't exactly proud of the General Ledger, but that was the beauty of being a privately held company. There were no shareholders to make happy and none of that awful SarbOx non- sense that big corporations had to deal with. Most of our money came from PUFF and they always paid on time. The hardest part was trying to track the expenses, since the various teams threw bags of money around in the course of completing their missions, and all of them were better at destruction than reliably e-mailing me their expense reports.

The stack of invoices had grown fat since I'd left for Mexico. As usual, the other Hunters couldn't be bothered to file anything correctly, and it all tended to just get dumped into one big pile right in the middle of my desk. This was going to take forever to book. The top sheet was labeled *Project Leviathan* in red Sharpie.

"Crap, Milo, ten thousand dollars for custom-machined harpoons? How many of those things do you need?" I muttered as I tossed the invoice aside. I had one expense account titled "Milo." It was filled with weird items.

Groaning, I flipped through the stack. My heart just wasn't in it today. I was too preoccupied with a death cult to get any work done. In my heart, I knew I should be out there, doing something useful. There were some framed pictures on my desk: me and Julie after hiking to the top of Mt. Cheaha together, the Amazing Newbie Squad posed with Friendly Fernando when we'd gone back to visit DeSoya Caverns as tourists rather than exterminators, and the only picture I had of Mordechai Byreika.

It was the black and white photo that Lee had found last summer from Mordechai's old journal, with the Hunter posed in front of something giant, scaled, and dead. I picked it up and sighed. It wasn't that I missed having a cryptic ghost hanging out inside my brain, but Mordechai would have known what to do. He'd always had the right answers, even when he was keeping them from me for my own protection. He couldn't have told me what to do, because I would've rushed to do it, and inadvertently opened the gate in the process. It had been a fine line to walk, but he'd been wise, careful, and thoughtful, all things that I sucked at. Mordechai died decades before I had been born, but he would always be my mentor.

"I wish you were around, Old Man," I said. "I could use some good advice right about now...." I didn't want to be special, but as Mordechai had said, I'd drawn the universe's short straw and been the one to decide the fate of worlds. Now I was paying for it.

I put the picture down and glared at the stack of invoices.

*Screw it.* The paperwork could wait.

At least I got paid to shoot, which, as a lifelong gun nut, is kind of a dream come true. From ten until noon I worked on marksmanship and manipulation with the Newbies. At this point they had already been here for two months, and this was the final week of training, so the dumb and dangerous had long since been rooted out and sent home with fat severance checks.

The remaining Newbies were pretty sharp. As usual, all of them were themselves survivors of brutal supernatural attacks. This particular class had a soldier who'd taken out an Akkadian storm beast in Iraq; a cabby who'd given a ride to a vampire (not only had it tried to eat him, it had been a lousy tipper); two brothers whose foundation business, Haight Brothers Construction, had unearthed a skinwalker; an archeologist who discovered that some things were best left undiscovered; and even a kid just out of high school who'd had a blood fiend climb in the drive-through window at the Arby's he'd been working at. And yes, it turns out that you can actually kill a blood fiend by shoving its face into the fry cooker and holding it there until it quits kicking.

I'd been tasked with helping on the range, but I had to admit that most of the Newbies were already proficient shots. One of Esmeralda's guys, a fellow hardcore shooter named Cooper, had done a good job getting them up to speed. But Cooper was primarily an explosives guy, a rifleman second, and I was able to contribute quite a bit of knowledge to teaching the Newbies how to improve with the shotguns and pistols. Not meaning to boast, but as far as I knew, nobody at MHI was as good as I was with a shotgun. Being good at something, and being a good teacher were not necessarily the same thing, and I could only hope that I would do half as good a job as Sam Haven had done for my Newbie class. Now, he had been one hell of a great instructor.

Grant was working with those chosen to be the sharpshooters. I hated to admit it, but he did know more about long-range precision shooting than I did—though in my opinion, he was a perfect example of a knowledgeable but lousy teacher, but then again, I was biased.

This was the largest Newbie class that had ever gone through training, and under Esmeralda's patient tutelage, it was also looking like it was going to have the highest graduation rate. She had better be careful. If she did too good a job, Earl would probably try to draft her to run every training class, and I doubted any of the experienced Hunters would want that as a full-time gig.

I walked back and forth behind the firing line of Hunters. I had approximately half of them today. Each Newbie was paired up, with one serving as coach and the other shooting. Today I was drilling them on transitions, running their primary long gun dry, then slinging it quickly to draw their pistols. Most of them were actually looking pretty damn good. Franks' Goon Squad had integrated seamlessly into the class. I had to hand it to the MCB agents. They were professionals. As far as the other Newbies and Esmeralda's team knew, they had been part of the last Newbie class but had pulled out early due to various training injuries. That also explained their above-average skills and knowledge. Watching them on the range, I learned that Torres was damn good, Archer was well-trained and methodical, and Herzog was decently proficient, but made up for it with maliciousness.

My protective detail hadn't liked me walking around a bunch of potential Condition assassins with guns, but I still thought they were full of crap. The undercover agents kept glancing my way, waiting for something terrible to happen. Sadly for them, nothing did. After transitions, shooting on the move, and shooting from various cover positions, we took a break to hydrate, snack, and reload magazines before moving onto the next series of more complicated exercises. Grant immediately began to tell most of the willing-to-listen about some story where he was the hero. He had lots of those. There was a tin roof set up for shade over the firing line, and I plopped down onto a concrete bench to suck down a Gatorade, seeking solitude away from the Newbies for a moment. Even spring in Alabama is hot when you're standing in the sun carrying a full combat load and wearing a Kevlar suit. My shadow, Franks, wandered off momentarily to answer a phone call.

One young woman broke away from the crowd and approached. She had to have been one of the youngest in the class, an attractive girl in a bouncy cheerleader kind of way, blonde and perky. "Mind if I sit here?"

"Sure," I gestured at the bench across from me. She flopped down, armor pouches banging. I noted Torres, Archer, and Herzog scanning her for threats and assessing if they needed to come over and protect me. I shook my head slightly. The agents went back to their snacks.

The Newbie held out a granola bar. "Want one?"

"No thanks." I mentally ran down the roll call of names. I had always sucked with remembering names. "Dawn, right?"

"Yeah," she smiled, then looked around to see if anyone else was listening. "Do you mind if I pick your brain for a second?" She had a cute Texas accent. I knew that one well from having lived in Dallas. I'd struck out with a lot of girls who sounded like that.

"Brain-picking. That's what I'm here for," I answered. I was, after all, supposed to be the experienced role model. "What can I do for you?"

She looked around to see if anyone was listening. I noted that a couple of other Newbies were watching, like they had dared her to come over here. Dawn leaned in conspiratorially. "You're the guy that destroyed Lord Machado last year, right?"

It wasn't exactly a secret, but it wasn't something I liked to talk about. Way too many things had occurred that night that I preferred to keep secret. "Where'd you hear about that?"

"Are you kidding?" She laughed. "Esmeralda told us about it during monster-lore class yesterday. That fight was the biggest bounty ever collected in MHI history! And you were the primary on the PUFF. One Master vamp by yourself, assists on a couple of others, and a solo takedown of a one-of-a-kind mega-bounty monster."

That was all true, and I had made serious bank off that particular mission, but I hadn't realized that it granted me celebrity status. "Yeah, that was me, but it was all a team effort. I was just in the right place at the right time."

"I knew it. I bet you made millions."

"Something like that." It had been a considerable chunk of money. I had actually donated most of my personal earnings from DeSoya Caverns to the families of the Hunters who had died there, not that I spread that fact around. It had just seemed like the right thing to do. I'd still made a ton. "It was a tough case."

"Wow," she batted her big blue eyes at me. "That is *so* hot!"

I had been taking a swig of Gatorade and nearly choked on imitation grape. "Excuse me?" I coughed.

"Oh, sorry." The way she looked at me said that she was anything but sorry. "I just love this stuff. You know, we should like totally hook up later and you could tell me all about it. I'd love to hear the story firsthand. Maybe over drinks or something."

As a man who'd spent most of his life ignored by pretty girls, it took me a moment to realize that she was actually coming on to me. It took my higher brain functions a few seconds to compose a response. "Uh, sorry, Dawn. I'm going to be really busy for a while. See, Agent Franks is here as a . . . goodwill ambassador . . . and I've got to stay with him." I casually pulled my shooting gloves off in the hopes that she would see my ring.

She saw it. "So, you're married, huh?"

"Engaged."

That didn't deter her either. "No biggie. I was engaged once, but he got decapitated by fish-men. Long story, but that's how I ended up here. You ever see what happens when you shove a humanoid fish monster into a propeller?" She gave me a smile that would best be described as *flirty*. "I'll have to tell you about it sometime. Maybe we can talk again." She got off the bench. Somehow females still managed to make body armor look good. "See ya later."

Dawn went back to a knot of Newbies. One of the other women giggled at whatever she'd said. What the hell was this, MH Junior High? I shook my head and went back to my drink. Of course, when you're single, pretty girls won't talk to you, but when you're in a relationship...*bam*, they come out of the woodwork. Fed business completed, Franks rejoined me. He looked down, saw the look of consternation on my face and shrugged.

After hours of yelling at Newbies and shooting cardboard targets shaped like various monsters, I grabbed lunch for two, ditched Franks at the agreed-upon base of the stairs, and met Julie in her office.

My fiancée's office suited her personality. One part order, one part chaos, but the chaos was a work in progress. She had painted the walls a kind of sea foam color, had hung up several nice paintings, decorated everything else, and then promptly buried it all in paperwork and MHI-issue equipment. She had a couple potted plants with flowers that she could rattle off by their Latin names (they all looked the same to me, and bothered my allergies, but I would never tell her that). There was a bulletin board behind her full of photos of friends and family, including a couple of me mugging stupidly for the camera. Her desk was covered in papers, and there were a few piles of strategic paper on the floor, stacked on top of the filing cabinets and in the corners.

The problem is that this kind of work never really

stops accumulating. Julie is in this for the love of Hunting, so when there's a job to do, that comes first. But as the designated heir to the family business, she still has to pay attention to the day-to-day crap that all businessmen do. She also has a really difficult time delegating.

As an experienced financial-type professional, I managed to help her out quite a bit between missions, but MHI really needed more full-time office staff. The plan was to wait for some really smart Newbies that we didn't trust enough to go on teams, but we were so short-handed in the field that our standards were low in that regard.

"What's up, sexy," I said as I entered.

Julie held up one hand to shush me. She was listening to someone on the phone. I set her lunch down on top of the pile of quotes, bids, invoices, reports, and a worn copy of a Jane Austen novel. Even Julie takes breaks now and then. She grabbed a pad of paper, pulled a pen out from behind one ear, and started making notes. "Yes . . . rubbery. Green . . . eight feet tall. Yes, sir. I know exactly what those are, and yes, we can handle them."

I pulled up a chair and flopped into it, still smelling of gunpowder and oil. It sounded like we got another job. *Sweet.* Business was hopping, and even if this was in a different team's area, the whole company still shared in the bounties. The last year had been record-breaking, but that had been due to the abnormally high rate of monster activity, not to mention the absurdly large PUFF bounties we had been paid after the Lord Machado case.

Julie was still talking. "No. No, sir. Do not, I

repeat, do not approach them. . . . *Why*?" She rolled her eyes as the person on the other end of the line asked something incredibly stupid. "Because they will eat you. . . . Yes. *Eat* you." She paused to cover the phone's receiver and said to me, "What is it with these people who want to *reason* with monsters? Morons."

"I blame it on *Twilight*." In real life, vampires only sparkle when they're on fire.

Julie went back to her call. "Okay, we'll have a team there in . . ." She glanced at her watch, and since she didn't have to call somewhere else to check on that team's readiness, I had to assume that it was our team's gig. "Three hours."

The person on the other end of the line freaked out at that. Julie drummed her fingers on her desk while she waited for the tirade to end. I had seen the same mannerism recently from her mother, but where Susan's nails were pointy and red, Julie's nails were kept short so they wouldn't interfere with her shooting. "Sir, listen. They'll still be there. As long as you don't approach them, or bother them, or look at them funny, they shouldn't attack. We'll expect the down payment to be in our account by the time we arrive on scene. Don't let anyone near that property in the meantime. Yes, thank you. Have a nice day." She hung up the phone. "Or as nice a day as you can have when you've got a troll infestation."

"Oooh, trolls. What's the plan?"

"We're driving to Bessamer. Skippy's off today for something, so no chopper. I'll have Milo and the others come over from Mississippi and meet us; hopefully they'll be there in time. That gives us most of the team. The trolls are holed up in a small abandoned building, so there shouldn't be too many of them. Nothing we can't handle. Bounty on a full grown one is"—she checked the PUFF table tacked to her wall—"fifty thousand a pop. Not bad."

"Awesome," I said, looking forward to grabbing Abomination and dispensing some monster justice. "I've never seen a troll before. Let me guess, cute little fellas with big hair?"

She smiled at me sweetly and batted her big brown eyes. "Bummer, you can't see one now."

"Aaahhhh man," I whined.

"I know, I know. Earl's orders though. You're safer here."

"Can I stow away in your luggage?"

"You're too big to fit. Look, honey, I know this makes you angry." Julie tried to be soothing, but she already knew she was failing miserably. I just leaned back in the chair and palmed my face. It was still weird to touch it and not feel a mass of scar tissue. This wasn't right. I should be there with my team. "But don't worry. Once we take care of this cult, life will get back to normal."

I snorted. "Normal?"

"Relatively normal. And speaking of which, in all the excitement, we forgot something," she said with a grimace.

I hesitated. Had I forgotten another stupid wedding thing? I had just wanted to elope, go to Vegas or something, but the Shacklefords insisted on doing everything in a big way. She waited, prompting me to guess. "Pick out napkins?" It was a stab in the dark, but all of these things tended to run together to me.

"Already done. Yellow and lavender. How could you forget?"

"Uh...death cult?" I said in my defense. I didn't even know what color lavender was. I think most men would consider it light blue, or something.

"No. I'm supposed to meet *your* family. You were going to call them, remember?"

I smacked my forehead. *Of course.* I didn't really talk to my family very often. The last time I had seen them was when they had come out to visit after Mr. Huffman had torn me apart. I had called Mom and told her about the engagement, and she had gushed and cried on the phone for about an hour and a half, but because of various Hunting gigs, I'd kept postponing an actual visit. As far as my parents knew, I was still an accountant.

"And you were supposed to call your brother too."

"He's still on tour." I had spoken to my brother, David, or Mosh as the rest of the world called him, more recently, but that was to arrange VIP concert passes for some friends, and even that had been a real brief conversation. The Pitt family loved each other, in their own dysfunctional way, but it wasn't like we communicated a lot. "He's really busy."

"He's also coming through the state this week," Julie pointed out.

"Too late. He's already here, and playing Buzzard Island tonight. I got tickets for Skippy and his people. I was going to go too, but I guess that's out of the question now," I muttered.

Julie was perplexed. "You got tickets to a heavy metal concert, in public, for a tribe of orcs? How's that supposed to work?"

"Private sky box," I explained. "You know how they are with crowds. I told my brother I'm doing volunteer work with the local burn ward, so that explains all the masks and goggles. He was totally down with that." He had also been very suspicious as to when I had become the volunteer-at-a-hospital type, but there was lots of stuff Mosh didn't know about me.

"Well, I don't know, as long as Skippy keeps everybody out of trouble..." Julie said, concern evident in her voice. Orcs were still PUFF-applicable so the ones living with us were, technically speaking, illegal aliens. "Thanks for lunch, but I have to find Earl. We've got to hunt some trolls and I need to draft some extra gunmen to fill in for you."

"Esmeralda's good, so are the guys that she brought along. Cooper's hell on wheels with a FAL. I'm sure they're just itching for an excuse to get out of training. I can handle the Newbies."

"Okay, we'll take Esmeralda's team too. It'll be fun for me to get to work with my little brother. That way if Milo's held up, we can still move on those trolls as soon as we get there. This should be pretty straightforward. How's the training going anyway?"

"Good, but I think one of the Newbies just tried to flirt with me," I said. "You know, us ugly guys aren't used to that kind of thing. Gets us all flusterpated."

"Uh huh, sometimes young impressionable Newbies fixate on their more experienced instructors... oh wait. Why does that sound kind of familiar? How was it we met again?" Julie gave me her best playing-dumb look. "Which bimbo was it?"

"Dawn the Texan."

She nodded. "Oh, she *is* pretty. She was like Miss Houston or something. Pity, I have to murder her now."

"Don't worry, you're the only one for me," I

responded dryly. "Even if I am a dashing specimen of manhood and there's plenty of Owen Pitt to go around. You guys take care of the trolls. Grant and I can hold down the fort here."

"You promise to play nice with him?"

I raised my hands defensively. "You have my word, no assaulting Grant." *Unless he gives me a good reason*, I added mentally. "Seriously, I think we're cool. Seeing him was a surprise though, wasn't it?"

Julie shrugged uncomfortably. "I didn't expect to ever see him again, especially not here. Not after what happened to him and the way he left so suddenly."

I turned serious. "You okay?" She and Grant had been pretty tight last year. It was still an awkward topic of conversation for us. I knew that there was still a part of her that felt guilty about the timing of our getting together so shortly after we'd assumed Grant was dead.

She stood, came around the desk, and kissed me lightly. "I'm fine . . . Now those trolls aren't going to off themselves. I've got to go before the client calls back and screams some more. Love you." That was code for *I don't want to talk about it right now.*

"Love you too," I responded. "Be careful."

"I will. And don't forget to call your parents." Julie Shackleford smiled her perfect smile as she left the office. "Stay out of trouble!" she shouted from down the hallway.

"Always," I responded, but she was already gone.

It was approaching sundown when I was finally able to break away from the routine. I had been out on the obstacle course assisting while Grant Jefferson yelled at the slower Newbies. Agent Franks stood just outside of bad breath distance the entire time. The trainees kept casting a fearful eye at the brute behind me. Even among brand-new Hunters, Franks was already a legend.

The compound seemed relatively quiet without Team Harbinger and Team Paxton. Skippy's tribe was gone too, but they were virtually invisible even when they were here anyway. The Alabama spring air was thick with enough pollen to make my eyes water and fireflies were beginning to flicker through the chain-link-and-razor-wire fence surrounding the compound. Since it was relatively peaceful, I decided to call my folks while sitting on one of the benches outside the main building. I would need to think of another excuse as to why they couldn't meet my bride-to-be yet, but with a bunch of psychos stalking me, it was pretty rotten timing.

The ever-present Franks sulked ten feet away. He crossed his arms and scowled as I pulled out my phone. "Can I have some privacy?" I asked in exasperation.

He looked around. We were alone. There were no possible threats in view. He looked back. "No."

"You're such a douche bag." I sighed as I pulled up my folks' number. Franks didn't bother to respond. He was the immovable object.

It wasn't that I didn't love my parents. We just didn't communicate well. My mom tended to talk a lot, but seldom about anything important, and my father talked *at* me, rather than *to* me. Speaking with him was always awkward, as I was more used to him giving orders and training me for the inevitable fiery apocalyptic end of the world than anything approaching a normal relationship. I had to admit though, if my war-hero father hadn't spent all those hours teaching me to fight, then I wouldn't be alive today. Thank goodness for paranoia.

It rang three times before someone picked up. The voice was raspy and unfamiliar. "Who's this?"

"Who's this?" I responded, glancing automatically at my BlackBerry's display. Sure enough, it read *Mom*, so I hadn't misdialed.

"Well, hello, Mr. Pitt," replied the man with a chuckle. "That's some good timing. Your parents have a nice little home here in the country. You really should visit more."

A cold lump formed in my stomach. The look on my face must have telegraphed my distress, because Franks immediately perked up, one big hand unconsciously moving under his coat. "Who are you?" I demanded.

"No one important." There was a hoarse laugh. "I am but a mere acolyte of the shadows, but I bear a message from the High Priest of the Dread Overlord. We have your parents. He is willing to offer a trade: your family, for you." There was a shout in the background, an impact thud followed by a crash, and a woman cried out in fear. Somehow I knew it was my mom. "If you don't do exactly as we say, we'll feed them, bit by bit, to the mighty shoggoth."

My stomach lurched. I was speechless. Franks realized what was going on, pulled out his radio and started barking commands, but that was just a gray, background, buzzing noise as my world spiraled out from under me. "I...I..."

"You will do exactly as I say, Mr. Pitt, for we are the spear of the Old Ones' righteous fury. We— Hey, watch the old guy!" Glass shattered, there was some crashing, then something that could only have been a gunshot, and the phone went dead.

"NO!" I shouted, but the signal was gone, and I was only screaming at the silence. "Damn it! Franks! My parents! They've got my parents!"

"On it," he said calmly as he listened to his radio. Apparently their vast files told them right where to go. "Local law enforcement has been dispatched."

Panicked, I redialed. The phone just kept ringing, but nobody picked up.

I found myself pacing back and forth. This couldn't be happening. They had nothing to do with this. This wasn't their fight. They didn't even know what I really did for a living. They were hundreds of miles away. The feeling of helplessness hit like a sledgehammer. A painful minute passed, and I honestly didn't know what to do. I wanted to puke.

"Agent Myers," Franks said, holding out his radio.

I snatched it from him and slammed down the transmit button. "Myers, you son of a bitch, you better go get them!"

"Calm down, Pitt. My men are on it. If they escape before we arrive, we'll cordon off the area. My chopper is warming up now. I will personally oversee the search."

"Damn right you will. This is your fault!" I raged.

"Just stay calm and *stay* at the compound," Myers ordered.

I hurled the radio back to Franks. He effortlessly snatched it out of the air before it hit him in the face. I started running for the main building.

"Where are you going?"

"I'm going after them," I shouted back.

"It'll take hours to get there," the giant stated.

"Shit!" He was right, of course, but that didn't change the fact that I had to do something. *Who did MHI have in the area?* Julie would know. I pulled out my phone and hit speed dial J. I walked in a circle as it rang repeatedly.

"Hi, you've reached Julie Shackleford, business coordinator for MHI. Please leave a detailed message at the beep."

I swore. Of course she wasn't answering her phone; she was hunting trolls. At the tone, I left what I was sure was an incoherent and panicked message about cultists kidnapping my folks.

My phone chirped. I switched to the incoming call. "Hello?" I said quickly.

"Son?" The gravely voice was winded.

"DAD!" I shouted. "Are you okay?"

"Yeah," heavy breathing, "some assholes kicked the door in, started tying us up. Talking all kinds of craziness. Fucking amateurs."

It was like I could breathe again. "Is Mom okay?"

"Sure, she's fine."

*Oh, thank you God.* "What about the cultists?"

"Cultists? These punks? Well, I got three of them. The last one's crawling down the driveway, but he isn't going very fast with all those holes in him, so I'll mop him up in a second. What the hell's going on?"

I let out a huge sigh of relief. He had survived everything assorted communists and terrorists had thrown at him in twenty-five years of warfare, both official and unofficial. He wasn't the type to scare easily.

"Dad, listen carefully. Hang tight, cops are on

the way. You've got more guns, right?" I asked. He grunted, almost like that was insulting. "Okay, good. Grab some big stuff, just in case."

"How big?"

"Big as you've got." And I knew that for Dad, that meant some serious firepower. The militant apple didn't fall far from the militant tree.

Franks interrupted. "Cult survivors?" I held up one finger. "We need him." I nodded.

"Dad, don't shoot that last guy anymore. The cops want to question him."

"Well, they best hurry up then. I'll go toss him a towel and tell him to put some direct pressure on it and quit his crying. Now, you listen to me, boy. They were talking about you, that this is all about you. What kind of bullshit are you mixed up in? Is this some sort of mafia accountant thing?"

Of course he still thought I was a CPA. "I'll explain everything later, I promise. I need you to get to Alabama as fast as you can. The Feds will escort you here." I glared at Franks as I said that, but he nodded in consent. At some point he had summoned the Goon Squad, because Archer, Herzog, and Torres had come running, carrying all their equipment. "Did they say anything else?"

Dad gasped. "Damn, forgot. Yes. Your brother, they said that they were sending 'violence and evil' or something like that after him."

"Force and Violence?"

"Yeah. But then I went for the kitchen gun." Growing up, it had been Pitt family custom to stash at least one gun in every room of the house, so having a kitchen gun had finally paid off, "I shot the son of a bitch that said it in the face, so I was a touch distracted. We've got to get to David."

"He's near me. I'm on it, Dad. I'll see you in Alabama. Just hang tight." I hung up and scrolled through until I found my brother's number. My hands were trembling so bad that it was hard to work the little trackball on my phone.

"Yo?" Somebody unfamiliar picked up and my heart lurched. *Was I too late?*

"I need to talk to Mosh right now!" I shouted.

"Dude, he's going on stage in a minute. Call back later."

"It's a family emergency," I said forcefully.

"Well, I'm his manager. I'll pass it on when the show's over." The voice was very laid back, bordering on obnoxious mellowness.

"Mosh is in danger. You need to get him out of there, now!"

"Look, man, lay off the dope. It makes you paranoid. Call back in a couple hours." He hung up.

Bellowing something profane and incoherent, I started for the main building. I needed my gear.

"Where are you going?" Torres asked.

"They're coming for my brother. He's in Montgomery tonight. I have to get to him. We can be there in half an hour."

"Our strike team is camped at Maxwell," Archer said quickly, referring to the Air Force base in Montgomery. "I'll raise them."

"Myers said you weren't supposed to leave the compound," Herzog snapped.

"Our team is already there. They can handle it. Driving up there will just put you in danger. This is probably just what the Condition wants you to do," Torres suggested softly. "This could be a trap."

"I'm going," I spun around. "And I'll kneecap the first one of you who tries to stop me." I'm a physically intimidating specimen when I'm enraged. The three junior agents stepped back automatically. Franks didn't flinch. None of them said another word as I stared them down. "You gonna help me or not?"

Franks mulled it over, probably weighing the pros and cons of endangering his charge versus being able to go kill something. The decision didn't take long. "I'll drive."

# CHAPTER 6

The G-Ride speedometer pegged at a hundred and forty miles an hour but we were going much faster as we entered Montgomery and headed west on the 85. The black-armored Suburban had been delivered to Franks sometime in the last few days by some of his minions and I was glad we had it. Although MHI had a lot of vehicles, none of them apparently had a friggin' quarter-million-horsepower engine forged in the fires of Mordor like this thing apparently did. It normally took me forty-five minutes to hit the outskirts of town from Cazador, but Franks had done it in less than twenty, and I wasn't exactly averse to speeding. The demonic roar of the engine was almost as loud as the banshee siren that warned everyone else to get out of the way or be flattened beneath our armored steel bumpers. Our tax dollars had equipped Agent Franks with the SUV from Hell.

Franks was emotionless in the reflected flashes of blue and red, still wearing his cheap suit. A pine-tree-shaped air freshener bounced around under the rearview mirror. I was in the passenger seat, hunched forward by the armor and pouches on my back. Abomination was muzzle down, balanced between my knees. It had been almost impossible to get dressed while we had slalomed around the corners of rural Keene County, but I had managed. The Goon Squad was in the next row of seats, also armed to the teeth, each one intense and ready to fight.

I had run into MHI headquarters long enough to grab my go-bag and give Dorcas a brief rundown. She had been trying to raise the others as we had left. I shoved my MHI-issued earpieces in, partially to protect my hearing from the siren, but also to check to see if any of my people were in range. I was alone. The radio mounted on the SUV's dash was tuned to the Monster Control Bureau's encrypted channel, so I knew that their strike force had mobilized and moved to the Buzzard Island Amphitheater, now only a few miles ahead of us.

"Alpha Team is in position outside the concert and holding," said someone over the radio.

"Any suspicious activity?" Agent Myers asked over the airwaves.

There was a long pause of open air. "Uh, sir, *most* of the people here are suspicious looking." Apparently they had never been to a Cabbage Point Killing Machine show before. Their tours were legendary. You could drop all sorts of weird supernatural creatures into one of their average gigs and nobody would notice.

My phone rang and I hurriedly pulled it from the small pouch on the front of my armor. "Yeah?"

"Z?" It was Albert Lee. "Dorcas just got ahold of me."

"Where are you?"

"We're a couple miles north of Cazador."

"Who you got?"

"Me and Grant. Dorcas raised Harbinger. They turned back too." *Excellent.* Lee was a good man, and Grant, say what you would about him, was a known quantity, more than I could say about my current carpool. "Listen, I've got to tell you something. Dorcas said it was Force and Violence. I've been reading up on them. Be really careful."

Franks must have somehow, impossibly, heard that. "Put him on speaker."

I complied so the Feds could hear. "First, what can they do? Second, how do we waste them?"

"Nobody really knows what they are. The descriptions sound kind of like an ogre and an ogress, but they're too fast, too smart, and apparently indestructible. Esmeralda thought they were Greek, and they've been seen in that part of the world a lot, for at least three thousand years, but from the descriptions, I think they're *oni.*"

"Three thousand years?" Herzog said incredulously. "Bull."

Franks held up one hand to silence her.

"What's an oni?" I asked.

"Far Eastern legends talk about them a lot. They're evil spirits that have gained a physical body, usually really big and strong. They suck the life out of other things in order to power their own bodies indefinitely. That's probably what Skippy meant by getting paid in souls. I don't see why some of them couldn't wander over to Europe and end up in that area's folklore."

Some Hunters just seemed to geek out at monster factoids. "That's great. Now how do we kill them?"

"Beats me," he answered. "MHI has never killed

an oni that I can find record of. Esmeralda said that bullets bounced off of them."

"Great . . ." I muttered. "We'll improvise."

"Electricity," Archer chimed in. "Enough current will stun an oni. That's what the field manual says."

"There's more. When MHI went up against them last time, they had a hard time tracking them, which is weird since witnesses say they're huge. But they would suddenly appear, kill something, then *poof*, they were just gone. So I'm guessing they're either able to fly or teleport. The Fed file said the necromancer can create shadow portals, so maybe they can too. They might even shape-shift, so who knows . . ."

"Well, that narrows it down. Thanks, Al. See you there. Go to the radio band when you reach Motown." I dropped the phone back in its pouch. This wasn't shaping up to be a fun night.

Updates continued to come in from the strike force as they surrounded the concert. They were all in position. "Stay low profile and hold your position for now," Myers ordered his teams. "Wait for the Condition to make their move first. Our primary concern is capturing a Condition operative. Civilian casualties are secondary. Myers out."

"What?" I shouted and slammed my fist into the glove box. Mosh was a sitting duck up there on stage. "Tell them to go in there and grab my brother now!"

Franks shook his head. "That's not the mission."

"Bullshit it's not. You're using him as bait, like you used me. He's not part of this." I reached over for the radio, but suddenly Franks' ham fist clamped around my left hand, immobilizing it as easily as if I were a child.

"He is now," Franks said, blank eyes never leaving the road as he steered with one hand between freeway traffic at absurd speeds.

"That's my brother out there. Don't you have any family, Franks?"

He scowled. "Yeah. Big family."

"Would you just leave them to die?"

"Not my problem . . ."

Something broke. I'd had enough. Mosh wasn't going to die if I could help it. Fury bubbled up from the pit of my stomach, as my STI .45 cleared its Kydex drop leg holster with a snap. I screwed the fat muzzle into Frank's ear, hard, and snapped, "Order them to get Mosh, right now."

It only took the Goon Squad a second to react. There was a click of a manual safety as Herzog put her HK .45 against the base of my skull. "Drop the gun, Pitt! Drop it!" she screamed. Archer was a split second slower but he slammed his Sig 229 into my head as well.

"Shut up!" I shouted. I wasn't going to let my brother get killed for their stupid mission. My finger was on the trigger and blasting Franks at this speed would surely end us all. "Call Myers!" Spit flew from my lips. "Now!"

Franks didn't take his eyes off the road, but he did unconsciously squeeze my left hand harder. Bones creaked and I grimaced. "Negative," he said.

"Owen, put the gun down," Torres urged softly. "Use your brain, man. We warned you about the Condition. They'll just keep on attacking everyone you've ever loved until they get you. We have to capture some of them or this will go on forever. Please, put the gun down."

Franks was utterly calm, even with a silver .45 slug aimed down his ear canal. "Do it."

My brother was going to be killed and there wasn't a thing I could do about it from here ... *Damn it.* I couldn't threaten Franks. Shooting him wouldn't accomplish a thing. Deflated, I thumbed the safety back on and slowly lowered my gun. Franks let go of my aching hand and went back to 10 and 2 on the wheel. Archer and Herzog kept their guns trained on me.

"Hand your piece back, slowly!" she shouted, voice shrill in my ear. "Do it or I'll blow your brains out! You're under arrest."

"Screw you," I said. She pushed even harder with the muzzle. I knew that I'd gone way too far this time. "All right." Slowly, I passed the custom long-slide, double-stack pistol, turning it back butt first. She thumped me again, and I handed Abomination over my head, the stubby and bulky shotgun and grenade launcher combo difficult to pass between the seats. Another thump and I sent back my secondary STI off my left hip, this one a compact, bobbed and chopped .45.

"Everything." She whacked me again for good measure.

I slowly passed back the two Spyderco knives I kept on each hip pocket, then dragged out the 21" Chitilangi heavy kukri that replaced my lost Ganga Ram. MHI was one of Himalayan Imports' best customers. "Careful, that one's sharp," I said as I passed it back. Hopefully one of them would cut their fingers off by accident. *Another thump.* I was going to be covered in lumps from that hag. "Damn it," I muttered as I reached down to my ankle and pulled out the snub-nosed .357

Airweight Smith & Wesson that I kept stashed for worst-case scenarios. Now the three of them had a pile of weapons to contend with.

"How many guns do you have?" Torres asked in exasperation.

"It's a Second Amendment thing. You wouldn't understand."

"You're under arrest for threatening a federal agent, Pitt. Put your hands on your head," Herzog snarled.

"Uh . . . he's still got hand grenades," Archer pointed out.

"Stand down," Franks ordered his men, sounding exasperated. It took them a moment to respond. "I said STAND DOWN." That time both metallic weights left my head. Franks turned and looked at me, not paying any attention to the freeway that was flying past. For once he actually showed some emotion, and unfortunately for me, it was anger. His black eyes burned a hole through my soul as he sedately said the most words I had ever heard from him at one time. "Primary mission. Keep Pitt alive. We need live bait, so I can't twist your head off. But if you ever point a gun at me again, you'll pray for the Old Ones to take you away, because compared to what I'll do, the Elder Things will be a fucking picnic." He veered us past a semitrailer without looking, and it zipped by so quickly that it was just a silver blur. Franks just kept staring, his black eyes containing nothing but barely controlled rage. The three agents tried to shrink back through the seats. "Got it?"

"Yes."

"Good." Then he slugged me.

It was so unbelievably fast, so staggeringly hard,

that I didn't even see it coming. A big fist crashed into my cranium like a lightning bolt from a clear blue sky. A bomb went off inside my gray matter. My head rebounded against the bulletproof glass of the passenger side door hard enough to crack it. He didn't just hit me in one place, but it was like he had somehow punched my entire face at once. My eyes automatically filled with tears and blood billowed out my nose in a froth of bubbles.

I was stunned, reeling, my brain trying to process what the hell had just happened as I came back to full consciousness either a minute or maybe a day later. "Ouch," I croaked, with the ultimate of understatements.

Franks was back to driving insanely through the evening traffic. The bright lights of the state capitol and downtown Montgomery were off to our right. He took one hand off the wheel long enough to crack his knuckles. "Now we're even."

The Buzzard Island Amphitheater was a new facility, just across the Alabama river, north of Montgomery. It had been a narrow patch of damp, low dirt for most of recorded history, but they had built it up with oceans of concrete, and put in a top-of-the-line convention and concert facility. It was a large, oval building, with a bulging glass dome for a roof, and giant, stainless-steel spires that were probably supposed to be some sort of industrial-modern-art thing. Tonight there were several large spotlights staggered around the amphitheater, casting giant beams seemingly forever into the clear night sky in big circular patterns. We tore into the parking lot at just under eighty miles an hour, leaving a thick parabolic curve of rubber as we left the main road and got serious air off a speed bump. Our sociopathic driver nearly ran down the orange-vested traffic directors, ignoring all rules of both safety and courtesy, as he searched the lines of vehicles for his target. Apparently Franks found it, because he gunned the engine, cut off another car, and hammered the SUV across the pavement, only to hit the brakes at the last possible second and slide in sideways behind a large, black, SWAT-style van at the far end of the lot. The giant unmarked van seemed appropriate, because that was Myers' idea of low profile, after all.

We piled out of the SUV and around the back of the van, where several black-clad agents were clustered out of sight of the people walking around the lot. Still dizzy from the sucker punch, I stumbled around the vehicle, holding one arm up to my face to pinch off my bleeding nose. Agent Myers was sitting on the back steps of the van, listening to a radio with one ear and to his phone with the other. He was nodding, and it wasn't in time with the music throbbing from the far end of the lot either. Franks put one massive hand on my chest and shoved me back against the passenger side door. "Stay here."

*He didn't want to get in trouble for bringing me.*

"Watch him," Franks told the Goon Squad, then he turned and went to his superior's side. Torres took the front of the vehicle, Herzog the rear, and Archer stayed right by me. The three agents folded their arms, rifles dangling from their tac-slings, as they waited for me to try something else stupid. I suppose at this point I should consider myself in custody, though the MCB weren't the kind of cops who read people their rights... Last rites, maybe. Myers glanced up, obviously surprised to see his subordinate. They were far enough away that I couldn't hear what they were saying, but Myers appeared really ticked when he saw me. He began to shout and gesture wildly, but Franks said something that seemed to placate his boss momentarily.

I had to do something. We were just going to sit out here until the bad guys attacked. Mosh was toast. I could probably kick the crap out of some of them and make a run for it, but even if I were to somehow ditch them, my guns were sitting in the back seat, and I would have to run across a couple hundred yards of parking lot, only to arrive unarmed where Condition assassins were stalking Mosh. So scratch that plan. Maybe I could pull it off if I had some help. Torres seemed like the least obnoxious of the bunch, but he was further away. "Archer," I whispered to the nearest agent. "Those hit-monsters are going to murder my brother. We've got to get in there and save him."

"Shut up," he said angrily, apparently still offended that I had threatened to shoot his commander. "We're following orders."

"Is that why you volunteered for this? Letting civilians get slaughtered right under your nose, so you could follow *orders*? Come on, man. Do the right thing." We were at the far side of the parking lot, well away from the crowds, but I nodded toward the throngs on the steps of the amphitheater. "How many of those kids have to die tonight?"

Frustrated, he grabbed me by the straps of my armor, "As many as it takes, damn it! You don't know what the

Condition is capable of. They have to be stopped!" Then he tried to shove me against the SUV, but apparently he had forgotten that I was a giant brute of a man. I outweighed the thin agent by probably a hundred and thirty pounds. He barely succeeded in budging me.

"Yeah, Franks makes it look easy," I said.

Feeling stupid, Archer let go. His Adam's apple bobbed nervously, but his eyes were cold, angry, and he kept one hand on the pistol grip of his M4 carbine. "Just shut up, okay." He jerked his head toward the improvised command center where his superiors were conferring. "Agent Myers knows what he's doing. He's a pro. Look . . . I don't want your brother or anybody else to get hurt, but this is bigger than he is. This cult, they're trying to awake something evil." Archer realized he was talking too much. "Never mind. Just shut up."

The Fed wasn't going to budge. I had to think of something else, fast.

There was movement over Archer's shoulder. Something small and black scurried low between the tightly packed rows of cars, then another shape, and another. *How could I have been so stupid?* I had forgotten all about them. A goggled head poked up over a Volkswagen's hood, scanned the contingent of Feds and then glided back down, unseen by everyone but me.

I softened my tone. "Look, Agent Archer, I'm not trying to be a jerk, but can I get a Kleenex or something? I'm bleeding all over my armor." I gestured at my swollen nose. It really hurt, so that part wasn't an act.

"Serves you right . . ." He hesitated, scowling, but finally relented. "Okay, hang on a second." He reached down and pulled open the Velcro tab on his first aid kit. He didn't see the thing crawling out from under a nearby car, then rising silently behind him. The orc grabbed Archer by the strap on the back of his armor while simultaneously kicking both knees out from under him. The agent fell backward, pulled by the weight of his armor and equipment, crying out in surprise.

It was my old pal, Edward. I only recognized him because he moved so smoothly that he made Bruce Lee look rickety. The orc didn't even slow. He covered the distance to Torres, leaping into the air at the last second as the younger agent turned to see what the commotion was about. Edward's heel collided with the Fed's chest, kicking him back. Torres collided with the hood of a car, tripped, and sprawled onto the pavement. There was a thud from the other direction as another black shape cracked Herzog over the head with a club. Gretchen didn't have Edward's moves, but she was mighty handy with her totem stick. The female agent went to the ground in a heap.

The passenger door of the SUV from Hell flew open. "Noble One, hurry fast," Skippy ordered. Franks had left the keys in it. I jumped into the seat as Gretchen climbed into the back. Still on the ground, Torres pulled his pistol, but Edward was on him in an instant and kicked the HK across the lot. The orc bent over and slugged Torres in the face, knocked him silly, spun him on his back like a turtle, and dragged him effortlessly over to Archer. He kicked the first agent again as he was struggling to rise, snatched a pair of handcuffs off Torres' vest, and locked one agent's wrist to the other one's ankle.

Skippy cranked it and the demon engine roared

like a Tyrannosaurus Rex. He slammed it into reverse and the tires spun as we flew rearward, smashing the back armored bumper into a parked Corvette. The Corvette lost.

Thirty feet away, Franks' head snapped up. His hand flew under his coat and came out with a fat Glock. Skippy put it in drive and the massive vehicle jumped forward, Gretchen holding the door open as Edward dove through to safety. Franks aimed at Skippy but hesitated, probably more worried about his truck than violating his primary mission. Then we were speeding past. "Big Fed. Look mad," Skippy grunted as he put the hammer down.

I whipped around to see Franks sprinting after us, gun in hand. Skippy wasn't kidding. He looked pissed.

All orcs have gifts. I don't know how it works exactly, but each of them has a unique ability. Edward's was kicking ass. Gretchen was a remarkable healer. And Skippy, leader of the MHI orcs, brother of Edward, and husband of Gretchen (wife one of five), was a helicopter pilot of almost supernatural skill. However, that ability apparently didn't translate into driving ground vehicles, as Skippy smashed the SUV brutally right down a line of parked cars, flinging headlights, glass, and bits of plastic in every direction. Concertgoers were forced to dive for safety as Skippy high-speed crunched his way toward the amphitheater entrance.

"I'm glad to see you guys!" I shouted as Skippy drove over a parked Suzuki motorcycle. Our shocks absorbed the impact rather well. "We've got to get to my brother. Mosh is in danger."

The orcs in back just started passing my confis-cated weapons back to me. They never talked much anyway. Skippy piped up as I tucked various guns and knives—even a kukri!— back into their respective spots. "Yes. Joo-Lee call. Say, Great War Chief...in much danger. Twins come. Take soul." His super-gravelly voice sounded angry. His people venerated metal and its musicians above all. A threat against my brother, whom they called the Great War Chief, was serious business. "Twins kill many Urks before...now Urks turn. We go find...Brother of War Chief. See gub mint." He lifted the base of his hood, revealing his tusks, and spit on the steering wheel. Orcs were probably the only people I had ever encountered who had more issues with authority than Hunters. "Gub mint, take you prisoner. So we save."

"Who do you have here?"

Skippy shook his head. "Only few...*Grtxschnns, Exszrsd*, and—" he grumbled his real, incomprehensible name, reminding me again of why we called him Skippy. "With gub mint here, send tribe away to village. Go home. Be safe. We...we stay for help." He was right. Orcs, even the ones that stayed with MHI, were still on the PUFF list, and thereby fair game to the Feds. What these three were doing was incredibly brave.

"They're heading for the front entrance," said a voice on the radio. "Intercept! Intercept!"

"Belay that order," Myers said. "All units hold position. Wait until we get a shot at those monsters. Pitt, you obstinate pain in the ass, I know you can hear me. Don't you dare go in there."

I grabbed the radio and pulled the mike over to me. "Myers, that's my family we're talking about."

"They'll kill you," he said.

"Yeah, heard that before." I ripped the cord out of the radio. It felt good. Skippy held up his pointer finger and pinky and threw the horns. *Rock on.* "You guys armed?"

"No. Security," Skip's hood dipped toward the rapidly approaching concert entrance's row of metal detectors. Gretchen held up her totem stick, complete with feathers and small animal skulls, that she had somehow snuck in. There were two sudden clicks as Edward flicked open the ASP collapsible batons he must have lifted off of Torres and Archer. Edward was a lousy shot, but death incarnate up close. I pulled my big .45 and passed it over to Skippy. "Thanks," he said. "Hold to something, now."

We drove up the entrance stairs and slammed the radiator into a concrete wall right across from a giant bronze statue of Hank Williams, Sr. The armored Suburban was so heavy I barely felt the impact.

I leapt out, scanning the crowd. It was a diverse bunch watching the chaos of our car wreck. Most of them were pierced or tattooed, and there was a bewildering variety of hairstyles—everything from shaved heads all the way to long flowing hair and even a few old-school mohawks. They were pointing and laughing at the G-Ride, with its red and blue flashing wigwags perched lopsided on the stairs, which meant security would be here any second.

Skippy grunted to get my attention. "Disguise." He tossed me a blue windbreaker that said DEPARTMENT OF HOMELAND SECURITY in giant gold letters on the back. It was huge, big enough to fit over my armor even, so must have belonged to Agent Franks. I tugged it on and clumsily hid Abomination under one armpit. It was then that I noticed for the first time that all three orcs were wearing Cabbage Point Killing Machine shirts over their usual baggy, black clothing. Skippy's boldly read HOLD THE PIG STEADY. So the orcs were in disguise too.

"Get inside," I shouted, and the four of us ran for the entrance. The concert had been going on for a while, so there weren't very many people standing in line, and we rudely shoved past those that were. "Out of the way. Homeland Security. Coming through!" I bellowed. Having already committed assault with a deadly weapon and grand theft auto in the last ten minutes, what was a little impersonating a federal agent?

*Oh crap. The Law.* "Who the hell are you?" asked the uniformed cop pushing his way through the sea of tattooed skin. He must have seen the G-Ride.

"Agent Franks. Homeland Security!" I shouted, still trying to get to the entrance. "We've got a terrorist incident."

Apparently me and my bloody nose didn't make the most convincing Fed. He held up one hand to stop me, his other hand came to a rest on his holstered sidearm. Alabama cops do not screw around. "Let's see some creds."

"Edward, my credentials please," I requested. The orc smoothly melted through the crowd and batoned the cop to the pavement before anyone could react. The two figures went down and were lost in the churning mass. "Don't hurt him," I ordered, not slowing. We made it around the corner and away from the Suburban. I broke into a run.

There were four people wearing yellow SECURITY shirts taking tickets and manning the metal detectors at the gate. "No weapons, no drugs, only eight ounces of sealed bottled water, no flash photography..." the first guard droned automatically. "Ticket, please." I ignored him and strode right through. The detector started beeping like crazy. "Hey, asshole." One meaty hand fell on my shoulder. I instantly grabbed it and twisted, putting the man in a wristlock. He screamed and went to his knees. My jacket fell open, revealing my shotgun.

"Anybody else want my ticket?" I asked.

"Naw, that's cool," said the second guard slowly, hand unconsciously reaching for his radio. There wasn't much I could do about that, short of shooting everybody, and being one of the self-proclaimed Good Guys, that wasn't an option. I let go of the first guard, put my boot on his shoulder, and shoved him out of the way. "Enjoy the show..." said the calm one. The three orcs came next, each one taking the time to politely display their VIP wristbands to security people that weren't really paying attention at that point.

Then we were inside the concourse. This place was huge, with lots of ground to cross, and I knew I didn't have much time. Regular cops would be looking for a big dude in a blue jacket, and a show like this had to be crawling with cops. A giant row of vendors selling souvenirs, tee shirts, beer and food, stretched for what looked like a quarter mile before the building opened up into the actual hall. There were probably a thousand people wandering around, clustered in talkative knots or buying various things between us and my brother. They would have to serve as cover.

"Walk fast, but try to look like we belong," I said, realizing how stupid that sounded as soon as I said it. A man walked past wearing a Viking costume with lit sparklers on his helmet, and in the other direction went two young women whose only clothing on their upper halves was strategically placed, black electrical tape. Yeah, it had been a long time since I had been to one of my brother's shows. Edward suddenly bolted off to the side in the direction of the restrooms. Either he had seen something, or orcs had easily excitable bladders. I kept moving.

*Damn, more cops.* A few of them were running down the concourse back toward the entrance. I bowed my head so I wouldn't appear so tall and got into a line that was either for funnel cakes or nose rings. The Montgomery PD went right past, but I knew that kind of luck wouldn't last for long.

There was a tap on my shoulder. Edward shoved a giant leather trenchcoat at me. I saw my reflection in his goggled eyes as he nodded at the restrooms. His English was worse that Skippy's. "Fat man. Go pee. No need coat." Then he emitted a low-pitched noise, like shaking gravel in a bucket, that could only have been a hearty orcish laugh. I pulled the DHS jacket off and tossed it on the floor, exposing piles of guns for just an instant, before quickly donning the massive garment, which I discovered came with chains and a row of spikes down each shoulder.

"Sweet," I said. Gretchen handed me a ridiculous cowboy hat, complete with a swath of what I assumed was real armadillo that she had lifted off of somebody else. Orcs were damn sneaky when they put their minds to it. Living in the shadows of humanity for centuries had that effect. I pulled the hat down low, even though it was way too small, and headed for the show.

In the main hall, the music was deafening, driven by a giant wall of speakers behind the band. The place was packed. The floor was a sea of bouncing bodies, hands raised, moving in time with the music, a veritable sea of hands and heads throbbing up and down. It was muggy from the body heat, and I immediately began to sweat under the layers of Kevlar and the absurd coat. The air was thick from glycerin foggers, as strobes and lasers cut confusing patterns above us. The three orcs began to bob automatically, unable to resist the instinctive urge to headbang.

A giant shape loomed over me. *Monster!* I started to pull out Abomination, only to realize that the huge thing tottering past was some awkward demon costume, made by a girl sitting on a tall man's shoulders, and draped in burlap and tarps. If it hadn't been such a dangerous situation, I would have stopped to admire the fact that they even had red LED lights mounted for eyes. I really needed to get to more of Mosh's shows.

My brother had always been musically gifted. Dad hadn't really appreciated it since it was a skill that wasn't directly useful for survival. But Mom had put her foot down and young David Uhersky Pitt had taken classical guitar lessons. Then one day as teenagers the two of us had snuck out to a Slayer concert and he had found his calling in life. The rest was history.

Brilliant spotlights beamed down on the stage as Cabbage Point Killing Machine played. The singer was moving back and forth, jumping up and down and screaming. Fireballs exploded and soared upward over the stage as the pyrotechicians earned their keep. Then I spotted my brother, the guitarist, just a silhouette standing out in front of a propane explosion, as he played his guitar like I shoot guns. He was one of most talented musicians in the world, in my humble opinion, and I felt pretty justified in that opinion as his fingers flew back and forth faster than the eye could track, coaxing chords out of his instrument not meant for the human ear. The boy could *shred*.

I tried to stick to the edge of the main floor, as the bodies were only tightly packed here, as opposed to absurdly packed into the center. I headed directly for the stage. There was probably a better way to go around, but I had never been here before and had no idea how the area behind the stage was laid out. Not to mention that there were bound to be more cops back there too.

It was deafening, but I heard a voice in my radio earpiece. I clamped one hand over it in order to hear. "—ing on the freeway. North side of Montgomery," it was saying. It was somebody else from MHI.

My microphone was in a strap that rode around my neck, a military design used so soldiers riding in turrets could still be heard over wind noise. Hopefully, it would work in here. "This is Z. I'm inside the concert."

"What is that noise?" I recognized that voice as belonging to Grant Jefferson. "Are the cultists attacking?"

"No, that's just the music." I had to remind myself that when I had driven Grant's car last summer, all of the stations had been programmed to opera or something. "Stay outside the concert. Feds are crawling all over the parking lot, and they're ticked. They'll probably just arrest you on sight."

"What? I can't hear you over that horrible racket." Some people just can't appreciate *good* music.

I started to reply, but choked it off as I saw them.

Two things were making their way toward the stage, parallel with me but on the opposite side of the floor. They towered over the jumping crowd, a pair of huge, slumped shapes, merely black outlines in the flashing lights. The first was much taller than everything around it, and the other was even larger, and unlike the flailing costumes I had seen so far, these were moving far too smoothly, cutting their way right through the unsuspecting masses.

Grabbing Skippy's arm, I pointed at the monsters. His goggled head swiveled back and forth. Finally, he shrugged. He couldn't see them. "Damn it, the two big things. They're huge. Right *there*." I pointed again. The other orcs looked as well, standing on their tiptoes to see, then glanced at each other, shaking their heads as thousands of sweaty bodies jostled around us. They couldn't see them either.

There was no time to ponder that mystery. I doubled my efforts to get to the stage, pushing and shoving, a big man on a mission. Across the hall, the ogres, or oni, or whatever the hell they were, were moving at about the same speed. Somehow, the people being plowed out of their way didn't even seem to notice.

An elbow caught my cheek and a heavy boot kicked me in the thigh. This was the kind of crowd that didn't react well to rudeness. I just kept going. Edward clotheslined a large youth to the ground when said youth took issue with me cutting in front of him. The closer I got to the stage, the more violent it was going to get. Anybody who has been to a show like this knows that the front few rows were not for the faint of heart. It was a downright Darwinian environment. The floor narrowed as it got down to

the stage, which was serving to funnel us closer to
the approaching monsters.

Risking a quick glance to the side, I could see
them clearly through the fog. The lead thing was at
least a foot taller than my 6 feet 5 inches and even
then, it seemed somehow hunched over. Its head was
covered in some sort of gray shawl. It collided with
the moshers, and they just parted before it, a few of
them getting confused looks on their faces, but none
of them seeing the creatures.

"See them now?" I shouted at Skippy.

"No," he said, while looking right at them. "Smell.
Smell monsters."

I don't know how Skippy could smell anything over
the odor of thousands of bodies and various types of
illegal smoke, but whatever worked. The first creature was almost to the stage as I reached the base.
More yellow-shirted security were standing behind a
row of aluminum rails separating the mob from the
band. I climbed over the rail, only to have several
pairs of strong hands shove me back. Only tough guys
got this kind of job. It was the kind of thing that I
probably would have done in the past and enjoyed. I
had always been about gigs that allowed me to punch
people *and* get paid for it.

So it wasn't anything personal when I palm-struck
the guard in the chest and launched him back into the
concrete. I just needed to get on that stage. The other
guard touching me went down with a flick of Edward's
stolen baton, crying out and holding his fingers. I was
over the railing and pulling myself up to the stage in
a second, losing my idiotic cowboy hat in the process.

The song finished in a flourish of guitars and

drums, along with a propane explosion right over my head. The lights twirled and flickered as they spun the spotlights like a kaleidoscope. I was up and over, rolling onto the hardwood planking as the crowd went insane, asking for, no, *demanding* an encore. I got to my knees as the lead singer tossed his microphone and leapt past me into the waiting arms of the crowd. He was surfed back and forth on the sea of hands, and I had to admit that at any other time it looked like fun. Mosh better not do that, because I didn't fight my way all the way up here just to have him go and jump the hell off. I headed for the guitarist. I sensed the orcs right behind me as one of them, Skippy, left us and sprinted toward the row of speakers.

My brother had pulled his instrument off, and was waving it over his head like some medieval weapon. People said that he looked a lot like me, but I never saw the resemblance. He was a few years younger, a few inches shorter, and a few pounds lighter. Personally, I thought he looked more like Mom, with me being darker, uglier, and more beady-eyed like Dad. He was wearing a tank top, showing off the typical Pitt family bulkiness and love of lifting heavy objects, and also demonstrating that three quarters of him was inked with various designs. You have no idea how angry that made my dad. Mosh had a long black goatee; his head was totally shaved and shiny under the lights. I was going prematurely bald, and my brother, blessed with a full head of hair, shaves his. *Jerk*.

For a second I thought Mosh was going to bring the guitar down and smash it on stage, but that would be like me smashing a perfectly good firearm. He was a rock star but we had been raised too cheaply to ever be wasteful. Finally, he lowered the guitar and shook his fist at the crowd, the wide grin of a man doing what he loves and knowing he's the very best at it on his tanned face.

Then he saw me. His mouth formed my name as he tried to process what I was doing here. Security was coming from offstage to get me, but he waved them away as I got closer. Confused, he was starting to ask me a question when the first monster hit the stage. A body in a yellow tee shirt flew twenty feet in the air, screaming, before crashing into an overhanging speaker and taking the entire assembly crashing to the floor in a shower of sparks. The crowd loved it.

The guard's impact caused a giant confetti dispenser to break open prematurely, spilling tons of reflective bits of white paper like snow. "What the hell, man?" Mosh shouted as a great gray mass vaulted effortlessly onto the stage, knocking over stands and crushing a huge bank of Digitech pedals. Through the wall of sparkling fake snow, the creature turned toward us. The face underneath the gray hood was human, mostly, but twisted, somehow too long, too pointy, with a mane of curly black hair framing bulging red eyes set in a purple hag's face. The shroud fell open as the monster rose to its full height, towering over us, spreading wide long purple arms, six-fingered hands opening into a bank of nails the size of steak knives. The form was that of a human female, but far too enormous, with skin the texture of punching-bag leather.

The audience cheered.

I swear it actually smiled—gleaming white pointy teeth poking out in an evil grin—turned, and bowed to the crowd.

"That's one *big* chick," the drummer said stupidly.

Then it was back to business, as the thing crossed most of the huge stage in two steps, curled toe claws digging splinters out of the floor. A black, forked tongue licked past lips as it spoke, with a voice that sounded surprisingly normal and feminine. "Come along, little performer. Show's over."

"Shit!" Mosh shouted, stumbling back, knowing full well that this wasn't part of the act. "What's that?"

"Oh, *now* everybody can see them!" I shouted as I pushed past my brother, shrugged out of the stupid coat, raised Abomination and flipped the selector down to full auto. The EO-Tech holographic sight settled on the creature's center of mass as I jerked the trigger. Abomination recoiled up and to the right as I stitched a line of buckshot impacts across the creature's torso. The purple shape jerked under the steady impacts, raising claws to protect its face as I blasted it with a continuous roar of ten magnum rounds. No normal being could have lived.

"Mosh. Run," I ordered as I dropped the spent magazine and pulled another one from my vest.

The clawed hand came down and belligerent red eyes focused on me through the swirling confetti. "You!"

New magazine rocked in, I jerked the charging handle to chamber another round, aimed and fired. The one-ounce silver slug could have blasted a hole through a medium-sized cow but it didn't seem to phase the oni. The projectile actually made an audible, buzzing, ricochet noise and there was a clang as the drum set took the hit.

She turned to the pit and shrieked, "Cratos! He is here. The Hunter arrived, just as they said he would."

The second monster lumbered up onto the stage, also cloaked in gray, but, *holy shit,* this one was huge. The arms bulging out the sides were bright red, big around as my waist, and rippling with veins as thick as garden hoses. The head rose, revealing a much more demonic visage, rhino-horn-sized tusks pointing up out of a jaw a foot across. Above that, tiny black eyes blinked stupidly. Squat, with thick legs and a stumpy torso, he was still twice as tall as I was, and every inch of him was coated in red hide and hard muscle. It was truly terrifying. "Master will pay many souls for this one, Bia," he bellowed, his voice shaking the foundations of the building.

The audience went nuts. Now this was entertainment. As long as they thought this was part of the show, they wouldn't kill each other trying to stampede out the exits. Edward swung his arms sharply downward, and the two batons extended with a snap. I pointed my shotgun at the big red monster. "Ready, Ed?" The orc spun both batons around him fast enough to make the air whistle, looked at me, and nodded.

One of the bouncers stared up at the giant in shock, backing away slowly, while the others had the sense to run like hell. "Yum...snack," Big Red said. The brute reached down, effortlessly picked the man up and casually bit his head off. Twitching and fountaining blood, the decapitated body was tossed fifty feet out into the audience by the monster like it was discarding an empty beer can. The nonchalant crunching of the skull as he chewed was audible across the entire stage. The purple one laughed.

Edward glanced down at the batons in his hands, then back at me, as if to say, *Screw this.* We both ran.

My brother hadn't listened to me, and he was watching the two giants, mouth agape, guitar dangling in one hand. "Come on, man!" I grabbed him by the arm and dragged him along as we sprinted for backstage. There was a massive roar and a harpy's shriek as the creatures followed, each one of their strides equivalent to several of ours. The other people in this general area were close enough to know that these were not special effects and were fleeing in every direction. My eyes were dazzled from the spotlights as we ran under the overhang supporting most of the sound equipment and into an unadorned concrete hallway. I crashed and tripped over a cart, dragging Mosh with me. Gretchen and Edward were now far ahead, as were the fleeing roadies and stagehands.

Skippy was pushing the metal container cart that I'd run into toward the stage. It took me a second to realize what it was. The black stencil read DANGER: PYROTECHNICS. Skippy gestured at my vest. Knowing automatically what he wanted, I pulled out an incendiary grenade and handed it to him.

"Owen, what are those—wait, is that a grenade?" Mosh asked as he pulled himself to his feet, still trying to figure out what was happening. *Welcome to the party, Bro.*

"Yes, and when the pin is pulled, Mr. Grenade is no longer our friend, so move your ass."

"Bia, here they are," the red oni said as he squatted on his haunches and peered down the hallway. "Filthy souls to eat...*he-he-he*." His giggle was unnerving.

The hallway was clear of innocents. Not that Skippy probably would have worried about it anyway. He tugged the pin, dropped the grenade on top of the cart, and both of us shoved as hard as we could, sending the heavy load down the hall with a surprising bit of velocity. *Five-second fuse on the white phosphorus ones.* The cart rolled haphazardly toward the huge figure now waddling, crouched, down the hall. "RUN!" Cratos smashed the cart against the wall, pushing his way past it to get to us.

The three of us made it down the rest of the hall and around the corner before the WP detonated. Willie Petes don't go off with a typical explosion—more of a *pop-fizz*, and then a layer of flame that sticks to everything and could melt steel goes shooting out in every direction. Cratos roared as phosphorus embedded itself in his hide. "Keep going!" I screamed. The pyro bundle detonated a moment later, not as massively as I hoped, but the shockwave traveled over us, raining dust down from the ceiling.

I hit the floor, sliding forward on my face, quickly rolling onto my back, and checking the way we had come. Smoke was billowing out of the hall.

"It burns me!" The idiot monster shouted as it blundered out of the inferno, still right behind us but now coated in living fire. Flames licked out around him; somehow they climbed the concrete walls and moved between the beams of the ceiling. An alarm began to wail as the fire sprinklers kicked on, pelting us with cold water. He blundered about, crashing into pieces of equipment and smashing the walls into powder, apparently blinded by the fire. The damn thing showed no indication of giving up.

This place was confusing, a maze of concrete halls. "How do we get out of here?" I shouted.

"This way." Mosh pointed down another corridor,

this one lined with green equipment lockers. He realized he was still holding his guitar by the neck and tossed it on the floor with a clatter. Too bad; that thing would probably be worth a bundle on eBay. We ran, leaving the burning oni behind, and raced past dressing rooms, equipment closets, and a table lined with all sorts of colorful food that was now drenched by the sprinklers. "Parking lot's this way." A bunch of people clustered ahead of us, mostly groupies hanging out for the afterparty judging by how trashy most of the girls were dressed. The groupies were every bit as soaked and terrified as everybody else and were all pointing down the intersecting hall.

"Why's everybody screaming?" Mosh demanded as we slid through the water behind the women. He got his answer as a small, black object came flying back through the sprinklers. Edward hit the ground rolling, splashing instantly back to his feet. The female oni was right behind him, claws swinging wildly. Somehow she had gotten ahead and cut us off.

Edward dodged under the black claws. Long divots were ripped from concrete behind him. He spun, nailing the creature in the body with the batons: *pop, pop, pop*. The impacts sounded like solid hits and he was moving unbelievably fast, striking over and over, but she didn't seem to notice. Bia lashed out with one taloned foot, raking a hole in the carpet where Ed had just been.

I pushed past the groupies. "Edward, down!"

"Everybody, this way," shouted Mosh, grabbing some of the women, and physically propelling them through a door that he'd jerked open. Luckily it appeared that all Pitts adjusted quickly under stress. "Move!"

The purple creature ducked under the overhanging lights, which were flickering and shorting in the artificial rain. Orange emergency lighting suddenly kicked on along the floor. Edward dove aside, giving me a clean shot. Bia had protected her face earlier, so I put the holographic reticle on her skull and pulled the trigger. Her head snapped back under the impact as the slug bounced from her forehead. Skippy materialized at my side and my loaned .45 barked as he opened fire. Bia snarled and lifted her gray tattered cloak as if to protect her face. I kept firing as she ducked her head and retreated back the way she had come. Skippy quit shooting. "Where she go?" he grumbled.

*They could turn invisible.* That's how they were able to move through the audience. But how come I could still see them? Maybe this Chosen One business did have a few perks after all. "Her head is vulnerable," I told Skippy.

"Garage is this way," Mosh shouted from the door. Water was running in thick rivulets down his goatee. There was a mighty roar from the direction of the burning Cratos. He was on the move. "Let's get out of here."

I followed my brother, walking backward, waiting for that horrible purple screechy thing to charge back into view at any second. The innocent bystanders had used the time to run like crazy and there were a bunch of discarded high-heel shoes on the floor. Mosh, Gretchen, Edward, Skippy and I ran down a steep ramp that had to be at least fifty yards long before we entered the huge open space of the parking garage. The sprinklers in this area hadn't activated, so at least there was plenty of traction. There were several semis and trailers parked here as well as a bunch of miscellaneous cars.

"Pitt! Status!" shouted the voice in my earpiece.

"Busy right now, Grant," I gasped as I kept on running.

We passed a pillar and I was suddenly jerked off balance as someone grabbed my arm. Slamming into the pillar nearly knocked the wind right out of me. I tried to bring up my shotgun but it was swatted aside. Agent Franks shoved me back into the wall, hard, and held a single finger up in front of his lips, indicating the need for silence. The reason quickly became apparent when the wall twenty feet over the ramp exploded in a shower of fragments, dust, and flying rebar shards. Cratos slammed his fists right through the wall. The great red beast launched himself flailing into the room, landing on the floor hard enough to shatter it in a ten-foot circle.

Franks pushed me back even harder with his left hand, raising a stubby FN F2000 rifle in his right. He was still in his suit, and hadn't even taken the time to remove his clip-on tie. Cratos immediately focused in on my fleeing brother and the orcs and took off in pursuit. "Filthy souls to EAT!" He kicked a parked car and rolled it onto its side, scattering a cloud of safety glass. The screech of metal was obnoxious. Earth shaking with each step, the monster ran right past us. Smoke rose from his flesh but he looked no worse for having been doused in chemical flames.

"Now!" Franks shouted, spinning out from behind the pillar and leveling his rifle at the back of the running monster. A dozen other Feds appeared from behind various vehicles and opened fire, filling the garage with the deafening chatter of automatic weapons and the thumps of grenade launchers. Cratos was caught in the fusillade, hundreds of rounds and supersonic fragments impacting his armored hide. He momentarily disappeared in a cloud of smoke and flashes, spinning, off balance. I caught a glimpse of him as he reacted to the onslaught and covered his head. The monster tripped, toppled forward, and crushed a pickup truck beneath its bulk. Mosh and the orcs were nowhere to be seen.

The fire let up as the final guns ran out of ammo. Then came the simultaneous clatter of the well-trained agents quickly reloading. The oni wasn't moving. Nothing normal could have lived through that, but these things were not normal. "Cables," Franks ordered as he jerked the mag from his bullpup carbine and pulled a fresh one from inside his coat. "Go."

Wiping the water from my eyes, I stared in disbelief as four agents sprinted to the downed monster. Each one was carrying a giant steel manacle, thick steel cables strung between them. Several other Feds ran up behind them, carrying some sort of spear trailing a fat electrical cord. A generator roared to life. It was some sort of monster taser. "You've got to be flipping kidding me," I muttered. "Go cut its head off or something."

"Orders said take them alive," Franks replied.

That was stupid. Taking a cultist captive was one thing. Getting close to that downed monstrosity was idiocy. "There's another one around here," I warned.

"Bia," Franks said, indicating that he knew a lot more about these things than he had ever let on. *Son of a bitch.* "We'll take the big one first."

The red form stirred, the metal of the pickup truck

grinding beneath it. The agents began to shout and they hit it with the metal spear. Electricity crackled and the oni jerked and twitched, thrashing violently, smoke rising from the impact with a smell like burning rubber. "Bag him!" one of the men shouted and they started locking the giant manacles around Cratos' thick wrists and ankles. Every time it began to move, the agents on the cables would step back, and they would hit him with the spear again. I had to admit, the MCB was effective. MHI would just have chainsawed the beast as soon as he was down.

Franks got on his radio. "This is Delta. We're taking Force into custody. Violence unaccounted for."

"Excellent. Research was positive that oni were vulnerable to electricity." I could hear Myers reply. "Is Pitt still alive?"

Franks scowled. "Yeah..."

"So, you got your monster to interrogate. I'm guessing we're square?" I asked hopefully.

"I've got three injured men because of you," the big man replied. "We're not done yet..."

"Movement. Shock him!" One of the agents shouted from Cratos' side. The men on the manacles stepped back and the spear was driven in, but nothing happened this time, no arc, no sparks, nothing. "Malfunction! Hit him again." The spear was jabbed again but with no effect. The agents cried for help with terror in their voices.

Franks stepped forward, trying to discern the problem. The red hulk started to rise. The men on the manacles retreated, yelling for assistance. I glanced to the side. The electrical cable leading from the portable generator to the spear had been severed. "Bia!"

I shouted, as the purple figure threw off its cloak behind the men providing covering fire. Cackling, she slashed into the agents, ripping through their armor, blood spraying. They died quickly, having never even seen her coming.

"Aim for her eyes!" Franks shouted, but she was already gone, moving behind some parked trucks.

My attention snapped back to the big red one. An agent was shouting, "Sir, Force is—" but he never got to finish the sentence. The massive oni rose, bellowing, cables twisting and snapping, and one huge fist clocked the man, launching him across the garage in a cloud of bodily fluids. The other men started shooting, but they were too close to the beast now. With a roar, Force laid into them, living up to his title. With each movement, another agent went down, and in a matter of seconds, the survivors were retreating in disarray.

"All teams converge on the garage now!" Franks ordered into his radio. He put his rifle to his shoulder and aimed carefully at the twisting and jerking monster, searching for the eye. I put Abomination to my shoulder and centered the sight on the moving target. It was an exceedingly difficult shot. Franks fired and missed. The oni whipped one strand of cable wildly, cracking the air like a bullwhip, and a nearby agent went down. The man screamed incoherently, both of his legs severed at the knees. I tuned that out and exhaled. The eyes were moving. Focus on the holographic dot. The trigger pull was smooth and straight back to the rear.

My slug struck Cratos in one diminutive black eye. The giant paused stupidly, as if thinking about something exceedingly complicated. He stumbled and went to one knee. Something that looked like thick steam came pouring from the now-open socket. He put one meaty palm on the floor to steady himself and shook his head. When he looked back up through the rotating cloud, the eye had returned. His red lips pulled away from his tusks, and he snarled at me as the smoke dissipated. "Filthy souled Hunter!" He came off the floor and charged like an enraged bull.

Franks shoved me aside at the last second. Cratos flew past and collided with the pillar, blasting a giant chunk from it. Franks spun one way, I sprawled the other, frantically dragging myself on my butt through the debris. The giant came out of the dust, shaking himself violently. One piece of rebar, unnoticed, was impaled through his chest. "Lose some souls because of you. Replace it with yours!" he growled, bearing down on me. I kept scuttling away, but he was right there, and I could taste his horrible sulfuric breath pouring down.

His tiny eyes bore into me and the blackness behind those lenses seemed to stretch on forever, inky pools from a horrible place, utterly devoid of light. He extended one giant red hand toward me, palm as big as my chest. I felt myself growing weaker, like all of the warmth was being sucked out through my ribs, leaving my limbs numb and cold. I couldn't breathe.

The life was being pulled out of me . . .

Suddenly, it was as if I could see through his skin. The oni's body was just a shell, a constructed mass of false tissues, and underneath was the real creature, a swirling demonic bag of stolen souls.

The oni licked his lips hungrily.

Then he was gone. The rear end of a bus smashed

into Cratos, driving him back into the pillar with a brutal crunch. I shook my head as air filled my lungs and blood flowed back into my extremities. It hurt. I stumbled to my feet. The door of the Cabbage Point Killing Machine luxury tour bus slid open with an automated hiss. Mosh sat behind the wheel. "Get in!"

One giant red arm was already flailing about, pinned between the pillar and the bus. The rear tires began to slide forward against his pressure. *That's one tough monster.* I ran and jumped into the vehicle. The three orcs were clustered behind Mosh. Edward had gotten cut on the arm at some point and Gretchen was ministering to him. Somebody pushed in behind me. Franks.

"Get on the freeway," he ordered. There was a huge gash across his chest, and his white shirt was hanging open and soaked with blood. I didn't know if it was his or somebody else's. Franks didn't indicate that he was in pain, but then again, I didn't know if he could feel pain. "They'll follow Pitt."

"Me?" Mosh asked in confusion.

"No, him." Franks jerked his thumb at me. "Drive."

I ran down the aisle of the tour bus as Mosh ground the gears. The bus was so opulent that if it hadn't been such dire circumstances, I probably would have stopped to gawk. It was like a death-metal version of *Lifestyles of the Rich and Famous.* "You've got a Jacuzzi in this thing?" I shouted.

"Hell, yeah," Mosh said. "Hold on. I've only driven this once before."

The bus lurched forward, stopped, lurched again, and then was building up steam, heading for the garage exit and the open night. The rear end was crushed and a giant red visage was glaring at me through the broken back window. Cratos' tusked face curled into a snarl as we pulled away, freeing him. I raised Abomination, aimed carefully, and put my finger on my gun's second trigger. These things absorbed people's souls, and somehow that's how they had lived for thousands of years. I'd seen the pressurized bag inside them. Apparently the gateway to that was in their heads. If he lost some energy from a .68 caliber slug through the eye, let's see how he did with a 40mm grenade up the snoot.

"HUNTER!" Cratos roared.

I shot him in the mouth as we drove away.

The explosion blasted his head wide open, unhinging his jaw. There was a billowing cloud of that same white smoke as the giant toppled over and thudded to the earth.

That had to have finished him. The oni shook on the ground, facedown, head deflated like collapsed dough as the false body seemed to shrink. "No backstage pass for you, jerk-off." I laughed.

But then the head puffed back up. The skull was briefly soft as it bulged and throbbed but then it seemed to instantly harden. Re-formed, he looked up and focused right in on me, black eyes filled with simple hatred. Cratos lurched from his knees and started running after us, each step like thunder.

"Step on it, Mosh!"

# CHAPTER 7

We tore out of the Buzzard Island Amphitheater parking lot and up onto the freeway heading south. There were a ton of flashing lights, ambulances, fire trucks, and police cars arrayed around the hall now. Thousands of people were wandering around, aware that something weird was going on, but not knowing what exactly. And it was about to get a whole lot weirder for them when that unkillable red bastard came running out after us.

"Head for the Air Force base," Franks directed Mosh.

"Listen, big scary dude, I don't know where the air base is," Mosh said. "Owen, who is this asshole?"

"He's my bodyguard..." My brother started to turn around. I knew he had a lot of questions at this point, and the look he gave me indicated just how pissed off he was. "Just... Never mind... Keep heading south. I'll tell you where to turn." I held onto a stainless steel pole by the driver's seat as the bus jerked violently through the gears.

Franks keyed his radio. "This is Delta lead. Southbound in the black bus with the primary."

Myers came back. "Are you all right, Franks?"

"Yes, sir. But Alpha Team was rendered combat ineffective." Apparently "combat ineffective" meant that most of them had just gotten dismembered. The quiet man stated it with less emotion than the average person expressed over stubbing their toe.

"Evacuating them now. Apaches' ETA ten minutes," Myers replied. I breathed a sigh of relief at that. There was no way that Cratos could catch up to us on foot before we had some serious firepower overhead. "We've got a level-five containment problem here, a couple hundred viable witnesses." The senior agent sounded really upset.

"Did you get Violence?"

"Negative."

Franks started scanning through the darkened windows. "Roger that."

"Owen, we've got to talk," Mosh said as he painfully ground the bus into a higher gear. He turned and looked at me. "Okay, what the hell were those things? What are you doing playing *commando*? You're an accountant! And these weirdos keep bowing and calling me *War Chief*." He waved his hand at the orcs. All three bowed simultaneously. "See? *See*!"

"I'll explain everything."

"No. You won't," Franks ordered. I had to remember that part of his job was murdering witnesses who couldn't keep their big mouths shut.

"Wait," Skippy interrupted before I could tell Franks to go screw himself. "Smell monster." He lifted up the base of his mask, revealing his face. The wide nostrils in his piglike snout flared as he sniffed the air.

"Aaaahhhh!" Mosh screamed when he saw Skippy's

face, jerked the wheel of the tour bus, and clipped the rear end of a passing car. The car careened off the freeway and out into the wetlands. He barely regained control before we went off the road, all of us being slammed back and forth, and stumbling in the aisle. "What the *fuck*!"

Skippy dropped his mask. "Sorry...War Chief." Then he bowed an apology to Mosh. "Sister here."

There was a thump on the roof.

I raised my shotgun and started blasting random holes through the ceiling. Franks had lost his rifle at some point. A Glock appeared in his hand and he started shooting. Skippy raised my .45 and popped off the remaining rounds in the magazine. The roof was Swiss cheese in a matter of seconds. A purple hand smashed through the roof and wrapped around the shoulder of my armor. Bia hoisted me from floor as if I weighed nothing. My head slammed into the sheet metal as she tried to tug me through the gap. My boots kicked uselessly. Franks maneuvered for a shot. I levered Abomination up and emptied the rest of the magazine through the roof and right into Bia's body. She didn't let go.

Skippy and Gretchen grabbed my legs and pulled down. *Monster tug-of-war.* I screamed as my head slammed into the roof repeatedly. Ditching the totally ineffective baton, Edward leapt up and pulled the kukri from my vest. He swung, embedding the blade deep into the oni's arm. She shrieked and the claws released.

I landed on the minibar, shattering a bunch of expensive booze bottles and a fancy mirror. The arm disappeared. I hit the floor hard but my new angle gave me a clear view of the freeway ahead. "Mosh! Look out!"

My brother, distracted, had turned toward the action. He swiveled back just in time to see the rear end of the semi we were about to collide with. All of us were flung about as Mosh cranked it violently to the right and stomped on the brakes. We tore one of our headlights off against the rear of the trailer. The bus bounced wildly as we went off the pavement, tearing huge swaths out of the grass. We slid, somehow moving sideways in the mammoth vehicle, then jarred violently back onto the pavement.

We were on an off-ramp.

Mosh righted the vehicle, but now we were curving back, heading to the northeast. We began to climb up an overpass, going back over the freeway. We were in too high of a gear, and the engine made a gurgling noise as Mosh downshifted.

"Wrong way," Franks said simply as he shoved a fresh magazine into his 10mm.

"Maybe we knocked that bitch loose!" Mosh said hopefully.

Bia crashed through the side this time, a purple blur swinging down from the roof. The oni's massive fist hit Franks square in the chest and he just *disappeared*, his body flying through the glass on the opposite side.

"Franks!" But he was already gone, blasted right out the moving vehicle and into the night. Struggling, I pulled another Saiga magazine from my armor. A long purple arm stretched forward, searching for me, ripping up shards of thick carpet. Edward stepped forward, kukri swinging, and nailed her again. The blade bit deep but no fluids came out. Bia screeched, swinging at Edward, and without room to maneuver he couldn't dodge. The orc sailed down the aisle, colliding with the dash. Ed tumbled down the stairs, landing against the door.

Abomination reloaded, I put a round of double-aught buckshot into Bia's face. She turned away from me, and noticed my brother steering, eyes on the road, a bunch of orange flashing lights pulsing through the windshield past his bald head. Bia crawled further into the bus. "Mosh, move! Move!" I screamed.

But she wasn't going for him. She knocked Mosh from the driver's seat. Claws reached for the wheel and I realized what was happening, but too late to do anything other than shout something unintelligible about holding on. Purple fingers clenched and jerked, the wheels screeched in protest, and the orange flashing lights rushed up to meet us.

We hit the construction equipment at about forty miles an hour.

I woke up.

It must have only been a moment later. I tasted copper. Blood was running freely from my scalp and down my face. I wiped it away with one sleeve, smearing it away from my eyes. The bus was resting at an angle, the right side and front end a lot higher than the rest of the vehicle. The door was open. Edward was still stirring slowly on the steps. The door was open. My brother was gone.

"Mosh?" I sat up slowly, feeling the urge to puke. No answer. "You okay, Ed?" He gurgled. But he always sounded like that. I started to call for Franks, my brain needing a second to realize that Bia had already murdered him. The hole through the side of the bus was splattered with Franks' blood. "Skippy? Gretchen?"

"Pretty bus...all smash," Gretchen said sadly.

"War Chief?" Skippy asked. The two of them had ended up further back toward the Jacuzzi.

"Mosh?" I asked again, pulling one leg out from under me. Dizzy, I crawled down the stairs, past Ed, hands crunching bits of broken safety glass into the thick carpeting, and tumbled, facefirst, onto the pavement. Bia had steered us into a giant orange vehicle labeled Alabama Department of Transportation. Judging by the front of our bus, it was one solid chunk of machinery. Other orange vehicles were parked behind it. One lane of the overpass, the one that we were currently in, had been blocked off by rubber cones. Glancing back, Mosh had managed to run over at least fifty of them. I pulled myself up the side of the bus, and tucked the butt of my shotgun against my shoulder. "Mosh! Can you hear me?"

We were on the edge of the overpass. Southbound vehicles flew past beneath us, in the direction we were supposed to have been going to meet air support. Would the Apaches know where to find us? Gun raised, I stumbled around the side of the bus. That evil she-demon had to be around here somewhere.

"Pitt. Come in, Pitt." It was Grant.

"Listen, we're on the overpass about two miles south of the concert, just north of the river," I replied. "We need immediate extraction."

"Damn it, that was you behind us." His voice became quieter as he said, "Flip around, head back to the overpass," then returned to normal volume. "We're on the way."

The construction crew was on foot, running for their lives down the edge of the overpass, scared to death of something. A car zipped past in the open lane. Every passenger in the vehicle swiveled their heads in the same direction, a family of four, each of them with mouths wide open, all staring at something just around the end of the bus.

*Bia!* I flew around the corner, Abomination up. I was going to pop her in both eyes and kick her ass off this bridge.

"Hey, Bro..." Mosh croaked, "...could use a hand."

My brother was dangling over the edge of the overpass, Bia's claws encircling his throat. Mosh was holding onto her wrist with both hands, arms bulging, legs kicking futilely as vehicles screamed by below. The oni smiled, her sharp white teeth a brilliant contrast to her leather skin. She was standing on the raised concrete barrier to keep cars from driving off the side. If the drop didn't kill him, a passing car would.

Bia dipped her head in greeting. "Greetings, Hunter."

"Let him go," I ordered.

She ignored me and continued speaking. My brother had to weigh at least 250, but she didn't seem to even notice his struggling weight. Her focus was entirely on me. "I should have pulled you out of there instead of this one, but you humans all smell the same when stinking with fear."

Grant's voice sounded in my earpiece. "We're south of you. What's that purple thing?"

I keyed my radio as discreetly as possible. "Snipe her," I whispered, hoping that the throat mike would pick it up.

The oni didn't seem to hear me. "The old gods have smiled upon us tonight. I was afraid we would have to harm you. The Shadow Lord's contract specified that our payment would be halved if you were injured. Luckily, the foolishness of humans knows no bounds when their blood kin are threatened. When the Shadow Lord's minion reported that you had left in such haste to come to your brother's aid, I knew we would surely capture you tonight."

That staggered me. *There is a spy.* I had a clean shot at her eyes, but I was terrified she'd drop Mosh. "I don't care about your contract, just my brother."

Bia cackled. The unnatural sound caused the hair on my arms to stand up. "The contract is everything. Would you break a contract, my fellow Hunter?"

"Fellow Hunter?" I snorted, never letting the muzzle of my gun waver. "I don't think so."

"Oh, we're very much the same, we are. My brother and I deal in the same trade as you, only we're not picky who we work for." She reached with her free hand into her gray cloak and pulled out a tangle of rope. She tossed it at my feet. "Just like you, we have contracts to fulfill, and now I must fulfill mine."

It was just a small bundle of hemp rope. Then suddenly, it twitched. I took a step back. The rope moved on its own, uncoiling into a memorized circle. As the ends met, there was a flash of fire, and the cement inside the radius disappeared into nothingness. It was like there was a black hole in the floor of the overpass.

"The portal will take you to the Shadow Lord. You will step into it willingly."

"Fat chance of that."

"Or I drop your blood kin to his certain death." She shook Mosh painfully. His eyes were shut tight as he yelped in pain. "Then I will *make* you get in the portal. If I cannot, then my brother will be here in a moment. You would much rather do it my way than his. Cratos will simply pull your limbs off and toss you in. I would rather not lose our bonus. Either way, you will be at the feet of the Shadow Lord before this night is through."

"Violence . . ." The ragged voice came from slightly behind me. I turned.

*Franks!* He was alive, barely. Blood was running freely from a dozen lacerations. His suit had been reduced to rags. He must have lost his gun, because now all he had in his right hand was a folding fighting knife. He limped right past me, one foot dragging on the pavement.

He was seething.

"We have no quarrel with your kind," Bia said. "This is not your concern."

"Bullshit," Franks muttered, closing, as he left a splatter trail behind.

Bia was distracted by Franks. "Grant, you got a fifty?"

"Yeah. I've got my McMillan."

He'd been working on precision shooting with the Newbies today. I could only pray that he had a good zero. There was no wind. "Head shot. Don't miss. Wait for my signal."

"I'm three hundred yards away," he protested.

"It's a big head, asshole," I hissed.

Bia shook my brother again. Mosh was struggling to hold onto her arm, slipping. "I only want the Hunter."

"You can't have him," Franks said slowly, still drawing closer to his target. I had to do something before he got close enough to attack, because I knew he wouldn't care if Mosh was splattered into road kill.

"Have you grown so weak, so jealous, that you would live as a slave?" She extended one huge hand toward Franks, pleading. "The Shadow Lord understands the fallen. He can grant you true freedom. Join us." Bia said something else in a strange, almost musical language.

Franks stopped, turning his head slightly, as if thinking about her offer, whatever the hell all that weirdness meant. There was a bellowing cry in the distance. Car horns were blowing. Cratos was almost here.

"Ready," Grant said in my ear. "Hostage is blocking the shot."

"Hey, Bia!" I shouted. She turned her attention back to me. I was way too far to make a grab for Mosh. "I'd go with you to save my family. Your shadow guy was right about that. But you've got one problem . . ."

"Yes?" Her red eyes narrowed suspiciously.

"That's not my brother. You grabbed the drummer by mistake."

Curling her massive arm, she pulled Mosh closer for examination. Purple lips pulled back, puzzled, over those deadly sharp teeth. Mosh was suspended over the concrete now.

Grant was calm. "Clear."

"Send it."

The impact made a distinctive sound, like a watermelon being struck by a bat. The boom of the .50

BMG sniper rifle arrived a split second later. The bullet missed her vulnerable eyes but pierced directly through her ear hole.

Bia's head jerked violently to the side. Mosh was thrown against the concrete, landing hard on his shoulder and rolling away. A terrible whistle emanated from the oni as something unnatural ruptured. Her hands clenched spasmodically over her ears, trying to staunch the energy screaming from her collapsing skull. The inner creature had been ruptured. There was a vortex of white light and vapor shooting from her ears, eyes, and mouth, spinning, flashing upward under the halogen lights.

Franks covered the last few feet, stopped, and glared up at the monster as Bia added her inhuman shriek to the noise. "You always did talk too much," he said simply. Then he put one hand on her chest and shoved the oni over the side.

It was a twenty-foot drop to the freeway, but I couldn't tell if she actually hit the ground before the speeding 18-wheeler's grill struck her. The entire engine block of the semi instantly collapsed around her, driving steel through Bia's animated body. The truck turned brutally to the side, trailer jackknifing as the truck's weight slammed the oni solidly into the base of the overpass. The truck shuddered to a smoking-rubber halt. Suddenly a shockwave expanded outward from the impact point. Brilliant white light turned night temporarily into day. The wave passed and there were ghostly figures, literally hundreds of shapes, men and monsters, intelligences and lives that had been captive for thousands of years, now freed, leaping into the sky. They were gone in an instant.

"All those people..." I muttered as I walked to my brother's side, trying to comprehend the sheer horror of the creature we had just ended.

"What people?" Mosh asked hysterically, surely waiting for something else to try to kill him. "Where?" He hadn't seen them.

Franks regarded me suspiciously, shook his head, then stepped forward and peered over the edge. The truck was crushed below us. The trailer—a giant, stainless-steel tube—was sideways directly underneath the overpass, blocking two full lanes. It was tall enough that I probably could have just jumped down to the trailer and been fine.

Franks still had his radio. "We're on the overpass." I was far enough away that I couldn't hear the response. "Good. Evacuate the road." The southbound traffic was stopped by the wreck. The Feds must have blocked the northbound route, because nothing was coming from that direction either.

The orcs materialized, Edward balanced between his brother and sister-in-law. I checked Mosh. He was shaken, confused, but seemed okay. It was when I stood up that I noticed how badly Franks was injured. His left arm had been ripped apart from hitting the road, flesh shredded and hanging in strips, splintered bone shards visible through the welling blood. His clip-on tie had been applied as a tourniquet around the top of his bicep.

He caught my shocked expression. "Just a flesh wound," he said nonchalantly.

"BIA!"

The cry was so loud that the halogen lights overhead exploded. All of us flinched. Glass rained from the sky.

"SISTER!" Cratos was crashing down the freeway, colliding with the stopped cars. His gray cloak was flapping behind, rendering him visible to all. People ditched their cars and fled screaming from the red nightmare giant. "Filthy souls! Filthy souls must die! Kill! Killed SISTER! NOOO!"

"Oh, man. We've made him mad," I said.

Franks scowled, doing the math. The oni was a few hundred yards away and closing quickly. "Go," he ordered without looking. He limped to a nearby construction vehicle and retrieved a length of heavy cable from the back with his good arm.

I didn't know what Franks was planning, but anything involving staying and fighting was suicide. "Come on!" I shouted at him as I ran to one of the Alabama DOT trucks. Of course, there were no keys in it. I swore.

"Primary mission, protect Pitt from the Condition," Franks stated as he pulled out the cable. His injured arm was leaking everywhere, but he still managed to use his left hand to open the steel clip on the end to fashion a loop. Franks tugged out the other end of the cable, pulled it over to the bus and crawled under. He started wrapping the cable around the frame.

"Pitt! We're below you," Grant screamed in my ear. A horn honked on the freeway just south of the wrecked truck. "There's a big red thing coming this way, and I think I just killed its sister or something."

Franks was going to sacrifice himself to slow down Cratos. He looked up from his work long enough to glare at me. "I've *never* failed a mission."

In other words, it was time to go.

The fastest way down to Lee and Grant was to go right over the edge. Skippy was way ahead of me. He climbed over the concrete ledge and jumped down to the top of the trailer. His boots bounced, and he fell, but managed not to go over the side. He stood and gestured for his wife. Gretchen was much more nimble and she had somebody to help catch her. Ed, weaving badly, but still managing more dexterity than I would ever have, went over next. I helped Mosh to his feet and we wobbled to the side. "You've got to be shittin' me," he said when he looked at what was still a pretty darn scary leap down to a narrow, stainless-steel catwalk. Cratos roared again, much closer now. "Point taken." He jumped, landing awkwardly. I waited for Skippy to help him before I went over.

The yellow sign said that this was a 20-foot overpass. It felt like ten times that when I stepped into space. My boots hit the trailer just as the smell hit my nose. *Gasoline.* Pain surged up through my ankle, still tender from Mexico. Strong hands grabbed my arm. Mosh shoved me toward the ladder. "Gas truck!" he shouted.

I slid down the ladder, past a bevy of red signs saying DANGER/PELIGRO and FLAMMABLE, and landed with a splash. I was standing in gasoline. The tanker had ruptured on impact. My brother was down a second after me. Lee laid on the horn. "Come on!" But then Mosh was running in the wrong direction. "Damn it!" I shouted as I followed. He was running toward where Bia had died. Didn't he realize we had to get out of here, either before this thing caught on fire or before Cratos got here? *Stupid idiot.*

Then I felt like the idiot as Mosh scrambled his way up to the wrecked truck. He was trying to get the driver. The engine block was completely smashed into the wall and fragments had been hurled a hundred feet but the trucker could still be alive. Mosh jerked on the door but it was crumpled tight. I reached him just as he crawled, headfirst, through the broken window.

"Hurry, man. We've got to go," I insisted.

"Working on it," came the muffled reply.

"KILL! KILL!" Cratos screamed.

I saw Agent Franks standing at the top of the overpass, perched in the exact spot that Bia had been in only a minute before. He held the thick loop of cable in his hands, noose ready. Was he going to actually try to lasso the thing? The rear of the tanker shook as Cratos slammed into it, pushing past, splashing into the gasoline. He was so absurdly tall that his head terminated nearly three quarters of the way to the overpass above. He saw me.

"FILTHY HUNTER DIE!"

Franks waited patiently for the monster to step into view.

Force roared. The sound began as a rumble, but then rose in intensity, until it was a primal scream of pure hate. He lowered his head and charged.

Franks tossed the makeshift noose. The oni's head passed right through and he made it three more steps before the cable jerked tight. The bus was jerked several feet. His beady eyes bulged as the cable tightened around his throat. Too enraged to stop, he kept tugging inexorably toward me, dragging the bus with him.

The ground was littered with wreckage, gasoline quickly spreading and washing over it. I realized with a shock that much of the debris was actually what was left of Bia. The purple bits looked like dried clay. "Grab my feet and pull!" Mosh shouted. I grabbed him, glad that he was wearing those giant lineman boots that laced all the way up to his knees, and yanked as hard as I could. The adrenaline was surging through my system and I pulled my brother back out the window. Mosh saw Cratos struggling less than a hundred feet away but he was a man on a mission. "Help me with this guy."

We both reached through the window. I found an armpit, and we pulled, lifting the unconscious man through the gap. Of course, he had to be a big, heavyset guy, too. *No*, it would have been too much to ask to have to carry a petite person out of a probably soon-to-be-exploding truck with an angry giant *thing* trying to eat your soul. No, Owen Z. Pitt, *you* get a three-hundred-pounder. It took two strong and desperate men to pull him through the window. I slung the trucker over my back in a fireman carry and ran for our lives.

Cratos was trying to scream, but the sound was choked off by the cable. The harder he pulled, the tighter it got, but he was still getting closer. Driven by supernatural strength, he had dragged the tour bus partway over the cracking ledge. If that thing went over it was bound to spark and blow us all to kingdom come.

Then I heard the choppers. The MCB's Apache gunships were coming in, low and fast, from the west side of the island. Their mission was to put some hurting on this monster.

*And they didn't know about the fuel tanker.*

What Franks did next absolutely stunned me. With his knife held in his good hand, he leapt over the edge, not to the trailer top, but rather, straight to the ground, directly behind Cratos. Franks landed on his feet, automatically rolling to absorb the impact, but still surely breaking his legs. He tumbled through the gas, coming up in a petrochemical splash, right beneath the oni's leg. Franks slashed the knife brutally, chopping through whatever served as the unnatural beast's ligaments, hamstringing it. Cratos collapsed to one knee, the cable pulling even tighter.

The beast swung, tearing one mighty fist at Franks, but hitting only gas and pavement, as Franks had rolled behind the other leg, and struck deep there as well. This time Franks wasn't fast enough, and a backhand landed hard enough to tear a cloud through six feet of road. Franks was flung into the darkness, disappearing into the trees along the river.

Now, with both legs damaged, the oni toppled, hanging itself entirely. It struggled, twisting, legs flopping, as it swung back under the overpass.

The gasoline was everywhere, soaking my legs, as I lumbered up to the MHI van. Grant was holding the back door open. "Toss him to me!" he shouted. I shoved the injured trucker in before clambering up behind. Grant and Mosh were in a second later, and Lee had us moving before we could even get the rear door closed. An angry dragonfly shape passed overhead as the first Apache took aim.

"Gun it, Lee!"

"Going as fast as I can," the little man stated calmly, as he put all of his weight and will on the gas pedal. The MHI vans were all supercharged V8s, and that was a good thing.

"Go! Go! Go!" Grant shouted.

Behind us, Cratos raged and fought. The millennium-old killer was hanging, thrashing, tiny eyes bulging with hate, when the chopper fired. The 30mm cannon struck him in the torso, depleted uranium shells exploding out his back in a shower of fragments and white light. Rocket pods launched, lancing fury under the overpass. The gasoline caught, flames tearing across the freeway, leaping back up into the emptying trailer, igniting the massive amount of fumes in a conflagration that was probably visible in Cazador.

A wall of heat and pressure rocked the van, blowing the rear windows out in a spray of hot glass. I covered my head. A killing wind smashed through the interior, super hot and stinging. The exterior paint caught on fire.

But we made it.

A roiling red-and-black mushroom cloud rose behind us, hundreds of feet into the air. Somehow I alone could see through the conflagration to see the ancient oni's final moments. Through the curtains of fire and smoke and howling wind, the beast hung by a fraying cable, false flesh boiling away, energy fleeing, until finally in a flash, he was consumed. The container was destroyed, freeing thousands of trapped souls as his body exploded into clay dust that was sucked upward into the flaming vortex.

"You okay?" I asked softly.

My brother had spent the last fifteen minutes doing CPR on the trucker. The two of us and the rapidly cooling body were the only ones left in the van. He had done his best, and his chest heaved from the stress and exertion. He smelled like evaporating gasoline.

After we had stopped the van, Gretchen had examined the man for only a few seconds, shook her head sadly, then walked away. If Gretchen had said nothing could be done, then truly, it was over. Mosh didn't know what I knew about her healing powers and had continued trying to resuscitate, pumping the man's chest over and over, stubbornly trying to work a heart that was just plain done, then filling the lungs with air and trying again.

The back of the van was bare. It made a decent work space for first aid. Mosh leaned back against the wall and rubbed a filthy hand over his face.

"You okay?" I repeated, a little louder this time.

The trucker was a big old boy with a Charlie Daniel's beard, with those kind of thick arms that bordered on fat but were amazingly strong, and he had LOVE tattooed on one set of knuckles and HATE tattooed on the other. It was cheesy, but it didn't matter now, because he was dead, and it was my fault. College kids in Mexico, who knows how many innocents tonight, my family put in danger, and it wasn't going to stop. . . . All because of me.

Mosh gave a sad little laugh. It was a pathetic sound. "Hell of a night."

"Yeah . . . Listen, dude, I can explain everything."

He just shook his head. "Shut up."

"No, really. Everything you saw, I can explain."

Mosh lowered his hand. His face was bloodstained and scratched. "Just leave me alone right now, okay?" His eyes got a dangerous squint to them and just for a second I could see that family resemblance that everybody always told me about.

I nodded. I could understand. There was a helicopter

landing outside. This particular talk could wait. The back doors of the van were pulled open. Grant was standing there in his perfect black armor. "Feds are here," he stated, though it was pretty obvious with the black helicopter settling on the freeway a hundred feet away.

"Hey, Grant."

"Yeah?"

I clapped him on the shoulder. It was kind of awkward. "Good shot back there."

Grant just nodded, his expression inscrutable. It was no secret that he disliked me. "Just doing my job." Saving my life was a professional courtesy, nothing more. "I suppose that makes us even."

He was talking about me pulling him out of DeSoya Caverns. Technically I figured I was still ahead by one, but I had broken his nose for that incident. "Fair enough."

The fire was still burning in the distance. We were parked on the bridge between Buzzard Island and Montgomery. State police, by order of the Feds, had blocked the bridge into town. This area was now quarantined, certainly as part of what Myers had referred to on the radio as a Level 5 Containment Event. Agent Myers, trailed by Agents Torres, Herzog, and Archer, approached as Grant and I waited. The Goon Squad looked pretty beat up. Archer had a black eye and a Sig 229 dangling from one hand. Skippy, Gretchen, and Edward were nowhere to be seen, which was probably real smart right about now.

"Pitt...Jefferson," Myers addressed us, anger barely contained. I was waiting for him to explode. I was going to jail, if I was lucky.

"Myers," I said gravely. "Have you found Franks yet?"

"We will find him," Myers stated matter-of-factly, somehow talking while keeping his jaw clenched. "As for you . . ."

I waited patiently for my arrest.

Agent Myers hesitated, obviously waffling between having the cuffs put on or ordering his agents to just shoot me to get it over with. The look he gave me was a mixture of anger, frustration, and something else that I wasn't sure about. He turned from me, studied the surviving members of my protective detail one by one, and then scowled back at me, deep in thought. Finally he seemed to deflate. His teeth unclenched and then Myers just seemed like the tired, middle-aged, glorified bureaucrat that he was. "You, I'll deal with later. Go home . . ." He waved his hand. "Just . . . go home."

That was a surprise. "Seriously?"

"But, sir!" Herzog shouted. "He attacked us."

"I never touched you," I said, which was true. The orcs had beat the hell out of them—not me.

"He pulled a gun on Agent Franks." Archer said. "That's—"

"Enough!" Myers cut his subordinate off. "Pitt, if I thought it would benefit my mission I'd have you locked up for eternity. Your actions jeopardized my men."

I had no idea why he was letting me go. A smarter man would have kept his mouth shut, but my temper tended to run faster than my brain. "You knew more about these oni than you let on. I had nothing to do with your trap failing. Did you expect me to just let them kill my brother?"

"You're a free man for one reason only. You're still our only in against this group," Myers spat. "Don't mistake my actions for mercy. I need all of my available men for this containment but I'll provide another protective detail shortly. We'll assess how tonight's setback affects our case against the Condition. Hopefully, the cultist your father shot will survive and we can get some information out of him."

"How are my parents?" I asked.

"Fine. They're on a flight now."

"Parents?" Mosh spoke up from behind Grant, concern evident in his voice. "What happened?"

Myers gestured into the back of the van. "One of your people?"

"That's my brother, the one you were going to leave to die," I said, pointing to Mosh, who looked really exasperated.

Myers sighed. "I meant the dead one."

"Driver of the tanker." Grant spoke for the first time.

"We tried to save him," Mosh said.

"I understand." The senior G-man nodded. "Men, carry this body to the chopper."

"What about Mom and Dad?" Mosh demanded.

"I'll explain later," I said. Mosh scowled in a manner that suggested he was giving serious thought about attempting to kick my ass. I was bigger and had a lot more experience but I knew my brother was damn tough when he got angry. "Chill out, dude. They're fine." Mosh punched the side of the van and stomped away. I waited until the Goon Squad had picked up the trucker before returning my full attention to Myers. It took all three of them to hoist the body up and shuffle away, each of them telegraphing their distaste for their superior's decision not to haul me off. "Any idea how many more dead?"

"Not as many as you would think," Myers replied. "We got lucky. Some civilians at the concert and I have four men dead and several more wounded." I didn't know if he was counting Franks in that quantity. "We got most of the cars stopped away from the tanker and the people stuck behind the crash were smart enough to run when they saw Force drop his invisibility. As far as we know, nobody else was caught in the explosion. In the meantime, I've got hundreds of witnesses and a slew of damage that I have to explain. Some idiot is going to talk about this and that means they'll have to be dealt with . . ." He trailed off, finding the idea distasteful.

"Wouldn't it be better if we just let the truth be known?" I suggested.

"Not my call, Pitt. I just enforce policy. I don't make it." He began to walk back to the waiting Blackhawk.

"You murder survivors and witnesses!" I shouted. "You destroy lives to keep up this illusion of safety! People should know what's really out there."

Myers paused, turned, and shook his head sadly. "Can you imagine what would happen if the world found out the truth? Chaos. Pandemonium. No. People need to be kept safe from themselves, and I'll do whatever I have to, lie, cheat . . . kill . . . anything, to keep my country safe." The professor was a dedicated man.

It was disgusting. "How do you sleep at night?"

Myers actually chuckled, his normally bureaucratic demeanor apparently damaged by his losses. "I don't. If you knew what was coming"—he resumed walking, the wind from the rotors snapping his cheap tie over his shoulder and making it difficult to hear—"you wouldn't sleep anymore either."

"What's that supposed to mean?" I shouted after him.

But he didn't answer. The chopper lifted off a minute later, leaving me to ponder what it was that Myers thought was coming. Clearly there was more to this cult than the Feds were letting on. Lee hobbled around the side of our van. He was in jeans and a Schlock Mercenary tee shirt. He had bailed out of the compound so fast he hadn't even had time to gear up. Grant must have gotten dressed on the road. The sight of Lee in normal attire made me especially thankful for my friends. They hadn't hesitated to go after me any more than I had for my own brother. "Z, I've got Harbinger on the phone. He's been trying to reach you."

I pulled out my cell phone. It had gotten cracked at some point during the evening's excitement. "Piece of crap!" I cocked my fist back and chucked it far out into the Alabama River. That small bit of random violence made me feel better.

Lee shook his head and grinned. "You know the company phones have a warranty on them, right? You could have got that replaced for free. Now you'll have to buy a new one."

I groaned. "What did he say?" I knew it had to be some variation of *Pitt, you suck. Go hide at the compound*. Lee handed me his phone.

My boss actually sounded concerned. "How're y'all doing?"

"We're good. Only minor injuries." I hurried, knowing that he was going to rip me for disobeying his orders. "We got to my brother in time. Agent Franks is dead." Saying that sounded weird. Franks had always seemed so stoic, so invulnerable, that it was hard to imagine anything being able to end his life.

"He was a jackass but he was a pro," Earl said simply.

I turned away so the others wouldn't hear. Something that Bia said had been gnawing at me. "The creatures knew I was coming. Somebody told them I was on my way. There *is* a spy at the compound."

There was a long silence at the other end while Earl mulled that over. "Either there or it could have been somebody who's with me right now. Julie got your message and told everybody else. We're on our way back. I've got an idea. I want you to meet me someplace. Can you ditch the Feds?"

"Already done."

"Okay, Lee's driving? Pass the phone back to him."

I walked back to the others and handed the phone to Lee. "What's going on?" Grant asked. Lee was listening to instructions and went forward to program an address into the onboard GPS.

"Earl wants us to meet him somewhere."

"I don't like it. Myers said we should go back to the compound," Grant said.

"Screw him," I said automatically. "When did you start caring what the Feds say?"

Grant snorted like that was absurd. "I don't."

"You're just worried that you're too pretty for prison." They'd have loved Grant in Tijira. Lee came back. "Where to, man?"

"Birmingham. Harbinger gave me an address for a house in a neighborhood called Hensley." Lee said.

"Never heard of it, but cool." So Harbinger had something up his sleeve after all. The whole "hide and wait for the bad guys to kill me" plan hadn't gone real well so far, so hopefully he had found a way to go on the offensive.

I *like* being offensive.

# CHAPTER 8

Birmingham was the next big city north of Montgomery. It took us awhile to drive the van through all of the various detours that popped up in the aftermath of the concert. It gave Gretchen a chance to bounce around between the seats, applying greasy, smelly ointments to all of our various injuries.

"Yes, damn it, Tim. The tour bus exploded... Yeah, you heard me. Ex-*Plode*-Ed," Mosh said into Lee's borrowed cell phone with quite a bit of consternation. He had wanted to contact his band to let them know that he was still alive. "No, I don't know what's going on... Atlanta? Hell, I guess we're probably going to have to cancel it, don't you think? Since the bus *exploded*." He shook his head sadly. "Okay, whatever, I'll call you back as soon as I can." My brother handed the borrowed phone back and then banged his forehead against the window.

Yep, I've had nights like that before.

Mosh wasn't very responsive and appeared deep in thought. He hadn't even commented as Gretchen had applied a paste made out of old squirrels and herbs to the scratches on his face and arms. I had thought about taking him to a real hospital but I knew that he was a lot safer with me than floating around out there, alone and a target.

The worst injury to our contingent had been to Edward. Bia had clubbed him pretty good. He was resting in the back, and Gretchen informed us that he would be just fine. Orcs were built tough.

The broken windows made conversation difficult but at least the airflow made the evaporating gas stink from my soaked boots bearable. Grant rode shotgun, literally in this case, with a 12-gauge FN auto-loader sitting across his lap. It was still unknown just how much info the Condition had about us but we were a relatively small and vulnerable force out here on our own.

Lee had asked for details on the monsters while Gretchen pasted an inch-long cut on my scalp shut. I had lost a lot of scars because of the magical healing at DeSoya Caverns but I was having no problem picking up new ones. Lee had pumped his fist in the air when I had told him the details of Force and Violence's demise. "Yes!" our librarian shouted. "The clay, the explosions, the ghosts, that's textbook right there. They were giant, animated, soul containers. I was right. They were definitely oni, disembodied spirits living inside a created form. That's awesome." He turned to look at me over the seat. Apparently I gave him a stupid look. "Don't you get it?"

"Uh, no? And watch the road, I've already been in two car accidents tonight. Don't make me make a tacky comment about Asian drivers."

"Puh-leeze, like I've got a Camry with a giant spoiler on it."

Lee flipped back around. "PUFF on an ogre is only like twenty grand, depending on the breed. They're big but they aren't anything special. The PUFF bounty on an oni is in the hundreds of thousands."

Grant perked right up at that. "You all saw it. I got a confirmed on the purple one. So I'm the primary," he said smugly. At MHI, the entire company shared bounties, but the team, or in this case, the individual who did the most work, got the most pay. "And to think Earl left me behind to train stupid Newbies while he wasted his time on some wimpy trolls. How many hundreds are we talking about?"

"I'll have to look it up. It's not like anybody has killed one of these in a long time." Lee almost giggled. He was such a dork when it came to monster lore. "And the best part? The Feds smoked the big one, but the law says that government representatives can't collect PUFF."

"Really? Agents don't get PUFF?" Grant was incredulous. "That's . . . that's crazy. Well, good thing I'm not a Fed! We'll file the paperwork for an assist on the red one in the morning." He had been MHI's golden boy once, but had left in disgrace. Pulling off a great kill in his first few days back would probably help his reputation. "They couldn't have got him without our providing a distraction."

"Oh, that'll piss off Myers, but good." Lee held out his fist for Grant to bump knuckles. Grant looked at him awkwardly for a moment and then did so.

"On a personal note, it sucks to be the number one target of a godlike interdimensional being, but it sure is good for business," I added.

"That's it." Mosh finally spoke up. "I've had about enough of this shit. PUFF? Ogres? Oni? Who the hell are you people?" He jerked his thumb to where the orcs were sitting quietly in back. "*What* the hell are those people?" He turned toward me and stabbed one callused fingertip into my armored chest. "And *you*. You owe me an explanation or you can pull this thing over and let me out right now."

I glanced out the window. It was the middle of the night and we were in the country. "Not the best place to hitch a ride, bro."

"I swear I'm about to beat you like a tetherball," Mosh said.

"Well, it's a long story," I began.

"Give me the short version."

"Monsters are real. We make lots of money killing them," Lee piped in.

"I didn't ask you. I asked my stupid brother, who I'm guessing isn't really a CPA." He thumped me in the armor. "I want answers."

I laughed. "Short version?"

Mosh gave me a dangerous look. "Break it down for me."

Well, if he wanted to be that way… "Cool. Remember last year when my accounting supervisor turned out to be a serial killer? Nope. Werewolf. Remember last time we talked and I told you about my new finance job? Nope. Monster Hunter. These guys are some of my coworkers." I waved toward Grant and Lee, then I jerked my thumb to the rear. "Those folks back there are orcs, but it's all good, they're on our side. That muscle-bound guy who got killed back at the overpass? He was my bodyguard, assigned by a shadow government agency that keeps monsters secret from the public. The things at the concert were mythical creatures hired by a death cult to sacrifice me to a giant space mollusk because they think I poked it in the eye with a nuclear weapon last summer...Any questions?"

Mosh glared. "You always were a dick."

"You ready for the long version now?"

I wrapped up as much of my story as possible by the time our GPS guided us to the location that Harbinger had given Lee. It was in an old, rundown, kind of scary area on the northwest side of Birmingham. We pulled onto a narrow street. To our immediate left was a series of fat, rectangular, red-brick buildings. Each identical building was aesthetically awful, with barred windows and knee-high brown weeds in the neglected yards. We were in the Projects.

"So, what do you think?" I asked my brother. "We cool?".

Mosh had been stroking his goatee and quietly looking out the window for the last little while. He turned back to face me. He was still incredulous, but taking it well. "Why didn't you tell me this before?"

Honestly, I had wanted to. I shrugged. "If you hadn't seen what you saw earlier, would you have believed me anyway?"

"No. I would have told you to put down the crack pipe. But now? Hard to argue with what I saw tonight." When I had first joined MHI, Harbinger had told me that Hunters' greatest weapons were the flexibility of their minds—their ability to take in situations, no matter how weird, and just deal with them. I had made a pretty good Hunter, and judging by my brother's reactions, flexible minds ran in the family.

Hensley had the look of a tough town. The streets were mostly deserted at this late hour, but there were still knots of rough young men standing under the streetlights on various corners. They glared at us suspiciously as we drove by, not recognizing us as part of their regular customer base. "Friendly place," Grant said, clutching the shotgun. Now this would certainly be the wrong vehicle to carjack.

"Come on, trust fund baby. You haven't been in the 'hood before?" I asked sarcastically. "This is the kind of place that me and Mosh grew up in. Right, bro?"

Mosh raised a single eyebrow. We had grown up in a middle-class suburb, but he was quick enough to play along. "Hell yeah, straight up ghetto. Right out of Compton. Slinging...gats. Yeah."

"Word," I said.

"Pimpin' ain't easy," Mosh stated, dead serious.

Grant shook his head, having his negative opinion of me confirmed again. Lee stifled a laugh, realizing immediately how full of crap we were.

The GPS computer voice told us to make a turn and head down under a railway into an even older neighborhood. Lee had to hit the brakes to keep from creaming a nasty-looking Chow dog that blundered stupidly in front of us. To the right was a street of small frame houses, each one with a tiny front yard. The indicated address was the only one with lights on. An MHI vehicle was parked in the driveway and another was in the street. We pulled in behind it and stepped out.

I heard deep barks coming from a dog in the

fenced-in backyard. Other than that, this particular street seemed eerily dead. Trash and broken bottles were scattered in the other yards, and every single lawn was dead. There were a lot of smashed windows on this street. It looked like most of the surrounding houses were long since abandoned, leaving this one particular home isolated. It felt good to stretch my legs. There were a few random gunshots in the distance.

"Owen," Julie cried as she stepped out of the other MHI vehicle. She ran over and engulfed me in a hug. The Hunters from Esmeralda's team piled out behind her. I kissed her forehead as she held me tight, almost like she was afraid to let go of me again. "I'm glad you're okay."

"No biggie," I said modestly.

Mosh cleared his throat.

"Oh, Julie, this is—"

"David!" Julie said, letting go of me, and grabbing Mosh by the hand. She was almost as tall as he was. "Oh, I've heard so much about you!"

Mosh looked surprised, first because of the use of his real name, and second because of how strong her handshake was. I'd had that reaction the first time I'd met her too. "You must be Julie ... You know, I've never dated a Julie," Mosh smirked. "But I did date Ms. July once and you are way prettier."

Julie hesitated, not sure how to take that particular compliment. "He actually did," I explained with a sigh. My brother had dated centerfolds, supermodels, and famous actresses. Where I turned into a stammering moron around women, Mosh had always been smooth.

Mosh grinned. "Z really talked you up."

"I bet. He's a regular poet," she said. "I've wanted

to meet his family forever. We've got so much to talk about, but first—" She jerked her head toward the house. "Owen, Earl's waiting for you inside."

"What is this place?" I asked.

"I don't know. He wouldn't say. He was adamant: just you, and..." Her pause indicated that the next part was going to suck. "You need to leave your weapons out here." She raised her hands defensively. "Yes, yes, I know. He knew you'd freak out, but he said he didn't want to offend *them.*"

*Them?* "Oh, what now?" I groaned. I hated being unarmed on principle, let alone after the week that I'd had, but I trusted Earl. I unslung Abomination. "Fine..." It took me almost a minute to completely disarm.

Skippy joined us. He took one glance at the lit house, then shook his head sadly. "Trouble," he muttered before wandering off.

Under the orange streetlights, Mosh looked a bit apprehensive about being left with a bunch of heavily armed strangers. He grabbed me by the arm and leaned in close. "Where are you going?"

"Just hang out, man. Besides, Julie can explain all this stuff way better than I can."

"Yeah, about that, you said she was hot, but... *damn.*" He whistled. "How the hell did someone like *her* go for someone like *you?*"

"My charming personality." I shrugged his hand off. "Now back off before I scissor-kick you in the neck. I'll be back in a minute. Just relax."

A moment later I found myself at the waist-high chain-link gate in front of the house. There was a plastic sign with a cartoon pit bull printed on it saying

BEWARE OF DOG. I lifted the latch, and walked up the path. Nothing came out to bite me. This yard was free of trash but the grass was just as brown and dead as the neighbors'. The streetlights were blocked by a few overgrown trees, and most of the yard was cloaked in shadow. There was one of those cheesy garden gnomes in the desiccated bushes of the flower bed but nothing else that gave a clue to the personality of the residents. Light was coming through the window but the blinds were drawn, so I couldn't see a thing inside.

This place gave me a bad vibe. I stepped up onto the porch and went to ring the doorbell, but paused as there was a flicker of light from the flower bed. I glanced down and realized it was orange ashes from the end of a fat cigar. The lawn ornament returned the lighter to the inside of its blue shirt, dusted the ashes out of its white beard, and swiveled its head toward me. Beady eyes peaked out from under a pointy red hat.

I stood there awkwardly. "Hi."

"What you lookin' at?" the tiny little man said. "Got a problem?"

"No."

"Damn right, punk-ass bitch, best step off my porch," he said around his massive cigar. He was a stocky eighteen inches tall, not including the hat, but his attitude indicated he meant business. "Hunters think they're tough, actin' up in here like they run the place? Ringin' that bell's gonna wake up Momma, and you don't wanna wake up Momma." He lifted his shirt, exposing the butt of a small pistol shoved in his waistband. "You hear me, big man?"

"Hey, I don't want trouble."

"That's right, you don't. I don't take nothin' off no Hunters," he snarled around the cigar, one diminutive hand landing on the gun. "Move."

I stepped off the porch, my hands still held in front of me defensively. This was a strange encounter, even by my admittedly jaded standards. "I'm looking for Earl Harbinger."

"Your boy's around back with my homies. We owe him a favor, only reason I don't go upside your head and show your crew what's up. I'm addicted to killin', so don't go temptin' me."

"Gotcha," I said slowly, extending one finger and pointing around the side of the yard. "I'll just go..."

The gnome let go of his gun and let the shirt fall. He blew out a huge cloud of smoke. "S'all good. Follow me. Your boy probably get pissed if my dawg ate you, know what I'm sayin'?"

"Uh...yeah."

The little man swaggered around the side of the house, and I tagged along obediently, following the cloud of smoke. There was a taller gate to the backyard. He pushed it open and entered. The source of the barking was back here. The backyard was even more barren than the front. There was a long steel cable running from the house to the kennel with a length of heavy chain dangling from the middle. But there was no animal currently attached to the dog run. The grass had been packed down into nothing but hardened dirt. The barking picked up and something large crashed into the kennel's sheet metal wall.

The gnome went back to the kennel, paused to unlock a big padlock, then opened the chicken-wire-and-rebar gate. "Down, boy," he snapped, his voice way too deep for such a little creature. The barking obediently stopped. He disappeared inside. I paused, confused, outside the kennel. It was too dark to see in. His red hat popped back out the door. "You comin' or what?"

"What's in there?"

"Our secret hideout, what you think this is?" The red hat disappeared back into the shadows as the gnome continued to mutter. "Tall people is stupid."

I ducked my head to keep from stabbing it on the makeshift structure. I had a sneaky feeling that any cut I got from this thing would result in tetanus. I had to crouch to fit. The inside of the shack smelled like wet dog and poop. There was a huge animal curled in shadows of the corner. The surly gnome paused long enough to move a water bowl aside, then pulled up a hidden trapdoor. The bowl read FAFNIR. A ladder led down into darkness.

The gnome simply stepped into the hole and disappeared. My attention snapped toward the dog as it growled. It sounded unbelievably scary in the dark. The shape moved slightly with the rustle of chains and brute strength. The gnome shouted from down the hole. "Better hurry 'fore he gets hungry." Then he laughed. I shuffled over to the hole and glanced down. I couldn't see the bottom, and it looked like an absurdly tight fit. *Screw that.*

The dog moved forward slightly and now I could see it better and I immediately wished that I hadn't. It had the thick face of a Rottweiler and solid black jowls pulled back to reveal a row of sharp teeth and dripping saliva. Then two more heads appeared on each side. Each one was big enough to gnaw my arm off, and all three necks terminated on the same muscular body.

All three heads growled.

The hole was barely wide enough to fit my shoulders but it beat staying up here with Super Dog. I was down the ladder in a second. I landed hard and the trapdoor fell shut above me with a slam. A small flame ignited, revealing that we were in a brick room. The gnome snarled at me over his lighter. "Watch it, stupid human, big old feet stompin' on everything. Scuff my shoe and I'll go psycho on your ass."

"Better put that out. I'm covered in gas."

He appeared to think about immolating me for a moment. "Yeah, I thought you smelled funny." The lighter snapped shut, leaving me blind again. He rapped his fist on something steel. A slit of light appeared at knee level and another set of beady gnome eyes peered out at us. A moment later the slit slammed shut, and there was the sound of metal on metal as bolts and locks were undone. The door, which was thankfully normal-sized, opened with a creak.

A second gnome, complete with red hat, white beard, and sawed-off, double-barreled shotgun, was waiting for us. He cradled the shotgun in his arms, and the short weapon was longer than he was. I couldn't imagine what would happen to the little guy if he touched it off but the look he gave me indicated that he wouldn't hesitate to use it on me to find out. My guide passed some complicated signs with his hands and asked "Wuzzup?"

"Chillin'." The shotgun bobbed as he nodded his red pointy hat down the dimly lit hall stretching behind him. He looked me up and down. "The boss is waitin' for you, so hurry up. You disrespect the boss, and we bust a cap in you, big human. Know what I'm sayin'? You're on gnome turf now." He leaned his shotgun against the wall and picked up a metal detecting wand and swiped it over my lower half. He could only reach up to my stomach, even standing on his tippy-toes and stretching. That seemed to really piss him off. "You gonna bend over so I can finish this, or am I gonna hafta whup your ass and bring you down here?"

Putting my usual sarcastic comments in check, I knelt down so he could search me. I got the impression that these guys had zero sense of humor. The only thing that beeped was a couple of buckles and some pocket change, and seemingly disappointed that he didn't get to blast me with his 20-gauge, the guard signaled for me to continue. My guide walked down the hall. Judging by the size of the hallway, this had been a normal human structure until they had taken it over. The brickwork was old and crumbling. Naked light bulbs flickered and dangled from exposed wiring. We turned the corner and entered a large room.

A stereo was playing gangsta rap. There were at least two dozen of the diminutive creatures in here. All of them were tiny, with long white beards and pointy red hats. There was furniture scattered around, and I was guessing that it had originally been intended for little kids, as it was all plastic and in festive colors, but these certainly weren't little kids, and they sure as hell didn't look festive. One of the gnomes had his shirt off and was laying on a plastic stool, bench-pressing a single forty-five-pound dumbbell. He had *Thug Life* tattooed on his chest. Every other gnome had an alcoholic beverage in his hands and these were full human-sized drinks. The smoke was thick enough to constrict my lungs. And guns, man, these guys were armed to the teeth. Everybody was packing, mostly a bunch of cheap .25s and .22s, but with an occasional larger gun shoved awkwardly into a waistband.

The gnomes glanced up as I entered. *Way up.* Every one of them tried to appear as threatening as possible. A few passed complicated gang signs at me. One little guy raised his arms out wide, as if to say, "You want a piece of this?" Then he jerked his head toward me to see if I would flinch. Since he was small enough that I could probably kick a field goal with him, I can honestly say that I didn't show any fear.

"Word up," my guide said to the largest gnome, who had to be all of two and a half feet tall, including the hat. They performed a complicated handshake, and then did one of those man hugs where they pat each other on the back once. During the ritual, I noted Harbinger waiting at the back of the room. My guide put one hand on my calf and shoved me forward with a remarkable amount of strength. He laughed as I stumbled, and I resisted the urge to toss him across the room.

Harbinger nodded when he saw me. Someone had brought out two adult-sized folding chairs, and he motioned toward the other one. He was sitting at a wooden table that had its legs sawed off. On the opposite side of the table was another gnome, dressed identically to the others, except for the giant, golden, bejeweled dollar-sign necklace he was wearing. The necklace sparkled in the dim light. The room was large enough that we had a little bit of privacy from the other gnomes now. Other tunnels led off in various directions, suggesting that this place had a lot more to it than what you might first expect. I took my seat.

"Owen, this is Sven Bone-Hand, leader of the Birmingham Gnomes. Sven, this is Owen Pitt," Harbinger said to the boss gnome. "He's the one."

The two of us, sitting hunched forward, across the short table from the gnome, made it feel like we were playing tea party with stuffed animals. The creature sized me up. "He's extra big," the gnome said slowly, like that was a bad thing. "Real tall."

Harbinger nodded. "I know, but he's okay. I vouch for him."

"You didn't say nothin' about him being *tall*," the gnome said. "This changes the game, man. I don't trust tall humans."

"You don't trust any humans." My boss leaned forward. "You going back on the deal?" He reached into his leather jacket and pulled out a stack of rubber-banded currency. It was fat, and the visible bills had Ben Franklin's picture on them. He put the cash on the table and slid it toward the gnome.

Sven picked up the money and thumbed through it. He smiled. His teeth had diamonds embedded in them. "Harbinger, my brother . . . I'm a hustler, but I keep my promises. Let me do my thing." Then he vanished.

Literally vanished, he was there one second and then just *gone*. His chair was empty. The money was gone too. I blinked. Earl didn't seem surprised.

"Where'd he go?" I asked.

"Gnomes can do that. That's why they come in handy. They have a gift for not being seen." Somebody had given Earl a beer, and he tilted it at me like it was a toast. "You didn't stay at the compound like I told you to."

"No. No, I didn't."

He took a theatrically long pull from his drink. I had disobeyed his orders, but he knew me well. He knew I was borderline suicidal when it came to loyalty. "With family in danger, I would've been surprised if you had." At least he wasn't mad at me.

I glanced around the basement. "So, what did you just buy?"

"Information."

"Oh, good. I thought you were branching off into wholesale drug distribution or something," I said. "What kind of info?"

He didn't respond directly. "At first, I thought Myers was a liar. There was no way we had a mole at the compound, but if those things knew you were coming, then we've got to face facts. We've been infiltrated. So now we're bringing in a secret weapon. You've met some of the other races that live in mankind's shadow, but they live on the outskirts. Gnomes have mastered living right under our noses, thousands of years, damn near in plain sight. Gnomes are sneaky. Every city has them and nobody ever knows."

"They're urban?"

Earl glanced at the crowd of little creatures watching us suspiciously as the rap music thumped. "Well, duh." He went back to his drink. "Scandinavian originally, but everybody adapts. In the old days they hid on farms, cursing the animals if the owners didn't leave them good offerings. Basically an old-school protection racket, they've just gone mainstream over time.

Unfortunately, these learned American culture from watching TV...rap videos mostly."

I lowered my voice, "I thought gnomes were supposed to be like all quaint and cute. You know, rosy cheeks, big smile, chubby little guys you put on your lawn. These guys aren't nice...They're freaking *scary*."

"Humans love to take terrible things and make them cute," Earl said. "Read some of the old fables, before they got prettied up for little kids. If you left your farm's gnome a bowl of porridge and you forgot to add butter, he'd get mad and slaughter all your cows. That sound cute to you?"

"No. That sounds like the kind of thing somebody would hire us to blow up. Can we trust these things?" I whispered.

"Of course not, they're crooks. But this bunch owes me a favor...Let me do the talking."

There was a shifting of the air in front of us and suddenly Sven was back in his chair. His "grill" gleamed when he smiled. It was slightly unnerving.

"We good?" Earl asked.

"It's like this...I got a business to run, Harbinger. Sparing a soldier? B'ham's up for grabs, my man. I need strong arms to hustle. So it's gonna cost you. Dog-eat-dog world, you know what I'm sayin'?" Almost on cue, the kennel above us shook and the three-headed mutant started barking at something. "West Coast Gnomes tryin' to move in on my turf. Punks gonna get took down."

My boss nodded at me, apparently feeling the need to explain. "The Southern gnome families are from Sweden. The ones from California are Norwegian. That side wears blue hats."

"We got no beef wit' 'em, but these gnomes is straight off the boat, tryin' to muscle in on my turf. Ain't gonna happen. This is the dirty South, know what I'm sayin'?"

Earl smiled. "Consider what I gave you the first half. Second half when we catch the rat. And I know you're up to it. Did I ever mention that I worked with Al Capone once? You remind me of him."

The gnome boss beamed at the compliment. Apparently being compared to Al Capone was pretty darn neat for him. He snapped his fingers. Instantly another gnome materialized at his side. That freaked me out. "This my boy, Heimdall Thorfinn Flargin, but we call him G-Nome, 'cause he's a straight up killa'. He's like a gnome Tony Montana. He's got your back." The new arrival puffed on his cigar. I recognized him as the one that had threatened me on the front porch.

"He'll do," Earl nodded.

"He'll do what?" I asked in confusion.

"Find your snitch. Take care of *biz*-ness." G-Nome lifted his shirt and flashed his gun again. In the better light I could tell it was a chromed Walther P22.

"No. You'll stay invisible at the compound. Keep an eye out until you find out who's talking to this Condition. And you only talk to me or Owen, that's it."

"Shit, whatever, dawg. Long as I get paid."

"The sooner you find the spy, the sooner I give you the rest of your money."

Sven seemed to take exception to this. "G-Nome's so good, I think we need the rest of the dough up front, know what I'm sayin'?"

"I know what you're saying, and it sounds like you're trying to take my money without showing me any results. No. Half up front, half when you find the spy." Earl acted like dealing with criminal scum was something that he had done a few times, but hell, apparently he had known Al Capone. I had to remember that my boss had been around for a long time.

"Harbinger, my dawg, G-Nome's my main gnome. My main *tomte* like we say in the old country. He'll get it done. Even if we have to lower ourselves to dealing with"—he sneered at me—"tall ones."

I was getting tired of these little bullies and their lame tough-guy act. "At least I'm not a lawn decoration," I muttered.

"*What?*" Sven shouted as he shoved away from the table. "What'd you say?"

"Oh hell," Harbinger muttered.

There was a huge chorus of clicks and rattles as a dozen guns were tugged from various waistbands, safeties removed, hammers cocked, or slides jacked. I was sitting down, so G-Nome was able to reach my neck. His little Walther jammed painfully under my ear. "You got a death wish, bitch?" he shouted. The entire gang of gnomes surged forward, guns extended, most of them held sideways and I was about to expire in a slew of small-caliber gunfire.

Apparently I had just made a serious breach of gnome etiquette.

"Do it and I'll get angry," Harbinger stated. "I dare you."

That caused the gnomes to hesitate. Apparently they knew just what my boss was capable of. A dozen little muzzles hovered around my skull as Sven huffed and turned increasingly dark shades of red. "You know how insultin' it is to be stuck out on a yard to keep away

Fey? Do you, punk? You ever have a wizard hex you and plant you out in the grass, huh?"

"Sorry. I didn't know!" I cried, hands raised in the surrender position.

"You come in my house, and think you can get away with calling us *lawn* gnomes? I don't think so. Waste him, boys," Sven ordered.

"Hold your fire." My boss stood, towering over the diminutive gang. "He doesn't know Scandinavian fairy lore. Give the kid a break. He's had a tough day."

G-Nome snarled. "I demand respect!"

"Shoot him and you've got to deal with me, and even if one of you little bastards was smart enough to load silver bullets, then my great-granddaughter and a bunch of Hunters are parked outside. They hear gunfire, they come down here, and Julie will kill you all."

One of the gnomes piped up. "I saw her. She's really *tall* for a girl!" Several other gnomes nodded at this, as if that fact was somehow extra terrifying. It was a really tense moment.

"Your man has to pay for dissin' my boy in our own house," Sven stated.

"Hell no," Earl said.

"You know I can't lose no face in front of my crew, comin' in here and callin' my *tomte* a lawn gnome. So either we get some respect, or we're gonna have us a gunfight. He's at least gotta get a beatdown."

Harbinger appeared to mull that over for a moment. "Sounds fair."

"Earl!" I shouted.

"I told you to let me do the talking," he told me calmly. "A beating's better than getting shot. Okay,

Sven, but let's make this sporting. Make it a fair fight. My man wins, you still do the job, and it's half up front, half on completion. Your gnome wins, you get it all up front, plus I'll throw in another ten grand as a bonus."

The gnome leader thought about this, stroking his beard slowly. "But it has to be a *fair* fight . . ."

"Fair?" I asked in confusion. Fairy-tale creatures or not, I was a three-hundred pound former, illegal pit fighter. I bench-pressed over four-hundred pounds and had once beaten a gargoyle to death with a tire iron. I was having a hard time seeing how me fighting somebody the size of a Cabbage Patch Kid could be construed as fair.

Sven held up both hands, fingers splayed open, displaying them to Harbinger. Gnomes had six fingers on each hand. "Twelve."

My boss shook his head. "Eight."

Did these guys have to haggle about everything? He turned down two fingers. "Ten. Or somebody's takin' a bullet."

"Fine, but no weapons. And you're not allowed to kill him. I need him on my crew. Once he's out, you leave him alone, or I step in."

"Deal." The gnome clapped his hands together. Suddenly it seemed like there was at least another thirty gnomes in the room. Money immediately began to change hands as they started taking bets.

"Seriously?" I asked in total bewilderment. G-Nome pulled his pistol out of my neck. He was grinning savagely as he passed his .22 off to another little guy, and then started signaling specific other gnomes. Those tossed their pieces also. The shirtless *Thug Life* one dropped the dumbbell with a clang, stood, and cracked his knuckles. Other gnomes began to efficiently remove the plastic furniture from the center of the room. I had a feeling they'd done this before.

"Don't hold back. They're tougher than they look. Sam Haven got drunk one time and picked a fight with half this many gnomes and got his ass handed to him. It was hilarious. Don't worry about murdering any of them. They're magical, so they don't die easily. And try not to lose, 'cause it's gonna cost the company another ten thousand dollars." Earl clapped me on the shoulder as I stood. "Though, personally, it's worth it for me to watch you fight ten gnomes at one time."

"But, but . . ." Somehow this had all just spiraled totally out of control. "I've already had a really crappy day!" There was a huge quantity of gnomes in the room now, as a veritable sea of red hats formed a large circle around us. Ten of the little buggers were waiting for me. G-Nome was stalking back and forth, high-fiveing the others. "I can't hit them! They're tiny." The audience began to boo.

"Owen, there ain't no rules. Don't forget to protect, well . . ." Earl waved toward his crotch. "You know, they're gonna hit you low."

This was ridiculous. I couldn't hit them. They'd like *explode* or something.

"Get It On!" Sven Bone-Hand shouted from his vantage point on top of the table.

"Welcome to my Thunderdome, bitch!" G-Nome bellowed.

"Oh, this just sucks," I muttered as ten gangster gnomes charged me simultaneously.

I've been in a lot of fights, but I can honestly say that this was a new experience. It was like a wave of meat collided with my kneecaps and I was instantly swept to the ground in a sea of white beards. Tiny fists began to slam into me with the speed and intensity of a tropical rainstorm, only each one hit like a rock. I screamed something incoherent as I tried to protect my vital parts. They were remarkably strong for their size.

"I told you not to hold back!" Earl shouted from the sidelines as a child-sized leather boot smashed into my larynx. "Get up and fight, damn it! I've got money on this."

I was on my back. There were three of them sitting on my chest and stomach, doing the ground and pound, punching like tiny little jackhammers, while the rest were in a circle kicking me. I reached up and grabbed the only thing I could, which turned out to be a handful of beard. Then I pulled as hard as I could. The gnome flew off my chest and disappeared.

"No fair!" The audience cried. Apparently beards were sensitive. Well, screw 'em. This hurt like hell. I snagged a kicker on each side by their beards, and yanked them together over me. They only weighed about thirty pounds each, and collided with a great deal of force. I rolled over, tossing gnomes in every direction as the beating continued.

Roaring, I squished one underneath me, and the little bastard just kept hitting me in the kidneys. I sat up, a gnome on each shoulder. One of them tried to fishhook me while the other one bit my ear. "Aaarrrgghh!"

I slugged that one in the face and he was airborne. I

struggled to my feet, gnomes hanging off of everything, all of them punching, kicking, kneeing, elbowing, biting, and just being a general obnoxious pain. Standing now, I started tossing gnomes into the audience. They landed, got pats on the back from their brethren, and got right back into the fray.

It was G-Nome himself that maneuvered right in front of me and threw an uppercut into my testicles. A wave of unbelievable pain followed by nausea surged through me. I went back to my knees. "Oh . . . it's on now . . ." I gasped through the continuous stream of impacts. All thoughts of fairness went right out the window as righteous fury bubbled up from my core. G-Nome's smiling face appeared in my view, beady eyes searching for another good strike. That smile disappeared as my massive hand clamped around his throat. His eyes got very wide.

I picked G-Nome up as I stood, grabbed one kicking leg with my other hand, and slammed him up into the brick ceiling. He disappeared in a cloud of brick dust. The audience made a noise that sounded like "ooohhh." I brought him back down, let go of his neck, and swung him around by his leg. Half a dozen gnomes were knocked spinning out of the circle. At the apogee of the arc, I let go of G-Nome's ankle and he flew down with the hallway. The gnomes surged back toward me, and it was a swirl of violence. I remember gnomes hanging onto each of my feet as I dragged them across the brick floor, gnomes crumpling under my fists with every swing, and gnomes twirling through the air in every direction. But then somebody shattered a beer bottle on the back of my head, and it got kind of blurry.

"I said no weapons!" Earl bellowed. "That's it!" I stumbled back and fell on my butt, a literal pile of moaning gnomes scattered around me. The audience was booing and throwing trash at me, but luckily no more bottles.

Mad as hell, I stumbled to my feet, disoriented and ready to go beat the entire audience to death. I could feel hot blood spilling down the back of my neck. More miscellaneous objects flew at me. "Hey! Watch it, you little assholes!" I grabbed a passing gnome by the neck and lifted him overhead.

"Enough!" Sven shouted and the missiles quit flying and only one, last, empty soda can bounced off my boot. My chest was heaving from exertion, my brain ached from the shattered bottle, every inch of my body pulsed with bruised tissue and firing nerves, and I felt an unbearable urge to vomit. But mostly, I was really *angry*. I was ready to go another round. I cocked my fist back. The gnome I was holding squealed in fear.

"Owen, drop the gnome," Earl ordered.

I slowly lowered my fist and let go of the little man. He scrambled back into the audience. Sven shouted over the noise of the booing crowd. "All right, Harbinger. You win. Deal's a deal."

G-Nome reappeared, missing his hat, blood and dust staining his white beard. He walked back into the circle and spit on the floor. The audience got really quiet. He glared at me dangerously as he flexed his muscles and I got ready for him to charge. "You done yet?" I gasped.

The dangerous little creature eyed me for a moment. "You know what? You're all right for being so *tall*." Finally he grinned, showing off his bloodstained teeth.

"Best damn rumble I've had in years." He turned to Harbinger. "We still on?"

Harbinger held up the roll of bills. "If you're *gnome* enough?"

"Hell yeah," G-Nome answered as he caught the money.

. The gnomes all cheered.

Julie asked what had happened when she saw me come out of the gnome house, battered and bruised. Unfortunately, Earl and I hadn't thought to come up with a cover story, and lying to Julie, especially after sustaining a minor brain injury, seemed like a really bad idea. So I told her it was a secret and that I would explain later. I don't think she liked that one bit, but was enough of a professional to understand that Earl and I had our reasons. On the bright side, I didn't really want to tell her about how I had gotten beaten up by a gang of garden decorations.

Mosh had been on the phone again, trying to explain how the tour bus had exploded to somebody else. Apparently, rampaging monsters was a bit beyond his PR firm's regular duties. I crawled into the back of the van and Gretchen began sewing up the back of my head to match the repair she had made on the front earlier. *Ahh . . . symmetry.* Earl signaled for us to roll out and our convoy started back to Cazador.

Julie and Mosh were in the same vehicle, and as I lay there, incoherent, a bone needle and thread being run through the fleshy part at the base of my skull, my fiancée tried to explain to my brother how he was currently a lot safer hanging out with us for a while. Obviously, *safe* was a relative word.

After a few minutes their conversation was just background buzz.

It probably wasn't a good idea to take a nap after receiving a serious blow to the head, but I was exhausted, sore, and was asleep by the time we got on the freeway.

# CHAPTER 9

Brilliant sunshine scalded my closed eyelids. I must have slept for hours.

*Nope.*

I was dreaming. My surroundings were a city park, but not one that I recognized. The trees were thick, brilliant green, and the grass was manicured to perfection. The air was clean and fresh. It was a huge city. Tall buildings rose above the leaves on all sides, but the skyline was unfamiliar. Children ran, laughing, playing, while a nearby street vendor peddled food that smelled really good. Everyone looked happy and the walkways were clean of grime and garbage.

Must be Canada.

I wandered down a stone path, not sure where I was going. In my dream state I noted that I was still dressed exactly the same as I had been when I was awake, complete with armor and weapons. None of the attractive locals seemed to notice. Everyone greeted me with a polite smile, guns and all, so that definitely ruled out Canada.

"Hello," the Englishman said. He was seated on a wooden bench at the edge of a pond, looking as rough as the first time I had met him, lean frame hunched forward in a bulky gray hoodie, head and cheeks bristling with brown-gray stubble. He was a relatively average-looking man, the kind of guy where you would never guess that he had a demonic leach monster living inside of him. His cold eyes had that same deadly focus as when he had tried to kidnap me, only now he was holding a loaf of bread and tearing off pieces to chuck into the pond. A rioting crowd of ducks clustered there, fighting for crumbs. "Have a seat, mate. We need to talk."

"Uh, no," I responded as I automatically pulled my .45 from the holster. I raised it in one hand and cranked off four quick shots into the side of his head. The gun recoiled and noise blasted my eardrums but nothing struck him.

"Don't be like that. This is neutral ground," he said, sounding unperturbed, still not looking at me, all his attention on the ducks. I stupidly lowered the STI as a bunch of kids ran past carrying balloons that had been twisted into various animal shapes. Not even the ducks had seemed to notice the sudden gunfire. He pulled off a big chunk of bread, crumpled it into a hard ball, and pitched it far out into the pond. The ducks swam after it, quacking angrily. "You're safe here. You've parlayed before."

I had spoken with Lord Machado in my dreams once, and that hadn't turned out particularly well. "I'll stay over here, thanks."

"Suit yourself, but we do have business to discuss, you and I. Circumstances have changed since we last met."

"Met? You tried to eat my brain and murdered a bunch of innocent people."

"My apologies. I'm working for the Dread Overlord itself. One can't hesitate when fulfilling the orders of something so epic and terrible that even saying its true name can cause insanity in mere mortals."

"Well, you can take those orders and shove them up your Dread Overlord's ass, or whatever orifice crustaceans have."

He ignored me. "But that was before that meddling vampire exposed you to a shard of the sacred artifact. Events have been set into motion and I'm afraid it may be too late for us all." The Englishman finally turned to face me. His eyes pierced through me with an unnerving cold. "I need your help."

I actually laughed out loud. His expression did not change. "Wait . . . you're serious? Hell no."

"You think I'm evil, that I'm some sort of monster, don't you?"

"They teach deductive logic at Necromancer College?"

He shook his head. "I'm no monster. I'm just like you."

That ticked me off. "You're *nothing* like me. I don't go around murdering innocents."

"Yet," he muttered, his voice hoarse, "you murder every day to earn your living. Innocence is such an *arbitrary* thing to a Hunter. Where you see creatures of evil, I see wonders of the unnatural world, yet you destroy them out of fear and greed."

"And I'm damn good at it. Get to the point."

"Remember your search for Machado's Place of Power? You learned that they only existed at certain junctures, certain specific places and times, and that they were oh so rare. Well, it isn't just places, mate. It's people as well. People like you and me. Destiny falls like a mantle on very few of us, and we're given the power to shape the world, whether we like it or not."

Or as Mordechai would have said, *I had drawn the short straw*. I knew this part pretty well. "Yeah, yeah, I'm the Chosen One. Whatever."

"Yes, a Chosen, but not the One, rather one of many. We are the artists, and this reality is our canvas," he began to pontificate, reminding me why he was the leader of a religious nut cult. "We're brothers, pawns in a cosmic struggle, where only—" I lifted my gun, centered the front sight on his forehead and pulled the trigger. *BOOM*. Still no effect, but it was strangely satisfying. That seemed to annoy the Englishman. "Oh, piss off then. I'll tell you why I'm here."

"About damn time."

"I'm not as simple as you might think. Yes, I do work for them but only because I was able to see the future. The greatest Old One will return, no matter what mankind does. It's inevitable."

"Inevitable?" I was unable to accept that. "We've beat him before. I stopped him last time. He'll try again in another five hundred years and somebody else will stop him then."

"You think that's the only way? Do you honestly believe it's so easy? No. There are other plans, other ways back. And it's only a matter of time before he returns. I was *exactly* like you once. I learned about the Old Ones, and I thought that I could stand against them. I studied their ways, their power, originally with the noblest of intentions, only to discover it was futile. I could not stop them, so I joined them."

"So you wanted to kiss up to the winning side? Noble," I spat. "Selling out humanity so you don't end up as dinner? I got the same offer from Machado, and my answer stays the same as last time. Go to hell."

"Machado was a fool." He went back to the bread and ducks. "You can think that if you like, but I'm not 'selling out' humanity. No, I'm the *savior* of humanity. If I can conquer this world and present it to them, then we will be spared from their full fury. Those are the conditions of my employment." It was totally insane, but I could tell that he actually bought what he was shoveling. He was a true believer. "If I fail, then eventually they will win, only they won't be as merciful as I would be."

"You're nuts."

He chuckled. It was a rough sound. "Perhaps. But there's a war coming, a war that man cannot win. The only question remaining is how brutal will be our defeat. Your way, your struggle, it only ends in death, the eradication of all life on this world. My way, many will perish, so that many more will live. It will be a time of rebirth, renewal, where man will take his place as righteous servants of the great Old Ones." I started to raise my gun again. "Okay, okay. You're so bloody impatient. I'm making you an offer..."

"I won't join you."

"Join me?" he said incredulously. "Why would I do that? I'm asking you to surrender." Right about then I found myself really wishing that this wasn't the dream world, and this wasn't a dream gun, filled with dream bullets, because I'd blow his brains all over the duck pond. "Hear me out. The Dread Overlord has never been personally offended by a human before. He called you by *name!*" He said that like I should be proud. "His fury is infinite. By sacrificing yourself, you will salve his anger. The longer it takes for me to bring you to him, the more the entire world will pay for your insolence."

"That's one hell of an offer."

"I'm a humanitarian. Think of your friends, your loved ones... You've personally spit in the eye of the deadliest being in the universe. He will get you. It's only a matter of time. But it's my job to make sure that your meddling doesn't endanger us all. I'm trying to protect the innocent. Your irresponsibility threatens my plan to save the world."

He was telling the truth, but there was something more. I thought of what Susan said. "There's something else... Something in it for you."

"I have made a deal, yes. The great gods of the beyond do not give power easily. It must be earned. You will be traded for something that I, and my father before me, have yearned for. You are the key to achieving my life's work, the merciful domination of this world. "

"You're as deluded as Machado was. I've seen what those things want, and mercy isn't part of the equation," I said.

"The Old Ones don't want to destroy this world. They're ambivalent masters. They only destroy that which they can't have." He tossed more bread on the water. The ducks quacked and fought for the crumbs. "There are many factions of Elder Things. They don't care about us. They only want to control as many worlds, as many souls, as they can, and deprive the others of their ownership."

"Nice touch." I pointed at the duck pond. "So, are these like some sort of symbolic illusion of great warring interstellar beings and we're the bread?"

He looked at me like I was dense. "No. They're just ducks."

"Yeah, I'm not real good at this whole metaphysical dream thing. How about we hook up someplace out in meat-space so that I can shoot you with real bullets?"

"Owen, I'm begging you. Help me present this place to them. It's the only way to save us all. Fighting only makes them mad." He gestured around the city. For the first time I noticed some sort of massive, alien *tree* amidst the skyline, as tall as the skyscrapers around it. The branches were segmented, twisted, unnatural and black. There were no leaves, rather strange membranes, shimmering like locust wings, stretched between the insectoid branches. It was wrong. It did not belong on this world.

"What is that?"

He was rather proud. "The key to man's unity. The key to our survival. Under its boughs, there is only peace."

The beautiful city had been built around the tree, for the tree. I shuddered.

"This is my world. My world will be a utopia. No more war. No more starvation, strife, or disease. I will *banish* death. But if we continue to struggle, their patience will wear thin, and their methods will turn from subterfuge to brute force . . ." As he said that, the sky darkened. The nearby leaves and grass turned brown, wilted, and died. The giant buildings twisted and collapsed in gushing clouds of dust, but the great tree remained unharmed, standing alone on the burning horizon. The sky turned blood red with smoke and fire. The sounds of laughter in the distance mutated into screams of pain and the wails of torture. "And this will be the result..." The clean water of the pond turned to black pollution. The feathers burned off the ducks in a stench of acid and bile. Oily purple tentacles the size of spaghetti noodles encircled the frantic birds and sucked them down in a spew of harsh bubbles. "My way is the only way. Help me stop *this*."

Glancing around the terrible landscape, I knew he wasn't exaggerating. I had seen this before, different variations of this vision many times. The Old Ones were coming. This was the future...

*No*. This was *a* future. I strengthened my resolve and gave my final answer. "I've already picked my side."

"Your side?" he replied derisively. "Oh, I'm quite familiar with them. Your side is made up of ghosts and fools. You ally yourself with the Hunters, yet Harbinger's a liar and a murderer. You think the government can protect you from my religion of truth, yet Myers is a traitor and a coward. The vampires Shackleford offer you an out, but my own sins pale before Susan's ambitions and Ray's pride. Your side is an alliance of flawed convenience, and it will shatter at its first test."

*He spoke like he knew them...* "Who are you, really?"

"I'm your friend. I'm the only one who'll tell you the truth." His voice raised in volume and intensity. "I am the Lord of Shadows, High Priest of the Sanctified Church of the Temporary Mortal Condition. I am the first Horseman of the Apocalypse, the herald of the burning sunset of one age and the dark dawn of a new."

My grip tightened on my pistol. A hot wind blew through the destroyed park. I had had enough of this nonsense. "No. You're just another pain-in-the-ass psycho screwing around with magic shit that shouldn't be screwed with. Listen real careful, you quisling fuck, I'm coming for you and your little church, and I'm going to *end* you."

"I was afraid of that, but I had to offer. I'm not by nature a violent man," the Englishman responded, but the steel in his voice indicated that was a lie.

"Well, I am," I responded.

We were plunged into shadow as a huge shape blotted out the reddened sun. I glanced up, my brain unable to comprehend the massiveness of the creature swimming through the air above us, trailing streamers of flesh, thorns, and a thousand eyes for what had to have been a quarter mile. Part blimp, part squid, all gut-wrenching terror. I knew that there were hundreds more just over the horizon.

"You've made your choice," the Englishman said, but when I turned my attention back to the park bench, the thin man was gone, and now it was a hulking shadow shape there, a formless mass with the consistency of oil-fired smoke. It tossed the rest of the loaf of bread into the bubbling tar, which disappeared with a hiss. The shape moved, flowing up from the bench, towering above me as it prepared to leave. "When we meet again, expect no mercy."

"Likewise."

❖          ❖          ❖

By the time we rolled into the compound, the sky had reached that kind of muted, quiet gray that came just before dawn. Most of the occupants of our vehicle were asleep at this point. An exhausted Lee was still driving. Julie was out, somehow actually using the butt stock of her M14 to prop up her head, and snoring loudly, which she did quite a bit, though I would never let her know. Mosh had finally passed out, having called his PR firm, manager, agent, and band mates before the borrowed cell phone battery had croaked.

My muscles groaned in protest and my ankle burned painfully as I stepped onto the gravel outside the office building. I was still hurting from Mexico, let alone wrecking the tour bus and getting my ass kicked by gnomes. I had removed my stinky gas-soaked boots, and the little rocks jabbed painfully into my too-soft soles and still-bandaged heel. I didn't really think about the pain, which was nothing a handful of aspirin couldn't dull, but rather I was preoccupied about my meeting with the shadow man.

He had known Harbinger, Myers, and Julie's parents. There was just something about the way he had mentioned them that indicated some familiarity. I had a higher opinion of Earl than murdering liar, of course, but I couldn't really fault his assessment of the Fed or the vampires. If he knew them, then they might know him, and at this point, any intel was good intel. I intercepted Harbinger as he was stepping out of the passenger side of the other MHI vehicle. "We need to talk. I just had a psychic meeting with the bad guy."

It was a testament to the weirdness of our job that

he didn't even bat an eye. "No shit? Okay, conference room in five minutes. Just me, you, and Julie. We don't know who else we can trust."

"Make it ten. Give me a chance to scrub the gas off before I get foot cancer or something," I said quickly as the road-trip weary Hunters from Esmeralda's team began to pile out and unload their gear. I had to keep in mind that one of these people could be the traitor.

"Well, that was a waste of time," Cooper said as he pulled a rifle case out of the back of the truck. "Didn't even get to shoot any trolls."

"You're such a glass-is-half-empty kind of guy," his team leader said, stifling a yawn. Esmeralda didn't manage to look any more intimidating wearing all her gear than she did wearing a sweater with kittens on it. "Think of that as a chance to drive around scenic Alabama."

"It was dark. Then we stopped in the ghetto," Cooper muttered. He was a relatively new Hunter, about my age, a few inches shorter than me and stocky, with square glasses and short dark hair. He had been an explosive ordnance disposal tech before joining us last year. He'd just gotten off active duty and gone on a road trip when he had encountered a winged terror eating travelers at a rest stop on I-15 in middle of nowhere, Nevada. The manner in which he'd shoved an illegal hand grenade down the creature's mouth had gotten him recruited. "Yeah, that was awesome."

Nate Shackleford unfolded himself out of the driver's seat. He was the junior man on the team, but men of our stature always got the front seat. I did not know Julie's little brother very well yet, but he really seemed like a likable, energetic, humble kid. Like Julie, he took more after Susan than Ray, though I could see the resemblance to his father, only without all the crazy. "I can't believe that Milo took out the whole infestation."

Cooper snorted. "Infestation... It was *one* troll!"

"I warned you guys that eye witnesses always exaggerate," Esmeralda chided them.

Julie joined us. "The client was pretty excited on the phone."

Esmeralda automatically lapsed into teacher mode. "You never know what's going to happen when you meet a new client. Most of the time they're pretty normal, but every once in a while, one answers the door and tries to chop your head off with an ax."

"Wow, has that ever actually happened?" Nate asked.

"No... but it could."

Mosh was trailing along behind Julie, looking around in confusion at the paramilitary compound. "Oh, man..." His jaw fell open when he saw our red and white MI-24 Russian attack helicopter parked in front of the hangar. I suppose that my workplace was a bit different than the average. "You guys have a *Hind*?" He had always appreciated anything with an engine more than I had. "That is so awesome!"

"That's Skippy's baby," Julie responded.

My brother turned to the orc. "Can I have a ride?" Skippy began to nod vigorously, eager to please the Great War Chief.

"Shhh..." Earl held up his hand. I couldn't hear a thing, but he was the one with the werewolf hearing, so I shut up. "Chopper coming in." He paused. "Blackhawk."

It could only be the government. With the huge debacle of the freeway explosion and the hundreds of witnesses to the oni there, I had been sure that the Feds would have been too occupied with damage control to dispatch new babysitters. Apparently I had been wrong. With Franks dead, I had no idea who they would send this time. Unfortunately, after my talk with the Englishman, I wasn't feeling real optimistic for the fates of those assigned to guard me.

It took another thirty seconds before anyone else could hear the Blackhawk. It came in low over the trees, circled the compound once, then set down in the parking lot in front of the office building. The blades kept turning as the door slid open. A Fed in a jumpsuit and helmet exited from the side. He positioned himself to help the next person out, which turned out to be a burly, older man.

"Oh crap," I said. "I forgot."

"Dad?" Mosh asked in confusion.

My father had exited a few helicopters in his day, and even had one shot out from under him once in 1968. We had heard all of those stories as kids. He glowered at the agent attempting to assist him until the man shrank back under that intimidating stare. Keeping one hand on his head to keep his hat from blowing off, he extended his other back inside and—

"Mom?" My brother was really flustered now.

My mother was really excited to have ridden in a helicopter. We were far away, and the rotors were beating, so we couldn't hear her, but she was animatedly talking to the agent, probably about the weather, or her book club, or trying to find him a wife, or who knows what, because Mom was *always* talking about something. The agent actually took the time to snap a crisp salute to my dad. Probably a former military man himself, and *everybody* saluted my father once they knew who he was. Dad did one of those "whatever" salutes in return, grabbed Mom by the arm, thereby interrupting her conversation—not that anybody could have heard her over the rotors anyway—and steered her away from the chopper. The crew began to unload luggage onto the parking lot.

Dad saw us and approached with that bulldog walk that only men with really thick necks and big shoulders can pull off and still look tough. Mom paused to point at the chopper as it lifted off because, despite the inconvenience of being evacuated from her home after a kidnapping attempt by rabid cultists, riding in a chopper is pretty darn cool any time you get to do it.

"Mom and Dad?" I think Mosh had been less surprised to have an oni dangle him from an overpass than to see our parents get out of that Blackhawk.

"Mom, Dad!" I waved.

"Oh, shoot. Your mother ... oh, crud, I wish I had a chance to change," Julie began to fidget. I thought she looked perfectly presentable, since she was wearing armor and carrying a sniper rifle, which I personally found to be remarkably hot, but women are weird like that. "Why didn't you tell me?" She didn't add *you insensitive jerk* but I could tell it was implied.

"Lot of stuff on my mind," I muttered out the side of my mouth.

"Like that's an excuse." She was trying to decide what to do with her rifle. Finally she just slung it, and let it hang behind her. She always wore her long hair pulled back when she was working, but that didn't stop her from patting her head to make sure it was still there.

My parents stopped right in front of our group. Dad was angry. Of course, he had just shot four men and knew it was somehow my fault. Mom looked kind of confused. She pointed at my feet. "Where are your shoes?"

"Uh . . ." With all of the weird things that were going on for them right now, that wasn't one of the questions that I had been mentally prepared to answer.

"You'll wear holes in your socks!" Mom had immigrated to the U.S. a long time ago, and you could barely hear her accent, except when she got excited. Apparently my socks were very exciting. My mother was white-blonde, pale, tall and, shockingly enough considering the man she had married and the sons that she had spawned, skinny.

Dad just scowled. His skin was dark, wrinkled and creased from years of sun and wind. His once-thick, curly black hair was gray. He was wearing a hat, mostly, I knew, because it hid his bald spot. That killer gaze swept over our crew. All of the miscellaneous Hunters took an involuntary step back, then quickly decided that they were better off unloading the rest of their gear later, and dispersed without further comment. Dad just emanated this attitude of *the only reason I don't kill you all is because it would be illegal.* Only Mosh and I were immune to *The Look*, and that was only because of overexposure.

"Boys," Dad stated.

"Owen blew up my bus," Mosh exclaimed, as if that explained everything. I had to remember that my brother hadn't actually spoken to our folks for several years, and their last parting hadn't been friendly. Despite Mosh's massive success, Dad had never approved of his decisions. This reunion had to be kind of awkward.

"The government blew up your bus," I explained calmly.

Only Earl and Julie had stayed. Julie elbowed me in the ribs. I grunted, realized that I was supposed to introduce her, and stammered, "This is Julie. My girlfriend. I told you about her . . . and stuff. I guess." I had to remember that pretty much everything I had told my folks about the two of us had been fabricated, because, at the time, I had no intention of ever telling them how we had actually met or what we did for a living. This complicated matters.

"Yay!" my mother exclaimed, and immediately wrapped Julie in a hug. "She's beautiful. Let me see the ring! Oh, I'm so proud, Owen." Apparently Mom didn't even notice that Julie was dressed for combat. She was probably just glad that I had found a girl at all. She had certainly hounded me enough on that subject my entire adult life. Mom had probably been suspicious that Julie was imaginary, and I had just made her up to stop the nagging.

Dad scanned Julie once and nodded in approval. "M14. Nice rifle." My father was a practical man. Then he gave Earl *The Look*. Earl didn't flinch. That alone should have alerted Dad that Earl Harbinger wasn't actually human anymore. Dad stared at my boss for a long time, bit his lip, looking confused for a moment, almost perplexed, like a bullfighting bull that just got poked and was trying to figure out whom he needed to gore. Mosh and I glanced at each other. Dad perplexed was scarier than normal Dad. "Do I know you?" the senior Pitt asked.

Earl shook his head. "I don't believe so."

"Yeah...yeah I do." Dad was positive. "But it can't be. You're too young. Was your father in Vietnam?"

Earl paused for a long moment. "No," he said calmly.

"You wouldn't happen to be related to some guy who worked for the CIA, went by the name...what was it...Mr. Wolf?"

*Mr. Wolf?* If that was one of his pseudonyms, it was pretty damn lame.

Earl frowned slightly. "Never heard of him."

"Good, because he was a real jerk-off. But damn if you're not like his twin. Good thing you're not, 'cause me and him have a disagreement to settle." Dad was obviously suspicious. Mosh, Julie, Mom, helicopters, compounds, assassination attempts, everything else was forgotten as Dad focused in like a laser beam on Earl. "What's your name, buddy?"

"Harbinger. Earl Harbinger. Your son works for me." He stuck out his hand to shake. My father took the smaller hand in his catcher's-mitt-sized paw and I knew that Dad was going to try and crush him.

"Auhangamea Pitt," Dad said as he squeezed. "This is my wife, Ilyana."

Earl smiled slightly and squeezed back. Dad's brow furrowed and I could tell that he wanted to cringe. Most normal men would have. Earl let go and nodded. "Nice to meet you, Mr. Pitt. I'm sure you've got a lot of questions for your boy that I'm sure he's just itchin' to answer. I can assure you this inconvenience will be temporary. We'll find you a room and get you settled in for your stay. Welcome to Monster Hunter International."

The best available room at the compound was on the first floor of the main building, near the stairs to the basement and the archives. It had been set up for clients and VIPs, but since visits like that were extremely rare, the room, though nicely furnished, smelled a little musty.

"Beats a hotel," I suggested helpfully as I put Dad's suitcase on the bed. I still stunk of gas and had quite a bit of my own blood dried on my clothing. Dad just glowered at me.

Mosh was getting cleaned up. It had been about fifteen years since we had last been forced to share a room, but it was either bunk with me, or sleep in the barracks with the Newbies. He'd dealt with enough weirdness so far that the last thing I wanted to do was stick him with a bunch of really gung-ho, brand-new Hunters.

Julie had tagged along. My mom hadn't stopped talking to her since she'd gotten off the chopper. Julie had dropped her vest and rifle behind Dorcas' desk, so now she only had her form-fitting and, in my opinion, very flattering, Under Armor shirt on. Julie was nodding her head patiently as Mom continued to ramble on about her day's adventure as she carried more bags through the door. She gave me a patient look that basically said *you weren't kidding about your parents*.

Dad waited until all four of us were present. His deep voice indicated that he wasn't messing around. "All right then, I want some answers, and I want them now. There's some strange business going on here. First off—"

"How did you two meet?" Mom asked, clapping her hands together excitedly. Dad rolled his eyes and groaned.

Julie gestured toward me. "Well, we had a contrived story to tell you, but I guess we can tell you the truth now. We work together. The first time Owen and I met was when I interviewed him for this job."

Mom covered her mouth, like me dating the boss' great-granddaughter was the most scandalous thing ever. Hell, like Mom even knew what I did for a living. "You're his supervisor?"

"Technically, yes, but he doesn't take well to supervision," Julie laughed. Mom laughed. Mom began to ask Julie for details. They both plopped down on the edge of the bed. Dad and I exchanged glances. He signaled for me to pull up a chair to the side so we could address *man business*.

Mom was so personable that when she entered a room, she created her own gravity field that dominated everything. Once free from Mom's sphere of influence, my father turned stern. "I killed four people today. I haven't done that for a while. I'd like to know why."

"So the last guy died too?" I had really been hoping that the Feds could have gotten something out of him.

Dad shrugged. "Looked like a liver hit. I'd be amazed if they got him to the hospital before he croaked. I'm getting sloppy in my old age. Mozambiqued the other assholes. Don't dodge my question, boy." He glanced at his watch. "I'm missing a fishing trip today because of this."

"Okay..." I had thought about this moment, and

the best way to convey it, for a long time, but all of my practiced lines were forgotten under the stare of those hard eyes. My entire life, this man hadn't ever really approved of me. He had always been gruff and cold. The closest we had ever come to bonding was him teaching me to kill stuff. Well, when all else fails, go for brevity. "I'll get right to it. Monsters are real. I'm one of the people who hunts them."

Dad nodded slowly. "Pay good?"

"Pay's awesome."

"Monsters?" Dad took off his hat and set it on the small table between us. He scratched his bald spot. "All right then. I'm glad we got this all cleared up."

*That's it?* He showed no emotion. That wasn't one of the outcomes that I had imagined. "Uh . . . cool. Any questions?"

He intertwined his fingers, put his elbows on the table, and studied me silently. I never could read him, and now was no different. It was like being under an electron microscope as he stared right through my façade of confidence. This man could read me like a teleprompter. "Oh, I got questions—lots." Then he went back to glaring at me. It was extremely awkward. I shifted uncomfortably in my seat.

I've died twice, traveled through time, stopped an alien invasion, and battled just about every terrible being that hell could puke onto the surface of the Earth, but despite those facts, this man could still make me feel like a pathetic fat kid. It really pissed me off. My entire life I had striven to make him proud. I had failed every step of the way. No matter what I did, I would never measure up to his impossible ideals of what it meant to be a real man.

But no more. I knew what I was. And I didn't have to take his shit anymore. I was going to *make* him understand. He was on my turf now. "Listen, Dad," I said as I reached across the table and grabbed him by the arm. "I—"

*Black energy crackled inside my skull.*

"Damn it, boys. That was pathetic," I shouted at my sons as I threw my own pack down. Personally, I was exhausted, but I wasn't about to let them know it. They could never see weakness as an option. The boys were big and strong for their ages, but I had overloaded their bags on purpose. I knew that they had to be hurting bad by now. "That was slow." I made a big show of looking at my dive watch. "We only averaged thirteen minutes a mile. Thirteen!"

"It was straight uphill!" Owen protested. He had to pause, pull out his asthma inhaler and take a deep puff. He didn't use it nearly as much as he had when he was younger, but we were several thousand feet higher in elevation than he was used to.

"And the ground was all loose," David whined. "My feet hurt."

Damn right their feet hurt. My feet were killing me, and I had done forced marches most of my life. They were only fourteen and eleven. Their pack straps had probably abraded right through the skin of their shoulders by now. "You think if the enemy were right behind us they'd be complaining? Hell no, they would've chased us down, raped us to death, then cut us into steaks and eaten us."

"But 'the enemy' aren't chasing us, Dad. This was supposed to be a camping trip." My oldest gestured around the mountainside. He had always been a smartass. The kid was incapable of knowing when to shut up. Despite how I was always farming him out to the neighbors for adult-level manual labor, and he was strong as hell, the boy was still pudgy. He paused to wipe the sweat off his face with his tee shirt, not that it would do much good, since his shirt was already totally saturated.

David started crying. "I can smell Mom's cooking. Camp's right there. Can I go sit down now?"

"Yeah, go," I jerked a thumb back toward camp. I could smell it too, and my stomach rumbled. "And don't be such a baby." I felt like a complete asshole as I said it, but I had started having the dream again, at least once a week now. Some nights I couldn't sleep at all, even when the dream didn't come, just because I couldn't get it out of my mind. I didn't pretend to understand the dream, but I knew it was true. My children couldn't afford to be weak.

"Dude, drop your pack. I'll take it," Owen offered to his brother as he glared at me. Yeah, the boy may be chunky, but he'd inherited my mean streak. *Good.* Let him be angry. It gave him something to focus on. David shrugged out of the pack and handed it to his big brother. Owen cradled it in his arms as David ran for our campsite.

"This was supposed to be a fun weekend," he said.

"Fun is relative," I answered. "Having the strength and the knowledge to survive anything the world throws at you isn't supposed to be fun. But it makes you a man. So man up and quit your crying."

"You don't always have to be such a jerk." Owen spat as he walked away.

*If only you knew, boy... if only you knew.*

I took my time following them into camp. The forest was actually very peaceful as sunset approached. He was right. This was supposed to have been a vacation. I had retired from the Army a few years ago, and was now working as a bookkeeper, of all the idiotic things... So it wasn't like I got to spend a lot of time in the great outdoors anymore.

My wife was waiting for me, arms folded, scowling, her blonde hair pulled up underneath a handkerchief. She smelled like wood smoke.

"Keeping the home fires burning, huh?" I joked.

She didn't think I was funny. "Ten miles? You made them walk ten miles, and after *skipping* lunch?" She had grown up in a home where they often went hungry because of Communist ineptitude. To my wife, missing a meal as an American was a serious offense, because this was the Land of the Free, damn it.

"I have to do stuff like this... You know it."

God bless her, she at least believed me. "You've been distant lately. The dream again?"

"It's been bad." The sound of an acoustic guitar started back at the tent. It was actually rather good. David certainly had a gift for that silly thing.

Ilyana nodded slowly, understanding. She was as pretty as the day I had first seen her, sneaking her dissident family over from the wrong side of the Iron Curtain. "You know that I trust you, but what if you're mistaken? Your children think you're a beast, you know. You push them too hard. And what if you're wrong?"

"I pray every day that I'm wrong." I bit my lip. Saying this made my voice tremble and break, and tears welled up involuntarily in my eyes. "But I know

I'm not. I hear the war drums. Some day one of those boys will be known as the god slayer and that's before it even gets really rough."

No father should have to know that it is his son's job to die saving the world.

*Dad can cry?*

I was back in the room, still clutching Dad's arm. I let go, shocked by how hard I had been squeezing. There was an imprint on his forearm and he looked at me, stunned.

"Son, what's wrong?"

It was the same thing that had happened a few days ago with Agent Myers. Somehow I was seeing other people's memories. I shook my head. Only a few seconds had passed. I was nauseous and dizzy. When I closed my eyes hard I could still see the lightning shapes moving in the corners. They slowly dissipated. *Stupid artifact.* This vision brought to you by the Corporation for Public Broadcasting and the Forces of Evil.

*One of his sons had to save the world?* I already had. Mordechai had told me that I had been picked before I was born for that job. How had Dad known so long ago? "You had a dream?" I asked. "What's this dream show you?"

Dad was confused. "What are you talking about?"

I began to babble. "All these years, the way you treated us, the stuff you taught us. The shooting, the fighting, the survival skills, it was all because of a *dream*? God slayer?"

My normally imperturbable old man suddenly looked like he had stuck his finger in a light socket. "How do you know about that?" he demanded.

"Tell me!" I shouted. This startled Mom and Julie.

Dad shoved himself back from the table and stood. "No!" he bellowed. "You can't know about that. You can never know."

"Calm down, dear, remember your condition," Mom scolded.

My father began to pace like a caged bear. It was almost like he was *nervous*. But that was impossible. "I kept it from you, because... I was *scared*." He had never said that phrase ever before. Auhangamea Pitt was scared of nothing, or at least that's what I had told myself my entire life. "I was scared for you, even before you were born. I didn't want to believe the promise. It was just too terrible, but in the back of my mind, it was always there, so I tried to get you ready. That was my duty. The dream taught me what I had to do. Preparing you boys was my calling. That's why I've done what I've done. That's why I got so mad at David when he ran away. I was so fixated on this that I chased my own son away, and when that happened, I swore that I would forget about the damn dream and never talk about it again. You were grown, and I'd done my best, so my job was finished."

I placed my hands on the table to steady myself. "Dad, listen, it doesn't matter now, but I need to find out what you've seen."

He shook his head. "I'm... I'm not ready."

It was my turn to be the bossy one for once. "Well, you damn well better get ready then, because some serious shit is going down."

"Don't cuss," Mom snapped automatically.

Dad quit pacing, returned to the table, and slowly sank into the chair. He seemed to shrink. That scared me. "I've had this dream for decades. In it, one of my sons has to die to save the world from something terrible...." He sounded tired as he revealed his burden.

This whole thing was so damn shocking that I actually laughed out loud. "Dad, it's okay! The stuff you taught me paid off. I've already saved the world. It's okay. We beat the terrible thing last summer, and I'm still alive."

"No," he stated solemnly, like a man who knew his torment wasn't yet over.

"Mr. Pitt, really, it's okay," Julie said soothingly. It was weird to hear her call my father "Mister," but it wasn't like she knew him at all, and she still didn't know how to pronounce his first name properly anyway. Too many vowels. "Owen's telling you the truth. I was there. He did what he was supposed to, and we all lived."

"No." Dad shook his head. He looked like he was going to cry. I had never seen that before. It was making me very uncomfortable. "What I've seen hasn't happened yet. What you've seen so far is *nothing*. There are still a few signs left."

"What are you talking about?" I had done my job. I had stopped the Cursed One. What else did they want from me? "Signs?"

My father began to speak, but there was a commotion out in the hall, and a sudden banging on the door. The door flew open, revealing Trip Jones. He was really excited, and his appearance indicated that he had run here. He must have just gotten back from exterminating trolls. "Sorry to interrupt, but you guys need to come with me right now. Z, Julie, you've got to see this. It's really important."

"Damn it..." I muttered. Mom scowled. "Sorry."
I stood and pointed at my father. "We'll talk later."

Dad pushed away from the table. "Owen, son..."
And then he surprised me. He grabbed me awkwardly
by the shoulders, pulled me close, and gave me a
hug. He had never actually done that before. I was
25 years old, and had never actually been hugged by
my father that I could remember. I was too shocked
to respond. Finally I patted him on the back.

"Ahh...how nice," Mom said.

After a brief moment, he let go. "Give me time to
think, then we'll talk. I didn't know if this time would
ever really come. I'll tell you everything."

Trip jerked his thumb down the hall. "We've got
to get to Milo's workshop."

# CHAPTER 10

Apparently Trip really did believe it was important, because he full on sprinted across the entire compound to Milo's workshop. Trip had played college football and could run unbelievably fast. I, on the other hand, am a sluggish brute, and preferred only to run when something was chasing me. But apparently this was a big deal, so I hauled butt, yelling hoarsely for various Newbies and Hunters to get out of my way. Unfortunately, Milo's workshop was set out by itself, most likely isolated to protect everyone else in case one of his inventions went horribly wrong and turned our gear man and his shop into vaporized atoms.

By the time Julie and I got there, Trip was already inside, and I was panting. Julie looked fine. "You should do more cardio," she said patiently as she opened the door for me.

"Punching bag's cardio," I gasped.

"Only when you do it for more than a minute."

"If I have to punch something for more than a minute"—*panting*—"it's time to go to guns."

"Wait." She grabbed me by the arm. "This business with your dad..."

"I don't know, but I intend to find out. Come on."

The inside of Milo's shop was a mess of machinery of every type: welders, lathes, mills, drill presses, and things that I didn't even recognize. Miscellaneous guns were piled in every corner and on every shelf. There was even a rocket launcher of some type dangling from a strap hung over the antlers of the crocodile head mounted on the wall.

We stepped past the biggest harpoon gun that I had ever seen. It was the size of a riding lawn mower, all stainless steel with a spool of cable thick enough for high-power lines, loaded with a spear as big around as a fence post, and painted on the side was a picture of a creature with a shark's head ending in squid tentacles with a big slash through it, Ghostbusters' style. So that's where Milo's discretionary budget had gone lately. If I wasn't in such a hurry, I would have stopped and admired the monstrosity.

Milo saw me looking at his invention. "Yeah, it is pretty freaking cool. I'm done messing around with stupid luskas. Next time we have to hunt shark-krakens, we do it in style. This sucker could harpoon Godzilla! The guys in Miami are going to love this baby. I call it *Leviathan*." He had been waiting for us, pacing, his long red beard bouncing with each step. He had undone the beard braids and the entire thing was in a giant puffy mass that extended halfway down his chest. "Well, anyways, you aren't going to believe this, but I think I've found a way to track down the Condition." He gestured for us to follow as he headed for the back of the workshop.

There was a roll-up door, and an MHI Crown Vic was parked in one of the few open spaces. Holly was standing near the rear, casually holding her .308 Vepr carbine pointed at the trunk. She smiled when she saw us. "Z, you're all sweaty. Did we interrupt you two at something?"

I was too out of breath to respond, so I flipped her the bird. She winked. Trip appeared with a ring of keys and moved to the trunk. "Ready?" he asked Holly.

"Born ready," she said as she planted the big AK against her shoulder and took aim. "Open it."

"Slow down," Milo urged. The short man paused to push his glasses back up his nose before getting down to business "You guys have no sense of presentation. Young Hunters are so excitable. You can't just spring it on them. You've got to work up to it. It's all about presentation."

Julie groaned. Milo's ideas were often good, sometimes bad, usually weird, but always with the best intentions. He was constantly thinking outside the box. *Way* outside the box. "I swear if there's Powerpoint involved, someone's getting shot."

I was a little impatient, considering that my father had been about to tell me something that was probably really important concerning my destiny and all that jazz. "Come on, Milo. Spill it. How are we going to find the Condition?"

Milo smiled broadly. "You sent the three of us out to shake down the elves to see if we could find out anything—"

"Useless as usual," Holly interjected. "Though the Elf Queen asked how the Dreamer was doing. I think she's got a crush on you, Z. She's kinda cute for a four-hundred-pounder."

"But then we get the call to head over to Bessamer for a troll infestation. You guys had to bail, so we took care of it on our own," Milo said proudly. "How much do you know about trolls?"

"I've killed..." Julie paused, thinking, "five of them on two separate cases. They're rubbery, super resilient, heal fast, are very vulnerable to fire, eat anything, but prefer children, and they're smarter than they look. It's always best to engage them from a distance, then when they're down, burn them."

"Yes, yes," Milo steepled his fingers, looking briefly like he was teaching elementary school, obviously leading up to the payoff. "All true, but more important... what do they do for *fun*?"

"Hang out under bridges and harass goats?" I asked.

Julie hesitated, flustered. "Well...I...I don't actually know."

"Aha!" Milo shouted, grabbing a bunch of printouts off a nearby table. He shoved the papers into her hands. Julie glanced at them, frowning, then started to pass them off to me.

"Hot stock tips? Free iPods? Discount Viagra? Enlarge your— What the hell?" I asked, as Julie handed printed e-mails to me. *Dear Sir, I am Barrister Kojima Loima of Nigeria and I must approach you concerning an opportunity of extreme urgency. My client former Prime Minister Katanga has requested that I safely move his fortune from our country to the U.S. in secrecy. I must transfer a sum of sixty-two million dollars to your bank account—* It just went on and on. "What is this?"

"Spam," Milo said solemnly.

"Trolls are spammers?" Julie asked.

"Oh, and so much more!" Milo exclaimed. "Open it, Trip."

Holly tightened up on her rifle. Trip turned the key and popped the lid. The trunk appeared to be filled with a bunch of greasy rubber hoses. Suddenly, the pile moved, revealing it to be one solid mass curled into an uncomfortable fetal position. Giant clawed hands and feet had been chained together and padlocked. Two round yellow eyes opened and blinked at us. It had a pointy nose, hooked over a mouth full of dingy blunt teeth.

"You are the suck!" the creature hissed. It started to rise. Trip moved forward, cocked one fist back and slugged the monster right in its massive mouth. The creature winced back.

I looked at Trip in surprise. He was normally the nicest person I knew. "I hate spammers," he explained as he shook his aching hand.

"Milo?" Julie asked slowly. "Why is there a troll in your trunk?"

The little man was really excited now. "When we hit the target, we were expecting a bunch of these things, and instead only found this one. He'd fallen asleep with his head sitting on a desk with a bunch of computers running on it."

"There was a pile a foot deep of empty energy-drink cans and Ho-Ho wrappers on the floor," Holly added. "He'd been playing online games, arguing with random people on like fifty different internet forums, writing spam. It was really pathetic. Most of it was totally incoherent."

"And the punctuation..." Trip muttered, obviously offended. "According to his MySpace page, he's a sixteen-year-old girl named Brittany who likes to post pictures of herself in her underwear."

The thing in the trunk stirred, glaring at each of us angrily. It was an intimidating beast, lean, with limbs that even though they were crammed into the trunk, were obviously too long. "So internet trolls... are really *trolls*?"

Julie folded her arms. "No, Milo. You can't keep him as a pet."

Milo was indignant. "Of course not; I remember what happened when I tried to raise that sasquatch. How was I supposed to know it was going to eat Sam's dog? Poor Squeaky..." I didn't know if that was the name of Milo Anderson's bigfoot or Sam Haven's deceased pooch. Milo lifted one last bunch of papers. "Anyway, *this* is why I brought him back."

The logo on this e-mail was the same sky squid as the Condition handout Myers had presented to us. I took it from him and read. The message was brief.

*Attention creatures of the darkness, the Shadow Lord, High Priest of the Sanctified Church of the Temporary Mortal Condition, extends his benevolent hand in friendship. Join our mighty legion. No longer must you live in secret beneath the blighted cancer of humanity. A new age is coming. A dark new dawn breaks.*

It was an invitation. It was dated several weeks ago.

The troll continued to glare at me and gnash its dirty teeth. "Are you a member of the Condition?" I asked.

"No," it hissed. "Condition is not to be trusted." The troll's voice was wheezy, like its lungs were filled with cobwebs and its vocal cords were coated in rust.

I distrusted it immediately. This thing was just plain icky. "What's your name? And I know it isn't Brittany."

Air escaped from its mouth in a series of puffs. Laughter. "Tell you nothing, human."

Holly leaned forward and jammed the muzzle of her AK into the side of his head. "Start talking, spam-boy, or I'm going to let out some pent-up aggression on your face!"

That got its attention. "Okay...okay. Don't let the pretty one hurt me!"

"Aw...he likes you," Trip said.

"Melvin, humans call me Melvin," the troll said quickly, raising one chained hand to protect his face. The dirty claws extended from the end of each fingertip at least half an inch. "My pack joined Condition, but Melvin stayed. Not trust Condition."

"Where's your pack now?" Julie asked.

"They go to join army. But trolls are lazy. He not want lazy servants. Dead servants never lazy. So he made them all dead. Now Melvin is alone. All alone..."

That almost made me sad. *Almost.* "Do you know where to find them?"

He shook his head. "Let me go free. I tell you, then you kill poor Melvin."

Poor Melvin was an eight-foot-tall, carnivorous killing machine. Letting him go wasn't really an option. But I needed him to talk. Maybe if I treated him with a little respect, he might open up. If that didn't work, we could always let Holly have a crack at him. She seemed the least morally adverse to beating the truth out of something. "Let him out."

"What, Z?" Trip asked. "Serious?" Julie looked at me like I was nuts, but didn't say anything. She drew her .45 from her holster and held it low by her side.

Milo stepped off to the side and retrieved a Mossberg

shotgun from one of the many racks. He pumped a shell into the chamber. "Don't trust him, Owen. I'm a moderator on a forum. You can't ever trust a troll."

"Listen, Melvin. We're going to let you out of the car. If you try anything stupid, we're going to shoot your arms and legs off and then we're going to burn you to ashes. Got it?"

"Melvin play nice," the troll promised. He began to slowly unfold himself out of the trunk. First one long leg came out, chains clanking, until claws clicked on the concrete floor, then it took a minute to get his spindly torso out of the narrow space. Finally the troll stood, all twisted and gangly, wrists chained together in front of its narrow chest. His flesh really did look like row after row of dirty garden hose stacked into a rough humanoid shape. I had to crane my neck to look him in the eye. There was a mass of stringy black hair matted together on his head. The other Hunters kept their guns trained as I stepped closer.

"Okay, Melvin. I'm going to level with you. I really need to know how to find the Condition. Help me avenge your pack's murder."

He laughed again. "Not care about rest of pack. Pack was stupid. Got turned into zombies. Now they not hog Melvin's bandwidth." His breath stank of stale Red Bull and his teeth hadn't been cleaned lately, if ever. "They are the Fail. No, Hunter. You let Melvin go. Then I tell you where pack went."

I was afraid of that, but I had an idea. Twice in the last few days I had been able to live somebody else's memories: Myers', and only a few minutes ago, my father's. Susan had exposed me to that cursed artifact so that I would have the ability to fight this

Condition. If it worked on people, maybe it would work on monsters. If he wouldn't tell me what I needed to know, then maybe I could just take it. It was worth a shot. I extended one hand slowly toward Melvin's clawed hand.

"What are you doing?" Julie asked.

"Trust me."

The troll regarded me suspiciously. Finally I touched his hand. He felt warm and *squishy*. Nothing happened. No black magic lightning. Nada.

Melvin screamed. "It burns! It burns!" I jerked my hand away. The other Hunters took an involuntary step back. The troll smiled, showing off row after row of rotten teeth. "I kid. I kid." Then he head-butted me.

His rubbery skull rebounded off mine, flaring pain through my brain, sending me flailing back, blocking Julie's shot. He moved with surprising speed for his size. One fist swung out, slamming into Holly's stomach and knocking her to the ground. Milo blasted him in the back, the buckshot sending chunks of green meat in every direction. Melvin didn't seem to notice. He surged forward, grabbed Trip by the shirt and tossed him headfirst into the trunk of the Crown Vic. Then Melvin slammed it shut.

My eyes were watering as I stumbled out of Julie's way. She opened fire on Melvin, her bullets tearing into the troll. I swear he giggled as he reached past Milo, grabbing onto a huge shelf of tools, guns, machinery, assorted widgets, and pulled. The heavy shelf teetered for a second before falling over.

"Move!" Julie shouted as all of us dove for cover. The shelf came crashing down, bits and pieces flying in every direction. I rolled out of the way as a chainsaw spiraled past. Milo cried out as something landed on him.

Ankles chained together, Melvin hopped for the open roll-up door and the freedom of the forest. Trolls were amazingly fast. "Ha ha. You got pwned, bitches!" He laughed as he cleared the exit. Milo was trapped underneath the shelf and thrashing about. Julie was cursing and reloading her 1911. Holly had the wind knocked out of her and was gasping for breath. Trip was beating on the inside of the trunk. I drew my STI .45, wiped my watering eyes, and started after the escaping troll.

"Witness my perfection, newbs!" Melvin shouted as he hopped down the pavement. If he reached the fence, we were going to lose him.

Suddenly a figure appeared around the corner of Milo's workshop and intercepted the bouncing troll. With his back toward me, I couldn't tell who it was. A boot smashed into Melvin's knobby knees as a large hand grabbed him by the neck. The troll went down with a screech, "No fair!" as the man wrapped his other hand around Melvin's head.

"Wait!" I shouted, but I was too late. With a brutal twist, the troll's neck snapped, and Melvin flopped twitching to the pavement.

The figure stood, dusted himself off, and nonchalantly turned around. The big man was wearing a black suit, black sunglasses, and black strangler gloves. I gasped.

Agent Franks nodded slightly in return.

The Goon Squad rushed around the corner and joined him. Torres, Archer, and Herzog looked exhausted. They'd apparently had a long night. "Burn it," Franks ordered as he strode forward, gesturing back at the troll.

"How? But you . . ." I stammered.

Franks stopped in front of me. "Mornin'...sunshine," which was exactly how I had sarcastically greeted him every morning since he'd been here. I think he was enjoying my discomfort.

Julie pulled the shelf off Milo. He was flustered, but okay. Holly had gotten unsteadily to her feet. Trip was still banging on the inside of the trunk and shouting. "Would one of you guys let him out?" I asked.

"Trip's got the keys," Holly responded.

Archer, who struck me as the most efficient of the Feds, entered the workshop and spied an acetylene torch. "Mind if I borrow this?"

"Be my guest," Milo responded. Archer wheeled out the torch, turned on the gas, and ignited it with a striker that was chained to the dolly.

"Who's pwned now, punk?" Holly asked rhetorically as she rubbed her bruised stomach. "Aww, hell, that didn't work out like we imagined."

Milo shrugged. "Capturing him seemed like a good idea at the time."

Trip yelled something unintelligible from inside the trunk.

"Good idea. Hold on," Julie shouted at Archer. "Trolls regenerate. Let's haul him down to the basement and lock him up. We can still interrogate him later." Archer looked disappointed as he twisted the knobs and closed off the torch. It made a popping noise.

Franks glanced around at the destruction. "I can't leave you alone, can I?"

I had always suspected that there was more to Franks than met the eye. He was unbelievably tough. Despite my background as a fighter, he had beaten me soundly and had taken inhuman amounts of damage at Natchy

Bottom before going down, but that proved nothing. The fact that he was standing here now, after I had seen some of his bones sticking out twelve hours ago, indicated that he was definitely not human. "What are you?" I asked.

Franks' face was emotionless behind those tinted sunglasses. "Hungry. Let's get lunch."

Franks, showing no indication that he should have been dead, ate about 7,000 calories worth of MHI's food, while his men wandered back to the barracks to get some sleep. Apparently, threatening as many witnesses as there were during a Level 5 Containment was hard work. I was feeling it myself. I had slept for less than one hour in the last thirty, and I had met with the shadow man during part of that, so I was nearing a terminal crash, and was damn loopy at this point.

I moved the ice pack to a different spot on my face. I had a nasty bruise. "So, Franks, seriously, your arm was hanging off in pieces last night. And now you're sitting here, all fat and happy." I've had a werewolf for a boss, twice, and had seen some really bizarre stuff over the last year, so I was flexible, but I was also curious. "What the hell are you, really?"

Franks chewed his fifth microwave jumbo burrito. MHI's stockpile of cafeteria food wasn't exactly gourmet dining. He still hadn't removed his sunglasses or gloves, even though we were indoors. "I'm a representative of the United States Government, here to protect you."

"Yeah, whatever, but you aren't *normal*."

He chewed with his mouth open. "Don't be such a racist."

I slammed my fist into the table and left. If he possessed any emotions at all, I knew he was doing this just to tweak me. Franks grabbed his last few burritos and followed.

I needed to get some rest, but Harbinger had wanted to discuss strategy first, and had called another meeting since the arrival of my parents had blown away our original plan. Julie and Earl were already there when I arrived. Milo, Holly, and Trip arrived once they succeeded in picking the lock on the trunk lid. Because the three of them had been on the way to Bessemer for the troll hunt, and nobody had ever notified them about my leaving the compound to go after Mosh until afterward, there was no way that any of them could be the spy. Which was great, because right about now I needed all the friends I could get. I had ditched my uncommunicative bodyguard at the base of the stairs and headed for the conference room. I wanted to make this quick, because I still wanted to talk to my father. I had a lot of questions, but first things first. I had to figure out a way to hit back at these cultists.

"What happened to your face?" Earl asked as we sat down.

"Head-butted by a troll," I grumbled.

Earl laughed at me. "I heard. I see Franks is back."

"I thought you said he was dead," Julie said.

"His arm was almost torn off and that's before he got punted across the freeway, so you tell me." I turned to Earl. "Is he like you?"

"No. I'd smell that," he answered.

"So, what does he smell like?" Maybe Earl's supernatural senses could give us a clue.

"Old Spice." Earl shrugged. I put my face in my hands and groaned. "What? He does."

"He's scary is what he is," Trip said. "Honestly, that man gives me the heebie-jeebies. There's something about him that's just not ..." He trailed off, looking for the right word.

"Human?" Holly interjected. "He's nominally on our side, and we're stuck with him, so we might as well just ignore him. But yeah, I agree with you. He gives off a bad vibe. Too bad he broke Melvin's neck before we could make him talk."

"Because that was going so well ..." My face really hurt.

"The troll will wake up eventually, though he'll probably be useless." Julie got us back on track. "So you spoke with the leader of the Condition?" I filled them in on the conversation, down to every detail I could remember, ducks and all. Earl frowned when I got to the part about how the Englishman seemed to know him personally.

He stood and walked to the wall, where the sketch artist's rendition of our enemy was tacked. "I honestly don't know this guy."

I kept on. Right now it was our only lead. "It was like he slipped up. Like he knew you, Ray, Susan, even Myers. You all used to work together. Did any of you work with somebody from England?"

"Yeah, lots. We've worked cases over there and we've worked alongside Commonwealth teams like the Van Helsing Institute and even their governmental units, but I can't think of anybody in particular." Earl was quiet for a really long time as he studied that picture, running his hands through his thin hair. He started to speak, then shook his head, as if the idea was just too stupid to contemplate. He grew frustrated and turned away. "Hell if I know."

"Well, what's the plan then?" Julie asked.

"I don't have one!" Earl snapped, which surprised me. He never raised his voice at any of us, let alone his great-granddaughter. That was really out of character. He immediately apologized. "Sorry, I'm just tired is all." He reached into his ancient leather jacket and pulled out his cigarettes, once again breaking his normal self-prohibition on smoking inside the main building. "This whole thing is pissing me off, and tomorrow's a big day."

"What's tomorrow?" I was too tired to remember.

"Newbie class graduation," Julie answered. "Esmeralda says they're ready to go. Most of our team leads and whoever else can get off are flying in to interview and pick which ones they want." Even as busy as our teams were right now, the leaders were going to make the time to come, because if they didn't pick their own Newbies, then they got the leftover ones, and nobody wanted to be *that* team.

"Well, that'll be fun," I suggested.

"Too bad one of them is probably a spy," Earl spat. That was probably what was eating him up. The very idea that one of his Hunters was working for the bad guys was blatantly offensive. In a group like this, we had to have total trust in each other. Hunters depended on their team, and by extension their whole organization, to have their backs.

"What did that oni thing tell you again?" Milo asked.

"She said that the Shadow Lord's minion had reported that I'd left the compound in a hurry to go there. So take that for what it's worth."

Milo stroked his beard contemplatively. "Maybe they just have somebody hiding out in the forest with binoculars." The idea of having a spy obviously seemed farfetched to him. He had lost his family at a young age, and had practically been raised by MHI. "Well, except that Skippy's people hunt the forest, and they'd spot anybody who hid out there for very long."

"We have to assume the worst," Julie stated. "We've got to think about who the possible leaks are."

"All the Newbies," Trip supplied. "How many of them saw you leave, or heard about it after you left?" Going through that group seemed daunting.

"Esmeralda's team. She and Cooper were with us, and one of them could have made a call when we weren't looking," Earl added. I noted that he didn't mention Julie's brother, Nate, because that was family, and therefore impossible to him, despite Nate's father's record for betrayal. "But I've known Esmeralda forever, and I just don't see that. Cooper seems like a good kid, but he's only been with us for a year."

"Dorcas," I said. Then all of us laughed. *Not very likely.*

"What about Grant and Albert?" Holly said. "They were right behind you."

"Al? I don't see it." Just because I held myself responsible for Lee's injury didn't mean he held any grudge. He was too honest a guy to fall in with the likes of the Condition. I paused. On the other hand, Grant had been gone for some time after leaving the company, only to come back just when this craziness started. "What was Grant up to all those months?" I asked.

Julie shook her head. "No way. He's a lot of things, but he's no cultist."

But it was obvious. Grant was our prime suspect. "Think about it. He's perfect. The timing just fits. Why else would he come back when he did?"

"A fat paycheck, for one thing," Holly suggested. "Man, I wish I had been along for that stupid oni instead of a lame troll."

"It'll be a cold day in hell before Grant Jefferson has to worry about money. His folks own, like, Delaware or something," Milo pointed out.

"You sure you're not letting your personal feelings get in the way of being objective?" Trip asked. "He did save you from the monster that was trying to kidnap you, which would make him a pretty lousy double agent."

"Or a really good one!" I insisted.

"You just hate his guts. It can't be Grant," Julie responded.

"And why are *you* defending him?" I shot back, and then immediately regretted saying it. Julie glared at me.

"Well, it's somebody," Earl stated. "And until we find them, we're not safe. Eventually this shadow freak is gonna lose his patience and just have the spy shoot Owen in the back."

"And if I leave, then he'll find me with magic and throw an army of undead at me. Great. At least here I'm safe from the dead."

"On the bright side, if it's a Newbie, then we'll farm them out to somebody else in the next couple of days," Holly offered helpfully.

"Unless I pick the spy for one of our vacancies. I'm a team lead too, and I'm still short since I sent Sam off to form Team Haven out in Colorado," Earl muttered.

"I do miss the big lug," Holly admitted.

"And then what about the next class, and the one after that? No, we can't risk filling MHI with a bunch of nut jobs. Not with the kinds of things that we're running up against all the time. Our people have access to every evil widget that comes down the pike. We have to end this now."

As if on cue, a small figure popped into existence, standing in the middle of the conference room table. The gnome tilted his pointy red hat at Earl. "'Sup, dawg. G-Nome, reportin' for duty."

Julie, startled, went for her gun, but I grabbed her arm. "He's cool," I said.

"Damn right, I'm *cool*. Cool as ice," he said. His face was badly bruised, and he was wearing a few Band-Aids. I had at least given as good as I had gotten. The gnome turned his attention to Holly, leering down her tank top. "Hey, baby. Lookin' fine. I do like them blonde human chicks."

"Who the hell are you," she demanded, before adding, "Shorty?"

"Hey now, baby. It's all good. I'm G-Nome, out of B'ham."

Holly was just confused now. "Genome?"

"No...G hyphen Nome, straight-up gnome killa from the North Side." He flashed a gang sign, then folded his arms. "Yeah, that's right. I'm Tony Montana, baby."

Julie pulled off her glasses, cleaned the lenses on her shirt, and then put them back on. *Nope.* He was still there. She glanced at me, and I gave her the *I'll explain later* look.

"You were only supposed to appear to me or Owen, remember?"

G-Nome shrugged. "Y'all didn't seem to mind sharin' no secrets with these."

"You find anything yet?" Earl demanded.

"I'm just gettin' the lay of the land, know what I'm sayin'? Seein' the sights. Speakin' of..." He looked back at Holly and raised his eyebrows up and down quickly. "You know, they say once you go *gnome*, you'll never go *home*."

"Ewww," she responded, too grossed out to come up with one of her usual rebuttals.

"Back off, stubby," Trip said.

"Oh, you want to go, homie? Thinkin' you all bad?" G-Nome said, puffing his chest out.

"Don't go there, Trip," I warned. "Trust me on this one, man."

"Get back to work. Report in when you've got something," Earl ordered.

"Peace." And he was just gone. It was really unnerving.

"So, that's the secret weapon you were telling me about? One of the guys from the Rice Krispies, only psychotic," Julie muttered. "What's this place coming to?"

Milo harrumphed. "And you made fun of me for bringing home a troll," he said with a great deal of indignation.

Earl tried to placate his people. "He'll find the spy. Gnomes are sneaky. In the meantime, I'm going to bump up our security here. That attack on the concert was too brazen, too crazy. Monsters don't normally operate in the open like that. It brings down too much heat, but those just didn't seem to care."

"Undead and transdimensionals can't enter the compound because of the warding, but he may try to attack us with his human followers or other types of monsters," Julie said. "Obviously it doesn't work on lycanthropes..." She waved at Earl. "It probably won't stop anything that was born on Earth."

"So something direct from the Old Ones couldn't come here either?" I asked, thinking of the swarm of Christmas Party monsters we'd fought in Natchy Bottom.

"As far as I understand how the ward works, it's basically a focus point for our reality. Like a magnifying glass under the sun. Undead are an unnatural thing in this world, so it just blasts them. Things from outside this reality can't take the heat," she explained. "Its part magic, part physics, and way over my head."

"Groovy," Trip said. He loved the magic stuff. It came from being a fantasy geek.

"We've got the security room in the basement. The whole perimeter is wired with cameras and motion detectors, but we hardly ever man it," Julie suggested. "That should give us plenty of early warning."

Earl nodded. "I want somebody in there, around the clock."

"I'll make up a schedule," she answered. "I'll have to cycle through the Newbies too, which means some of them will have to get limited basement access."

"Just keep them away from my *personal* space. Well, that's it for now then. Let's get some rest. I know none of us did last night." My boss yawned as he said it. Hunters tended to work really weird hours, but even we had our limits.

I raised my hand. "We're not done yet, Mr. Wolf."

He groaned. "I didn't get to pick the name. I thought it was goofy as hell. Hey, let's name the lycanthrope Mr. Wolf, because nobody will ever see through that. The government spooks love naming supernatural assets like that. I knew this one poor weredolphin in the Pacific that got coerced into working for the OSS doing naval recon back in '44. They designated the poor girl Ms. Fish."

"Dolphins are mammals," Milo pointed out helpfully.

"Exactly. And yes, Z, I have met your dad. I didn't ever know his real name either, so I never knew you were related, though I can see the resemblance now."

"You actually worked for the CIA?" It sounded surreal in a black-helicopter, conspiracy-theory kind of way.

"I'm the only non-PUFF-applicable werewolf in the world. They didn't grant that status for kicks. I've been called up to serve my country twice, three times if you count back to when I was just a poor human kid. People like me got to earn PUFF exemption, and sometimes earning it means working the occasional odd job for the Man, like you have to go somewhere nobody else can and eat a specific bad guy's face. Got it?"

"You were an assassin?" Trip asked in disbelief.

"It's hard to run a guerilla war when there's a werewolf sharing your jungle," Earl sighed. "I did what I had to do. Y'all would've done the same. I'm just not proud when I have to let the beast run free. Maybe that's why I've been such an effective Hunter. I understand both sides, *real* good."

That gave me pause. The Englishman had said Harbinger was a liar and a murderer. That put the murder part into new perspective. I let it go though. I was too tired to exercise any critical thinking skills right about now. "Sorry, Earl. None of my business."

# CHAPTER 11

Grant had to be the spy.

Maybe I *was* biased. We had butted heads ever since I had been recruited. I had never liked him and the feeling had been mutual. The fact that I'd had a crush on his girlfriend hadn't helped things, and then when he'd screwed up on the *Antoine-Henri*, it had pretty well sealed the deal. I had learned later that he had regretted his call to abandon me so much that it had made him doubt his abilities as a Hunter. That, coupled with the brutality of his time being a captive of the Seven, had led to him leaving.

Just because I was biased didn't make me wrong.

Grant Jefferson was staying in the barracks temporarily. He would be assigned to another team within a few days. I'd told the others that I was going to bed, but had immediately gone for a stroll. I figured it wouldn't hurt to go talk to him first. I mentally justified the lie, as Earl Harbinger had put me in charge of rooting out the mole, after all.

I was just going to talk to him and see if his story

made sense, nothing more than that. If he slipped up and said something suspicious, I would just take it back to Earl. The fact that I had stopped long enough to sling Abomination over my shoulder was just a *coincidence*. It wasn't like everybody around here wasn't always armed to the teeth anyway. This was just a friendly little social call. .

As usual, Franks had tailed me. I still didn't know how the hell he was alive, but I didn't really have the energy to dwell on it. This conversation was none of his business.

The main room of the barracks was filled with Newbies taking a break. The recreation room was actually a rather nice facility, complete with a pool table, big screen TVs, and lots of video games. We were a paramilitary organization, but we certainly weren't into that whole Spartan thing. Dawn, the Newbie who had spoken with me yesterday, was playing a game of pool. She perked right up when she saw me. That girl's default setting was *flirt*. She batted her eyes. "Hey, Z. Care to join me?"

Oh, so it was "Z" now? "Naw, I'm on business. Have you seen Grant?"

Her expression changed when she saw the hulking form of Franks fill the doorway behind me. For a second, she actually looked frightened. Maybe Franks had paid her a visit after her first monster encounter too. "No, haven't seen him," she answered quickly. "I've got to go." She tossed the pool cue on the table and walked away.

Some Newbies playing a game of Guitar Hero pointed me toward the correct room. Too bad I was a man on a mission, because I was the reigning company champ on that game. And to think that everybody thought my brother had inherited *all* the musical talent. The Newbies got really quiet when they saw that I had Agent Franks with me. I couldn't say that I blamed them. He just had a kind of dampening effect on people.

"Yo, Franks," I said. "You mind hanging out here for a minute?" He just stared at me blankly. "Private matter." He didn't even bother to respond. I leaned in closer so that the Newbies wouldn't hear. "I need to talk to somebody, alone."

Franks looked at me like I was an imbecile. I couldn't tell him that I thought Grant was the spy, since there was no way in the world he was going to leave me alone with somebody who might be a member of the cult he was supposed to be protecting me from. Franks glanced around the room, studying the inhabitants. He seemed awkward in a place dedicated to recreation.

"I've got to talk to Grant Jefferson. He... saved my life last night. I need to thank him. And I need to apologize for being a jerk to him." Franks raised an eyebrow. The concept of saying "thank you" or "I'm sorry" probably did not compute, but for whatever reason, he nodded. "One minute." Leaving Franks to watch the Newbies try to beat *Arterial Black* on "Hard," I went down the hallway and knocked on Grant's door.

"Yes," came the voice on the other side. "Who is it?"

"It's Owen Pitt."

There was a long pause and the noise of a drawer closing. Finally the door opened. Grant's black armor was hanging in the closet behind him, and he was wearing normal clothing for once. "Is there a mission?" he asked hopefully. I shook my head in the negative. "Does Harbinger need me?"

"Naw, man, I . . . uh . . . I just wanted to . . . talk."

That confounded him. "Talk?"

"Yeah, about . . . stuff. Can I come in?"

"I guess." Grant stepped out of my way. Harbinger had at least given him one of the private rooms so that he wouldn't have to share with a Newbie. There was a desk and I pulled out the chair and sat, casually letting my shotgun dangle at my side. Grant, puzzled at what I was doing here, closed the door and sat on the bed. "What can I do for you?"

I hadn't really thought through my plan. Planning's not the kind of thing you do when you're exhausted and just got beat up by gnomes. Might as well try to be nice, lower his defenses. If that didn't work, I would probably just start punching him in the face until he talked. "I just wanted to say thank you for saving my brother's life. That was a good shot."

"Yes, it was," Grant replied. "And?"

*And?* "Well, I just wanted to tell you I appreciate it." I paused. "And I wanted to welcome you back," I lied. "We never really got along before. I wanted to get us off on the right foot this time."

Grant was smart enough not to buy that. "That's nice. I'm glad to be back."

"Yeah, about that . . . why?"

"Why?"

He knew damn good and well what I was asking about. "Why'd you come back? I heard you'd moved out to Hollywood, and were living large, hanging out with movie stars and all that. Hell, I've been told that you're already worth a fortune. Your family are like billionaires. Why give up the sunshine and the babes and come back to this?" I gestured around the rather plain little room. He didn't respond, so I continued. "Slogging through the blood and the guts, risking life and limb. Most of us are doing this to make the kind of money that you've always had. Why risk that?"

"True, I've been financially blessed, just a happy circumstance." He regarded me suspiciously. "But Hunting was never about money."

"Why then? Why'd you come back?"

There was quite a bit of hesitation. *Got you sucker, you were coerced into it by a giant squid cult. Admit it.* Finally, Grant cleared his throat. "It isn't any of your business."

"I think it is," I answered, then corrected myself. "Not just for me, but for everybody in the company. You're going to get asked eventually, so what are you going to tell them?"

"I'll tell them what I just told you. That it is none of their damn business . . . So, is this an official visit or personal? Did Harbinger send you to check on my level of commitment or is this because you don't like having me around Julie. Are you worried about something?"

*What?* "That's just stupid."

"Is it?"

"Epic stupid. She has nothing to do with this."

Grant smiled. Holly had told me that he had a *disarming* smile. I found it rather patronizing. "You know what I did before I was a Hunter?" I shrugged. Julie had said that he'd gone to Harvard. "I was a new attorney at a very prestigious firm. I'd won every single case that I'd had, and some of them were rather impressive. You know why?"

"Because you're just that good?"

"Yes, that and because I can always tell when someone is lying to me, and you, Pitt, are a terrible liar. You're worried that your future *wife*"—he practically spat the word—"still has feelings for me. Before you came along, we were close. We had a real future together. You screwed that up. You feel inadequate, and now you're scared that I'm back—"

I cut him off. "Don't flatter yourself, dude."

"Well, don't worry about it. I'm done with her. I don't know if she had an aneurism or what to distort her judgment enough to fall for somebody like you, but it doesn't matter. Damaged goods now. If you think that I came back to MHI like some lovesick puppy, then you're a fool."

This was certainly spiraling in a direction that I had not expected. *Might as well run with it.* "Why'd you come back then, Grant? What pushed you to swallow your pride? Was it that hard to admit that you were wrong?"

Grant stood. "Wrong?" he shouted. "I was a *snack* for a nest of vampires. Do you have any idea what that's like? Quitting wasn't a mistake. It was what any sane person would do."

"So you quit because you were scared?"

He went to the door and jerked it open. "Get out."

I slowly stood. I had two options. Continue to push it, or let it go for now, and I hesitated, undecided. If I was wrong, I couldn't just start kicking the crap out of another Hunter in the barracks, but if he was the spy, then the longer he was free, the greater the danger to everyone. I split the difference. Stopping in the doorway, just inches away, I asked one final time. "I just wanted to know the real reason why. That's all. I'll never bug you again."

Grant was seriously angry. His face had turned a shade of red I'd not seen before. Something must have snapped. "I came back because I've never failed at *anything*. I don't know how to *fail*. Of course I was scared; only idiots like you are immune to fear. But I let the fear win, and I ran away, and I hated myself for it. Every single day, I'd read the papers. I'd recognize the cover stories. The missing persons, the obvious tricks to hide monster attacks, and the anger just *filled* me."

"Hunting's in your blood," I answered slowly.

"That's Shackleford myth," he hissed. "There's no such thing as a born Hunter. The only thing in my blood now is the curse of the vampire, and when I die I've got to get my head sawed off because of it. Nailing supermodels and going to all-night parties is great, but every morning I got to look at a failure in the mirror. I'm here for one reason and one reason only. I'm the best at *everything* I decide to do, and I can't quit until I prove I'm the best at this too . . . I can't quit until I beat this. I will be the most effective Hunter in the world or I'll die trying. Do you have a problem with that?"

*Damn it. He was telling me the truth.* I could see it in his eyes. This was a man who was just as driven as I was. No wonder we never got along. "No," I answered. I walked out the door and he slammed it shut behind me. I gave a long sigh. "Welcome back, Grant," I muttered to myself.

❖     ❖     ❖

"Owen, I'm glad to see you," Mom said as she answered the guest room door. "I'm afraid you woke us up. I know it's the middle of the afternoon, but we didn't sleep a wink last night."

"Sorry, Mom, but I need to talk to Dad. It's really important."

"What happened to your face?"

"Sucker-punched by a troll . . . Really, I need to ask him some questions."

Mom looked me over. I really wasn't in a state of grooming that was up to her usual standards. I was actually impressed that she didn't whip out a cloth, spit on it, and start rubbing my face. She had gained some self-control over the years. "Why do you have that big gun on?" She pointed at Abomination.

"Protection," I shrugged. I had been ready to shoot Grant with it, but that was too long of a story. Now that it looked like he was just another emotionally deranged Hunter, I was back to square one. "I use this for work. You know, my *real* work."

"Ooohhh, that must be your Abominator. Julie talked about it."

"*Mom* . . ." Leave it to your parents to screw up even the coolest stuff. "It's Abomination. And quit stalling, I need to see Dad."

She turned and looked back into the darkened room. I could hear Dad snoring. She moved out into the hallway, barefoot and in a borrowed bathrobe. She closed the door softly behind her. "He needs his rest."

"But—"

"No, you *But*. Your father needs his rest. He's been sick."

I had no idea what she was talking about. "Sick?"

"Oh, hello, young man. I didn't see you there." Mom smiled politely at Agent Franks, who as usual, was following me around. "I'm Ilyana Pitt. You must be one of Owen's friends."

I snorted. *Friend . . .*

"Ma'am," Franks nodded.

I cut her off before she could start to harass Franks. I knew even the most stoic man I'd ever met couldn't withstand her, and within moments she would beat his life story out of him and probably enroll him in her book club or something, but I didn't have time for that. "I've got to talk to him right now." I put my hand on the door and started to push.

One surprisingly firm hand landed on my chest. "Oh, no you don't, mister." Mom shoved me back. She was angry now. "You can talk to him when he's rested. I've been listening to this magic prophecy dream business for the last twenty-five years and I've had to put up with all sorts of strangeness and nonsense, and stockpiles of guns cluttering up my basement, and you two fighting and being obnoxious to each other that whole time. The *very* least you can do is come back later."

"But, Mom, it's important!" I'm afraid I whined; parents can do that to you.

"And it'll still be important in a few hours when we're not all cranky and stressed. Now go before I get mad."

I couldn't believe this. We're talking about the end of the world, and I was getting kicked out by my *mother*. This was embarrassing. If I hadn't been exhausted and injured, I probably would have pushed it, but as it stood, all I wanted to do was flop into bed and not get beaten up by oni, trolls, gnomes, or zombies for a while. "Fine," I muttered.

She actually patted me on the cheek. "Good. See you later. Love you." Then she slipped back inside the guest room and closed the door.

I groaned. Franks' emotionless mask almost appeared to be smirking. "Your mom seems nice," he said.

I sank onto my bed, frustrated, exhausted, and with no clear idea of what the hell I was going to do about the problems facing us. We had a spy, this shadow cult had shown they were willing to pull out all the stops, my family was now involved, and I was once again experiencing strange, Old One-related abilities. Normally I would have just lain there, too spun up to sleep, but I had gained a roommate.

"Okay, so what was the weird chick in the ninja outfit that put that smelly grease on my cuts?" Mosh asked. He wouldn't know just how effective that "grease" was until morning. "With the tusks?" He had been asking me monster-related questions for the last hour.

"Orc. They're distantly related to humans. Most of them never speak. They always wear masks, but even then they're painfully awkward. Each one has some sort of gift that they're magically good at. Gretchen is a healer. Skippy is the best pilot in the world."

Mosh was nodding thoughtfully in the dark. "So *that* explains the Stig."

"Who?"

"Never mind..." Mosh muttered. "I thought orcs were the bad guys and elves were good."

"It's complicated. This particular tribe is good."

"Are there elves then?"

"Yes, the local ones live in a magic trailer park. Go to sleep, Mosh."

I had killed the lights, but I could sense the shifting on the cot on the other side of the room. It was quiet for a long time.

"So, the reason Dad's always been a jackass is because of a *dream*? And because he's been *afraid*?"

I sighed. I still hadn't really absorbed that yet. All these years I'd just assumed my father was a paranoid jerk by default, and now it turns out that he had reasons. "I suppose so, but I don't know yet."

"I can't believe he told you that.... Dad only ever told me stories about murdering communists. It's not like he ever talked about his feelings. Hell, I didn't know he even had feelings.... So it turns out that Dad was right the whole time?"

"Huh?"

"You don't get it, do you? Ever since we were little, he's put us through Pitt boot camp and treated us like crap, and we hated him for it because we thought he was crazy... But now you're some sort of top secret badass fighting evil death cults, and you're using the exact kind of skills that Dad tried to beat into us. Hell, if it wasn't for Dad being such a dick, we'd probably be dead. So I guess that means that he was right all along.... That's some mind-blowing shit right there. I'm going to have to tell my therapist about this one."

*Crap.* Mosh was right. Talk about a paradigm shift. It can be really difficult to admit that you've had such a fundamental misunderstanding about someone. "Well, he's still been a jerk about it," I muttered.

"A prophetic jerk, though... Man, I can't believe Dad actually told you any of that."

I rolled over and stared at the ceiling. "He didn't tell me. I read his mind."

Mosh grunted. "You read minds?"

"It's a long story."

It was quiet for almost ten seconds that time. "Okay, what am I thinking right now?" my brother asked.

He was probably thinking that I had ruined his life. I still don't think he grasped the full implications of what was going on here yet. "You're thinking about how you're finally going to get that operation you've always wanted, and how you'll be a lot more comfortable as a girl, and not having to live a terrible lie, and how you can't wait to get a pretty blue sundress to go along with your new spring wardrobe. Now go the hell to sleep already."

"Blue isn't my color... Night, bro."

My brain finally gave up. I finally started to drift off. Tomorrow we would figure out something. There had to be a way to defeat the Condition.

"So... are dragons real?"

*We need to talk.*

The whisper startled me awake. I blinked the heavy sleep from my eyes. My alarm clock display read 3:00 A.M. on the dot. For a long moment I lay there, trying to decide if I had been dreaming or if somebody had actually spoken. There was an unfamiliar shape on the cot on the other side of my room, and it took me a moment to remember that my brother was crashing here too.

My whole body ached despite Gretchen's efforts. I had been physically abused over the last few days and I was feeling it right now. Every muscle protested as

I sat up. *Stupid monsters.* There was nobody else in my room, so I must have been dreaming. I needed to get up and use the bathroom anyway.

I walked barefoot into the hall and headed for the bathroom. It was quiet. The other doors were closed. I took care of business and headed back to bed.

*We need to talk.*

I froze, positive that I had heard that. Scanning both ways, I couldn't see anyone. I was alone in the hallway. It had been a woman's voice, I was sure.

*Meet me at the front gate. Neutral ground.*

What the hell? I was definitely hearing a voice, but I couldn't figure out where it was coming from. This was weird, and weird was usually bad. I flipped on my light, causing Mosh to snort, grunt, and roll over, pulling his blanket back over his shaved head. I picked up Abomination off my dresser and waited. I was wide awake now.

*It's telepathy, stupid. I'm trying to send you a discreet message.*

"Susan . . ." I said slowly, tightening my grip on my weapon.

*Yeah. Now pay attention. Broadcasting is hard work. Meet me at the front gate. Come alone. We need to talk. If I wanted to kill you, there are lots of easier ways to do it.*

"Bullshit," I stated. I didn't know vampires could do this kind of thing, but I guess it went back to the whole foggy night, hypnotize the victim, and have them walk outside kind of bad Dracula movie thing. This certainly wasn't nearly as smooth as the movies made it look.

*You have my word. I need to talk with you, not*

*murder you. It's about our mutual enemy. Time's getting short.*

"You can say what you've got to say just fine like this."

"Dude, shut up and kill the light." Mosh muttered. "You're having a bad dream."

*I'm trying to help you, moron.*

I laughed. "Maybe I don't want your help?"

*Oh, so that's how it's going to be. Fine, be stubborn. Don't come alone then. Let me wake up somebody with half a brain and see what they say . . .*

Then the voice was gone. I sat there, my shotgun cradled in my lap, waiting, but nothing else came. "Damn it," I muttered, realizing that if Susan really was at the front gate, then I needed to sound the alarm.

Mosh sat up, finally awake, and obviously frustrated. "Man, you're pissing me off. You've always talked in your sleep and—" He stopped when he saw I had Abomination ready. "Whoa . . ."

"Naw, it's cool. Stay here." I stood up and stuffed my big feet into my sandals.

"What now?" he asked, rubbing his eyes, suddenly worried.

"Nothing. Go back to sleep," I ordered as I opened my door.

"Oh, yeah, because that'll be easy," my brother responded.

Further down the hall, another door creaked open and Earl stepped out, tugging his leather jacket on over a shirt, Thompson subgun dangling in one hand. He saw me.

"Susan?" I asked.

"Yep," he responded.

"Plan?" I closed my door behind me.

"See what she's got to say, I reckon."

"And what if it's a trap?"

His eyes seemed unnaturally golden in the dim light. "Then I tear her apart."

Earl Harbinger and I moved hastily to the back stairs. We were assuming that Franks was camped out at his usual position and wanted to avoid him. My boss stopped me with a raised hand while he listened down the stairwell. "All clear," he said before padding down. I hadn't realized that Earl was barefoot.

Rather than stopping on the main floor, we continued to the basement. I had no idea where he was leading me. Earl walked quickly through the lower floor, past various storage rooms and the entrance to the archives before turning a corner and heading back into the deepest area of the basement, where I had never really explored. The building really was vast, and I just never really had the time to screw around in the dusty, unused sections. I knew that down here somewhere was Earl's cell for full moons. He finally paused before a closet door.

"What're you doing?" I whispered.

He didn't respond, just unlocked the door with one key from a fat key chain and went straight to the back of the room. He walked to a shelf of cleaning chemicals and shoved it aside. It was on casters and rolled smoothly out of the way to reveal a heavy iron door. He unlocked a padlock, then had to tug the door a few times to get it to open. It creaked on rusty hinges.

Stone stairs led into the darkness.

"You've got to be kidding me..."

"This whole place is riddled with secret passages," he responded. "Every major building in the compound is connected. This will take us right up to the gate. Come on." He started down the stairs.

"Why don't we just walk out the front door and across the parking lot?" I asked, as I examined the cobwebbed rock walls. "That'd be a lot faster." *And less creepy*, but I left that unsaid, because I didn't want to sound like a wimp. I really didn't like being underground.

"If we do have a spy, I don't want them seeing us meeting with a vampire," he said simply. He had a point. The less the Condition knew, the better off we were.

The tunnel was pitch black. I turned on Abomination's attached Surefire flashlight and the brilliant beam flooded ahead of us. Dust swirled through the light as we disturbed the ground underfoot. The tunnel was at least seven feet tall and four feet wide. "I didn't know about any secret passages."

"There's lots of stuff you don't know yet," my boss replied. "No offense, but you're still new at this."

"Relatively speaking," I responded as we walked. "What's to keep undead from using these to sneak in here?"

He shook his head. "The warding extends underground and into the air above us. It's kind of like a bubble in all directions. That's why I've got it hidden dead center in the middle of the compound for maximum coverage."

"Why don't we just take it with us whenever we go on a case? We could be blowing up undead left and right. That'd be sweet."

"Like I said, you've got a lot to learn. Wards aren't mobile. You can take them someplace and turn them on, but you can only do that so many times before they're worn out, which would be a waste. You've got to tune them for a location, but lots of important places get warded: the White House, the Vatican, NORAD, that kind of thing. But they're rare and expensive. The science of making them has been lost for hundreds of years. There's probably only a dozen ward stones in private hands in the world. I picked ours up off a guy that didn't need his anymore."

We turned a corner. There was an intersection that branched off in different directions. There were a surprising number of tunnels. I was totally disoriented but could tell we were trending upward. "Where'd you get ours from?"

"I looted it from Adolf Hitler's bunker. . . . Ah, here we go." He gestured at a rusty metal ladder sunk into the wall with heavy bolts. He immediately started up, not leaving me a chance to ask if he was pulling my leg or not. "Kill the light."

I shut down my Surefire, dropping us back into darkness. I was blind. There was a scraping noise from above as Earl moved some sort of cover out of the way. A small bit of light cascaded down the hole. It was blocked momentarily as Earl climbed through the gap. I followed.

It felt good to be in the open air. Crickets were chirping everywhere. It took my eyes a minute to adjust. We were just inside the chain-link fence, twenty feet from the front gate and main road. Earl was squatting to the side. He touched my arm and signaled for me to stay low. We were surrounded by kudzu. I sat in the slightly damp vines and waited. The nearest light came from the fat bulbs over the gate, hazy behind visible humidity. Swarms of miscellaneous insects buzzed around the lights, casting hundreds of tiny dot shadows.

"Where is she?" I whispered.

"Shhhh," Earl hissed.

Then the crickets stopped chirping. I realized the temperature was dropping. Suddenly it was abnormally cold and prickles of discomfort moved across my sweat-damp body. A feeling of dread and discomfort settled into my bowels. She was here. "About time." Susan's voice came from somewhere inside the shadowed forest. I scanned the trees but couldn't make out anything. "It's good to see you again, Earl."

"Hey, Granddad," Ray said. "Been a long time." I couldn't spot him either but I kept scanning.

"Make it quick," Earl responded, his voice sounding strangled. This was very hard for him.

"You don't have to be such a prick," Susan responded. "I'm trying to do you a favor. We were family once."

Earl stiffened. "No. A human being named Susan Miner married my grandson, Ray. They were good people. I loved them. But they're dead and gone. You're just an empty shell with no soul and all their memories. So cut the bullshit, and say what you've got to say, you worthless monsters."

Red eyes winked into existence through the fence. They were coming right at us. "You don't want to hear what I've got to say, old man," Ray was mad. "You left me to rot in Appleton for something that wasn't even my fault. You've got more blood on your hands than a legion of vampires. Which one of us is the real monster?"

Harbinger stood. "Well, why don't you just come across this fence and show me what's up then, boy?"

"I would," Ray spat. The red eyes stopped, hovering a stone's throw away. "But I don't feel like dying once and for all. Remember, I know all about your magic rock. Why don't you come over here and we'll finish up some family business."

"Knock it off," Susan ordered. She sounded just like Julie when she said that. "We're not here to fight. I offered a truce, and I'm standing by it."

"You've got your truce for now, but mark my words: I'm going to end your miserable non-lives eventually," Earl vowed. "You threatened my family, so you have to die."

Susan was livid. "I promised I would leave Julie alone."

"We'll see . . ."

"What do you want?" I asked, speaking up for the first time.

A second pair of eyes approached, swaying through the trees. She stepped from the shadows, an eerie mirror image of Julie, wearing the same dress that she had in Mexico. Her white teeth cut a razor line through the darkness. She was hauntingly beautiful as the humidity turned into swirling fog around her legs. "I want this necromancer gone. He knows I've helped you, and now he's trying to destroy me."

"Help?" I spat. "You can't call anything tainted from the Old Ones *help*."

"What's it done to you?" Ray asked eagerly. "What did it unlock?"

"Don't answer him," Earl ordered. "Ray talks a big game but he sucks at black magic. Damn near tore an interdimensional hole out Alabama's backside. Caused the death of his own son. He always let his pride blind him to danger."

"I told you that wasn't my fault!" Ray shouted. "I did the best I could."

"And little Ray got his guts torn out for it, as well as over a hundred and twenty other innocent people, including ninety-seven of *my* Hunters. Appleton was too good for you. I should have left you in that rift with those Old Ones you love so much."

"I was lied to," Ray insisted. "The spell should have worked."

"You can't blame anyone for that but yourself. Nobody lied to you. You dabbled in things no man should, and we all paid for it. If I had known what you were doing, I would have taken you out myself, blood or not. The only person lying here is you. You even set the archives on fire to keep us from finding a way to close your precious gate. You knew exactly what you were doing."

Ray laughed. It was an angry, bitter sound. "I didn't torch the archives, you old fool. I was at Gulf Shores getting ready for the party when that bomb was set. I got suckered, just like you, just like everybody else."

Earl hesitated. I could tell he was angry, itching to fight, but that had thrown him for a loop. I realized with a shock that this was the first time the two had actually spoken since the Christmas party that had almost ended everything. "We always thought you were working on your own."

"I promised Owen I'd tell him as soon as I knew for sure. The same man, or used to be man, that we're fighting now arranged it all..." Susan said. "My poor, distraught husband did what he did out of love. He just wanted to bring me back. If only he had known I was a vampire, and being kept as a slave, unable to contact him— No, Earl, save that anger. Ray was used. This damn necromancer preyed on his weakness, his mourning for me, and twisted it to his advantage, used him in an attempt to establish a bridge to the other side. That's your real enemy, and he's been your real enemy all along. He hates MHI for what it stands for, and he hates you personally, as he has for years."

"No," Earl stated. "Enough of your lies. Don't make excuses for Ray's bad decisions."

"What? You can't handle the truth? You don't want to hear that you punished your grieving grandson, when he was only trying to do the right thing? You don't want to hear that you've been wrong all this time? Well, too damn bad," Susan said. "You screwed up. The real bad guy was under the nose of the mighty Earl Harbinger for years."

"Who then?" he demanded.

"The man who arranged for me to be enslaved in '90. My death was part of his plan. Oh yeah, he was thinking that far ahead. He needed Ray broken and searching for something. The man who orchestrated the destruction of your company and the deaths of all your Hunters in '95, and when you stopped him there, the government completed his job and shut you down anyway. But it goes back even further, and you were too stupid and guilt-ridden to see it. You lost an entire team of Hunters to him before that, simply because one of them knew too much."

"Give . . . me . . . a . . . *name*. . . ." Earl said through clenched teeth. His eyes were bright gold now, and he was barely containing his rage. I honestly thought he was going to hop that fence and go toe to toe with both of the vampires.

"What's the matter?" Susan chuckled. "Losing your cool?"

The forest suddenly ignited with light. A red parachute flare was drifting through the sky. The vampires were both clearly visible now. The alarm began to sound, an old-school air raid horn blaring one harsh note across the entire compound.

"It's a trap!" Ray shouted as he moved back into the darkness.

"Damn you," Susan said as she melted away. "I was trying to help."

"No! Give me a name!"

But the vampires were gone.

"What did you do?" I shouted.

"Nothing," he replied. "Somebody must have picked us up on camera. I've got to go after them."

"You'll never catch them. They're way too fast."

"Watch me." He dropped his Tommy gun on the ground and shrugged out of his jacket. "A human couldn't track them, but I can."

"You're going to change?" And not on the full moon? That was insanity. He never did that. It was utter and reckless stupidity.

But Earl was desperate. "I've got to catch them. They're too damn evil to live." One impossibly strong hand grabbed me by the shoulder. The hair on his arms was now carpet thick and his fingernails were abnormally long. "Don't let anybody follow. Get them inside the main building. It's too dangerous out here."

"We can take Susan."

"No." He smiled beneath glowing eyes. All of his teeth were razor sharp and pointy now and his words were slurred and hard to understand. "Because of me." He took three steps, leapt effortlessly over the eight-foot fence and disappeared into the forest.

"I want everybody evacuated from the barracks and into the main building, now!" I shouted at the approaching Hunters. Esmeralda's man Cooper was in the lead. He had his FAL shouldered, was fully geared up, and was sweeping his rifle from side to side. Behind him were a couple of real Newbies, one of the Haight brothers from Utah, Dawn the beauty queen, and one make-believe Newbie, Herzog, still trying to be incognito.

"What's going on?" Cooper asked.

"Doesn't matter. I want everybody inside. Button the place up. This isn't a drill." I must have looked kind of weird, since I was just wearing shorts, a tee shirt, and sandals, but carrying Abomination in one hand and a Thompson in the other. I had tossed Earl's leather jacket over one shoulder, figuring that if he didn't end up committing any atrocities out there tonight while he was shape-shifted and insane, he'd probably want his stuff back in good shape.

All of us started back across the parking lot to the main entrance. Cooper was excited. "Yesterday Julie started having us take turns, working in pairs, monitoring the security system. She told us to be ready for anything. We caught a couple of figures on thermal and went to check it out. We were just getting off shift and these guys were coming on. When we saw the undead we sounded the alarm."

"How'd you know they were vampires?"

"I had two on thermal, but four on night vision," Cooper explained. "No body heat. Dude, that was like an 'oh shit' moment."

I bit my tongue. He had done exactly what he was supposed to have done. The timing had sucked, but it was what it was. "You did good. Head that way and clear out the barracks. And no word about vampires to anyone, got it?"

"Sure thing." Cooper ran off with the two Newbies in tow. Dawn hesitated, like she wanted to talk to me, but I had to hand it to her, she followed orders. Herzog, on the other hand, didn't give a damn about my MHI seniority and stayed with me.

"You better go keep up appearances."

"Shut up, punk," the undercover MCB agent snapped. "What were you doing outside without coverage?"

"Taking a stroll," I replied. "I do love spring nights." In the distance there was a terrible noise. A wolf's howl, but it was unbelievably loud and the pitch sounded too *human*. I had to remember that Earl wasn't just a werewolf. He was the friggin' *king* of werewolves, the ultimate alpha male.

Herzog almost leapt out of her boots. "What the hell was that?"

I was terrified of werewolves myself because of personal experience, but I didn't let it show. "That there is why I want everyone inside. For an agent, you sure are jumpy."

The noise startled the stocky woman from her usual hard-core façade. "Screw that. I'm no field agent! I'm not used to this crap. Let's go." She took off, moving with the speed of somebody who figured they were about to be monster chow, stubby legs pumping.

*Not a field agent?* I frowned. That didn't make any sense. She'd been assigned to protect me. Myers had said they were some of his best men...handpicked. We were about a hundred feet from the front door and Hunters were piling out, throwing on weapons and gear in response to the alarm. I caught the short woman in a couple of steps, let Abomination hang by the sling, grabbed Herzog around her bicep, and spun her back to face me.

"Hey!" she shouted.

"Not a field agent? What are you?" I demanded.

She began to stammer something. I squeezed harder. "I'm a clerk!" she squealed. "Admin clerk. But... but I'm a fully sworn agent. I've been through MCB school. Let go."

"A clerk?" I released her arm.

Her face fell. "I was at the IRS and I came across some top-secret returns about PUFF. I did some poking around and that's how I found out about monsters. I've never actually *seen* one. Even the MCB needs somebody to shuffle paper, so they offered me a job and sent me through the academy." Harbinger howled again. He was fully transformed now and he sounded relatively close. "Please, let's get inside!"

"Why are you on a protective detail?" This didn't make any sense at all.

"I don't know. Agent Myers assigned me to Agent Franks' command for this mission." Her beady eyes darted around nervously. She was really freaked out.

"What about Torres and Archer?"

"Oh no, Anthony's a full-on pro. He's been on all sorts of missions. But Henry's more like me. He's a crypto-commo geek. That's what he did in the Army.

But he's cool and he's actually been on a few missions with real monsters, but I don't know if he's actually ever killed any. Please, let's get out of here, before whatever that is comes and gets us."

She sure had been a lot tougher when she had been threatening *me* with a gun. "Go." I nodded toward the door. Something was fishy. Franks was a one-man wrecking crew, but the Goon Squad weren't the hardened killers that I had been led to believe they were. Torres had been by far the nicest of the bunch but he was the only one who had actually seen the elephant.

I would have to think about it later. A bunch of Hunters were fanned out, covering the entrance, weapons pointing outward in a rough semicircle of potential destruction. I had to remember that only the old-timers and the ones wearing Happy Face team patches knew about Earl's little secret. The alarm died off and two giant spotlights ignited on the roof, sweeping randomly across the perimeter.

It was a relief to see Julie come trotting out, brutal M14 in her lovely hands. "What's going on? Are you okay?" Herzog's stocky form pushed past Julie and retreated inside the relative safety of the fortress.

"I'm fine. Your parents are here."

"Damn *them*!" she shouted. Several other hunters jumped at that.

"And . . ." I raised Earl's empty jacket. She knew right away what had happened.

"Everybody inside now!" Julie ordered. "Move! Move! Where's Dorcas?"

Our receptionist was leaning in the doorway in a flowery, old-lady nightgown. Her hair was up in curlers. The reason she was leaning was because she hadn't had a chance to attach her artificial leg yet. It was tucked under one arm. A massive stainless-steel revolver hung loose in her hand. "Yep?"

"Once everybody's in, I want a full head count. We've got a Code Silver." She gestured at Earl's leather jacket.

"Aw shit. Not this again," Dorcas muttered. "Let's go, kiddies." She pushed off from the doorframe and hopped out of sight.

I stayed with Julie at the entrance until the last of the Newbies was roused from the barracks and herded inside. She glanced around, careful to make sure that there was nobody close enough to overhear us. "Why'd he do it? The full moon was a week ago. He didn't have to change."

"He did it on purpose. He was going after your folks," I whispered. "I think he was dead set on not letting them get away."

"That was stupid." Julie shook her head. She hadn't had a chance to tie her hair back, and it was so dark and shiny that it reflected the spotlights. "Well, at least he should have some judgment right now. The closer to the full moon, the more out of control it is. He shouldn't wander into town and eat anyone. Sometimes I'm really glad we're in the middle of nowhere."

"What about Skippy's village?"

"They know to get inside when they hear the alarm. Skip knows what to do and they've all got silver bullets. Earl goes in there and they'll shoot him. Nothing personal, that's just how it is, and Earl would understand. Their wargs will give them plenty of early warning. Let's get inside."

The two of us were the last ones in. We pulled the massive doors closed behind us and threw down the bar. There were a bunch of really confused, half-asleep, heavily-armed, almost-graduated Newbies wandering around the reception area. The Hunters experienced enough to know about Code Silver were busy getting everybody calmed down and oriented. Julie rested her head on my shoulder briefly so she could whisper, affording us a tiny bit of affection amid the chaos. "I hope he catches them..."

Wrapping my arms around her, I squeezed her tight. It would be really nice to have the curse of Susan and Ray removed once and for all. "Me too." Damn it, we had almost had a name. I had been right. The shadow man was somebody from MHI's past. If we knew who he was, we could find and destroy him, but that was assuming Susan was even telling the truth to begin with.

I let go of Julie so she could get back to damage control. Monster Hunters by their nature are not an easily riled bunch, but they were also intensely curious, and with Earl out running naked and hairy through the woods chasing vampires, that left Julie as the de facto head of operations. She needed to get everyone taken care of.

Dorcas had finished taking a quick roll and reported in. "Your grandfather's upstairs, has his hearing aids out, so slept through the alarm. Milo's in Cazador at his house. Everyone else who should be here is accounted for." She added the next bit with extra volume for anyone listening. "Oh, and Earl Harbinger is in Montgomery on business."

I noticed my folks standing near the wall of memorial plaques; they'd apparently been woken up by the alarm. Mosh was coming down the stairs. So I had some explaining to do myself. I started toward my parents and was almost there when a whisper filtered through my mind.

This message from Susan was weaker than the others. She was either further away, or hopefully busy getting her arms pulled off by an angry werewolf. It was a single word.

...*Hood*....

That sounded familiar. I paused, turning slowly. The wall of plaques stretched before me under the Latin *Sic Transit Gloria Mundi*. My hand automatically flew to the silver surfaces, passing quickly through them, each cool to the touch. I found the one I was looking for within seconds.

A. MARTIN HOOD
1/14/1960-10/17/1986

# CHAPTER 12

3:45 A.M. Back in the conference room, with the only people who I knew I could trust: Julie, Trip, Holly, and the absent Milo on the speaker phone.

"Do you remember this guy, Hood?" I asked. "Supposedly he died in '86."

Julie shook her head. "Kind of, but I was too young. I know I met him, but I couldn't tell you anything about him. Milo?"

"You sound funny on speaker. You aren't that high-pitched in real life, Julie," he replied. "He was the one who made the balloon animals at your birthday party a couple of years. He was really good at that."

"Oh! Dad's pudgy friend."

"Yeah, Marty Hood. The fat funny guy. He was on Earl's team when I first joined up. Couldn't ask for a nicer Hunter. I was a really young Newbie and he was always helpful. He had a reputation of being smart. One of the nerdy, brainy types, rather than the kick-in-the-door-and-blast-everything kind of Hunter. No offense, Z." That made me smile. I had a bit of a reputation. "Julie—him, your dad, and Myers were good friends, like brothers. Earl loved him like a son. I didn't know him that well, but I really liked him. He died not too long after I came aboard."

That didn't sound at all like the hyper-intense religious fanatic I had met.

Holly cut in. "Yeah, he was man of the year, but was he British?"

Milo answered immediately. "Yes, he was. I remember that. I thought it was funny, because he was from Birmingham, only the England one, not the Alabama one."

Holly sat back in her chair, looking smug. "Bingo."

"Looks like we've got our wizard," Trip replied. "He must have faked his own death."

The speaker-phone box was a triangular plastic thing and the noise that came through it had to have been Milo Anderson clearing his throat. "Uh . . . that's not real likely, Trip."

"So you had a body?" I asked.

"Well . . . we had *most* of a body. But it was obviously him. And we gave him a Hunter's Funeral, so there's no way you can fake that." Milo had a point. A Hunter's Funeral featured a decapitation. When you had to deal with the icky, contagious things that refused to die as often as we did, beheading and cremating your dead was a good habit to get into. "I saw the body, so did a bunch of others. No, Marty Hood died, and it was really horrible, and permanent . . . and messy."

Holly was nonplussed. "Magic."

Trip shook his head. "Real magic isn't just where you can wiggle your fingers and say some words and then break all the laws of physics. There's got to be another explanation."

"Yes, there is," Julie added. "My mother's a liar, and she picked a random dead British Hunter to make us waste our time." The hate in her voice was obvious. "We can't trust her." That explanation was plausible. Susan's motives were murky at best and only a fool would trust the dead. Julie unconsciously rubbed the mark on her neck, reminding me again of how Susan had said that the mark was eventually going to kill the love of my life. I needed to believe that Susan was a liar.

"So how did he die then?" Trip asked. It took my tired brain a moment to remember that Trip hadn't been there when Harbinger had admitted to killing Hood by accident, thereby earning Myers' eternal animosity.

The phone was quiet for a real long time. Finally, and with obvious reluctance, Milo began to speak. "I don't know if I should be telling you this. It's probably something that you need to talk to Earl about, not me. I wasn't there when it went down. I just helped clean up."

"Earl's a little busy and can't come to the phone right now," Holly said. "You know, blood-lust rampage . . ."

"It was an accident," I added, prompting Milo to go on. "It was Earl's fault." The others looked at each other in confusion.

"You know already?" Milo asked, sounding relieved. "Well, in that case, yeah, it was a terrible accident. I got there too late to help. Dorcas had already been taken to the hospital. Ray had gotten it under control and barricaded the door while he regenerated."

"Huh?" Julie asked. "While who regenerated?"

"Earl," Milo responded like this was the most obvious thing in the world. "Dwayne wanted to finish him off, go in there with a 12-gauge and some silver double-aught, but Ray pulled a gun on him. They got into a big fight. Dwayne was really mad."

Milo's stories tended to jump around a lot. "Dwayne?" Trip asked.

"Myers..." I responded. "Back when he was with MHI. Right?"

"Yeah, he was going nuts. Wanted to go in there and take Earl out, walked right up to the door with a shotgun, only Ray just laid him out cold, then stuck a .45 in his face. Hood's blood was everywhere. It was really intense."

"Okay, you need to back up a whole bunch," Holly suggested. "You lost me a while ago."

"Just like tonight. It was a Code Silver," Milo said.

There was a hard knock on the door. It immediately opened and Dorcas, still wearing her flowered nightgown, was standing there, out of breath. She had finally gotten the chance to strap her leg on. The old lady slammed the door behind her, seething, hobbled right up to the table, pulled up a chair next to me and flopped into it with a grunt.

The four of us exchanged glances. Dorcas didn't speak, she was breathing too hard. I suspected that she had actually *run* up the stairs. Her face was red beneath her white hair and pink curlers. "What? Who's that?" Milo asked.

"I caught part of your call when I picked up my phone downstairs," the crotchety old lady said. "Y'all need to remember to use the secure line if you're gonna be talking about secret stuff." She gave us all a withering death glare. "Spies and whatnot all around this place, and you use an unencrypted line?"

"Sorry," Julie responded, looking embarrassed. In the rush she had just called Milo directly. Even somebody like Julie could slip up when in a hurry at three in the morning. She started fiddling with the phone.

"Milo, you've got no business sharing this story. It ain't your story to share. You weren't there until the end."

"No, ma'am," Milo automatically replied. His response to cranky, scary old ladies was exactly the same as mine. "But they need to know."

"Damn right, they do," she answered. "But let somebody who was there tell it. I earned that much." Dorcas leaned way back in her chair, reached under her nightgown and pulled on a couple of straps. Her plastic leg popped right off. She tossed the prosthetic on the table with a clang. It had a fire-breathing warthog engraved on it and there was a pink slipper on the foot. "I earned it."

"Yes, ma'am. Yes, you did."

"That's right, that's why I'm gonna tell it." Dorcas gestured at Holly. "Get me some coffee, girl. Black. Move." Even Holly knew better than to argue with that. Then Dorcas turned to me. "You, what did I tell you about werewolves when we first met?" She stabbed one bony finger at me like an angry question mark.

"That you used to kill them yourself . . . before one took your leg."

"That's right, Z, my boy. Those of us who've got torn up by those things understand. Only you got all cured up by those Old Ones and lost your scars. Well, I got to keep mine. I *earned* my scars." She reached over and poked me in the forehead, right where my big scar had been.

The conference room disappeared.

◆     ◆     ◆

*What's that ruckus?* It was coming from the old slave quarters. I sat up in bed and listened. Earl was unnaturally agitated. Hell, he sounded right crazy. My watch said it was just shy of two in the morning. I got out of bed. The guestroom of the Shackleford place was real nice, but there was no rug in here, and the wood was October cold under my feet. I winced a little. Wide awake now, I pulled the curtain open and looked outside.

The little building that they kept Earl locked up in during the full moon was right under my window. The old slave quarters they called it. Damned bunch of scratched-up rocks I called it. The moon was bright and there weren't no clouds in front of it right then, so I could see somebody standing outside the door of that little prison fiddling with the chains. Damn idiot. What was he trying to do? Let loose a werewolf? Best put a stop to this nonsense real fast. My armor was sitting on an old chair by the bed, but I didn't have time for that. My team patch, Sparky the Warthog, was on the sleeve, but I probably wouldn't need ol' Sparky. Probably just some stupid country kid trying to figure out what kind of animal the crazy old Shackleford family kept locked in that little outbuilding. I stopped to get hold of my Ruger Redhawk and my flashlight, because my momma didn't raise no fools, and nobody ever said that Dorcas Peabody was a fool.

I hurried downstairs. I always was a fast runner. Even though I was starting to feel the age and the pains and whatnot, I could still show up those youngster hotshot Hunters. There were a bunch of us staying at the old Shackleford place tonight, Hunters from all over the damn place. Big case just got wrapped up, and it was nearing Halloween, which was always our busy season, so we'd celebrated, and I had drunk a little too much with dinner. It had been good to see so many old friends. I suppose I had probably drunk less than some of the other Hunters, though, which was probably why I was the first one to get my ass downstairs and out the back porch.

The soles of my feet were hard as leather. Where I grew up in Tuscumbia on the Tennessee River, shoes were for church and that was about it. Even though I could afford real nice shoes now, I still had country feet. I didn't even notice what was under them as I walked to the old slave quarters. All I was thinking about was somebody messing with Earl's door and how nobody was fool enough to let loose a werewolf.

A big cloud moved in front of the moon, making it dark. *Looks like rain.* I turned on the flashlight and pointed it at the slave quarters twenty paces away, lighting up the man by the door. *I'll be damned. It's a Hunter.* It was that dumpy limey kid, the one that Dwayne trained, and from what I'd heard, he was supposed to be smart enough to know better than to screw with Earl in this state. The kid had just got moved to Carlos' team back east, what the devil was his name again?

"Hood?" I asked. "What in the hell are you doing with that lock?"

He turned, looking at me, and he had a real funny look on his moon face. "I can't stop it." He had a ring of keys in his stubby fingers and I noticed that all the chains to Earl's door had been unlocked and were laying in a big mess at his feet. Werewolf Earl was just plain crazy, slamming into the door, sensing meat and blood right on the other side, just taunting him into a frenzy. The only thing keeping the door closed now was the big block of wood barred across it. "I can't stop it," he said again, sounding all sorts of crazy.

"Boy, you gone nuts? Get back from that door!"

"He's in my head!" His big eyes blinked at me, real stupid, like there was something wrong in his head. He was scared, and damn well he should be, because werewolves were some scary shit! He was bawling and tears were pouring down his face. "I can't stop it." Earl slammed into the door, hard enough to shake the entire building. But the Shacklefords had reinforced the door with bands of iron years ago. It would hold, unless Hood lifted that bar.

"You open that door, and Earl's gonna put a stop to you, right quick," I said, not even thinking about the .45 Long Colt in my hand. This was a fellow Hunter. No way he could be stupid enough to open that door. That'd be suicide.

Hood committed suicide.

The fat kid turned around, hooked his fists under that big old bar and lifted it real hard. It popped out and fell on the ground.

I was surprised. Hood stepped back. "It's done," he said, smiling, then started to say something else, but that's when the door flew open with a bang, and there was just this bunch of pale fur and golden eyes flashing 'round under the moon. Hood started to scream as claws lit into him. He got opened up. Guts spilling out, flying all over, and then he went down, the werewolf on top of him, arms and legs just a-kicking, blood spraying. He just kept screaming for what seemed like forever, but probably was only a couple seconds, before Earl sunk his teeth into Hood's throat and went to town.

"Oh, no," I said. I was pointing my big old .45 right between those golden eyes. We had talked about this. Everybody that knew about Earl's condition knew what to do. We weren't supposed to hesitate, just shoot him. That's what Earl wanted.

I hesitated. The werewolf was squatting on the body, just ripping and eating and tearing. Hood was sprayed all over as sure as somebody had stuffed a grenade in him. Blood and snot was just pouring off Earl's teeth and dripping all over Hood's face. The kid's eyes were open. His neck was gone and blood was all over the ground. Earl looked right at me, then took a slow step off the body, coming closer. Then he took another step. And another.

I had killed more werewolves than any other Hunter ever. I thumb-cocked the hammer. *Kill him!*

But I didn't. For the first time in my life, I didn't have the guts to do what needed to be done. I had known Earl for thirty years, met him clear back when I had been a pretty young thing. I had loved him once, but I had kept on getting older while he had stayed the same, and that kind of thing could never work right. He'd known that. He'd convinced me, a silly girl with a crush, of that. But I just couldn't shoot Earl.

"Earl, it's me. Dorcas. You listen up. You stop right there."

Another step.

"Don't make me kill you. Listen to me. Stop—"

Those eyes were glued to me. He moved so fast . . .

Earl hit me in the chest. I was flying through the

air, then I landed on my face. A big old claw landed on my foot and pulled me back to him, filling my mouth with dirt. Then he flipped me over. My gun came up for shooting, but he knocked it out of my hand. One claw slammed my thigh to the ground while the other one lifted my foot right straight up. My knee broke and I hollered.

It came right off. My leg tore right off! He just pulled so hard in both directions at one time that the muscle just ripped apart. It hurt so bad, Christ Almighty, it hurt bad. I must have passed out for a second, because next thing I knew, I was crawling, squirting blood all over, and Earl was back there, squatting, holding my leg in his hands and eating it. The son of a bitch was eating *my* leg, just chewing away. *Where'd my gun go?*

Then he tossed my leg over his shoulder and came at me on all fours. This time I knew he was gonna eat my guts and for the first time in forever, I was scared, damn scared, piss your pants, know you're gonna die scared. He stopped, and those yellow eyes got all scrunched up, and then I heard the gunshots. Earl turned to see who was shooting him, but a big old chunk of meat flew out of his chest, and he went down. *Silver bullet.*

"Dorcas! Are you okay? How'd Earl get out? Oh shit! Your *leg!*"

It was Dwayne Myers. I tried to tell him what happened, but my head hurt too bad and the words wouldn't come out. I had this damn ringing in my ears and I felt real cold.

Somebody else grabbed hold of me and I felt something hard twist around my leg. Hunters were here and they were all jabbering now. I wanted them to shut the hell up so I could close my eyes, but I knew that was probably just the blood loss talking. I started to come in and out. Black and then moonlight, stuff happening, all confusing, then back to black. Ray, always so damn brave, grabbed one of Earl's hairy arms and dragged him back inside the slave quarters, then came back out and slammed the door shut. Black. Dwayne was crying now, holding what was left of Hood in his arms and rocking back and forth. Dwayne was all covered in blood.

I finally managed to say something, but I wasn't sure who I was talking to. "Don't kill Earl. It ain't his fault."

Black.

*Black.*

I opened my eyes. I was myself again, Owen Zastava Pitt. This magic stuff was one bad trip. I had just lived for a moment as a middle-aged woman, and experienced having my leg torn clean off by a vicious beast. My knee hurt with a phantom pain from over twenty years ago. Glancing around, conference room, same people, Dorcas was talking, but it was just a background buzz. I had just *lived* the story as she'd brought the memory up. I closed my eyes, and all I could see was a much younger Agent Myers, kneeling, with half of a torso in his lap, exposed ribs in mangled flesh, and a flopping, nearly decapitated head cradled in his arms, his white shirt soaked red, as he cursed Earl Harbinger to hell.

The other Hunters were enthralled as Dorcas told her story. Gradually the humming in my ears tapered off, and the black flashes inside my eyes died down. I could hear words again.

"So that damn fool, Hood, lifted the bar, and Earl flew out and tore him apart. I went for my gun, but Earl came over and ripped my leg off. Then Myers came out and shot Earl a couple of times with silver bullets."

"I never knew..." Julie said. "That's horrible."

"Why didn't you shoot him?" Holly asked.

"He was just too damn fast, and I was sleepy and not paying attention," Dorcas lied.

"No," I said without thinking. "You didn't want to shoot him..." My head was still really clouded.

Dorcas glared at me, eyes like dangerous little pinpricks. "What was that, boy?"

"Nothing, ma'am," I responded quickly.

"Thought so," she snapped. "If you're ever close to him on the full moon, remember, he ain't got no control then. A real Hunter don't hesitate. You put him down. Put him down hard. Got that?"

"Yes, ma'am," all of us responded in unison. Dorcas continued to eye me suspiciously. Maybe she wasn't really lying. Maybe she had told this story enough times that she honestly didn't remember about how as a young woman she had once been so in love with Earl Harbinger that she had almost let him murder her decades later.

Either way...none of my business.

"Are you positive that it really was him?" Holly demanded.

"Yeah, I'm positive. Everybody was positive. Earl near tore his head off. That's hard to fake. Now where the hell's my coffee?"

"Sorry..." Holly murmured and returned to the coffeepot.

"That doesn't make any sense," Trip said contemplatively. "Did he say anything?"

"The whole thing was kind of fuzzy," Dorcas answered. She had undergone an intense trauma, so that was understandable. "He said he couldn't stop. Like he had no choice, like he had to open that door. It don't make no sense to me, but that's what he said."

"Why'd he do it? Did you guys investigate?" I asked.

Milo chimed in. "Of course. But we never found anything. He was totally normal one minute, then he did something monumentally stupid. It was like he was trying to kill himself, but he never gave any indication beforehand. His teammates were more surprised than anybody. Hood wasn't the suicidal type."

"He was on Carlos' team. Is he still around?"

"How'd you know that?" Dorcas asked. She had been suspicious before, and that had just confirmed it.

"Don't matter," I replied quickly, and I could tell she didn't like that one bit. Well, I didn't like being telepathic either, so too damn bad. There wasn't time to be polite. "Can we talk to this Carlos? Maybe a Hunter from that team will know something about this shadow man."

Dorcas shook her head. "Carlos Alhambra's team was lost." She thought about it for a moment. "Probably about three years after Hood got eaten. Like '89, I figure."

"A year before my mom disappeared," Julie added.

"How do you *lose* a team of Hunters?" Holly asked slowly.

Dorcas made a motion with her hands like a magician doing a trick. "*Poof*. Just gone. They were working a case and they just never came back. Five good men missing."

"Carlos was the only survivor," Julie said. "I remember because I was young and it terrified me. All I could think was that could have been one of my parents lost like that. They found him wandering through the forest weeks later, dazed, half-dead from exposure, his mind totally gone. No sign was ever found of his team."

"I've heard that story before somewhere," I said.

Julie nodded. "You met him. He's still a patient at Appleton."

"That's right." Dr. Nelson had showed me on the tour. Carlos had been in the wing of the Appleton Asylum reserved for the seriously damaged cases. That wing of the place had haunted me, noises of gibbering madness coming from behind every steel door while the good doctor had lectured me about the dangers a Hunter's mind could be exposed to. "Susan just said that Hood had taken out a team of Hunters and we had never even suspected . . . She said that they had learned too much."

"We've got to go talk to him," Trip said.

"Carlos hasn't said a word to anybody since they found him . . . All he does is sit there and hum children's songs and shit himself. His brain turned to mush. Whatever he saw messed him up something fierce," Dorcas said sadly. "He was a good man."

"Too bad," Holly muttered as she shoved coffee to Dorcas. "If he could talk, he'd probably lead us right to this shadow freak."

*There might be a way.* I glanced at Julie. She must have known exactly what I was thinking, because she shook her head. I didn't need psychic powers to know that she thought it was stupid and dangerous. We had no idea how these weird powers worked or what side effects they might have. All I knew was that anything that came from the other side had to come with a price. And dredging through the memories of a madman was probably not the best idea anyway.

"Don't you even think it," Julie said. "I'm putting my foot down."

"What?" I asked with feigned innocence.

"Huh?" Trip asked.

"Nothing," Julie responded. "Owen was just thinking of doing something asinine."

"What'd I miss?" Milo asked.

"Nothing. Sleep on it, and we'll see you in the morning." Julie stabbed the button and ended the call. "Dorcas, would you mind going back downstairs and checking on the Newbies? It isn't safe to send them back to the barracks yet, so we'll probably need to think up a story. I'll be down in a minute."

The old lady grumbled as she pulled her leg off the table and strapped it back on. She was the only one here who didn't know about what I was experiencing. Dorcas stood with a wobble, snatched up her Styrofoam cup, and headed for the door.

"Hey, Dorcas," I stopped her. "Thanks for telling us about that."

The old lady gave us a bitter smile. "There's always been too damn many secrets around this place," she said, knowing full well she was getting left out of something. She was on the list of potential spies, though personally I really doubted that. It would be a cold day in hell before I could imagine that woman signing up with a death cult. "Do what you gotta do, kids. I'd do the same if I were you." Then, in a flash of pastel bathrobe and the slam of the door, she was gone.

"Well, now we know why she's MHI's little cup of sunshine," Holly said.

"Like you've got room to talk," Trip responded. "That's you in a few years."

Holly reached over and punched him in the arm. Trip flinched.

This whole thing sucked. Earl had been right from the beginning. The very idea that a fellow Hunter could be betraying us was painful and damaging. I swore to myself that I was going to catch the son of a bitch so we could get back to normal. But first things first... Julie didn't waste any time. She turned to me. "You can't try to read Carlos' mind. That's suicide."

"You got a better idea?"

She paused, rubbing her neck. "Not really. But you don't know what you're doing. Do you honestly think you can control it?"

"Sure I can," I said with false confidence. "Compared to time travel, it'll be a walk in the park.

Holly laughed. "Then you're an idiot. You just had an episode when Dorcas was talking, didn't you? You got all glassy eyed and stupid for a second. I thought you were going to drool on the table."

"Again?" Julie asked with alarm. "How many more times has this happened?"

"Just a couple little ones," I lied.

"I don't like it, man. You're messing with things you don't understand," Trip said. "There's got to be another way. We've got his name."

"The Feds have more resources," Holly added. "They can probably find him better than we can. Like with secret databases and the Patriot Act or something."

"Do you really think the Patriot Act has a clause

for necromancers?" I asked pointedly.

"You know what I mean. We should tell Franks, and let them handle it. It's not like we're getting paid for this."

Julie agreed with Holly. "They're right. It's too dangerous."

I didn't say anything, but my friends knew me far too well, surely understanding that I'd had enough. They continued to come up with reasons why I should just stay safe. But I was tired of waiting. *Screw it.* I stood, placed my palms on the table, and raised my voice. "These assholes have tried to kill me and my entire family. As long as they're out there, everybody I love is in danger, and that includes you guys. Sitting around powerless is pissing me off. You want to sic the Feds on him, fine, whatever, but this is my fight. This is personal. So now it looks like my enemy is this Hood guy and we've got a lead. Yeah, it's a pretty iffy lead, but it's what we've got. So I'm going to Appleton, and I'm going to find out what those missing Hunters learned, even if I have to rip it right out of his brain."

The others were quiet after my outburst. Finally, Julie broke the silence. She folded her arms and leaned back in her chair. "You're the most stubborn man I've ever known."

"And that's why you love me. Look, I'll just sneak out. Nobody will even know I'm gone. You guys cover for me, tell everyone I'm asleep in my room or something. If the Condition thinks I'm here, then they won't even know to grab me."

"You're not going anywhere alone," Trip said. "I've got your back, Z."

That wasn't a surprise. Trip was probably the single most honestly noble person I had ever known. He typified all that was heroic about Monster Hunters.

"*We've* got your back," Holly added.

"I thought you didn't want to get involved if you weren't getting paid for it?" I asked, knowing that Holly talked a big game about being the hard-ass, but deep down, she was just as loyal as Trip.

"Don't be such a douche bag."

If I told them it was too dangerous, then I suppose that would make me a hypocrite. Trying to talk them out of it would be as futile as them trying to talk me down. So I said what I could. "Thanks. You guys up for a field trip to the insane asylum?"

After changing into street clothes, concealing some guns, and grabbing our gear bags for a worst-case scenario, Trip, Holly, and I snuck down the back stairs. In theory, if nobody saw us leave, then we wouldn't have to worry about the spy. Unfortunately for Julie, with Earl currently indisposed, she was in charge, and in a couple of hours most of the MHI team leads from around the country would be arriving to sort through and pick out their favorite Newbies, so she was stuck here being managerial. For the rest of us, our absences wouldn't be missed, but no Julie would be glaringly obvious. She didn't like it much either.

There was no sign of Franks or the other Feds. There was no way that he would let me go, short of me beating him unconscious, and from I'd seen, I didn't even know if that was possible. The front area was still packed with Newbies. Some had found spots to go back to sleep, but most of them were still milling around because of the excitement and the fact that they were still guessing about why they had been rousted out of the barracks. Julie was just going to have to deal with that problem.

I made eye contact with Grant as we were leaving. He'd been on Harbinger's team and knew the drill. He went back to feeding some line of bull to the Newbies. The three of us just kept walking. He was still a jackass, but it was nice having another experienced man on hand.

We gathered by the back door. The coast was clear. The plan was to discreetly grab a car from the lot and head for Appleton. It wasn't that far a drive, and we should be able to get there before sunrise. Hopefully Earl was still chasing vampires, so we wouldn't run into him. Julie was supposed to be covering for us right now and taking care of whoever was manning the security room. With luck, the Condition would never even know I was gone.

*I hoped.*

"You ready?" I asked, heavy bag shouldered, hand on the latch.

"Let's get out of here," Holly said. Trip gave me a thumbs-up. I patted my pocket to make sure I had the car keys. *Still there.* Good to go. A hundred yards to the car, and we were gone. I shoved open the heavy door and stepped into the night, only to immediately come to an abrupt stop. "Aw hell . . ."

Agent Franks was sitting on the concrete steps directly in front of the back exit. His face was emotionless behind his sunglasses as he fiddled with his fancy PDA. His gloved thumbs moved across the keypad. He was a surprisingly fast texter for a man with such large digits. "You think I'm stupid?" he asked, not bothering to look up.

"Is that a rhetorical question?" Holly responded.

"What are you doing out here, Franks?" I growled. I didn't have time for this nonsense.

"Checking my e-mail," he said. He finished what he was doing, closed the device and dropped it into a suit pocket. Now he turned his head slightly to study me. I could see my reflection in his shades. I had no idea why he was wearing them in the dark. It took him an infuriatingly long time to phrase his next question. "Going somewhere?"

"No," I answered, giant canvas bag large enough to hide a dead body slung over my shoulder, proving me an obvious liar. This was really making me angry. I was tired of this oppressive jerk getting in my way, because regardless of whatever the hell he really was, man or monster, Franks was above all a pain in my ass. "Didn't you hear there's a werewolf out? There's safer places for you to hang out while you download porn."

"You probably shouldn't do that on a government computer anyway," Trip pointed out. "That's a misuse of taxpayer funds."

Holly's voice was flat. "Naw, I'm cool with it. The more time federal agents spend masturbating, the less time they have to screw around with us."

The muscular Fed slowly stood, drawing himself to his full height, nonchalantly dusted his pants off, and then got right up in my face. He was remarkably intimidating, but I didn't blink. A giant vein pulsed in his forehead. "Where are you going?"

I'd had enough of this clown. If he wanted to throw down, now was as good a time as any, and I wasn't going to go out as easy as the last time we had tangled. I dropped my gear bag on the concrete at Franks' feet. "Wherever I damn well feel like."

"Is that so?" Franks responded slowly.

Always the peacemaker, Trip stepped forward. "Listen, Agent Franks, we've got a tip about the Condition. This is our chance to find out what's going on. Let us go take care of business. Anything we learn helps your mission just as much as it does ours." Leave it to Trip Jones to resort to reason when I was all ready to get my violence on.

"A tip?"

"The kind that only I can access," I responded. The silent jerk wasn't going to let us pass, there was no way. But I would be damned if I was going to be his prisoner in my own home while a gang of psychotic cultists plotted against my family. My pulse quickened. *If I sucker-punched him I'd have a chance . . .* Right in the nose, then push him down the stairs, kick him while he was down, and run for the car. Franks probably wouldn't shoot me since he was tasked with protecting me. *Probably.* "The kind of tip that leads us right to the shadow man."

Franks appeared to think about it, wheels ponderously turning. "You aren't going anywhere—" Decision made, my right hand flew up, fingers tightening into a fist the split second before impact, three hundred pounds of muscle driven by righteous fury and years of mixed martial arts experience, in a brilliant sneak attack maneuver—

*Blocked.*

Not just blocked, but somehow Franks actually raised his hand and caught my fist an inch from his shades. He shut me down so hard that it was like a kindergartener trying to fight back against a fifth-grade bully. He twisted, using my leverage against me, tendons crying in protest, as he bore down on my joints. I squealed like a little girl and went automatically to my knees. His other hand flew under his suit coat and came out with a Glock that he promptly stuck in Holly's face. She stopped doing whatever it was that she was doing, probably reaching for a weapon, and calmly raised her hands.

"Ow ow ow ow..." I said, my elbow touching my forehead and my wrist bent at an impossible angle somewhere behind my neck. The pain was unbelievable. For a second, Franks seemed to ponder what would happen if he just tossed me facefirst down the stairs, but then the pressure let up.

He kept the Glock on Holly, which was probably wise. "As I was saying, you aren't going anywhere..." He let go of my wrist and tingly nerve fire shot down my arm. I fell on my butt. Franks lowered his gun. "...without me."

Trip extended one hand to help me up. "Really?"

I groaned as my friend assisted me off the stairs. *How embarrassing.* Franks had read me like an open book. "You're letting us go?"

He nodded once, keeping one eye on Holly, as if waiting for her to attempt something nefarious. She tried to look innocent. "This better be good," Franks muttered as he turned his back and started down the steps. A werewolf howl reverberated across the compound. "You drive. My truck's in the shop."

# CHAPTER 13

It was a long, hushed drive to Appleton. Trip drove and I rode up front, with Holly and Satan's G-man in the back seat of the MHI Crown Vic. Since the last time I had gone anywhere with Franks I had actually shoved a .45 in his ear, I could understand why he chose to sit directly behind me. The mood was unnaturally somber as Franks' presence had a stifling effect on our normal conversation. I bet he was just a blast at parties.

I had asked him at one point if he was going to contact his superiors or the rest of his protective detail to notify them of our destination. He had responded with a single raised eyebrow, which indicated to me a big negative on that idea. Because not only would he get ordered to turn around, he didn't like his current assignment any more than I did, and the sooner he could wrap this case up, the better. It was kind of frightening that I got that from a single eyebrow, and indicated to me that I was spending way too much quality time around Franks.

"Does anybody have the Nelsons in their address book?" I asked as we neared Camden. The good doctors probably deserved a warning about our visit. The last time I had been here to see a patient, gargoyles had destroyed half the place, smashed a few patients into mush, and given the husband of the Nelson team a heart attack.

Holly responded. "I do. I'll call them."

I had no idea that she even knew them, though it made sense. The Nelsons were former old-school MHI members, one psychologist and one psychiatrist, who specialized in helping the victims of monster violence. Of all of us, Holly Newcastle had experienced the most brutal and unforgiving introduction to the real world of any Hunter I knew, as a captive in a vampire feeding pit. Even after all this time, she had still never confided her whole story to even her closest friends.

I caught Trip glancing at the rearview mirror to sneak a look at Holly. He was probably thinking the exact same thing I was. Was she getting counseling or something? If so, good for her. This stuff was brutally hard on the brain and I would never fault anybody for wanting to talk to a professional about it, especially somebody that actually *got* it, like the Nelsons. "Have you been visiting Appleton?" Trip asked. Even Hunters had days off, and it wasn't like we didn't have personal lives that the rest of the team didn't know about.

"Yeah . . . that offend you?"

"No. Of course not." He quickly snapped his eyes back to the road to avoid Holly's ire. I chuckled to myself.

"What?" Holly asked me suspiciously with her phone against one ear.

"Nothing," I replied quickly. I was saved when somebody picked up on the other end. Apparently the Nelsons, whichever one she had reached at least, were early risers. She warned them that some Hunters were coming on business, but didn't want to give any specifics over the phone. She thanked them and hung up.

Twenty minutes later, we were there.

The front gate of Appleton was new, made up of freshly painted iron bars riding on smooth hydraulics. Julie had driven a van through the old one. Trip braked at the intercom, hit the button, and stated that we were MHI. A moment later we were heading down the lane. The sun was rising over the gothic spires of the asylum, a gray hulking shadow of carved stone and bleak walls. It looked really terrible considering the good work that went on inside. The Appleton Asylum was the home to many survivors of monster attacks, shunned and considered delusional by the rest of the medical community, but welcomed with open arms here. We parked in the nearly empty lot. It was early enough that the day shift employees hadn't yet arrived.

There were new doors installed at the entrance, and it was obvious, since the stonework didn't quite match, that repairs had been conducted here as well. *Stupid gargoyles.* Both of the Nelsons were waiting for us.

Lucius was portly, short, with wispy gray hair in a halo around his mostly bald head, and suspenders keeping his pants up over his belly. Joan was taller than her husband, thin, gangly, and brought to mind a stork or other long-legged bird. Both were in their sixties, and both were wearing absurdly thick glasses. I loved the Nelsons.

We piled out of the car. "Hello, everyone!" Lucius bellowed with a voice that belied his age. It was rare for Hunters to come visit and we were always greeted with some enthusiasm. Apparently, those of us who made it as Hunters tended to find this place, and its residents, kind of unnerving. There was a fine line between a survivor who became a Hunter and a survivor who lost their marbles. "Good morning!." He came down the stairs remarkably fast and intercepted me with a hearty handshake. "Well, Owen, my boy, it's been a long time," he said, which made me feel even guiltier for not visiting.

"Holly, it's wonderful to see you," Joan exclaimed excitedly as she virtually tackled Holly in a hug. "And this young man must be..." She turned to Trip. "Jones. Let's see, James, no, John. It was something biblical."

Trip smiled and extended his hand. "They call me Trip, ma'am." She grabbed his hand and pumped vigorously.

The male Dr. Nelson let go of me and surged toward Trip. "Ah, yes. I've heard about you. Read your file, zombie attack survivor out of Florida. You were the school teacher who was forced to dispatch all his students with a sledgehammer!"

"Pickax," Trip corrected, slightly embarrassed.

"Marvelous! That must have been very distressing..." The Nelsons were looking him over excitedly, just sensing that he had to have all sorts of angst and trauma that they could write a paper on. They couldn't help themselves. They had done that to me the first time I had met them too. "Really, you need to sit down and have a chat with us...time permitting, of course." They simultaneously glanced over as the car door slammed. Franks had gotten out and was adjusting his clip-on tie. Lucius was flummoxed. "It can't be..."

"What's he doing here?" Joan demanded, pointing at the Fed. She raised her voice. "I want him off our property immediately!" Franks approached, scowling. She increased in volume and pitch. "Get him out of here before any patients see him."

"Doctors," Franks stated coldly, "I'm here on official business."

Both Nelsons were clearly agitated at his presence. "Your official business can kiss my old white ass, you simpering feculent, no good, hell-spawn fascist!" Lucius shouted. "You have no business here."

"I see you guys have met..." I said.

"You disgusting pig. You filthy murdering bastard!" Joan shook her fist in the air. "I'm calling security."

"Forget security. I'm getting my rifle," Lucius shouted, turning back into the asylum. "Jackbooted Nazi!"

"We gonna do this the hard way?" Franks asked.

I had no doubt that he wouldn't hesitate to pummel two senior citizens just for kicks. "Whoa!" I shouted loud enough to scare some birds out of a nearby tree. The Nelsons stopped yelling. "Everybody calm down. What's the problem?"

"He's the problem!" Joan shrieked.

"Yes, I caught that part. I already know he's an asshole, but *specifically*."

Lucius was enraged. "Half our patients wouldn't even be here if it wasn't for this man and the others like him. The MCB intimidates witnesses and survivors. They murder anybody who dares spill the beans about their little secret. Monster victims need love, and support, and therapy, so they can return to their lives. But the MCB takes survivors and punishes them instead."

Joan cut in. "The last thing these people need is for their own government to come along and tell them they're insane, that they imagined the whole thing, or if there's any forensic evidence, they cajole the victims into silence. Do you have any idea what kind of damage that does to people?"

"It's like locking up a rape victim because she might make the town look bad!" Lucius sputtered. "It's preposterous. It's absurd!"

"It's policy," Franks answered.

"That didn't work at Nuremburg and it won't work for you," Joan spat. "I may not know everything, Agent Franks, but one thing I do know for certain is that you're going to burn in hell."

Franks nodded, ever so slightly. "Been there. It's overrated."

"Enough," I said. "Lucius, Joan, please. I know this sucks, but we really need your help. I need to speak with somebody in your care. I'm stuck with Franks."

"It's really serious," Holly said apologetically. "We wouldn't ever had brought him if we had realized."

Joan shook her head. "I know you didn't realize what you were doing, because you're far smarter than that, Holly. I have patients inside, patients whose loved ones *this* man has actually murdered. I took an oath not to do any harm. I can't let him inside my facility." She was adamant.

This was getting nowhere, and I had to get to Carlos. "Franks, I need you to stay in the car."

"No."

I knew better than to waste my time arguing with him. Cutting down a redwood tree with my teeth would be more productive, and probably faster. "Doctor, please, we'll go fast. Your patients will never even know we're here."

"He's not coming in here without a warrant," Lucius stated.

"I don't need a warrant," Franks responded.

"Why you rotten—"

"Okay!" Holly jumped in. "How about this? While we're sitting out here making a scene, some of these patients you're worried about are going to come and see what's going on, and they're going to see this scumbag," she jerked her thumb at Franks, "and they're going to freak out. So how about we go someplace else, with no witnesses, and you bring out the one patient we need to speak to? Everybody's happy."

The Nelsons looked at each other, obviously not happy.

"It isn't to help the government," I said. "It's to help me, personally. A Hunter named Martin Hood has returned from the grave. He's already tried to kill my entire family and he will not stop until he gets me too."

That confused them. "Marty?" Lucius said. "Marty Hood? There's no way. He was one of the good ones. He was a great kid. You must be mistaken."

"Well, that's what we need to find out. This might be for nothing, but I have to know the truth. Please help me."

Joan sighed, exchanging glances with her husband. Lucius adjusted his mighty suspenders. They had been married for forty-plus years, and had reached that point where a lot of communication was unspoken. Lucius responded for them both. "Very well, Owen. We'll bring the patient outside. Whom do you need to speak to?"

"Carlos Alhambra."

Joan crossed her arms. "Then I'm afraid you're wasting your time. Carlos hasn't spoken to anyone in decades."

"He'll speak to me."

The spot that the Nelsons picked for our use was a gazebo on the far side of the lawn. None of the patients would be outside this early, and if any patients were at the windows, we would be far enough from the building that they wouldn't get a clear look at us. Franks would be just a random big dude in a bad suit, not the man who personally murdered their fellow survivors who couldn't keep their mouths shut.

A morning mist was rising from the Alabama River. Separating it from us was a wrought iron fence. Most of the patients at Appleton were here voluntarily, but there were a few who weren't, and there were others screwed up enough to decide that the river was a great place to take a header into. Tall trees, draped in Spanish moss, surrounded us. It was actually a very peaceful moment and I took the time to savor it, because what was coming next was probably going to suck.

"So, how have you been?" Lucius Nelson asked.

"Other than the whole death cult thing, pretty good actually." The two of us were sitting on a bench inside the gazebo. Franks was wandering through the trees, probably checking the perimeter. Holly was fifty feet away, throwing rocks over the fence into the river to watch them splash. Joan had left to retrieve Carlos, and Trip had gone with her. "You guys are coming to the wedding, right?"

"Yes, yes, of course. I've known Julie since she was a baby. We wouldn't miss it for the world. We're rather fond of her, you know. And I would probably be dead if it weren't for you."

That was embarrassing and I felt that it was mostly untrue. "I didn't do anything that any Hunter wouldn't have done."

"Exactly," he smiled, then gestured toward Holly. "And how has she been? We haven't seen her in months."

"Holly? Well, as far as I know, she's okay . . . I didn't know she was getting professional help. I know you probably can't talk about it, doctor-patient privilege, and all that, but if there's ever anything that I can do to help her, just let me know. She's my teammate and my friend, and finding out that she's still hurting, still needing help . . . is just terrible," I said truthfully. "Though after what she went through, who could blame her?" I added quickly, not wanting to offend the good doctor over the importance of his counseling.

He laughed. "Getting help? Son, she *is* the help."

"Huh?"

"That young lady is a volunteer on her days off. She comes in and helps out with the patients, visits, listens to them talk, plays Ping-Pong and checkers. She's especially good with the little children. She's wonderful, really brightens everyone's day, and we've been sad that she's been too busy lately, but such is the life of a Hunter. She understands these people, and they love her for it."

"Holly? Really?" That was a new one on me. It sure didn't fit the image that she tried to cultivate. I wondered why she never told us.

"Oh, here they come," Lucius pointed back toward the asylum. Joan was leading the way, and Trip was pushing someone in a wheelchair. "Now don't be disappointed when this doesn't work. If Carlos actually communicates I'll be absolutely shocked. He's been in a total stupor for decades."

"How bad is it?"

Lucius shook his head. "In layman's terms, he's checked out, toasted, brain turned off, a borderline vegetable. All he has done for years now is hum simple children's songs. Carlos was one of the smartest, bravest men I've ever known. I was proud to consider him a friend. And then one day, this happened. No medical explanation for it, no brain damage, no serious physical trauma, nothing."

"No idea what caused this?"

"No. He went on a mission, but only his body came back. I don't...I..." He lifted his glasses and wiped under his eyes. "Sorry."

"I understand."

Trip pushed the wheelchair up the ramp and into the gazebo. Carlos was wearing a red bathrobe over a white gown. He was frail, with atrophied muscles, hands so thin that you could see bones through the papery skin, and hair that was buzzed short on his pale skull, probably for ease of maintenance by the staff. His head was lolling slowly from side to side as he stared at his lap. He was humming but I did not recognize the tune.

222

Doctor Joan took a cloth from the back of the chair and wiped the drool from his chin. His blank eyes gave no indication that he was aware of any of this. I got off the bench and squatted in front of the wheelchair.

"Hello, Carlos. My name's Owen Pitt. I'm a Hunter too. We need to talk." No response, obviously. "I need to talk to you about Martin Hood. I believe that he's the one who did this to you and I need your help."

"I don't think he can even hear you, dear," Joan suggested gently. "He's shown zero reaction to stimuli since he's been here. We've run every test you can think of."

I reached out my hand to touch his, but hesitated. I had talked about ripping the memories right out of his head, but now that I was in his presence, I didn't feel so confident in my rightness. It seemed awkward and invasive. This was a man, a fellow Hunter, and I had no clue what I was doing.

"You think this is a good idea?" Trip asked, sensing my hesitation.

"No, not really," I snapped. "You got a better idea?"

He shrugged. "Well, if you're going to do it, do it before Franks comes back." Trip was right. I didn't want the government to know that I had inherited any abilities from the artifact.

"Do what?" Doctor Joan asked, concerned for her patient.

"Owen can read minds," Trip said, then held his finger in front of his lips to indicate that it was a secret.

"Really?" Lucius was fascinated, probably sensing another paper.

"I don't know how it works. It isn't every time I

touch somebody. It seems to be a combination of when they're thinking about a particularly strong memory while I'm also interested in that same memory. I think...I picked this up from the Old Ones somehow."

"Well, scientifically, that sounds like a crock of shit," Joan said.

"But we've seen some weird things," Lucius added. That was the beauty of working with former Hunters—very flexible minds. "Is it dangerous?"

"I have no idea."

"If they need to be remembering, how's that supposed to work with somebody who doesn't think about anything?" Joan asked sensibly.

I didn't really know that either. Maybe if I wanted that memory enough for both of us...

"Franks is coming back," Trip said.

*Aw hell.* I touched Carlos' skeletal hand.

*Well, this is certainly different.*

The world was vast, only there was no world. Just a void. An infinite space of nothingness. The void had no boundaries, no beginning, no end. There was no light, no dark, no color. Infinity stretched on forever.

"Who are you?"

"I'm Owen," I answered. "With MHI. Who are you?"

"I don't remember," the voice was male. "What are you doing here?"

"Where is here?"

"I don't remember that either..." the voice answered, confused. "But I'm not alone. *It* lives here too."

"Carlos, is that you?"

But then that first voice was gone. And something hideous took its place. This voice was different, screeching like bagpipes made out of rotten entrails and filled with broken glass. My mind rebelled against the unnatural force.

THIS IS MY SHELL. FIND YOUR OWN.

"What are you?" I challenged.

No answer.

Talk about weird, but I didn't have time for this. I needed to find information on Hood. Just having that thought seemed to cause the world to change. "I know that name," said the first voice. "I know *Hood*."

Now I could see; there was light, space, dimensions and gravity, as a blurry scene unfolded before me. A group of people, obviously Hunters, though their gear was outdated and their team patch was unfamiliar. There was no sound, but the scene was obviously one of welcome, as the group greeted a new member. The extraneous details of the scene were fuzzy gray blotches. The Hunters' faces were just...*blank*. Pasty blurs of flesh where their features should have been. Only one of the men was clearly visible, the new guy, and the scene focused in on him. He was an overweight young man, with a mop of curly hair, wearing a vest that barely fit over his stomach. His attitude was jovial as he smiled and laughed with the others. The scene slowed, the Hunters' movements became sluggish, until they quit moving entirely.

I had a physical form again. I walked between the frozen Hunters, a three-dimensional snapshot from time. Stopping in front of Hood, I studied him. I recognized him from Dorcas' memory. He had acne scars and looked nothing like the tough guy who had attacked me. In fact he didn't look like much at all, just a fat, goofy dude about my age.

"I remember this..." said the voice, and this time it came from directly behind me. I turned. One of the Hunters in the scene was speaking. Unlike the others, he still had details. His armor was olive drab, criss-crossed with leather bandoleers of shotgun shells. He was fit, strong, with a skinny beard and a thick head of dark hair just peppered with gray. Hispanic, probably about forty, he was a handsome man, but his eyes were sunken, haunted. I could only barely recognize him as the fragile person who I had met in the real world. "I remember this. It hasn't taken them all away."

"What hasn't taken them?"

"Feeder," he answered, as if that were obvious. "Are you here to help me?"

"Yes," I answered, not having any clue how I was supposed to do that. "Where is this Feeder?" Carlos held one finger up and placed it against his temple. I nodded.

"Don't worry. It'll come for us soon. Whenever I remember something, it comes and eats it. I have almost nothing left."

"It *eats* your memories?"

"More like it consumes, partially digests, and then pukes them back in pieces all over my brain. I've only saved a few. I've forced myself not to think about them, but I know they're there. When I remember something, it's gone forever. All the happy ones are gone." He held up his left hand, indicating a wedding ring. "I was married, I think, but I don't remember her. He destroyed those early, since they were the first ones I thought of when I was trapped. Once those were gone, then he took the regular ones. I couldn't fight him. He's too strong. He's always hungry."

I could only listen, horrified, wondering if my own were in danger while I was here.

Carlos stepped between the frozen bits of memory. His whole body was trembling. "I don't remember any of my life. I know what things are, and what words mean. I guess he can eat the meat, but not the bones. I don't remember ever experiencing anything. I know what food is, but I don't know how it tastes, you know what I mean? I've got almost nothing."

"How'd you save this one?"

"Oh, he let me keep the bad ones, the ones to taunt me, to laugh at my failure. Everything else I've ever experienced is all twisted and broken, but not these. I can relive the mistakes leading up to the end of my life whenever I want. In fact, that's the only thing that I can do. This thing living in my head is a malevolent motherfucker, that's for sure. If I could take any joy out of the ones he's left me, then I'm sure they'd be consumed along with all the rest."

"Once he takes everything, what'll happen to you?"

"Maybe then he'd just let me die. . . ." he said wistfully.

This poor man's mind was being devoured, but the thing doing it was leaving the memories about this one particular Hunter for a reason. "Martin Hood did this to you, didn't he?"

He walked past me, through the crowd of distorted figures, and stopped, staring into the frozen eyes of young Mr. Hood. "Will you help me?"

"What can I do?" I asked.

"I'll show you these scraps, these things that Feeder's left to toy with me. In exchange, I want two things. I won't help you until you swear you'll help me."

"Name them." I expected for him to ask me to free him, to destroy this demon in his head, but not what came next.

"Kill me."

I was shocked. That's not why I was here. I couldn't do that. I started to respond, but choked. The frozen Hunters surrounded me, their faces scratched out of existence like a pencil drawing brutally scrubbed with an eraser until the paper tore. All happiness had been blotted from this man's existence, his body was nearly a lifeless husk... No. I understood the request.

I nodded. "And the second?"

He glared at the jolly, fat Hunter so long that I started to think I was another forgotten memory.

"Avenge me."

This was different than the other times that I had lived through others' memories. This time I didn't see through his eyes or feel with his senses, because those were long since muted and passed. Carlos no longer knew what it was like to experience such things.

Rather it was like I was a bystander as a partial scene unfolded in front of me. Details were few, sounds were painful and flat. The colors had bled into grays and shadows as even simple things like that had been stolen from him. What a horrible way to exist and this was all that he'd had since 1989. I was watching the welcoming of the new Hunter. Hood smiled and laughed as Carlos' team greeted him, slapped him on the shoulder, and shook his hand. The only two who had faces were my host and his future nemesis.

"He came highly recommended. A good friend of mine said that he was talented, that he would be an asset to our team," Carlos spoke to me, even as he shook phantom hands with Hood. "My friend was a man named Harbinger."

"I know him," I said.

Carlos shook his head. "I don't. I only remember what little bit is connected to these few things. That's all. But I *hate* him for bringing this monster into my life. Feeder let me keep my hate. It makes him warm."

Then we were in an unknown place, an intersection of two streets. A team of Hunters had taken up position around a few cars and were firing into a crowd of shambling zombies. There were hundreds of undead. It was a huge outbreak. Carlos and I walked between the flying bullets and the crowd of rotting undead. He gestured to where his mirror image was leaning over the hood of a car and blasting round after round of buckshot into the approaching mass. "Business was really good. I didn't realize at first that it was a little too good."

A zombie made it over the hood of the first car and Hood took it apart in a spray of machine-gun fire. "It had been kind of slow. We didn't really have much to do, and my team was getting the least business of any team in the country. Just bad luck I suppose. But then, within a few weeks of Hood's arrival, we were getting undead outbreaks constantly. Suddenly my team was raking in the dough. We were the stars of the company."

A zombie hit Memory Carlos from behind, taking him hard to the pavement. The nearby faceless Hunters were in no position to help and it looked like certain death. But the zombie froze, an inch from taking a bite out of Carlos' neck. It stayed there for a moment until Carlos could roll over, draw his .45 and put a round into the creature's brain. The splattered team leader caught a brief glance of Hood, hand extended, two fingers pointing at the frozen zombie. Hood went back to the action as if nothing had happened.

My host shook his head sadly. "That was my first clue, but in the excitement, I missed it. It went on. Every time we had nothing going on, more undead would pop up somewhere in our region. I was thinking that we had some hardcore necromancer living in the neighborhood, but he was always one step ahead of us. I was too stupid to realize that I saw him every day."

More scenes flashed by. Several months had passed since these Hunters had started working together. "By that time, I was a wealthy man, not that I can remember what I did with it. He's let me remember that I was like a damn superhero to the other Hunters, just to rub it in. Really, I was just a chump. Hood came across as a nice kid, a real joker, a bookworm, an intellectual, and a dork. Everybody loved him. It was a lie, an act. We didn't realize what he was fixated on." There was a vision of the two men, sitting on a bench on an ocean pier, drinking and telling stories, unwinding after a long day at work. "It turned out that Hood's parents were killed when he was just a boy. They were occultists, and had been messing around with the Old Ones back in England. He confided this to me one night. That's why he became a Hunter. He wanted to fight those things. He was obsessed with them."

"Why'd he tell you?"

My host laughed. "You'll see . . ."

Hood took a long draw from a cigarette before

flicking the butt into the ocean. "See, boss, that's what got me thinking..." It was obvious that he'd had too much to drink. "There's a lot of information about the Elder Things floating around. Why not, and this is just a hypothetical, use their own weapons against them? Harnessing magic is no different than harnessing electricity."

Carlos openly scoffed. "That's insane."

"No. Hear me out, mate. You're a smart chap. It's like the war, the big one. My grandmother lived through the Battle of Britain and she told me what those V rockets sounded like when they flew over. Pure terror. Evil stuff, right? But as soon as the war was over, bam, the Allies grabbed up every German scientist they could, right? That's how we put a man on the moon."

Carlos took a long drink. "I suppose."

"This is the same thing. Just because knowledge originates from a bad use, doesn't make it bad. It's still knowledge. We owe it to ourselves to study the Old Ones, not just shun them. Think of what we could do." Hood grew somber. "Imagine if a group of us, people like me and you, who knew what was really out there, worked together and harnessed that power...We could banish death itself!"

"That's not how it works. Anything those things touch is tainted. Stay away from it, Marty." The Carlos of memory tossed his now-empty bottle out into the waves and stood to leave. "You're drunk and talking stupid. I'll call you a cab. Go home and get some rest, man."

"I thought maybe you would understand..." Hood muttered to himself as Carlos walked away.

Carlos continued his narration as the pier dissolved. "I figured it out eventually. Hood had found something in the archives back at headquarters. Some old book, picked up from who knows where." The next scene was in a room filled with many shelves, lined with row after row of books. At first I thought we'd come to a library, but then I realized that it was a small apartment, literally packed with books. The titles on the spines were all blurry and forgotten. Hood was sitting at a table, giant tome open before him, a single small bulb providing light enough to read by. The book must have been etched into Carlos' memory, because it was crystal clear. A massive, leather-bound thing, the pages ancient and covered in symbols and geometries that suggested madness in whoever inked it in blood millennia before.

"Hey, Marty. Nobody's been able to get ahold of you. I was getting worried so I had your landlord let me in. Are you okay?" Carlos called as he entered the room, only to jerk to a halt when he saw the open book. "Is that— What are you doing with that thing?"

"Learning . . ." Hood mumbled as if he was in a trance, not looking up as he traced his hands over the words. The crazed scribbling seemed to move. There was a drawing of the monstrous alien tree, branches like twitching cricket legs. A black smear had been rubbed onto the page above it, like a cloud rising from the tree.

"Damn it!" Carlos shouted as he shoved the book off the table and onto the floor. The pieces had finally clicked into place for him. The book landed with a *thump*, open to a page with a picture of a giant squid thing that I knew all too well. He reached across the table and grabbed Hood by the shirt and jerked him forward. "It's you! You're behind these outbreaks, aren't you? Answer me, you son of a bitch!"

"I don't know what you're talking about," Hood stammered. Then Carlos slugged him in the face, brutally hard. He grabbed the fat kid by his curly hair, yanked him out of his chair and shoved his face down against the open book. Blood dripped onto the pages.

"Liar!" Carlos shouted, enraged.

"All right, all right!" Hood cried. Carlos jerked him up and brutally shoved him back into one of the shelves. Books crashed to the floor. "Let go of me, please," he sobbed.

"It was you all along. I can't believe this!" Carlos released him and stepped away, hurt and disbelief obvious in his voice. "Why? Why'd you do it?"

"I had to! You don't understand what's at stake. We have to learn the mysteries or we're doomed."

"You're doomed all right. How many innocent people have died because of you? You know what the Feds are going to do when they discover you've been raising the dead? You're going to prison for the rest of your life."

Suddenly Hood went from simpering to in command. The change was shocking, like somebody had flipped a switch and another personality stepped forward. "Oh, that's where you're wrong, mate. You won't tell the Feds a word." Blood ran down his nose and dripped down the crease of his double chin but he didn't wipe it away. His eyes burned with the fervor of a true believer and for the first time I saw the man who would become the Shadow Lord. "Because you're going down with me if you do. I'll say that you ordered me to raise those zombies for the PUFF bounties."

"Oh, I am, huh?" Carlos responded as he pulled his pistol from inside his waistband. "We'll see about that."

"You won't shoot me," Hood stated flatly. "If I die, then I've left evidence for the authorities that not only did I create those undead, but that I did it on behalf of not just you, but all of MHI. The government will destroy you all for that. You love this company too much."

"Bastard!" The angry Hunter raised the gun and pushed it into Hood's cheek.

"Do it. I dare you," Hood snapped. "Kill your teammate. Murder your friend. Then explain that to the authorities. Explain that to the others while you try to convince them I wasn't making enough zombies to make you a millionaire."

Carlos hesitated, doubt creasing his features. "Damn!" he shoved the fat kid to the floor and stomped away, trapped. He paced back and forth for a moment. "You idiot. What've you done?"

"I'm fulfilling my destiny. I'm going to stop the Old Ones, once and for all." He finally paused to wipe his nose. "The bounties are funding my research. Animating the dead is letting me hone my skills. This is just the beginning of an epic work. You'll see."

Carlos shoved his pistol back into its holster before grabbing Hood by the neck and dragging him toward the door. "No. You're coming with me. We're going to see Harbinger. He'll know what to do."

We were back in the original void. Darkness in every direction.

"I didn't know what else to do. He was my responsibility and I failed. I turned to the one man who I knew would have the answers. We left that night,

me, Hood, and that infernal book, and caught the
first flight. I remember that he came along willingly,
telling me the whole time about how he was right
and how he would persuade Harbinger to see. I think
he wanted me to dwell on his argument...When we
arrived, there were a bunch of Hunters there, and
unfortunately, it was the full moon. I had been too
preoccupied to even realize that, so we weren't able
to speak to him."

*The night Hood died,* I thought to myself.

"Exactly," he answered. There was a terrible, rending
sonic wail. It came from the distant void. "Feeder's
coming. I have to finish this."

We were standing on the edge of a circle of chaos.
The little stone shack, the old slave quarters of the
Shackleford family estate, was before us. Hunters were
milling around. There was blood everywhere, stark red
against the black and white of the rest of the world.
Hood's dismembered body was at the entrance. A
faceless Hunter was holding the body, trying in vain
to help. I knew that the erased man was Myers. Other
unknowns attended to a second injured person. A leg,
severed at the knee, lay half chewed off to the side.

"He committed suicide."

"So I thought. Nobody but me knew about Hood's
crimes. I felt terrible. I blamed myself for his death
and the whole situation. I had failed."

I walked through the carnage. Hood was obviously
dead, literally torn apart. There was now a struggle, a
fight, between Myers and someone else who could only
have been Ray Shackleford. The words were erased,
but I knew that Myers wanted nothing more than to
avenge his friend's death. "You never told the others."

"No. I didn't. I thought that Hood had killed himself out of guilt. Everyone loved him. What good would tarnishing his memory serve? Plus, I was afraid . . . somehow I could have done something different, somehow it was my fault. No, it was my secret to bear. No evidence ever arose after his death, so Hood must have been bluffing about that, so I just left it alone. I hid his stupid book."

"You didn't destroy it?"

"I couldn't. It wouldn't burn. I should have tried harder."

Suddenly, something rose over the Shackleford ancestral home, above the slave quarters, a shadow as big as the house, only shaped like an earwig. The sonic wail tripled in intensity as the shadow of pincers covered the full moon.

FOOD. The scream slammed through my skull.

"Holy shit!"

"Feeder's here," Carlos said nonchalantly. "Good. I won't miss this one anyway. Come on, I've got one more. Three years later."

A new place, a large older house in a pine forest, on the top of a hill. A team of Hunters were moving quickly through the darkened trees, weapons hot. They were sweaty, panting, a few of them had sustained injuries. This memory was the clearest of all. The others even had faces.

Carlos must be reading my mind. "Yeah, Feeder hasn't touched this one. This is the worst of all. I couldn't tell you who any of these people are, but it likes to let me watch them die, again and again."

"I'm sorry," I said.

"Don't be. This is now the only memory I have

left of my entire life. Well, there's actually one other. I can remember *mi madre* singing nursery songs to me when I was little. I think that's the oldest one I've got. For some reason, Feeder has left that one alone. I think he likes the music . . . Please, don't forget your promise."

"I won't."

"Good," he said. "Watch."

There were six of them. They were coming up on the house in three pairs, moving fast. They stopped in the trees just outside the yard. I focused in on their leader as he tried his radio, frustration was plain on Carlos' face. "We lost radio contact as soon as we arrived. Then we were cut off, surrounded, driven through the forest by undead. It wasn't until later that I realized we'd been herded to this place. He wanted it that way. He wanted us on our own at the end. He knew our methods, our procedures, he knew exactly what we'd do."

The Hunters hit the house. One pair on the back door, one on the front, the final held the perimeter. The teams cleared the Victorian-style house, finding it empty, boarded-up, furniture sitting under tarps, covered in dust. The first pair discovered the stairs to the basement.

"He lured us in. We were surrounded, no comms. The case was supposed to have been straightforward, basic monsters on the property, not that I can remember what they were supposed to be at this point, or where this even is, but we sure weren't prepared for what we found."

The basement was utterly normal, except for one concrete wall where the foundation had been chipped

away to reveal a hole. The ancient tunnel wound down
into the earth. The Hunters prepared to check it out.

"No escape, so I decided to try the tunnel. It
might have led to a way out, or it might have led to
whatever was controlling the monsters attacking us.
I was such a fool. I let my ego cloud my judgment.
I remember that I only made three big mistakes in
my career. First was ever trusting Hood. Keeping his
secret was number two. Going down that hole was
my last."

Time passed as the Hunters went steadily downward, their unease growing at each step, noise of the
undead trailing behind them a constant companion.
They set ambushes, slowed their pursuers, but there
were always more. At the end, the tunnel opened
into a large, artificial room. Creatures—impossible
creations of mismatched body parts from various
animals, armor-plated monstrosities—rose up around
them and cut through the Hunters with ease. They
put up an amazing fight but were finally overrun. The
memory was allowed to linger on the final suffering
of each individual, chopped to bits at the ends of
meat-cleaver arms or lacerated by serrated-steel teeth.

Carlos awoke a short while later, bound to a table
with leather straps, someone calling his name. I recognized who was speaking immediately. The shadow
man's appearance in the memory was the same as in
the present. He hadn't even aged. This time he was
wearing a white rubber butcher's apron, splattered
with blood. He smiled broadly at Carlos.

"Hey, mate. How have you been?"

"Where are my men?"

"Recruited into my army." The necromancer paused

to pull a sheet off of another operating table. Carlos screamed when he saw the bodies of two of his team in the process of being stitched back together into something else. The Hunter thrashed against his bonds in vain. "I'm improving on God's creation."

Carlos continued to struggle, insane at the sight of his friends. "I'll kill you! I'll kill you! You son of a bitch! I'll kill you!"

"Please . . . You didn't have the stomach to do it before and that's what brings us here today, I'm afraid. It pains me to do this, but I gave you an opportunity to see my side of things, only you wouldn't listen. You had to be self-righteous and stubborn. So now, the time has come for you to pay for your mistakes. But take comfort, your sacrifice will not have been in vain."

"Who are you?" Carlos demanded, still straining to free himself, wanting nothing more than to rip the man before him limb from limb with his bare hands.

"Come on, Carlos." The shadow man shook his head. "Do I really look that different now? The old body was so soft . . . It was a liability. When you forced my hand, I had to go with one of my contingency plans. The spell had already been prepared, but it was something that I had lacked the courage to implement on my own. There are many things that can go wrong when you swap bodies. Really, I should thank you. I found a way to trade up to something better, switch places if you will. I took this body from a poor addled nitwit, an easily manipulated man-child. I moved in and the poor sod got my old body. Lucky for him, he only had to put up with it for a few minutes before Earl ate him!"

"M-M-Marty?"

Hood pointed at his chest with both hands and

smiled. "In the *flesh*! And the ladies love this body a lot more than the old one, I'll tell you that."

Painful realization hit. "But . . . but you're dead!"

"See?" Hood laughed. "I've conquered death, just like I told you I would, all those years ago. You shouldn't have mocked me . . . Nobody should have mocked me."

Carlos screamed. It was pure, primal hate. It went on for a long time as he struggled, futilely trying to break his bonds. Finally, rationality returned. "Marty, you worthless sack of shit, those were your friends." He jerked his head painfully toward the other table. "We were your family!"

Hood spread his arms wide. For the first time Carlos noticed the rotting things standing in neat rows behind his captor. The creatures had been spliced together, bones screwed to steel plates, bolts and wires criss-crossed, ivory, muscle, and iron conglomerated into a grotesque parody of life. "This is my family now."

Rage turned to fear. "You're insane!"

"That's a matter of perspective. I'm rather sure that I'm the only sane one here. See, things have changed. I was naïve. I thought I could beat the Old Ones at their own game. But I realized the truth. They *can't* lose. So I cut a deal to benefit us all. And now you're going to help *me* help *them*."

Carlos' eyes flicked back and forth across the line of slavering monstrosities. "What do you want from me?"

Hood chuckled. "After I 'died,' " he made quote marks with his fingers, "you kept something of mine. I need my book back. It holds information that will allow me to open a portal to the other side."

"You can't do that!"

"Actually, you're correct. Very few people have the

potential to unlock that kind of mystery. Sadly, I'm not one of them. I'm going to arrange for it to fall into the hands of someone who can. He's not even aware that he's helping me yet. He needs to be broken first, but I've already arranged for that."

*Devious bastard*... It all made sense. Hood was behind what had happened at the Christmas party. He was responsible for Susan's turning. He'd tricked Ray into opening that rift.

Hood leaned in close, stopping his face inches from his old leader. Carlos remembered it so clearly that he could smell Hood's aftershave. "So, where did you hide my book?" he whispered.

Carlos spit in his face. "I'll never tell you anything!"

The shadow man nodded slightly, not noticing the saliva in his eyes. "And I wouldn't have expected anything less from you. So once again, we'll do this the hard way."

"You going to torture me, *pendejo*?" Carlos demanded in typical MHI style defiance. "Bring it!"

"You wish. Torture would be easy. See, working for the Old Ones does grant you a few perks, a few abilities, if you will. They've sent some friends to... how should I say...*live* with me. Sure, I could torture you, knives, hot pokers, electric shocks, all that nonsense, but that would take time, and I don't have the stomach for such things." He gestured at the operating table full of mismatched body parts. "I'm a creator, not a destroyer. Rather, I'm going to send something to root around inside your brain and take what I need. So to answer your question, no torture. This is going to be much, much worse."

"What are you talking about?"

"Good-bye, Carlos. I learned so much from you, and really enjoyed our times together. You were one of my best friends. It really was a pleasure." His neck swelled as something crawled up from inside his torso. Hood opened his mouth. It was like staring down a deep well. Two tiny red eyes opened and blinked in the inky blackness. Miniscule pincers extended past Hood's lips. Carlos began to scream.

The tiny creature latched onto the Hunter's face, soft, black ooze crawling into his eyes, up his nose, down his throat. The screaming turned into choking and convulsing. I had to look away.

The scene went black. We were back in the void.

"It was a little thing at first. Like a headache. But it grew, and grew, and grew. The more it ate, the fatter it got. Everything I thought of, destroyed, torn apart. Just bits and pieces of me. It found what it was looking for, but it didn't stop there. No...it's just been taking ever since."

I had narrowly avoided the same fate in Mexico. I shuddered. The bagpipe howl arose as the mind demon approached.

"You better go now. Please, keep your promise. I'm begging you. Finish this."

Feeder surrounded us, a bloated, disgusting thing. Slobbering, chewing, tearing and flinging, as the last few visions of a mortal life were rendered into nothing.

"And this is the way the world ends...." my host said.

Back in the real world, I gasped and jerked my hand away from the wheelchair. Carlos' head was still rolling around weakly from side to side as a puddle of drool collected on his robe. He was humming softly.

"What happened?" Lucius Nelson demanded, concerned for his patient.

Glancing around, the doctors and Trip were still in the same spots in the gazebo as when I had left. Franks was approaching up the path at a brisk walk.

"How long was I gone?" I asked.

"You didn't go anywhere," Joan replied.

"Five seconds, tops," Trip answered quickly. "Did it work?"

"Yeah, kind of." I stood. "Doctors, we have to let Carlos die."

"What?" both of them responded simultaneously.

"Please, believe me. There's something terrible living inside his head. It's devouring him, piece by piece. He made me promise to kill him."

"Owen, that's ridiculous."

The wheelchair began to vibrate. I looked down. Carlos was going into some sort of seizure. It stopped. He was no longer humming. That too had been taken from him. His final memory was erased. The shaking ceased.

Joan knelt beside the chair and placed her fingers on Carlos' neck. "I think he's dead."

Suddenly the patient's head snapped up. His eyes opened, revealing blood red orbs. One thin hand locked around Joan's wrist with bone-crushing force. He jerked her to her knees.

My STI came out of the holster so fast that it practically materialized in my hand. I clicked the safety off as the front sight landed between those red eyes. "Let her go!"

"Noooo," the thing inhabiting Carlos' body hissed. Joan cried out as it squeezed her arm. "Feast is over. . . . Need new shell to live in."

"What's going on?" Lucius cried out. "Carlos, let her go. We've been trying to help you."

"That ain't him, Doc. This thing is from the other side. Isn't that right, Feeder?"

The body wheezed. "Not true name. Name given by weak fleshling." The voice was raspy, not used to creating speech. "So hungry. Must feed." His other hand reached toward Joan's face, as if to caress it. Nostrils flared as it drank in her smell. "So many memories in this one...to feeeaaassst."

His wife in danger, Lucius Nelson's reaction was a split second faster than mine. Carlos' head jerked one way and then back as our bullets crossed an X through his skull. Joan fell. I stepped forward and booted the frail body in the chest, sending the wheelchair rolling back down the ramp and into the sunlight. The chair toppled over.

Even with the back of his skull missing, the animated body tried to rise, atrophied muscles driving forward, in search of another host. The movements were jerky, awkward, painful to watch. "Feeeaaassst..."

Trip had drawn his Springfield XD .45. Doctor Lucius stood at my side, stubby Colt Officer's model at the ready. The three of us looked at each other, knowing what had to be done, then we opened fire. Dozens of bullets tore through Carlos. A few seconds later, our slides were locked back empty, my ears were ringing, and the riddled body was absolutely still, blood pouring into the grass.

"What the hell!" Holly shouted as she ran toward the gazebo. She paused long enough to pull her STI Ranger and train it on the blood-soaked mess on the lawn like the rest of us. "Everybody okay?"

"We're fine," Joan answered calmly. "I think my wrist is broken though." The birdlike woman had pulled herself onto a bench. From somewhere she had produced a .380 PPK and was holding it shakily in her left hand, her right resting awkwardly in her lap. She saw me looking at her. "Old-school MHI, kids. Shock is nature's anesthetic. Give me five minutes and I'll be crying like a baby."

I dropped my spent mag, slammed a new one in the gun, and dropped the slide. "See to your wife," I ordered Lucius. "Trip, Holly, on me." I approached Carlos' body slowly. The three of us covered him, pistols ready, but there was no movement.

The Hunter was dead, freed from his torment at last.

Agent Franks nonchalantly joined us a moment later. The big man studied the three of us, guns hovering over the ventilated corpse and his wheelchair. He shrugged, removed a candy from his pocket, unwrapped it, tossed it in his mouth, and threw the wrapper on the lawn. "Brutal...even by my standards," he said, chewing loudly as he walked away.

"What's that?" Trip asked, gesturing with his gun. "On the sidewalk?"

A tiny, black, glistening, earwig-slug thing was oozing away from the shattered skull. I moved so that my shadow wasn't protecting it. The tiny beast rolled over, revealing a pair of red eyes and a mouth with hooked teeth. It screeched in pain when the sunlight hit it.

I raised my size 15 boot. "Good-bye, Feeder." It smashed with a sickening wet pop. I ground it in. Black smoke hissed from the pavement.

First promise kept.

❖　　　❖　　　❖

"You know, you're no longer allowed to visit here, Owen," Lucius advised me. We were in the Appleton parking lot, getting ready to leave. "Every time you do, we lose patients. At this rate you'll put us out of business in no time."

"I'm really sorry...."

"I'm seriously thinking of having a restraining order drawn up," the doctor said with grave sternness. I suddenly felt like I was going to puke. He thumped me on the arm. "Ha. I'm just kidding, boy. Relax. It comes with the business."

Joan shook her head. "Forgive my husband. His idea of humor's a little skewed." Her sprained wrist had already been wrapped. She held it up. "But then again, I just took some Lortabs, so everything seems a little funny."

"Seriously, I wish we would have known about poor Carlos sooner. We kept him alive for all these years, when all we were doing was prolonging his suffering."

"You did the best you could," I responded. "There's no way you could have known."

"No medical textbook I know of has an entry for what crawled out of his head, I'm afraid," Lucius answered, "unless we write it ourselves. Maybe now you understand why when it comes to interviewing survivors, Joan and I can be a little..."

"Pushy?" I interjected.

"One way to look at it, I suppose," he chuckled. "Listen, I do want to help you. When Marty Hood first joined MHI, I did one of those *pushy* interviews. Here's the file. Maybe something in there will come in handy."

I took it from him. "Isn't this like privileged information?"

He smiled. "My Hippocratic Oath goes out the window when you sign up to help the Old Ones. I wouldn't piss on him if he was on fire."

Holly joined us. "We're ready to go. We took the body down to the basement like you asked. None of the other patients saw us."

"Good, good..." Joan said. "Thank you, dear."

Lucius smiled sadly. "This place was built eighty years ago to house tuberculosis patients. We have an excellent crematorium. Morbid, yet so very effective. Necessary, given the things that poor man was exposed to. Don't worry, we'll say a few words over him."

"Thank you for your help," I told them sincerely.

"We're always here to help, and we only ask one thing..." Joan said. Agent Franks, apparently tired of our good-byes, began to honk the horn. She groaned. "Don't ever bring that man onto our property, ever again."

"Deal. I don't like him, don't trust him, and the sooner we're done with this, the sooner I can get rid of him."

"Hmm...Franks is obnoxious. How many people *can* you fit in that crematorium at one time?" Holly batted her eyes innocently. We all looked at her. "What?"

"Anything helpful?" Holly asked.

I handed the file across to the back seat so she could see it. "Well, Doctor Nelson figured Hood was driven, obsessed with success, and couldn't tolerate failure. As a boy, he was deeply traumatized by watching his parents' deaths, and was fixated on preventing that kind of thing from happening to others."

"Sounds like a pretty typical Hunter," Trip said.

"Yeah, I suppose." Fanatical and traumatized by something and doing their best to protect the world. "Hell, I bet he fit right in."

"Except for this part where Doc says that Hood had a genius-level intellect. No offense, but I'd say most of us don't set the bar that high," Holly pointed out.

Trip responded. "I went to college."

"I took an IQ test once. It said I'm all sorts of smartified," I joked.

"Okay, so Trip got through school by catching footballs and you beat up some nerds for a certificate. But according to this file, this Hood guy's brain is wired like Stephen Hawking... Like an evil Albert Einstein or something. This is one smart dude we're talking about, with real obsession problems, and now he's locked onto you."

"He's smart, but I'm no slouch," I said. Franks snorted. *Man, I hate him.*

"Just because nobody will play against you in Trivial Pursuit anymore doesn't mean you're a match for this guy, Z," Holly pointed out.

"That's just because Julie's always on his team, and she knows all the artsy questions," Trip muttered.

Holly continued. "What I'm getting at is that we've underestimated this guy. When we first learned about him, we thought we were just facing another bad guy, another monster. But this one's different. He's a former Hunter, so he already knows how we roll. He's patient enough to fake his death and plot craziness for decades. This man outwitted Earl Harbinger and all the Shacklefords, all while right under their noses the whole time. We already knew about the cult, but we've underestimated their leader. The idea of a spy inside MHI seemed stupid to me at first, but this Hood's some sort of chess master, and he's thinking ahead. This man will not stop and he'll pull out all the stops. We've got a lot bigger problem on our hands than we thought."

She was right. The car was quiet while I mulled that over.

"What do you think, Franks?" Holly asked. I was surprised that she would actually try to involve him.

Franks had to have realized by now that I had somehow read Carlos' mind, but he didn't indicate that he cared one way or the other. He was quiet for a long time, shaded eyes staring out the window. "I'm not paid to think."

"Helpful, ain't he?"

Franks turned forward. "*But* . . . I doubt you're ruthless enough to survive." He went back to the window.

We drove the rest of the way in silence.

# CHAPTER 14

It was well after noon when we pulled into the compound. There were several extra vehicles in the lot, some rental cars from the airport and a few other MHI vehicles from the team leads who were stationed close enough to drive.

"I wonder if Earl's back?" Trip asked.

"We need to talk to him. And keep this on the down low. If the Condition's infiltrated headquarters, then they might have gotten people onto the other teams too." Hell, Hood had actually approached Carlos about working together. Who knew if he had tried that with anybody else?

"That really pisses me off," Holly said. "I hate traitors."

Franks actually murmured agreement as we got out of the car. "Me too." He held back as the rest of us got our gear bags out of the trunk, then walked up the stairs. Could Franks sense just how unwelcome he was going to be inside a building packed with the most experienced Hunters in the country? *Doubtful.*

He probably had some other nefarious, inexplicable reason. It wasn't like Franks cared if he was welcome or not.

The office building was busier than it had been since last summer. There were Hunters everywhere. Dorcas was at her desk, angrily answering questions and shuffling papers. She was surrounded by Newbies filling out requisition forms so they could take equipment with them or harassing her for their last training paycheck. They were out of here, ready to start life as real Hunters, and the atmosphere was kind of like the last day of high school before summer vacation. It was downright festive.

"Z!" somebody shouted. Suddenly I was engulfed in a rib-crushing bear hug, which smashed my arms to my sides, jerked my feet off the floor, and popped my vertebrae. The man was a little shorter than me but strong as an ox. He bounced me around for a moment, knocking his black cowboy hat off; his giant mustache tickled, and I could smell the Copenhagen chewing tobacco. Sam Haven was home.

"Hey, Sam." He dropped me back to the ground. Our old teammate then turned his attention to Trip and Holly. They got the same enthusiastic treatment. "How's Colorado?"

Sam grinned. "The finest warriors in history trained me to fight from the sea. I'm a master of maritime mayhem, a Son of Poseidon," he loudly proclaimed. Sam had been a Navy SEAL. He paused to pick up his hat and smashed it back onto his mullet. "So of course, Earl puts me in charge of a team stationed five thousand feet above sea level in the middle of the damned country. Denver's lousy with hippies. I mean, they're *everywhere*. But the women are smoking hot and there are some good local beers. So overall, it's a wash." He turned his shoulder so we could see the patch on his armor. "Check it out. Pretty cool, huh?" The Team Haven patch was a walrus with a banjo. "Maybe you kids will get your own someday. Holly could have a stripper on a pole. That'd be sweet."

"I'll save you a copy," Holly patted him on the back. She'd missed him too.

"That looks great." It really did. The walrus just kind of suited him I suppose. "Sam, listen, it's urgent. Is Earl back?"

He leaned in conspiratorially, glancing from side to side to make sure nobody else was listening. "He wandered in this morning. That skank-whore, Susan, got away."

"Figures."

"Don't worry, one of these days, we'll take them down. And I just hope that it's one of us old-timers. It should be our job, our responsibility." Sam had served with Ray and Susan when he had been a young Hunter and he had been on the team when Susan had disappeared. For Sam, having one of his team end up playing for the other side was a personal insult. "Come on. Earl's downstairs recuperating." Sam bulled his way through the crowd. Other leads intercepted us, greeting, visiting, all of them exceedingly friendly. I knew most of them from last summer or from Milo's wedding. It was kind of weird, but among all of these more experienced Hunters, I was sort of famous. I noted that Sam was the only commander wearing his full uniform. He was just that proud of his new patch that he had to show everybody. "We've been interviewing Newbies all morning, and after lunch we get to fight over who gets who. But I get the first-round draft pick."

"Because you're the newest team?"

"No, because I'm that awesome. Boone thinks he gets first pick, since he says he's short-handed. Hell, I've got the same number of men he does. We'll have to wrestle for it." Still being relatively new to the ways of MHI, it wouldn't have shocked me to discover that feats of strength were a recognized method of solving human resource issues. "I'd whup his ass."

"Hmm . . . Maybe I would make a good team lead," I muttered. I had, after all, beaten people up for money for a few years. Between that and the fact that I could actually do a budget, I might be able to get myself a promotion. As we approached the cafeteria, I heard the sound of an acoustic guitar. Glancing inside, I noticed my brother sitting at one end of the room, borrowed guitar in hand, as he cranked through something familiar. Several of the single female Newbies were sitting at the next table batting their eyes at him, as well as half a dozen masked and hooded orcs who were just happy to be in the presence of greatness. It was rare for any of the orcs to want to be around humans, even us, but they made an exception for our celebrity guest. "He always did get all the chicks."

Holly listened for a moment as Mosh's fingers flew back and forth. "Damn, he's really good."

"Some say the best in the world. We are a talented family."

"His talent's cooler though."

I shook my head. "Fine, don't come crying to me when you need help with your taxes next year."

Mosh saw us standing in the doorway, stopped playing mid-lyric, dropped the guitar, jumped up, and started toward me. The orcish contingent immediately began to boo loudly. He ignored them and focused in on me with an unnerving intensity. He must have picked that up from Dad. "There you are. We need to talk. Have you seen the news?"

"Been too busy."

"The official story is that I caused all the crazy stuff at Buzzard Island! Out-of-control special effects and lame-ass shit like that. When can I get out of here?"

"Dude, chill. I'm working on it." I raised my hand defensively. "I'm taking care of this as fast as I can."

"Not fast enough. Mom keeps trying to *talk* to me. I don't have any of my stuff. We've already had to cancel some shows, and if I don't get out of here soon, we're going to have to screw the whole tour. You know how pissed the fans are going to be when I have to refund ten sold-out concerts? I've got bills to pay."

"Aw man, you might have to sell that Ferrari you just bought," I said.

Mosh snorted as if I had just given him a grave insult. "It was an Aston Martin."

"Whatever. Look, it just isn't safe yet. You go out in public, and you might as well strap a big target to your forehead."

"I can get security."

"Now you're being stupid. Bodyguards aren't up to this gig."

Sam raised his hand. "Hey, if I can butt in, I know a little company that can pull security..." Mosh and I both scowled at him. "Oh, fine. Just trying to scare up some business. Alrighty then, I'll be waiting downstairs when you drama queens are done having your slap fight." He spun on his boot and left. Trip looked uncomfortable. Holly appeared to be enjoying the show.

Mosh moved in closer and poked me in the chest. I was certain he remembered just how much that bugged me. "Listen, people are already starting to talk. The fan sites are saying that I had to check into rehab. And one of those government guys was on the news saying that the big explosion was because I personally wrecked the tour bus into that gas tanker. He didn't come out and say it, but he was trying to make it sound like I was totally wasted or something. It was the one who looks like an English teacher, the dirty, rotten, lying, sack of shit."

"Oh, you mean Agent Myers. Yeah, that's what he does for a living. He makes monster attacks go away." I steered his hand away from me. "Look, I feel your pain, and I'm sure this will all make a great episode of *Behind the Music* someday, but in the meantime, you're stuck."

"I should so kick your ass." Mosh was ticked. "Am I supposed to be a prisoner here or something?"

"No, feel free to walk out that front gate and let me know what kind of monster manages to eat your brain first. See if I care."

"Damn it!" he shouted. "This is really screwing up my career."

"You think a bunch of fanatics and their squid god give a crap about your *career*? Quit being such a baby."

Holly stepped gently between us. "Okay, guys, calm down. Yes, this is all Z's fault." She gave me a look, indicating that I had just better shut it. "And I'm sure he's *really* sorry. But we're resolving this situation as quickly as possible."

Mosh stepped back, still huffy. He turned his attention to Holly for the first time. "And who are you?"

She stuck out her hand. "Holly Newcastle. Monster Hunter. I'm on your brother's team."

It was almost as if I could see the mental shifting of gears. Mosh went from *Angry Important Guy* to *Player* mode. He took her hand, and wasn't very discreet as he checked her out. And Holly was a *very* attractive woman. "Well, nice to meet you, Holly. I'm Mosh Pitt, international superstar." He was such a cheese ball.

*Oh, barf.* I waited for Holly to throat-punch him.

She giggled. Tough as nails, killer of monsters, Holly Newcastle actually *giggled*. Like a...*girl*, or something. Trip and I looked at each other in confusion.

"You know, Mosh, I'm sure you've got a lot of questions that just haven't been answered. And your brother's been too busy to help you, so I can totally understand your frustration. I'd be glad to take the time to explain everything."

He nodded. "Yeah, there's been a lot going down. Maybe we could talk about this...over some lunch."

*Oh my gosh.* Holly was flirting with my brother. "Sure, that's a great idea. We're not exactly equipped for fine dining, but I could probably whip up a little something.... Z, Trip, why don't you guys go talk to Earl. I'll catch up." She took Mosh by the arm. "Right this way."

Mosh winked at me. "Maybe this place doesn't totally suck."

They left for the kitchen. The female Newbies looked offended and the orcs were fighting over who got to keep the guitar that Great War Chief had actually used.

"What just happened?" Trip asked.

"Hell if I know. Either Holly's covering for us, or she's actually attracted to goofy-ass, bald men, with lots of tattoos and really stupid pointy goatees... My money's on getting him out of the way for me. I owe her one."

Trip folded his arms. "Well... I don't like it."

He actually sounded... jealous? *Naw, that was absurd.* "Come on, man. We've got to take care of business."

Earl leaned back in his chair and lit his fourth cigarette since I had begun my story. It was a good thing his tissues regenerated supernaturally or he surely would have died of lung cancer eons ago. He put his bare feet on the table and pondered on what I had said.

"I just can't believe it..." He shook his head. "All these years..."

Trip and I had found Sam and Earl in the basement office outside of Earl's prison cell. This was the place in which he usually cleaned up and calmed down after a werewolf stint. It was more of a bunker than an office, with some thrift-store furniture, a shower, and a door that looked like it had come from a bank vault. I knew behind that vault door was an even plainer room, with a tiny drain hole in the middle, and hundreds of thousands of scratches etched into the concrete. Sam was sitting off to the side. "All these years you've been beating yourself up about killing the little punk and it turns out he deserved it anyway."

My asthma was tearing me apart. There weren't any windows in the basement, and the air was thick with secondhand smoke. "Except it wasn't even him you killed."

Sam leaned forward. "So let me get this straight. Hood swapped bodies with some other dude, and it was that dude, in Hood's old body, getting mind controlled or something, that opened Earl's door?" I nodded. Sam paused to spit his chew in a Styrofoam cup. I was surrounded by nicotine addicts. "Man, that's some messed-up shit, right there."

Earl talked to the ceiling. "Why didn't you tell me, Carlos? We could have figured this out together."

"I'm sorry about your friend," Trip said.

"He was like a brother," my boss said simply. He lowered his head and faced us. I was glad that the anger in that look wasn't directed at me. "Marty Hood . . . It sounds stupid, but the more I think about it, the more it fits. He was always into that stuff. Him and Ray were always poking around the archives. Trying to *understand* monsters. You don't understand them . . . you understand how they think enough to track them down and destroy them. There's a big difference."

"So the necromancer was a Hunter. He knows our capabilities. Did Hood know about the compound's ward stone?"

"Ward what?" Sam asked. If Sam Haven didn't even know about the warding, then that meant very few Hunters did.

"Long story, Sam." Earl shook his head. "Hood shouldn't. I never told him. The last time we fiddled with it, he had already been moved to Carlos' team. We kind of take it for granted, don't really talk about it much."

"So now what do we do?" I asked.

Earl appeared exhausted, with black circles under his eyes. He pulled a pair of socks out of the desk and started putting them on. "Let me think on it. We'll talk again later. Right now, I've got to get presentable. I need to play referee while the team leads fight over who gets which Newbie."

"I want the Haight brothers," Sam said quickly. "I need more shooters, and those boys are tough." I knew which Newbies he was talking about right away. They were two brothers from Utah, whose construction crew had accidentally dug up the resting place of some evil spirit while laying a foundation. Both were rodeo tough guys and longtime varmint hunters; they had also been by far the best gunmen in this class.

"I can't give you both of them," Earl said.

"Aw...come on, man. They made a bomb out of five hundred pounds of ammonium nitrate fertilizer on the spot and blew up a skinwalker. That's the kind of initiative I need!"

"You and everybody else, Sam. I give you both of them, and I'll have to listen to the others complain about favoritism."

Sam smirked. "Well, I am your favorite. Okay, if I can't have them, then I want that Torres kid." Trip and I snickered. "What? Something about him I don't know? He seems squared away."

"He should be. He's one of Franks' men," I replied. "He's one of my protective detail."

Sam scowled. "Now you're just messing with me."

"No, I'll explain later," Earl said as he tied his

boots. "You can't have Archer or Herzog either. They're Feds too."

"Well, Archer had struck me as a good support guy. Those anal-retentive OCD types usually are, all organized and shit. But Herzog..." He grimaced, "I don't know why anybody would pick her. During the interview she went off about how a centralized government is the best way to hunt monsters. What a hag."

That reminded me of something. "She's not an operator. She's a clerk."

Earl looked up. "What?"

"She's not a Hunter at all. But she was assigned to this job by Myers himself. Herzog slipped up and admitted it because she was worried about you eating her. No offense."

"She's not my type," my boss responded dryly. "That doesn't make any sense. Why would Myers send a desk jockey on a protection job?"

"Beats me," I responded. "But Myers picked those three to back up Franks for a reason. And I can't figure out why."

Earl stood and threw on his ancient bomber jacket. "I want to speak with Myers anyway. He needs to know his old buddy is our bad guy...I'm sure Franks already reported in, but I can't wait to rub it in personally." He smiled maliciously. "Good old Myers wanted to kill me for that night, and when he didn't get his wish, he tried to ruin this whole company instead. He's screwed us every chance he's had, and it turns out that he was just as big a sucker as the rest of us."

There was a knock at the door, and Julie entered, only to stagger back as she hit the wall of smoke. "Oh wow, how can any of you guys breathe in here?"

"Man business," Sam stated. I coughed painfully.

Earl poked himself in the chest. "Regeneration. What's up?"

Julie saw me and grinned, forgetting Earl for a moment. "You're back." Her smile brightened my day. I'm such a sap. She got down to business. "We need you upstairs. VanZant is arguing with Mayorga again about who gets the top support person. Hurley's adamant he wants both techs, and says he needs another Spanish speaker. Esmeralda's taken a bunch of folks out to the range because Eddings thinks she's fudged the shooters' scores. He says there's no way that she can be graduating this many Newbies and more probably should have flunked."

My boss groaned. "That's because last time he trained, we only passed six people and he can't admit she's a better trainer than he is. These guys are the best killers the world has ever seen, but I swear sometimes running this show is like herding manticores." There was a sudden banging from inside Earl's cell. "And another thing, why is that *thing* in here?"

"Oh, I almost forgot about him. What's his face . . . Melvin. We needed to stick him someplace secure," Julie explained.

"Great, now my cell's gonna smell like troll," Earl muttered.

"He still might know something," she said. "I figure give him a few days without internet access and he'll be ready to talk."

Earl shook his head. "I'll have Milo order some air fresheners before the next full moon. Okay, everyone, that's all for now. We'll talk again later." The group dispersed.

Eyes watering, lungs burning, I stumbled into the hall. Julie took me by the hand as the others kept walking. "You okay?"

"Asthma," I replied.

"No, I mean, about everything. Something bad happened at Appleton, didn't it?" she asked.

"How can you tell?"

Julie was worried about me. "You seem...distant."

She was right to be concerned. She didn't know just how much I had been using the power that I had gained from that artifact shard. I stroked her hair, and as it parted, the black mark on her neck was revealed. There were a lot of things I hadn't confided to her yet, but since she was the most important person in my world, I needed to. "Everything's going to be fine. Don't worry. Come on, I'll tell you all about it. But let's get some fresh air."

"Oh, it isn't that easy," Julie said. "You forgot something. You've still got another challenge to face."

"Oh, man, what now? Walk the Hell Hounds? Clean the pterodactyl cages?"

"Not quite that terrifying. But still, he's pretty darn scary."

I had totally forgotten. "Dad."

I found my father sitting on a bench outside the main building next to a larger man who I recognized as one of our senior team leaders. His name was Benjamin Cody, and he was leading the team that was currently fulfilling our contract with the Department of Energy. Their patch was a molecule with fangs under the words EXITE! CHEMICUS SUM! Which was Latin for, *Back off, man! I'm a scientist!* That team had the proud history of having cleaned up Los Alamos after the Manhattan Project had unfortunately dabbled in other, less successful, types of weapons projects. Cody was one of the oldest active Hunters, and you had to be damn smart to get assigned to that contract. They were our specialists when it came to taking care of science projects gone bad. Julie had mentioned recently that Cody was mulling over the idea of retirement.

He had also served with Dad in Vietnam. I had learned that fact last summer when he had tried to pump me up to go kick Lord Machado's ass. So at least Dad had found a friend. I approached them from behind. They apparently didn't hear me, but what could you expect from two guys who had spent the best years of their life surrounded by explosions? Cody was telling a familiar story. "So, then they find this back door into the cavern . . . it's some sort of magic portal. No hesitation, balls to the wall, your boy actually jumps through it, grabs the hostage, and runs out, with like fifty wights right at his feet."

Dad stopped him. "What's a wight?"

"Think of a zombie on steroids that paralyzes you with a touch. But anyway, that was just the beginning. The rest of us were busy fighting these Master vampires, and we were running out of time, when the kid went back through the portal with a small group to take on the head asshole himself."

I swelled with pride. Everybody in MHI knew about my exploits at DeSoya Caverns.

"Brave and stupid. Sounds like my offspring," Dad grunted.

*Never mind.* I cleared my throat so they would know I was present.

Cody turned around. "Well, afternoon, Z." He extended one callused hand. I shook it. "I was just telling your father about the last time we worked together."

"That was a tough day," I replied. My dad scowled at me, as if to say that I wasn't qualified to judge such things.

"A bunch of us didn't come back," Cody replied as he stood. He was a burly man, thick-shouldered, with a gray beard and mane of hair that made him look vaguely like an old lumberjack. "Well, I've got to get back to work." He turned his attention back to Dad. "It was good to see you again, Augie."

"Likewise, old friend," my father replied. "It makes me feel a little better to see that this outfit isn't entirely staffed with nut jobs."

"Who said that it wasn't?" Cody smiled. "It takes some getting used to, but this is as good a group of men as I've ever served with. And we've got a hell of a good CO."

Dad's brow creased. "You mean, Mr. Wolf?"

Cody didn't show any reaction, even though all of the team commanders were aware of Harbinger's condition. "I wouldn't know. But if Earl Harbinger came to me and said he needed volunteers to follow him on a suicide mission into Hell's bathroom, I'd go in a heartbeat, just for the chance to watch him kick Satan off his crapper. Don't worry, Aug, your boy's in good hands." The two old vets shook hands and said their good-byes. I waited patiently.

After Cody left, Dad gestured at the empty spot on the bench. I took a seat. "We've got some things to talk about," he said simply, eyes staring into the distant forest. There was a constant rattle of gunfire coming from the shooting range as the Newbies showed off what they'd learned.

"Mom told me you've been sick. She wouldn't let me talk to you yesterday. What's wrong?"

"She's protective like that," he responded, avoiding the question. "That's not why you're here."

"I want to know about this dream of yours."

He shook his head sadly. "You wouldn't understand. . . ." My laugh was so sudden and bitter that I must have surprised him. "What?"

"Wouldn't understand?" My voice dripped with anger. "Don't treat me like I'm a stupid kid."

"Listen, boy—"

I cut him off. "No, you're going to listen to me for once. I've stood at the edge of the universe and seen what's on the other side. I've faced off against evil that most people couldn't even comprehend and I shot it in the face. I've traveled through friggin' *time*." A lot of pent-up aggression fought its way to the surface. "I've read people's minds. I've seen some things that no sane person would ever imagine. I'm not here for you to bully, and push around and scare. So don't you treat me like I'm your fat, dumb, never-good-enough child, Dad. I've had enough of your crap, and it's time I got some straight answers. Man to man."

Dad waited. "You done?"

I realized I was breathing hard. "Yeah."

He smiled slightly. "Cody was right. You do take after me. Stubborn. Now put a sock in it." He reached into his shirt pocket and pulled out an envelope that had been folded neatly in half. He handed it to me. My name had been scribbled across the front in bold black letters. "You know I've never been much of a talker, and Lord knows you aren't a very good listener, so I wrote it down for you. I spent all last night and all morning putting down every detail so I wouldn't forget anything."

I took the envelope. "This is the dream?"

"You could say that. Vision, prophecy, whatever." I started to open it, but his hand landed on mine. Dad started to speak, but hesitated.

"What?"

"Once you read that letter, my life will be over."

That sounded ominous. He was dead serious. "What do you mean?"

His voice was strained. "I've been living on borrowed time for over thirty years. My life was a loan, and once you read that," he gestured at the letter, "the loan can get called. So humor me."

"I don't understand."

My dad chuckled. "See, I told you so, Mr. Know-it-all. There's a place, a terrible place inside the border of the old Soviet Union. The coordinates are on that sheet. I was sent there on a black op a long time ago. Some really shady stuff was going on, some weird weapons' project, and we needed to find out what it was. I didn't survive..."

"Huh?"

"I was murdered. Dead. Done. Literally, a hole blown through my skull. But I was sent back, healed, given that dream and a charge that I couldn't fail. See, I wasn't done yet. I was told that I was going to have a son, and I had to prepare him for something unthinkable."

I didn't know what to say. It sounded so farfetched,

so impossible. But then again, I had experienced the same thing myself. Mordechai had told me I'd drawn the short straw and then sent me back to slug it out with the Cursed One to see who got to decide the fate of the world. You could say I was pretty open-minded.

"I never knew if it was going to be you or David, but one of you was chosen before you were born. But from what I've heard over the last few days, you must be the one. I'm sorry, son."

"I am the one," I responded. "But I did the job, and I'm still here."

He spied a stick on the ground, bent over, and used it to draw a design in the dirt. He tore at the ground furiously. The symbol was unfamiliar.

When he was done, he asked, "Have you seen this before?"

Looking at it left me strangely queasy. It wasn't like the Old Ones' writing I had seen in Lord Machado's memories, or like Hood's grimoire, nor was it like anything I had seen in the regular world. But at the same time, it seemed like something I should recognize, but it was just beyond the edge of my consciousness. "No. I haven't."

"Then it isn't time yet. When you see that sign, the time has come."

"What does it mean?"

"It's a name." He kept the stick in his hand and absently poked it at the dirt. "There were a few other signs. Some that I could see happen and others that I wasn't sure about. The five minutes of backward time. That was one of them. Before it happened, I had almost been able to convince myself that none of this was real. You kids were grown-up, leading your own lives, the dream wasn't coming as often, and maybe I had imagined the whole thing, you know. But the five minutes, that settled things."

My father didn't know that that had been my doing. There was no way he could know that. "That was my fault."

He nodded, unsurprised. "That was part of it. In the dream, time is like a tube filled with water. As time goes by, the water freezes. The past is frozen solid, unchangeable, but the future is fluid until it happens. We live at the surface of the ice, the present. The water goes on forever. Whatever you did flash-melted a tiny bit of that water, moved us back in time. You woke him up."

"Who?"

He gestured at the symbol, an unknown player in this game. Then he erased it with his foot, blotting it out with a look of disgust on his face. "You had no choice. There are multiple sides at work, and if any of them win, we lose. This is the first and the last. That jackass that's messing with us right now? He's with one faction, but his side isn't the worst. Not by a long shot."

"How do you know this stuff, Dad?"

"It's all in the note. And once you read it, my job will be done." He sighed. "I had a good run."

I lifted the envelope. "You make it sound like as soon as I look at this, you're going to just keel over or something. What's going on?"

Dad paused. "Nothing."

I groaned. "You're the worst liar ever. It has something to do with Mom saying you're sick, doesn't it?"

He smiled. "When I died, I got shot here. Boom.

Headshot. Asshole with a Dragunov." He tapped his finger to the base of his skull. It was utterly improbable, but I lived in a world of improbabilities. "Then I met the *others*. They stuffed my brains back in, fixed me up, sent me back, and I woke up on a mountainside covered in my own blood, with the understanding that when my mission was complete, when my son was prepared and taught, it was time to go home. A couple of years ago, guess what a physical turned up? Right in the exact same place..."

His words hung in the air. My world came crashing down. It was impossible. It couldn't be. "Oh no, please, no."

"There's no way to operate without killing me. The mass is at the base of my brain. But it hasn't grown or changed since the doctors found it. It's just sitting there, waiting. Just a lump of abnormal cells. Usually it don't bother me. I know it's not going anywhere until my job's done. That's a lot more assurance than a man can ask for."

"Does Mom know?"

He nodded.

His life had been prolonged to give me this? I shoved the letter toward him. "Take it back."

My dad didn't move. "I can't. The time will come that you'll need it. See, I'm not the only dead man walking here. Your fate is sealed as much as mine. Only you can't be weak. You can't fail." He grabbed my arm, hard, and shoved the letter back against my chest. His eyes bored into mine. "You have to be *strong*."

I didn't know what to say. Stunned, speechless, his hand crushing mine and the letter, I sat there. All these years, all the things that he had taught me, it was all for this. "Don't do this to me."

He let go. "Son, I'm sorry. But we're both soldiers. We didn't pick the job. It picked us. It isn't like I'm going to live forever anyway. And now that I know you're the one, there's no time to waste. The longer you hesitate, the stronger he'll become. Read the note. It'll tell you what must be done."

"That's insane. I can't kill you."

Auhangamea Pitt, war hero, man of courage and honor, father, wiped his eyes and turned away from me. "My job's done. I just hope that when you read this, you can know that I was just doing what I felt was right."

It wasn't right at all. For the first time in my life I finally felt like I knew where my father had been coming from. We'd talked, finally as equals, hoping to come to terms, to understand him, not this. It wasn't right. It wasn't fair. But I knew what Dad would say to that, the same thing that he'd told me for years. *Life isn't fair.*

But I was tired of being a pawn in some cosmic game. I stood and dropped the note on the bench next to Dad. He just looked at it, then back at me, disappointed. I had to get out of here. "Well, who-ever this scumbag is, he can get in line. Dream your dream, and tell the people who sent you back that I'm not ready yet."

"It won't work, son. This is inevitable."

"I'm getting real tired of that word," I spat. "I'll find a way to beat this. My father didn't raise any quitters...I'll talk to you later, Dad."

*Inevitable.*

There had to be a way to fix this. That's what I do.

I fix things. I find ways to make them right. There had to be a way.

I half walked, half stumbled, away from my father. I wandered aimlessly across the compound. There was a spot of shade under the roof of the barracks. It was a secluded spot, and I leaned against the wall, head in my hands. Before I knew it, my knees had weakened, and I sank to the ground, shaking.

I couldn't wrap my brain around not having my dad around. He had always been a rock. What was going to happen to Mom? Hell, somebody had to tell Mosh. I needed to talk to him, to somebody, but I couldn't find the strength to rise. So I sat there for a long time, just tired, too dumbfounded to string a coherent plan together, feeling stupid and guilty for not staying with my father.

Finally, something woke me from my stupor, a hard tapping on my arm.

"What're you crying about?" G-Nome was standing in front of me, partially hidden in the shadows of the barracks. The sky behind him indicated that dusk was approaching. I had been sulking for a long time.

"I wasn't crying..." I rubbed my face. "What do you want?"

"Sissy," he answered. With me sitting down, I still towered over him, even if you counted his pointy hat. "You humans get all emotional about shit.... Well, I done found your spy."

That got my attention. "Who?"

"It wasn't easy. But I caught him. He's been texting on his phone. I been readin' over his shoulder. He's been tellin' somebody where you at all the time."

"Who?" I demanded.

The gnome smiled, eyes twinkling over rosy cheeks and puffy white beard. He took his time answering, taking a cigar out of his shirt and lighting it. He must have realized that I was about to wrench his head from his shoulders and finished quicker than he started. "That pretty-boy human, Grant."

"Grant Jefferson? You're sure?"

G-Nome took a long puff, then blew it out in a perfect ring. "Sure, I'm sure. Last night, when you left with that blonde hottie and your homie, he waited till you got outta sight and then he was all like textin' some fool about it. I read it, sayin' you had bags packed, like you was escapin' out the back, know what I'm sayin? But I been followin' him to make sure and he just got called by somebody checkin' on you."

"No chance you're wrong?"

"Hells yeah. He texts in all the time. Always sayin' where you're at and who you're talkin' to. When you went to sneak out last night, he'd sent the message before you'd even made it out the back door! Ain't just about you all either. He's been tellin' them all about MHI business."

*Bastard.* All that talk about needing to succeed, not being a quitter, and I had bought that, hook, line, and sinker. He had totally snowed me. I should have trusted my initial instincts. My legs had fallen asleep, and tingled painfully as I stumbled to my feet. Coldly, I drew my .45 from my inside the waistband holster and pulled back the slide slightly to make sure I had a round chambered. "Where is he?"

"In the big building. My dawg, Harbinger's talkin' to his peeps, some graduation ceremony or somethin',

I don't know. That's why I had to find you. You gonna bring the pain?"

"I intend to kill him if that's what you mean." I shoved my gun back in the holster.

"Sweet!" G-Nome turned his head to the side, as if listening to something I couldn't hear from inside the barracks. His nose twitched, like he was smelling the air, and he suddenly frowned. "That ain't right. Gotta bounce. Have fun." And with a *pop*, he disappeared from sight.

I started toward the main building, murder on my mind. Thirty yards away was a figure leaning against the trunk of a tree, waiting. Franks had been following me the entire time, fulfilling his duty, but keeping his distance while I had my emotional collapse. I passed him without a word. I didn't turn my head to look, but I knew he followed.

As long as he didn't try to get in my way for what was about to come next, I didn't care. The traitor had to die.

The rational part of my mind urged caution, that maybe I should slow down, think it through, get some help first . . . Maybe it was because of my dad's terrible news, maybe it was because I somehow knew with absolute certainty that the gnome was telling the truth, I didn't know exactly, but rationality went right out the window and I was in a red haze of anger that could only be cured by facing the traitor.

The main building was busy. Everyone was congregating for the graduation ceremony that Esmeralda had organized. Earl was going to say a few words, and then announce where the Newbies were going.

The atmosphere was one of excitement. Nobody else was aware that I was a man on a mission as I barged through the entrance. Dorcas was behind her desk, being harassed by joyous Newbies. From the look of her, I was guessing that for the special occasion there was more in her coffee cup than just coffee. She saw me and started shooing the others away. "Z, where've you been? Julie's looking for you, but your phone isn't picking up."

That's because my BlackBerry was at the bottom of the river outside Montgomery. "Have you seen Grant?"

She must have realized from my expression that this was serious. "No. What's going on?"

I glanced in both directions, just a bunch of Newbies walking toward the cafeteria. Earl was about to speak. "Has anyone seen Grant Jefferson?" I asked loudly. The Newbies shrugged and continued on.

Franks tapped me on the shoulder with one gloved hand. "What are you doing?"

"Taking care of some personal business," I responded as I kept walking.

Franks began to say something, but paused as his phone started buzzing. He looked at the display in frustration, then stopped to read the text. I took the opportunity to head down the hallway after the Newbies.

The cafeteria was packed with folding chairs and loafing Hunters. The leads were all sitting in front, joking and heckling each other. The Newbies were filing in, taking their seats. Earl was pacing back and forth, waiting for everyone to gather. Not being the kind of person to go for a lot of ceremony, he was wearing his regular scuffed bomber jacket and looked agitated that he was doing this kind of thing. I'd heard him refer to his little talks as dog and pony shows more than once, but he was a hell of a good motivator. Julie was seated next to her grandfather. She waved when she saw me.

I was too preoccupied to wave back. Scanning the crowd, I saw just about everyone I expected to. Even my parents were there as guests watching the spectacle, but no Grant. I hadn't formulated a plan yet. Dragging him out of the room by the hair was probably not the most discreet tactic, but it was the one that I was currently running with.

I waited. Maybe he was coming. The Goon Squad was there, still pretending to be Newbies. Torres was the last of the undercover Feds to arrive, and when he saw me standing at the doorway, he paused and waited next to me. "You okay?" he asked, ever helpful. He must have seen the expression on my face, and grew worried. "Owen?"

I didn't answer. The last of the Newbies pushed past me, looking for seats. The gang was all here, over sixty Hunters. Julie handed Earl a microphone and he rapped it sharply. The intercom speakers thumped.

"Sorry, but I have to use this thing," Earl said, "Julie didn't think that it was fair that the Hunters manning the security room couldn't listen in. I don't know what she's thinking, because it ain't like I'm much of a talker." The room laughed.

*The security room.* Julie had scheduled it so that at least two people were in there manning the cameras continuously since Susan's visit. I exited and ran down the hallway. Grant might be there, and if he wasn't, I could use the cameras to find him.

I had always suspected it could be him, the slimy little prick. He had left the company with his tail between his legs. I bet he had been an easy mark for the Condition. I didn't know what they were paying him, but whatever it was, wasn't enough. He had come crawling back at such a convenient time... We were such suckers. Grant had probably jumped at the chance to betray us when he had found out it was all about killing me. Black anger welled up in my heart. Knowing the kind of evil we were fighting, it wouldn't surprise me in the least if his payment was in the form of Julie. Oh, this was personal now.

Earl's voice was tinny over the intercom as he got down to business. *"Welcome, Hunters. And I can actually say that now. Hunters. Because there aren't any Newbies in this room now, just equals."* The sound that came next had to have been applause, but it was hard to tell.

I flew down the stairs to the basement. The door to the security room was straight ahead down a long hallway. I stuck one hand under my shirt and put it on the butt of my gun.

*"No need to clap. Besides, if you get Boss Shackleford clapping he's likely to hurt himself with that hook."* More laughter. *"Just kidding, Boss."*

My blood was pounding in my ears. If Grant was in that room, I was going to end his miserable life. At the end of the hall, the door was closed.

*"Young Hunters, look at these people sitting in front of you. These are the finest leaders MHI has ever had. I've worked with every single one of them, and wouldn't hesitate to trust my life to their hands. Regardless of who you're assigned to today, you can know that you're with*

*the very best. Well, except for Sam...for those of you
stuck with him...sorry about that."* There was a loud
response, but it was indecipherable over the intercom.
More laughter. *"I'd put the microphone there, but I
don't think that's legal in Alabama."*

My boots skidded across the concrete as I reached the
security room. I grabbed the doorknob. It was locked.

*"Before Esmeralda reads off your name and your
assignment, let me just say that this is the most successful
training class we've ever conducted. I've interviewed you
all. I've seen your records. I've watched you improve.
I've been impressed, and I don't impress easy."*

I rapped on the door. "Come on..." I whispered.

*"When you came here a few short months ago, you
were all survivors. That's what set you apart from the
rest of the world. A survivor has heart. A will to win.
A desire to live. You were survivors, but now you're
something more..."*

My pounding increased in intensity. Nobody was
answering.

*"You are Hunters."*

Something was wrong. I stepped back, and with a
roar, slammed my boot into the steel door. Pain shot
up my injured ankle. The frame cracked, but it held.

*"Survivors take care of themselves. Hunters take
the fight to the other side. We are the final line
against evil."*

I stepped back again, readying myself to kick the
door again. Somebody shouted from down the hall.
"Owen!" I spun to see who it was.

*"We will hold the line."*

It was Grant. He was walking down the hall toward
me, five yards away. His arms were held wide and he

had his phone in one hand. "What the hell are you doing to that door?"

My .45 appeared in my hand and I punched it toward him. "Don't move! Don't you fucking move!"

"Whoa! Whoa! Calm down!" Grant cried. He was wearing his armored suit so I aimed at the junction of his nose and eyes.

"What are you doing down here?" I shouted.

"Somebody said you were looking for me," he said calmly. "Now put the gun down. You're acting nuts."

"I'm nuts? I'm not the traitor, you son of a bitch."

Grant paused, a painful look crossing his handsome features. "I don't know what you're talking about." Earl's voice was just background noise now.

My gun didn't waver. If he so much as twitched I was going to blow his brains out. "Don't you lie to me," I hissed. "I know all about your messages." I nodded at the phone. "Why'd you do it?"

His eyes flicked unconsciously to the device in his hand. "Just calm down, Owen." He slowly put the phone back into his pocket, then put his hands back up.

"Why, Grant? Do you hate me that much? Do you hate Julie that much? Are we talking jealousy, or is it something worse? Do you actually believe what the Condition stands for? Tell me, because I really want to understand before I kill you."

He was blinking rapidly, knowing that I wasn't bluffing. "It isn't what you think."

That sealed his fate. I tightened my grip. The safety was off. My finger was on the trigger.

"Wait!" someone ordered from the direction I had come.

I kept the gun on Grant, but turned my head slightly

to see. It was MCB Agent Herzog. Directly behind her was Agent Torres. They must have followed me downstairs. "Get Franks. I found your spy." I turned my attention back to Grant. "And tell him to hurry, because if he wants to interrogate him, he'll need his own necromancer."

"Listen to me," Grant pleaded. "Yeah, I've been spying on MHI, but for a good reason. Let me explain. I'm trying to help."

"I've heard that line before, you sack of—" Then I thought of something. Nobody had answered the door to the security room, even after all the noise I had made. I lowered my gun slightly, and threw a brutal side kick into the steel. This time the bolt tore through the frame. "Don't try to run or do anything stupid. You know I don't miss," I ordered.

I risked a quick glance into the security room.

There was blood everywhere.

"Son of a bitch..." I covered the distance to Grant quickly, my gun on him the whole time.

"Wait. What's going on?" he asked. "I don't—"

I struck him in the face with the butt of my compact STI. He stumbled back into the wall. I hit him again, slamming his head into the concrete. He raised his hands to protect his face, but I swatted them down and smashed my gun into his temple. Then I rammed my knee into his ribs repeatedly with savage fury. He slid to the ground. I jerked his pistol from its holster and tossed it down the hallway. I grabbed him by the boot and dragged his semiconscious weight back to the security room.

The agents were still standing there. Herzog was shocked. Torres had drawn his sidearm and was pulling something out of another pocket, probably his radio. "Sound the alarm," I ordered as I dragged Grant through the door. Herzog glanced inside, saw the carnage, turned a ghastly shade of green, and stumbled back.

I turned my attention to the security room. Blood was splattered all over the bank of monitors. There was a single Hunter on the floor, facedown in a giant red puddle. Adrenaline and fury were pounding through my veins. I rolled him over. It was one of the Newbies. The taxi driver. I couldn't even remember his name. His throat had been cut.

Flat on his back, Grant groaned.

I kicked him in the side. "Why? What'd he do to you?"

"Wasn't me!" he cried.

I squatted down. It was time to end it. "You want to worship the Old Ones? Well, tell them hi for me." I placed my gun against his temple.

Grant sputtered something. It took me a second to realize he was laughing at me. His teeth were red with blood. "Old Ones? God, you're a moron...Sure, I'm a spy, but not for the Condition."

*What?*

"He's working for the Monster Control Bureau," Agent Anthony Torres said from the doorway. "Myers recruited him after he left MHI."

"Are you serious?"

Grant gasped as he looked over my shoulder. "It's you!"

Torres was standing over me, collapsible baton extended above his head. "Yes." Then he cracked me hard, lights exploded in my skull, snapping my head around. The floor came up and hit me.

"Anthony! What are you doing?" Herzog screeched. I couldn't see what happened next, but there was a sudden *whump*.

Sitting up, I raised my gun but another quick strike of the baton knocked it from my hand. Torres kicked me in the chest, sending me back to the ground.

"Stop right there," he stated as he raised his HK in his other hand. A fat sound suppressor had been screwed onto the muzzle.

My head hurt. That baton had nailed me good. The spinning room lurched to a stop. "What are you doing?" I grunted.

"I'm completing my mission," Torres said calmly. His normally cheerful disposition had been replaced with something cold. He stepped completely into the room and closed the damaged door behind him. Back against the wall, he kept the gun pointed at me. I realized with a start that Herzog was also down, a gaping hole in the side of her head, brains dripping down the wall behind, eyes like glass, open and staring at nothing. "I never did like her," Torres said. "Too bossy." Then he lowered his gun and shot her twice more, each round from the suppressed pistol sounding like the slamming of a thick book. It was back on me before I could do anything.

Grant struggled to sit up, but began coughing. I had really hit him good.

*"Hunters, as you enter the world, your greatest weapon is the trust you have in your team,"* Earl said over the intercom. The intercom speaker was next to Torres and he turned it off.

"I've listened to enough blowhards for one night," Torres said. His demeanor had changed. The friendly act was cast aside, and now I could see the crazy in

402           Larry Correia

his eyes. Damn, he'd been a good actor. "You know, you look confused, Owen. Let me try to help you out here. I'm an acolyte in the Exalted Order of the Shadows, that's who I really work for. Jefferson here is pretending to work for MHI, when he's really working for Myers. His assignment was to help Franks catch which of your detail was the spy."

"Traitors," I muttered. "Both of you."

"I was trying to serve my country...." Grant said, spitting a gob of blood on the floor. "Unlike this piece of shit."

Undeterred, Torres' HK kept floating between Grant and me. If either of us moved, we were dead. "Well, you did find me finally, *Agent* Jefferson. I'll give you that." Torres smiled. "Maybe you'll get a posthumous promotion for catching me...."

"Squid lover," Grant spat.

"Don't knock it until you try it." He turned his attention back to the door, and peeked through the crack down the hallway. The gun was still pointed in our direction. Torres was a pro. "Don't try anything stupid, Pitt."

"Grant, what the hell's going on?" I hissed.

"I was trying to help you, moron." Grant moaned as he sat up. "Myers knew the MCB had been infiltrated. I was supposed to watch out for you and back up Franks. When one of Myers' people, Patterson, was killed trying to infiltrate the cult, there were only a few agents who knew about her cover."

My head was spinning, and not just from Torres' baton. Myers had shown me pictures of Agent Patterson. She had been the one chopped into pieces— Franks' friend. Torres was still listening and turned his attention back to us, grinning.

"Served the bitch right, trying to lie to the sacred Order. There were only a handful of us who knew about Ashley's assignment. Archer took care of her comms. Herzog"—Torres gestured at the dead woman— "processed her reports. And I was her field backup. Myers could only narrow it down to the three of us. He was suspicious, but couldn't be certain if he'd been betrayed or if the Order was getting its intel some other way. When the Dread Overlord sent his request for your *utter destruction*, that toad Myers saw his opportunity. He knew if one of us was a spy, we'd surely reveal ourselves to take a shot at you."

It made sense. That's why Herzog was just a clerk. They had never been here to protect me. They had been here simply to see which one tried to kill me and then Franks or Grant could capture them. I didn't know if I was angrier at Torres the traitor or Myers for bringing this down on our heads.

"You weren't supposed to figure that out. . . ." Grant said.

"I wasn't supposed to know about you either. Looks like Myers underestimated the Order again." Torres went back to watching the hallway. He was waiting for something.

I had to keep him distracted. I had to go for that gun. "So this whole thing about MHI having a spy was a lie?"

"Oh, no," Torres said. "You've got bigger problems, an actual doppelganger." He gestured at the blood-soaked Newbie, almost reverently. "This is its work. In fact . . ." He glanced absently at his watch. "We both have our missions, and our assignment is almost done. Check out the monitors."

Beneath the blood splatter were twenty different black and white ten-inch screens. The compound was well covered. The one of the cafeteria was packed with Hunters as Earl wrapped up his speech. The other views were mostly empty, but movement caught my eye on one of the central ones. A group of shapes were moving toward the barracks. Men with guns.

"Fellow acolytes," Torres said proudly.

"Half a dozen ass-wipes aren't going to stand up to a bunch of pissed-off Hunters," I said. "Hell, Earl will probably just eat them."

Torres was enjoying himself. He turned away from the door. "Our doppelganger will neutralize your little werewolf at the proper time, with MHI-issued silver bullets even. My brothers are here to destroy your ward stone." The look on my face must have betrayed my surprise. "Oh yes, we know all about that. Harbinger thought secrecy would protect it. Not even our High Priest was privy to that. But Myers knew, and he filed it in his official report on MHI." Torres shrugged. He was feeling smug. "Just another thing I was able to pass on to the Order."

The monitor that covered the front gate showed movement also. A semi pulling a huge cargo trailer rolled to a halt, then another parked beside it, and another pulled up behind. The drivers got out and moved to open the rear doors. More trucks were pulling up behind. You could pack a lot of dead stuff into that many trailers.

"With your shield gone, a veritable ocean of the righteous dead will flood this place. Once the Hunters are gone, I'll deliver you personally to my Master."

"What about me?" Grant asked.

Torres scowled. "You? I just wanted to gloat for a minute. Might as well pop you now." He moved the gun back toward Grant. "All that I'm going to ask is that I'll be the one to animate your corpse afterward."

Grant gave Torres a bloody smile. "Good thing I texted Franks when I found Pitt."

Grant had been holding his phone when I had spotted him.

Torres' eyes flicked to the door just as it exploded inward. He opened fire. The flash-bang grenade went off a split second later.

My eyes were scalded with light and my ears rang with a deafening screech. Head swimming, I struggled to my feet. I had to reach Torres. I misjudged and crashed into the wall. A strong hand grabbed my neck and shoved me out of the way. I tripped over Herzog's corpse and went to my knees.

A moment later I could see again. Bright purple ghosts floated across my corneas, but I could at least tell what was going on. Torres was facedown on the floor. Franks was kneeling on his back, handcuffing him. Archer stood in the doorway with a Sig 229 pointed at Torres' head.

Then I could hear. Torres was screaming, thrashing. "The High Priest is coming! His legions are coming! You can't stop him! It's the dark new dawn! Do you hear me?"

Franks jerked Torres to his feet. He towered over his prisoner. "Yeah. I hear you." Then he slammed his giant fist into the side of Torres' head with a brutal hook. The cultist collapsed, unconscious. "So shut up."

I got unsteadily to my feet. "Where's the alarm button?"

Franks pointed at Torres' limp form. "Get him out of here." Archer looked confused. "I'll explain later. Contact Myers. Tell him we got the spy." Franks glanced down at Grant. "Nice work, Agent Jefferson." He was smug, mission completed, no idea what was coming our way fast.

There was a large red button on the control desk. I mashed it repeatedly. Nothing happened. I looked under the desk. The wires had been torn out. I swore.

Franks' blunt features were perplexed. "What?"

Grant had gotten unsteadily to his feet. He pointed at the monitors. "The Condition's attacking!"

The acolytes had pulled up a hidden hatch near the barracks and were entering the tunnels. The view of the front gate showed the trucks and the movement of some vast beast tottering down the trailers' ramps. On the cafeteria camera, Earl finished speaking. He was stepping down. Esmeralda was taking his place. Someone stood in the audience, back toward the camera, a gun extended forward. It was utterly silent. Earl jerked as a hail of bullets tore into him. There was a loud noise down the hallway as something exploded.

The power went out.

# CHAPTER 15

A brilliant flashlight beam clicked on. Franks flashed it around the room.

"Status?"

"Commando team is trying to destroy our ward stone. And when they do there's at least four truckloads of undead waiting to charge in." I pulled out my own Streamlight and shined it around the room. I spotted my compact STI .45 and picked it up. "We've got to protect that ward."

Grant, stumbling from the beating, retrieved Torres' suppressed HK and looted some extra mags from the unconscious traitor. That's right, I had tossed Grant's gun down the hallway. Franks was a hulking shadow behind his light. "Archer, request reinforcements. Jefferson, call the Shacklefords and warn them what's coming."

Archer came back immediately. "I've got nothing."

"No signal," Grant said. The Condition was jamming us somehow. This was a full-on assault. Hood had set it up perfectly. He must have been planning this forever. Like Holly had said, this was a chess game to him.

"You know where the ward stone's at?" I asked. Grant had been around longer than I had.

"No idea," he answered. I shined my flashlight on him. He was bleeding from his nose and one eye was swollen shut. I had really clocked him. Served him right, just not for the reasons I had imagined. If we lived through this, I was going to find out why Grant had turned snitch and then I was going to beat him to death.

"The bad guys were heading into the tunnels by the barracks. Earl said that the stone was centrally located," I said.

"Probably in the middle of the property," he responded. The main building was toward the front. We had some ground to cover.

The compound was connected to the regular electrical lines. Those must have been cut by whatever that explosion was, probably set by the doppelganger. But we had our own backup generators in the basement. I could hear them begin to whine from down the hall. They were up and running within a minute. The lights came back on.

The cultists were in the tunnels. Luckily Earl had given me a brief tour. "I know about an entrance to the tunnels. We're close. We can intercept them. We've got to hurry." I started from the room.

"Wait," Franks said as he blocked the exit. "I'll handle this. My mission is still to keep you safe."

"No, you lied. Your mission was to capture your traitor." I pointed at Torres' unconscious form. "Now get the hell out of my way."

"You were both part of my mission."

"You son of a bitch..." He had brought a murderer right into my house, and put all of us at risk, just to accomplish his mission. Unfortunately, I couldn't even afford the luxury of being angry. There was work to be done. "We're out of time."

He contemplated that just for a second. After all, with the warding down, we were probably all going to die anyway. "Fine. Let's go. Archer, warn the Hunters. Find a way to contact Myers."

"Yes, sir!" Archer shouted, whipping out a pair of handcuffs and securing one of Torres' already cuffed wrists to the heavy desk. Then the efficient agent sprinted from the room, shouting back at us. "I'll get help."

Franks raised his Glock 10mm. He was wearing a suit, and other than what he had stashed in his pockets, probably didn't have a lot of extra firepower. All I had was my compact pistol, two extra 10-round mags, and a Spyderco folding knife. The rest of my gear was upstairs, fat lot of good that did me right now. Grant had Torres' piece, but at least he was wearing armor. So it was up to a brute, a snitch, and me, armed only with handguns, to defeat a commando force of heavily armed and amped-up cultists. I led the way toward the tunnels. "Hurry."

We reached the storage closet that Earl had showed me. The door was locked. I kicked it open. My ankle was really burning now. Shoving the shelf of cleaning supplies aside, I realized that there was no way I was going to batter this massive door open. The padlock hanging from the massive latch was a serious piece of steel. "Crap! I can't open it."

"Move," Franks ordered as he shoved past me.

"Well, that was stupid," Grant said.

"Shut it, you *rat*."

"You have no idea what you're talking about it, so shove it," Grant returned. "I saved your life."

"I can't believe you're a Fed. You lied to us all."

"I've got my reasons," Grant replied as he took a handkerchief out of his pocket and wiped the blood from his forehead. "I told you the truth earlier. You think this is all about you? The world doesn't revolve around you, Pitt."

Maybe Grant just brought out the worst in me, but I wasn't in the mood to listen to his crap. "Well, yeah, it does. So screw you."

Franks studied the big lock for a moment. Maybe he was planning on shooting it. Realistically, as solid as that chunk of steel was, we were going to run out of ammo and die from ricochets long before we broke it. Franks put his gloved hands around the lock, braced one big foot against the door and pulled with all his might. He roared as the metal bent, tore, then broke free. He fell back. Whatever the hell Franks really was, he sure was handy to have around.

Franks tossed the broken lock on the ground. He cracked his knuckles. "Go."

I pulled out my flashlight as we entered the tunnel. I remembered how to get to the intersection, but the only other time I had been down here, I had gone in the opposite direction than we needed to go. But rough estimation should get us toward the barracks.

The tunnels were cold, and without Earl to lead me, they felt strangely eerie. I set off in the direction of the barracks. Running with pistol in one hand, light in the other, I almost missed the turn. Franks collided with me. I picked the direction that seemed correct.

"Booby-trapped?" Franks asked.

"Uh . . . I don't actually know." Earl had never mentioned it, but all things considered, that seemed like a definite possibility.

"They should be. Stay behind me." Franks took the lead. He raised his light and scanned ahead. The big man took off at a run. It was a struggle to keep up. Franks was fast. I followed the bobbing light. It paused as he came to another branch. I guessed approximately where we were and shouted for him to keep to the left. Franks disappeared again.

"Damn, he's quick," I gasped. "What the hell is he?"

"I don't know either," Grant answered. "That was classified."

"Well, you're about useless."

We had to be getting close now. Suddenly the tunnel ahead of us was plunged into darkness. Franks had killed his flashlight. There had to be a reason, so I did the same. My eyes were not adjusted to the dark at all, so I placed my hand against the cold wall and shuffled forward blindly. My heart was pounding. I could hear Grant breathing hard behind me.

Something large and warm bumped into me. I almost shot him. "Suppressed weapon," Franks whispered. There was some shuffling as Grant handed off Torres' gun. "Count to thirty, then follow."

I counted. I got to twenty-five before I heard a pair of thumps that could only be the silenced .45. I moved forward.

The tunnel curved, and my boots collided with a large soft object. I knelt down. My hands landed in something sticky and hot. *Blood*. In utter darkness, I felt around. The body was wearing a tac vest covered with MOLLE pouches full of equipment. My fingers landed on lips and teeth. Goggles. The man had been wearing night vision goggles. I tore the device off his head and held it up to my eyes. The world was immediately bathed in a brilliant green glow. I flinched as I realized Franks was squatting a few feet ahead, looking right at me. Alien and terrifying in the unnatural light, his eyes glowed. He held up one finger in front of his lips to indicate the need for silence. Apparently he could see in the dark too.

The Condition did not skimp. These were at least as good as the third generation monoculars that MHI issued. I pulled the strap and chinpiece over my head. It was absurdly tight, and immediately began to hurt my face and cut off the circulation to my throbbing scalp. But I have an enormous head, so what do you expect.

Grant bumped into me. I put my head next to his ear and whispered for him to stay here. The cultist had an Uzi subgun with a massive sound suppressor at his side. I pressed it against Grant to replace the HK. He clumsily found it in the dark and took it from me. The goggles cut down my field of vision so much that it was like looking through a toilet-paper tube. When I looked back up, Franks was gone. I followed.

I heard voices. "We've retrieved the stone, Mistress. The warding is down."

"Excellent, take it to the surface. The Shadow Lord wants it immediately."

We were too late. The voices were getting closer. I reached another intersection. *How big was this place?* Maybe if I could put the stupid thing back, it would turn the shield back on. I was drastically turned around by now, but I could clearly tell which direction the sound was coming from. Franks materialized through the pixilated glow. He held up both hands. Five fingers on one, three on the other. Eight men.

"Where's Harris?" Sound carried strangely down here, so I couldn't tell how far away the voice was.

"I sent him to cover that tunnel," the woman said.

"Wait . . . I smell his blood."

I rubbed my sticky fingers together. I had wandered right into the dead cultist's body. I was covered in his blood. But how could he smell it? *Damn it*. They weren't all normal. . . .

"Hunters! They're here. I can smell them now. They're close. Let me transform and hunt them. Please?" The voice sounded eager, hungry. "Pretty please?"

"Be careful. I'll take the humans up to secure the stone. Kill them all, my love."

I saw Franks' pixilated face mouth the word *were-wolf*. Of course. It couldn't ever be easy, could it? I hoisted my STI and gave him a thumbs-up. *Silver bullets*. Franks pointed at me, then pointed down one passage. I nodded and proceeded in the indicated direction. Franks disappeared down the other.

I hate werewolves. Werewolves are what got me involved in this business to begin with. I'm scared shitless of werewolves. But there was no time for fear. I could dwell on the absolute bowel-clenching terror of trying to take on a ball of razor claws and fury in this enclosed space, or I could man up and go kill him. Less than a minute later a howl reverberated through the tunnel.

That transformation had been quick. This wasn't some wimpy young werewolf like the one that had almost ended my life. *But even tough lycanthropes weren't immune to silver.* That thought immediately made me think of Earl. If he had been hit with MHI-issued ammo, he might already be dead.

I kept swinging my head back and forth in wide arcs, scanning through the narrow field of view, gun trembling in my hands, waiting for the cultist-wolf to appear. When he did, it was unbelievably fast. One second the tunnel was open, the next, something was in front of me, a massive, hairy shape, with eyes glowing over a gaping maw full of teeth. The tritium night sights on my little pistol glowed like road flares in the night vision. I jerked the trigger twice.

The noise was brutal in the confined space. Smoke floated in front of the lens. The werewolf was gone. I'd missed.

*Damn, he's fast.*

The tunnel walls seemed to press in around me. I moved forward, gun up. If he reappeared, I wouldn't have much time to put him down. I had to incapacitate him quickly, because if he got in range, I knew that he'd tear right through my unarmored vitals.

Waiting, I covered the corner. He had to come through here. If I rounded the edge, he could be right there. I listened for breathing, but my ears were still ringing. I didn't have time for this. If the cultists got away with that stone, we were going to be up to our ears in dead things. They were probably already swarming over the fence. *Crap.* I surged forward, pistol raised. The hall was empty.

I ran in the direction that I thought the voices

had come from. The werewolf was still out there somewhere in the darkness, but I had to reach that stone first. My enhanced vision revealed a larger open space ahead of me. I came up on the corner ready to shoot, but there was no movement.

There was a big steel portal in this room. It was an old-fashioned vault door with a giant spinning wheel in the center. There was a perfect circle cut through the side of the door. I touched the edge. Several inches of steel had been cleanly sheared. It was cool to the touch. They had used some sort of magic to bypass Earl's security, and judging from the shape, it was probably another one of those magic ropes. Inside the room was a concrete pillar, looking almost like a speaker's podium, but with an empty indentation in the center about the size of a softball.

There was a scraping noise behind me, claws on rock. I spun, but couldn't see anything. *Stupid werewolf's stalking me.* Well, let him come. One of us would be faster than the other. It was that simple. I ran after the cultists. This tunnel was trending upward, but we seemed to be circling back toward where I had left Grant. I was so lost.

*Scritch.*

I spun on the ball of my foot, gun punching out. A black shape barreled toward me, eyes glowing like green balls of fire, saliva flying from rows of teeth. I fired.

We collided, slamming me painfully down. There was a flash of heat and fur rubbed across my face. I rolled over, gun tucked in tight against my body. My goggles had been knocked askew. I couldn't see anything. Something moved before me. There was a tearing of wind, and claws ripped four lines through my shirt. I opened fire.

A shriek of pain. I'd got him! The last shots in my pistol were gone in a split second, my slide locked back empty. I automatically dropped the mag and jerked another one from my belt, slamming it home and chambering a round. Claws scratched and I cranked off ten more shots in that direction, as fast as I could pull the trigger, muzzle blast creating a strobe effect as the shape rolled away from me.

It was quiet except for my breathing. Adrenaline was pounding through my system. I reached up with my shaking left hand and jerked the goggles back into place.

Agent Franks towered over me. I jumped. He had the suppressed HK in one hand. The werewolf was curled into a fetal position between us, a bristling mass of hair and muscle. Air hissed from its perforated lung. I'd nailed the werewolf repeatedly. Franks raised the pistol and put a final round through the creature's skull, splattering the tunnel floor. Franks nodded. "You got him . . ." Then he pointed at his abdomen. "And me."

It was hard to tell through the night-vision, but there was a leaking hole low in his side. *I'd shot Franks!* "Oh, man, are you okay?"

He appeared to think about it as he stuck one finger in the entrance wound, not feeling any pain. "Bullet struck my pelvis below my vest. Glanced upward . . . Hmmm, hit a kidney. You owe me a new one. Come on." He turned and stalked after the cultists.

Now that was tough, even by Monster Hunter standards.

"I'm *sorry!*" I exclaimed as I stepped over the dead werewolf. I'd never shot anybody by accident before. It was humiliating. Even if it was a pretty intense situation, I was still supposed to be the master of this stuff. I shoved my final magazine into the smoking STI and followed Franks.

Twenty feet of tunnel later, there was a chattering of submachine-gun fire. I pressed myself against the carved stone, but it wasn't directed at us. It was coming from just ahead. Franks surged forward. I followed. Grant was kneeling at the corner, metal Uzi stock at his shoulder, firing blindly down the hall. He must have stumbled around totally in the dark until he had heard the cultists. There was a ladder leading up into the night. There was one body at the base, and another one dangling with an arm trapped through the rungs. *Way to go, Grant.*

Somebody stuck an arm down the hole and muzzle flashes sparked as they shot at us. Franks extended the HK and fired. There was a scream of a pain and a clatter as the man dropped his gun down the hole. Franks hit the ladder and began to climb. He jerked the dead cultist off and let him drop. "Grant, follow us. We're heading up!" I shouted.

"I'm blind, idiot!" he responded.

"Head toward the gunfire," I suggested as I started climbing. Franks was nearing the top. There was a sudden *boom* as something detonated above him. He fell a couple of rungs, and I cringed, waiting for him to land on me, but he caught himself with a grunt. The cultists had grenades. Franks growled in frustration, blood falling from him and splattering my upturned face as he shoved himself up and through the hole.

I was out a second later, a cloud of dust and smoke still hanging in the air from the explosion. I tore off the goggles. The sun had just gone down, but it was brilliantly bright compared to the stifling tunnels. Franks was already moving, firing the suppressed pistol through the swirling dust. It ran dry, and he dropped it, automatically drawing a Glock. I couldn't see what he was shooting at, but I took off after him.

It took me a moment to orient myself as the dust cleared. We were at the north corner of the barracks. I ran, subconsciously crouching over as bullets crashed through the dirt at my feet. *Somebody was shooting at me!* I hugged the wall behind Franks, safely around the corner. I'd never actually been in a gunfight before. It was certainly different than fighting monsters!

Franks nodded at me. "Five left."

I was gasping for breath. I glanced down at my gun. "I'm down to my last ten rounds."

"So shoot each one twice," Franks replied. He reached down and checked his side. Blood was drizzling out from under his suit and soaking his pant leg. "I've got to stop this."

"Sorry," I stammered. I had often dreamed of shooting Franks, just never by *accident*. He had lost his sunglasses and in that brief lull I noticed something strange under the lights of the barracks. His eyes had changed. They had always been dark, almost black, and one still was, but the other was light blue.

Franks caught me staring and turned his head away. He pointed at the door the cultists had entered. "They're covering that entry. Is there another way in?"

It took my brain a second to process the request. There were windows, and they slid open, but like

everything at the compound, they were barred. I
had lived in the barracks while I had undergone my
Newbie training. Yeah, there was an entrance on both
sides, and one in the middle to the rec room. I found
myself nodding.

"Flank them," Franks ordered.

I didn't know at what point in time he had become
in charge, but I had never actually fought human beings
to the death before, so it seemed like a reasonable
request. I moved quickly down the wall, but just as I
did so, a massive fireball rose from the main building,
highlighting strange, disjointed shadows scaling the
walls. The undead were here. We were under siege.

The barracks was a very basic building. It was a
prefab, shaped like a big H, with a row of sleeping
quarters down both sides along a hallway, showers
on the end, and the recreation room in the center. I
paused outside the side door.

This was nuts. I shouldn't have been scared. I'd
risked my life dozens of times now, but facing people
was different. Well, they had at least one werewolf, so
I guess I couldn't assume the rest of the cultists were
human either. I had killed a man but I didn't really
know if the reborn Machado counted. I checked my
gun and took a deep breath. *Screw it.* Monster, human,
whatever, put a bullet in the right place, and they all
go down the same. People are just softer. The knob
was cool under my hand as I pulled the door open.

Nothing moved in the hallway.

I moved slowly, setting each boot down carefully so as
not to make too much noise. The doors to the Newbies'
rooms were all open, everyone having cleaned out their

stuff in preparation for getting the heck out of here. Luggage was stacked by each door. The walls had once been boring beige, but just about every inch had been covered by tacked-up posters, pictures, notes, Sharpie autographs, or even graffiti from years of new Hunters.

There was a noise—a crash as something fell over. There was movement in the room to the side. I raised my compact STI and covered the doorway.

A man stepped out, dressed entirely in black, wearing a balaclava and a pair of night-vision goggles pushed up on his forehead. He had the butt of an MP5 against his shoulder, muzzle down, as he swept into the hallway. They were clearing the building, probably getting ready to hole up and defend this place until the Condition secured the compound.

His eyes widened as he saw me five feet away, but it was too late to matter. The bullet passed cleanly through the cultist's face and he dropped in a spray of blood droplets.

"Contact!" someone screamed from the rec room. I leapt over the cultist's body and into the room he had just exited. Someone took the opportunity to fill the hallway with lead, emptying a magazine in a rapid buzz. Projectiles flew through the walls as I flung myself facedown on the carpet. I rolled over and covered the doorway.

The gunfire stopped. I got to my knees and took the corner. Another black-clad cultist was crouched just inside the rec room. He was fumbling, trying to shove a magazine into his subgun. He was mostly hidden, but prefab walls are thin. Since I couldn't see his head and he was probably wearing armor anyway, I aimed low, and cranked off four rounds through the wall.

He bellowed in surprise and fell out of sight. I got up and moved to the back of the room. Sure enough, another cultist responded, tearing the space that I had been inhabiting into splinters. The bars of the window collided with my back. Terrible noises reverberated through the glass, audible even over the gunfire and the angry shouting of the injured cultist. An epic battle was being waged outside.

It was with some shock that I realized that this was my old room. Right there on the wall was my own autograph. OZP: COMBAT ACCOUNTANT. I had been sitting on that bed right there when Trip had talked me out of giving up and quitting after I'd injured Green in training. My autograph disappeared as a bullet plowed through it. I hit the deck. These were high-powered rifle rounds, and they were zipping right through the walls like they were made of paper.

"Hold your fire!"

"I'll hold mine if you hold yours!" I shouted back.

It was a woman's voice, coming from the rec room. "I know that smell. We're supposed to take that one alive."

*Great, another werewolf.* "No, wrong guess," I replied as I crawled across the floor of the tiny room. There had been a mirror on the wall. I was lying in broken glass. Hands trembling, I picked up a giant shard and angled it so I could see down the hallway. It was clear.

"Yes, it is Pitt. The Master retrieved some of your clothing when you escaped from him in Mexico. I know your scent well, Hunter."

"How many werewolves does your boss have anyway?" There was someone moving just inside the rec room, but I didn't think it was the speaker.

It took her a moment to respond to me. She was

busy whispering orders to the remaining cultists. Where was Franks? I really could use a hand right now. But he was probably passed out from blood loss because I'd shot him in the kidney. The woman shouted back at me. "Just me and my mate, and since he's not rejoined us, I can only assume he's dead."

"Yep, I murdered the shit out of him."

She was quiet for a long time. When she spoke again, her voice was filled with fury. "Then that was a mistake. Kill him."

One of the other cultists piped in. "But the master said—"

"I said *kill him!*" the werewolf shrieked.

The reflection in the broken mirror revealed the cultist poking his head around the corner, barrel of a rifle just below. I threw myself into the hallway, front sight snapping into place instantaneously. I stroked the perfectly polished trigger to the rear, launching a 230-grain silver bullet, striking him in the throat. He didn't go down, so I shot him again, and again. He flopped backward in a heap, combat boots kicking stupidly into the air. I scrambled back into my old room before somebody else could jump out to shoot me.

There was more shooting from the rec room. Franks must be making his move. I got ready to charge. If I could hit the hall while they were distracted, I could pop the last few and get our ward back. I'd lost count, but I had a few shots left. Then I realized I was covered in blood, and with a panic began to look for holes. *Wait. It's not mine. . . . Awesome.* I moved for the hall.

But the werewolf had come to me.

We almost collided. She was a short woman, appearing physically young, but with unnatural silver hair and eyes that were glowing an angry gold. I jerked my gun up, but her hand slammed into my forearm, blocking the shot. It was like getting hit with a pipe. The STI dropped from tingling fingertips. She moved insanely fast even in human form. A punch landed against my ribs, slamming hot pain through my entire body. She wrapped petite hands around my throat and crashed me into one side of the hallway, smashing me through boards and drywall, only to jerk me out, and sling me around into the other wall. She tossed me headfirst toward the rec room. "He was a good man!" she screamed in my ear. "A good man!"

I came off the floor. I was pissed. "Now he's a dead man, bitch." I slugged her in the face, my massive fist curling tight at the last possible instant. It was the kind of hit that I had used to knock gigantic brutes into unconsciousness. Her head snapped around, silver hair flying.

My hand stung from the impact. But she didn't go down. When she looked back, silver hair parted, revealing a mouth that was now full of impossible incisors. She snarled as she swiped her open hand at me. Fire lanced across my chest as her lengthening fingernails tore through my skin. I leapt back, more of the wild swings tearing at me. I was too slow, and she raked lines of blood down my left cheek.

Rage washed over me then and it was *on*. I caught her by the wrist and pulled her forward. I jerked my knee up and hit her in the stomach. She slashed me again in the side, but fury cleansed the pain. With her bent over, I grabbed the back of her head and shoved down as I brought my knee into her face. Some of those sharp teeth shattered as I hit her again. I was on her, launching a flurry of attacks, meaty blows hammering into her like I was beating a hundred-pound punching bag. She flailed back and I straight kicked her in the chest. Supernatural powers aside, I was three times her size and weight, and physics beats magic. The werewolf flew down the hall.

But she landed on her hands and knees, her head flying right back up. "Is that the best you got?" she snarled with an inhuman voice as bones crackled and twisted. She ripped open her tac vest with claws that were now long enough to eviscerate. Silver hair was growing from her skin. She screamed as her teeth extended past her tearing lips.

"Yeah, it was." I spun and ran for the rec room. I didn't know where my gun was and I could only pray that the cultists I had shot had silver bullets loaded, too. The werewolf shrieked and jerked as she continued her transformation.

I hadn't really thought about what to do with the remaining cultists though....

Two were covering the other entrance, shooting at something that I assumed was Franks. One of the men I had hit was lying flat on his back, dead. The other one was leaning against the pool table, trying to stop the bleeding from his legs, and judging from the puddle, he was losing badly. None of them saw me enter.

The dead one had an AK-47 next to him. Even if it wasn't loaded with silver, 7.62x39 ought to tear some serious holes in a werewolf. I reached down—

But the werewolf intercepted me first. My feet flew out from under me as she collided with the backs of my knees. I landed on my back. The injured cultist cried out when he saw her, still more human than beast, but distorting rapidly. Distracted by the noise and driven into a frenzy, she leapt on her associate and lit into him with unbelievable ferocity. Blood and entrails sprayed across the pool table. The two others guarding the door turned to see what was going on, and lurched upright in fear.

"Claudia, no!" cried one of them. This was the kind of fury that Earl had warned me about. Her face had extended into bloody jaws. Golden predator eyes locked on them and lurched forward.

Both of the cultists jerked as projectiles ripped into them through the doorway. Franks had used the lull to his advantage. The werewolf leapt on top of the nearest and sunk her teeth into his throat, taking them both down in a jumble of arterial spray. They crashed into the 56" flat-screen and tore it from the wall.

I slipped in the warm blood, trying to find traction to rise. The werewolf looked up from her victim, the part of her mind capable of rational thought surely remembering that I was the one who had killed her boyfriend. I slid toward the pool table, latched onto a handful of felt and pulled myself up. Grabbing one of the solid balls off the table, I cocked my arm back and launched it at her. It hit her in the snout. She yelped, and I immediately chucked another pool ball. This time I missed.

She slunk forward. I grabbed the only other weapon that was in reach, a pool cue. It looked so skinny and feeble, but it beat harsh language. I raised it overhead and brought it down with a bellow. It snapped in half.

The werewolf was not amused. She stood upright, and now with her warping bones, she was my height, but gangly and misshapen. I held out the broken haft, ready to stab. Frothy bubbles blew from her nostrils as she backed me into the corner. Her silver mane was streaked with red. She closed in, instinct demanding to rip me to bits.

"Bad werewolf," Franks said from the entrance. "Sit."

The werewolf swung her head to assess the interloper. I slammed the jagged end of the pool cue into her throat. It was like a blood explosion. She howled in sudden agony, claws flying to the wound. Franks raised his Glock and calmly put a single round of silver 10mm through her brain, ending the scream forever. She collapsed.

"Stay. . . ." Franks walked up, assessed the body, then fired two more rounds into the corpse, just to be sure. "Good werewolf."

I was out of breath and covered in dripping blood. "Was that your idea of a joke?" He cocked his head to the side, inscrutable as ever. "Never mind. What took you so long?"

Grant answered that. He came running into the room, smoking Uzi in hand. "Help me barricade the door!"

"From what?" I asked.

Something *gigantic* roared outside. "*That!* Hurry!"

Franks got on one end of the pool table that had to weigh a ton, lifted it with a grunt and started dragging it across the floor. I threw my shoulder into the other side and shoved. Muscles straining, we got it next to the door, moved to one side, heaved, and tipped it over with a crash. We shoved it against the entrance.

The table shook as the giant beast collided with the doorway. The impact shook me to the bone. "What is that?" I shouted.

"I think it's a zombie bear," Grant said as he reloaded

the Uzi, putting his shoulder against the table to help hold it.

Franks braced himself against the table. "*Armored* zombie bear," he corrected.

"I tried to shoot it in the brain, but it's got a helmet or something," Grant shouted. The creature crashed into the table again, sliding all three of us back a few inches. "A helmet! Who puts buckets on zombies' heads? That's not fair! Where's the ward?"

The werewolf had been the leader. I hurried from the table, slipping on the bloody tile. The silver-haired woman was facedown. Her clothing was hanging in tatters. I had no idea what the stone looked like, but I assumed it was substantial. There was a black satchel on the floor. I ripped it open and my hands landed on something hard and cold.

It looked like a perfect granite sphere, about the size of a Magic 8 Ball. I rolled it over in my hands and discovered that there was a row of archaic letters carved into it. It looked like gibberish.

"Make it go!" Grant shouted. The zombie bear was crashing rhythmically into the table. My companions were sliding back against the relentless hammering.

"Turn it on," Franks ordered. A massive limb erupted through the center of the table. It was hairless, pink exposed muscle, with steel spikes bolted onto the end of the paw in lieu of regular claws. The paw swung about, searching, then jerked back out when it didn't catch us. Franks poked the muzzle of his Glock through the hole and cranked off half a dozen rounds. "Turn it on *now!*"

I touched the letters. Somehow, they turned like a combination lock. The letters were old-fashioned and spelled nothing. I randomly swiped my fingers across them, and they spun, symbols magically materializing on the smooth stone, spelling more nonsense. "I don't know how!" Earl had said that it needed to be tuned for a location. The cultists must have moved the combination when they picked it up.

The zombie bear had a running start this time. This time the table blew right in half. Franks and Grant were sent sprawling. I dove for the AK-47.

The beast was gigantic, big as a friggin' cow, hairless and pink, corded muscles bulging, with bands of steel and spikes welded together across its body. It was already riddled with puckered bullet holes, but showed no indication that it even knew. The head was an armored monstrosity, battleship plates bolted together into an armored box, then laced in razor wire and scalpel blades.

It was blind.

Now inside, it shuffled forward, clumsy limbs tearing rusty holes in everything, a snorting noise echoing from inside the helmet as it smelled us. It couldn't bite, but we were sure to be crushed or cut to ribbons as it stupidly tried. I hoisted the AK, jerked it to my shoulder, and fired at the helmet. The gun was set on full-auto, and the 30-caliber bullets bounced off in sparks and fragments. The best way to take out zombies was to destroy the brain, and that didn't look like an option here, not to mention it was covered in blades and weighed a thousand pounds. Catching my scent, it lumbered at me.

Franks intercepted the bear. He had his fighting knife in one hand and a grenade in the other. He dodged under the swinging blades, cut a long gash between the monster's ribs, then slammed his fist through the gap, sinking clear up to his shoulder in organs. It dragged him along toward me. "Back," Franks ordered, jerking his gore-stained arm out of the hole with a disgusting squelching noise and falling away from the deadly legs. The grenade was gone. The zombie bear's roar reverberated inside the helmet. I sprinted down the hallway.

The explosion was muffled inside the bear carcass. When I opened my eyes, a red cloud filled the recreation room. It was literally raining meat. Bits and pieces fell from the ceiling with wet thumps.

We certainly wouldn't be using the rec room anytime soon. The armored zombie bear had been blown apart. The head and shoulders were filling the bullet-riddled doorway. The head was still moaning, but it didn't have any limbs to drive it. I kicked the box.

Franks stepped out of the blood cloud. He was entirely coated in a viscous red slime. He was terrifying to look at, but I'm sure I didn't look much better. "Jefferson, get weapons. Pitt, ward."

I tossed him the ball. He caught it with one hand. The noise from the compound indicated that there were more of these things out there, and MHI was responding with explosives, *lots* of explosives. Franks scowled as he studied the letters. Apparently he was as stumped as I was.

"Let's get to a more defensible position while we figure that thing out," I suggested, jerking my head back the way I had come.

Franks put the ward stone to his ear and shook it. "I *hate* puzzles."

# CHAPTER 16

The most defensible rooms in the barracks were the bathrooms. There was only one entrance and no windows. If the cultists had grabbed this instead of the rec room, we wouldn't have been able to dislodge them. We took the women's instead of the men's because it was on the side away from the main building, where the undead seemed to be focusing their attention.

Franks held the ward stone in his big hands and studied it with one black eye and one blue eye, unblinking. The letters were not cooperating. Grant and I covered the doorway. Grant had picked up another Uzi. I had kept the AK-47 and stuffed magazines into every pocket until the weight threatened to pull down my cargo pants. I had found my pistol in the hall and returned it to its holster, but it only had a couple of shots left.

"Any luck?" I asked. Franks didn't answer, intent on the code. "What, they don't teach you this stuff at your fancy academy?"

"Shut up," Grant muttered.

"No, you shut up," I snapped. "I'm not done with

you yet. We live through this and I'm going to beat your ass. The last one was just a warm-up."

"You sucker-punched me at gunpoint. Try me in a fair fight, and we'll see how tough you are," Grant responded. He was delusional if he thought that would make a difference. "Torres would already have turned you over to his church if it wasn't for me."

I turned back to the door. "Traitor," I muttered.

Grant was ticked. "You've got no clue. I joined MHI to make a difference. But MHI's all about making money, not about making the world a better place. Myers was just like me once, disillusioned by MHI. He gave me a chance to do something important. MHI let me down, not the other way around. I thought that I had failed you guys, but it was the organization that failed me."

"So you took Myers' job offer?"

"Yes, I did. Best decision I've ever made. He needed somebody who could get on the inside, help catch his spy, and if that didn't work out, at least he had someone undercover to keep an eye on MHI before they did anything really stupid. I got into this to help people. The Monster Control Bureau represent the real heroes. They do a dirty job to protect this country. MHI is just out to make a buck."

"Make a *buck*? That's right, that doesn't matter when you're born rich."

"Quiet," Franks ordered, tired of our bickering.

I glared at Grant, then went back to watching the entrance. He was a traitor, pure and simple. Myers had used me as bait to clean his own house, and now my friends were paying the price. When this was over, there were some accounts that needed settling.

My face hurt from where the werewolf had clawed me. Touching it indicated that the flesh was rent open in a few parallel strips down my cheek, and I was bleeding badly. Grant had the door covered while Franks fiddled with that stupid thing, so I made my way over to the sink and turned it on. The cold water burned.

Franks looked up from his task and saw me splashing the claw marks. "If you're infected, I'll have to—"

"Kill me? Yeah, I know. That's how we met, remember?"

Franks nodded and went back to the ward.

It was when I looked back in the mirror that I noticed something amiss in one of the stalls. The door was closed, but there was a shadow dangling just under it. Shutting the water off, I approached the stall. I used the muzzle of the AK to push it open.

"G-Nome?"

The gnome had been shoved in the toilet. He was so small that most of his body was squished into the water, and it was awfully pink. One boot was dangling down, and that was what I had seen. His red hat was crunched low on his head, and his white beard was smeared with blood. His breathing was rapid and shallow.

I knelt next to the toilet and removed his hat. His eyes fluttered open weakly. He was badly injured. "'Sup, tall one," he sputtered.

I reached out and touched his hand. "What happened?"

Black lightning struck and the bathroom vanished.

This time was different than the others. It was the first time that I'd experienced a nonhuman's memories.

The thoughts were subtly alien, and it took a moment for my brain to adjust and it couldn't quite settle into the first person, rather I was a spectator in G-Nome's head. He had confided in me Grant's treachery, and he'd left me, confused by how such a physically tough human, a man-mountain of ass-kicking, could be crying and moping like a baby. No self-respecting gnome badass would ever let his homies see him cry. Tall humans were so *weird*. He knew it came from all of that banging their heads on doorways and ceiling fans and shit.

G-Nome had heard the shower turn on in the girls' bathroom, and though he enjoyed spying on human girls as much as the next gnome, he was excited to watch the Tall One shoot the Snitch. He was from Birmingham, so he'd seen plenty of humans shoot each other, and that never got old. But when he caught the smell of killing on the air, he knew something wasn't right. Suspicious, he'd left the tall human to his business and ported through the wall.

The shower was on when he popped into the bathroom. G-Nome held extra still so the invisibility would hold. He knew from experience that humans freaked out when they caught you looking at them. He could smell which human it was immediately. There was something special about this one. He'd seen her around the compound, and she'd stuck out for some reason, even for a human. It was that younger human hottie, with the redneck accent . . . *Dawn*. He'd overheard that she was a human beauty queen, and he could see why—that human was *smokin'*. Momma had warned him about the dangers of human women, what with their tallness and lack of facial hair.

G-Nome noticed Dawn's discarded clothes and he was reminded of the death smell that had gotten his attention to begin with. They were piled up at the foot of the shower, and they were all messy. She'd been splashed with blood. He got closer and checked them out. The red was in splatters, like she'd slaughtered a pig or something.

Now that didn't make no sense. That red beard, Milo, wasn't having anybody do any work with bodies and guts today. And it was the day of the Hunters' big ceremony. So why was Dawn here, covered in blood, and not in the big building with everybody else? She had been up to something.

G-Nome was known as the sharpest gnome on the North Side for a reason, and he knew right away that something was up. He snuck over real quiet and picked up her shirt. He sniffed it. The smell told him that it had come from one of the other new humans, but he couldn't remember the dude's name. G-Nome didn't know how much blood was inside a normal human, but if this much got spilled at one time, he was probably dead. He had to tell Harbinger.

The shower turned off. G-Nome dropped the shirt and padded quickly to the corner. He was extra careful to stay still so the invisibility would hold. Dawn stepped out of the shower.

The sight was enough to take his mind off the murder. *Aw hells yeah, baby...* She had the longest legs of any human he'd ever seen. G-Nome knew he better be paying attention now that he knew some weird shit was going down. She didn't bother to cover herself or dry off. Instead she picked up the clothes and stuffed them into the garbage. Then she stopped and lifted her pretty face to smell the air . . . He'd never seen a human do it like that before. Humans had terrible noses. G-Nome thought about just porting through the wall and getting the hell out of here, but he was too curious. Dawn's nostrils flared. She spun around, wet hair flying around her shoulders and she stared right at him.

How could she see him? Humans couldn't see gnomes when they were still.

Dawn blinked and then her eyes were solid, colorless, clear as ice cubes. *"Tomte,"* she hissed, and her voice was all wrong, low and scary, and she used the old word for gnome. It took him a second to realize that he was dealing with a Fey and another second to realize that it was the worst kind of Fey of all.

"Doppelganger!" G-Nome sputtered as he reached for the gun in his waistband. But by then it was too late. The creature descended on him.

I jerked my hand away, a trail of black light drifted from his arm to my fingertips. It held for a moment, then drifted off like smoke. I could still feel the pressure of the shapeshifter's hands around my throat.

"Yeah, crazy, huh?" G-Nome smiled weakly. "That was whack . . ." He trailed off.

He was dead.

I pulled his sopping body out of the toilet and set him gently on the ground. He didn't weigh much.

"Where'd you get a gnome?" Franks asked.

I shook my head. "The Condition has a doppelganger here. That's what Torres was talking about."

"Who?" Grant asked.

"The girl from Texas, Dawn. She must have been

on guard duty and killed that other Newbie, then she came back to clean up here and murdered G-Nome." I knew almost nothing about doppelgangers, except that they were some kind of rare shapeshifter. "Then she went back and shot Harbinger."

"So that's how you caught me." Grant muttered. "A gnome. . . ."

"If the doppelganger got away, it could be anyone now," Franks said, not looking up from the ward stone. "I can't figure this out. You have to know the inventor's codes." There was a massive *bang* as something landed on our roof. Grant and I flinched and raised our weapons, but with a sudden tapping, the noise retreated. There were all sorts of undead out there. "Who could make it work?"

I shrugged. "Earl, of course." I didn't add *if he's still alive*. "Maybe Julie, or one of the older Hunters, but they're all at the main building. Let's get back there and find somebody." Apparently Franks agreed. He handed the ward to me. I stuffed it in the bag and hoisted the stolen AK. "Tunnels?"

Grant stood. "I don't really want to try the front door right now."

The compound was a war zone. A few hundred yards away the main building was under siege. Black shapes were clambering up the walls. Occasional explosions highlighted more dimly-visible things moving in a circle around the structure directed by robed figures. Muzzle flashes flew from every window on the top floor. Continuous streams of tracers rained from the roof into the surroundings and a few worked patterns across the night sky.

"What are they shooting at in the air?" Grant asked hesitantly.

The three of us were clustered, kneeling next to the opening into the tunnels. The ladder stretched into the darkness below us. "I don't know," I said quickly. This asshole was creative enough to animate bears, so who the hell knew what he had for air support.

Headquarters seemed to be holding its own. The heavy portcullis had been dropped over the front door. A mass of misshapen bodies was piling up at the entrance. Hammering and hacking could be heard even over the gunfire. Suddenly a brilliant streamer of fire ignited from the narrow windows above the door, as someone used a flamethrower to hose down the monsters at the gate. Flaming bodies stumbled about before collapsing.

The flamethrower revealed something else charging out of the darkness. A massive shape, big as a truck, plowed through the burning dead and collided with the gate. The crash echoed across the entire compound.

"What's that?" I hissed.

Four streams of tracers lit into the giant, followed by more fire, and what had to be a chain of 40mm grenade detonations. The now-burning beast backed up for another run. "Hmmm . . . zombie elephant," Franks answered thoughtfully. "Unless it's a dinosaur. Hard to tell with the armor."

So Hood had either murdered a zoo or he'd pulled a *Jurassic Park*, but either way, this was really bad. "Back door it is," I suggested, shining my flashlight down the ladder.

Two dozen white eyes blinked back at me.

"Shoggoth!" Franks bellowed. His palm struck me

in the shoulder, knocking me aside. A black tentacle exploded from the hole, splitting the air where I had been standing. It snapped back into the dark with a bullwhip crack. Franks yanked another grenade from his damaged suit coat, pulled the pin, and tossed it down the hole. "Back."

I ran toward the barracks. I could hear Grant huffing along beside me. The grenade detonated, but rather than a boom, it was a hiss. Thermite. The shoggoth made an unbearable noise, a terrible distorted wail, like somebody had overloaded a bank of speakers by having an insane howler monkey attack the microphone. We clamped our hands over our ears. The noise faded away.

When I turned around, smoke was pouring from the hole. "Is it dead?"

Franks looked at me like I was stupid. *Of course not.* Harbinger had said that the warding kept out undead and transdimensional creatures, which apparently included the Condition's pet shoggoth. With the shield down, it must have burrowed right into our tunnels. "We've got to get back down there."

"No more grenades," he replied.

They were only vulnerable to fire. Now there was no way to get into the main building. "Damn it!" That thing would own us in the tunnels.

"Quiet!" Grant exclaimed, holding up his hand. Large wings batted above us in the night. The shoggoth's scream must have gotten its attention. The three of us ducked back under the overhanging roof of the barracks. The thing circled for a moment, each beat of the wings ponderous and slow. As the noise stopped, something landed on the roof above us with a crash of breaking shingles.

I held my breath. I was screwed. Monsters below us, monsters above us, monsters all around us. We were armed with a few stolen small arms and a magic rock that we didn't know how to work. We had nowhere to go, and my companions were a snitch and a psycho. Talk about bleak. Dust fell from the overhang as the winged monster above us shifted.

There was a flash from the opposite side of the compound. There was a violent impact overhead and whatever it was above us crashed into the roof. The mystery creature leapt upward, visible for just a moment as a gray mass, before two wings spread wide and it jerked straight up and out of sight, absurdly fast.

*What was that?* Grant mouthed, obviously afraid.

I shrugged, *hell if I know,* then pointed in the direction of the muzzle flash. It had come from Milo's workshop. Either Milo was at his shop and had sniped the thing, or somebody else had done us the favor. Either way, it beat sticking around while other things came to see if there was anything edible over here. Franks realized what I was thinking and nodded. There were a few terrain features we could use for cover between us and the shop, but there was a long expanse of open ground at the end. Sticking Milo clear out there made sense when he was playing with explosives and deadly chemicals, but didn't seem so clever right about now.

"Leapfrog," Franks stated. He pointed at Grant, "One," then at me, "two," then jerked his thumb at himself. "Three. Move."

If something spotted us, we were as good as dead. Grant took one quick look at the dark sky, then back at the fires leaping up around headquarters. Nothing seemed to be coming this way. His Adam's apple bobbed visibly as he swallowed hard, then he took off at a full sprint for the next building. It was a Tuff Shed we stored maintenance equipment in. He reached it, then spun around, jerking his head in every direction. He waved for me to come, then raised the Uzi and waited.

I leapt to my feet, moving as fast as I could. My blood was thundering in my ears as my big boots slammed into the gravel. I made it halfway before I heard the wings. Grant was looking right over me, eyes unbelievably wide, as he jerked the Uzi up and opened fire. I fell on my face, sliding across the dirt like I was trying to steal a base. The winged monster zipped past me in a blast of wind. Jerking my head up, I saw the wings spread as it soared upward again, giant three-toed talons trailing behind. I wanted nothing more than to lie here and try to hide, but that was suicidal. Clambering back up, I ran the rest of the way to the shed.

Grant was stammering. "Okay, walking dead, that's fine. Running dead, I can handle. But the flying dead? Hell with this. I quit."

I gasped for breath. "Too late. You're fired." Franks had seen what had happened to me, but went for it anyway. He moved unbelievably fast for such a big dude, arms and legs pumping like an Olympian. "Here it comes," I said, as I caught sight of the flying monster banking around. It was trailing Franks now, high in the air. It tucked its wings in and plummeted like a missile right at him. The AK's iron sights were rudimentary at best, and I could barely see them in the dark, but I did my best, pumping round after round at the speeding target. We weren't going to stop it in time.

Franks must have known that. He suddenly stopped, throwing his weight back, skidding through the gravel as he turned, raising his own stolen AK one-handed and firing, a long strobe-effect burst of full-auto right into the creature. It flared its wings at the last moment, then Franks was simply gone, scooped right off the Earth and sucked into the sky.

They passed right over us, and the last thing I saw before they disappeared over the top of the shed was Franks crawling up the monster's legs and actually *punching* it in the face.

The land-based undead had heard the gunfire and shadows were moving in front of the flames, lumbering our way. Grant and I looked at each other, then at the direction Franks had gone. That was the direction we were heading anyway. Tactics were out the window, and now it was time to haul ass. Correction—speed is a tactic. "Run!" I shouted.

We cornered the building, moving fast for the relative safety of Milo's workshop. Grant is a lot lighter than I am, and even wearing his armor, he quickly left me in the dust. When you're getting chased by a zombie bear, I guess you don't need to be faster than the bear, just faster than your friends. I briefly contemplated shooting Grant in the leg.

Then I heard the beat of wings again. *Damn it, not now.* This time the beating seemed somehow lopsided and unbalanced. The gray shape appeared out of the sky ahead of us, ungainly, with one wing fluttering. A darker shape that could only be Franks was dangling from one side, slamming a fist repeatedly into the monster. It spiraled down, out of control, and crash-landed into some kudzu-coated trees.

I veered slightly off course, heading for the trees. The noises were clear. Somebody was administering a severe beating. The monster was on its back, Franks was astride its chest, raining hammer blows down on its mutant skull, beating the hell out of a creature that was approximately the size of a living-room couch.

One giant claw shoved Franks off and the creature sat up. It was a zombie, but a zombie of *what* I couldn't tell you. Its legs ended in raptor claws, but its upper body was that of a man. Leathery bat wings extended from each shoulder, one clearly crushed and broken by the fall. Its face was a skull now, but about the size of a five-gallon bucket and filled with teeth that looked like rusty nails. Blank eye sockets swiveled toward me.

It took me a couple of shots in the dark before the skull exploded into powdery fragments. It dropped.

Franks appeared. His breathing was ragged. "I hate flying coach."

"Man, you're a regular comedian tonight," I said as I jerked another magazine out of my pocket and reloaded. "We've got to keep going, more bears coming fast." But he didn't respond. When I glanced back, he was facedown into the kudzu. "Aw hell."

Grant had kept on running for the workshop and I could no longer spot him in the dark. I could, however, hear the undead getting closer. Franks weighed a ton. The smart thing to do was leave him here. It wasn't like I owed him any mercy. This whole thing was his and his stupid organization's fault.

I actually made it a couple of steps toward the

workshop before I stopped. *He wouldn't have left me.*
"ARRGHH! Stupid Fed. Stupid Franks." I scooped
him up, got one arm over my shoulder, and shouted
in his ear, "Move your ass!" His big head lolled to
the side. He was unconscious. "Oh, it can never be
easy. Never! Easy!" I heaved him into a fireman's
carry. The kudzu vines dragged at my boots. The
shuffling, metallic snorting of the undead was getting closer. Safety was still a hundred yards away. I
kicked my feet through the thick plants and tripped
and stumbled for safety.

I could see the workshop clearly now. Someone was
moving in one of the windows, a long tube on their
shoulder. I cleared the kudzu and could run again,
slipping through the dirt, ankle throbbing with each
step. A terrible noise came from the workshop and a
streak of fire tore past. The trees behind us exploded.
*Rocket launcher.* Oh, these monsters had picked the
wrong place to mess with.

More rockets followed. Judging by the rate of fire,
Grant had reached the workshop and was joining in.
Milo had a ton of stuff stashed.

"Pitt!" A voice bellowed behind me. "I'm coming
for you."

*The Englishman.*

I risked a glance back. A towering thing was making its way through the smoke and falling debris,
each footfall shaking the very earth. It had been an
elephant once, and a big one, a majestic beast, but
now its ivory tusks were sheathed in iron, its head
plated in steel, its bones wrapped in wire and Kevlar
sheets. Riding on its back was my nemesis. He was
no longer wearing simple clothing, but had dressed

for the occasion with an ornate black robe, a golden pendant of his squid god on his chest. His rough features shifted under the shadows of his cloak.

"Hood," I spat.

He raised one hand, signaling a halt. The zombie elephant reared up on its hind legs, rising high into the air, blowing air through its dusty lungs like a damaged tuba. It came back down, forelegs slamming into the dirt with an impact that shifted the ground underfoot. "So you know my name . . . There's power in knowing one's name." There was another bear, and something that looked like it had been stitched together out of a German shepherd and a goat, and behind them were at least a dozen humanoid zombies, all in various states of augmentation. His troops began to fan out in a circle around me. "How did you find out?"

Franks was dead weight on my back. There was no way I was going to reach the workshop now, so I slowly lowered him to the ground. "Carlos Alhambra told me."

The shadow man nodded, unsurprised. "Killing him would have been smarter, but he deserved to suffer." There was another concussion from the workshop, but Hood merely waved his hand in the direction of the oncoming rocket. The darkness seemed to coalesce and solidify, and the warhead detonated harmlessly well short of us. "Destroy that nuisance," he ordered, and several of his minions immediately charged the workshop, scampering off through the swirling wall of black.

The wall blocked the lights of the workshop, but Milo's rocket fire had ignited the small copse of trees, and I had some flickering light to work with. But it was even dimmer than what I had in Mexico, and he had been virtually unstoppable there.

"You got what you came for. Let the others go and I'll come with you."

He laughed above me. "Oh, come on, mate. You had your chance to do it my way. I've squandered years of work for this moment. Do you have any idea how much time it takes to put together an army of the dead? I've been collecting corpses like some people collect stamps." He stroked the mottled, rotting back of the elephant. "But tonight has put quite a dent in my collection. So, no, I'm going to see the heart torn out of MHI before I go."

"Where the hell do you get dead elephants anyway?" I asked.

"The internet," Hood responded. "Zoos, circuses, that sort of thing."

"Oh . . ." I still had the AK in one hand. He saw me thinking about it, and shook his head.

"I wouldn't do that if I were you."

"If you were me, I'd kill myself," I responded. "And you know . . . that's not a real bad idea. . . ." I raised the hot muzzle and stuck it under my chin.

He stood on the back of his mount. "Wait!"

"Delivering me with half my head missing might piss off the Dread Overlord, don't you think?" I stuck my finger on the trigger. I wasn't bluffing. "Call off your army and I'll go with you. Otherwise I blow my brains out and you've got to break the news to your super oyster."

"Hold on," Franks whispered from the ground. He'd woken, and had reached into his suit, pulled out a flask, and was unscrewing the lid. Hell of a time for a drink. . . .

Hood's voice was soothing. "You don't want to kill yourself. Suicides go to hell, you know."

"Oh, like you believe in hell," I muttered.

"Got me there, but we can still work this out. Alive is preferable, just for the amount of suffering that he can inflict on you, but dead? I could probably clean you up right well, if you leave me no other choice." He seemed to grow angrier the more he thought about it. "You think you can threaten me with your death? I'm a king of death! Look around you! Death is my servant! Death is my *art*!"

Franks put the flask to his lips and poured the contents down his throat. He grimaced in pain as if the liquid really burned going down. Some of it spilled out and dripped down his face. It glowed blue in the dark.

That got Hood's attention. "Well, well, well... Special Agent Franks, I'd almost forgotten about you. I see that you've some of the Elixir of Life. I always wondered how something like you managed to stick around for so very long. Personally, I'd thought that *Herr* Dippel had taken the formula to his grave. You really must give me that recipe." Franks dropped the flask and began to convulse in the dirt. Hood shook his head sadly. "Painful, and wasteful. You can't expect a dosage of the Elixir to save you now."

Franks was shaking badly as he struggled to his feet, using my belt for help. I kept the AK pointed at my brain. I could *hear* his body reacting to the potion. Franks' bones were popping. The veins in his face were pulsating. The shadow man was obviously surprised by this development. Franks smiled, teeth white in the dark. "One dose? Try *five*, asshole."

Hood paused. "Impossible... No flesh could withstand that level of purification."

"You've got to work up to it." My protector shrugged

out of his coat and yanked off his clip-on tie, Glocks dangling on both sides from a double-shoulder holster. His shirt hung in a blood-soaked ruin. The firelight flickered across his body. The muscles in his neck throbbed and pulsed. He pulled off his strangler gloves and tossed them to the side, the bones in his hands cracking as he rolled them into fists.

His left hand had HATE tattooed across his knuckles...

The dead trucker in Montgomery had that same tattoo.

*No.* That *was* the dead trucker's tattoo... That was the dead trucker's *arm.*

My mouth fell open and I almost dropped the AK. Franks spoke quietly, "Primary mission. Protect Pitt from the Condition." He glanced over at me, one blue eye reflecting the firelight and nodded through gritted teeth. "I've never failed a mission."

*Franks was built out of spare parts....*

The shadow man, suddenly afraid, gestured at his undead. "Take them!"

The monsters surged forward. I jerked the AK down and opened fire. Franks crossed his arms, then whipped them outward, a Glock appearing in each hand, firing with terrifying accuracy right through the joints in the zombies' helmets. The elephant bellowed, stampeding forward, coaxed on by its master. Hood shouted a maniacal cry as the elephant bore down on us.

There was a blur of motion as something leapt through the air onto the elephant's back. Earl Harbinger landed directly behind Hood, dumping an entire magazine of .45 from his Tommy gun into his enemy's back. Hood's body rippled like water. The gun emptied in seconds, Earl Harbinger grabbed the shadow man by the robes and flung him from his perch. Hood fell hard in the dirt. Earl jumped after him, landing in a crouch. The elephant was heading right at me, and I dove aside, tree-trunk legs crashing past like thunder.

"You!" Hood spat from flat on the ground. The robes shifted as his flesh turned to molten shadows. They swirled and re-formed. Now he was standing. He calmly brushed the Alabama red clay from his fancy outfit. "So my assassin failed."

Harbinger stood. "Shot the hell out of me with silver bullets." He raised his arms, displaying his battered leather bomber jacket. "You should have told her to shoot me in the head. I don't just wear this coat 'cause it looks cool. This is one-hundred-percent-genuine minotaur hide." He thumped it for emphasis. "Bulletproof." Earl smiled his predatory grin. His eyes were glowing gold. "You're looking good, Marty, for a dead man."

Undead were swirling all around. The humanoids were wearing helmets of hardened steel, only their lower jaws open and chomping. I shoved my muzzle into an onrushing zombie's mouth. The jaws clamped down automatically and I fired, the bullet ricocheting around inside the bucket, pulping the skull to bits. A zombie bear intercepted Franks, knocking him to the ground, slicing him about between the razor sharp legs. The Fed, unperturbed, jammed his guns into the intersection of the bear's protected head and body and severed the neck with a slew of 10mm rounds. The bear collapsed, crushing him beneath.

Hood and Harbinger were circling each other. The

Condition's high priest was speaking. "A dead man, Earl? On the contrary, I've never been more alive." He waved one hand, and it warped into a foot-long shadow blade. His other hand twisted into a three-fingered claw, wide as a shovel head.

"I'll have to remedy that," my boss replied. "I'll get it right this time."

"You destroyed my old body. Rather admirably at that, but the spirit that was residing there came from this vessel. Think of it as trading up for a new model car." Hood swung the shadow blade and Harbinger ducked under it.

I kicked the legs out from under another zombie, slammed the AK under its chin, and blasted it. I moved to help free Franks, but with a bellow, he pushed the giant bear off him and heaved it aside. He sprang to his feet and slammed his fist *through* an approaching zombie's helmet. HATE came out clutching a handful of brain and the zombie dropped like a sack of potatoes. A goat-dog thing charged Franks, snapping at his legs, but he punted it across the clearing and into the burning trees.

"I'm invulnerable in the dark, and this little fire isn't nearly enough," Hood stated proudly as he swung his blade hand. Harbinger bounded over it, flying through the air at his foe, his own hand opened into a claw, swinging with a roar through the ornate robes. Earl rolled through the robes, crashing into the ground as all resistance gave way. He was up, bewildered at the empty fabric in his hands. A twelve-foot solid shadow rose behind him, and he screamed as a black spike was driven into his back.

"Earl!" I shouted.

"Stay back!" he ordered, bloody spittle flying from his mouth. Harbinger spun, tearing through the shape to no effect. One whipping tendril struck him across the abdomen, launching him back into the darkness. He hit the ground closer to the fire.

The shadow surged under the robes, the fabric rising into a man shape, and then settling into the form of Hood as he strode toward Harbinger. "You have no idea how much I've looked forward to this." I shot Hood square in the back of the head. The bullet zipped out his forehead. He paused, looking back at me slyly. "Patience. I'll be back for you."

Earl rose. He was shaking badly. There was a hole in his chest, and it gradually closed, pinching off a trail of blood. There was a loud series of *booms* from the main building, like the sound of launching fireworks. "This whole owning-the-night thing ain't fair," Earl said as he pointed at the sky. "And if you find yourself in a fair fight, your tactics suck."

The sky lit up with a brilliant fireball. It drifted slowly toward the Earth. Then there was another, and then several more, appearing in rapid succession. The compound visibly brightened as the parachute flares and star shells floated downward. The compound's mortars were filling the sky with burning phosphorus light.

"That's cheating, Earl." Hood smiled, seemingly eager for this fight.

Flickering shadows played across Earl's features as more shells rained from the sky. "My daddy always said that if you ain't cheating, you ain't trying hard enough."

Franks twisted the head off of the last zombie, and immediately began walking toward Hood. The shadow man paused between the two foes, glancing warily between them. The new illumination revealed that the zombie elephant was turning around, coming back for another pass.

Hood nodded slowly, determination hard on his craggy face. He studied the sky, watching the fireballs. "This won't be enough to save you." He wrapped his hand around his talisman. It glowed with a black lightning that was eerily familiar. He seemed to grow in size, density and darkness, like he was sucking energy from his surroundings. His voice was low and terrifying. "A bureaucrat's Frankenstein and the redneck Wolfman are no match for the Lord of the Shadows, High Priest of the Dread—"

"Shut up already," Franks said as he walked forward. Tendrils of blackness shot from Hood's hands, lashing into the Fed, knocking him easily aside. The ground swelled under Hood, like a rising bubble. The dirt ripped wide open, revealing a giant rolling slug of tar. Packets of reflecting eyes glared in every direction. The shoggoth had returned.

"Owen! Get the ward to Milo. He knows what to do!" Earl shouted as he ducked and dodged under waves of black energy. "Go!"

I did as I was told and ran for the workshop. It was our only hope. No matter how tough Earl and Franks were, I knew they couldn't defeat Hood and his minions. The roars and crashing intensified behind me. Gunfire and explosions continued to rock the main building as the bulk of the undead kept up their assault. I sprinted through the artificial wall of darkness, holding my breath like it was a poisonous vapor. I cleared the wall within a few steps, and there was the workshop. I leapt over numerous undead that had been blasted or scorched into pieces. "Milo! I need your help!"

Milo's head popped up on the roof from behind a stack of discarded LAW rocket tubes. "Owen, what's going on?" he shouted.

I reached into the satchel that was bouncing against my side and hoisted the stone above my head as I ran. "Activate this thing!"

"I'm on my way down," Milo exclaimed.

I started to lower the stone, but it disappeared from my hand in a blast of wind. *The stone was gone!* Jerking my head up in surprise, I was shocked to see one of the flying undead, the stone encircled in its talons, as it beat its mighty wings and gained altitude. I screamed in frustration.

*BOOM!*

The creature's leg exploded with a terrible impact. The entire talon fell, severed, still clutching the ball. Running, I caught it all in my outstretched hands. I looked up to see Grant on the rooftop, his head poking up from behind the scope of a Barrett M82A1 .50 caliber. "Move your slow ass, Pitt!" he shouted.

The roll-up garage door was closed. The man-door next to it flew open, and Milo was there, holding a giant flamethrower that had THE BURNINATOR and a cartoon dragon painted on it. "Let me see it," he cried as he shrugged out of the flamethrower straps.

*BOOM-BOOM-BOOM-BOOM!*

Grant had opened fire on something. I turned to see the zombie elephant come swirling through the black wall like an undead freight train, lumbering right at the workshop. I slammed the ball, severed talon and all, into Milo's outstretched arms, and pushed through the door. I closed it behind me and, for some unknown reason, threw the dead bolt. Milo gave me a look that indicated the idiocy of what I had just done, then he snapped out of it, and started swiping his hands over the numbers.

"Hurry," I suggested.

"You think?" he responded, beady eyes intent behind his glasses. "Oh, it's been a long time."

I began looking for something that could stop a zombie elephant. There had to be something. I paused in front of Milo's giant wall of weapons. *What gun for armored zombie elephant? Man, what kind of messed-up job do you have to ask yourself that kind of question?* Then I had my answer, sitting right in front of me on a giant wheeled tripod. I grabbed the handles of the device and began to push the heavy weight across the linoleum. "Is this loaded?"

"Of course," he responded absently. Milo stood in the center of the room, studying the ward intently. "The ward is like a puzzle, but with coordinates based on ley lines, and the letters are substitutes, but the hard part is that it's in German . . . Now what was that—"

The roll-up door collapsed as the pachyderm from Hades rammed its way through. Milo looked up in time to see the looming threat bearing down on him, 15,000 pounds of undead fury. I cranked the mighty harpoon gun toward the beast, grabbed the trigger, every bit of the circular sight filled with gray rotting flesh, and pulled.

Leviathan discharged. The concussion of the harpoon gun actually lifted me off the floor. Driven by a mighty charge of gunpowder, the six-foot, machined-steel spear drove right through the armored bucket of the monster's head, a roll of cable unspooling through its entire body and out its backside. The beast jerked as the harpoon embedded itself in a steel support pylon. The huge weight dropped instantly, cable pulling right through the decaying flesh, and it fell to the side, taking down row after row of shelves in a mighty crash.

I picked myself up from the floor. The room was filled with smoke from the gun's charge. I coughed. "Milo?"

*No response.*

The elephant's head had been torn off, rotting neck no match for gravity, and was dangling like a piñata on the taut cable. The body was on its side, limp, storage shelves crushed beneath it. Right where Milo had been standing—

*He was under it!* I ran over to the monster, trying to figure out some way to get under the body. If he was between the metal shelves, he might still be alive. There was no way I could reach him. I needed something to pry up an edge of meat. "Hang on, buddy! I'm coming for you." I spotted a crowbar, and started to work it under one leg.

Then I heard a strange noise, muffled beneath the corpse. Like somebody was trying to start a lawnmower, or a weed whacker, or...

*A chainsaw.*

I automatically stepped back as the powerful device caught with a roar. There was a terrible racket as Milo attacked the elephant from underneath. Thirty seconds later the chainsaw erupted out the elephant's flank, spraying fluids, and a disgustingly coated Milo came crawling out from the stomach. He took a mighty gasp of air as his head pushed through the skin. He killed the chainsaw and tossed it. I grabbed him by the hand and tried to pull. Milo pushed me back, reached deep inside the guts, and pulled out the ward stone.

"You okay?"

"Shush!" he sputtered through a face full of rotting elephant blubber. His fingers flew across the stone. There was movement at the torn-open door. I glanced over to see more undead coming. A winged beast landed right in the entrance, hopping forward on its one remaining leg. This was it.

"Bingo."

Milo moved the last letter into place. A visible shockwave traveled outward from the stone. The air bent in a violent oval. It washed across my body, but I felt nothing. The wave hit the undead and they simply exploded, flesh parting, bones and sinews flying like shrapnel. The wave expanded outward, surging across the compound, a tsunami of destruction, obliterating undead on impact.

There was a terrible wail, a scorching-evil distorted cry, like when we hit the shoggoth with thermite, only far worse. The shoggoth fled before the wave, screaming in pain the entire way.

That left just one thing...

Milo tumbled out of the elephant, sliding in a pile of squishy entrails. "Ew...this is karmic payback for making Newbies do the Gut Crawl, that's what this is."

I picked up the discarded flamethrower, hoisting the heavy pack onto my back. A thick tube led from the pressurized napalm pack to the heavy-duty nozzle gun labeled THE BURNINATOR. Its operation seemed pretty self-explanatory. I snagged a portable spotlight with my other hand and headed for the exit. "Grab anything that makes light and follow me."

The star shells were slinking across the sky. The noise of the battle was tapering off, gunfire and explosions ceasing as the undead on the outer edge of the ward's area of effect were driven off and their cultist handlers retreated. The wall of artificial darkness was still standing and I ran straight through it, heedless of danger. I tripped over a dismembered zombie and fell, sprawling over more bodies. Struggling upright with the heavy flamethrower in one hand, I turned on the brilliant spotlight and shined it outward.

Franks was on his hands and knees directly before me, lacerated, torn, holding one hand to his abdomen. He was coughing blood. It shone red and frothy in the light. I shouted at him as I approached. He looked up, unable to speak, but pointed. I followed his finger with the beam of light. There was a mighty thing there in the shadows, two hulking hands clamped down on a seemingly tiny object. The thing was bent over, like it was devouring whatever it was holding. When the light struck, the giant shape was replaced with Hood's normal form. He was holding Earl's head in his hands. When Hood lifted his hand to shield his eyes, Earl fell over, limp.

I set the spotlight on the ground, still covering Hood, and hoisted the flamethrower. He had to step away from Earl before I could use the deadly Milo-designed weapon. "Come and get me, Hood! Bring it!"

He stepped away from Earl and walked toward me, using the sleeve of his robe to protect his sensitive eyes from the light. "You're a brave man, Pitt." He swung his hand downward and the spotlight exploded into shards of glass and plastic. His body was instantly replaced with the towering solid shadow. "It's over, though. Your protectors are finished."

He drew nearer, but I hesitated, I couldn't risk immolating Earl. Werewolves couldn't regenerate from fire. "What'd you do to him?" I demanded.

For the first time I thought I could make out facial features on the shadow blob's head. Hood was *smiling*. "I'm assuming since you spoke to Carlos, you met the little imp I put in his head? Well, the thing that I just set loose in Earl's mind is much, much worse. Serves him right." Franks surged to his feet, charging past me with a roar. Hood swatted him down, brutally hard. "And as for you . . ." Franks hit the ground, and the shadow man paused long enough to kick him in the ribs, launching him across the clearing. "I have dominion over everything without a soul. I don't know how you're managing to resist my commands, but I'm going to drag you home and dissect you until I figure it out."

Unable to wait any longer, I pulled the Burninator's dual triggers. The first one ignited a pilot light while the second opened a valve of pressurized napalm. A wave of intense heat washed over me, singeing the hair from my arms. The fire lanced out in a fifty-foot beam, exploding right into the hulking shade.

Hood howled in rage, the shadow shape shrinking into a human form in the firelight. He extended both hands, palms open toward me. The fire seemed to wash over him, around him, but didn't burn him to a crisp. He grimaced as black energy crackled from his squid amulet, down his arms, and out his hands. The energy collided with the fire, pushing it back. Sparkling bits of napalm fountained into the air, hissing and burning as they fell to earth.

I kept the triggers mashed down, but I could see the wall of flame being pushed back toward me. The heat rose. The moisture was torn from my skin. I gritted my teeth as it began to cook my flesh and burn my clothing. Milo's flamethrower was no match for Hood's magic. The heat was unbearable. I couldn't breathe. The black magic was pushing the fires ever closer, and finally with a scream of heat-exhausted frustration, I was forced to release the twin triggers. I collapsed to my knees. The shadow shape loomed overhead.

Then the world exploded in light and eye-searing agony and an ear-rending screech. Hood screamed with real pain. I was instantly blinded. It was like somebody had driven ice picks through my eye sockets. It was so bright that it threatened to overload my brain. "Owen, get down," Milo ordered. I was too stunned to comply. Hands hit my back and shoved, slamming my face into the cooler dirt. "Secret weapon time!" Milo shouted. I covered my head as the intense flashing barrage continued.

Thirty seconds later, the terrible noise stopped. I looked up, but all I could see were flashing lights and purple spots. Then some rectangular shape was looking down at me. It was a blank, faceless monster. Milo flipped back the welding mask and grabbed me by the arm. "Let's go!"

I could barely see. Hood was still shouting, the light having actually seared his shadow flesh. There were other sounds now, a chopper overhead, surely using a spotlight, and the voices of approaching Hunters.

The purple blotch that must have been Hood was moving, staggering about. "It's not over, Pitt!"

"You lose, Hood!" I bellowed.

"But even in defeat, my servants have secured your fate. I'll see you soon." There was a scrambling noise that ended in a *pop* as he used one of the magic portal ropes, and then he was gone.

I collapsed to my knees. "What's going on?"

Milo yelled in my ear. "My secret weapon!"

"I'm blind, not deaf, damn it."

"Sorry. I just made the world's biggest flash-bang. That was a whole bunch of magnesium and aluminum powder there! I didn't know if I had the mixture right either, but we didn't all blow up, so I guess I did. Come on." He helped me up. Stumbling, led by Milo's elephant-blood-covered hand, he led me away from the noise. He found a clear spot, and had me sit.

I could barely see my hands. "What's going on?"

It took him a moment. "Hunters are securing the area. The crazy shadow dude is gone. All the undead are blown up. Fed choppers overhead."

"Where's Earl?" I asked. Milo hesitated. "Milo? Where's Earl?"

"They're working on him, but . . . he's not moving."

I was still blind. "Take me to him!"

"You're not a medic. Let them do their thing," he said calmly. I reached out and grabbed his wrist, hard. "Ouch!"

"No time to explain. Get me over there quick, or he's going to die."

Milo might not have understood, but Hunters were

flexible under pressure. He pulled me back the way we had come. I was starting to see shapes and color further away. There were a group of Hunters clustered over a still form.

"He's not responding," someone said. "Physical wounds are regenerating, but something's wrong. Temperature's dropping rapidly."

"Let me through," I said. "I can help."

"Z, what're you doing out here?" It was Holly. She sounded shocked to see me. "What happened to—"

I cut her off. "No time. This is like what happened to Carlos." Milo guided me closer. I knelt at Earl's side.

Holly understood. "Everybody step back," she ordered.

"What're you talking about?" a purple shape that sounded like Cooper asked.

"Z knows what he's doing," Holly said tersely. "You Newbies get ready in case something bad comes crawling out of Earl's head. And come with me, Coop, we've got a rat to catch."

I had no idea what she was talking about. I touched Earl's chest. His breathing was almost undetectable and he was utterly cold to the touch. Blood drizzled down my lacerated face and onto my open hand.

*I have to save him.*

Having no real clue what I was doing, I concentrated, trying to remember what I had felt before when I had activated the power. I could sense it. I could feel the alien presence. Hood had called it an imp, a demon. Whatever the hell it was, I had to figure out how to evict it, and fast.

The world blinked out of existence.

# CHAPTER 17

My eyes no longer hurt. I couldn't feel the aches, injuries, or fatigue. I was standing on bright white sand while powerful waves crashed ashore at my feet. A brilliant blue ocean stretched for what seemed like forever. It was gorgeous, a veritable tropical paradise. For whatever reason, it really wasn't what I had pictured the inside of Harbinger's head to be like.

"What's going on?" Earl asked from behind me. I turned. He was standing there, looking pained and confused. Behind him was a black rock cliff, and atop it was a rough shack of some kind. "Marty knocked me out and now I'm here."

"We're inside your memories," I responded. "Hood put a demon inside your brain to devour them. We have to stop it before it kills you."

He didn't seem surprised, as if my explanation made perfect sense, flexible minds, and all that. "Did you get the ward activated?"

"Milo did, but why isn't it chasing this thing off?" I asked.

"Maybe it's safe as long as it's in somebody's head?" Earl shrugged. "You got any idea what you're doing?"

"No. The last time I did this, the monster killed the host, then animated the body and tried to eat Doctor Nelson. But if we attack it before you get too weak, we might be able to throw it out and step on it."

"Well, that sounds like a hell of a plan," Earl replied sarcastically. "Remember when I told you not to screw around with this Old Ones' magic bullshit?" I nodded. "Belay that order. Let's go kill this little fucker." He suddenly grimaced, raising his hands to his temple. "Oh damn. That hurts."

I looked around for a giant earwig. "Where is it? Show me."

"Near," Earl said through gritted teeth, glancing from side to side. "I know this place. It's attacking where I'm most vulnerable."

Obnoxious seagulls were wheeling overhead. "Where are we?"

"This island is where I learned to finally control the beast. This was my exile."

"Nice exile," I exclaimed.

"It wasn't my first choice," he muttered, swaying a little, as he put his face in his hands. "I can feel it . . . in my head . . ." The sky was darkening rapidly. I could no longer tell where the horizon ended, as it all turned to an ugly shade of purple, like a spreading bruise. Earl cried out and went to his knees. I moved to his side to help. He gasped and shoved me away. "No. This was where I became a man again . . . I came here, where there was no one to hurt. I can't let him have this."

Werewolves were normally borderline psychotics. Earl was an exception. He exercised unbelievable mental control over his state and had done so for the better part of a century. If you were an evil force intent on destroying his mind, you would go right for where he had learned that control. With that iron will broken, the demon would be sure to win.

"It's here," Earl growled.

A purple dome appeared, rising over the horizon, dwarfing the cliffs, the shack, then the sky, and finally the entire world. "You've got to be kidding." It was far bigger than Feeder had been. It made the other creature look like a pathetic bug by comparison. A single giant eye opened in the center of the dome. It blinked once, the lid slamming back and forth with a concussion like a hundred sonic booms. A shockwave traveled down the beach. The seagulls exploded.

The unspeakable entity of the Old Ones, summoned by Hood, and dumped into Earl Harbinger's skull to devour his mind addressed us solemnly. *Greetings. I am Rok'hasna'wrath, reaper of souls, devourer of worlds.*

The thought hit our minds like a battering ram.

"Aw hell," Earl muttered.

There was a terrible screeching noise as the creature said its master's true name. ———— *ordered me to this world long ago to serve its mortal priesthood. The High Priest has commanded me to rend this mind to pulp. Already I can see that this is a strong mind, hardened through strife and honed in conflict. I shall consume your memories one by one, growing stronger with each victory. You will attempt to defeat me. I welcome this challenge. This will continue until your spirit departs this shell or the Dread Overlord's servant no longer requires my services and I return to my home plane. Only one of us can survive.*

"Aw hell," Earl repeated himself. The sky began to spin violently, a maelstrom centered on this one place in his memory.

"How the hell are we supposed to fight that?" I shouted.

*This is not your fight.*

It was addressing me.

*BEGONE.*

A wave of force struck me, bludgeoning my consciousness. The world dimmed as the pressure increased. He was banishing me. In this realm, the thing was unstoppable. I could feel my connection slipping. "Earl! He's too strong. He's kicking me out!"

Harbinger nodded into the wind. "I've seen weirder." He turned to me, deadly serious. "I'll hold out as long as I can, but if he wins here, then the beast might end up in control. If I start to change and anyone else is in danger, shoot me. You have to find Hood and kill him to stop this."

I was sucked upward into the vortex.

*Let the battle commence.*


My hand burned as I took it from his chest. Earl was convulsing violently, icy sweat pouring from his face.

"What's going on?" somebody shouted in my ear.

"He's fighting . . . something," I responded. My eyes had recovered from Milo's lights sufficiently that I could see who I was talking to. Esmeralda was at my side, holding a large syringe. She was using it to pull some liquid out of a vial. "Wait, what're you doing?"

"Horse tranquilizer. If Earl transforms out here, we're all in danger." Her forehead had been bandaged and she appeared absolutely exhausted. "I've already lost too many kids tonight. We can't risk it. I have to knock him out."

"You can't." I put my bloody hand on hers. Esmeralda stared at me in disbelief, but she didn't plunge the needle in. "He has to be focused if he's going to have any chance at all. We have to get him back to his cell."

Esmeralda hesitated. She had ten times my experience. If I was wrong, and he started to turn, then we'd have to shoot him or risk all of our lives. "You better be right, Z. Let's get him out of here fast."

Hunters were scurrying in all directions, securing the compound. A hairy shape lumbered up to us, red eyes glowing. A giant red tongue flopped out as it panted. It was a warg. "Need ride?" Skippy asked from the giant wolf's back. The orc's goggled face swiveled to indicate the others behind him. "See dead things. Clan help."

"We've got to get him back to his cell," I said. Esmeralda and I lifted Earl's shaking body and put him over Skip's legs. The orc was fearless, despite the twitching man on his lap who might quickly turn into a ball of teeth, claws, and fury. "Do you know where that is?" Skippy nodded. The warg immediately launched itself forward, moving with unbelievable speed for the main building.

More warg riders were arriving. Esmeralda turned to me. "Owen, go with him. You need to get back right away."

I didn't know what she was talking about. "Why?"

"Julie was hurt during the attack."

My heart lurched into my throat. "How bad?" *Oh no. Please no.* I grabbed Esmeralda by the shoulders. I towered over the tiny woman. "What happened?"

She hesitated, not wanting to answer. "Just go. Hurry."

A second warg and rider padded up to us and stopped. I had never ridden a giant wolf before. The orc extended his hand. The beast tilted its head and examined me quizzically. Hell, I didn't even know how to ride a horse, and this thing had jaws that could bite the head off a cow, but I needed to get to Julie fast. I grabbed the orc's gloved hand. With my other hand I got a handful of fur and pulled myself onto the wolf's back. It yipped as my weight settled and then immediately took off at a run. I hugged my arm around the orc so hard that I probably cracked his ribs, but I was frightened that I was going to bounce off.

*She's going to be fine. She's going to be fine.* I kept repeating that mantra to myself, too scared to think. The ride was surprisingly smooth as the warg ran across the compound. Shocked Newbies raised their guns as we passed but the more experienced Hunters shouted them down. I kept my face pressed against the warg's fur the whole time. It smelled like coconut shampoo. We reached the main building in a matter of seconds.

I slid off and landed, wincing, on my injured ankle. Skippy was already pulling Harbinger off his warg. "Help Skip," he grumbled at the Hunters that came running down the steps. I recognized the shortest one as the team lead, VanZant. Two Newbies were behind him, obviously frightened by the snorting warg. "Take Harb Anger...safe place."

Skip knew right where to go and the Newbies took Earl's convulsing arms and legs and followed. I grabbed VanZant by his sleeve. "Where's Julie?"

He was a stocky man: the other team leads jokingly referred to him as the Hobbit. He was also a no-nonsense, former Army mortar man and a welterweight champion fighter. He seemed surprised to see me. "How'd you get... Never mind. You better come with me, Z," he responded, then hurried up the stairs. I followed him in a daze. The injured Hunters had been moved into the cafeteria. Those with medical training were tending to the worst hurt. Three female orcs had arrived and were lending their supernatural healing skills to the cause.

There were too many wounded, moaning... This was my fault, all my fault. "Where is she?" I asked.

"She was right here." He pointed at an empty spot on the floor. All that was there now was a bloody towel. "We were on the roof when one of those flyers attacked. I was setting up an 81mm and she was directing fire and then it was right on top of us. It clawed through her armor." He ran his fingers across his stomach quickly. "She was hit... bad. I carried her down here myself." He started to choke up. "There's no way she walked off."

I picked up the towel. It was sodden, dripping.

VanZant was an experienced Hunter. He knew a severe injury when he saw one. "Julie!" I shouted, panicking. But everyone else down here had their own concerns right now. The nearest Newbies were utterly shell-shocked and didn't even look up to see who was yelling. This assault had cost us dearly.

There was a tap on my shoulder. I turned and stared down into Gretchen's reflective shades. Her manner was inscrutable as usual, but she jerked her head for me to follow. I did so. She led me to the nearest women's bathroom and held the door open. I was confused. She nodded that this was where I was supposed to go.

I entered to the sound of running water. Julie's green armor vest was discarded on the floor. It was soaked in blood and there were three vertical slash marks on the front, each one an inch wide, right through the Kevlar.

"Julie?" I asked hesitantly, knees weak, voice trembling, as I stumbled around the corner.

*She's alive!*

Julie was standing in front of the sink, back toward me. Her head was down, long dark hair covering her face, and her hands were flat on the tile, as if holding herself up. She had taken her shirt off and was only wearing her bra. The tile around her was stained pink with blood.

She was sobbing.

"Are you okay?"

She lifted her head slowly. "I shouldn't be." My fiancée turned, lifting her head and revealing her tear-stained face. "Look." She pointed at her stomach. Julie had abs of steel. Currently those abs were pink from half-washed blood. There were three dark horizontal lines down her stomach, but other than that, she looked fine. There was no wound at all.

"I don't get it." I said quickly. "Esmeralda made it sound like you were dying. VanZant was freaked out."

"Look," she ordered again. Puzzled, I bent down. The three lines were black, like a smudge from a piece of charcoal. The skin around the lines was healthy. The lines looked...*familiar*.

"No way!" I leapt back in shock. "No way!"

She pulled her hair away from her neck. The line from last summer had more than doubled in size. Now it was a thick black streak. The tattooed man had saved her life with that gift but we didn't understand a thing about it. "I should be dead. I never saw it coming. The claws went right through me."

"This is impossible."

"Impossible?" Julie screamed. "I *shoved* my own guts back inside while they carried me away. Fifteen minutes ago I was disemboweled and now I'm fine." I went to put my hands on her shoulders, but she jerked back. "Don't touch me!"

"It's okay," I said soothingly.

"I don't know what I am!" she cried. Julie turned away, unconsciously touching her neck, then realizing what she was doing, snapped her hand down in disgust. With a shout of pure anger she slammed her fist into the mirror, shattering it. She realized what she'd done and stepped back, quivering, blood tricking down her knuckles. She stared at the fresh cut in terror, waiting for something awful to happen.

I stood there, useless, helpless. The pain seemed to calm her down. The blood just kept trickling from her hand. Nothing happened. It was just a normal cut. She slowly unclenched her fist and sighed. Her fingers were shaking badly as blood dribbled down them to splatter the tile.

"Oh, Owen, what's happening? What's inside of me?"

I couldn't answer that. I grabbed her and pulled her close. She struggled at first as I kept saying that it would be okay. Finally she relaxed and just sobbed into my chest. "It's all going to be okay."

But all I could think of was what Susan had told

me in Mexico. *You know that it'll eventually kill her, don't you? It's from the other side, where everything comes with a price.* I stroked my filthy hand across her cheek. "Everything will be fine."

Finally she quit sobbing. Her voice cracked. My heart cracked. "I've got to get out there. They need me." I wanted nothing in the world more than to disagree with her, and tell her that she just needed to rest, but she was right. We did need her. She pushed away. "I need a shirt. Can't rally the troops like this...."

I pulled a bunch of paper towels from the dispenser and passed them to her. She took them and pressed them against her injured hand. It was then that she stopped to look at me. She seemed surprised. "What happened to your face?"

I hadn't looked at it yet, but I knew the silver-haired chick had cut me good. I could feel the flap of skin dangling wetly. I pushed it back into place and held it there with the rest of the paper towels. "Werewolf in the barracks clawed me."

"Barracks?" she asked, confused. "When? How'd you get there?"

"Franks, Grant, and I went after the ward stone," I explained.

Her brown eyes went hard behind her glasses. I'd seen that look before. The sadness, the shock, the fear, it was all gone, replaced with hard determination. Usually when Julie got that look, something was about to get killed. "Hand me my armor. We've got to go."

"Where?"

She threw the blood-soaked vest on, not even bothering to buckle it closed. "To have a talk with somebody." She pulled the door to the hall open. "You coming?"

We almost collided with a very excited Cooper entering the cafeteria. "Oh man," the young Hunter sputtered when he saw me. "I was supposed to find both of you. Holly says you need to come quick."

"Where?" Julie asked.

"Basement." He hoisted his FAL and ran. Julie was right behind him. I had no idea what was going on, but followed. Cooper was headed for the stairs. Several Hunters stopped to point at Julie, surprised to see her alive, let alone running through the halls. Everyone who tried to talk to her was dismissed with a wave. She was too focused on whatever it was that we were doing. We went down two stairs at a time and found Holly Newcastle waiting for us at the base.

"He went that way"—she pointed—"looking non-chalant."

"Heading for the tunnels probably, trying to get away," Julie replied. "Come on."

The four of us moved quickly. There was a massive hole punched in the wall next to the archives. Broken cinder blocks were scattered everywhere and piles of loose dirt had spilled onto the floor. "What happened?" I asked.

"The shoggoth dug right up to the basement. Then undead crashed through. They were under us, above us, and outside. It was nuts," Holly said. "Lee held them at this one. He wasn't going to let anything hurt his precious books. Trip stopped them at another breach by Earl's room. We tossed some explosives down each and collapsed the walls."

"And *you* were with the group that stopped the breach next to the control room," Julie said.

"What?" Then it hit me. "The doppelganger!"

"So that's what it is," she replied. "After Dawn stood up in the meeting and shot Earl, the lights went out, and she vanished in the confusion."

"Why would she take my form?"

"I intend to find that out right now," Julie responded as she jerked open the janitorial closet door. She held up one hand for the rest of us to stop. "Owen, honey, where are you going?"

I heard my own voice reply. "Oh, hey, Julie. I was just checking to make sure this door was secure. What's with the gun?"

"Don't move!" Julie shouted. "Take them both."

Cooper leapt through the door after her. I froze as a cold steel muzzle was jammed into the base of my neck. Holly's voice was totally calm. "Z, I'm pretty sure that you're the real you, so this is nothing personal, but if you so much as twitch, I'm going to blow your head off, got it?"

"Got it," I responded. I knew better than to argue with Holly, and I had taught her to shoot that .45 currently aimed at my medulla. Holly would not hesitate.

A large man stumbled into the hallway, thick arms raised, hands placed on top of his short hair, the muzzle of Cooper's FAL covering him. Except for the fact that he was wearing *my* armor, carrying *my* weapons, and was far cleaner, it was like looking in a mirror. "Against the wall," the young Hunter ordered.

"Watch it, kid," the duplicate replied.

"Do I actually sound like that?" I asked. "Man, I sound goofy."

The doppelganger looked up, seemingly surprised to see me. "What the hell is this?"

"Cut the crap, Dawn," I responded.

My beady eyes squinted back at me. "No way. This is some Condition trick. Blast it, Holly."

"Both of you, shut up," Julie ordered as she came out. Her 1911 was at her side. "One of you is my boyfriend, the other one's dog food."

"See you in hell, dog food," the doppelganger said. *Dang, that was a good impression.*

"So, how do you want to figure this out?" Holly asked slowly.

"We could get Earl to sniff them both, see if they smell different," Julie said. Cooper looked confused at that. Apparently he wasn't part of the in-the-know clique.

"Yeah, go get Earl. He'll know," my double said.

"Except your stupid boss put a demon in his head and Earl's busy fighting for his life right now," I said. Julie frowned. "I didn't get the chance to tell you. I tried to help, but he's on his own for now."

"Personally, I'm thinking this one's the real one," Holly tapped me on the back of the head.

"Why?" I asked.

"Because the real Z's strategy is always to get right in front and let the monsters beat on him until they get tired. The other one's too clean."

Julie nodded. "Valid point . . . but . . ." She turned back to me. "How'd you know to say that it was a doppelganger?"

"I found G-Nome stuffed into one of the toilets in the barracks. He saw Dawn cleaning up from murdering whoever was on guard duty in the control room. I read his mind before he died."

"You *what*?" Cooper was really confused now.

I heard approaching footsteps, and turning slowly, so Holly wouldn't get jumpy, tried to see who it was. Trip was leading the way with a massive, hulking shape loping along right behind him. It was the troll, Melvin. "What the hell?" the doppelganger and I said in perfect unison. What was that monstrosity doing loose? And armed? He had a sawed-off, 10-gauge Browning BPS in one hand.

"Hey, guys," Trip said. "Z...and Z." He was unperturbed. "So I guess one of these two is Dawn." He must have witnessed the shooting during graduation. He stopped and looked between us, trying to guess. "You know, that is some creepy stuff right there."

"Oh! Oh! Melvin help," the troll wheezed eagerly. "Trolls have good senses. We can smell evil Fey."

"You can't trust that thing," the doppelganger said.

"Okay, I've got to agree with the shape-changing monster on that one," I pointed out. "I missed the part where he joined our side."

Trip smiled and jerked a thumb at the troll. "The undead were breaking into the basement. I was outnumbered and desperate, so I made Melvin a fast job offer. He saved my butt. Say what you will, trolls are mighty handy in a fight."

"Melvin Monster Hunter now!" the troll said proudly. "Old clan all dead, because stupid. Melvin have nowhere else to go. MHI is my clan tag now."

Julie pushed her glasses back on her nose. "Trip, we're really going to have to have a discussion about this."

"He's agreed to certain terms of employment," Trip responded. "No eating people."

"Melvin not like eating people anyway. Like snacky

cakes better." He smiled, showing off rows of rotting teeth. MHI did at least have a good dental plan. "Melvin will make badass IT department for you. You can pay Melvin in Red Bull and internet connection."

"No spam or fraud," Trip continued.

"Aaahhh . . ." Melvin whined. "Fine. Whatever."

Julie just shook her head in resignation. She'd had a very long day. "All right then, which one is the real Owen?"

The giant troll stood between us, swiveling his head back and forth. Melvin's nostrils flared. He pointed one clawed finger at me. "That one."

"Julie!" the fake cried. "You can't believe that thing! It's a monster."

"Keep your hands on your head. Coop, take his guns," Julie said.

"I can't believe you'd fall for this," it grumbled, as Cooper lifted Abomination's sling. "This is such a crock of—" The doppelganger moved suddenly, slamming his armored elbow back into Cooper's face, smashing his glasses. The Hunter crashed back into the wall. The doppelganger reached across his chest and yanked out my kukri. Julie calmly shot it in both legs. The bullets didn't penetrate the Kevlar weave, but struck like hammer blows. My duplicate dropped to its knees.

"Ha! Melvin just guess! Monster go all dumb! Ha ha!" The troll bellowed, then looked stupidly down at his hand as it separated from his arm. The rubbery appendage hit the floor. "Hey!"

My double had swung the heavy blade right through Melvin's arm. Julie shot the doppelganger in the hand and it dropped my knife. She shot it in the other hand just to be sure. Two fingers flew down the hall. It was kind of unnerving how little hesitation Julie had to shoot something that looked exactly like me. The creature tumbled to the floor and glared up at her with four injured limbs.

I was closest and grabbed Melvin. His rubbery skin squished under my hands as I caught him. "Are you okay?"

"Stupid monster. How can Melvin type now with one hand? *Poor* Melvin!" It sobbed as it sank to its knees. "How can play video games? Life is ruined. Noooo!"

"Somebody get me a tourniquet!" I shouted.

The troll emitted a strained wheezy noise. He was laughing at me. "I kid. I kid. Melvin grow new arm by tomorrow. Trolls very resilient."

My duplicate struggled to rise. It still spoke with my voice. "Fools. You can't stop the Condition. The time of man is done."

Julie strode over and snap-kicked it in the face, putting it solidly down. "Drag it inside. Let's see what it knows."

I used the opportunity while we taped the doppelganger to a chair to strip it of my gear. It felt good to have my armor back on. I used a bandage from my first aid kit and patched my cheek. I needed to have Gretchen look at that, but she had serious injuries to deal with upstairs, and I didn't want to bug her about my cosmetic boo-boo. It would probably leave a terrible scar. I had gotten used to having werewolf scars once before. No big deal. I had more important things weighing on my mind.

Cooper was in over his head and had a broken nose to boot, so he went back to join up with his team. Melvin got put back in the cell while he regenerated a new arm. We didn't really know what to do with him yet anyway, but Trip was a man of his word, which in the best case meant that we couldn't just shoot him, and worst case meant we probably owed him a job.

We stuck the doppelganger in the next room where it couldn't hear us while I caught the others up on Earl's state and what had transpired during the fight for the ward stone. We were using Earl's office, and just on the other side of the vault door, he lay alone and twitching, fighting an improbable battle against some shade of the Old Ones. With the possibility of him losing control and reverting to his werewolf state, we didn't even dare leave anyone inside with him. This shape-shifter could hold the keys to finding Hood, and if I could find him quickly enough, we might still be able to save Earl.

I debriefed them as fast as I could. Julie patted me on the shoulder when I was done. "Doppelgangers can read minds a bit. That's why they're such effective mimics, so it'll know exactly how far you're willing to go to find the truth. It'll play with us, mess with our minds. This is a job for somebody who knows what they're doing."

"Earl doesn't have time." Every second we waited put him one step closer to ending up like Carlos.

"I know," she said. "Do what you can. I'll find Sam, Boone, or Cody. All of those guys have had to get information out of actual human beings back when they were military. This won't be a problem for any of them."

*Or my dad*, I thought to myself. The will to do awful things was never something that he had lacked. And right now I just prayed that I could live up to what he'd tried to teach me.

Julie hadn't spoken any more about the marks on her stomach, not even to Trip or Holly, though the two of them had surely noticed the ruined state of her vest. "I've got to get a sit rep and headcount. I'll be back as soon as I can." Her voice was strong, the fear compartmentalized and shoved away to be dealt with later. With Earl down, and her Grandpa too old, Julie had to run the nuts and bolts of this show. Her people needed her. She left the room without another word.

God, I was terrified for her. I watched her leave, wanting nothing more than to never let her out of my sight, but Earl was counting on us, and our only lead was this doppelganger. She'd find us some experienced help from the chaos above, but in the meantime, that left Trip, Holly and me to deal with the doppelganger duct-taped to a chair in the next room.

"We should interrogate Torres too," I said as I unrolled the hose that we used to spray down Earl's cell. I had no idea what I was doing but beating the monster with a hose had definite possibilities. "Where's he at?"

They looked at each other in confusion. "We stopped the undead in the basement, but we never saw him," Trip said. "I'm assuming that other Fed, Archer, picked him up."

"The place has got to be swarming with Feds up there by now," Holly said. "I hope they've got the jerk in custody and they're about to put the screws to him. You know, I never liked him."

I hoped they were right. If he'd escaped, then Myers' stupid escapade had been for nothing. I hadn't had time to consider what I was going to do about that yet, but Myers deserved a shallow grave for what he'd brought into our house. "We better hurry. When the Feds hear we've caught this thing, they're going to haul it off."

"You guys ever done anything like this before?" Trip asked slowly. We all knew that this had the potential to get real ugly.

"Dude, I was an exotic dancer. How often do you think we had to torture information out of shapechangers?" Holly responded.

"Weekly?" I answered. I held up the hose, immediately felt stupid, so dropped it. "Don't look at me like that. I was an accountant. We didn't go over water-boarding in school either, okay?"

Trip looked a little queasy. "Maybe we should wait for Sam or one of those guys."

"We don't have the luxury." I could tell that this was really not something that Trip was mentally prepared to do. He was just too kind-hearted to contemplate torture, even against something like this. I, on the other hand, had just shot a few actual human beings, and it didn't seem to bother me at all. In fact, I felt strangely justified. I could handle this. "Get your game face on. Earl's counting on us. There's a literal demon inside his head, and it's going to rip him apart until we stop it. We can't let him down. You with us, man?"

Trip nodded with more vigor than he felt. "Yeah, let's do this."

"Holly?"

She snorted. "I'm tougher than you are."

No disagreement there. "It can read minds, so don't

think weak. Think _mean_." I jerked the door open and
we went in to question the creature.

We had used an entire roll of tape to secure the
shape-shifter to a heavy wooden chair. The three of
us stood in a row. If I was smart, I probably would
have brought a big lamp or something to shine in its
face like in the movies.

"You're out of your league," it responded, still wearing my face. "None of you _children_ have the guts. My
master holds the keys to life and death and walks in
the shadows between worlds. How could you possibly
expect me to betray him? My god is a wrathful god!"

"So is mine," Trip answered.

"You're Baptist," I pointed out.

"Exactly." Trip surprised me. He stepped forward
and backhanded the creature in the face. "Where's
the Condition?" my friend shouted.

The head rocked back, but slowly returned, laughing. I have an evil laugh when I'm angry. No wonder
people consider me intimidating. "Come on, Trip, you
can do better than that!" Trip hit him again, harder
this time. He cocked his fist back for another shot.

Suddenly the doppelganger blurred and re-formed.
The transformation was nearly instantaneous. Now it
was Holly that Trip's fist collided with. She squealed
in pain. Trip jerked back, shocked. The fake Holly
cried, hot tears pouring down her bruised cheek.
"Don't hurt me, please!"

Trip raised his hand again, but he was shaking. The
doppelganger shifted again, and now it was an older
black woman with white hair. "John, how _dare_ you
raise your hand to me!" She had a Jamaican accent.

Trip closed his eyes and gritted his teeth. "Where's the Condition?"

When he reopened his eyes, his mother had been replaced with a teenage girl with red hair and freckles. She batted big sad eyes at him. "You promised you'd protect us, Mr. Jones. But you let those zombies get to us anyway. You got scared. You lied! You couldn't protect us! Sure, you came back and saved the others, but you were too scared to save me. I hate you!"

"I . . . I'm sorry . . ." Trip stepped back from the creature.

"Enough," I said. "Dude, it's okay."

"Sorry." Trip was wiping his eyes as he left the room. He closed the door behind him. I glanced over at Holly. She was leaning against the wall, impassive and cool. The doppelganger turned its teenage girl face and spoke, only using my deep voice. "Your friend has a soft heart. I'm sure it'll be delicious."

"Your turn," Holly stated.

The doppelganger studied me for just a moment. Its changes were almost so quick that it was hard to believe my own eyes. For just a moment, the face would be slack, almost squishy, then it was somebody else entirely. Mannerisms, speech patterns, even size. It would have been impressive if it wasn't so disgusting.

Julie Shackleford looked up at me, fearfully, as I approached. "Don't hurt me, Owen, please," she pleaded. *No. Not she. It.* I kept walking.

"I'm going to figure out how to hurt you. Then I'm going to hurt you until you tell us exactly what we want to know," I stated. I repeated those words in my mind. I could afford no weakness.

"Very good, Hunter. Harden your heart," the fake

Julie said. Then my girlfriend was gone and it was my father. "You always were weak, soft; it's good to see you man up and take care of business. Come on, fatty, show me what you've got."

I balled up my hand into a fist and slugged the doppelganger in the face. My whole body shook with the impact. "That's the spirit, boy!" It laughed with my father's voice. Then he was gone and it was Mordechai Byreika, old and frail. "Boy, what are you doing! Why do you hurt me?"

*It's not him. He's dead.*

"Smart you are, boy. But proud, and proud will hurt everyone you love."

"It won't work!" I spat.

Then it was Julie again. "It doesn't have to. I just want to enjoy the damage you're doing to your soul," it hissed. "Beat your wife, Hunter. Come on. This is what I do for fun." Then it shifted into the form of a little girl. "Owen, don't let them hurt me! Don't let them take me away. Not again!"

I paused. I had no idea who this was. She was probably seven or eight years old, with dark hair in a ponytail and blue eyes. "So, is this like a test to see if I'm willing to beat little kids or something?"

The little girl stopped her crying. "You don't remember me?" she asked incredulously.

It had to be a trick. I had never seen this kid before.

The girl giggled. "You really don't. You, the Chosen with the ability to see everyone else's memories has his own locked away... How ironic. So much power but too stupid to use it," the little girl said. "Past, future, it is all so linear to you pathetic mammals."

"Who are you supposed to be then?" I asked.

It read my hesitation. "Apparently that's a secret. Too bad for you. It's really a sad story."

"Z," Holly spoke. "It's messing with you. Step back."

"I've got this!" I shouted.

"Step back," she said again.

"Fine!" I stomped away, seething. This stupid monster was pissing me off.

Holly stopped in front of the doppelganger. The little girl face studied her. "Now you ... you're dangerous," it said. "Your edge, it is not an act. There are two sides to you, human. Burning hot or freezing cold and somewhere in the middle innocence dies. Delicious."

"You can read minds?" Holly asked.

"Sure can, kiddo," it replied. Now the doppelganger was an older man with wispy hair and the flushed face of a terminal alcoholic. "You're never gonna amount to nothing. You're just like your mom, the tramp. No good slut—"

Holly cut it off by slamming the ridge of her hand into its throat. The creature coughed and wheezed, writhing against the duct tape, like the old man was having a heart attack. "You gotta try harder than that," Holly replied. "I've watched episodes of Doctor Phil that were more emotionally wrenching."

It changed again. Now it was a young woman. It was hard to tell what she looked like because every inch of her was coated in dried blood, dirt, and filth. "Holly, you bitch. You left me alone in the pit. I'm dead because of you."

My teammate snorted. "Worked through that, chief. Cindy died because she gave up. Vampires killed her. I didn't do it. Is this supposed to make me feel guilty?"

"Guilty? You should. You could have taken me with you! Whore!"

The doppelganger began to thrash, swearing and crying hysterically. Holly turned to me and shrugged. She went back to the creature, walking a slow circle around the chair, studying the mirror image of somebody who had apparently been a fellow prisoner in the vampire feeding hole. "I think that we're going about this all wrong," she said slowly.

The creature continued to curse her. I couldn't tell if the fear was genuine or fake at this point. Holly paused in front of it and pulled out her folding knife. The Benchmade flicked open with a snap. "Let me test this theory." The creature flinched and thrashed away. "Hold still, or I'll really screw this up." She slowly poked her blade into the creature's face. A clear fluid began to bleed from the cut. The woman screamed. I turned away involuntarily.

The screaming stopped. I risked a peek. Holly was holding up the dripping knife. "Yep, just like I figured. The tissue is all soft underneath, malleable. Like the fingers Julie blew off."

Holly had carved a chunk out of the thing's face. The flesh underneath had the consistency of raw dough and was leaking a viscous juice down its neck. "Oh, gross."

The doppelganger hissed. "You think you're so clever."

"Yes. Yes, I do," Holly responded. "See, I don't know how your biology works, but I'm sorta like what passes for a medical professional around here now, so I'm just going to keep cutting pieces off until I find something important."

It had reverted back to the form that it had been in most of its stay at the compound: the Newbie, Dawn. The young woman looked terrified. "Please . . . please don't hurt me. Owen, don't let her hurt me."

"Hurt you? You killed Billy Tanner in the control room. Slashed his throat wide open. You set up an attack that cost us I don't know how many more Hunters dead and injured. You tried to assassinate my boss." Holly smiled maliciously. "Hurt you? Dawn, you can read minds, so I want you to read what I'm thinking about doing *right now*." Holly closed her eyes.

The creature flinched.

Holly's smile was terrifying. "Think that'll hurt?"

"Okay, okay." Dawn blinked, and her eyes were suddenly clear orbs. Her entire face went slack, the color seemed to fade, the features just sloughed away, leaving a blank mass of goo where the head had been. The hair retracted as those ice cube eyes watched us. There wasn't even a mouth, just an indentation in the doughy mass. It puckered inward as it spoke with Dawn's voice. "So, you want to see what I really am?"

"What the hell?" I muttered.

It was some sort of . . . well . . . I didn't know, doughy asexual humanoid blob, utterly pale and damp. It seemed to shrink inward, as if it had been artificially inflating itself to reach correct human proportions. The fingers exposed from the end of the tape were stubby little white sausages that wiggled like hooked nightcrawlers, except the end of each one terminated in a hard yellow point. "Happy now?" Its voice was utterly bland, toneless, accentless, neither masculine nor feminine.

"Yeah, that's much better," Holly gagged.

"Maybe you should go back to the beauty queen," I suggested. How had this…*alien* made it through the warding? Damn, the Pillsbury Doughboy had come on to me.

"Shove it, human," the doppelganger said, hissing bubbles through its face. One crystal eyeball swiveled to study me, bulging out of the lumpy head, independent of the other. Apparently it had read my thoughts. "Your ward meant nothing to me. I was born on Earth. There are more of us here than you expect. We're everywhere, preparing the way for the great and inevitable return of—"

"Shut up, Gumby." Holly silenced it by shoving her knife against the creature's chest. "Where's the real Dawn?"

"Dead," it answered. "Replaced not long after Harbinger and Shackleford made her a job offer. We did not even know of this one at the time." It twitched one eye at me. "I was just to observe. The High Priest believed that MHI might pose a future threat to his plans."

I stepped forward. "Where is this High Priest? Where's Hood?"

The creature shook as it laughed. The sound was utterly emotionless. "He's with your brother."

*What?* Holly and I exchanged glances.

"I hid during the initial assault. My attempt on Harbinger had failed and I waited for an opportunity to redeem myself rather than return to the Exalted Order in shame. I sensed the presence of the acolyte known as Torres. So I freed him. In his wisdom, he suggested that I take your form so we could get close to one of your loved ones. Torres will go far in the

Order. I found your brother and asked him to follow me to the basement. Torres led him into the tunnels. They are gone now, surely reunited with the High Priest by now."

I stumbled back in shock. *Mosh?* Gone. I could envision this creature leading him away. Mosh would have trusted what he thought was me. He would never have even guessed. It had to be lying. Mosh had to still be upstairs. "You bastard. I don't believe you!"

"Believe it, hairless monkey. I'm sure he will be contacting you soon. I returned here to try and finish my assignment. I was to neutralize Harbinger. When I found that the High Priest had already dealt with him, I fled. That's when you caught me."

It was telling the truth. Mosh was *gone*. They'd taken my brother. Rage darkened my vision. My boot collided with the doppelganger's chest. It flew back, crashing violently into the floor. The creature emitted a high-pitched squeal. I kicked it again, shattering the back of the chair against the concrete. "Where?" I put the boot to it, stomping the monster over and over. It felt spongy, but something hard cracked on the inside. "Where's my brother?"

"Z!" Holly shouted. "Calm down. We don't know what kind of abuse this thing can take."

"Where's Hood?" The impact of my steel-toed boot slid the doppelganger across the floor. I kicked it again.

Holly grabbed one of the straps on my vest and tried in vain to pull me back. "Stop it!"

I paused, fists clenched tight, breathing hard, seeing red, stomping back and forth, hot air blowing through my nostrils. This thing had my brother.

Slumped on the floor, it laughed at us one final

time. "Go suckle your warm-blooded young, filthy mammal," it hissed. "My work is done." It made a rattling noise and the protruding eyes flopped limp.

Unclenching my fists, I glanced at Holly. She looked back at me, shocked. "Did I kill it?" She shrugged. It was more like it had just given up the ghost after taunting me. "Oh crap...what do we do now?"

There was no time to contemplate that question. The door flew open with a bang. It was Sam Haven. Trip was right behind him. "We've got a problem," the burly Hunter said quickly. He didn't even seem to notice the doughy monster lying dead on the floor.

"Sorry, Sam, I think I killed it," I responded.

"No. Some of the cultists survived. They've regrouped the remaining undead."

But that didn't make any sense...with the ward in place they couldn't touch us.

Trip was panicked. "They're burning the orc village!"

# CHAPTER 18

A horn was blowing.

The sound echoed across the compound, a plaintive wail, coming from the direction of Skippy's village. The sun was rising over the hills and a thick plume of black smoke was rising from the nearby forest. I leapt into the back of a waiting pickup truck. Trip, Holly, and Sam were right behind me. I slammed my palms down on the truck roof and shouted, "Go! Go!" to the unknown Hunter who was driving. The truck lurched forward, threatening to knock us down. We tore across the red dirt, dawn's first light turning us into long shadows. Dust hung in the air from vehicles that had left moments before us.

I stared at my companions. All three of them were dazed. An attack on us was one thing, but the orcs? There were *children* there. We bounced onto a narrow forest road, forcing all of us to duck to avoid the stinging branches.

Sam caught my glance. "A bunch took off as soon as we heard the war horns. Skippy and their warriors weren't home. They were helping us," he shouted. "Cheating, rat-bastard sons a bitches!" Furious, he slammed one meaty fist against the side of the truck.

The tribe had lived with MHI for years, they could have settled inside the boundary of the compound and the protection of its warding, but they were too uncomfortable around humans to ever live inside our walls. Their people had been persecuted for generations, and even though they considered themselves part of our clan, they preferred solitude.

They just wanted to be left alone.

The air smelled like smoke.

The orc village was just a circle of simple prefab houses, decorated with antlers, animal skulls, and feathers. It was where Skippy's people lived under the protective umbrella of their adopted clan, MHI. They had come here as refugees, and Harbinger had taken them in. They had made this their home, safe from the world that saw them as freaks and monstrosities. I had been here many times. I'd eaten their food, drank their drink, played with their kids, and listened to their music.

It had been a peaceful place.

*Not anymore.*

The truck locked up the brakes as we entered the clearing. I leapt over the side before we had even slid to a stop, Abomination ready to dispense some vengeance. The wooden homes were burning, crackling as the flames devoured everything in their path. A giant warg lay dead at my feet, eviscerated by steel claws. Hunters were moving around the houses.

There were more corpses near the homes. Most were Hood's automatons, as even orc women and children knew how to defend themselves, but some of the crumpled bodies were smaller and dressed all in black.

"Status!" Sam shouted.

A Hunter, so covered in soot, ashes, and blood that I couldn't even recognize who it was, stepped forward. "Undead destroyed. A handful of cultists are escaping through the forest. We've got men after them."

"Casualties?"

His name tag read SOUTHUNDER. "I . . . I don't know how many people lived here, but it looks like most of them escaped into the woods. But some tried to stay and fight. They . . . they . . ." The Hunter couldn't finish his sentence. He had a Utah County MHI patch on his arm, a werewolf with a gun. I'd heard that our Utah team had an orc volunteer on it too, someone who'd grown up in this very village. "I can't believe this."

"There were probably two dozen kids that lived here," Trip said slowly.

I stumbled toward the bodies. Other Hunters were efficiently chopping the heads off the undead and checking for survivors. There weren't any so far. The smoke was burning my eyes, and involuntary tears cut a path down my cheek.

*This was my fault.*

A warg and rider tore into the village. The black-clad figure leapt from the beast's back and ran, tripping, and sprawling next to one of the dead. The orc clawed his way forward, lifting the lacerated little body into his arms. He let out a howl of anguish.

It was a massacre.

"Survivor!" a Hunter bellowed from the far side of the clearing. She was carrying a small form in her arms. Holly, who was a decent medic, ran to help. I watched helplessly as she applied a tourniquet to the young orc's leg. The foot was just *gone*.

In an utter state of shock, I found myself trying to assist. Someone pressed a plastic five-gallon bucket into my hands. We managed to use the orcs' well to douse the flames. I kept throwing water onto the fires in a complete daze, bucket after bucket, in a futile attempt to do *something*.

The warriors and healers who had come to help at the compound returned, all of them in various states of despair, fury, and grief. Skippy immediately began to bark orders in their hoarse language and the others responded quickly, fanning out into the trees to search for more survivors.

They were a simple people. Brave, good, strong, kind... They didn't deserve this. No one deserved this.

There was a shriek as someone made a discovery in the trees. One of the wargs had picked up the scent and tracked down some of the fleeing orcs. A figure came out of the forest, waving at us, and I could tell it was a female only because of the burkha. A group of short, stubby children emerged behind her. Some of them had lost their masks, and tears rolled down their green cheeks. They were terrified, disheveled, clothing torn and dirty from their flight through the trees.

Skippy ran forward and engulfed her in his arms. One of his wives had led most of the children to safety. Three of the kids charged forward and hugged Skippy's legs. I tossed one more bucket of water onto the smoldering ashes. The fire was under control, but it was too late for the once-proud village. My injuries were just a dull background throb over the hurt in my soul. My brother was gone, Julie was cursed, Earl was dying, Skippy's people were decimated, and all because of one fanatic on a mission. All because of me.

Sam grabbed me by the arm and pointed back toward the road. "Feds are coming."

"The orcs have been through enough. I'll keep those assholes out of here," I spat as I threw the bucket on the ground. A black Suburban was pulling into the clearing and I moved to intercept it. The last thing these people needed was the presence of an entity that terrified them—the government.

The passenger door opened and Agent Myers stepped out. It took every bit of self-control I had not to snap Abomination to my shoulder and pump a round of buckshot into his face.

"Pitt! What's going on here?" he demanded.

"Turn around and get back to the compound," I ordered. "Now."

Archer got out of the driver's seat, obviously shocked at the carnage. Myers glared at me. "My men are in control of the compound. This is an official investigation, and I need to know what's—"

I got right up in his face. "Get out! Don't you get it? These people are scared of you. They've got more important stuff to deal with right now."

"Stand down," Myers said, eyes narrowing dangerously.

"No! You stand down!" I shoved him back into the Suburban. Myers was shocked that I dared to lay hands on him, and the evidence was in the two soot-black handprints on the breast of his cheap suit. "I'm done standing down, asshole!"

Archer moved his hand to his gun. Sam cleared his throat, and the skinny agent glanced over his shoulder to see the big Hunter standing there with a .45-70 cradled in his arms. "Let's let those two settle their beef. Know what I mean, kid?" Archer nodded slowly as he let go of the butt of his Sig.

Myers tried to dust the ash off his suit. He failed. "I can understand the anger, but if you touch me again, I'll make sure you go to prison forever. Do you understand me?"

I jerked my thumb toward the grieving orcs. "This is your fault. You took your problem and made it ours, you coward. You lied to us, used us..." I was enraged, shaking. I shoved him again. He collided with the Suburban. Myers flinched on impact. "Torres, the asshole scumbag *you* brought here, he took my brother. *My brother!* You—"

Despite his mild appearance, Myers was shockingly fast on the draw. The barrel of his revolver appeared under my chin. I froze. He cocked the hammer. *"Calm down."* The muzzle was cold against my skin. I was breathing hard, nostrils flaring with each breath as I contemplated snatching his gun and killing him on the spot. The hardness in Myers' eyes indicated that I would fail. "Listen to me very carefully, Pitt. This isn't a game. You think I wanted this? You think I wanted these creatures to get hurt, for your family, for MHI to lose men? Of course not. But this is bigger than that, bigger than you, bigger than me. You have no idea how *hard* the choices are that I have to make."

"Only when you choose wrong, you're not the one paying the price."

"I'll pass that along to Agent Herzog and my men

who died at the amphitheater." He slowly removed his Smith & Wesson 610 from my neck. A crowd of orcs were regarding us warily. I had no doubt that if Myers had shot me, they would have torn him limb from limb, and he knew it too. He carefully lowered the hammer. "We'll leave your precious monsters alone. I know I'm their bogeyman. Take a walk with me, Pitt. I think you need to understand what's at stake here."

Myers and I stopped at the entrance to the clearing. It was quieter here, but I could still hear the lamentations of the tribe. I was furious. Myers holstered his revolver and pulled out a pack of smokes. He offered one to me. Resisting the urge to cave his skull in, I shook my head.

"I'm trying to quit," he explained as he lit the cigarette. "Ironic. It was working with Earl that got me hooked on these stupid things. The *good* old days..." Myers chuckled. "Looks like they've come back to haunt us."

"You know about Hood, then?"

"Franks briefed me." He shook his head slowly. "I can't believe it."

"Well, you better."

"No...That's impossible. Marty Hood was a good man." I could sense the consternation in his voice. He really couldn't wrap his mind around the truth. Myers continued, "He was my friend. Nothing like this cult leader. The Condition is brutal, efficient, psychotic. They'll stop at nothing to reach their goals."

"So that's why you stuck one of their acolytes with me?"

He shrugged. "I saw an opportunity and took it.

There were only a handful of my men who could have sold out Agent Patterson. Investigating them turned up nothing. If I questioned them outright, then they'd know I was onto them, and we'd lose our opportunity. But I knew that they wouldn't be able to resist taking a shot at you." He waved his hand across the clearing. "I just didn't expect this level of response."

I had to fold my arms across my chest. Every fiber of my being wanted to murder him. "You just expected them to pop me. Not a full-on assault."

"Correct." Myers said, stone-faced. "Don't look at me like that. You would have done the same thing."

"No. I still have my soul."

Myers tossed his smoke down and ground it out with his wingtip. "When the President himself tells you to stop a death cult, no matter what the cost, then your perspective changes a bit. The Condition is getting ready for something big. Something devastating, called *Arbmunep*. We don't even know what it is, some sort of secret weapon, but it's coming soon. All our intel indicates that this is an Extinction Level Event. Do you know what that even means?"

I shrugged. It sounded pretty bad.

"Poof. Done. Mankind's done. We're like the dinosaurs. I'm personally responsible for the defense of my country, and I've got the things from Lovecraft's worst nightmares knocking on the door ... A soul? You say I don't have a soul? That's a luxury for people who don't have my responsibilities. People who live in the suburbs and take their kids to Little League and walk their dogs have those. I can't afford a soul."

There was more yelling from the direction of the village as some of the Hunters returned with more survivors. "What are you going to do about my brother?"

"My men are interrogating some of the surviving cultists now. I've got others tearing apart the trucks and undead looking for forensic evidence. All this material came from somewhere. We have access to the best intelligence databases in the world. The Condition's tipped their hand. You can't stage an operation of this scale and not leave clues. We'll track them down for sure."

That wasn't what I wanted to hear. I wanted results now. "Earl will be gone by then. Mosh will be dead."

"I'm sorry about them, really I am. But we're doing everything we can. I can promise you this: we will bring these people to justice."

"Justice isn't good enough."

There was a sudden commotion from the orc village. A group of Hunters walked out of the trees, dragging a few robed cultists behind them. Myers perked up. "Good. More people to question."

There were three prisoners. Their black robes were torn and muddy. One of them was obviously injured. The Hunters stepped aside as several orcs approached. One of them had a pair of swords on his back, so I recognized Edward immediately. One blade flashed from its sheath as Ed stalked forward with single-minded determination.

"You want to question them, you better hurry," I suggested. Edward looked like he was about to do the slice and dice.

"Stop! Stop right there!" Myers shouted as he ran back toward the village. "Stop that orc!" Edward either didn't hear him or didn't care. The sword sang through the air and one man went down in a spray of blood. Ed was a super-efficient killing machine, but that wasn't his goal today. The cultist dropped to his knees, one arm missing at the shoulder. He started to scream and Ed took his other arm. "I need them alive!"

Ed paid him no heed. He drove his blade through the pelvis of the next cultist. These men had hurt his tribe. He was their best warrior, and default executioner. The Hunters understood this and stayed out of the way. That didn't help me get Mosh back though. Ed jerked steel through bone, grinding his sword back and forth, before tearing it violently free. That cultist fell, thrashing.

"Skippy, stop him," I bellowed. Skippy's goggled head dipped once in agreement. He raised his gloved hand and Ed complied immediately, perfectly still, sword tip inches from the last cultist's nose.

"Make this ... good ..." Skippy grunted.

I reached them a moment later. Myers was hesitant to get too close to Ed, who was like a statue, one sword unmoving in the last standing cultist's face. A single drop of blood fell from the tip of the steel. The one with no arms had passed out in a puddle. The other's bowels had been opened in half a dozen places. He was still crying, and probably would for quite a while.

Myers addressed the last uninjured man. "Tell me where to find your High Priest, or I'll give you to these ... creatures."

He was a young man who looked more like a frat pledge than a cultist. His eyes flicked nervously to his dying companions, to the faces of the impassive

Hunters, and then to the masked and circling orcs. Obviously terrified, he stammered, "I...I...can't."

"Yes...can," Skippy stated over the screams of the dying. The orc chief glanced down at the disemboweled cultist. The cries were annoying him. "Quiet bad human."

Edward responded instantly. His sword swung down, severing the injured man's head cleanly from his body and sending it bouncing across the dirt. The blade returned immediately to its space before the young cultist's nose.

Skip looked down at the twitching body. "Not mean for kill him, *Exszrsd.*" He finished the sentence in his own incomprehensible language.

Ed shrugged, as if to say *whoops*. Ed was a literal kind of guy.

"Okay, don't hurt me, don't hurt me!" the cultist stammered.

"Talk!" Myers shouted. "Where is he?"

"If I tell you, he'll hunt me down. You can't stop him. He walks through the shadows! He owns the night."

"We can protect you," the senior agent said calmly. "I represent the government. We've got places that even he can't go."

There was a glimmer of hope. "You...you do?"

"Yes," Myers responded soothingly. "You help me and I can help you. What's your name, son?" Myers was a sly one, but then again, he had plenty of practice playing good cop to Franks' bad cop.

The cultist was terrified. His eyes crossed a bit as he looked down the length of the sword. "Chad. My name's Chad. I didn't know what I was getting into.

You've got to believe me." He began to babble. "Some other guys told me about this church, and they could do all sorts of cool stuff, and if you did what they said, then you wouldn't ever die! And I saw it with my own eyes. You've got to believe me. I just wanted to have that power. But then they were doing all sorts of crazy stuff. I was scared of the High Priest, so I went along. I never wanted to hurt anybody."

Skippy shook his head. I had serious doubts that no matter what Myers promised, Chad was not going to leave this village alive. I almost felt bad for the guy. He was probably younger than me, inexperienced, stupid, and suckered into something way over his head. I noticed that he had a squid necklace, like a smaller version of the one Hood had been wearing. Maybe it was just the light, but it seemed slick and alive.

Myers continued, being as unthreatening as possible, which for him was saying a lot. "I understand. Chad, I give you my word. You give me a location, and I'll get you right into protective custody. I promise. Okay?"

Chad had started blubbering. "Okay." He nodded, obviously broken. Watching Edward mercilessly chop two of his buddies into bits probably helped. "I'll tell you everything I know." He took a deep breath and wiped his nose on his sleeve. "There's a place in New—" Chad looked down in sudden confusion. He tried to speak, but no sound came out. He clutched at his throat.

The squid amulet's chain was shrinking. "The necklace! Get it off!" I shouted. Chad stumbled, fingers trying to get under the chain. I grabbed the cultist by the neck and tried in vain to grab it, but it slipped right through my fingers. He fell, eyes bulging out of his head, skin turning blue. He began to jerk as all the oxygen was cut off from his brain. The chain was slicing through the flesh of his neck like piano wire. "Damn it!"

It just kept tightening. The squid seemed to wilt and die. A few seconds later, the convulsing stopped. Chad's muscles tightened in one final spasm, then it was over.

I was on my knees next to the cultist, surrounded by Hunters and orcs. "What happened?" Sam Haven asked.

"Non-disclosure agreement from hell," I responded. Disappointed, Ed poked the cultist in the leg with his sword. No reaction. I knelt at his side, pulled my glove off, and felt for a pulse. He was dead.

Myers was rubbing his face in his hands. "He was about to talk."

"Apparently," I muttered. "You better warn your men before anybody else gets somebody to roll over." The senior Fed pulled out his radio. "Hood is in New something or other." I glanced over at Holly and Trip. They were looking to me for ideas, and I was fresh out. "Call headquarters. See if they—" A terrible pain tore up my arm and I shouted in surprise.

Chad's dead eyes were staring at me. His mouth was clamped onto my left hand. Blood was gushing past his teeth as he rent it from side to side. My blood.

"Aarrgh!" I jerked my hand away, tumbling to the ground. The zombie began to rise. Edward cleaved the top of his head off in a cloud of red and white.

"Z!" Holly screamed. I grabbed my hand. Blood drizzled down my arm. Trip tore my hand away and began dumping a bottle of water on the wound. There it was, clear as day, a serious bite mark.

*Stupid, stupid, stupid.* "Oh man..."

"Skin's broken!" Trip shouted. "Gretchen! Help!"

*Zombie bite. One hundred percent fatality rate.*

The healer pushed her way through the crowd. I started to rise, but she pushed me down with shocking strength. I could see the reflection of the wound in her mirrored glasses.

*Impossible. It can't be.*

"Can we cut his arm off?" the Utah Hunter asked.

"Oh, hell," I whimpered. But it beat the alternative.

Edward stepped forward, sword in his hand. I cringed, knowing that with that two-foot razor blade I wouldn't even have to take my armor off. The orc warrior looked to Gretchen for wisdom. If she gave the go-ahead, there would be no hesitation.

Gretchen shook her head. Ed lowered the sword.

"Amputation doesn't work," Holly said, her voice flat. I knew that she had an eerie ability to fall into a state of utter calm when she was really freaked out. "Just causes blood loss that kills the subject faster. The contamination spreads instantly through the nervous system."

I was hovering between disbelief and panic. Such a stupid Newbie mistake...

Sam kicked the body. "Maybe it wasn't a zombie," he said hopefully. "I've never seen a zombie animate that fast after death."

There was laughter. It seemed strangely out of place. The crowd around me all turned toward the unnatural sound. The group parted enough that I could see. The cultist with no arms was sitting up. "Of course you haven't seen anything animate that fast, fools." The squid amulet on his chest was glowing. His eyes were open but rolled back sightless into his head. "You've never dealt with my *art* before. Well, well, well, now isn't this just a happy bonus."

*Hood.* Somehow he was channeling himself through the dying cultist. Multiple guns lifted to eliminate the new threat. "Hold your fire!" I screamed. The Hunters didn't shoot, but they didn't lower their weapons. "What do you want?"

"I warned you, Pitt. Now you're coming into my world, whether you like it or not. The plague is in your blood now, chap. Game over." The voice came from the cultist's mouth, but the lips didn't move.

I struggled to my feet. "Liar!"

"Your body will try to fight it at first. As we speak, your temperature is rising, trying to battle the infection. Within a second of introduction it began taking over, traveling down every nerve, every vein, artery, and fiber. Your very DNA will be torn apart. Once your brain tissue is overwhelmed, the transformation will be complete. Your heart will stop and the only thing that will matter then is finding your next raw-flesh meal... Welcome to the family." I stumbled toward the cultist. "Look at that, dead man walking." Hood laughed again.

"Marty?" It was Myers.

The lolling head turned vaguely in the direction of the Fed. "Hello, Dwayne."

"No, it can't be," Myers sputtered. "What are you doing?"

"Fulfilling my destiny. You were my best mate once and one of the few who truly mourned me. I appreciate that. I always will. But you're in my way now, so you'll step aside if you know what's good for you." The cultist's head flopped forward, chin against his chest. "Nothing personal."

Hood wasn't here just to gloat. "What do you want?" I asked.

The body jerked, throwing the head back hard on the neck, rolling around on the shoulders. "Perceptive. I've won, but now the question is, to what degree will be my victory? Killing you, especially in such a horrid way, fulfills the letter of my orders, but I want to also fulfill the spirit. I have a covenant to live up to, and I don't make promises lightly. Come to me, Pitt. That way I can turn you over to the Great One itself. In exchange, I'll return your brother."

"How do I know he's still alive? I don't even know you've got him for sure."

The blood-soaked mud before the cultists ignited in a small flame. The flame traveled in a circle, like an old-fashioned dynamite string. The flame reached its starting point, forming a tiny circle. There was a pop and a splash in the mud. The flames flickered and died in the breeze. There were several small objects resting in the puddle.

*Fingers.*

"I'm sure Dwayne can print those for you if you like, but trust me, they belong to your brother. And he certainly won't be playing the guitar ever again. I never liked that kind of music; too—oh, what's the word I'm looking for?—Brash? Offensive? I prefer the classics.... Your call, Pitt. Die alone, hiding in your compound, or die for something useful. Give your life in one final act of mercy to free your brother and slake the thirst of my impatient god."

My pulse thundered in my ear. My face was flushed with heat. "Where?" I hissed.

"Return to this place in exactly one hour. It will

take that long to prepare a portal large enough. Do not attempt any trickery. Only one person will be able to pass through the portal. Don't bother sending through a bomb—I'll see it coming and not open the gate on my side. Personally, I won't be close enough to the portal for it to matter anyway. I'll only open the portal for you. And as punishment I'll send your brother to the other side for the amusement of the Dread Overlord in your place. Do you agree to my terms?"

I was going to die. Mosh didn't have to.

"See you soon," I answered.

The cultist dropped limply to the ground as Hood's consciousness left him. Just to be on the safe side, several Hunters shot the body in the head.

It was quiet for a long moment as everyone in the clearing stared at me. It was just starting to sink in. I'd been bitten by a zombie.

"You can't do this," Sam said. "It's suicide."

Agent Archer joined us, pushing rudely past the orcs. He had a device similar to the blood sugar testers diabetics used in hand. "Hold still," he said as he pushed the needle against my neck. It made a hissing noise at it stabbed me. He pulled it away and studied the little screen, biting his lip. The whole group was totally silent, watching Archer and his little box for about thirty painful seconds. My stomach hurt from the fear. All I could hear was my breathing. A little red light began to flash on the tester. I lowered my head as the group began to murmur.

*I'm dead.*

Strangely, I was calm, staring at the mud. "No such

thing as suicide if you're already dead, Sam. How long do I got?" I asked. The Hunters exchanged glances. "How long?" I shouted.

"Calm down, Z. Maybe it was...something else." Trip said. "Maybe it's wrong."

Archer cut in. "It's not a lycanthropy test. The zombie infection tester is always accurate."

My mouth was totally dry. I was so terrified it hurt to talk. "How *long*?"

Myers spoke up. "The longest a healthy person has ever lasted after being bitten was five hours. Most are done in under two depending on the severity of the...well, you know..." He wouldn't look me in the eye. He studied his shoes. "Sorry."

The old Hunter, Cody, carefully picked the fingers out of the mud. He also pulled up a short piece of rope. It had to be related to how the Condition's teleportation magic worked. "Maybe we can use this somehow?" I had no idea how, but he carefully stowed the rope too.

It was settled. "I'm going after my brother. Can you put a tracking device on me?" I suggested. Maybe my sacrifice didn't have to be in vain.

Myers pointed at my armor and then at my shotgun. "Already done. That's why we gave your gear back to you in Mexico."

I should have known. Any act of kindness from them had ulterior motives. "Well...hell..."

My friends were scared. They all knew that I was doomed. Nobody knew what to say.

"Let's get back to base. I've got an hour. I'm not going out without a fight."

◆          ◆          ◆

Time was running out.

MHI had taken a beating. Several Newbies had died during the attack, as well as one team lead, Williams, out of Kansas City. We had six others with serious injuries and over a dozen with various degrees of damage. The injured had been evacuated to the hospital in Montgomery. We were also missing our most experienced Hunter, since Earl was down with a demon trying to devour his mind. A group of us had gathered in the conference room to come up with ideas. Frankly, I didn't have any. More Hunters arrived every second. Word had spread quickly.

I hadn't even had a chance to explain to Julie what had happened, but by the time I had gotten back to the compound, somebody had already informed her of the zombie bite. She hadn't left my side since. It was a good thing that we were so preoccupied, because I honestly had no idea what to say. *Sorry, honey, gonna die soon. Gotta go take care of some business. Sorry you're cursed by evil.*

Instead I was standing at the front of the room while Milo used black electrical tape to tie row after row of green glow sticks to my armor.

"Telekinesis keeps taking out flashlights, but if he pops one of these, it just covers you in more diphenyl oxalate and hydrogen peroxide," Milo explained.

"Glowing crap," I said.

"Yes, glowing crap. Remember, you'll need to crack and shake when you need them."

"How am I supposed to do that?"

"Roll around or something."

"You look ridiculous," Sam said.

"Got a better idea?" I snapped. Knowing that

you're counting down toward certain death makes you tense.

"Three hundred pounds of C4 shaped into a giant Owen doll," he muttered.

"Hood won't go for that. Nothing big or elaborate. We've already shot him, burned him, and blown him up. Even if he sees I'm armed, he's cocky. He'll think he can take me, so he'll let me in. Then maybe I can figure out a way to kill him." It was stupid, but it was the best that I had, and going quietly wasn't my style.

Holly had cleaned the bite, applied a bandage and wrapped my hand. It was an utterly useless gesture. What was I going to do, get an infection?

"Has anybody ever lived through a zombie bite?" asked Trip.

"Never..." Julie said. "I've never...never heard..." Her voice broke badly. "Sorry."

I reached over and squeezed her hand. I only had to be strong for an hour. She had to be strong the rest of her life. I was trying to not show it, but I was already feeling the effects of the bite. My stomach ached and my head hurt. My eyes grated in their sockets as they moved. It was like I was coming down with a bad flu.

The small length of rope was lying on the table. I had no idea where the fingers had ended up. On the bridge at Buzzard Island, Bia had thrown a bigger piece of rope on the ground, and it had turned into some sort of portal. That piece had also apparently led back to the shadow man's lair. Esmeralda was studying the cord intently.

"Do you really think we can figure out how to activate that thing?" I asked.

"Maybe," she replied. "I've heard of these things before. I read about them somewhere in the archives a long time ago. Where's Lee, already?"

"I'm coming," he shouted from the hallway. Our librarian hobbled in a moment later. He dropped a heavy book and a bunch of half-burned papers on the table, so preoccupied that it was as if he didn't even notice the rest of us. "I've got it. I cross-referenced it under dimensional gates." He opened it with a thump. "It works on the same principle, like a portable version of the door in DeSoya Caverns."

"That's awesome," Sam responded. "Can we turn it on and dump a strike force in the bad guy's lap or not?"

Esmeralda held up the rope and touched the ends together. It only made a tiny circle. "You got a team of attack leprechauns around here I don't know about?"

Sam punched the wall. He wasn't taking this very well. I was still strangely calm. Julie's little brother entered the room. He paused long enough to nod at me, but then looked away uncomfortably. It was like being a guest at your own funeral. A lot of people were struggling right now.

"The damaged papers are what's left of Ray Shackleford's notes that got burned during the Christmas party. There were things in there about portals. And this old book has a section on them too." Lee began flipping pages. "I'm trying to figure out if we can tweak this one, make it bigger or something, or even if we can turn it on, but this book was written hundreds of years ago. It's not exactly easy to understand, and I'm having to use a computer translator, unless any of you guys speak Renaissance German."

Milo looked over. "At least that one's got pictures..."

There were other pictures before Lee got to the magic rope section and one of them looked familiar. "Lee, stop. Go back a few pages... There. Milo, check that out."

Milo looked up from his glow sticks as he bit the end off the tape roll. "Hmmm... that's kind of like our ward stone."

Lee looked at it, puzzled. "That's what that is?"

Of course, he had never seen it. "Yeah, that's it. What book is that?"

Lee flipped it over. "If I'm reading this right, *Principles of Alchemical Artifacts and Unnatural Philosophy.* It has stuff about teleportation, animating corpses, alternate dimensions, immortality potions, that kind of thing.... It was written by somebody named Konrad Dippel."

That name rang a bell.

Julie might have been in a state of shock, but she was also our best historian. "He was an alchemist, one of the really talented ones, a peer of Isaac Newton. It's possible that he would know how to make this teleportation thing work, if we could just decipher his notes."

"That's just awesome trivia, but it doesn't help us save Earl," Sam spat. "Sorry, Z, I appreciate what you're doing. Futile noble gesture, man, but I can't stomach letting you do this on your own."

"I know, Sam. If we're lucky the Feds' tracking device will work and you can come avenge me." I grimaced. I had to hang in there; everybody here needed me to stay tough. I couldn't break down yet. "Wait a second." I raised one hand. That disturbed

Milo, who was busy shoving road flares in every pouch on my back. "Why's that name familiar? Dippel?"

Julie thought about it for a moment. "Well . . . Dippel's experiments on cadavers were carried out at the castle with the same name as the doctor in the book. A lot of people think he's the man who inspired Mary Shelley."

"Who?" asked Holly.

"The woman who wrote Frankenstein," Trip answered.

It clicked.

"Get Agent Franks."

We located Franks at the hangar where the Fed choppers were currently parked. The MCB had taken over the building and turned it into their command post. This pissed off a lot of Hunters, but the Feds played by their own rules and we were in no shape to argue. The main doors were open and I barged directly past the guards there. One of them moved to stop me.

"I need to see Agent Franks."

He automatically looked back into the open space. A twenty-foot-wide white tent had been put just inside the hangar door. There were figures moving around on the other side of the thin fabric. "I'll have to check."

A voice came through the fabric. "Let them in." Myers appeared around the corner of the tent. "How are you feeling?" he asked awkwardly. Knowing that I was ready to kick the bucket any minute had at least made him slightly humble.

"Oh, I'm just peachy. Thanks for asking." The dead automatons had been stacked neatly on the hangar floor in rows. Multiple agents were ripping them apart, looking for clues. "Where's Franks?"

Myers studied me for a moment. "He said you

knew . . ." Then he glanced at the half-dozen or so Hunters standing behind me. "They wait here." Julie stepped up to my side. She didn't need to say a word as she gave Myers a look of utter coldness. He nodded once, understanding that she wasn't ready to leave me yet. "Fine, but what you're about to see is classified way beyond top secret. You have to take this to the grave with you."

"At least that won't take me long!" I exclaimed sarcastically. Julie visibly flinched. It made me feel guilty.

We followed Myers into the hospital tent. Several gowned and masked individuals were clustered over an operating table. Around them were beeping machines and a cart with various clean red organs stacked on it. The medical team parted as I approached. Franks was on the table. Myers had to look away.

The big man was a mess. His chest was cracked wide, held open with some sort of stainless steel device. A doctor stepped back, holding what appeared to be a damaged lung. Shockingly enough, Franks was awake and propped up on pillows. The fact that I could see his internal organs didn't seem to bug him any.

He slowly turned, eyes lingering on the bandage encircling my left hand. "Looks like I failed."

"Yeah, you did," I responded. "But let's make it count for something."

Franks dipped his head slightly. That was probably the closest thing he'd ever made to an apology.

"I need someone to help Lee and Esmeralda figure out how to reactivate Hood's teleportation device. We have a book that talks about that kind of device, written by somebody named Dippel. I have a feeling that you know something about his work."

The big man closed his eyes for a moment. When he opened them, I could see that they were still different colors, the blue one probably donated by some poor sucker from the concert. "Know his work? I *am* his work." Franks then addressed the doctor. "Wrap it up."

"But, sir, you still need another kidney, and you've also sustained damage to several major muscle groups. We need more time."

Franks looked at my hand again. He knew we were out of time. "Start stapling." The medical team complied immediately. Before they folded his chest closed, I noted that his physiology diverged wildly from anything I had ever seen in a biology textbook. There appeared to be extra organs and his ribcage was more of a hardened plate with flexible bits than separate bones. It was seriously weird. Franks caught me staring. "The taxpayers paid for some upgrades."

"So that's what you are . . ." Julie said. "You're Frankenstein's Monster."

"More than that," Franks snorted. "I *hate* that book. I'm no whiner."

I glanced at my watch. I had about forty minutes before I had to be back to the village. "Do you know anything about the magic teleportation rope?"

"No. But I understand his writings. Had to figure them out to stay alive. Good alchemist . . . Terrible father."

"It looks like he might have been the guy who built our ward stone too."

"Hmmm . . ." Franks frowned. That had thrown him off. "I didn't recognize it. I remember all the doctor's codes . . . Even the offensive ones." His thick brow furrowed in thought as the medical team literally screwed his chest together with terrible cracking noises. My already-nauseous stomach threatened to empty. "Sir, I have an idea."

Myers looked up from his corner. He was holding a handkerchief over his mouth. "You can't be serious."

"What are you thinking?" Julie asked. "Is there a magical way to save Owen?"

Franks' face was impassive as he squashed Julie's hope. "Nothing I know can help Pitt."

"I know what you're getting at...." Myers stepped forward, surprised. "The wards were manufactured as focal points of reality, deadly to other dimensional creatures. Isaac Newton and the alchemists created them to protect mankind from the Old Ones and..." He trailed off. "Are you saying what I think you're saying, Agent?"

"A ward is a shield *and* a sword," Franks said simply.

Whatever he was suggesting rocked Myers, the man who had once ordered a nuclear bomb dropped on Alabama. "That could disband all cohesion!"

"Exactly," Franks responded. Whatever the hell that meant. Slowly he raised one big hand and held it out to me. "I can avenge you."

I shook his hand. He was unbelievably strong. "Kill them all."

Less than thirty minutes left.

Franks, Lee, and Esmeralda were working on the magic rope. MHI and the Feds were surrounding the village just in case. I had just enough time to make a few final preparations. I was strapping on every weapon in my arsenal when Milo lifted one final item from the table.

"This one is exactly like the one we used earlier when I fried Hood's butt," he explained as he pushed the sack into my hands. "You know those nasty little things kids use on the Fourth of July, the little hockey pucks that flash like a strobe light and hurt your eyes? Think of this as one of those on steroids from hell, only *angrier*. Don't look at it directly, or you *will* go blind. Well, it is pretty close to what we used earlier, so there should be about a twenty-second flash, but I was kind of surprised that one was actually a controlled burn and didn't just explode and roast us."

That made me feel particularly safe as I put the satchel over my armor.

Milo paused awkwardly. Then he hugged me. He patted me on the back a few times before breaking away. He looked like he was going to cry. "I'll go get the rest of your gear."

"Yeah, thanks, man."

Julie and I walked into the hall. My mind was reeling. This was the end.

"You okay?" I asked. It was an idiotic question.

"Of course not," she answered. "But it is what it is."

We stood there for a few seconds, huddled together in silence, which is an eternity when your remaining life is measured in minutes. But we were Monster Hunters. It wasn't like either of us hadn't ever thought about this before. I had always figured it would have been sudden though, with no time for long good-byes. This was much harder.

"There's something I have to tell you," I said softly. "In Mexico, when I talked to your mother, she warned me about the mark on your neck." Julie stiffened against me. "She said that it was going to kill you eventually. I didn't say anything because I was scared and I thought that she was just lying to us again...But with what happened last night..." I couldn't help but think about the three new marks. There was something terribly wrong, and I wasn't going to be around to help her through it.

Julie gave me a pathetic smile. "You've got other stuff to worry about right now, Owen. I'll take care of it."

I knew she would. Julie was strong, far stronger than me. No matter what happened, she would always find a way. That was just her nature. The year that I had known her had been the best year of my life, and I had somehow believed that it would go on like that forever. I held her tight as my heart ached.

Unable to contain it any longer, Julie began to sob. "I'd trade with you if I could."

"I know..."

In a little while, I would be dead and she would be alone, but I knew that she would survive. She would get on with her life without me, and someday, she would be happy again.

And knowing that gave me the strength to go on. *It was time*.

Hunters were standing in a line down the hallway to see me off. Everyone was somber. Julie's grandfather saluted me with his hook. "Good luck, Hunter." I paused in front of the memorial wall. I was going to have a plaque up there soon.

Shit. I didn't want to die. I wasn't ready to have a plaque yet. This wasn't *fair*. I tried to think of something memorable to say, but didn't have the words. "Thanks, everybody. I'll try not to let you down." It was stupid, but it would have to do.

My mom came out of nowhere and intercepted me. She almost took me down in a tackle. She was totally hysterical, and her accent was extra thick when she was this freaked out. "What are you doing?" She pointed at my shotgun. "Where are you going with your Abominator?"

"Abomination," I corrected her. "Never mind. Look, Mom, I've got to go after Mosh. It's me for him."

"They told me you're dying, that something poisonous bit you. Why can't we go to the hospital?"

"It doesn't work like that, Mom. I have to do this."

She wouldn't let go of my arm. "No! Owen, please." Hysterical tears streamed down her cheeks. "No, son, please, no."

I wasn't tough enough to do this. I grabbed my mom by the shoulders. "Listen. I'm doing what I have to do. If I had any other option, I would be doing that instead. I'm already dead, but Mosh isn't. I'm going to get him back."

Then Dad was there. He took Mom in his arms and guided her away. He studied me while Mom screamed and thumped her fists into his chest.

"I'm sorry, Dad," I said.

"Don't worry. It isn't your time yet."

He was delusional because of that stupid letter. But at least he was calm while he kept Mom restrained. "I love you, Dad. I love you, Mom."

"We'll talk about it when you get back. Bring your brother home."

"I will," I promised. I just wouldn't be with him.

There was a grumbling noise off to the side. Gretchen was standing there, a tiny black shape squished between the hulking Hunters. Her totem stick was in hand, dangling feathers, beads, and small animal skulls. I had no idea why she wasn't with her people in their time of need. She spoke directly to Julie. It must have been something too complicated for Gretchen's poor English.

"Gretchen says we're part of the clan too..." Julie seemed puzzled, trying to keep up with the rapid-fire Orcish. She actually gave a very sad little smile. "Thank you, honey. That's really sweet."

"What's she saying?" I asked.

Gretchen switched to English. "Marry." She shook her totem stick. "Marry. Sad to die... alone." She reached into her burkha and pulled out a sheet of paper. She unfolded it. The notarized letter bore the state seal and declared that Gretchen F. Skippywife was an ordained minister in the state of Alabama.

"She's offering her services as a priestess of *Gnrlwz*," Julie nearly choked trying to say it correctly, "the orc god of war, to perform a wedding before you go." It took me a moment to digest. It was so absurd, so sudden, that despite everything else, all the fear, anticipation, and dread, I actually laughed. Julie started to giggle along with me. "You want to?"

It was just the kind of thing that Monster Hunters would do. Even when death was staring us right in the face, we'd still give him the finger. "Yeah. Yeah, I do."

Julie shrugged. "Well, this isn't how I imagined it at all... Do your thing, Gretchen. Grandpa, would you do the honors of giving me away?"

The old man stepped up, proud of his granddaughter. "Of course. And I was worried I'd have to wear a tux for this..."

The Hunters gathered around us in a circle, seemingly just as surprised as I was. Gretchen hissed and the crowd fell silent. Trip stood just behind me and off to the side, appointing himself as my best man. Holly, apparently, was Julie's maid of honor, only instead of flowers, she had a .308 Vepr carbine.

Ironically, this was the spot where we'd shared our first kiss, right under a Latin phrase warning about the dangers of fleeting glory.

Gretchen had us get on our knees in front of the wall of memorial plaques. I took Julie's hand. This wasn't how I'd expected it either. My mom started to cry even harder and my dad put his big arm over her shoulder. Gretchen tapped us both on the forehead with her stick as she started grumbling something memorized and incomprehensible. She kept it brief. Orcs weren't big on ceremony.

I glanced over at Julie, she looked back at me, eyes shining bright. I loved her. And that one split second was *exactly* how I'd imagined it, and that made everything okay.

Gretchen thumped me on the forehead with the stick. *"Grok?"*

"I do."

Gretchen thumped Julie. *"Grok?"*

She looked into my eyes. "I do."

Gretchen raised her stick high overhead and screamed her devotion to the god of war. It was actually almost musical. She slammed the tip of the short staff hard into the floor, the impact resonating through the entire hall. I think that was when she pronounced us man and wife. She took the stick, pointed it at my nose, and gave me an order. I didn't understand a word that she was saying.

"She says that it is orcish tradition that the more you

love your wife, the bigger the thing you need to kill for her as a wedding night offering," Julie translated. "She says Skippy killed a seventy-foot lindwyrm for her." Gretchen said more and Julie giggled again. "So she *bore* him many sons."

And just like that, I was a married man. I couldn't kiss the bride, because I was infected by a zombie, but other than that, it was actually a pretty happy moment. One of the Hunters even thought to take a picture.

Somebody started clapping. The two of us made our way through the cheering crowd. Dorcas was at her desk. I had never seen her cry before. She blew her nose with a sound like a trumpet. "Congratulations, I guess. See you 'round, Z." I got outside before anyone could see me completely break down. A mess of other Hunters were going to follow us to the village to provide backup. There was a car waiting.

Trip and Holly were riding with us, of course. I held the door open for my new wife. Trip reached over and thumped me on the arm. Holly gently rested her hand on my shoulder. Trip put the car in gear and we headed for the village. "It's been an adventure, guys," I told my best friends.

"It isn't over 'til the fat lady sings," Holly stated.

"Why all the tears then?" I asked.

"I always cry at weddings."

I stood in the spot where the last teleportation effect had taken place and checked my watch. Hood better not be late. I wasn't feeling very well. My head had started throbbing in the car and wouldn't stop. Cold sweat was leaking from every pore.

The orc village was deserted. The tribe had retreated

to the relative safety of the compound. A dozen Hunters had formed a perimeter around the village and were just waiting. MCB agents had massed in force at the entrance.

My friends didn't want to let go of me. Trip had started to babble. "Dude, we'll be praying for you. I know that you're going to come back. It might take a miracle, but it's not like we haven't seen miracles before. God's on our side, man."

Holly was tougher. "Be strong, Z."

I stumbled away. Saying my farewells to the Amazing Newbie Squad of Yesteryear had been particularly painful. Trip was hurting. Holly was too, but she kept it bottled up behind a stoic mask. I noticed Trip starting to shudder, and Holly took his hand as they walked away.

Now it was just me and Julie.

"No matter what happens," she said. "I'll always love you."

"You were the best thing that's ever happened to me, you know that, right?"

"Yeah, I know." She tried to smile, but failed. "I can't . . . I don't know what to . . ."

"It's okay," I assured her. I stroked her face. My hand was trembling.

The earth shuddered. A few feet away, flames erupted from two points in the dirt, quickly burning outward, forming a circle just big enough for me to stand in. The ground inside seemed to disappear into darkness.

*This was it.*

"I love you." I couldn't even kiss her good-bye.

I broke away from Julie and stepped into the circle. It was the hardest thing I've ever done.

# CHAPTER 19

Now I was alone.

I fell immediately as I entered the portal. It was as if the world just vanished, leaving me in a violent freefall. I hit the ground on my side, cracking a bunch of glow sticks. I lay there disoriented for a few seconds. Gravity seemed to be coming from a different direction, and it took me a dizzy moment to orient myself.

The circle I had stepped through was there, but instead of being above me like it felt it should be, it was off to the left. A beam of sunlight came through the hole, like a window into a pitch-black room. Wherever I was, it was nighttime, and we were outside. There were stars in the sky, and I was no astronomer, but I could tell I was nowhere near Alabama. I lumbered to my feet. "Hood! I'm here. Let Mosh go!"

"You're armed I see. I expected no less from someone so stubborn, but at least *I* am a man of my word." The voice of the shadow man came from all around me. "Free the brother."

Lights ignited atop several tall lampposts. I was on an asphalt path through an old cemetery. The mausoleums were gray and crumbling. Every path was surrounded by ornate wrought-iron fences, speckled with rust. Mosh was there, and directly behind him were two hooded acolytes. My brother was shaking, held up by the cultists. His left hand had been wrapped in a towel, but he'd already bled through it. The acolytes pushed Mosh toward the hole.

"Dude? What's going on?" he cried. He looked terrible, pale from blood loss.

Relief flooded through me. At least he was still alive. "I'm trading myself for you. Go through the portal."

"I can't leave you, man. These guys are nuts. They cut my fingers off! They're going to kill you."

"I can take care of it. Go."

One of the cultists shoved Mosh. He tumbled forward and simply disappeared when he hit the hole. It closed behind him, taking the sunlight with it.

That left just me and the crazies. *Monster Hunter Solo*.

"Come with us, please," one of the cultists said nervously, glancing at my shotgun. "The High Priest awaits." There was a large building at the end of the path. It looked like a really cozy house, but somehow it had an industrial feel at the same time. I scanned in every direction. There were no other lights anywhere near us. Hood was nowhere to be seen. If I made a run for it, I'd die from the bite before I made it very far.

"Does he await over there?" I nodded my head toward the building.

"Yes, please allow us to escort you."

"Naw, I think I can get there myself." I flicked off Abomination's safety as I raised the stubby weapon. *BOOM.* I blasted a round of buckshot into the chest of the first cultist, then jerked the muzzle onto the next one. *BOOM.* Both of them went down like the sacks of crap that they were.

"It's on now, Hood!" I shouted as I stepped over the bodies and walked toward the building. I was missing my honeymoon for this.

The lights all died at once. His voice came from the air itself. "Of course. I'm impressed that you're still able to walk. Usually by now the bitten is nearly comatose. I can see it though. The fever is burning you up. Your muscles are weakening. You're bleeding internally. It won't be long now."

I'd managed to smash most of the glow sticks by the time I reached the manicured front lawn. I activated the brilliant flashlight attached to my shotgun's rail and swept it over the front of the building. There was a sign: MORTUARY.

"Oh, that just figures," I muttered, clambering up the steps.

"Yes, I own twenty of these around the world, as well as several dedicated crematoriums and livestock-rendering factories. It gives me plenty of raw materials. Art supplies, if you will."

The double doors at the entrance were beautifully carved wood and stained glass. I smashed them open with my boot. I moved through, my shotgun light pulsing. I checked to see if the flashlight was malfunctioning, but I realized it was because of how badly my limbs were shaking. It was a nice waiting room. Large displays of flowers were set in vases under the stained glass windows. Nothing moved in here. My illuminated green reflection bounced back from the glass.

His voice came from just ahead of me. "Nice glow sticks. Are you going to a rave?"

The chapel was one of those bland, nondenominational types, but with one obviously recent addition. The flashlight beam illuminated a giant-golden-squid idol tied to the wall. I swept the light back and forth. The room was huge and there were deep shadows everywhere. The tremors in my legs were making it difficult to move quickly. I had to pause and lean against a pew to catch my breath. Something hot and wet dripped down my face. I wiped it away, then studied my glove under the glow sticks. My nose had started bleeding.

"Show yourself!" I screamed.

"Certainly," the response came from directly behind me.

I turned, whipping Abomination around. There was nothing there.

"Why must we fight, Owen? Why do you rage against your destiny?"

"Face me," I hissed. "Let's finish this like men!" A finger tapped me on the shoulder. I spun and blasted a round of buckshot through a stained glass window. A curtain moved and I shot it too. "Damn it!" There was movement overhead, a massive shadow slinking across the ceiling.

I raised my gun as it dropped. The light caused the shape to shrink. Jerking the trigger, I managed to pump several rounds upward before impact. It slammed me into the carpet. I kept firing. The shape rose. My flashlight beam cut a path through the shadow, leaving nothing but a man in a robe. I shot Hood repeatedly in the chest, silver buckshot tearing right through him. I kept on shooting even as my flashlight exploded.

He disappeared into the darkness.

Now all I had was the pale green glow coming from my armor. I dropped Abomination into its sling. "You killed me, Hood. I'm going to return the favor!" I reached for the pouch on my back and pulled out a pair of road flares. They ignited with a hiss of flame and sparks. "I'm gonna burn this motherfucker down!" I laughed maniacally as I tossed the flares to the far end of the room and reached back for more. Once I had thrown a flare into each corner I drew another magazine from my chest rig and reloaded my shotgun. One of the curtains was on fire and the carpet had caught at the far end. Now that was more like it. Flames licked up the wall, casting flickering light across the chapel. I glanced back and forth, searching for my target.

"Monster Hunters are always hell on the furniture," he whispered in my ear. I turned, too slow, and he blocked my shotgun. Hood's sneering face was inches from my own. He head-butted me. Stars exploded in my vision. Then he hit me, once, twice, fists colliding with my face, robes snapping around his arms, and finished it off by kicking me brutally hard in the stomach. I collided with a pew, flipped over it, and landed on my back.

Gasping for air, I started to crawl. I was so weak. Water began to fall from the ceiling. Fire sprinklers. I coughed uncontrollably. My body was tearing itself apart.

"You have any idea what this'll do to my insurance?" He leapt onto the top of the pew I had gone over, and crouched there, watching, enjoying my plight. The light from the flares was dying, extinguished by the sprinklers. As the light dimmed, Hood seemed to blur and grow. I flipped Abomination to full auto and emptied an entire magazine through his body. He leapt from the pew, splinters flying in every direction, and vanished back into the shadows. I rolled onto my stomach and clawed my way across the carpet beneath the other pews. It wasn't like I could hide. I glowed in the dark.

"I defeated Earl Harbinger *and* Agent Franks simultaneously. What exactly do you think *you're* going to accomplish? Part of me exists in a dimension beyond your understanding. You couldn't stop me in broad daylight on your best day, let alone half-dead and in the dark."

I found an open space between rows and rolled into it, whacking my head in the process. I reached for the satchel with Milo's super flash-bang. I could barely feel my hands and they blundered about clumsily like they were asleep.

"You still haven't wrapped your brain around what's really going on! Come on, Owen, don't disappoint me like this."

It hurt to move, but I raised my head and looked. I could make out Hood, in human form, leaning against the far wall, arms folded. "Okay, then why don't you educate me, asshole. What's your master plan, besides feed me to your stupid god?"

"That's the spirit." He chuckled. "As you learned last year, it's a real chore for an Old One to enter our world. They exist in a reality different from our own. The rules of our existence are fatal to them. The few trapped here are dead yet dreaming. Their spawn can only exist inside a body created in this world or as disembodied spirits. The Elder Things are far too great to lower themselves in that way. For them to exist in this plane they must first bend our reality to match their own."

"Yeah, I know, and they need somebody like me to do that for them." I had to keep blinking. I didn't know if it was because of the sprinklers, or if my eyes had started bleeding. No time to worry about it. I had to focus. When I set this thing off, I would only have a few seconds to take him out.

"Very good. You're a very special man. Preordained before your birth to wield the key to the planes, the Avatar of Chaos himself, blessed with powers beyond that of any mortal man."

"Blah, blah, blah," I gasped. "Get to the point. I ain't got all day."

"That's your gift, your curse. Lord Machado was the last, but he was too weak. But then you were too strong. You have no idea how jealous I am of you." He pushed away from the wall and walked casually down the aisle toward me. "If only I had been born with your blessings . . . If only you knew . . . But I do go on, and your time is so very short. To achieve my life's work, I needed something to appease the Dread Overlord. Sacrificing you will suffice, and I needed the means to control his gift, which in a way, your side has also provided me." He snapped his fingers. "Torres, my son, would you bring in our guest, please?"

There was the sound of doors opening. I jerked

around toward the front of the chapel. It had opened into a viewing area. Fifteen feet away, half a dozen robed acolytes stood beside an ornate coffin.

"Anthony..." I hissed, raising my shotgun, my feverish mind forgetting that it was empty. The former Fed dipped his head at me. There was a hint of madness in his eyes. They opened the casket's lid, revealing the occupant. Falling water beat a cadence onto the silk.

*Julie?*

My laboring heart skipped a beat.

No. It wasn't her. The figure was perfectly still, hands folded peacefully across her chest, just below where someone had driven a wooden stake through her heart.

*Susan...*

"Susan Shackleford stole the artifact. She took it from DeSoya Caverns after you so carelessly discarded it. She kept it, like a common thief, stupidly thinking that she could learn to use it for herself. It was *mine*. I earned it. I was the one who should have inherited the key after Machado failed. Who was this stupid vampire to think that she could take my honor? She'd made herself unbelievably strong by feeding on unholy monsters of every kind, stealing their precious lives, their energy. The ghastly hag. I offered her an alliance, but that wasn't good enough. No! Susan dared think that she could take over the Condition, the church that I built with my own hands, the flock that I'd tended! She thought she deserved my glory!" Hood's voice was bitter. "That's why she came to you with a piece of the key. She knew she was no match for me, but my dear old friend, Ray, believed that you, one of the Chosen, might actually have a chance. He's as big a fool as he's ever been, thinking he could keep it from me."

"The artifact?" I gasped. It was too powerful. I couldn't begin to imagine what it could be used for in the hands of a loony like Hood. "You have it?"

"After Susan dared to interfere in Mexico and then again in Cazador, I tracked her down and took back what was rightfully mine. She escaped Earl only to run into me. I'm not done with her yet, either. I've never been able to use such a powerful vampire in my experiments before . . . She's always been beautiful, but I could *improve* her."

He was closer now. He reached into his robes and pulled out the small piece of stone. About the size of a pack of cards, it looked innocuous enough, but I knew that it held the end of the world inside. "With you, with this, my dream will be complete."

It wouldn't do him any good. The big gate could only be opened once every five hundred years. He couldn't let the Dread Overlord in. "You're too—" I had to stop as a fire rippled up from my abdomen, burning through my throat, and bloody vomit spilled involuntarily past my lips. I retched and cringed while Hood waited patiently for me to finish. "Late . . ." I finally gasped.

He was only a few feet away. "Of course. This isn't about letting them in. I'm trading you for something special. I've proved my worthiness to awake the *Arbmunep*, and the artifact will allow me to utilize it to its full potential."

Myers had said that name. "What now, you sick freak?"

Hood grinned. It was terrifying. "Eternal night.

Beautiful eternal night. The world will wilt and decay until they surrender to their rightful king."

"You're insane."

He didn't like having his sanity questioned. "I'm the Lord of Shadows!" he shouted.

I was growing weaker by the second. I didn't know if I could do this. Cold water rained down on my face. The giant flash-bang was in my lap. It was now or never.

Gathering up what strength I had left, I pulled the cord and tossed it. The Frisbee-sized chunk of lethal chemicals sailed down the aisle toward Hood. Sparks shot from the top as it landed on the sopping carpet at his feet. He frowned at the device. "Delaying the inevitable with a mere distraction," he said as he raised his cloak to shield his face. "Pathetic."

I forced myself upward as it ignited. Scalding light burned across the room. The cultists covered their eyes and cried out as the light bombarded them. The chemicals burned with an unholy screech. Blind, desperate, I drove myself forward. I had to reach my target.

Maybe it was the water soaking the explosive into mush, but this one didn't last nearly as long. Hood, unfazed, lowered his cloak, grinning. "You didn't even reach me." He stopped when he realized where I had gone. "Oh, bloody hell."

"Ha!" I responded, still blind, but I had found what I was looking for. The wooden stake embedded in Susan's chest brushed my numb fingers. I forced my hands to curl around the shaft and I tugged. It grated against her ribs.

Stakes through the heart don't permanently kill vampires. They just shut them down, their supernatural regenerative abilities unable to heal as long as the foreign object is there. When the stake comes out, the vampire heals. I wasn't strong enough to do this on my own. I needed help. She was evil incarnate, but the enemy of my enemy was my friend.

"Stop him!" Hood bellowed at his blinded minions.

The stake wrenched free with a sickening *pop*. Someone crashed into my back, taking us both to the ground. I rolled over, weakly trying to defend myself. A cultist was on top of me, trying to hold me down. I got one arm free and slammed the stake upward. The man made a terrible gurgling noise as the sharpened wood pierced his throat.

Susan rose from the coffin with shocking speed, perfectly straight, the hole in her chest still closing. The vampire was eerily still for a long moment, arms demurely folded, false rain cascading around her. Her dress was torn and filthy from the flight through the forest. Her black hair hung like a veil over her pale face.

One of the cultists moved.

Her eyes opened, a sick shade of red. One delicate hand swept down, cleaving like an ax through an acolyte's face and out the back of his skull. The other cultists retreated. Susan growled at them, raised her hand, and licked the blood from her fingers. It took a second for Susan to get oriented, taking in me on the ground, the huddled nut jobs, and her nemesis.

The Master vampire growled at the necromancer. "Marty..."

"Susan," the shadow man responded.

"We have a score to settle, you and me," she said, showing off her fangs.

"Indeed we do. You thought you could best me, take over the empire that I built. That was your last mistake."

"And your first was having me turned into a vampire to begin with, you limey bastard." Susan stepped out of the coffin and floated to the floor.

I shoved the dying cultist off me. "Get him, Susan! Kick his ass!" I shouted. I tried to sit up, but was too weak, and sank back to the floor.

For a second, I thought we might just have a chance. She was powerful, mean as hell, but then Susan shook her head. "Sorry, hon. I tried that once, didn't work out. That's why I hired you, remember? Thanks for saving me though. Much appreciated." Then she was just *gone*.

"No! No! Damn it! Damn it!" I screamed in frustration. The tattered dress hit the floor, empty, as a white mist rolled across the ground and out the broken window. *Stupid! So much for that idea.* Never trust the undead. "You better run, you bitch!" It figured that the last thing I'd accomplished in my life was to save the life of a vampire. *Way to go, idiot.* I collapsed into a pathetic coughing fit.

Unbelievable pain shuddered through my body. The undead curse was shredding my cells. As a reminder of things to come, the cultist with the wooden stake jammed in his neck sat up, corpse already animated. Struggling to rise, I made it only a few feet before falling on my face. I was just too weak. A boot splashed right in front of my nose.

"Somebody shut off the sprinklers already," Hood ordered. Strong hands landed on my back and rolled me over. I tried to reach for my pistol. That same boot collided with the side of my head. "Determined bloke, isn't he? Disable the tracking device."

"I've been jamming the signal since he came out of the portal." Somebody took my shotgun. Someone else began pulling on the side of my armor. I was too feeble to do anything about it. "What now?" Torres asked.

"Watch him. I'll prepare the sending. Young Mr. Pitt has a very important appointment to keep."

Consciousness returned in tiny bits. First came the terrible aching in my bones. My body felt like an old garment that had been eaten thin by moths. Next I became aware of the taste of blood, my own blood. I gagged. My head rolled to the side so it could spill out. My eyes opened. Everything was blurry.

"Well, look who's awake." Torres was sitting across from me. One of his eyes was bruised and swollen shut. That's what you looked like when Agent Franks knocked you out. "How are you feeling?"

I couldn't respond. My face hurt too much.

"Figured as much. Well, you look like shit." He was leaning back in his chair, enjoying himself. He had Abomination resting on the chair next to him. "In fact, let me show you." There was a small mirror on the table between us. He picked it up and held it so I could see my reflection.

My skin was utterly pale. There were red blotches on my skin from blood vessels breaking just under the surface. The whites of my eyes had taken on a sick yellow tone and they were circled by blackened sockets. The fresh wound on my cheek from the werewolf was festering and leaking pus.

I closed my eyes. I had killed zombies that looked healthier than that. Not too much longer now.

Torres put the mirror down. "You were always ugly. Hell, I wondered how somebody like you wound up with a hot piece like that Shackleford chick. But now? Damn, you're ugly. About to get uglier too. But don't worry, the High Priest says that you'll hang on long enough to make it to the other side."

I tried to tune out the pain but it was all-consuming. I had no idea that it hurt this much to turn into a zombie. All I could feel was agony. One part of my body would just hurt, until another part started to hurt worse, and that would briefly take my attention, until the next bit topped it. The traitor continued to drone on. He was really enjoying himself. There were three other men in the room with us. They would occasionally laugh at something Torres said. I fixated on him. I failed to take out Hood because of my stupidity. Trusting Susan... What the hell had I been thinking? Not only was Hood still alive, which meant Earl was doomed, I had also managed to let loose another devil into the world. Maybe I could partially atone for that and somehow take *this* piece of trash with me.

I forced myself to pay attention to my surroundings. It was a comfortable but plain apartment, probably attached to the back of the mortuary. There was one closed door and a curtained window off to the side. I was in a heavy wooden chair. They had put down a tarp to protect the carpet. My wrists had been tightly bound to the chair arms with orange twine. The cord was frayed, but strong, and had already cut deeply into my flesh. Looking at my hands made me sick. Blood was seeping around my fingernails.

"I will say this for you, Pitt. You're a man after my own heart, somebody who can appreciate the finer things in life. Good-looking women, good-looking guns." He lifted one of my .45s. "Just so you know, I'm keeping your gear. Don't worry. I'll give them a good home." The others laughed. "And look what else I've got." He stuck out his chest. He had pulled the Velcro MHI patch off my armor and pinned it to his robe. The happy face with horns didn't mean much to him, but he knew it did to me. "I figure I played Monster Hunter long enough to earn this bad boy. Pretty sweet, huh?"

"Screw..." I was too tired to finish the sentence.

"Poor, Pitt. You'll be on the other side, suffering for an eternity. And we'll be here, living like kings, running the new order."

"The dark new dawn," said one of the cultists.

"Amen, brother," Torres replied. "And we owe it all to Owen Pitt." He pushed the .45 into my forehead with a sneer. "Don't we, you zombie fuck?" He pulled the gun away and snickered. "Don't want to get a bunch of scabs on my new gun. I want to keep this baby nice. I'll probably use it to put a bullet into some of your friends. We're not done with MHI, oh no. When the sun doesn't rise tomorrow, the payback begins. We clean house, and nothing will be able to stop us."

"You'll...die...too..." It took a moment for me to register that the horrible scratchy noise was actually my voice. I sounded worse than an orc.

"Unbelievers are already dead, they just don't know it yet. The faithful will live forever." Torres slouched in his chair, carelessly gesturing with my gun. "We're not as crazy as you think. The master's one smart dude. Look at me. He's been grooming me for years, knowing that he'd need men in the MCB eventually. I worked hard, got into federal law enforcement. He arranged a monster encounter for me to survive, bam, and next thing you know, I'm one of America's finest ... Don't worry. We're not shutting the sun off. Just blocking it until everyone's ready to fall in line. But it's going to get real cold and people are going to get real hungry before they have the sense to do that."

"Convert or die," recited another cultist.

"Holy shadows will engulf the earth. Nations that convert will get to see the light, pardon the pun. Those that don't ..." He shrugged. "Too damn bad for them. We'll animate their starved dead and turn them loose on the survivors. When it's over, we'll build a perfect society from scratch."

Torres kept talking. He was really enjoying himself. These lunatics were actually going to go through with this. It sounded preposterous, but I had seen the gate that had opened over Alabama. After that, I could believe just about anything. The Old Ones could do it.

I closed my eyes. I just wanted the suffering to end. Maybe if I hurried up and died, then Hood's squid god wouldn't be satisfied with just a zombie. I found myself wishing for death, and death drew even closer, like a black wall. I touched it.

"Poor boy. Hurt to look at," a familiar voice said. "It makes an old man's heart hurt to be seeing such pain."

It took a second to recognize the voice.

"Mordechai?" I whispered.

"What?" Torres asked. When I opened my yellow eyes, Torres was regarding me suspiciously. "What did you say?"

I ignored him and tried to lift my head higher. "Mordechai? Is that you?"

It was. Old, bent, leaning on his cane, small glasses perched on his nose, Star of David hanging in front of his battered shirt. He was not young and healthy like the last time I had seen him, but in the form from the time of his death in 1944, just like how I'd gotten to know him originally. He was standing directly behind Torres, between two of the cultists. They didn't appear to notice him.

"Yes, boy, I am here for help," he said with a slight smile. "Others felt you need some wisdom. They say, boy very strong, but not always smart. Others can be mean like that." His Polish accent was as thick as ever.

"But...you moved on...I freed you."

He shrugged his bony shoulders. "Eh...what can say? I moved on, but veil is thin for you now. Close enough to death that we can talk so easy. Not exactly a long trip for me to get here! This more important now, so I come back. You need smarts." He tapped his finger on his temple and smiled. "I have smarts. You have guns and magic. Should blow up *many* crazy people together."

Was he really here? Had he come back to help me again? "Are you an angel?"

Torres turned back toward his henchmen. "He's hallucinating. Get the stimulant, now. We can't afford to lose him yet."

The ghost of Mordechai Byreika lifted his cane. It looked exactly like the one I'd driven through Jaeger's torso. "This look like flaming sword to you, boy? Of course is not angel. Angels? They're more formal. Kind of, how you say, stuffy. Now listen close. Time is short."

"Too late." I tried to show him the bandage on my hand, pulling repeatedly, forgetting that I was tied down. "Dead . . . soon."

Torres took my jerking against the bonds as a seizure. "Hurry with that potion, damn it!"

"No!" Mordechai admonished sternly. "You not die yet, boy. More work to do. For something more important than you. Not like this."

I tried to speak, but the pain was too great. *Nobody has ever been bitten by a zombie and lived.*

"You are not *nobody*, boy. You are *somebody*. You are one picked to finish fight. Good has said you are their champion. Bad's champion is waiting for you. Champion of Good not die because of stupid zombie! That's crazy talk."

*I can't. Dying.*

A cultist had removed a vial from his robes. He shoved a syringe into it and began pulling out a thick red liquid. "Give me that!" Torres ordered as he snatched the syringe away.

"You not die until I say so," Mordechai insisted. "Listen to your elders, boy. You have power to fight off zombie bite, just like you fight off werewolf when we met first time."

*That was different. That was something I could fight with my hands. I was never infected by the werewolf.*

"Of course not infected, because you are not monster now. You are Monster Hunter. Quit being stubborn and listen. Werewolf can't turn you. Zombie can't turn you. Vampire can't turn you, if stupid enough to get bit by vampire too you are. Regular Hunter, yes, but you? Different you are. You only turn if you give up."

*So I can't die until I give up?*

"No, that's just dumb. Turn, not kill. They can kill you just fine. Cut head off or blow up or set on fire, maybe shoot you in face, you die." He spread his hands as if balancing the scales. "Sploosh. Dead. Just like everyone else. But you are Chosen. Harder to kill Chosen unless he is being big baby. Certain things only you can do. Old Ones not realize who they're fighting with."

Torres jammed the huge needle into the nerve bundle between my ear and jaw and slammed the plunger down. The thick clump of liquid burned. Every muscle in my body automatically contracted with brutal force. The legs of the chair slammed back and forth on the floor. "Hold him!" Torres and one of the others grabbed me by the shoulders to keep me from flopping over.

Mordechai walked right through Torres as if he wasn't there, and I suppose in the twilight spirit world that my old mentor currently inhabited, he probably wasn't. Mordechai leaned close to my ear and whispered, "Don't give up."

The drug, or potion, or whatever the hell it was they shot me with pummeled my central nervous system like a jackhammer. The now-familiar black lightning was not just in my vision. It was colliding back and forth between the very fibers of my being. My body was a battleground, an undead virus was my enemy, and the prize was my soul.

"Never give up."

*I won't.*

"I know. That's why *you* are one who drew short straw."

Then I died. I think.

❖        ❖        ❖

I'd done this kind of thing enough times that nothing could really surprise me at this point. I was standing in the ornate ballroom at the Shackleford family estate. I was either in the past, before we'd blown it up and set it on fire while trying to kill Susan, or in the future, when we'd finally gotten it fixed, because the room was absolute perfection. The walls were covered in mirrors, giving the illusion that it was much larger than it really was, as each view doubled and tripled onto itself. The massive chandelier reflected the sunlight from the tall windows, causing the crystals to sparkle brilliantly. The hardwood floor had been polished until I could see my bedraggled reflection in it.

There was a man waiting for me in the center of the room. I did not know him. He was a head shorter than I was. The stranger was lean, but muscular, with long brown hair, muttonchops, and a mustache that extended to the end of his square jaw. He was in his forties. His uniform was made of creaking leather, with thick protective pieces over the torso and wrists, and a guard that pulled up over the throat to shield from bites, similar to our modern suits. While his archaic armor was battered, his guns were not. He had a pair of Colt Peacemakers with ivory grips holstered on a heavy-duty gun belt. The ammo stuck in the cartridge loops of the belt shined with old-school silver bullets.

The way he carried himself seemed vaguely familiar. "Who're you?"

"Somebody who's been sent to help. Mordechai kindly asked that I not let you pass." He had a very pronounced old Southern accent. "You ain't done yet. There's a mess of folks counting on you."

"I know."

"You best not fail them." He glanced around the ballroom, as if taking in something familiar. "I never liked this room. It felt snooty. It was for bunches of rich folk, gallivanting around in their fancy clothes, telling each other how important and pretty they were." He snorted. "But you know that it was always the most special to her, ever since she was a wee little thing."

He was talking about Julie. This was her favorite room in the old Shackleford plantation house. This was where we were supposed to have gotten married. The stranger hadn't picked this backdrop. I had.

"What am I supposed to do?" I asked.

"Damned if I know. Get back there and take care of business I suppose."

"I'm dying. I got bit by a zombie."

The stranger shrugged. "Cheat death then."

"Cheat?"

"If you ain't cheating, you ain't trying hard enough. That's what I always say. So pull your head out of your rear, get righteous mad, and get to killing."

"I will."

"Then what're you doing giving up and dying?" He pointed for the door, not that I'd walked in, but I got the idea. He was sending me back. "Them monsters ain't gonna kill themselves! You a Monster Hunter, or not?"

"I'm a Monster Hunter!"

"Good!" The ghost had a mischievous grin. "My boy always had a good eye for talent."

Okay. I was back. I inhaled for what seemed like the first time in eternity.

"Hang on," Torres said. "He's still breathing."

I wasn't normal. I knew that. That point had been driven home a long time ago. I had no idea what I was. All I did know was that I didn't want to die. Especially not like this.

The pain returned like a crashing tsunami. It was like being on fire and electrocuted and drowned at the same time. The virus, an incomprehensible curse from outside the boundaries of this world, pushed one last time to finish me. I screamed at the top of my lungs, a combination of fear, agony, and fury. My thrashing increased in intensity. The joints of the chair cracked. "Get help!" Torres cried as he tried in vain to restrain me.

The black energy swept through my body like a flash flood, burning, purging, cleansing, only this time I was the one in control. The lightning clashed with the virus. Then as quickly as it started, it was done.

The war was over.

The shaking stopped. My head flopped limply onto my chest.

"Wait!" Torres commanded.

The pain was still there. But now it was different, the fever had passed. I flexed my hands on the arms of the chair. I could *feel* again.

"Is he dead?" a cultist asked hesitantly.

"If he is, it's your fault for not getting the needle fast enough," Torres snarled. Fingers stabbed my neck. "Wait...I've got a pulse. And...it's really *strong*."

*Thanks, Mordechai.*

He was still in the room, waiting patiently. "Don't thank me yet, boy. Life ahead of you is hard one. Much work to do. Much sacrifice to make. Sometimes

I see what's coming, and I feel very bad for you. No, no thanks for me. Someday you probably curse me for not letting you just die."

I heard the door open. It was a young woman's voice. "It's time. My father needs the sacrifice."

"Yes, mistress," Torres responded.

"What happened here? What was that noise?" she asked with a very proper, high-brow English tone. "Did you harm him?" That one question held a lot of menace.

"No, but we had to give him the shot your father gave us. Pitt was beginning to turn. He's passed out now."

"Lucky for him, pity for us. Come along then. Time is short." The door closed.

*What now?*

The ghost laughed. "Do what you do best, of course!"

"Come on, guys. Let's go." The chair lifted from the ground. There were three of them carrying me, and since I'm a big boy, they were still struggling. "Great Dagon, this son of a bitch weighs a ton. Careful," Torres admonished. "If you piss off Lucinda, she'll skin us all. Get the door."

*Mordechai?*

But there was no answer. He was gone.

I could think again. Had he even really been here? Had I been hallucinating? Had I really died again? Had I beaten the zombie infection, or was I just feeling better because of the shot?

*Hell if I know.* But I was about to get FedExed across the universe to be dissolved for eternity by a creature so evil that just saying its name caused madness. I had to move *now*. My eyes were closed and my head was lolling side to side as they carried me, boots dangling. They were too sure of my weakened, soon-to-be-zombified state to bother with securing me that well. Their mistake. I just needed a chance to get my hands free. The chair was solid, but I could probably break it. What I needed was a distraction. "Anthony . . ." I croaked. "Wait . . ."

"Hold on," he barked. He was holding the chair on my right side. "He's awake."

"Did you take Myers' treasure?" I kept my voice weak. "He told me to . . . keep it safe . . . from you."

"What treasure?"

"Some powerful . . ." I mumbled something else, too faint for him to hear. He leaned in closer. I risked a peek. He was at bad-breath distance. "Can you hear me now?" I whispered into his ear.

"What did Myers say?"

I bit his ear. I really chomped down on it as I jerked my head away. Torres screamed. The chair toppled, sending me crashing to the floor. Spitting his ear out, I jerked violently against my bonds, pulling with every bit of strength I had. The twine held, but I tore the arms right off the chair. I was free.

Cultist on my left, one behind me, one at the door. I swung my left arm, leading with a big chunk of splintered wood and slammed the nearest bad guy in the crotch. He doubled over and I threw an uppercut into his throat. My fist never contacted, but the chair arm did. He went down, choking.

A weight collided with my skull. I was too furious to slow down. I was up, driving my shoulder into the next cultist, taking us both across the room. I threw the smaller man into the wall, crushing him into the paneling. I slammed him in again, breaking his ribs. The last cultist rushed me, but ran directly into my boot as I side-kicked him in the stomach. Since I was twice his size, the kick put him on his back.

All four of them were hurt. I had to press my advantage quickly. Even as experienced as I was, there was no way I could take on multiple assailants in my sorry state. The one against the wall was wheezing, gasping for breath. I brought the chair arms down on his skull with terrible force, striking until the wood was nothing but splinters. The man I had struck in the throat didn't look like he was moving, but the cultist I kicked was trying to rise. Abomination was still sitting where Torres had left it. I scooped it up and charged.

He reached for his squid necklace, either to signal for help, or to activate some sort of magic, but I never found out what exactly, as I flicked open Abomination's silver bayonet and slammed it through an eye socket and into his brain. I yanked the bayonet out and he toppled, twitching to the carpet.

That just left Torres.

He was crawling across the floor, panicked, disoriented, holding his hand against the side of his head, blood streaming between his fingers. There were still loaded magazines in my pouches, so I reloaded, worked Abomination's charging handle, and put a round of buckshot into the chamber. Torres wasn't currently a threat, so I risked a quick peek out the curtained window. We were on the third story of the mortuary, overlooking the back of the graveyard. It was dark, but I could see quite a bit of the cemetery below. There was a lot of movement, robed figures with torches and flashlights moving between the mausoleums. Something big was going down out there. I let the curtains drop and got back to business.

"Hey, Anthony," I said, my voice cold and detached. My pistol was on the ground. He had seen it and was trying to reach it. I didn't plan on letting him. "Stop right there. Yeah, I'm talking to you." He kept crawling, making a kind of whimpering noise. Furious, I walked ahead of him and put my boot down on his hand. "Try listening with your *good* ear."

"How...how did you..." he gasped. Apparently that kind of injury was very disorienting. "You should be..."

"Dead?" I asked, as I tugged the cords from my wrists. "Eventually, but I'm busy right now. What's your boss up to?" I ground down on his hand. He cried out. "Start talking"—I put my bayonet against his back—"or I start stabbing."

Torres raised his head. He looked pathetic with one ear. "You can't stop us."

"Maybe, but I bet I can kill a whole mess of you in the process." There was a groan. I glanced over. Two of the cultists were stirring. Apparently every member of the Condition animated as an undead as soon as they expired. The one that I had stabbed in the brain wasn't going anywhere, ever, but the other two were going to be an issue here pretty quick.

"See...already my brothers are rising. The Exalted Order will never stop—"

I swung Abomination over and blew both zombies' heads off. The blasts were deafening in the small room. "They look stopped to me." If that didn't raise the alarm, nothing would. I bent down, grabbed Torres by the back of the neck, and jerked him to his feet. My strength had returned. In fact, I was feeling pretty damn good. Good . . . and *violent*. "I've just got one question, Anthony. Why? Why'd you fall in with these people? Why'd you betray your friends, your country? Why?"

His eyes were windows into insanity. "I had a revelation. I saw the majesty of the Old Ones. I heard their songs. Their mysteries were—"

*Screw this*. I squeezed the back of his neck harder as I dragged him across the room. "Yeah. You know what? Never mind." I paused long enough to rip the MHI patch from his robe before shoving him against the window. The glass shattered, and he tumbled headfirst and screaming out of sight. There was a tearing noise and the screaming stopped abruptly.

I stepped forward. The damp night air was refreshing. The curtains billowed around me. Torres' crumpled body was impaled on multiple fleur-de-lis tops of an iron fence. Several other surprised Condition members had rushed to the body. One of them looked up and pointed my way. "It's the Monster Hunter!"

"Damn straight," I responded as I stuck the Velcro patch back on my armor. "That's more like it." Then I shoved Abomination out the window and fired the 40mm grenade launcher directly into them. Everything in the blast radius was torn apart by shrapnel. I turned away from the window, picked up the rest of my gear, and headed for the door.

I wasn't done yet.

Oh, no, not nearly done. I was just getting warmed up.

# CHAPTER 20

Several Condition members tried to stop me inside the mortuary. I cut them down without remorse. Compared to monsters, whack jobs were soft targets. There was a phone in the hallway but it was as dead as the cultists. I was rocking another magazine into Abomination as I cleared the stairs and reached the back door. The cemetery stretched before me. A fog was rolling in and mist was collecting between the mausoleums. Spotted throughout the fog were bobbing lights, cultists moving to intercept me, and who knew what else was out there. The smart thing to do was probably run and hide, maybe find a phone and make a collect call to the Department of Homeland Security. Anything but go out there where the unkillable Hood and his minions were lurking.

But at the same time, if Mordechai had just been a figment of my feverish imagination, and the only reason I was operating at this tempo was that shot Torres had given me, that meant that as soon as it wore off, I would go back to joining the ranks of the undead. For all I knew, I was going to keel over any second. I had to take my chances. Whatever Hood meant by eternal night was already starting.

I went straight forward with no real strategy in mind other than shooting anything that moved. And there was lots of stuff moving. The grass was thick and wet, sliding around under my boots. The names on the tombstones seemed English, but I still had no idea where in the world I actually was. It was cool, but not cold. Looking at the stars, they were weird enough that I figured I was in the southern hemisphere, not that it mattered now. I was on my own. I headed in the direction with the most lights. Hood could see in the dark but most of his followers were human and could not.

Shapes appeared through the mist and then retreated from view as I swung to face them. I knew that things were watching me from behind every stone wall. I could only imagine what kinds of horrid beasts had joined up with the Condition for their big moment. It made perfect sense. In a world without daylight, the creatures that we hunted would have an absolute vacation.

But nothing attacked. Cultists and creatures both hung back.

I reached the lights. They were the giant, portable, construction kind. Some huge project was taking place in the middle of the old cemetery. Bulldozers, dump trucks, and backhoes were parked off to the side. A giant hole, at least as big across as a football field, had been dug here, and it was obviously a rush job, completed recently. The ground had been churned into mud. Tombstones had been carelessly smashed into bits. The machines had cleaved right through the earth and I could see where they had just dislodged or cut cleanly through old coffins. Skeletal limbs were discarded and forgotten like bits of trash.

I approached the edge of the hole and looked inside. The mist was swirling in weird patterns. Strange insects cast giant shadows as they flew in front of the huge lights. There was something in the hole, something odd, but it was still covered beneath loose dirt and broken coffin bits.

Hood was standing in the center of the hole, waiting for me, arms folded. Standing at his side was a young woman, also wearing intricately decorated robes. Both of them had put on elaborate golden headpieces with all sorts of squiddy goodness and were wearing amulets that just felt unbelievably ancient.

"You didn't have to get all dressed up," I said.

"Those who mock shall mourn, unbeliever!" the girl shrieked. She was the one who had bossed Torres around. She was actually kind of cute, if you disregarded the whole diabolical, crazy-fanatic thing. "Your fate is sealed. Your time is done!"

Hood smiled and patted her on the arm. "You must forgive my daughter. The exuberance of youth, you know." She scowled but he ignored her with parental smugness. "Lucinda, my heir, meet the man who's been a thorn in my side. I'm happy to see you came here voluntarily. So you've decided to fulfill your destiny?"

"If my destiny is killing you, then yeah, guess so." There was motion behind me. Things were circling, surrounding the hole on all sides. I risked a glance over my shoulder. Cultists had approached from behind. The fires that I had earlier thought were torches had been other teleportation devices. All of his worldwide church had gathered for this event. "Nice hole. You dig this for me?"

He shook his head. "No. Sending you back to the Old Ones will be simple enough. There are thirteen small gates scattered around this world and we are fortunate to have one at this sacred place. It is already prepared." He pointed to my left.

I took a few steps to the side to see better. Some of the excavation had unearthed a stone circle. A sick red light flickered from the hole and unearthly music drifted forth. The notes made my sanity hurt.

I turned away. "Oh, I thought maybe this construction project was some sort of secret weapon so you could finally defeat me," I said sarcastically. "For somebody who's supposed to be so friggin' bad, you've certainly sucked at it." I lifted Abomination and launched a grenade at them.

Hood extended his hand and the 40mm shell detonated on an invisible wall, temporarily obscuring them in a cloud of smoke and fragments. They were untouched. He smiled. "I could kill you with a fluffy pillow, Pitt." He gestured around the giant hole. "*This* is an ancient living device. The last time it was used was before man even walked the Earth, in a war beyond your comprehension against the mighty Yith. I've known about this place for years, but lacked the ability, the permission to use it." The shadow man reached into the sleeve of his robe and pulled out Machado's artifact. "With this, I can guide it. With the Dread Overlord's blessing, I can awaken it."

I heard hundreds of voices raise a cheer around me. I looked up from shoving another grenade into Abomination long enough to mutter, "Shit."

"Awake and arise, my legions!" Hood raised his voice to shout at his followers. The sound reverberated across the cemetery. "Let there be NO LIGHT! Rejoice, my children, for THE DARK NEW DAWN BREAKS!"

His followers roared in excitement.

The earth shook. The dirt beneath the sod rolled like the waves of a turbulent ocean. The tremor increased in intensity. My equilibrium was gone and I fell to my knees. The shaking grew in intensity. I had lived through some decent earthquakes, but this was just crazy. This was something way off the Richter scale. The earth screamed in protest. I had to scramble away from the edge as dirt began to cascade downward, the pit widening. The old mausoleums cracked, blocks shattered, and they collapsed on themselves. Levees of dirt erupted upward in places and wide cracks spread outward from the epicenter. The creatures and humans in the dark cried out in fear.

Something was coming out of the hole.

A hundred yards wide, dirt falling off in streamers, a tower rose. It was misshapen, twisted, unnatural, and it continued to grow higher and higher into the air. Hood stood on top of it, laughing maniacally, his daughter clinging to his arm in sudden terror. The two of them were lifted upward, riding the surge of something completely alien.

It was a structure, but it seemed to be organic, living, a sick, green, mottled thing. It stopped climbing, and then the top began to flow outward, snapping and unfurling. Branches stretched laterally overhead, raining dirt down against our upturned faces as the thing filled the night sky. It was part plant, part insect, and something that the human mind had never been meant to comprehend.

The earthquake subsided. The towering entity shuddered, freed from a million years of slumber. It seemed to click and twitch, pulsing with an unnatural life. I couldn't even estimate how tall it was, but it was like standing on the sidewalk and staring up at a high-rise.

It was the tree from Hood's utopian vision. It was the tree from the grimoire Carlos had taken from him. It was sick, wrong, and bad, and it was right here, right fucking now.

"BEHOLD. I GIVE YOU *ARBMUNEP*, TREE OF ETERNAL NIGHT!" Hood cried from a platform three hundred feet in the air. A cone of utter darkness began to grow from the branches, climbing into the atmosphere. It spread like a canopy, blotting out the sky. The cloud grew rapidly, like some sort of festering cancerous sickness.

"Mighty *Arbmunep* will consume the radiance of the heavens. We will blot out the light, darken the sky, erase the dawn. The night will rule. No sun, no moon, no stars. Only utter darkness. Absolute night, my children, and in it, I will rule. WE WILL RULE!" Hood screamed as the cloud grew larger. It wasn't just blocking the light, it was eating it. *Arbmunep* was alive and it was hungry.

There was a sound from the portal to the Old Ones' universe. Something was laughing. It was like running fingernails across a chalkboard multiplied a billion times and then driven through your ear hole with a variable-speed electric drill. I clamped my hands over my head involuntarily. The Dread Overlord was watching, fueling the monstrous tree, and it was positively giddy. Denied entrance to our world, it could at least enjoy the destruction of that which it couldn't possess.

Even something that incomprehensibly vast could be petulant.

"Thank you, noble and great master, for this ultimate gift. I will not fail you," the Shadow Lord cried.

The Condition came out of the shadows, hundreds of them. All had donned the ceremonial robes and raised their cowls. I couldn't tell what they were, most were certainly human, but there were many that *felt* unnatural, various types of intelligent undead probably, and several of the robed shapes were too large, too cumbersome, too *wrong* to be people. Stitched together automatons stood guard in the background, unthinking killing machines, simply here to observe. The cultists went to their knees or whatever else their equivalent was, and prostrated themselves before their false god and its blasphemous tree.

The shadow man spread his arms wide and leapt from his perch, plummeting toward the ground like a missile. At the last possible instant he stopped, then stepped lightly to the earth, his cloak settling around him. He walked straight at me. "Ready for your trip?"

"Ready to die?" I responded, my pulse quickening, adrenaline and energies I didn't understand flowing through my veins.

"Get in the portal, Pitt." He was getting closer. The Dread Overlord laughed. Someone killed the generator powering the portable lights, leaving us with nothing but the red light coming from the portal and a faint phosphorus gleam of the Tree's skin-bark as it fed. "I will not tell you again."

I gripped Abomination tighter. I had no clue what I was doing. I bellowed incoherently and charged. Hood lowered his head and did the same. His human form disappeared and a twelve-foot shadow took his place. The shadow bore down on me, cheered on by his followers and the king of pain itself.

I opened fire, the shells nothing but a futile gesture. The shadow crashed into me, knocking me down, and slapping me incoherent. Now, at his triumphant moment, there wasn't a damn thing I could do to hurt Hood. He grabbed me by one foot and dragged me through the dirt toward the portal. My fingers tore through the ground but I didn't even slow him down. He was going to toss me into that hole. Panic ripped through my guts. "You've been a worthy adversary, I must admit. I have no idea how you defeated the virus. I wish I could put you under a microscope and figure out just what it is that makes you tick but this is much more important."

*I had survived the zombie's bite.*

I had somehow found the strength to do the unthinkable. I had survived something that no human ever had before. I had generations of dead Hunters rooting for me. *I was special, damn it!* There had to be some way to hurt him. "No!" I rolled over and pulled my kukri from its sheath. Now he was just pulling me along on my back. I swung the blade through the black mass holding my boot. The knife ripped through with no effect. I kept swinging. The stone circle was only a few feet away. I could see down into the red light, coalescing shapes and impossible geometries, songs of dead civilizations and abstract realities.

The Dread Overlord was waiting.

The shadow man lifted me into the air. I was still thrashing, kicking, screaming, cursing, swinging my knife, all to no avail. I was upside down, blood rushing to my head, suspended over the portal, the Old Ones below, the Tree blotting out the stars above. The Condition members edged closer, chanting in unison, excited to see me, their Lucifer, thrown to his eternal condemnation.

Hood paused, leaving me dangling over the portal. Something vast shifted on the other side. "Dread Master, accept this humble sacrifice. I will prove worthy of your power."

"*Arbmunep F'thagen. Arbmunep F'thagen,*" the cultists chanted, hundreds of them, increasing in volume and intensity. Hood raised his shadow arm triumphantly, holding me up as a trophy as I continued to swear and hack at him. "*Arbmunep F'thagen! Aaiii!*"

Then Hood paused, letting me dangle. "Oh, what now?" he asked in exasperation. I glanced up from the Dread Master's realm. The shadow shape moved and I could see what had attracted his attention.

Some distance away, probably where I had first teleported in, there was a tiny flicker of fire in the dirt amongst the Condition. The minions were stepping aside to get out of the way as the portal opened. It was only a foot across as the two small flames intersected. The dirt disappeared and a brilliant shaft of daylight pierced upward. A head popped through the hole, wearing round, bug-eyed aviator goggles with a long red beard underneath and a stubbly cranium. I recognized the interloper immediately. "Milo?" I asked in disbelief. The head swiveled around, casually studying the various monsters and cultists, took in the unbelievable alien tree, then focused in on me upside down in the air and the shadow man that was holding me.

"Hey, Z. Hang on just a second," Milo responded from Alabama, as if this was a totally unremarkable circumstance. His goggled head bobbed back through the hole and disappeared. I could still hear him as he shouted. "It worked *and* it's outdoors. See, I told you we'd figure it out. Let her rip!"

There were two more flickers of flame. They ignited and spread outward in a circle, just like before, only this time they were traveling in a much wider arc. This circle was going to be huge. A bunch of cultists belatedly realized that they were standing in the area of effect and rushed to escape, tripping in their clumsy robes, or getting knocked down by their fellows in a panic to escape. MHI must have not only figured out how to make the magic ropes work, but they had stitched together one hell of a big one in the process.

"You guys totally rock!" I bellowed.

Within seconds the two flames met and with a horrendous air-suctioning *pop* a giant circle of dirt disappeared. Several cultists simply vanished. My eyes had adjusted to the bleak dark of the cemetery and underside of the Tree, so it was painful when a massive blinding circle of Alabama daylight appeared. A portal doesn't just let matter through; it is a direct doorway to someplace else, and this particular place was sitting under the afternoon sun. Light exploded all around us.

Hood's mighty shadow form wilted and shrank under the onslaught. The alien Tree shuddered and actually screamed as the light struck it. The undersides of the branches were now shockingly well lit. Vampires amongst the crowd of cultists burst into flames, screeching as their flesh bubbled and melted off.

There was a terrible mechanical wail, growing closer and louder by the instant. It was a rhythmic beating noise, and accompanying it was a loudspeaker, blaring music at such impossible decibels that it could even be heard above the noise of the approaching rotors. A red-and-white dragonfly shape blasted through the portal, pointed so that it was shooting straight up into the beam of light.

*Up* in our current location was apparently *sideways* in Alabama, and the MI-24 Hind attack helicopter blasted skyward. The nose jerked down as MHI's crack pilot immediately adjusted. Wind tore at us as the blades fought the new direction of gravity. Within seconds Skippy had oriented the chopper so that it was moving predatorily under the branches, surveying the graveyard. The painted shark jaws swiveled in a circle, taking in the target-rich environment.

The speakers were blaring "More Human than Human." It cut out long enough so that Skippy's gravelly voice could come over, electronically amplified until the orc was as loud as Hood had been when he had activated his evil Tree.

"MONSTERS . . . TASTE VENGEANCE . . . OF SKIIIPPPYYY!"

Skip had broken the FAA regulations about arming MHI's helicopter. Rob Zombie came back on just as the GE 7.62 miniguns mounted on both sides of the Hind opened up at 6,000 rounds per minute, stringing lines of tracers into the cultists; 20mm cannon shells thundered into the creatures as Skippy rotated the flying tank's nose gun. Rocket pods ignited like chains of Roman candles and bits of undead were flung everywhere. Winged beasts leapt into the air to attack the chopper and Skippy scythed them down methodically.

It was terribly impressive.

Another helicopter flew out, then another—MCB Apaches—ready to add to the carnage. There was noise and fire from the portal as Hunters and Feds poured out over the edge, guns blazing. Flamethrowers ignited, spiraling out napalm in swaths of burning destruction. Apparently the Condition's ceremonial robes weren't fire resistant either. Stop, drop, and roll doesn't work with napalm.

"Protect *Arbmunep*!" the shadow man screamed. "Stop them! Protect the Tree, damn you!"

Julie stepped into this place, M14 at her shoulder, hair blowing in the fire-laced wind, screaming orders like some sort of Amazon warrior queen, blasting monsters left and right. She saw me, saw Hood holding me over the portal, and a look of fury so intense and pure crossed her face that even I was afraid.

"You're screwed now!" I shouted at Hood.

The shadow shape was twisting, wilting in the light. The side of his face toward the MHI portal was human, the side in the red light of the Old Ones' portal was demonic. "But so are you," he hissed.

Then he dropped me.

Screaming, I caught the edge of the pit, rock tearing my fingers, body jerking past, wrenching my arms in their sockets, my legs dangling downward into red infinity. Hauling myself up to my elbow, I flipped my kukri around in my hand and slammed the tip into Hood's foot, anchoring it to the ground. He bellowed and jerked back, his boot parting like smoke around the blade. I used the knife to leverage myself away from the hole.

Deprived of his prize, the Dread Overlord let out a terrible wail.

I rolled to my feet and swung the giant knife through Hood. He grimaced as the steel parted his robes and whatever served as his flesh. The sunlight from Alabama was enough to allow me to damage him.

Hood sensed that as well. He leapt back through the air, away from my blade. "Destroy that portal!" he ordered as he levitated out of my reach. "Kill the light!"

The cemetery plunged into utter pandemonium. Monsters were everywhere, throwing themselves at the flaming circle of Hunters. The pillar of sunlight was our only hope. MHI had formed a perimeter around it, hunkering down behind broken tombstones, piles of earthquake dirt, and collapsed mausoleums, lancing bullets outward, cutting down targets with every burst.

Hood was retreating toward the Tree, trying to marshal his forces. I started after him. "Owen!" I jerked my head toward the sound. Julie and a squad of Hunters had fought their way to me. She had Trip, Holly, Sam, her brother Nate, Cooper, and a couple of Newbies I recognized as the Haight brothers. They immediately surrounded me, crouched down, and started firing their weapons at the approaching automatons. "You're alive!"

Holly must have thought I didn't look very alive. She stuck the muzzle of her .308 close enough to my face that I could feel the heat rising from the metal. "Say something!"

Smiling made my face hurt. "Took you guys long enough." I sheathed my knife. The Hunters exchanged glances. There was no way that I should still be moving, unless I was undead.

"But...how?" Holly asked.

"I'm the Chosen One, remember?"

"I told you there were such things as miracles," Trip shouted over the chattering bolt of his subgun. He glanced over into the still-open chasm to the Old Ones. "Is that...*Hell*?" All of the Hunters looked in, then looked away just as quickly. You didn't stop to gawk at that kind of thing.

"Close enough. Come on, Hood went that way." I pointed toward the Tree. We had to get him before they could kill the sunlight.

Julie was surely glad to see that I was still alive but right now was not the time to celebrate. She got on her radio. "Skippy, this is Command. My team's heading for the big...tower *thing*. Cover us." She didn't have to wait long. Within seconds the Hind dipped from its position over the pillar of light and headed right over us, expending hundreds of pounds of munitions in the process. Dirt rained down as rockets blasted through the cemetery. "Go!"

I led the way, firing Abomination, lumbering forward through the clouds of smoke. An automaton rose before us, probably something that had been a troll once, but was now covered in spikes. I pumped several rounds into it before I had to duck under the swing of one arm. Cooper stepped past me and slammed the steel butt-plate of his rifle into the off-balance body, taking it down. The Haights were on it in a split second, jamming their weapons through the unarmored joints and hammering it to bits.

One of the brothers shouted in pain as something struck him in the back. There was a noise like angry bees buzzing through the air. "Down! Down!" I shouted as the bullets zipped past us.

"Son of a bitch shot me!" the Newbie bellowed as he slid behind some rubble. Nate picked out the muzzle flash and returned fire.

There was a line of cultists moving through the dust ahead of us, covering Hood's retreat. There had to be dozens of them and judging from the volume of fire coming our way, they were heavily armed. Our squad of Hunters took cover behind whatever was available. Bullets ripped through the dirt between us.

"Surrender, Hunters!" one of the Condition ordered as the gunfire tapered off. "You're outnumbered."

Sam Haven bellowed back from behind the safety of a marble headstone. "How many of you fucking lunatics do we have to kill before you get out of our way?"

The same cultists responded. "The Exalted Order stands as one! Even in death, we shall live to fight. We—"

Sam cut him off. "Well, you could have just saved some time and said all of y'all." He lowered his voice and spoke into his radio, "Skippy, targets at the base of the tower, twenty yards ahead of our position. Waste 'em."

Almost instantly there was the thunder of an airborne minigun as Skippy tore the bad guys to pieces. Tracers zipped back and forth ahead of us until nothing could possibly live. Julie stood. "Keep going." The Hunters were up and running in seconds.

Something strange was happening. There was chanting, growing in intensity. I immediately recognized Hood's amplified voice, speaking in an incomprehensible language. The alien limbs overhead began to twitch, clicking in their unnatural joints. The *Arbmunep* emitted a keening rattle, like a swarm of cicadas, as it began to move. "Tell Skippy to watch out!"

But it was too late. One of the segmented branches crashed downward. Somehow Skippy saw it coming and jerked the chopper out of the way, narrowly missing the rotor. The branch creaked in protest and rose back into place, moving with a lumbering ferocity. One of the Apaches wasn't as lucky, and a limb slammed through its rotor. The chopper spun wildly through the air, billowing smoke, and crashed onto its side near the portal. The blades snapped off and flew through the army of monsters.

"What the hell's that?" Sam shouted.

Before I could answer, the ground beneath our feet surged, hoisting all of us into the air. Some of us went tumbling down, others managed to hold on. I was in the center where it was relatively flat, and was barely hanging on when the hill started to move. Julie was next to me, and went tumbling over the edge as the ground disappeared. I grabbed her wrist and held on for dear life. I was twenty feet over the ground, the other Hunters being knocked away, before I realized what was happening. The *Arbmunep* was moving.

The entire world was spinning, shaking, and there was a vast tearing noise. Trenches and hills were exploding up through the dirt all around us. Nate Shackleford disappeared into the ground as a crevasse opened up beneath his feet. Julie screamed something incoherent. The hill we were on lurched forward twenty feet, screeched to a halt, almost dislodging me, then surged again.

*Roots.* The giant tree was *mobile.* And it was heading right for the portal and the Hunters who were defending it. I pulled until Julie scrambled up beside me.

The other Apache was torn in half in a cascading gout of fire as a limb crashed through it. Skippy was staying just ahead of the shockingly fast branches, zipping about in a way that was surely impossible for the bulky chopper, clouds of ancient dirt falling with every swing. Explosions ripped across the trunk with no effect. He should have gotten the hell out from under it, but he was still firing, trying to provide cover for the humans on the ground.

"Skip, get out of here! Fall back!" Julie ordered. Another branch struck, and Skippy barely avoided it. The next sparked against his tail rotor, blowing it to bits. The Hind began to rotate violently, puking smoke, and it sank out of view into the cemetery. "No!" There was a terrible crashing noise.

I was barely hanging on. The root we were on top of would rise quickly into the air, then slam back down seconds later. There were dozens of these appendages, all driving the Tree onward, each movement surely shaking the earth for miles. As it neared the portal, whichever Hunter was in charge was smart enough to order everyone to retreat back toward the mortuary. The dirt we were hanging onto dislodged and Julie and I tumbled to the ground.

"Move!" I shouted as we hit, still holding onto her wrist, trying to stay ahead of the giant flailing appendages. Each root was as big around as a car, and they slammed around us with terrible impacts. Both of us were knocked on our faces as another root landed behind us.

The Tree shifted as it hit the portal, slamming its roots into the ground, breaking the magic cord and severing the connection to Alabama. The pillar of light disappeared and we were plunged back into absolute darkness. The Tree was still.

It was silent except for our frantic panting in the dusty air, and then an insectile chattering noise as the Tree settled into its new position. I couldn't see my hand in front of my face. It took us a moment to catch our breath. "Come on," Julie hissed. She grabbed the front of my armor. "We've got to go back for Nate."

I could barely make out her figure in the dark. Then three dozen bright white eyeballs opened in a wall behind her. "Shoggoth!" I raised my gun and triggered my flashlight. One tentacle impacted my chest, pinning my weapon and crushing me down. It encircled my arms and cinched tight. It was immensely strong. Another tentacle zipped around Julie's waist and hoisted her into the air. She swore at it. More eyeballs blinked in my face as I struggled helplessly.

"CAPTURED SACRIFICE," it wheezed in an impossible bass from half a dozen mouths. It was so loud that wherever Hood was, he had certainly heard it. The amorphous blob seeped across the ground, Julie held in the air, me dragging along on the dirt, disoriented, but seemingly going back in the direction we had come from. No matter how hard I fought, I was stuck. I tried to yell for help, but a wet appendage slapped shut over my mouth. It smelled like hot tar.

It dragged me for about a minute, only slowing when

the light visibly turned red. The shoggoth had brought us back to the portal to the Old Ones. It spilled us to the ground, leaving us both coughing and gagging in a puddle of ooze, our arms still leashed to our sides. The necromancer was standing there, waiting, a giant undead automaton flanking him on both sides. The hole to the Old Ones' universe stretched before us, cloudy and red.

"You're dead, Hood," I gasped. "The Feds know where we are. They've probably got nukes inbound already. They'll never let your stupid Tree live."

He nodded. "Obviously. But this is just the first of many. On my own, I was barely strong enough to unleash one. In return for your sacrifice, my Lord will awake the others. This is the first and greatest, but there are hundreds more seedlings buried across the world." Hood smiled. "And even then, an attempt to cleanse the mighty *Arbmunep* with nuclear fire will just end up bathing this entire part of the world in a cloud of perpetual night. The Yith made the same mistake sixty-five million years ago."

"You'll never get away with this," Julie said. The wall of eyeballs turned on her, blinking suspiciously. "My men will make sure of that."

"Well, little Julie Shackleford is all grown up." Hood laughed hard. "Your men? That's a good one. Your Hunters are running for their lives, my minions at their heels. And even if they do manage to interfere, it won't do you two any good." He clapped his hands. "Great shoggoth, send these mortals to meet your almighty maker!"

But the blob didn't toss us into the portal. It hoisted Julie with one dripping arm and turned her upside down, studying her with lots of curious eyeballs.

"What are you waiting for?" Hood demanded. "I command you to put them in the portal!"

Julie's hair was dangling in the tar. It was like she was having a staring contest with the blob. "Mr. Trash Bags? Is that you?" she asked quietly.

The eyes all blinked at once. "CUDDLE BUNNY?"

Julie grinned. "It *is* you!"

I could feel the surge of emotion through the dripping tentacle as Mr. Trash Bags remembered. This time the dark lightning struck like a bomb.

"Hi," said the grubling. "I'm Julie."

"FILTHY MAMMAL," the Exile replied. The mammal grubling was to be devoured. The Exile was shamed. The Exile had failed—*TERRIBLE SHRIEK-ING DOOM*—the Exile had come here to devour the mammals that had battled the other servants of Horde. The Exile would please the master and no longer be Exile. Again it would be Number 786 of Horde. "CONSUME!"

"You're funny," said the grubling. Air passed over the grubling's vocal cords and made a melody, not unlike the shrike-hounds of the howling gates and it made the Exile feel stop. New sound, word list on mammals called it *giggle* made the Exile feel not to devour the grubling. The grubling held up with its opposable thumbs an image of a tiny earth beast, made of cloth, stuffed with fibers. "This is Cuddle Bunny. Want to play?"

"CONSUME?"

"No. Play, silly." The grubling used its pathetic leg limbs to hop away. "Come on. You're my friend. You're like a big trash bag."

The Exile was confounded. The other mammals were made of hate and burning. The master—*TERRIBLE SHRIEKING DOOM*— was made of pain and orders. This grubling was of not kill. Suddenly the grubling changed to the Exile's current eyes and the Exile saw that this mammal was made of stars.

Confused. The Exile followed. The Exile became Friend.

At the time I had thought that the gnome's memory had been slightly alien. Mr. Trash Bags had just shown me what a real alien was. My head ached with haunting sounds, thought bubbles that popped like dynamite, and the lingering image of a tiny, perfect, glowing angel, with pigtails and a stuffed rabbit.

"Destroy them!" Hood shouted at the hesitating shoggoth.

"NOOO!" The simple beast remembered what was probably the only thing that had ever loved it. Two tentacles cracked like whips, splitting the automatons flanking Hood in half. The limbs tore through the shadow man, pulverizing the ground at his feet, but he merely re-formed in place.

Snarling, he extended one hand. "Traitorous amorph!" A bolt of fire leapt from his amulet, down his arm, and from his hand, bursting into the shoggoth, engulfing it in flames. "How dare you!"

"PROTECT CUDDLE BUNNY," the shoggoth thundered as it carelessly tossed Julie behind it. The burning blob surged over me, across the portal, and at the shadow man. I was released, and spun wildly through the tar. The flaming beast collided with Hood, burning bits flying in every direction. Already it seemed to shrink as it turned to ash. I slid through the goo, trying to get to my feet. The blob hardened and shattered into burning shards. There was a terrible piercing squeal as Mr. Trash Bags exploded.

Hood dusted the ash from his robe. "Never trust a blob to do a man's work." He took three steps and leapt across the portal, landing effortlessly beside me. I fired my shotgun into his head and he merely swatted it aside before grabbing me around the throat and lifting me off the ground. Half man, half darkness, the hole in his face quickly closed. "We already said our good-byes."

There was a mighty yell. "Pitt!" I glanced up in time to see Agent Franks sprinting toward us, leaping between the massive roots. He would never make it in time.

"Too late," Hood said as he heaved me into the center of the portal.

# CHAPTER 21

I broke the surface.

Time was different.

It was difficult to comprehend. Our existence doesn't really encompass this kind of experience. Time passed, but in different directions simultaneously. My brain hurt just trying to function.

My eyes still worked. The light was primarily red, but didn't seem to come from any particular source. It was utterly strange, alien. The air entering my lungs wasn't made of what I thought of as air, but it didn't matter, as enough time hadn't passed yet to breathe. I was floating in place, in a haze, almost like being on a cloud in some alternate hellish version of heaven.

Which according to the Condition, I probably was.

A creature made entirely of eyeballs floated past. It was tiny, but then I realized that with no scale, it might have been miles away and the size of a subway train. It was eating hornets made of razor blades and steam, but it didn't matter, because time wasn't passing. It just was.

*Oh God. I'm scared.*

The whole universe moved. It was the Dread Master blinking. A yellow slit appeared through the red. It was *looking* at me.

Time wasn't right, but at the same time I could see a million years in the past, and a million years into the future, and in other directions into dimensions that I couldn't comprehend, and I was going to die repeatedly through all of them, forever. This epic thing honestly believed that I was the first mortal being to ever harm it. I just knew that this being had waged millennia of war between stars against things even more diabolical than it was, but somehow a mere human had hurt it. And I was going to pay for that. A lot.

"That whole thing with the nuke, that wasn't me. The guy you want to talk to is Dwayne Myers. That's Special Agent Dwayne Myers of the Monster Control Bureau. M-Y-E-R-S." I didn't know if I just thought that, or if I could actually speak in this place, but even if I could, I'm sure my pitiful utterances were like a mosquito buzzing around its ear.

That giant eye kept regarding me. I could feel it in my mind, poking around as it figured out what would hurt me the most. I was a bubble of linear time in this ageless place, an oddity. My universe was poison to the Dread Master, but consuming me would be the equivalent of a healthy person eating a single jelly bean. Not exactly good for you, but it wasn't like you were going to notice.

Then it *spoke*. The entire universe thundered with its incomprehensible voice. All I could understand was the pain. The message itself was beyond me. But it didn't matter, because this was how I was going to spend eternity.

A few minutes in this place had shattered Ray Shackleford's mind before Earl had pulled him out. Ray had never been the same. For the first time, I had nothing but pity for him. The Dread Master said something else. I experienced agony beyond anything I had ever imagined. Turning into a zombie was Christmas at Disneyland with all-you-can-eat ice cream and a free ride on the space shuttle in comparison.

When it was done, I floated there, wishing to die.

I was mortal at home. Here I was an infinite chew toy. It hadn't even started yet. It got closer. Ten thousand feet of sleek carapace attached to millipede tentacles crackling with electricity. The eyeball creature was snagged by the forest of limbs and absorbed, digested for eternity to fuel the fires of chaos.

Then, in the abyss of confusion, there was a presence of something familiar, another bubble of familiar reality. A blue light intruded into the red, and it was as if time began to move again. It was coming from the opposite direction of the Dread Overlord. "I've never failed a mission," the presence said as I turned.

"Agent Franks?"

He was different here. The physical body was just a shell, housing a spirit that was clearly not that of a normal human, but rather something simpler and older. The recycled organs, bones, and sinew that served as Frank's avatar showed me the ward stone. It boiled with the power of pure reality. "Won't start now." There was a clear trail of energy connected to the ward stone stretching back to our universe.

Julie had explained it to me. *As far as I understand how the ward works, it's basically a focus point for our reality. Like a magnifying glass under the sun.*

*Undead are an unnatural thing in this world, so it just blasts them. Things from outside this reality can't take the heat.* And now that I could see what it really was, I could tell that it was far more powerful than any of us had realized. The ward was huge, crackling with potential. The alchemists of old hadn't just created a defensive device. They'd created a doomsday weapon. It was like the seventeenth century's version of Mutually Assured Destruction.

If our reality was poison to the Old Ones, then Franks had just brought a keg of VX nerve gas into their living room.

The Dread Master assaulted us both with hate. As alien as we were to it, it probably didn't even understand what was going on, but it didn't like it one bit. Terrible visions and alien memories pounded my psyche. Bombarded by pain, Franks still pushed toward me, finally shoving the ward stone into my waiting hands. "Break it," Franks ordered. "I can't."

Of course not. It had been built by a human, for humans.

The Dread Overlord propelled itself forward.

In this place, I could see the stone for what it really was, a mere shell, a container, harnessing a violent reaction of raw physics and possibility. Four hundred years ago, a combination of dark wizardry and powerful alchemy had bound it to the shell, letting just enough leak so that it could be used as a shield against the forces of the other side. Franks had prearranged all of the numbers on the sphere using his creator's mathematical codes. It was ready.

The Dread Overlord was right on top of us. I would never make it in time.

My fingers sunk into the stone as I wrenched it apart. The field fragmented and energy lanced through the spreading cracks. I let go of the stone and it floated away from me, power building toward a cataclysmic reaction.

"Take my hand!" *Julie* . . . She had come after me. I reached toward her voice. "Hurry!" Then she grabbed me, pulling me down the chain, back to the real world.

The container shattered. Unleashed, a blue tidal wave of linear time invaded the reality of the Dread Master. If consuming me was a jelly bean's worth of bad health to it, then this was the equivalent of suck-starting a double-barreled 12-gauge. The yellow eye focused on the approaching wall of deadly reality. Incompatible matter collided, splitting atoms and releasing energy in an algorithmic multiplying fury. Ageless infinity broke. Every bit of the ancient squid god became disjointed, fractured, down to the subatomic level. The galaxy quivered.

The Dread Master simply . . . ruptured.

The explosion billowed outward, consuming planets.

I gasped for air.

There was dirt under me, real honest-to-goodness dirt. Flat on my back, lying in the center of the now solid stone circle, the Tree blotted out the sky above. Gunfire and explosions came from all around. A ten-foot-tall ogre lumbered past, on fire. I was never so glad to be home.

One of my arms was stretched out. Someone was holding my hand. My head hurt and I was so dizzy that it took me a moment to roll over and see who it was.

"Julie?" I whispered. She was lying facedown, perfectly still, but she had a death grip on my hand. "Julie?"

Slowly, she took a deep breath, then finally raised her head. Tears stained her cheeks. "You came after me...."

Julie smiled weakly. "Well, duh."

"Thank you," I croaked.

She just pulled herself closer, resting her head against mine. "Don't ever make me do that again."

I didn't know if she meant the portal, or having me abandon her so I could sulk off to die. She'd had the courage to follow me someplace that nobody should ever have to go and had dragged me back out. "Deal."

"*Ever* again..."

Something stirred at my feet. Franks sat up abruptly. He looked around slowly before staggering to his feet. "Never killed anything that big before," he said, sounding almost, but not quite, proud of himself. "It was...satisfying."

*We had killed an actual Old One. We'd blown up the Dread Overlord!*

"Is it really dead?" Julie asked.

Franks didn't answer. He just pointed.

Illuminated only by the burning remains of the shoggoth, Hood was on his knees. His cowl lifted, revealing black-oil tears leaking from his eyes and dripping down his face. "Oh, Master, what have they done to you?" he cried. Behind him, the undead automatons were not moving, frozen perfectly in place like statues. Then one by one, the joints began to give away, and they toppled, metal screeching, into the dirt. The High Priest's body seemed to wilt as the shadow energy dissipated from him.

With their animated troops falling apart and the source of their magic gone, the Condition forces were done for.

I got shakily to my feet and picked up Abomination.

My nemesis seemed to be choking, clouds of flies spewing from his mouth with every heave. He retched, and a dead leech thing fell out of his mouth, fading away into nothingness on impact. Shadowy shapes rose from him like steam, red eyes blinking, before drifting off in fear. Hood was being abandoned by all of the Old Ones' servants. I stopped directly in front of him. Above us, the Tree still loomed; the gunfire suggested MHI was still battling the now outmatched cultists, but this part here was my job to finish. "Why?" He looked up, black fluids leaking from his nose and ears. The substance that had kept him immortal was dissipating. "Why has he forsaken me?"

"Because he's dead."

He gagged on the demon oil. "Impossible."

I shrugged. "Shit happens."

Hood was sobbing, shaking. He knew I was telling the truth. "I studied them for so long. They couldn't be defeated. Their victory was inevitable. *Inevitable!* I couldn't stop them, nobody could. I sold my *soul* to protect this world."

"You got a bum deal."

"Then you come along . . . so stupid. So nonchalant about the ultimate gift you've been given. I had to *work* for my gifts. I had to bloody sacrifice. Fight and scrimp for every last bit of knowledge." It was like his body was breaking down as the realization of defeat hit him. "Your way could only end in blood and fire. My way led to utopia. I did what I had to do."

"You're no martyr," I said, cradling my shotgun. "Don't tell me you did what you had to do. You did what you *wanted* to do."

"Curse you, Pitt!" He surged to his feet, stumbling at me. His hands landed on my shoulders but his black eyes widened in surprise as Abomination's silver bayonet was driven through his chest. "I...I..."

He rested his head on my shoulder and bled down my armor.

The funeral was on an appropriately rainy day. Grandmother stood at my side, never letting go of my hand, as Father and Mother's caskets were put in the dirt. The caskets were closed, since the acid of the thing inside the pentagram had burned their faces into nothing but strands of meat and jelly.

The priest continued his litany, droning on, saying the same thing that his ancestors had said since Martin Luther himself had last stuck men in the ground. Eventually he was done, and the sky over Birmingham erupted into a downpour. The pitiful few who had gathered for the ceremony bolted for safety.

The two of us stayed, watching the fresh dirt churn into mud. One old crone and one twelve-year-old child dressed in black, pathetic in the rain.

Grandmother bent down and whispered in my ear. "Let them go, Martin."

I shook my head, water running down my face.

She squeezed my fingers hard. "Listen to me, child. Your father trifled with things beyond his understanding, and he paid dearly. Don't make the same mistakes he did. Let it go. I know he educated you in his dark ways and his dark books, but he was a fool."

I thought about the thing coming out of the basement floor. Grandmother was the fool, not Father. He understood what was out there and he had passed that information on to me. The Elder Things didn't need to be feared, they just needed to be understood. And understanding could lead to control.

I could control them.

"Your parents reside with the devil now because of their terrible sins."

"Yes, Grandmother."

"I tried to burn your father's evil book, for your own good, of course, but it wouldn't burn. So I gave away all his things to those Americans who destroyed the creature. They said that they would put them someplace safe, where nobody else would meddle with them."

*Those were mine.* "Yes, Grandmother. What were those brave Americans called?"

"Monster Hunter International. You owe them your life, you know."

"I know." *And they owe me my father's book . . .* I vowed then on my father's grave that I would regain my birthright. Someday I would find these Monster Hunters and take back what was rightfully mine. "Can we go home now, Grandmother? I'm very cold."

"Yes, Martin."

I jerked the bayonet out in a flash of red human blood.

Martin Hood let go, stumbled back, and pressed his hands against his chest. The blood just kept coming. He sank slowly to his knees, staring at me in disbelief.

"I . . . forgot what pain . . . felt like . . ."

Pain was a burning village littered with orc bodies. Pain was what the families of his innocent victims were feeling. Pain was what my brother felt when his fingers had been sawed off. Pain was one of the many things he had stolen from Carlos. Pain was what G-Nome had felt when the doppelganger had ripped into him. Pain and death and suffering were all that Martin Hood had left in his wake.

Pain was his legacy.

"Sucks, don't it?" I whispered.

Then the High Priest of the Sanctified Church of the Temporary Mortal Condition fell on his face and died.

I stood over him, bayonet dripping. Julie approached with a limp, raised her M14 and mercilessly ripped an entire magazine of silver .308 into the body. I hate to admit that I flinched at the blasts. "Just in case," she said.

"Of course," I responded.

The Tree above us shuddered, insect limbs cracking. The blackness above the branches slowly dissipated on the wind, revealing stars. The nearby roots went from green, to brown, and then finally to gray within a matter of seconds, leaving the mutation with the consistency of cold stone. Mighty *Arbmunep* was finished, returned to the same hibernation that it had existed in for all of recorded history. Deprived of their magic and their undead war machines I knew that the cultists were now going to get the ever-living hell kicked out of them by a bunch of pissed-off and heavily armed Hunters.

Franks stepped up to the pulped body and thumped it with his boot. "Looks like shadow boy wasn't as *bright* as he thought he was."

Julie and I exchanged glances. "Bright?" I responded. "Look, dear, Franks made a joke."

"Fascinating," she responded, but she was mostly listening to her radio earpiece. "Sounds like the Condition is retreating, but our people are scattered and trying to regroup. A bunch are missing where the roots landed." I knew that she was thinking of her little brother. "We've got to find them."

There still had to be bunches of monsters lurking out there. Any Hunter who was alone was vulnerable. "We'd better hurry."

Franks rolled Hood over and began patting down the bloody robes. I knew immediately that he was looking for the artifact. I unconsciously stepped back. The Dread Overlord itself might be dead, but who knew what else that little thing was capable of. "Keep that damn box away from me."

The big man scowled. "It's not here."

"Looking for this?"

The three of us spun toward the voice. It was the girl, Lucinda, Hood's daughter. She had lost her ceremonial headpiece and her black robes were in muddy tatters. She was crying as she held up the artifact. It glowed with an unnatural black light in the fog. She was barely an adult.

"Drop it," Franks ordered as a 10mm Glock materialized in his hand.

"You killed him . . ." she wailed. "You murdered my father!"

"I did," I responded slowly. "And you'll die too, if you don't put that box down and step away from it."

"You'll pay for this. All of you will pay! He was a good man," Lucinda cried. "The Exalted Order will rise again and come for you."

"Gonna be hard since we just blew up your god."

"Lies!"

"Your father was an idiot. Now give up before you get hurt." I really didn't want to see Franks blow away a girl who was probably still a teenager. "Listen to me."

"My father was a *good* man!"

"Your dad was a complete psycho. Listen, girl, I can relate," Julie responded coldly. She had family missing out there amongst the roots. "But I really don't have time for this. Franks, you got the shot?"

"Affirmative," Franks responded. He put his front sight between Lucinda's eyes.

"Drop her," my wife said.

There was a gunshot. The bullet slammed into the dirt at Lucinda's feet. I turned in time to see a look of confusion cross Frank's square face, then his eyes rolled back in his head and he collapsed in a heap.

Ray Shackleford stood over Franks, blood-soaked hand open in front of him with a length of spinal column resting in his palm, torn cleanly from Frank's back. The vampire smiled as he dropped the vertebrae on the ground. "Well, that worked perfect! Hey, kiddos."

"Dad!" Julie gasped. She dropped her empty M14 and went for her pistol.

Lucinda Hood screamed. I jerked my attention back to her, only to see Susan Shackleford standing where she had been. The girl was scrambling away leaving a trail of blood behind her. Susan held up something and laughed. It was Lucinda's petite hand, torn clean off at the wrist, still holding the artifact. "About damn time!" Susan exclaimed as she examined the device.

"You'll all pay!" Lucinda whimpered, holding her bloody stump against her robes. She pulled out a length of rope and dropped it. The portal activated in a burst of flames and she fell headfirst through the opening.

"Hey, honey, you forgot something," Susan said as she tugged the severed hand off the artifact and tossed it casually through the portal. The opening snapped close behind. "Kids these days, I swear... Speaking of which... how're you guys doing?"

Julie and I stood back to back. She aimed her .45 at her father and I kept Abomination on her mother. If they attacked at this range we were dead meat. Susan was unbelievably powerful for a vampire of such young age and could move so fast that it was hard to watch.

"Been better..." I responded slowly. "We had a deal, Susan."

"Stay back!" Julie shouted.

"Whew!" Ray said as he raised his shoe and smashed Franks' torn-out spine. He ground it fiercely into the dirt until it broke with a sickening splatter. "Good thing he was distracted. Franks could totally have whupped my ass."

"Yes, we had a deal," Susan smiled, showing her pointed teeth. "You were supposed to take care of the necromancer for me. Check. Killing an actual Old One, though. I've got to hand it to you, *that's* impressive. Seriously, that's like some sort of record. My chief rival is dead, and I owe you one for saving me from his service. No, we're not going to kill *you*, Owen. I'm just here for what's rightfully mine."

"What do you want with that thing?"

"Oh, this little trinket unlocks all sorts of ancient goodies, and until the Others pick a new Guardian to protect it, I'm going to milk it for all it's worth." Susan shrugged. "But that's not what I'm talking about. Like I said, I'm here for what's rightfully *mine*... Like my children. Julie, honey... come with us."

"Never," Julie hissed. Her father shifted a bit and she tightened the grip on her gun. "Don't come any closer."

"You don't have a choice."

Ray twisted his head and smelled the air like the predator he was. "Hunters are coming...I can't tell how close. This stupid Tree messes with my senses. I smell...Copenhagen."

"Come with us, Julie. Your little brother is out there in the dark, hurt and scared. Only I can save him now." Susan's eyes were glowing.

"I should have left that stake in you," I spat.

"Your mistake," she smiled. "Take them, Ray."

We both opened fire, but the vampires moved so quickly that it didn't do us any good. It was like Susan just stepped between the shotgun slugs. I perforated her heart and lungs, but the wounds closed instantaneously. She slammed her open hand into my armored chest, launching me back into the circle of stone. I crashed into a rock and the air blasted from my lungs.

My head swam as I tried to rise. Julie screamed. Susan had her.

Filled with rage and fear, I pushed myself to my feet. Ray intercepted me. Our bulks collided, and he engulfed me in a bear hug, crushing my ribs. "Stay out of this, kid. This is family business."

I head-butted him in the face. His nose shattered. I hit him again, my forehead the only weapon available. Ray let go. He had superhuman strength and speed. I had desperation. I drew my .45 and shoved it into his chest, jerking the trigger as fast as I could. Ray looked at me in shocked disbelief as I tore his heart into silver-laced confetti. He grabbed me by the throat, hoisted me into the air, and then slammed me back down with a roar.

Susan had a handful of Julie's hair and had jerked her head back, exposing her throat. Julie was fighting, struggling against the iron-hard claws. Her mother's face distorted as she opened her mouth impossibly wide, razor teeth gleaming.

I shoved myself up, putting my shoulder into Ray, trying to drive him back. He clubbed me in the back with a blow that should have crippled me for life. I went to my knees. The vampire's mouth descended toward Julie's neck. Time slowed to a standstill. I could see the terror in her eyes, the pulse in her carotid artery, the unnatural black mark on her skin as Susan's fangs pierced her flesh.

"NO!" I jerked my kukri from its sheath and slammed it through Ray's stomach with all my might. He looked at me in shocked disbelief as I lifted him off the ground, blade tearing through half his torso. I hurled him over my shoulder, screaming the entire time.

Susan looked up, hot blood streaming from her mouth. Animal face contorted, she hissed. Julie's eyes were closed, her pretty face twisted in a grimace of pain. "She's mine n—" The vampire suddenly jerked, hands flying to her face, releasing Julie. Red steam rose from her open mouth. "What's happening? Her blood burns!"

Ray was pushing his guts back in as he struggled to rise. "The mark! The Guardian's curse!"

Susan clamped her claws down over her lips. Acid smoke was pouring from her face. The flesh on her chin and lips was peeling away, leaving nothing but exposed teeth. She tripped back, shrieking.

I leapt forward, trying to protect Julie, blade held high. Julie's eyes flashed open, and for a moment, they seemed to be pure black, but then she blinked, and they were normal. There was no wound on her neck, nothing. There was nothing on her skin except for the Guardian's mark. It flickered briefly with its own living movement, then it was still.

"I'm okay," Julie whispered.

Susan was shaking, in terrible pain. She lowered her hands. The bottom half of her face was nothing but glistening bone. "I can't . . . can't turn you . . ." the vampire stuttered, confused. "Why . . . why isn't it healing?"

Ray cried out. "Susan!"

"I'm not regenerating." She rubbed her fingers across her exposed jaw. "What have you done to me? I'm hideous!"

I rose from Julie, blade extended. It was time for Susan to die.

"Damn it." Susan raised one hand, pointing the artifact toward us. It crackled with black energy. I knew it was going to consume us both. "If I can't have her, nobody can." The air around the artifact swirled into a vortex.

"No!" Ray shouted. "Don't kill her!"

Then the artifact dropped harmlessly from Susan's stunned fingers.

Susan stumbled forward, white oak stake sticking out her back, black blood drizzling out. Sam Haven brutally slammed another stake into her. Heart ruptured, Susan went to her knees, paralyzed. "Leave them alone!" He backed up a step, raised his boot, and kicked the stake right through her.

"SUSAN!" Ray bellowed as he leapt right over Julie and me.

"It's over, Ray!" Sam yelled as he drew his bowie knife. He jerked Susan's head back as the blade came down.

Ray slammed into Sam. The two of them crashed and rolled across the dirt. I went after them. Ray was up first, his form twisting, muscles snaking across his vampire frame as bone talons burst from the ends of his fingertips. "Get away from my *wife!*" Ray struck with supernatural desperation. Struggling to rise, Sam grunted as the bone claws tore right through his armor and sent him sprawling.

The vampire hesitated, looking down at his former friend, then at the blood dripping down his arm. "I'm real sorry, Sam." Ray bent down, grabbed the stake from Susan's back and yanked it free.

With a cry, I swung my blade for the base of Ray's head. The blade struck and a tremor ran up my arm. The steel came to a stop most of the way through his neck. Black fluids came welling slowly out the cut. Ray stood there for a moment, his vampire features gradually softening, returning to a semblance of normalcy. He smiled slightly. "Good shot, kid...."

I cleaved the blade the rest of the way through his throat. Ray's head fell from his shoulders and bounced away. His body dropped a second later.

"Ray!" Susan cried. "What have you done?" She stood behind me, hole in her chest sealing shut, her lower jaw still nothing but white bone. She took a step forward. "What have you *done?*"

I spun my knife and got ready for her charge. "My job."

My father-in-law was dead. Ray's flesh was softening, turning to ooze, and dripping from his skeleton. I'd finally done him the favor that I should have fulfilled last summer.

Susan hesitated, shaking, looking down at her husband's body, then her red eyes locked on mine. "Oh, now I'm *mad.*"

"Dad's free, Mom," Julie said as she rocked a magazine into her rifle. There were flashlights approaching from all directions and the shouts of Hunters. Julie pulled back the charging handle and let it fly forward. "You're done here."

"Not yet, I'm not." Susan bent over to pick up the artifact, but Julie's bullet knocked it flying away from her hand. Susan snarled. "So that's how it's going to be?"

Julie took careful aim. "Yeah, I guess it is."

The bullet passed through nothing. Susan's bloody clothing fell to the ground as a thick gray mist rolled across the ruined cemetery. Within seconds the mist had mingled with the fog and rolled out of sight.

"Are you all right?" I shouted at Julie.

"I'm fine. Check Sam."

The burly Hunter was sitting down, pressing his hands against his side. I squatted next to him. "Sam? You okay?"

"Naw...." He moved his hands. Torn sheets of Kevlar parted, and I could see inside his chest cavity. Desperate to protect his wife, Ray's blow had been so powerful that he'd cleaved right through the armor. Sam coughed violently and blood drenched his giant walrus mustache. "Shit, that hurts."

"MEDIC!" I screamed at the top of my lungs. Julie spoke into her radio, calling desperately for an orc healer. I wrenched open my first aid pouch and pulled out a pack of bandages. I ripped them from the package and stuck them against him. It was soaked useless almost instantly.

"Gotta lay down," Sam wheezed. I put my hand on his back and gently lowered him. "We...win?"

"Sure did, man."

Julie knelt at his other side, shining a flashlight at the wound. The vampire's claws had torn four terrible lacerations deep through him. Blood was pouring out. I was shocked he was still conscious. Julie looked up at me, a terrible knowledge in her eyes. "Hang in there, Sam. Gretchen's coming."

Sam's strong hand grasped mine. "It's all good, guys." Other Hunters surrounded us. A group of Feds found Agent Franks and called for a stretcher.

"Not Sam," Holly cried when she arrived. I glanced around the assembled Hunters. None of us could do a thing. Sam could have taken an injury like this in an emergency room and still not have had a chance. Holly began desperately cutting the rest of Sam's armor away. There was no way she was going to stop the bleeding in time.

"Figures it would be Ray. He always was a dick." Sam closed his eyes. His breathing was rapid and shallow. "I taught you kids good, though. Where's Milo?"

"Right here!" the little man shouted as he sprinted up to us. "Oh, Sam, no . . ." Milo dropped down beside me. "What happened?"

His eyes opened. "No biggie." Sam coughed. "Listen . . . brother . . . I . . ."

Then he was dead. The great heart simply quit beating. The hand grasping mine was suddenly still . . . *just like that.*

"Sam?" Milo asked. "Sam?"

We were all quiet. Finally Milo, trembling, reached up and closed Sam Haven's staring eyes.

# CHAPTER 22

The mortuary became our temporary headquarters while we regrouped and figured out what was going on. Myers had not accompanied his men through the rift from Alabama but was in contact. With Franks incapacitated, Archer was in command. The thin man was pacing back and forth in the mortuary chapel, speaking excitedly into a satellite phone.

"No, sir. I don't see any way that we can cover this up. Negative. It's like twenty stories tall." The agent stalked back to the window. When the sun comes up, the town below us would surely see the giant alien tree. It was a secret agency's worst nightmare. Archer nodded as Myers gave him instructions. "Yes, sir. I'm on it." He closed the phone and started yelling orders. "Johnson, contact British MI4. They have an office in Auckland. They'll have to evacuate the town before dawn. Have them make up something about...anthrax or plague or something...hell, I don't know, maybe an outbreak of rabid sheep."

I was standing in the doorway, waiting. "Auckland?

We're in New Zealand?" That would explain why my watch was saying that it was afternoon in Alabama; it felt like we were getting close to sunrise. That, and it had seemed unseasonably cool.

Archer glared at me. "What? I'm busy."

"Yeah, Myers sure does make it look easy, doesn't he? Keeping all those lies straight and all that. The man has a gift," I said. Archer frowned, waiting. "I was wondering if Franks...is he okay?" We had blown up a god together, after all. Now that's male bonding.

Archer actually smiled. He really wasn't a bad sort. "Franks will be just fine. It takes more than getting his spine pulled out to kill him. He probably won't even take sick leave. I'll tell him you asked."

"Thanks." I turned to leave.

"Hey, Pitt..." He stopped me, suddenly uncomfortable. "Just so you know, man. I was just doing my job. I didn't know about Torres. I really was just trying to protect you."

I nodded once, then left the young Fed to his damage control.

The Feds had taken the comfortable waiting room, leaving MHI the soaking wet and partially burned chapel. Our people had moved in to tend to our injuries and check our gear. The mood was chaotic and somber. Julie was sitting on one of the pews, wrapped in a wool blanket. She looked haggard, with big dark circles under her eyes. She gave me a weak smile when she saw me. I flopped down next to her.

"I just got some good news," she said. "Nate's going to be fine. He broke his leg when he fell down that hole and took a good whack on the head, but other than that, Gretchen's not worried about him."

"Good thing Shacklefords are so hard-headed," I responded.

She didn't laugh. "I haven't told him about Dad yet."

"Oh...okay." That was going to be hard. This would be the second time they would have to deal with his death, only this time, it was permanent. "Have the Feds found the artifact yet?"

Julie bit her lip. She seemed deep in thought. "No...not that I know of."

"Well, when they do, they better stash it someplace that nobody will ever find it. That thing's too dangerous. I hate the idea of them even having it, because eventually somebody is going to use it again. Anything else?"

She shook her head. "Amazingly enough, we've got a ton of injuries, multiple gunshot wounds, and one Newbie lost a foot, but we only had the one fatality. The Feds lost two pilots, but the other two lived."

"How's Skippy?"

"He's good. He managed to put the Hind down right side up. Not bad considering the tail rotor was gone. Minor injuries on the orcs running the door guns, but that's it. Skippy even thinks that we can fix it, provided we can ship it home."

"We're in New Zealand," I pointed out.

She nodded. "We checked GPS as soon as we stepped through the portal. By the way"—she pointed at my armor—"your patch is upside down." Sure enough, I had stuck it back on wrong after tearing it off Torres. I had been a little preoccupied at the time. "Will you look at that? Upside down, it's a penguin... swimming right at you. Never noticed that before."

Milo arrived and sat down next to me. He looked

even worse than Julie. He and Sam had been friends since Milo had joined MHI as an orphaned teenager. He was holding together right now, but that was only because there was still work to do. "I checked. The magic rope's toast. Half of it is still stuck under that stupid tree, so I don't think I can turn it back on. Don't have the ward stone to juice it up either."

"How did you do that, anyway?"

Milo shrugged. "Couple of clever people, a killer deadline, and a mutant that happened to be familiar with the inventor's work. Esmeralda figured out how to turn it back on, and I said, why not splice it into a couple hundred feet of climbing rope and fly some attack helicopters through it... Seemed like the reasonable thing to do with a magic teleporter thingy. Then we took volunteers to go through it, and that turned out to be just about everybody who wasn't already banged up."

"Well, you guys saved my life. I'll never forget that."

"Don't ever forget *Sam*." Milo sniffed and blew his nose into a handkerchief. "Darn, I must be allergic to penguins or something, making me tear up and stuff. Well, if you'll excuse me, I've got to see about arranging transport out of here. I'm assuming most of us didn't bother to bring passports."

Milo walked away. I corrected my patch. "Does New Zealand have penguins?" I asked.

Julie shrugged.

The British Supernatural Service, commonly known as BSS, working in conjunction with the U.S. Monster Control Bureau of the Department of Homeland Security, was gracious enough to provide lodging and transport for the forty-some-odd members of MHI stuck in Pukerua Bay, New Zealand. Mostly I think they just wanted to get us out of the rapidly disintegrating situation. The small town had not been evacuated quite in time, and many photos and even cell phone video of the massive *Arbmunep* had been taken and dumped on the internet. People were freaking out. The Feds were scrambling to come up with a plausible cover story.

*Not my problem.*

Skippy had refused to leave until Archer had agreed to have the Hind crated up and shipped back to Alabama. I didn't know if Myers would allow his subordinate to keep that promise, but if he didn't, I figured the orc would probably just hunt him down, and it wouldn't be pretty. That chopper was Skippy's baby.

I was riding business class on a transoceanic flight when I got the phone call. My phone was still sitting at the bottom of the Alabama River, so Earl had finally managed to get ahold of Julie. She woke me up with a poke to the ribs and passed the phone over, violating the hell out of the airline policy about using electronic devices in-flight.

"You did it," Earl said. "As soon as the link with the Dread Overlord was broken, Rocky said he was done and went home."

"Rocky?"

"You know, *Rok'hasna'wrath*, devourer of worlds and all that crap. We spent a lot of quality time together, so we're on a first-name basis now. I think he was surprised to find that I was a little tougher than he initially figured. I didn't give up anything without a hell of a fight."

"Any permanent damage?"

Earl was quiet for so long that I thought I had dropped the connection. "Well, I lost a few things..." He didn't specify further. I remembered the terrible fate of Carlos, and was just glad that I had been able to spare one of my friends from that. "Thanks, Owen. Thanks for everything."

"I'm sorry about Sam." *If I hadn't freed Susan...*

"Don't be. *Sic Transit Gloria Mundi.* Sam Haven was a hero and one of the best friends I've ever had. He died how he lived, brave as hell, saving lives, and getting the job done. That's exactly how he would have wanted it."

"See you in a few, Earl."

The day after our return, I had been summoned to a meeting at one of the miscellaneous federal buildings in Montgomery. I was to come alone. It had not been a request. Apparently the MCB had a few questions they wanted answered about the events of the last few days.

I wore my only suit, which was normally reserved for funerals and weddings. There was still a very good possibility that I was going to be prosecuted for the various things that I had done. There was also the much smaller possibility that they were just going to make me disappear for being a general nuisance. My gut feeling told me that was unlikely though. If the government ever decided to just pop me, I knew that they would just send Franks.

Myers had requisitioned an office near the courthouse during his stay in Montgomery, and the receptionist pointed me in the correct direction when I got off the elevator. There was a single chair outside the office, and it was occupied by a fidgeting Grant Jefferson.

I paused, waiting.

He stood, adjusting his suit, which was much nicer than mine. He looked a little nervous, which was understandable, despite the fact that I'd had to go through a metal detector in the lobby. "I wanted to talk to you before your meeting."

I waited. I didn't really have anything I needed to say to him.

But he apparently felt the need to get something off his chest. "When you asked me why I came back, I wasn't lying when I answered." I didn't respond, so he gradually continued. "I did feel like a failure. I hated knowing what was out there, and I felt like a coward for not fighting anymore. I was bitter. I felt like MHI had let me down, not the other way around. When Myers approached me, I saw a way that I could do the right thing. I could protect people, serve my country . . . I saw a way that I could make a real difference."

*A difference? Hiding the truth, killing people who talked too much? All while deluding yourself that you're a hero?* "Why are you telling me this?"

He shook his head. "I . . . I don't really know. I just thought you should understand."

"You done?"

He stuck his hand out to shake. I just glanced down at his waiting hand. It would be a cold day in hell before I accepted his pseudo-apology. Finally, awkwardly, he lowered it back to his side. "Never mind then." He brushed past me and walked quickly down the hallway, footfalls echoing on the granite. I put my hand on the doorknob. Grant paused and glanced back. "One last thing, Pitt."

I waited.

"Be good to her. She deserves the best." Then he walked away.

Agent Myers was waiting for me on the other side of a desk. He had a file with my name on it sitting open in front of him. His fingers were steepled together and his elbows were resting on the desk. His cheap suit was wrinkled and I was willing to bet that he hadn't gotten much sleep over the last few days. "Have a seat."

I pulled up a chair.

He got right down to business. "The necromancer is dead. His plot to utilize the *Arbmunep* weapon, defeated. All of our intel indicates that the Condition is collapsing without him. There are a few splinter groups holding together, and one young woman claiming to be his successor—"

"His daughter, Lucinda."

"Correct. But we will find her before she causes too much trouble, so don't worry about that. I'm not too worried about a teenager with one hand and a shattered organization. That's not why I called you in here." He lifted the top page in my file. "In the last week, you've threatened one of my agents with lethal force, failed to cooperate in a federal investigation, lied to investigators, and hindered an ongoing operation. These are all very serious charges."

"I also killed one of your agents with a grenade launcher," I pointed out, "which I think I should get bonus points for, and not to mention that Franks and I blew up the Dread Overlord itself."

"I'm aware of that, and Agent Franks will be reprimanded accordingly. He was not authorized to enter another universe or to attack an unknown entity. The Congressional Subcommittee has ruled it an act of self-defense, however, so Franks will not be terminated."

Did that mean fired or dismantled? "You know that's absolute bullshit, right?"

Myers, unfazed, continued. "Even more troubling is that it seems like you've been keeping secrets from me. I have evidence here that you have some sort of psychic powers and that somehow you are the only person in recorded history to have survived a zombie bite."

"That's impossible," I said with no inflection.

"Indeed," Myers said. "Because that would mean that your continued existence could prove to be an important national security issue." I did not respond. If Myers wanted to just make me go away it was certainly within his power. "But I'm really doubting the accuracy of this report," he said as he waved the paper.

"Why's that?"

"Because this same intel indicates that the Condition's Shadow Lord was really a man named Martin Hood, who died quite some time ago. See, I happened to know Martin Hood, we were actually close friends, and I would hate to see his good name slandered."

I nodded. "And it would also call into question the judgment of the interim head of the Monster Control Bureau if it turned out that one of his oldest friends was really the leader of an evil death cult." Myers was concerned about his association with Hood coming back to haunt him...

*Unless...*

Could Hood have also approached Myers about working together, like he had with Carlos? It was a definite possibility. They had been best friends. Had Myers known just what kind of craziness Hood had been dabbling in? Had he known about Hood's father's book? Had he known, but protected his friend anyway?

I had to know. "Can I see that report?"

Myers extended it to me and I reached out and touched his hand instead. It wasn't so difficult to use the ability this time. After all, the memory was just sitting there, floated to the top by the pressure of Agent Myers' buried guilt.

Ray Shackleford was furious. His face was turning a shade of red that was normally reserved for when he was chainsawing a monster in half. He shoved the chubby Hunter against the wall, enraged. "Damn it, Marty! What the hell were you thinking? I told you not to screw around with this stuff anymore!"

Ray was such a brute that Marty's feet dangled a few inches off the floor and the big man didn't even notice that he was holding him up. But the smaller Hunter was undaunted. "Don't you get it? I figured it out! I've learned the language of the book. I've read the entire *Skia Thanatou!* I can control the dead. There's no limit to what we can do now," Hood gasped, trying to breathe past the meaty hands clamped around his throat. The wall of Shackleford family portraits was at his back. The family estate was packed with Hunters but we had this room to ourselves.

"You were animating zombies, you idiot, and Carlos found out, and in the morning when Earl wakes up human, he's going to know too." Ray let go and Marty dropped, gasping. "I got you transferred so you would quit dinking around with the magic shit in the archives. You weren't supposed to sneak the evilest book down there with you!"

"It was my book to take," Marty snapped. "It belonged to my father, and his father before him. You didn't think it was such a bad idea when I used it back here and was making us millions in bounties!"

Ray rubbed his face in his hands as he stomped away. "What are we going to do? Does Carlos know anybody else helped with your research?"

"Of course not," Marty snapped. "You think I'm stupid? Now lower your voice, or the whole house will know. I'll handle this. I'll tell Earl that it was all me. I'll take the heat. What's he going to do? Kill me?" Marty snorted.

"Yes," Ray snapped. "My dad and grandpa are a lot of things, especially old-fashioned, but they've got principles. They won't tolerate a Hunter using dark magic. One of these days, I'll be in charge, and that'll change. We all know that this stuff can be harnessed for good, but until then, we were supposed to keep our mouths *shut*."

Marty's fat face opened in a wide grin. "Don't worry, mate. I'll handle this. If there's one thing I can do, it's keep a secret. Nobody ever has to know who helped me."

"Damn right," Ray snarled, poking him in the chest. "We're done tonight. In the morning, you'll come clean and beg Earl for forgiveness. You're going to take your lumps. Earl will probably fire you, but at least he won't eat you, and it beats all of us going to prison, right, Myers?"

"Agreed," I said, speaking up for the first time. I hated myself for ever getting involved. It had been stupid, playing with evil for the greater good, and my best friend had taken it too far. We had been fools.

But I did know how to keep a secret.

Only a second had passed. I was getting better at this. I studied Myers' face for a moment. He still looked like a community-college English professor, not like the interim leader of a top-secret government agency tasked with protecting the United States from all supernatural threats. He was an easy man to underestimate, but now I knew why he was so doggedly determined in his work. Myers was seeking atonement.

"It would probably ruin your career if it also turned out that your best friend was animating zombies and studying the darkest of mysteries while you guys were hanging out. Some of the good congressmen might even get the crazy idea that you were somehow involved," I said.

Myers smiled nervously. "Yes, no need for the Subcommittee to even worry about such preposterous allegations. I think that it would be for the best if this erroneous report never saw the light of day, wouldn't you?"

"Martin Hood died in 1986. Werewolf accident," I said.

"And Owen Zastava Pitt is just an average man, with no magical gifts or anything absurd like that." Myers nodded. "That seems fair enough." He neatly stacked all of the papers, put them all back into the folder, and fed the entire thing into an industrial shredder next to the desk. We both waited for it to quit grinding. "Now that's behind us, I do sincerely hope that we never have to work together again. In fact, I damn well better never see your name come across my desk, ever again. You should just stick with *normal* monsters. It seems like every time I get a case that's almost impossible to cover, it somehow involves you. No more world-altering events, time travel, portals to the Old Ones, or giant super trees. Is that understood?"

"Of course, Agent Myers." I stood. "I can show myself out."

We held the funeral services three days later. The dirty but necessary work had been done immediately, so this part was only for the living, not the dead. During the attack on the compound we had lost a team lead, Adam Williams, and three Newbies: Drew Foster, William Tanner, and John Newton. We had lost Sam Roger Haven under the boughs of the Tree, and we were also honoring the sacrifice of Carlos Alhambra.

Everyone had gathered.

There was a small cemetery in the forest outside the compound and the place was packed. The only Hunters who were buried here were the ones who requested to be. Most were cremated and then sent back to their families with some sort of fabricated cover story. It was sad, but it was how we had to operate. There was only one person actually being buried here today, and that was Sam, because his only family had been his fellow Hunters. The casket was closed, as we had already cleanly removed his head. It was something that we all had to do eventually.

We had set up a little podium in front of the hole in the ground. Milo Anderson had been tasked with saying a few words. The little man looked terribly uncomfortable in front of the crowd, glancing nervously about the entire time. He had dressed up in his best purple suit and had carefully braided his beard.

The orc tribe had buried their dead in their own private ceremony, but three solemn representatives had joined us. Skippy, Gretchen, and Edward held back, uncomfortable around so many humans, but feeling the need to acknowledge their connection to us, their adopted tribe. Their people had suffered because of their friendship with us, and I felt like it was my fault.

Yet they didn't see it that way. The orcs had welcomed me back as the hero who'd avenged their village. Gretchen had been impressed that I'd provided Julie the biggest wedding night offering ever, and she had warned my new bride that she was now obligated to provide me many strong warrior sons. Given how big an Old One was, Gretchen estimated three dozen sons would be sufficient.

Every Hunter that wasn't currently in the hospital was here, and even a few of those had managed to limp in.

My family had stayed for this. They would be leaving this afternoon. They could have left sooner. The Condition was broken, their members scattered, their leader and their lord dead. But my father had insisted on being here for this. After all, he was a man who understood sacrifice.

I still wouldn't speak to him about his dream and I refused to take his letter. Yes, I was curious, but I'd be damned if my curiosity was going to kill him. Dad glanced down the line of Hunters directly at me. In his opinion I was being a coward by not reading his letter. That may be the case, but I felt like I actually understood him for the first time. He had been trying to do his best the whole time. Dad's tough love had enabled me to survive, and as a result I'd found my calling in life and the woman I loved. My father had done his duty. I would do the same, and that meant keeping him around as long as possible.

My brother had also stuck around and was standing next to Mom. His career was ruined. His left hand was still wrapped in a massive bandage. Cody had saved the fingers and after Mosh's return they had been surgically reattached. The best he could hope for was a tiny fraction of the strength and dexterity he had once had. His days of being the best guitarist in the world were over. The Feds had publicly smeared him as the person responsible for the Buzzard Island incident. The official story now was a load of nonsense about special effects gone astray while under the haze of illegal drugs that had left a lot of people dead. It was utter crap, but somebody had to be blamed, and the flood of lawsuits was going to leave him bankrupt. He could maybe hope to someday play again, but Mosh was like me, and if you couldn't be the best at something, why do it at all?

Yet another life ruined because of me...

But Pitts are flexible, he hid his bitterness behind an impassive mask, and besides, Mosh had seen the real world. He had approached me just this morning, curious about what it took to become a Hunter. He also said that if he joined, and that was a big *if*, he had dibs on Team Rock Star once he inevitably became the greatest Hunter alive. I had been glad to put in my recommendation to hire him.

The Feds had felt the need to send representation for some reason. Maybe Myers understood that this whole thing was his fault, or maybe he just wanted to tweak us because he was such a petty man. Two agents had been sent to represent, and judging by who had been sent, I was assuming it was out of pettiness. Grant Jefferson looked painfully awkward in his expensive Italian suit. Grant actually would have made a good Pitt. If he couldn't be the best, why bother? I had no doubt that he would be a very effective Fed, since being a lying, self-righteous bastard came naturally to him. He shifted nervously, as Hunters cast the occasional cold glance at him. But at the same time, he and Sam had been teammates. Maybe Grant hadn't been ordered to come. Maybe he had volunteered. I would never know.

Agent Franks was the other government representative. He was chewing gum. I was sure that he would much rather be somewhere else, killing something. I did not understand what made Franks tick. He had kept his word, though, and fulfilled his mission.

The other Hunters listened to Milo patiently. He wasn't the most eloquent of speakers, but he spoke for all of us. Grandpa Shackleford sat between his father, Raymond Shackleford the Second, whom we all knew as Earl Harbinger, and his grandson, Nate, who had a large cast on his leg. The Shacklefords had another person to mourn. One of their own turned to the other side had finally been set free. Raymond Shackleford the Third, or Boss as I called him, had cornered me the day I had gotten back. His only words had been, "Thank you for killing my son," and he had been sincere. It had made me cry.

Julie came from solid stock. The wall of family portraits had confirmed my suspicions, but even if I hadn't been able to recognize the very first Raymond Shackleford from his painting, seeing the generations of Shackleford Hunters here today would have clued me in. They all carried themselves with that same solid determination. The ghost who had sent me back had been Raymond "Bubba" Shackleford himself. The founder of MHI was still keeping an eye on things.

Holly was torn up, taking Sam's death hard. Trip put his arm around her and pulled her close, trying in vain to comfort her. The others looked away. They had been there for me. The threat had been against me specifically, but Hunters stood together. I was the least of them, but I knew that every single one of them would lay down their lives for me, and I would do the same for them. I loved them like family. Hell, they were family.

I was in the front row, uncomfortable in a black suit and tie. The day was beautiful. The sky was clear. The spring air was clean. Birds were singing.

Julie was at my side, wearing a black dress. She hadn't spoken much since we had gotten home, and I knew that she was still in shock about the final death of her father. She had a lot on her mind. The marks on her neck and abdomen had not changed since that night, but they were an indication that *something* was happening. While Milo told stories, I reached out and took my wife's hand. She gave me a nervous smile. Whatever was coming, we would face it together.

When Milo was done, he stepped away from the podium. Earl Harbinger stood, and without a word, placed two patches on top of the casket, a happy face with horns and a walrus with a banjo. The few of us who had been asked, helped lower the casket into the earth.

A baby began to cry. Milo moved to his wife, who was gently bouncing the squalling infant. Shawna Anderson had given birth the day after Milo had gotten back from New Zealand. It was a healthy baby girl.

They named her Samantha.

# EPILOGUE

The powerful demon crouched, unobserved, in the top branches of a distant tree, silently observing the Hunter's funeral below. It remained perfectly still, claws sunk deep into the bark to provide a stable platform as the breeze caused the branches to sway. The creature's third eye, etched deep into the plate of its skull, was able to clearly record the event for its distant master.

The mewling of the human infant caused the demon's belly to rumble with hunger, but meat would have to wait. Today it would watch. Tomorrow it would kill.

*The four have gathered*, the master projected his thoughts directly into the creature's mind. *Can you feel them?*

The demon scanned the crowd. It was said that four of these fleshlings had been to the Old Ones' dimension and returned alive. That alone was remarkable, but three of them had actually destroyed an Overlord. That was impressive, even by the demon prince's immortal standards.

The first was easy to pick out. It was one of the fallen, cloaked in a suit of flesh, animated by the Elixir of Life. Unlike most of its kind, this one pretended to be a man, living as a human. But even then, the demon could see the aura of violence this particular fallen wore like a cloak. It could play at being a human, but it would never succeed.

*They call him Agent Franks now,* the master confirmed. *He went to the other side out of a sense of duty.*

That made no sense to the demon. The fallen had no duty, no allegiance. They were damned for eternity, regardless. They had nothing to lose, no stake in this war.

*And that's why he is dangerous.*

The second was the werewolf.

*Harbinger entered the Old Ones' world to save his grandson several years ago. The grandson was chosen to be the champion of man, but he was weak, manipulated by the necromancer, Hood. He fell to the vampire and has been replaced.*

The demon could tell this was no normal lycanthrope. He was ancient by mortal standards and no stranger to battle, having hunted down nearly every type of beast. Killing that one would be an honor.

Many ghosts shared this forest. They too were watching. The demon was royalty amongst its kind, but the Hunters' unquiet dead left it nervous. These spirits had picked their side in the upcoming war. Many of the dead would not ally with his master this time. A particularly angry ghost was circling the tree, trying to pick a fight. It ignored the spirit and concentrated on the master's task.

It took longer for the demon to spot the next of

the four. It was a young woman sitting in the front row. A Guardian? It couldn't be, but as the third eye refocused, it could see the black marks of the Others beneath her clothes.

*Yes,* the master said. *She crossed over to bring back her lover. She is a brave one.*

The demon prince scoffed. The last Guardian had been an unstoppable warrior, finally killed only through treachery. This little girl would be easy prey.

*Do not underestimate her, child. Even now she has hidden the sacred artifact. The Others do not choose a new Guardian lightly.*

The last was the hardest to find. All of the Hunters at the funeral were dangerous, special in their own way, fearsome, honorable, creative, ruthless, or courageous. It recognized a few of them from prior battles, but none were the champion.

*There.*

The demon fixated on the young man holding the new Guardian's hand. He was a warrior, that much was certain, but the demon prince could not understand what was special, why this one had been chosen above all the others.

*He is the only one who did not cross over willingly, but even forcing him to do that ended the wretched Overlord. Before that the Old Ones could not tempt, coerce, nor trick him to do their will. When he destroyed the vampire Raymond Shackleford, the prior champion of man, he unwittingly took that mantle upon himself.*

It took a great deal of effort, but the demon began to really see. This human had been picked for a reason. It was in his blood. For generations the factions had steered events to this place, this intersection in time, for the great unsealing.

*This is the one who woke me. He who has broken time. He must be the champion. I will use him, then I will destroy him.*

Sudden forces shook the tree. Energy struck the demon in the chest. Claws tore through bark as it was knocked from its perch in the tree. Spreading leathery wings, it glided to the ground silently. Landing, hunched, it tucked its wings in tight and waited. The living Hunters had not heard the commotion.

A flickering ghost appeared before the demon, dressed in the leather armor of a turn-of-the-century Hunter. The spirit was ready to battle. "Y'all ain't welcome here. This is a private ceremony," he ordered.

The demon prince recognized the dead man. They had fought long ago. It spoke for the first time as it drew itself up to its full height, towering over the ghost. "I know you. I helped kill you."

The dead man gave a slow nod. "I reckon you did, but don't you worry your pointy little head on it. My folks will even up that score eventually." He pointed to the northwest, the direction the demon had come from. "So get off my land."

It weighed the options. There was not much that a lone spirit could do to harm it. Yet, the nearby Hunters with their physical bodies and silver weapons could prove troublesome. More ghosts had appeared and the prince realized it was badly outnumbered.

*It is not time, child,* the master warned. *The end of the world is near, but it is not yet upon us. Leave the Hunters to bury their dead for now. There is still much to prepare.*

Frustrated, the demon dipped its curled horns in acknowledgement to the gathering army of spirits, turned and stomped away, leaving nothing but a trail of cloven prints in the red soil. Along the trail, it passed the shimmering ghost of a bent old man, leaning upon a wooden cane. The dead Hunter was studying the intricate symbol branded on the demon's chest.

"Seen that sign before," the ghost said with a thick accent. "Drawn in the dirt by father of my friend, just the other day." He pushed the glasses back up his nose, hawked, and made a big show of spitting on the ground at the demon's hooves.

"We are not done here," the demon hissed.

"No. We're just getting started," the old man replied with a smile.

The Following is an excerpt from:

HARD MAGIC

Book I
of the Grimnoir
Chronicles

# LARRY CORREIA

Available from Baen Books
May 2012
Mass Market

# ⚐ Prologue ⚐

*One general law, leading to the advancement of all organic beings, namely, multiply, vary, let the strongest live and the weakest die. The appearance of esoteric and etheral abiliites, magical fires and feats of strength, in recent decades are the purest demonstration of natural selection. Surely, in time, that general law will require the extinction of traditional man.*

—Charles Darwin,
*On the Origin of Man and Selection
of Human Magical Abilities*, 1879

## El Nido, California

**"OKIES."** The Portuguese farmer spat on the ground, giving the evil eye to the passing automobiles weighed down with baskets, bushels, and crates. The cars just kept coming up the dusty San Joaquin Valley road like some kind of Okie wagon train. He left to make sure all his valuables were locked up and his Sears & Roebuck single-shot 12 gauge was loaded.

The tool shed was locked and the shotgun was in his hands when the short little farmer returned to watch.

One of the Ford Model Ts rattled to a stop in front of the farmhouse fence. The old farmer leaned on his shotgun and waited. His son would talk to the visitors. The boy spoke English. So did he, but not as well, just good enough to take the Dodge truck into Merced to buy supplies, and it wasn't like the mangled inbred garbage dialect the Okies spoke was English anyway.

The farmer watched the transients carefully as his son approached the automobile. They were asking for work. They were always asking for work. Ever since the dusts had blown up and cursed their stupid land, they'd all driven west in some Okie exodus until they ran out of farmland and stopped to harass the Portuguese, who had gotten here first.

Of course they'd been here first. Like he gave a shit if these people were homeless or hungry. He'd been born in a hut on the tiny island of Terceira and had milked cows every single day of his life until his hands were leather bags so strong he could bend pipe. The San Joaquin Valley had been a hole until his people had shown up, covered the place in Holsteins, and put the Mexicans to work. Now these Okies show up, build tent cities, bitch about how the government should save them, and sneak out at night to rob the Catholics. It really pissed him off.

It always amazed him how much the Okies could fit onto an old Model T. He'd come from Terceira on a steamship, spending weeks in a steel hole between hot steam pipes. He'd owned a blanket, one pair of pants, a hat, and a pair of shoes with holes in them. He'd worked his ass off in a Portuguese town in Rhode Island, neck deep in fish guts, married a nice Portuguese girl, even if she was from the screwed up island of St. George, which everybody from Terceira knew was the ass crack of the Azores, and saved up enough money doing odd jobs to come out here to another Portuguese town and buy some scrawny Holsteins. Five cows, a bull, and twenty years of backbreaking labor had turned into a hundred and twenty cows, fifty acres, a Ford tractor, a Dodge pickup, a good milk barn, and a house with six whole rooms. By Portuguese standards, he was living like a king.

So he wasn't going to give these Okies shit. They weren't even Catholic. They should have to work like he did. He watched the Okie father talking to his son as his son patiently explained for the hundredth time that there wasn't any work, and that they needed to head toward Los Banos or maybe Chowchilla, not that they were going to work anyway when they could just break into his milk barn and steal his tools to sell for rotgut moonshine again. His grandkids were poking their heads around the house, checking out the Model T, but he'd warned them enough times about the dangers of outsiders, and they stayed safely away. He wasn't about to have his family corrupted from their good Catholic work ethic by being exposed to bums.

Then he noticed the girl.

She was just another scrawny Okie kid. Barely even a woman yet, so it was surprising that she hadn't already had three kids from her brothers. But there was something strange about this one . . . something he'd seen before.

The girl glanced his way, and he knew then what had set him off. She had grey eyes.

"Mary, mother of God," the old farmer muttered, fingering the crucifix at his neck. "Not this shit again . . ." His first reaction was to walk away, leave it alone. It wasn't any of his business, and the girl would probably be dead soon enough, impaled through her guts by some random tree branch or a flying bug stuck in an artery. And he didn't even know if the grey eyes meant the same thing to an Okie as it did to the Portuguese. For all he knew she was a normal girl who just looked funny, and she'd go have a long and stupid life in an Okie tent city popping out fifteen kids who'd also break into his milk barn and steal his tools.

The girl was studying him, dirty hair whipping in the wind, and he could just tell . . .

"Fooking shit damn," he said in English, which was the first English any immigrant who worked with cows learned. He'd seen what happened to the grey eyes when they weren't taught correctly, and as much as he despised Okies, he didn't want to see one of their kids with their brains spread all over the road because they'd magically appeared in front of a speeding truck.

Leaning the shotgun against the tractor tire, he approached the Model T. The Okie parents looked at him with mild belligerence as he approached their daughter. The old farmer stopped next to the girl's window. There were half a dozen other kids crammed in there, but they were just regular desperate and starving Okies. This one was special.

He lifted his hat so she could see that his eyes were the same color as hers. He tried his best English. "You . . . girl. Grey eyes." She pointed at herself, curious, but didn't speak. He nodded. "You . . . Jump? Travel?" She didn't understand, and now her idiot parents were staring at him in slack jawed ignorance. The old farmer took one hand and held it out in a fist. He suddenly opened it. "Poof!" Then he raised his other hand as far away as possible, "Poof!" and made a fist.

She smiled and nodded her head vigorously. He grinned. She was a Traveler all right.

"You know about what she does?" the Okie father asked.

The old farmer nodded, finding his own magic inside and poking it to wake it up. Then he was gone, and instantly he was on the other side of the Model T. He tapped the Okie mother on the arm through the open window and she shrieked. All his grandkids cheered. They loved when he did that. His son just rolled his eyes.

The Okie father looked at the Portuguese farmer, back at his daughter, and then back to the farmer. The grey eyed girl was happy as could be that she'd found somebody just like her. The father scowled for a long time, glancing again at his strange child that had caused them so much grief, and then at all the other starving mouths he had to find a way to feed. Finally he spoke. "I'll sell you her for twenty dollars."

The old farmer thought about it. He didn't need any more people eating up his food, but his brother and sisters had all ended up dead before they had mastered Traveling, and this was the first other person like him he'd seen in twenty years, but he also hadn't gotten where he was by getting robbed by Okies. "Make it ten."

The girl giggled and clapped.

**New York City, New York**

**THE RICHEST MAN IN THE WORLD** stepped into the elevator lift and looked in distaste at the gleaming silver buttons. The message had said to come alone, so he did not even have one of his usual functionaries to perform the service of requesting the correct floor. Rather than soiling his hands or a perfectly good handkerchief, he sighed, tapped into the lowest level of his Power, and pushed the button for the penthouse suite with his mind. Cornelius Gould Stuyvesant, billionaire industrialist, could not tolerate filth. A man of his stature simply did not get his hands dirty.

He had people for that.

The steel doors closed. They were carved with golden figures of muscular workers creating the American dream through their sweat and industry under a rising sun emitting rays as straight as a Tesla cannon. He sniffed the air. The elevator car *seemed* clean. The hotel was considered a five-star luxury establishment, but Cornelius just *knew* that there were germs everywhere, disgusting, diseased, tiny plague nodules just itching to get on his skin. Cornelius understood the true nature of the man who was staying in this hotel, and he must have ridden in this very car. Cornelius shuddered as he squeezed his arms and briefcase closer to his sides, careful not to touch the walls.

He could afford the finest Healers. In fact, he was one of the only men in the world that had an actual Mender on his personal staff, but nothing could stop the blight of a

Pale Horse, and it was that foul Power that brought him here today, reduced to a mere caller. Cornelius had tried to seek out others, once under a gypsy tent on Coney Island, again in a tiny shack in the Louisiana Bayou, but those had been frauds, charlatans, wastes of his valuable time. He tapped his foot impatiently. After what seemed like an eternity, the doors whisked open.

A tuxedoed servant was waiting for him, an older negro with stark white hair. The servant bowed his head. "Good evening, Mr. Stuyvesant. Mr. Harkeness is waiting on the balcony. May I take your coat, sir?"

"Not necessary. My business will not take long."

The servant studied him with cunning eyes. "Of course, sir. Would you care for a drink? Mr. Harkeness has a selection of the finest."

"As if I would drink anything *here*," Cornelius sputtered. The notion of ingesting something from the household of a Pale Horse was madness. "Take me to him immediately."

"Of course, sir." The servant led the way down the marble hall. Carved busts of long-dead Greeks watched him from pedestals, judging. Cornelius hated statues. Statues made him prickly. Even the giant idolized bronze of himself at the new super-dirigible dock bearing his name atop the new Empire State Building bothered him.

Lots of things made Cornelius Gould Stuyvesant uncomfortable, including this servant. He did not like the way he had examined him, like he was being sized up. The information he'd gathered on Harkeness indicated that the man surrounded himself with other like-minded Actives. There were many who would kill a Pale Horse on basic principle, so it made sense to have loyal staff with Power for security. He idly wondered what kind of Active the old servant was. Probably something barbaric, like a Brute, or even worse, a Torch. That would seem to suit a race that was so easily inflamed by its passions.

"Mr. Harkeness is through here, sir." The servant paused at the fine wood and thick glass door leading to the balcony. He turned the knob and opened it. "He prefers the fresh air. Will there be anything else?"

Cornelius did not bother to respond as he stepped onto the balcony. His time was valuable, more valuable than any man in the world, more valuable than emperors, kings, tsars, kaisers, and especially that imbecile, Herbert Hoover, and the very idea that he was reduced to having to take time from his busy schedule to meet someone on their terms rather than his own was blatantly offensive.

To further the sleight, Harkeness was leaning on the balcony, overlooking the city, placing his back toward the richest man in the world, as if Manhattan were somehow more important than Cornelius Gould Stuyvesant himself. The balcony lights had been extinguished, so as not to hamper the view. The city was illuminated forty stories below by electric lights and flashing marquees. Thousands of automobiles filled the streets, bustling even at this hour, and overhead a passing dirigible train floated in the amber spotlights like a herd of sea cows. Cornelius snorted in greeting.

"Mr. Stuyvesant." The Pale Horse didn't bother to turn around. His voice was neutral, flat. "I was just admiring your marvelous city. Have a seat."

Cornelius felt a single drop of sweat roll down his

neck. It was shameful, but he found that he was actually frightened. He glanced at the pair of chairs, fine, stuffed leather things that in any other scenario would be inviting to rest his ponderous bulk, but at that moment, all he could imagine were the horrible diseases crawling on the cushions.

"I said have a seat," Harkeness repeated, still not turning around. His accent was indeterminate, his pronunciation awkward. "You are a guest of mine. I would not harm a guest. I am a civilized man, Mr. Stuyvesant."

Cornelius sat, vowing that he would throw this suit into the fireplace as soon as he got home, then he would have his personal Healer expend a month's worth of Power checking his health. He would probably burn the Cadillac car he had traveled in, maybe the driver too, just to be on the safe side.

Harkeness left the railing and took the other seat. He did not offer his hand. He was older than Cornelius had expected, tall and thin, face lined with creases, and blue eyes that sparked with an unnerving energy. His hair was receding, and what remained was artificially blackened. His tailored suit was as fine as could be had, and his tie was made of silk as red as fresh blood. He smiled, and his teeth were slightly yellow in the dim city light. "Smoke?"

Cornelius looked down at the wooden humidor on the table between them. The cigars were sorely tempting, but the very thought of touching his lips with an item tainted by Harkeness's evil made his stomach roil. "No, thank you."

Harkeness nodded in understanding as he puffed on his own Cuban. "Straight to the chase then. I was informed that you were looking for me."

"Nobody can ever know we spoke," Cornelius insisted. He was the founder and owner of United Blimp & Freight, the primary shareholder in Federal Steel, and the man that bankrolled the development of the Peace Ray. He'd sired children who had gone on to be ambassadors to powerful nations, senators, congressmen, and even a governor. A Stuyvesant could not be seen consorting with such sordid types.

"I assure you, I am a man of discretion." Harkeness exhaled a pungent tobacco cloud, not seeming to notice his guest's discomfort.

Cornelius cringed, trying not to inhale smoke that had actually been inside the very lungs of such a pestilent creature. "You are a hard man to find, Mr. Harkeness," the billionaire said, aware that he had to tread carefully. Even with eight decades of mankind dealing with the presence of Powers, of actual magic, to the point that they were just an accepted part of life in most of the world, the Pale Horse was such a rarity that most still considered it to be a myth, crude antimagic propaganda created to sow fear and distrust in the hearts of the masses. "Men of your . . . skills . . . are especially rare."

"Yes . . . What is it you were told I am?" Harkeness asked rhetorically, examining the ash on the end of his cigar.

Cornelius hesitated, not sure if he should answer, but growing tired off the awkward silence, he finally spoke. "I was told you are a Pale Horse."

Harkeness laughed hard, slapping his knee. "I like that. So . . . biblical! So much nicer than plague bearer, or grim reaper, or angel of death. That title has gravitas. Pale

Horse! You, sir, have made my day. Perhaps I shall add that to my business cards." His pronunciation was stilted, with pauses between random words. Cornelius found it almost hypnotic, and realized he was nervously smiling along with the other man's mirth. Then Harkeness abruptly quit laughing and his voice turned deadly serious. "So, who must die?"

"You presume much," Cornelius said defensively.

"If you just wanted to merely curse someone and make their hair fall out, or to give them boils, fits, or incontinence, there are far easier Actives to reach than I." Harkeness's smile was unnerving. "People come to me when they desire something . . . epic."

The industrialist swallowed and placed his briefcase on the table. He unlocked it, then turned it so that Harkeness could see inside. It was filled with neatly stacked and meticulously counted bank notes and a single newspaper clipping. Cornelius quickly snatched his hand away before the Pale Horse could touch the contents, as if his Power might somehow be transmitted through the leather.

The Pale Horse did not seem to notice the money. He gently removed the yellowed clipping, took a pair of spectacles from his breast pocket, set them atop his hawk-like nose and began reading. After a moment he removed the glasses and returned them and the clipping to his pocket. "An important man. Very well . . . What will it be? Bone rot? Consumption? Cancers of the brain or bowel? Syphilis? Leprosy? I can do anything from a minor vapor to turn his joints to sand while his skin boils off in a cancerous sludge. I am an encyclopedia of affliction, sir."

Cornelius bobbed his head in time with the litany of diseases. "All of them."

"I see . . ." Harkeness seemed to approve. "Very well, but first, I must know . . ."

"Yes," Cornelius answered hesitantly. The hairs on the back of his neck were standing up.

"Why? A man such as you has no shortage of killers to choose from. Why not a knife in the back? A bullet in the head? You yourself are a Mover, why not just invite him to a balcony such as this and shove him off? It would even look like a suicide, which would be particularly scandalous in the papers."

"How—" Cornelius sputtered. His Power was a secret. "Me? A Magical? Who told you such slanderous lies?"

Harkeness shrugged. "I have a trained eye, Mr. Stuyvesant. Now answer my question. Why do you need me to curse this man?"

Cornelius felt his face flush with anger. No matter how dangerous Harkeness was, Cornelius Gould Stuyvesant was not about to have his motives questioned by a mere hireling. He pushed himself away from the table and rose, bellowing, "Why you? I do not want him dead. That is far too good a fate for one such as he! I want him to suffer first. I want him to know he's dying and I want him to pray to his ineffectual God to save him as his body rots and stinks and melts to the blackest filth. I want it to hurt and I want it to be embarrassing. I want his lungs to fill with pus. I want his balls to fall off and I want him to piss fire! I want his loved ones to look away in disgust, and I want it to take a very, very *long* time."

Harkeness nodded, his face now an emotionless mask. "I can do this thing for you, but first, I must ask, what terrible thing did this man do to deserve such a fate?"

The billionaire paused, pudgy hands curled into fists. He lowered his voice before continuing. He had planned this revenge for years. It was only the purity of the hate for his enemy that drove him to this place. "He took something . . . *someone* . . . from me. Leave it at that." Cornelius tried to calm himself. He was not a man given to such unseemly outbursts. "Will that do?"

"It is enough."

Cornelius realized he was standing, but it did make him feel more in control, more in his element. He gestured at the open briefcase. "I was given your name by an associate. I believe that this is the same amount that he paid for your services." Rockefeller had warned Cornelius about how expensive the Pale Horse would be, but it would be so very worth the money. "Take it."

The other man shook his head. "No. I don't think so."

"What!" Cornelius objected. Was he going to try and shake him down for more money than Rockefeller? The *nerve*. "How dare you!"

Harkeness leaned back in his chair, puffing on the cigar. He took it away from his mouth and smiled without any joy. "I don't want your money, Mr. Stuyvesant. I want something *else*."

Cornelius trembled. Of course, he'd heard the odder stories about the Pale Horses, the rarest of the Actives, but he had paid them no heed. He was a man of science, not superstition. Sure, he had magic himself, nowadays one in a hundred Americans had some small measure, but it didn't mean he understood how it actually worked. One in a thousand had access to greater Power, being actual Actives, but men like Harkeness were something different, something rare and strange, themselves oddities in an odd bunch. Hesitantly he spoke. "Do . . . do you want . . . my *soul*?"

This time Harkeness really did laugh, almost choking on his cigar. "Now that's funny! Do I look like a spiritualist? I'm certainly not the devil, Mr. Stuyvesant. I do not even know if I believe in such preposterous things. What would I even do with your soul if I had it?"

That was a relief, even if Cornelius wasn't particularly sure that he had a soul, he didn't want to deed it over to a man like Harkeness. "I don't know," Cornelius shrugged. "I just thought . . ."

Harkeness was still chuckling. "No, nothing so mysterious. All I want is a *favor*."

That caused Cornelius to pause. "A favor?"

Harkeness was done laughing. "Yes, a favor. Not today. But someday in the future I will call and ask for a favor. You will remember this service performed, and you will grant me that favor without hesitation or question. Is that understood?"

"What manner of favor?"

The Pale Horse shrugged. "I do not yet know this thing. But I do know that if you fail to honor our bargain at that particular time, I will be greatly displeased."

He was not, by nature, a man who intimidated easily, but Cornelius Gould Stuyvesant was truly unnerved. The threat went unsaid, but who would want to cross such a man? The industrialist almost walked out on the absurd and frightening proposal, but he had been planning his revenge for far too long to turn back now. If the favor was too large, Cornelius knew he always had other options. Harkeness was deadly, but he wasn't immortal. It would not be the first time he had used murder to get out of an inequitable contract.

"Very well," Cornelius said. "You have a deal. When will he get sick?"

Harkeness closed his eyes for a few seconds, as if pondering a difficult question. "It is already done," the Pale Horse said, opening his eyes. "Isaiah will see you out."

Isaiah joined his employer on the balcony a few minutes later. Harkeness had gone back to admiring the view. "Could you Read him?"

"He's very intelligent. I had to be gentle or he would've known. He's got a bad tendency to shout his thoughts when he gets riled up." The servant leaned against the concrete wall and folded his arms. "He even thought I might be a Torch. Can you believe that?"

Harkeness chuckled, knowing that Isaiah was far more dangerous than some mere human flame hurler. "Was he truthful?"

"Mostly. He absolutely despises this man."

"For what he did to him? Wouldn't you?"

Isaiah sounded disgusted. "Stuyvesant is utterly ruthless."

*So am I,* Harkeness thought, knowing full well that Isaiah would pick that up as clearly as a high-strength radio broadcast. "You don't get to such lofty positions without being dangerous. I'll have to curse him quickly. Arranging a meeting should be easy enough. Stuyvesant will be expecting immediate results now."

Isaiah left the wall and took one of the cigars from the table. "I liked your little show, with closing the eyes and just wishing for somebody to die and all that. That's good theater."

Of course, even he had his limits. He would actually have to touch the victim, and it took constant Power thereafter to keep up the onslaught against the ministrations of Menders, which he already knew this man would have. This would be an extremely draining assignment. "Whatever keeps Stuyvesant nervous," Harkeness shrugged. "I do like the new term though. It suits me."

Isaiah quoted from memory as he clipped the end from the Cuban. "And I heard a voice in the midst of the four beasts, and I looked and beheld a pale horse, and the name that sat upon him was death . . ."

"And hell followed with him," Harkeness finished, smiling. "Appropriate . . ."

"If the favor you ask of him is too difficult, he'll have you killed."

Harkeness had suspected as much. "He could try. Wouldn't be the first."

"The man's got a phobia about sickness. The Spanish flu near did him when it came through, been worrying him ever since." Isaiah said as he lit the cigar. "He's scared of you."

"Good," the Pale Horse muttered, watching the people moving below, scuttling about like ants, ignorant little creatures, unaware of the truth of the world in which they lived. The Chairman was about to change the world, whether any of the ants liked it or not, and that meant war. Many ants would be stepped on, but that was just too bad. It was unfortunate to be born an ant. "He should be . . ."

## Billings, Montana

**EVERY DAY WAS THE SAME.** Every prisoner in the Special Prisoners' Wing of the Rockville State Penitentiary had the exact same schedule. You slept. You worked. You got put back in your cage. You slept. You worked. You got put back in your cage. Repeat until time served.

Working meant breaking rocks. Normal prisoners were put on work crews to be used by mayors trying to keep budgets low. They got to go outside. The convicts in Special Wing got to break rocks in a giant stone pit. Some of them were even issued tools. The name of the facility was just a coincidence.

One particular convict excelled at breaking rocks. He did a good job of it because he did a good job of every-thing he set his mind to. First he'd been good at war and now he was good at breaking rocks. It was just his nature. The convict had single-minded determination, and once he got to pushing something, he just couldn't find it in himself to stop. He was as constant as gravity. After a year, he was the finest rock breaker and mover in the history of Rockville State Penitentiary.

Occasionally some other prisoner would try to start trouble because he thought the convict was making the rest of them look bad, but even in a place dedicated to holding felons who could tap into all manner of magical affinities, most were smart enough not to cross this particular convict. After the first few left in bags, the rest understood that he just wanted to be left alone to do his time. Occasionally some new man, eager to show off his Power, would step up and challenge the convict, and he too would leave in a bag.

The warden did not blame the convict for the violence. He understood the type of men he had under his care, and knew that the convict was just defending himself. Between helping meet the quota for the gravel quarry that padded the warden's salary under the table, and for ridding the Special Wing of its most dangerous and troublesome men, the warden took a liking to the convict. He read the convict's records, and came to respect the convict as a man for the deeds he'd done before committing his crime. He was the first Special Prisoner ever granted access to the extremely well-stocked, but very dusty prison library.

So the convict's schedule changed. Sleep. Work. Read. Sleep. Work. Read. So now the time passed faster. The convict read books by the greatest minds of the day. He read the classics. He began to question his Power. Why did his Power work the way it did? What separated him from normal men? Why could he do the things he could do? Because of its relation to his own specific gifts, he started with Newton, then Einstein, finally Bohr and Heisenberg, and then every other mind that had pontificated on the science related to his magic. And when he had exhausted the books on science, he turned to the philosophers' musings on the nature of magic and the mystery of where it had suddenly come from and all of its short history. He read Darwin. He read Schuman, and Kelser, Reed, and Spengler. When that was done, he read *everything* that was left.

The convict began to experiment with his Power. He would sneak bits of rock back into his cell to toy with. Reaching deep inside himself, twisting, testing, always pushing with that same dogged determination that had made him the best rock breaker, and when he got tired of experimenting with rocks, he started to experiment on his own body. Eventually all those hours of testing and introspection enabled him to discover things about magic that very few other people would ever understand.

But he kept that to himself.

Then one day the warden offered the convict a deal . . .

# ◅ Chapter 1 ▻

*We now have over a thousand confirmed cases of individuals with these so-called magical abilities on the continent alone. The faculty has descended into a terrible uproar over the proper nomenclature for such specimens. All manner of Latin phrases have been bandied about. Professor Gerard even suggested* Grimnoir, *a combination of the old French* Grimoire, *or book of spells, with* Noir, *for Black, in the sense of the mysterious, for at this juncture the origin of said Powers remains unknown. He was laughed down. Personally, I've taken to calling them* wizards, *for the very idea of there being actual magic beyond the bounds of science causes my esteemed colleagues to sputter and choke.*

—Dr. L. Fulci,
Professor of Natural Science, University of Bern,
Personal Journal, 1852

## THREE YEARS LATER

### Springfield, Illinois

**THERE WERE TWENTY LOCAL BULLS,** ten state coppers, and half a dozen agents from the Bureau of

Investigation, and every one of them was packing serious heat. Jake Sullivan approved. Purvis wasn't screwing around this time. Delilah Jones was going down.

The lead government man was pacing back and forth in front of the crew assembled in the warehouse. "You don't hesitate. None of you hesitate even for a second. She's a woman, but don't you dare underestimate her. She's robbed twenty banks in four states, and killed five people." He paused long enough to jerk a thumb at his men. "When you see her, nobody makes a move until me or Agent Cowley says the word."

A second government man raised his hand. Sam Cowley's suit was cheap, but his 1928 Thompson was meticulously maintained. Sullivan knew he was a man who kept his priorities in order, so at least he'd been roped into working with an experienced crew this time.

There was a wanted poster stuck to the wall. Sullivan had known Delilah back in New Orleans. She was a dish, a real looker. He had to admit that the ink drawing was actually realistic, unlike his old wanted poster, where they had uglied him up for dramatic effect, but in the sketch artists' defense, somebody that could crush every bone in your body should look scary.

"How many men in the gang?" one of the locals asked.

Melvin Purvis paused. "I'm not expecting a gang. Just her."

The room got quiet. It normally didn't take thirty-seven men with rifles and shotguns to take down a lone woman, bank robber or not. They all realized what that meant about the same time, but nobody wanted to say it.

Finally the same local slowly raised his hand. "She got big Powers then?"

"Yes, McKee. She does," Purvis responded. "She's a Brute, and she's Active. Probably the toughest I've heard of." McKee lowered his hand. The sea of blue and brown uniforms all looked at each other, grumbling and swearing. "Yeah, yeah, I know. Listen, boys, when I got here, I asked your chiefs for hard men. I know you're all up to it, but if any of you want out, there's no shame in leaving."

"Is that why he's here?" McKee asked, since he'd somehow become the leader of the uniforms, gesturing to where Sullivan had been trying to remain unnoticed in the back of the room.

"He's with me," Purvis said. "We let Sullivan do his job, and none of you have to worry about dealing with a little lady who can toss automobiles at you. You got a problem with that?"

"He's a murderer," McKee pointed out.

"Manslaughter," Sullivan corrected, speaking for the first time. "And I done served my time. J. Edgar Hoover says I'm *reformed*."

There were no more questions forthcoming. Somebody coughed. Purvis folded his arms and waited until the count of ten. Nobody stood up to leave. "Good. We try to take her alive. My men go in first with Sullivan. The rest hang back outside and get the bystanders out of the way. Nobody shoots unless she goes Active."

"Then don't miss," Agent Cowley suggested.

They'd be moving out in a matter of minutes and Sullivan sensed the room was nervous, kind of bouncy and tense. It reminded him a little of the Great War, in those few awful seconds before the whistle blew and they'd jump out of the relative safety of their muddy trenches and run screaming into Maxim gunfire, barbed wire, and the Kaiser's zombies.

Jake Sullivan had gotten the call from Washington two weeks before, telling him to report to Special Agent Melvin Purvis in Chicago. The assignment came at a good time. His regular business as a private dick was floundering, and he had been reduced to pulling the occasional security gig, standing in as muscle during some of the labor strikes. He didn't like it, but just being special didn't pay the bills. At least he hadn't had to hurt anyone. Just his reputation kept the strikers peaceful. Nobody wanted to cross a Heavy, especially one that had served time in Rockville.

The government jobs barely paid a decent wage, but more importantly, this was the last of the five assignments he had agreed to upon his early release. The warden had appealed to his patriotism when he had transmitted the offer, telling Sullivan that it would be a chance to serve his country again. He had found that amusing, since his only desire at that point was to get out of that hellhole. He'd already served his country once, and had the scars to show for it.

As had been agreed upon, every single other Magical he had assisted in capturing had been a murderer. Jake still had some principles left.

And this one was no different, though he had been surprised to find out that he had known her once. Hearing the name of the target, and then the terrible crimes she'd

committed had left him stunned. Sullivan still couldn't
picture Delilah as a cold-blooded killer, but people could
change a lot in six years. He certainly had.

Sullivan sat uncomfortably in the backseat of the Ford
as they watched yet another dirigible drift into the station.
Purvis and Cowley were in the front seat. It was raining
hard, pounding mist from the pavement and creating
halos around every street lamp.

"This should be it," Cowley said from behind the
steering wheel. His Thompson was on the seat next to him
and he rhythmically tapped his fingers on the wooden
stock.

"The informant said she would be on the eight-fifteen,"
Purvis said, checking his pocket watch. "Must be running
late 'cause of the weather."

*An informant?* "So that's how you found her." Sullivan
wasn't surprised. He'd been ratted out himself all those
years ago. "Figures."

"I don't like this," Cowley said. "There's too many
people around if she goes Active. It'd be safer to tail her
to someplace quiet."

"We already talked about this. We can't risk losing her.
She's supposed to be coming here to do a job for the
Torrios. You want somebody like her working for Crazy
Lenny?"

Sullivan just listened. Strategy wasn't his area. He just
did what he was told. Nobody expected a Heavy to be
smart, so Jake found life went easier if he just kept his
mouth shut, but if it were up to him, he would have to go
with Cowley's plan. It wasn't like Magicals didn't catch

enough heat from a few bad apples as it was. The last thing they needed was stories in the papers about a Brute taking the heads off some G-men in public.

"You ready, Sullivan?" Purvis asked as he opened his door into the downpour.

"Yeah," he muttered. "This is the last time, you know. That was the deal. After this, I'm a free man. I ain't beholden to nobody."

"Over my pay grade," the senior agent responded before stepping out. He slammed the door behind him. All down the street other cops saw Purvis appear and the lawmen began to exit their cars as well.

"He better keep a leash on those bulls or this could get ugly," Sullivan said as he pulled a pack of smokes out of his coat. "Got a light, Sam?"

"You know I always do, Sullivan." Cowley turned around and snapped his fingers. A flame appeared from the end of his thumb. "Figures God would bless me with a little tiny Power, and he gives a magic lighter to somebody who doesn't smoke." He chuckled. Cowley was some religion that forbade smoking, a strange combination for a Torch.

Sullivan lit the fag. "Ironic." He took a long drag. Sullivan liked the agent. Cowley was homely and avoided the spotlight as much as Purvis sought it. They'd worked together before and Sullivan knew the agent was competent. "You know, you best not let your boss see you do that. I hear J. Edgar don't like magic."

"Lots of folks don't." Cowley turned around and opened his door. "We better go." He got out, pulling the Thompson with him.

Sullivan sighed. Cowley was the weakest kind of Magical, with just a flicker of natural Power, but even that could ruin a man's career in some circles. He tugged his hat down low and got ready, feeling the Power stored inside his chest. It took a lot of practice to build up that much and still keep it under control. He activated a small part and felt his body shift. For a brief moment the world around him seemed to flex. The springs on the Ford creaked. He cracked his knuckles, feeling the Spike, gently testing the tug of gravity around him.

Cigarette dangling from his lower lip, he opened the door and slowly unfolded himself from the backseat. Jake Sullivan was a big man, and he used a big gun. He reached back inside and maneuvered the long case from the backseat. The black canvas bag was enormous and he let it dangle from one hand.

Cowley looked over, rain running off his fedora, and pointed at the case. "I don't see how you can carry that thing around."

Sullivan took one last drag before tossing his smoke into a puddle. "Saved your life in Detroit, if I remember right."

"True, but it has to weigh a ton."

"Not to me," Sullivan said as he reached into the bag, grabbed the Lewis gun by its stock and withdrew it. Even twenty-six pounds empty didn't really concern somebody who could alter gravity. To him it was light as a feather and swung like a bird gun.

"Damn, is that a fence post?" Purvis asked, cradling a short barreled Browning Auto-5. "Put that thing back. This is an arrest, not a war."

"You don't know Delilah." Sullivan threw the sling over his shoulder and head so the massive machine gun could hang at his side. It wasn't exactly concealable, but his parole deal had specified he would help take down Active murderers, not that he had to be tactful about it. "You know, Purvis, I've never got in a gunfight and said afterwards, damn, I wish I hadn't brought all that extra ammo."

"Put it away, Sullivan. That's an order. I got lots of men who can shoot, and I've only got one that can do—" he waved his hands like a bad stage magician—"*whatever* it is you do."

"Where'd you get that monster anyway?" Cowley asked.

"Flea market," Sullivan answered as he unslung the mighty Lewis and put it back into its case. All the Spikers had been issued heavy weapons in Roosevelt's First Volunteer. He'd brought quite a few souvenirs back from France besides the shrapnel still lodged in his body. He might not be able to take the Lewis, but he still had a .45 auto riding his hip. Magic was great and all, but a lot of problems could still be solved faster the old-fashioned way, and Jake considered himself a practical man.

"Just do your job, and we'll keep you safe," Purvis promised. "I want this to go nice and clean. You just wrap her up."

At least Purvis seemed like the kind of agent who cared more about being effective than being popular in the papers, unlike the fiasco in Detroit six months ago. "Yeah, fine," he said, shoving the canvas case back into the Ford. He closed the door too hard. "You know, Agent

Purvis, I know Delilah pretty good. The dame's had a tough run. She's not the kind that'll go down easy, and she ain't going quiet, that's for damn sure. She's a fighter, but I never knew her to be the murdering kind."

"You saw the same file I did. I've got five dead men that say different. Necks snapped, one arm torn clean off." Purvis scowled. "I've got my orders. We take her alive . . . But I'm more worried about the safety of these boys than I am about orders. You getting me, Heavy?"

Sullivan preferred the more dignified term Gravity Spiker. Heavy was what you called the Passives who were employed in factories as human forklifts. Cold water was slipping inside his trench coat as he shrugged. He just wanted to get this last job over with and finally get the Man off his back. "I get you, Agent Purvis." The street was clear of oncoming headlights, so he started across, big boots splashing through the puddles. The six G-men followed.

The wedge-shaped dirigible was gradually slowing between the towers, and when it came to a rest, the passengers would begin to debark. It was slow going in bad weather, and this particular balloon was just a little two-hundred-footer hybrid machine, so it was getting kicked around quite a bit by the wind. The Springfield dirigible station was relatively small, nothing like the enclosed behemoth just constructed in Chicago.

Ground crews were braving the rain and catching the security lines. One man was giving them orders with a bullhorn from the tower, probably a Crackler, redirecting lightning and static electricity to keep the airfield's workers safe at the ends of those cables, but it wasn't like

Magicals like that got any credit in the press. No, everybody knew Hearst didn't care about working stiffs with Powers. He only wasted ink on people like Delilah. *And me . . .* Sullivan thought, *trouble makers*, but then shook his head, getting back to business.

He and the Bureau of Investigation men took cover beneath the overhang at the entrance to the waiting room. Through the glass he could see the room was nice, mosaic tile floor, all brass and glass on the walls, with lots of wood and iron benches for the commuters. There were a handful of people waiting. Purvis left two men outside, and the rest got out of the rain and entered the dry comfort of the lounge.

The lift was clearly visible. Sullivan noted that they'd be able to see the passengers before the passengers could see them, which was convenient for once. A United Blimp & Freight worker spotted the guns but Purvis flashed his badge and waved the man away. The G-men started ushering people out into the rain as fast as they could, and Purvis sent one to make sure nobody was loitering on the stairs. The uniformed bulls were out on the dark perimeter if Delilah somehow made it past or drew on her Power and turned it into a fight.

Most of the UBF employees didn't know what was going down, but word would spread quickly now. He stood with his back to the mirrored wall. The tower was four stories tall, and that was a lot of stairs, which meant that Delilah would probably come down in the elevator, especially if she had luggage. Either way, from this position he could watch both.

Everything in this place was mirrored and shiny—even

the ceiling had mirrors—but the mighty UBF budget had been cut because of the recent downturns, and the place felt kind of grimy. The Twenties had been a huge economic boom time, but Sullivan had spent most of those happy years doing hard time. The papers were calling it a depression, but compared to Rockville, Jake thought the whole outside world seemed pretty damn nice.

The dirigible's cabin made a strange clanking noise as it mated with the docking platform through the roof above. Sullivan closed his eyes and used a little more of his Power to feel the world around him. The giant reserve of helium felt unnatural, being lighter than air, and that always made accurate Spiking a little difficult. He'd have to compensate for it. He was supposed to capture Delilah, not splatter her into red mush.

It wasn't even five minutes after the dirigible had docked that the elevator came down with its first load of passengers. UBF was the model of efficiency. Like the ads said, they were the *Convenient Way to Travel*. The agents tensed up, but there were only a few passengers, none of whom were Delilah Jones, and a young UBF employee pushing a cart full of suitcases. The passengers looked a little wobbly, which was understandable since blimping wasn't exactly a joyride during a storm. Two of the G-men flashed badges and converged on the car before the employee even had a chance to raise the gate. They started herding the passengers outside while Cowley grabbed the UBF and showed him the wanted poster. The kid nodded his head vigorously and Purvis smiled. "Got her."

Cowley came back. "She's in a red dress, black hat, black furs, and she's in line for the next ride."

The gate scissored closed, the elevator lift clanked back up, and it was just then Sullivan noticed a shadow moving on the stairs above. The grey shape was there for a second, but when he looked harder, it was gone. "I think we got somebody up there," he said, pointing.

"Hollis, Michaels, check the stairs," Purvis ordered and his two men immediately tromped up the brass capped steps, guns in hand. They were out of sight in a few seconds but their footfalls could still be heard. The agent in charge turned back to the elevator doors, nervously bouncing his shotgun. "I thought they'd already cleared those," he muttered.

"There's nobody up here," one of the G-men called from the stairs.

The elevator was coming down. Sullivan got ready. He had to be careful. He didn't want to damage any of the other passengers, so he would have to be very selective. If there were people in there with bad tickers or delicate constitutions, it was far too easy to hurt them by accident, and that still mattered to him. The safest thing to do for the bystanders would be to get nice and close, but getting close to a Brute was a game for suckers.

*Guess I'm a sucker.* He tilted his fedora down, stuck his hands in his suit pockets, and strolled to the elevator. When the doors opened, he'd just be loafing around, as if he were waiting for the next one up. Hopefully she wouldn't recognize him until it was too late. His best bet was to overwhelm her before she could use her Power. Cowley and Purvis let him go. They'd worked together enough times before that they knew Sullivan was a pro.

The elevator appeared, and Sullivan scanned the passengers through the gate as they descended. Four more people and another cart full of suitcases, and there she was. Delilah Jones was in the front of the car, borderline petite, delicate hands planted on lovely hips, tapping one high-heeled shoe impatiently. Jake had a moment to admire her legs before he was forced to lower his head. *The girl still has nice gams.*

They'd met in New Orleans not too long after the war, only a few years before he'd gone up the river. Back then she'd just been a petty crook at worst, using her Power like a can opener to rip open cheap safes, and Jake had been an idealistic idiot, thinking that people like them could make the world a better place. They'd been tight once, maybe even something special, but Jake Sullivan didn't have friends anymore. A stint in the Special Prisoners' Wing of Rockville State Penitentiary had seen to that. Now he just had jobs.

One of the male passengers lifted the gate and the others began to file out. Jake reached inside himself and felt the Power. Reality faded into its component bits. His surroundings now consisted of matter, density, and forces. The Power began to drain as he willed the pull of the Earth to multiply over the form that was Delilah Jones. Selectively increasing gravity was one of the more challenging things he could accomplish. It took a lot of effort and Power, but it was darn effective. It was a lot less draining to just Spike something hard, whereas this was more like delicate surgery. She wouldn't be able to move, no matter how strong she could make herself, and after a few seconds he'd manage to cut off the blood flow and knock her out. Go too soft and she'd Power out of it, go too hard and he'd kill her, but Sullivan was the best Spiker in the business. She would never know what hit her.

There was a shout and a gunshot. Sullivan's concentration wavered, just a bit, and the real world came suddenly flooding back. The Power he'd gathered slipped from his control and the elevator gate was sheared from its bolts and slammed flat into the floor under the added pressure of ten gravities. A passenger screamed as his foot was crushed flat and blood came squirting out the top of his shoe. "Sorry, bud." Sullivan turned in time to see one of the G-men tumbling down the stairwell, a grey shape leaping behind, colliding with Cowley and Purvis and taking them all down, "Aw hell," he muttered, then spun back in time to see Delilah's lovely green eyes locked on his.

"You were trying to *smoosh* me, Heavy!" she exclaimed, eyes twinkling as she ignited her own Power. She grabbed the big man by the tie and hoisted him effortlessly off the floor, even though he was almost a foot taller. The tie tightened, choking him as he dangled, and she finally got a good look at her assailant. "*You!* Well, if it isn't Jake Sullivan. Been a long time."

Then she hurled him. Suddenly airborne, he flew across the waiting area. Instinctively, his Power flared, and he bounced softly off the far wall with the force of a pillow. Jake returned to his normal weight as his boots hit the floor. He loosened his cheap tie so he could breathe again. "Hey, Delilah."